THE Pitch SLAP

BEAUTY AND THE CLEATS BOOK 1

KRIS BUTLER

The Pitch Slap
Beauty and the Cleats Book One
Kris Butler

First Edition: December 2023
Published by: Incognito Scribe Productions LLC
Kris Butler
Copyright © Kris Butler

Proofreading: © 2023 by The Blue Couch Edits
Formatting: © 2023 Incognito Scribe Productions LLC
Cover Design: © 2023 Incognito Scribe Productions LLC
Photo Credit: © Cadwallader Photography
Model Credit: Jordan

❀ Created with Vellum

THE Pitch SLAP

BEAUTY AND THE CLEATS BOOK 1

KRIS BUTLER

BLURB

Growing up a baseball princess had taught me a few things:

- One, the only truly scary thing about ball players was their superstitions.
- Second, baseball always came first. It was their one true love.
- And third, never take your eye off the ball, or you just might get pitch-slapped.

The past three years I'd been licking my wounds in Greece after I ran away from my wedding, and somehow forgot all three.

Too bad the baseball gods weren't as forgetful.

Lured back home by my brother with the perfect job opportunity to photograph the YellowJackets baseball team, and I had no clue I'd step up to bat before even entering the stadium.

And the pitches just kept coming.

Strike one—a plane-night stand ghosting after being stranded in a storm.

Strike two—a grumpy ex who coincidentally was my brother's best friend.

Foul Ball—a mistaken text with two players saved me from striking out completely, especially when it turned into a sexy exploration.

But there was no doubt I had a full count and only one swing away from striking out.

My first mistake was taking my eye off the ball; the second was believing I'd ever come before baseball. But most grievous of all, learning that the scariest thing about ball players wasn't their superstitions… No, it was falling in love with them.

FOREWORD

This book has sexual scenes meant for adults. It's a why-choose romance that has bi-awakening themes. The steamy scenes are steamy and you might need new batteries by the end. Sorry, not sorry.

This book uses the F-word as well as other foul language. See the below for all the good stuff and things to be cautious of while reading The Pitch Slap.

TROPES AND CONTENT

- Multi-Pov
- Found Family
- Possessive, growly men
- Persistent Cinderella
- Bi-awakening
- Brother's Best Friend
- Baseball club
- Tattoos
- Cute Hamster
- Mistaken Texts
- Brother's Rival
- Comeback Queen

- Single dad
- Precocious four-year-old
- Threesomes
- Golden Retriever Energy (though he likes to think of himself as a golden doodle)
- "Can you be quiet?"
- Hate sex
- Quasi-public sex
- Grumpy/sunshine
- One bed
- Planegasms, busgasms, and stadiumgasms
- Anal
- Sexting
- Casual Exploration
- Sex positive
- Mental Health rep
- Queer rep
- No third act breakup, just some angst and mild anxiety about the status of the relationship

SENSITIVE TOPICS

- 'God, Jesus, Hell, Damn' used casually or in a sexual context
- PTSD/panic attacks
- Medical illness/history
- Pitch Slap disasters
- Depression/anxiety
- Alcohol recovery
- Homosexual slurs
- Self-doubt
- Negative thoughts
- Mild second-hand embarrassment
- Vomit (sorry)

TEAM POSITIONS

This book will revolve around the Blue Devils (Major League Team) in Columbus, Ohio and the YellowJackets (Triple-A Minor League Team) in Wilmington, North Carolina. There are 15 players on the YellowJackets that are considered part of the Blue Devils roster and can be called up when needed.

PITCHERS:

Austin Gibson, #5 (Blue Devils roster)
Tucker Jameson, #7 (Blue Devils roster)
Dalton Park, #3 (Blue Devils roster)
Jose Campos, #1 (Blue Devils roster)
Aaron Shortridge, #49

CATCHERS:

Shane Park, #15 (Blue Devils roster)
Graham West, #13 (Blue Devils roster)

FIRST BASEMAN:

Bryce Baker, #44 (Blue Devils roster)
Luke Olson, #24 (Blue Devils roster)
Pascal Lane, #16

SECOND BASEMAN:

Hector Ortiz, #21 (Blue Devils roster)
Sal Sandoval, #18 (Blue Devils roster)
Kevin Grant, #29

THIRD BASEMAN:

Seth Davis, #11
Emmett Michaels, #20 (Blue Devils roster)
Keith Delgado, #19

SHORTSTOP:

Levi Garza, #10 (Blue Devils roster)
Ledger Collins, #27 (Blue Devils roster)
Ewan McGuire, #43

OUTFIELDERS:

Johnny Lewis, #33 (Blue Devils roster)
Aaron Chang, #8
Tommy Williams, #22
Wyatt Hart, #2 (Blue Devils roster)
Noah Bowen, #41
Matt Gorski, #37
PJ Henny, #25

COACHES:

Eric Phillips
Hawk Anderson
Bailey Hank

OTHER TEAMS:

Omaha Sluggers
KC Tornados
Richmond Royals
Charleston Grizzlies
Salt Lake Rockets
St Paul Sliders
Bowling Green Bruisers

For a glossary of baseball terms, please check the back of the book.

PLAYLIST

Spotify Playlist for the book

To everyone who keeps persisting, especially when it feels like the pitch slaps keep coming with no end in sight, be your own fairy godmother and slay those dragons.

CHAPTER
ONE

BLAKE

"Come home."

The request had been innocent enough three days ago, but now, I questioned my brother's sanity. And perhaps my own, too.

But this job... it was the unicorn of jobs. My perfect mashup of interest and skills.

I clutched my ticket, my heart thumping erratically as I tried to slow my breathing. The intercom blared overhead, and I startled as it announced the last call for a gate a few feet away. My frayed nerves skyrocketed as everything around me went into hyperdrive, catapulting my overstimulated brain into a spiral.

It's too soon. You're not ready.

You can turn around now. Bryce will understand.

You're going to fail, and then everyone will know you're a flake and a loser.

What the heck, brain?

My breaths quickened, and the overhead lights brightened as sweat beaded my brow. Crap. I couldn't do this. Not here. Not with all these people looking at me.

I squeezed my eyes shut, the sounds of the airport intensifying as people shuffled their feet, their luggage clicking loudly as they hurried by. The smell of body odor and coffee beans filled my nostrils, and I swayed on my feet, dizziness wracking me.

How humiliating.

Speaking of humiliation… Remember when you couldn't say no to a wedding proposal, so you agreed to marry the most boring human ever and then ran away with your brother's best friend on your wedding day? Remember that?

That was humiliating.

Thanks, brain. Glad we're on the same page here.

If I was honest with myself, being an unintentional runaway bride wasn't the most embarrassing part of my past. I'd long gotten over the mortification with therapy and had talked to Brandon two years ago to clear the air. Things were okay with us. He'd moved on and was happy, living the life he wanted with someone who appreciated it.

No, the part I struggled with the most was losing my virginity to the boy I'd loved my whole life and then sacrificing my heart the next morning for my brother. Bryce had saved my life as a child by giving me his bone marrow; surrendering my heart had seemed like a fair trade at the time.

After three years in Greece, the place I retreated to after everything blew up in my face, I wasn't so sure.

At first, hiding out in a country where only one person had known me was the reprieve I'd needed to heal. Across the ocean, I could pretend it didn't hurt every time I breathed. That there wasn't a gaping hole in my chest where my heart had been.

Eventually it got easier. With therapy and new passions to pursue, I could ignore the heartache that had sent me running in the first place.

Standing in the airport now, it was all I could feel—everything I'd left behind.

The boy I'd loved.

The overbearing parents.

The fear of disappointing others.

Of never being good enough.

What if the work I'd done hadn't been enough? What if I fell flat on my face? What if I returned to a role I'd played my entire life, erasing the past three years?

What if, what if, what if!

Trepidation skirted up my spine as fear engulfed me, and I swallowed my rising panic. Clenching and unclenching my fists, I forced myself to open my eyes and slowed my breaths, calming my heart rate.

I would not have a panic attack.

Remembering everything I'd learned with my therapist, Delia, I centered myself. I focused on the wall, rolling my eyes up and down as I inhaled and exhaled deep breaths. After three more ups and downs, my heart slowed, my breathing evened, and my vision no longer blurred.

Okay, you did it. See…you did learn something. You can—

A bag knocked into my side, breaking my trance, and I stumbled as the air rushed out of me. My passport and ticket fluttered to the ground as I braced my hands out in front to stop my fall, my knees hitting hard.

"Ow. Son of a glove!" I rubbed my knee as I gathered my stuff, muttering curses under my breath.

"Shit, sorry. I didn't see you," a smooth voice said from above, halting my movements. No man's voice had the right to be sexy. It just wasn't fair.

However, my frazzled disposition and lack of sleep didn't appreciate it, and I scowled down at my hands and the items I'd dropped. I kept my eyes lowered as I stood, wobbling slightly from the sudden change of position.

"Whoa," he said, grabbing my arm to steady me. His hand

was warm, and goosebumps grew where his palm landed. His touch felt oddly safe, throwing me off and befuddling my mind.

"You okay?" he asked, and I finally looked up, meeting green eyes that reminded me of baseball diamonds.

"Um, yeah." I blinked, staring at the man who still held my arm.

Of course, he had to be gorgeous. He was the type of hot that almost hurt to look at for too long. Like he was the sun, and you'd burn your retinas if you stared directly at him. But the desire to test it out was there, and I wondered how long I could stare without ruining my eyesight.

Everything about this man was golden—sun-kissed skin, golden honey hair, and a smile that had to be worth millions. And all that goldenness was aimed at me like a solar eclipse, momentarily blinding.

"You sure? You seem out of sorts," he said, his brows furrowing in concern. "Do you need me to find a doctor?"

And just like that, a cold dose of reality washed over me, darkening the golden sun and plummeting me back to reality.

Helpless Blake. Sick Blake. In need of rescue Blake.

No. I wasn't *her* anymore; I couldn't be.

I snatched my arm back more forcefully than I intended. "I'm fine. *You're* the one who bumped into *me*."

The golden guy held up his hands in defeat, his eyes holding a pitying look I hated as he stepped back. "Apologies."

I pressed my lips together to stop myself from saying anything else. Years of pent-up emotion rose, and I would likely snap his head off unloading my baggage. I already knew I'd be the "kooky airport girl" to his friends. I didn't need to add "bitchy" either.

"All right, well…" He paused, rubbing his head as he watched me. "Have a good flight." The golden god cringed, hopefully realizing how lame that statement was. Like I had any power over how well the flight went.

He spun around, and I shifted over, attempting to leave his bumping area and reduce further incidents. I exhaled and realized there had been one positive thing from the whole ordeal—the rage had erased my anxiety.

"Flight B2384 will now begin loading. Please have your ticket and ID ready to be scanned when your group is called. We will now board group one."

He moved forward, his designer bag tucked over his shoulder as he handed the attendant his ticket and ID. Of course, he was in first class. His goldenness couldn't be diminished by the peasants sitting in economy. On the plus side, I didn't have to worry about sitting beside him on the plane. That would be just my luck. Ha!

Time passed slowly as passengers boarded, and I zoned out. Since I'd only gotten my ticket two days ago, I was in the last boarding group with a middle seat. Fun times.

I blew out a breath, tapping my foot as I waited to be called, my nerves resurfacing. Without any other distractions, my thoughts returned to him—the man I wasn't supposed to think about.

It had been easier to ignore my broken heart when I'd been thousands of miles away, and time had given me a false sense of security as I deluded myself I was over him.

But the truth was, I'd always loved Hawk Anderson, even when I claimed not to.

Not when I swore to my brother I was over my crush on his best friend at fifteen.

Not when he kissed me and then ignored me at sixteen.

Not even after taking my virginity and then denying my love the next day.

And now, after spending three years away, not only would I have to see him, but I had to work with him. It was a disaster waiting to happen, especially since he had a girlfriend.

He'd moved on, so I'd have to do the same, even if it seemed impossible.

The reality was that I'd set us on this course, so I had to live with the repercussions. There wasn't a world I knew where my brother could accept his little sister dating his best friend. Thus, I'd chosen for him so he wouldn't have to.

I just never expected it to hurt this much.

CHAPTER
TWO

BLAKE

"Group eight, you may now board."

Flinching at the sound, I glanced around me, noticing how few people milled around the gate now—nothing like reminiscing about the one you could never have to pass the time.

"Group nine, you may now board," the attendant said, her voice flat and lifeless, echoing the way I felt.

Me too, buddy. Me too.

The rest of the passengers filed into line, and I followed. Lifting my bag onto my shoulder, I shuffled my feet as I waited for the people in front of me to pass. Why did this part always feel the longest?

Maybe it was the jetlag, or that this was my third flight of the day, but I was over flying. My body ached from traveling, and all I wanted to do was curl up in my favorite hoodie with a book and ignore the world for a few days.

Instead, I had to board one last plane and pray the healing I'd done hadn't been for nothing. I refused to place the gratitude shackles back on, but could I really stop my people-pleasing ways? It had been easy to make my own decisions with an ocean between my family and me.

When your dad was a famous baseball player, everyone knew your name. From an early age, I had people calling me a baseball princess. I went to all of my dad's games that I could and would cheer and yell at the players, making everyone around me laugh. But then I became the sick kid, and no one laughed when I was around. They just stared and whispered, giving me pitying looks.

After that, I told my dad I hated baseball, refusing to go to his games anymore. I couldn't take the stares that had replaced the adoring looks. Eventually, my brother coaxed me back to the stadium, but the magic had gone.

By the time my parents divorced, I felt so let down by baseball that I no longer believed it could solve any problem like my dad did. I still went to games and volunteered, helping out over the summers I spent with my dad. But the real kick to the gut came when my boyfriend proposed with a flash mob at the World Series.

After running away from the stadium where my wedding was held, I'd decided it was time for baseball and I to take a break. Which, subsequently, had also meant my family.

Because not only was my father a former Major Leaguer who'd retired and managed the Columbus Blue Devils to a World Series title, but he'd also bought the club, making him the owner of the Blue Devils *and* their triple-A affiliate team, the YellowJackets.

My brother had eagerly followed in Dad's footsteps, playing baseball from an early age through college. He was drafted to the Blue Devils at the age of twenty-two. After an injury three years ago, he'd been dropped down to the YellowJackets where he played now.

Even my mother was dedicated to the sport. Candi Baker was among the league's most cutthroat and sought-after sports lawyers. She had several high-profile players, with a mile-long list of players wanting her to represent them.

The Bakers ate, slept, and breathed baseball.

I'd been the only one who had nothing to do with the game, yet it had still ruled and controlled my life. Even my disaster of a wedding had been scheduled around the season.

Hello, bitterness. You crept in there quickly.

Fortunately, with time away and therapy, I'd come to terms with the sport and was eager to find my footing in the game my whole family loved. While in Greece, I found a love for photography, especially sports photography. My two worlds were colliding, and I was eager to have them merge on my terms.

Thus, why this job meant everything to me. It was my ideal job, and I was ready to prove I wasn't the sick kid, the former baseball princess, or even the runaway bride. Instead, I was a strong and independent woman, ready to make her mark on baseball.

And only one more plane ride stood between me and it.

"ID and ticket," the attendant said, smiling softly as I handed my passport and ticket to her. I'd been gone so long that I didn't have a current driver's license. "Enjoy the flight."

"Thanks." I smiled back, hoping to capture some of her optimism.

Shoving everything back into my bag, I jerked in alarm when my phone vibrated in my palm. Expecting a text from Bryce or my mom, I furrowed my brows when an unknown number popped up. Even more when a second number quickly followed.

831-444-6543: Hey, thanks for last night.

831-945-4824: Yeah, it was great to get to know you more.

831-444-6543: I expected you to be more
intimidating. Thanks for taking it easy on us.

What in the world? My thumb hovered over the keyboard as I debated whether to tell them they had the wrong number, ignore them, or block them. I was back in America for a few hours and already getting weird texts.

My thumb hovered over the keyboard when the realization hit me. My brother's and my phone numbers were only one away from each other. These had to be for him. Unfortunately for me, it wasn't the first time I'd received a stray booty call text. Bryce had his fair share of cleat chasers, and some were a little stalkerish.

In my jetlagged and avoidance-fueled state, I decided to have a little fun.

Blake: Last night was great. I especially
enjoyed that thing you did with your tongue.

Chuckling, I glanced up to see how much time I had to respond. The line moved slower than molasses as people stowed their belongings giving me the freedom to chat.

Blake: We should do it again sometime.

831-444-6543: Baker, I don't think we were
at the same dinner.

831-945-4824: Unless he's talking about
how you licked the gravy off your plate.

831-444-6543: How else are you supposed
to get every last drop?

831-945-4824: You don't.

831-444-6543: Blasphemy!

> 831-945-4824: Pretty sure the waitress was going to give you her number until she spotted that.

> 831-444-6543: Newsflash, she still did.

I laughed out loud, causing a few people to turn and look at me. I didn't even care, enjoying the banter between the two.

> Blake: So, you're not my date from last night?

> Blake: Bummer. I thought we really hit it off.

> 831-444-6543: Do you usually date your teammates? Asking for a friend.

> 831-945-4824: Dude. No offense, but he's not my type.

> 831-444-6543: What? Baker's everyone's type.

> 831-945-4824: No offense, Baker. Like I said, happy to have met you and get to know you more this month during spring training, but I don't want to date you.

> 831-945-4824: Or to offend you by not wanting to date you.

> 831-945-4824: Or make you think I'm checking out your junk now in the locker room.

> 831-945-4824: Geez. Now, I sound like a rookie.

Oh shit. This wasn't a hookup. These were two players on my brother's team. The team I now worked for. My heart raced faster, and I knew I needed to say something. It would only be funny if I never saw this person again.

Blake: Well, I should tell you that you're not texting who you think you are. So, calm your mitts.

831-945-4824: Wait, what?

831-444-6543: This isn't Bryce?

Blake: Nope. Last time I checked, I had boobs.

831-444-6543: Boobs. I like boobs.

831-444-6543: And you spoke baseball. My love language.

831-444-6543: Do it again. I wield a big stick.

831-945-4824: Freaking hell, man. You can't say that to a girl you don't know!

831-444-6543: Why not? It's not like I'll ever see this person.

Knowing how untrue that was, I felt a twinge of guilt, but I still couldn't stop. Talking with them was fun, and I could use some fun. Plus, I felt included, and I'd done it on my own.

831-444-6543: Besides, I still think it's Bryce.

831-444-6543: He's pranking us.

831-945-4824: Oh, like a team hazing thing?

831-444-6543: Totes.

831-444-6543: Do you remember the last team we were on?

831-945-4824: Don't remind me. *shudder*

Blake: Still not Bryce.

831-945-4824: Prove it.

Blake: How?

831-444-6543: Show us your boobs.

831-945-4824: Dude! You can't ask for a boob pic.

831-444-6543: You can when it's not a girl.

Blake: Fine. I'll show you mine if you show me yours.

831-444-6543: Kinky, Baker.

I rolled my eyes, but I couldn't help smiling. I tucked my phone into my pocket and finally stepped onto the plane. I headed to the back and ignored the golden god, who already had his eye mask on, his head lying gently against the pillow in first class. The seat next to him was empty, and I suddenly wanted to dump the glass of water on his tray over him. Because yeah, he got an actual glass of water in first class. Jerk.

Keeping the urge to myself, I continued to the back and tried not to grimace as I found my seat. The one right between a toddler and an older man, the little boy's mother on the other side of him. She looked haggard and tired already, making me sympathize with her.

That was until he moved toward me with his purple-covered hands, and I barely managed to miss them as I leaned into the older man next to me. He smelled like body odor and cigars, and I felt him sniff my hair. Jumping away, I stowed my bag under the seat before me and buckled in, hoping if I ignored the people next to me, they would do the same. Pulling my phone out, I spotted a new message, and I smiled.

831-444-6543: You first. I don't want my dick plastered over the clubhouse.

Blake: Well, considering I'm on a plane, there's not much I can do to prove I'm a girl.

Blake: But hopefully, this will do.

Tilting my phone down, I took a picture of my cleavage, hoping it would be enough, and hit send before I could second-guess myself. Anxiety filled me that maybe I'd gone too far. Was I trying too hard? What if they thought I was dumb? Or that my boobs were small? Why was I talking to strangers? I should end it now before I embarrass myself further. I didn't need another scandal for my family to deal with. My phone vibrated, and I checked it despite my fear.

831-444-6543: Those are nice. If they're real, I definitely want to explore them.

831-444-6543: But how do we know that's not a picture you saved on your camera roll?

831-945-4824: Is this how you flirt?

831-444-6543: It's good, right?

Blake: What do you suggest then? Like I said, on a plane.

831-945-4824: Retake it, but write "catchers do it better" on paper and hold it in the frame.

831-444-6543: Hey, no, it's pitchers. Pitchers do it better.

Well, that gave me some clue about who these two could be, so I changed their names in my phone to pitcher and catcher. Leaning over, I dug out paper and pen from my bag and quickly wrote, "Photographers do it better" instead.

It wasn't that the catcher's part was untrue; Hawk had been the best sex of my life. Granted, I'd only had sex with two people, but it still held true. I ignored the older man as he leaned closer and tilted away as I held the paper and snapped another selfie. I hit send without looking, too scared I'd chicken out. The adrenaline felt good, and I wanted to ride it out as long as possible.

> Blake: There. The plane's taking off, so I better have some good pics when I turn my phone back on.
>
> Blake: Later, boys.

Sighing, I tucked my phone into my bag and sat back, smiling as I listened to the safety spiel. The plane took off a few moments later, and I realized I hadn't thought about Hawk for a while, and that felt like a big win.

The two mystery guys had been fun, and I hoped I would have some funny pictures when I landed. If anything, it gave me something to look forward to. I knew I'd have to tell them who I was eventually, but for now, it was a little secret that I got to have. It allowed me to be a different version of myself without all the "Blake Baker" baggage.

Closing my eyes, I was about to drift off to sleep when an awful noise hit my ears, followed by a foul smell as wet chunks landed on my lap.

"What the—?" I shrieked, opening my eyes to discover the little boy beside me had just vomited. All. Over. Me.

Like a chain reaction, the people around me gagged, and I was one second away from upchucking myself and recreating the pie-eating scene from *Stand by Me*.

"Oh dear, come here," the flight attendant said, unbuckling and pulling me into the aisle and the back of the plane quicker than I believed possible. Damn, she was good.

In a flurry of movement, powder was tossed on me, and liquid wiped off as flight attendant's worked around me in a coordinated fashion I could never dream of mimicking. Thankfully, it stopped the rest of the plane from losing their cookies.

"Here, you can change into this," she said, motioning for me to enter the lavatory.

In a daze, I stepped inside and grimaced as I pulled my shoes and pants off. I stuffed the soiled clothes into the biohazard bag she'd given me and tugged on the two sizes too-big sweatpants and a shirt that had shrunk a time or two.

Great, I had a giant's pants and a doll's shirt. Oh well, they were clean, and I had a jacket in my bag.

Washing the smell off as best I could, I prayed I didn't stink. Stepping out, I spotted my bag and pulled out the jacket, leaving it open for now.

"You okay, dear?" the flight attendant asked, her voice soft and caring.

"Yeah. Is there anywhere else I could sit?" I asked, hoping I didn't have to return to the crime scene. My eyes welled up with tears; the exhaustion of the day and the emotional energy getting to me. Thankfully, she took pity on me, patting my arm.

"It's a full flight, but there's one seat open. And after *that* ordeal, you deserve it. Follow me."

I sighed in relief when she swapped sides so we didn't have to walk directly past the old man or the vomit child. However, as we neared first class, a sense of dread rose.

One empty seat.

The golden guy.

My horrible attire and vomit smell.

Fuck my life.

"Here you go, sweetie. This gentleman was happy to give

up his extra seat," she said, beaming at the golden god, like he hung the moon. I mean, I got it. He was hot. But the arrogance on him made me want to shove his face in the dirt or something.

Wow, that's violent.

She patted my arm like I'd won the lottery and moved away before I could deny it. The guy smiled as he peered up. That was until he realized it was *me*, and his smile fell.

"*You?*" he gasped, his eyes bugging out of his head as he stared at me, a grimace forming at the realization we were about to endure this flight right next to one another.

Hard same, dude.

At this point, I seriously dreaded returning home. What else did the universe have in store for me? And the better question was, would I survive?

CHAPTER
THREE

LUKE

THE CUTE GIRL I'D SOMEHOW PISSED OFF EARLIER STOOD BEFORE me in the most ridiculous outfit. The sweats swamped her, but the tank top left little to the imagination. Even with the jacket on, I could see how it hugged her delicious curves, and I licked my lips, desire pooling in my gut.

What the fuck?

I blinked, wondering if I was hallucinating her effect on me. But I hadn't had a drink, so that couldn't be it.

The urge to order one slammed into me, the taste of sour mash tickling the back of my tongue as I worked to rid myself of the longing.

No. I wouldn't surrender to its call.

During my internal battle, the firecracker had taken the seat and yanked the jacket closed before cramming her bookbag under the seat. Her movements were charged with anger as she jerkily pulled on the sweatshirt jacket, almost knocking me in the face with her fist.

"Watch it there, little slugger. I need my eyes to see," I teased, hoping to lighten the mood. The scowl she directed at me told me I'd missed the mark. Majorly.

"I'm not *little*," she hissed. Her blue eyes burned hot like fire, searing me.

"Okay, touchy subject." I lifted my brows, holding my hands up in surrender.

She opened her mouth like she wanted to say something but snapped it shut, turning her head back to the front, ignoring me.

"Most people say 'you're welcome,'" I taunted, unable to let the conversation drop despite knowing better. I liked that she didn't fall at my feet or appear to know who I was. *Maybe that's what the desire's about?*

She turned to me, her blue eyes igniting something deep inside me. It was only a tiny flicker, but I felt my heart come alive, shocking me even more to my core. Outwardly, I kept smiling, while internally, I freaked the fuck out.

Feelings? Ew. Hell no. Desire was risky enough, but I could handle that. Maybe.

My eyes traveled over her, clearly not getting the memo to not engage. Her blonde hair was long, the ends a pale pink that I itched to spread through my fingers. It looked soft and shiny, and I desperately wanted to feel it against my skin. Seriously... What was wrong with me?

I sniffed my glass of water. Not vodka.

Her button nose scrunched up as her mouth gaped open, her pink and plump lips spread wide, and I instantly pictured them stretched around my cock. The member in question twitched, liking that idea, too. Her heart-shaped face drew me in, my eyes struggling to look at anything else. I watched in amazement as her full cheeks grew rosy, and I slowly became addicted as she stared at me.

I needed her to say something before I reached over and kissed her.

That would be bad. So, so bad.

So why did I still want to do it?

Finally, her paralysis broke, and she screamed at me, "You

want *me* to thank *you* for being vomited on?" Her voice was high, but I still liked it. I smiled at her cute outrage until I realized how douchey I sounded, and winced.

"Well, not *that* exactly," I backtracked, "but for giving up *my* seat."

She spluttered, making noises as she stared at me, mouth agape.

Noises that made me wonder how she sounded when aroused. *Bunting hell.* I needed to get laid if this angry stranger was making me this hard.

"Why did you have two to begin with? Huh? Seems a bit greedy," she huffed, crossing her arms over her chest and not helping my dick-uation. Her cleavage spilled over the top of the tight tank, her boobs screaming at me to touch them.

Shit, she had nice tits. I wanted them in my mouth.

"I have a valid reason," I said, fighting to keep my eyes north.

She lifted her eyebrows in a challenge, the blue of her irises swirling. She might act like she hated me, but the desire in her eyes said otherwise. I leaned closer, my arm touching hers, and I smiled when she didn't jerk away, proving my point.

Focus on the desire. I could work with desire. Ignore that heart thing.

Solid plan.

I slanted my head closer, my breath ghosting over her ear. "We can spend the flight fighting or getting to know one another. But we both know this is ending one way." I paused, licking my lips, her eyes tracking the movement. "What's it gonna be, *Slugger*?" I asked, emphasizing Slugger and leaving off the "little" this time.

See, I could learn from my mistakes.

"What makes you think I want to get to know *you*?" she challenged, her voice husky despite the glare.

"For one, our arms have been touching for a minute now, and you haven't moved away."

She glanced down at our arms and swallowed. To my surprise, she didn't jerk away but met my eyes with a steely confidence. It was hot as fuck, and I wanted to taste more of her fire.

My heart thumped again, clearly not caring, so I ignored it.

We held one another's eyes; a game of chicken I knew I could win.

"Fine. How about a game?" she consented.

"What kind of game?" I smiled; happy I'd won.

She rolled her eyes and sat back but leaned toward me in the expansive seats. Her arm didn't move; if anything, she pressed it harder against mine on the console between us.

When she said nothing, I wondered if she'd forgotten my question or changed her mind.

"As long as it doesn't involve drinking, I'm game." I snorted at my unintentional pun.

She swallowed, not noticing my joke as she thought. "I can agree to those terms. What about two truths and a lie? Never have I ever? Or just plain ol' twenty questions?"

Perfect. I pretended to think it over despite knowing which one I wanted to play.

"Hmm." I tapped her hand, loving all the ways I got away with touching her. "I like two truths and a lie. I'll even go first." I smirked as she narrowed her eyes, clearly not liking I'd taken the initiative.

"I'm an only child, I once got a tattoo on a dare, and I volunteer at soup kitchens."

Everything I'd said was true. I'd learned long ago to give people the truth, and they'd do with it what they wanted. It was much easier to surprise people if everything you said was true. It wasn't my fault they didn't believe me.

The cute girl narrowed her eyes at me, searching my face

as she deliberated. I didn't know which one I wanted her to believe was a lie. It said a lot about a person by what they judged you on in those first few seconds. I felt slightly guilty I was using this game to learn about her more than she'd intended, but I couldn't take things for granted in my life. So, for a few hours, I could pretend to be a regular guy and feel what it was like to be someone else for a plane ride. Just a guy and girl attracted to one another.

"I don't believe you have a tattoo," she finally said, surprising me. "You seem like you wouldn't like pain and wouldn't want to markup that perfect skin of yours."

Flutters danced in my belly at her response, my heart flipping hard again. I'd never told anyone I volunteered, preferring to do it privately so it wasn't used as a publicity stunt. I wanted to help people, not make it about me. And this girl with the pink-tipped hair and bluest eyes I'd ever seen believed it about me. My heart raced, and I struggled to get out any words.

"Was I wrong?" she asked, biting her lip.

That action snapped me out of it, and I gave her one of my genuine smiles, not the one I practiced for the cameras.

"Nope. You're right, Slugger. Your turn."

She scowled at the nickname but didn't correct me. Good, because she'd slugged the crap out of my heart. I wasn't sure if I'd recover from it. The name stayed.

"I have an older brother, I have two tattoos, and my favorite fruit is mango."

"Hmm," I murmured, searching her face for clues. Her eyes sparkled, and even the awful plane light seemed to shimmer off her hair, making it look like a halo. "I also don't think *you* have a tattoo, much less two."

"Wrong," she hummed, doing a little shimmy in the seat I adored. "I do have two tattoos."

"So, no brother?" I asked, curious, trying not to think about where she had tattoos and failing miserably.

"Also, true. It's the mangoes. Allergic to them, actually." Her face pinked at the information, and I squirreled it away, liking that she'd told me something real about herself. My heart beat erratically in my chest, my desire morphing into genuine attraction.

Shut up, heart. Go away.

"Your turn again since you stumped me," I said, when I couldn't shake my feelings.

She bit her lip, tapping her finger against her chin as she thought, slowly making me addicted to her little moves. She returned her other arm to the console, pressing it against mine after her victory dance. Her lips tilted as she decided, and I wanted to trace them with my fingers.

"My first time was on my wedding night, I've only been able to orgasm with one partner, and…" She paused, her blue eyes jumping up to mine. "I've never had a one-night stand."

I gulped, her eyes holding mine with an intensity I didn't know what to do with. Shit, she'd just upped the ante by making it sexual, and I was desperate to know the truth. My pulse jumped beneath my skin, and my palms sweated, itching to touch her.

"Your first time wasn't on your wedding night," I said, praying it wasn't true. I didn't want her to be married.

She grinned, my heart falling back into my chest at her nod.

"You're right. I actually left my groom at the altar. Ergo, no wedding night." She cleared her throat; something off about her statement, but I let it go. We'd both moved closer, our heads only a few inches apart as we shared our secrets.

"I can't believe you've only had one orgasm."

"Engh, I said *one* partner. There were *a lot* that night, and I'm very adept with my own hand, but no one else seems to have the magic touch." She blinked slowly, dropping her eyes to my lips. My cock jerked, liking her look. "Your turn," she said softly, her breath ghosting across my skin. I looked up and held her eyes as I thought.

"I'm not a player, I just learned I had a daughter, and I'm always the one dumped." I sucked in a breath, not believing I'd just shared those truths with her. It had to be this weird feeling between us, where our secrets felt safe in this little bubble of anonymity. Her eyes held mine, something shifting in them as the blue deepened.

"I… I'm not sure. They all feel…" She didn't finish, but I couldn't help the heart flutter I got at her words. They all felt true? God, I hoped that was what she meant.

"Take a guess." I shrugged, trying to act nonchalant, not holding my breath as I waited for the next reveal of how she viewed me. Did she see past the cocky guy I pretended to be?

"Hmm, I guess the daughter part. But, I dunno…" She shook her head, her hair flying and wafting an enchanting fragrance of floral and dark undertones into my nose and raising goosebumps all over my body. Damn, that smelled intoxicating.

My heart flopped in my chest, my stomach feeling tight and like a thousand ants were running through it. I wanted to correct her, for her to know this truth about me.

"Nope, that's true," I said before I could stop myself.

"No way!" Her eyes widened. "Are you… are you with the mother?"

My heart thumped, and I smiled, realizing she'd been worried about the same thing.

"No. I'm single. You?" I asked, deciding to put it out there.

"So single," she groaned but smiled for a second before it dropped. "That, um, sounds heavy. Do you want to talk about it?"

Her question surprised me. Yet it shouldn't have. Everything about this girl had been the exact opposite of what I was used to. Her question swirled around us, and I realized I did want to talk to her about this. She made me curious and I liked it.

"It's been an adjustment. I've been away for a few weeks, working on myself. Her mother's a girl I dated a few years back, and she only told me on New Year's Day."

"Wait, she just told you now? Years later?" If her brows could join her hairline, they would; they were that far up her forehead.

"Yep. Shitty, right? I wasn't in the best place when she told me. It was the punch to the gut I needed. I booked myself..." I trailed off, debating how much to share. Something about this girl made me want to blurt out everything. Which was so dangerous for me.

See, heart, go the fuck away. Dick, you're up.

"You don't have to tell me anything you don't want to, but I'll listen and not judge if you want a non-biased perspective."

How could I refuse an offer like that?

"I don't usually talk about stuff," I admitted.

"I get it. That marriage I ran away from? Yeah, well, that night, I slept with my brother's best friend and then denied it meant anything the next day to my brother when he found us in bed. I took my honeymoon time off and went to visit my aunt in Greece and kind of stayed there for three years." She cringed; her cheeks rosy as she divulged. "I went to therapy for over a year, so I get needing to work on things. No shame about it from me."

Her truth made me like her more, and her earlier behavior made more sense. She was nervous about returning home. I knew that feeling well. I nodded, accepting her answer.

"I was injured last year, but I didn't tell my job, afraid it would jeopardize my position. However, I was moved to a different location because I wasn't performing at my standard. I tried to manage the pain with booze, but that only made things worse. I had to eventually admit I needed help and come clean. The injury was worse than I thought, and they wanted me to have surgery, but I was stubborn and said no, that I didn't want to jeopardize everything for something that might not help." I shook my head, sighing at my arrogance. "Once Jas told me about my daughter, I booked the surgery the next day and haven't had a drop of alcohol since. It felt important to get my shit together before I tried to be her father."

"That's brave of you," she said, again shocking me.

"Thank you. It hasn't been easy, especially not drinking. Still, I pushed through the physical therapy and did all the rehab they wanted, even if it felt dumb." I rolled my eyes good-naturedly at myself. "I have a physical in two days to see if I can return to my old position. It feels like everything is hanging on that... if I pass it, my life will be back on track."

It felt wrong not to disclose my job as a professional athlete, but I didn't want to sully the intimacy between us with the knowledge I was a baseball player, even if that title didn't hold as much merit as it used to for me.

I was on the brink of being an injured, washed-up first baseman headed for retirement if I didn't get my act together.

"So, why did she wait so long?" she asked, pulling me back to our topic of conversation.

"Some bullshit about not wanting to interfere with my life, but now she doesn't want to be a full-time mom anymore. She has a modeling opportunity that will take her away for six months. So now, she needs me." I rolled my eyes at Jasmine's lame excuse.

"A model. Why am I not surprised?" She scoffed, but her earlier vitriol had disappeared. "It sucks that she stole those years from you. How old is your daughter?"

Hearing her say those words softened my heart more. How easily she accepted that I could be a father and had a daughter. Up until now, it had felt like a dream. A messed up one, but a dream nonetheless.

"She's four. Her name's Willow."

"That's a cute name."

"I didn't have anything to do with it, but I was glad it wasn't something cutesy like Braylin or anything that ended in Leigh."

She chuckled, making my insides all warm. My heart fluttered again, my pulse kicking up as I stared at her.

"Want to see a picture?"

"I'd love to." She leaned closer as I pulled out my phone and opened the album I'd made for Willow. Jas sent me pics when I asked, willing to give me whatever I needed if I agreed to take her. Willow's cute head of dark curls appeared, her smile big, and her eyes almost the same color green as mine.

"She has your eyes." Her voice was soft, her words more wistful than I thought possible. "Have you met her yet?"

"No. I'm meeting her in a few days. I'll admit, I'm a bit nervous. I don't have much experience with kids."

"She's probably just as nervous. Just talk to her and get to know her. Kids are a pretty good judge of character."

"I hope so." I put my phone away, the conversation going silent, but it didn't feel awkward.

"I—" Her words were cut off as the plane dropped, the turbulence coming from nowhere. The fasten seat belt sign flashed overhead as lights flickered around us.

My slugger's eyes were wide, the pupils so small I worried she was having a stroke or something. One hand gripped the armrest, the other my arm, leaving fingernail imprints. I peeled it off and put her hand in mine, squeezing it. She turned to me, her breasts moving with each breath she took. They were short and quick, and I knew she was on the verge of hyperventilating.

"Slugger, tell me something else that's true," I tried.

She shook her head, her hair sending that intoxicating smell to me again. Panic clawed at me, and the need to drink again hit me, but I pushed it away. I didn't need it. I could do this. I needed to get her out of her head. Anger and lust worked well for me.

"Are you sure you've only had one person bring you to orgasm?" I baited. "I'm not sure you were being honest."

She nodded her head, but no words came out.

"I dunno. I bet I could make you come," I whispered, putting our lips a centimeter apart. She stopped, watching me as she sucked in short breaths.

"I could get you off right here and prove it."

She looked around, her eyes growing more aroused as she calmed down. Her hand still gripped mine, but her other one wasn't as tight on the armrest.

"What do you say, Slugger? Up for a dare now?"

She shook her head, but I wouldn't let that stop me. I pulled the blanket out of the side compartment and dropped it over our laps like we were cuddling, adding a pillow on her other side to block the view.

"Doubt you even have two tattoos," I taunted.

She narrowed her eyes at me, but still, no words came.

"It's for the best that I don't make you come. Then you'd lose at two truths and a lie and have to tell me thank you again, and we both know you're incapable of doing that."

"Ass," she spat, her voice a hiss. "You couldn't make me come even if I was already turned on and ready to go."

"Is that a yes to the dare then?" I asked, lifting my brow.

The plane dropped again, and more screams and shouts sounded behind us. Slugger's eyes widened more, her breathing increasing as she held my hand to her chest, slotted right between her boobs. It was a nice place to be, but I was more concerned about her passing out.

"Say yes, and I'll make you forget about this, Slugger."

"Yes," she whispered, her eyes pleading to make the panic disappear.

Sliding my free hand under the blanket, it was easy to

reach beneath her sweats since they were so baggy. I brushed against her silk panties, wishing I could see them. Her body trembled, and she closed her eyes as I continued down. The front of her panties had a wet patch, and I prayed it was from me, from our banter. It had been sexy as hell, and I wanted to know I had caused that reaction for her.

Pushing aside the soaked material, my fingers skimmed over her, feeling her plump lips and the slight smattering of curls. I bent my finger, rubbing against her clit as she sucked in a breath. I leaned back against the seat, my mouth next to her ear. I hadn't even kissed this girl yet, but I wanted her, unlike anyone I'd ever wanted.

"You're drenched, Slugger. Have you been having naughty thoughts about me?" I asked, sliding my finger through her wetness.

"Mmhmm," she murmured, rocking on my finger, her eyes closed.

I took her earlobe between my teeth, sucking on it as I pressed in more, curling my finger as I pushed in and out of her wet heat and hit her G-spot. She whimpered, making my cock hard as granite from that slight sound.

"Fuck, you feel good wrapped around my finger. I bet you'd be even tighter wrapped around my dick. I'd fuck you so good, baby. We'd do it all night long in every position until our muscles hurt."

"Please," she whispered, her eyes opening and begging me for something.

"You want to come, Slugger?" I asked.

"Mmhmm," she hummed, tightening her grip on my forearm. The plane continued to dip around us, people shouting and cursing as we traveled through a storm, the overhead speaker crackling on and off.

I ignored it all, focused only on the girl in the seat next to me and wanting her to come. I needed it more than I ever thought possible, wanting to protect her and make her feel good at the same time.

"Can you take two?" I asked.

She nodded, her eyes not leaving mine, our hands still intertwined and held between her breasts.

Pressing two fingers in, I held back my groan at how good she felt. Her eyes closed, and her head fell back as I plunged into her, her arousal thick and covering my hand now. Flicking her clit with my thumb, I felt her body tense as her walls tightened around my fingers, clamping around them as an orgasm rolled through her. She turned, muffling her moan on my shoulder as she came.

It was hot as fuck, and I barely managed not to come in my pants.

She panted in my ear, her whimpers living on in my mind as she ground herself on my fingers. When she pulled away from oversensitivity, I withdrew my fingers slowly, lifting them to my mouth and hoping no one watched. Odds were they were too focused on their own panicked state to pay attention to us, but I didn't care enough to ensure it was true.

"Wow," she breathed, her eyes wide and blown. "That was… wow."

"You said that already," I teased, laughing.

"We've made it through that patch of storm, ladies and gentlemen, but we'll have to make an emergency landing. The storm's too unpredictable to continue. I'm sorry for the inconvenience. The flight attendants can help you find a new flight when we land. Hold on tight; it's going to be a bumpy landing."

My seat partner turned to me, her eyes wide at the news. I knew I should be more upset about the detour, but something inside of me felt excited about the opportunity that presented itself.

More time with my slugger.

My dick twitched, the tip leaking precum at the thought of more.

I didn't know when I'd started to call her mine, but she was, and I wanted to taste more of her, to see her naked, spread out for me, her blush traveling all the way to her toes.

And now it seemed I had a way to get it.

I might be a cocky asshole, but I was also possessive. I went after what I wanted. And there was no doubt I wanted her.

My slugger would be mine before the night was over.

"By the way, my name's Luke." I'd thought of giving her the fake one I used, but after what we shared, that felt cheap.

"Hi, Luke. I'm Bee."

She smiled, stealing my breath, and I knew I was so fucking doomed.

CHAPTER
FOUR

BLAKE

THE PLANE LANDED WITH SEVERAL HARD BUMPS. MY HAND WAS still firmly gripped by the golden god of seat 4A… Luke. Despite being terrified, my body was languid from the orgasm, at odds with how my nerves felt. I didn't know which way was up or down, but I couldn't muster enough energy to care.

Gah, I'd forgotten how good an orgasm could feel.

"We've arrived, ladies and 'gents."

Everyone clapped, sounds of relief echoing around us as people took off their seat belts.

"Where are we?"

"Somewhere in Georgia. I didn't get the city. I was a little occupied," Luke said, winking.

My face blushed, and I looked out the window. It was dark, rain pelting the side of the plane as lightning flashed in the distance. Despite all of that, I felt safe. Okay, even. It had to be the orgasm, right?

"Come on, let's stick together and figure out our options," Luke said as he stood, grabbing my bag from under the seat.

I took it from him in a daze and slipped it over my

shoulder. He grabbed his from the overhead compartment and reached down, taking my hand and linking our fingers. He did it so naturally that it took me a few seconds to notice.

The flight attendant who'd helped me with vomitgate gave me a knowing grin and wink as we passed. I returned a bashful smile, unsure I wanted to know what the wink was for. Was it just because he held my hand? Or had people seen us? Had I been loud? Did I have that 'I just had an orgasm' look? *Was there a look?*

As much as I hated that after only a few hours on my own, a guy I'd just met was rescuing me and taking charge, I couldn't drop his hand or step away. My golden god had a magnetism about him, and I'd fallen in head first despite all attempts to hate him.

Luke had felt safe from the first moment he touched me, even if I hadn't liked it. And while that underlying feeling was there, he also pushed me out of my comfort zone. I hadn't worried about what he thought of me for one second, telling him exactly how I felt from the get-go. It was refreshing.

And I wanted to keep feeling this for as long as possible. I'd take whatever I could until this moment between two strangers ended. Then we'd go back to our everyday life, never to see each other again.

Him to his new daughter, and me to my new job.

I didn't want to think how sad that made me. But on the flip side, it had been hours since I'd thought about Hawk. At least I'd been great at finding distractions with texting strangers and planegasms.

You know, easy stuff to replicate.

"Do you need to call someone?" he asked as we stood in line. The airport was small, with only a few airlines. They all had long lines, and I scanned over them, remembering he'd asked me something.

I met his green eyes, and he smiled at me, stealing my breath.

"Oh. Um. Probably my brother. He was going to pick me up."

I didn't know if I imagined it, but his shoulders dropped slightly at that news. The corners of my mouth lifted as I pulled out my phone, happiness flooding me that we seemed to be on the same page. A few text notifications lit up my home screen, but I ignored them and hit Bryce's number.

"Hey, Sis. Have you already landed? I'm just about to head to the airport," he said as he answered.

"Yeah, about that. We had to make an emergency landing."

"Shit. You okay?" The noise in the background stopped, and I had his full attention.

"Um, as good as I can be. There were some crazy storms. Lots of turbulence. It wasn't safe to continue."

"Where are you? Do you want me to come get you tonight?"

I looked around, trying to find a clue to what city we were in. I poked my new friend when I couldn't find out anything. He lifted his brow, his eyes sparkling.

"What city are we in?"

"Augusta."

"Georgia?" Bryce asked, apparently hearing the answer.

"Uh, yeah. How far is that?" I asked, feeling lost after being overseas for so long. Geography, smeography. Was it wrong I hoped it was far so he couldn't come?

"Around four and half hours." I could hear the grimace in his voice, but I sighed in relief.

"Oh, poo. That's far. It's totally fine. I can wait until the storm clears and get a plane out in the morning," I said quickly, hoping it wasn't obvious.

"You sure? Will you be okay there on your own? You know I'll drive through a hurricane for you, Blanket."

The warmth from my brother's admission had tears pricking my eyes, the emotions from the flight and orgasm swirling, pushing me to the brink of being overwhelmed. I sucked in a breath.

"I'm good. Promise. The airline's putting us in a hotel, so I'll be fine once I get some sleep and a shower." I rubbed my temples, the image of a bed and warm shower sounding like heaven. "Crap. I don't have any clothes."

"Um, do I even want to know?" I could hear the chuckle already in his voice.

"Let's just say it involved a messy child and vomit. I'm wearing what I can only assume are leftovers from flights, considering my pants were made for a giant and my top a doll."

"Why am I not surprised? You always seem to get yourself into the funniest situations."

"Not on purpose!" I laughed, feeling lighter talking to Bryce.

"Grab something from the gift shop?"

"I think you highly overestimate the capabilities of this airport." I glanced around, not spotting much other than a dead coffee shop. "It's fine. I'll figure something out. I'll let you know what I find out in the morning."

"All right. Be safe, little Sis. Can't wait to see you."

"Ditto, big Bro. Love you more than cheddar cheese."

"Pulling out the big guns! Well, I love you more than red gummy bears."

"Damn. That's a lot." I smiled, feeling better.

"You know it. See you tomorrow."

"Bye."

I hung up, taking a deep breath as I glanced back up. Luke, Mr. Golden from seat 4A, was watching me, a soft look on his face.

"You're close with your brother, huh?"

"Yeah. It's a long story, but he saved my life once, and it's always been us against the world. We haven't seen each other much the past three years, so I'm excited to be in the same city with him again for a change."

"That's nice. I never had that. I always envied people with close family relationships."

The reminder he was an only child surfaced, but before I could ask more questions, it was his turn. He placed his arms on the counter, his charming smile in full force as he addressed the airline attendant.

"Hello, ma'am. I hope your evening hasn't been too stressful with all this weather."

The harsh woman melted, her face changing into a smile as she listened to him. Even I wanted to lean forward and have him talk more. He had a voice that soothed something inside you while promising dark things. It oddly made you feel safe and warm. It was a dangerous combo.

"Really? That's unfortunate," he said, returning me to the present. I'd missed everything else they'd said. He turned, his eyes meeting mine.

"Um, so." His cheeks were rosy as he cleared his throat, some bashfulness emerging. "There's only one room left."

"Oh." I blinked. Shit. What was I going to do now? He took my hand.

"I don't want to presume anything or make you feel unsafe, but I don't think you should stay in this airport overnight. We could, um, share the room if you're okay with that?"

Relief surged through me at his offer. I noticed he hadn't offered to give it up for me, but I honestly didn't want him to. His solution was seductive, giving me the choice without putting me on the spot. Clever.

I cleared my throat, hoping my cheeks would cool off soon. He offered to share a room, but it didn't mean he wanted to have sex with me! One orgasm, and I was gaga for this golden guy already.

But... one bed? That was a sign. Just like in all those romances I read.

"I'd be okay with that," I said, somehow managing not to sound like a drowned cat.

His green eyes sparkled, sending tiny shivers through me, as they promised to make it worth my while. My mind blanked as he took care of the hotel and food vouchers, analyzing everything that could happen in a shared hotel room.

Was I ready for this? Could I have sex with a practical stranger? Was I a one-night-stand type of girl? What if it was terrible?

I shut my thoughts down. It was past time for thinking. I'd have to find out because this was exactly what I needed.

Once Luke had all the information, he retook my hand, linking our fingers like he'd done it all his life. His fingers were long, with a bit of roughness to them. But I didn't mind. In fact, I liked it. They reminded me of my dad's from wearing a glove and batting so many days out of the year.

The airport blurred as we walked, and the sounds and lights escaped my notice. It probably wasn't wise to stay with someone I'd just met. Regardless, considering he fingered me to orgasm as the plane went through turbulence, I didn't know if there were any reservations left for me to have. I guess orgasms were my test of character in a guy. It was a bit of an inconvenient way to measure, but I wouldn't complain about the results.

"Come on, Slugger," he said, smiling back at me as he pulled me out into the rain. We ran together, avoiding puddles, our bags smacking against us with each step. I didn't even care that he called me Slugger. I wanted to hate the nickname, but I didn't. I really, really didn't.

A bus was parked at the curb, and we climbed up on it, our clothes soaking wet from the little jaunt. Awesome. The only set of clothing I had to my name was now drenched.

Luke smirked as he took in my pebbled nipples, his eyes heating as they traveled over me. My second-hand tank top had suctioned to my body, exposing everything. I wanted to pull my jacket closed, but something about the look in his eyes stopped me.

I felt brazen as if I could do anything.

CHAPTER
FIVE

BLAKE

THE DRIVE TO THE HOTEL WAS SHORT, AND WHEN WE ARRIVED, I realized why there weren't many rooms available. Calling it a hotel was generous, and I wasn't sure if the term applied since this seemed more like a three-story home with rooms to rent.

But beggars couldn't be choosers.

We trudged into Triple Platypus Lodge with the other passengers stuck there for the night. Surprisingly, there was a gift shop, so I motioned to Luke that I would check it out while he went to the desk. The fact I didn't know his last name didn't bother me. It was the smart thing to do if I was spending the night with him. But something about not knowing felt more seductive in a plane-one-night-stand kind of way.

The gift shop didn't have a lot of options, but there were leggings, hoodies, t-shirts, and, blessedly, hygiene products. Nothing was sexy about traveling for a whole day. Grabbing a random magnet, chocolate, a stuffed platypus, and everything I'd need for the night, I took my purchases to the counter.

By the time I had everything bagged up, Luke waited for me at the entrance. He smiled as I neared, and I shyly held out the platypus for him, hoping I wasn't being too presumptuous.

"What's this?" he asked, taking it, giving me an odd look.

"Something to give Willow." I shrugged, my cheeks heating. I wondered if I'd overstepped.

"Oh." He swallowed, staring at the platypus with new eyes, and nodded. His green eyes were glassy when he looked back up. "Thank you, Bee. That's very kind."

Grinning, I wrapped my arm in his, feeling more confident as we climbed the stairs.

"What horrors do you think we'll discover in our room? Floral wallpaper? Porcelain dolls? Taxidermy?"

Luke snorted, shaking his head. "No clue. You have a creative imagination, Slugger."

I shrugged, liking he saw me that way. "Thanks."

We came to the door, and he held up the key, letting out a nervous chuckle. Placing it in the lock, he turned and pushed open the door. It squeaked and hit the wall with a thud. Complete darkness greeted us, and we turned to one another with wide eyes.

"Ladies first." Luke motioned for me to enter, a cheeky smile covering his kissable lips.

"Fine, use me as the sacrifice," I huffed, pulling my phone out and using the flashlight app to find the light switch. Flicking it on, the light cascaded around us and brought the room into view.

"Golf?" Luke's nose scrunched up, his brow pinched as he took in the decor. It had a wood lodge look with exposed beams, but the decor was all golf with platypuses mixed in. I didn't get it, and it hurt my eyes if I stared at it too long, but it could've been worse.

"It's different." I chuckled, no longer able to hold it back.

"At least it isn't dolls." I shuddered, and he nodded, agreeing with me.

"How about you shower and change, and I'll grab us some food in the meantime?"

"Sounds good." I smiled and stepped toward the bathroom, but Luke stopped me, placing his hand on my arm.

"Wait," he said, stepping into the bathroom. "Okay. It's safe."

"Oh, so now you care about the boogeyman?" I laughed, then patted his arm. "Thanks for looking out for me. *This* time," I teased.

"Anytime. You make it easy, Bee."

Despite my teasing tone, something in his was sincere. We stood staring at one another, the tension increasing between us like static coming to life. We both took a step closer toward one another, our bodies pressed together. The wetness of his shirt had me shivering, and I closed my eyes as I took a breath.

Luke's hand smoothed across my chin, lifting it. I kept my eyes closed, feeling his warm breath across my face. He pressed a small kiss on my eyelashes, then my nose, before rubbing his with mine. I'd never felt so precious before.

His lips softly caressed mine with the lightest pressure, as our mouths met. That slight touch lit a fire, sending warmth through me and jumpstarting my heart.

"I'll be back," he whispered, not taking anything else and leaving me a panting mess. The door shut a second later, and I opened my eyes, my breaths coming out of me in large gulps.

"Shit. I'm in trouble," I whispered, stepping into the comfort of the bathroom and shutting the door.

In a daze, I turned on the water and stripped out of my wet clothes, hanging them across the towel bar to dry. Steam billowed out, so I stepped in and warmed my cool skin, silently going through the motions. Thank God taking a shower was muscle memory. Using the kit I'd bought, I washed my hair and did a quick rinse of my body. The products smelled of citrus and vanilla, and while they were new, they had a clean and invigorating smell that I liked.

Once cleaned, I turned off the water, mindful that I didn't want to use all the hot water before Luke could shower. I had no clue what type of water heater lodges had. Using the tiny comb in the kit, I hacked away at my tangles, giving up halfway through them, and sat on the toilet, my arms aching. Nothing like brushing your hair to make your arm strength feel inadequate.

My phone vibrated on the counter, and I remembered I had messages earlier.

Opening it, I snorted and laughed at the pictures my accidental texters had sent. Pitcher sent a picture of a spotted dick fish over his drool-worthy abs, and Catcher's was a pile of junk over his butt that said, "I got all the junk in my trunk."

Covering my mouth with one hand, I laughed hard as my body shook from the force. When I recovered, I typed out a response, smiling the whole time.

> Blake: Well done, boys. I love the creativity.
>
> Blake: I'm slightly sad I didn't get the real things.
>
> Blake: But in due time.

Their message bubbles instantly danced at the bottom, creating the same feeling bubbling up inside me. I crossed my leg over the other, biting my lip as I waited. Part of me felt guilty for being flirty with two guys while another was outside the door, but I wasn't doing anything wrong since labels weren't used with us. Right?

Catcher: Due time. That sounds promising.
Did your flight go okay?

Pitcher: I tried to send the real thing, but the image was too big to upload.

Catcher: Really, dude?

Blake: Flight. Humph. That was an epic disaster.

Pitcher: Ignore my lousy attempt at humor.
Are you okay?

Blake: I think so.

Catcher: What happened?

Blake: First, there was vomitgate.

Pitcher: I'm gagging in response.

Catcher: That doesn't bode well for a plane.

Blake: Nope. My clothes were ruined, and I ended up with borrowed leftovers that don't fit.

Blake: Thankfully, I was given a different seat. Right next to the pretentious guy who had bumped into me earlier.

Catcher: Bumped how?

Blake: Knocked his bag into me, made me drop my stuff. Barely apologized.

It felt wrong to say that now, but it was still valid for that part of the story.

Pitcher: Did you put him in his place?

Blake: Yeah. I think so. We found a truce and talked.

Catcher: What else happened then?

Blake: Crazy storm. Lots of turbulence.

Pitcher: My stomach is already queasy. Hold me, G!

Catcher: There, there. Now, back to the mystery girl. You okay? Really?

Blake: Yeah. I am. We had to land at some small regional airport, and I'm staying with my seatmate.

Pitcher: As in overnight?

Blake: Yeah, there was only one room left.

Pitcher: Sounds fishy.

Catcher: Is this someone you trust? Do you feel safe?

I didn't know these two, but their concern for my safety was endearing.

Pitcher: Though, if it's a move, then baller on his part, but I'm suddenly feeling guilty.

Catcher: Give it a few minutes, and it will go away.

Pitcher: I'd be offended if it wasn't true. But what if I'm growing, G?

Catcher: In your pants? Doesn't count.

Pitcher: Come check to make sure.

Catcher: I'm not getting you anything. You have two legs. Get your own water.

Pitcher: Fine. Someday, I'll find a roommate who treats me like the princess I am.

Catcher: *eye roll* Got the princess part right.

Blake: I take it you're roommates?

Blake: And yes, I oddly do feel safe. Thanks for checking, though.

Catcher: Since freshman year of college. Going on seven years now. I can't seem to shake this fungus. I mean, Fun guy.

Pitcher: Haha. I am a fun guy and also a hallucinogenic like a shroom, so the joke's on you.

"You need anything, Slugger?" Luke asked from outside the door.

"Nope. Almost done. Sorry."

Blake: Be good, boys. I'll send a reward tomorrow. Night, fellas.

I turned off my phone before I became distracted and pulled on the new leggings and t-shirt I'd bought in the gift shop. The shirt was more see-through than I'd thought, my headlights on full display. Eep. I quickly brushed my teeth and grabbed everything, taking the evil comb.

"Hey," I said, halting at the glorious body on display. He'd changed into a pair of sweatpants, leaving his torso bare.

And fuck me. It was magnificent. I blinked, my cheeks flushing as I stared. Thankfully, my mouth hadn't fallen open.

He smirked, clearly liking my malfunction.

"They didn't have much selection in food; hope you like pizza." He patted the bed, giving me déjà vu from my night with Hawk.

A white dress. A wedding feast. A different hotel room.

Shaking my head to clear the images, I placed my belongings on the dresser and climbed onto the bed. It was now his turn to gulp as my nipples made their debut. Enjoying the attention, I attempted to comb the rest of my hair, getting frustrated halfway through.

"Would you like some help?"

"It's useless. I need a detangler or something, and this comb is for the creepy dolls missing from this room."

"Hold on, I might have something." He climbed off his side of the bed and bent over as he rifled through his luggage, giving me an excellent peek at his butt. He returned with a bottle and brush. "May I?"

"Um, sure."

I turned, uncertain what he could do, but was willing to admit my defeat with my hair. He sprayed the mist over my hair before he slowly combed through it.

"Another secret: I use a lot of hair products," he whispered, his hands soft in my hair.

"Well." I cleared my throat. "I'm happy for your high maintenance if it means my hair isn't a tangled ball. Plus, it smells good. I'll have to get the name of it."

He chuckled, the sound springing goosebumps across my body and making my nipples stand at attention, begging to be touched.

"There. Now, let's eat."

I turned, patting my hair, amazed at its silky smoothness. My cheeks blushed when I spotted the wet splotches on my shirt, making the material even more obscene.

"Fuck," he whispered when I turned, his eyes heating. "I'm suddenly hungry for something other than pizza."

His green eyes shimmered as he licked his lips, clearly implying me.

CHAPTER
SIX

LUKE

Despite my reputation as a cocky playboy, I didn't sleep around that much. Mostly because I didn't trust others easily, never had. Most of my life had been people using me for their gain, which had only increased as I became a professional baseball player.

Women wanted to bed me, not date me.

I became a square on their bingo card, a story to brag about to their friends. I wasn't considered a person, a man with feelings and my own insecurities—just a guy to fuck.

Most guys would guffaw at my plight, assuming I had it made and not understanding how meaningless sex took something from you that you could never get back. I hadn't cared in the beginning, but sex didn't heal me like I thought it would. Nor did having money and fame.

I learned the hard way what strings were attached and the lies people sold to get what they wanted. On top of the demons I already had, I'd turned to alcohol to drown it all away. I couldn't even remember the last time I'd had sex, sober.

Nerves shook me at that realization, hoping I wouldn't embarrass myself or, worse, suck at it now. My slugger blinked at me as I stared at her, hunger in my eyes for something other than carb-loaded cheese.

Bee's eyes were the prettiest blue I'd ever seen, and something told me even lousy sex with her would be better than my previous best.

It should terrify me to want her this much so soon when I didn't even know her last name. But it didn't. The connection between us went beyond names, and it felt, at this point, to learn more would only muddy what we had. The pureness of liking one another without the weight of who we were was breathtaking. Perhaps that was the chickenshit way of looking at this, but I wasn't brave enough to test my theory.

I wanted her, and breaking the spell felt like it would ruin it.

With my slugger, I wasn't Luke Olson—cocky first baseman, one wrong move away from losing his career.

I wasn't the son of an alcoholic or a codependent mother who couldn't stand on her own without a man.

Nor was I the man who did everything he could to change his past, hoping it was enough to remove the stench of not being good enough.

I wasn't even the soon-to-be-father of a four-year-old I hadn't met yet, scared shitless he would screw her up.

No, right now, I was just an average guy with a gorgeous girl in his room as they waited out a storm.

Moving the pizza to the nightstand, I watched her closely to ensure she wanted this. Her chest rose and fell in quick succession, her nipples on display with each lift. I knew it wasn't on purpose, her hair having soaked the material, but the view was the most erotic thing I'd ever seen.

"You're so beautiful," I whispered, cupping her jaw. She leaned into my touch, her eyelashes fluttering against her cheek. "I know we just met, but I feel this insane connection with you. Do you, Slugger?"

She nodded, humming.

"Look at me," I demanded, and her eyes snapped up to me. The dominant part of me preened at her obedience, and I barely held myself back from taking what I wanted.

Despite her not knowing who I was, I was still me and had to protect myself. I needed explicit consent so there were no misgivings.

"I want you, Slugger." I brushed her wet hair aside. "I've been thinking about you since you glared at me." I smiled as she leveled me with another. "Touching you on the plane and feeling you move against me was so hot, and I'm dying to feel more of that."

I moved closer, ghosting my lips against her neck. She whimpered, her fingers gripping my forearm. "I want to bring you to so many orgasms your throat is raw from screaming, and everyone on this floor, hell, in this lodge, knows how good I'm making you feel." She sucked in a breath, my cock twitching against my thigh at the sound. I swallowed down my groan, eager to see how much I could make her squirm. I tilted her chin back, holding her eyes.

"When you walk down in the morning, sore between your legs with my stubble burn all over you, I guarantee everyone will wish they were you. Because of the sounds you're going to make." I paused, licking my lips. "I can already tell they'll live rent-free in my head."

Her pupils dilated to the point the blue darkened like the bottom of the ocean. She stuck out her tongue to lick her lips, and that small peek of pink made me want to bite it. A growl vibrated in my chest without my permission.

"Before we get there, I need to hear you say you want that. That you're here with me in this connection and chemistry. Nothing is hotter than enthusiastic consent, and I need yours, Bee."

"I feel it, too. It scares me, but I want all of that, Luke. Even if my cheeks will be red in the morning." She blushed, giving me an idea of how she'd look, and the smug part of me relished in it, knowing it would be from *me*.

"Say yes, Bee."

"Yes, Luke."

The sound of my name on her lips made my cock twitch, and I couldn't hold back any longer. Sealing my mouth to hers for a real kiss this time, I didn't hesitate as I swirled my tongue and teased hers. She tasted like mint, the hint of her toothpaste lingering on her lips. I got lost in her taste, the kiss sending shivers through me with each swipe of her tongue.

Her mouth slanted over mine harder, pressing me back as she climbed into my lap, our kiss never breaking. With her straddling me, I could feel and touch her all I wanted, and I wasn't going to waste the opportunity. My hands tightened around her thighs before moving up her legs to her waist. Squeezing her hips, I slid my palm under her shirt. I swiped my thumb across the visible bare skin, and she sucked in a breath at the touch.

Taking the opportunity, I moved to her neck, leaving little nips and sucks as I traveled. The smell of the shampoo and body wash she'd used wasn't the same as on the plane, but it was still intoxicating, sending shivers of lightning through me as I inhaled it. My thumbs continued to trace her stomach, her skin soft and supple beneath me. She made little whimpers as I moved across her, but I couldn't stop. I needed to inhale everything about her.

My palms moved further up her shirt, coming into contact with the breasts that had been taunting me for hours. Tracing my thumb over her nipple, she sighed into my mouth, and I retook it, needing her lips back on mine. I cupped her breasts, their weight perfect in my hand, and squeezed and tweaked her nipples. Bee rocked into me, hitting my hard as granite cock in my joggers.

We moved perfectly together, instinctively letting our bodies take over the talking as we explored one another. Her hands landed on my chest, roaming up and down my muscles. I couldn't ever remember being this turned on, and we'd only kissed, barely even touched one another.

But I needed to feel her skin against mine, to see her tits in all their glory and not through the fabric of her wet shirt.

"Can I?" I asked, lifting the hem.

She nodded, and I narrowed my eyes until she responded, "Yes."

Removing the layer, I stared as her tits came into view. They were more magnificent than I imagined. They weren't large, but they were firm and soft, filling my hands perfectly. Her nipples were dark with a rosy hue.

"Wow," I whispered, my hands unable to stay put as I touched them, my thumb grazing over them. Her neck pinked, matching her cheeks at my praise and making me want to see her whole body in that color. She rocked into my touch, moaning, as I massaged her breasts.

Dropping my mouth down to one, I sucked it, biting the nipple lightly with my teeth. Bee's head tilted back, her wet strands tickling the tops of my joggers. Her nails ran down my chest, sending jolts of desire right to my cock, and it jerked again, precum wetting the fabric.

"Fuck, that feels good," I moaned, pulling off her for a second as I relished what she did to me. "I need more of you, Slugger."

Before she could respond, I stood with my hands under her ass and tossed her on the bed, my body covering her. I gripped her leggings, lowering them inch by inch as I took in the glorious skin it revealed.

Her tattoos came into view on her leg, and I paused, licking my lips. They were simple but hot all the same. I glanced up at her eyes.

"Color me surprised."

She giggled, the sound so pure and light that I lost my breath for a second. I wanted more of that sound. And despite deluding myself, I knew this wouldn't be enough. I'd only known this girl for a handful of hours, but I wanted more of her time.

So much more.

Once I had her completely free of her clothes, I scanned her entire body and committed it to memory. My dick tented my pants, my arousal evident as I licked my lips. Her pale skin was dotted with freckles, and I wanted to kiss every one of them. She was soft and curvy, her body beckoning me to worship her.

"Your turn," she breathed, sitting up and pushing down the band of my sweats. My cock bounced free, and she stuttered, licking her lips as her breathing hitched. She kept lowering my joggers, revealing my thighs, and stopping at the knees. Her eyes were big as she took in my full length; satisfaction and arrogance filtering through me at her look.

No matter how often a girl saw your dick, getting that reaction felt good.

Her hand reached out, gripping my length as she stroked me, her fingers barely wrapping around me. My head fell back as I let her take her time. Her hand was soft and smooth, her touch gentle.

"Um, do you have condoms?" she asked, her voice hesitant.

"Yes, but we don't need them yet. First, I need to feast on my meal."

Tackling her to the bed, I kissed her as I lost myself in her taste. Pulling apart was torture, but I had another destination in mind. I took my time as I mapped out her body, leaving my mark all over her. I didn't want this to be the only time, but I wanted her to never forget me if it was. I knew I wouldn't forget her. She'd imprinted on my heart, and I wasn't sure how to act like she hadn't.

But that was future Luke's problem. Right now, I needed to taste her.

I finally reached the apex of her legs, her body writhing and trembling on the bed from my torture. Her pussy glistened, and I'd never seen anything as tempting in my life. My cock pressed into the mattress, and I moved to get some friction on it, the need to rail into her stronger than I'd thought possible.

Diving in, I licked up her center as her taste exploded across my tongue. I held her thighs down, my hands clamping on them as she moved, leaving fingerprints in their wake. Sucking and thrusting my tongue, I devoured her as cum covered my face. Her panting and moans filled the room, and I ran my thumb over her clit, her back arching at the touch. Plunging one finger in, I wasn't shocked when she spasmed around me, her orgasm hitting her at full force.

"That's two," I said, smug as fuck.

Lifting, I pushed my joggers the rest of the way off and reached for the condom. Rolling it on, I lifted her hips up to me. She seemed dazed but let me position her as I notched my dick at her drenched entrance. In one move, I slid in and stilled as she squeezed me. It was the best feeling in the world.

Better than winning a game. Better than a home run. Better than drinking.

Being inside my slugger was a heaven I hadn't known existed until right this second. If I could stay right here in this moment, I wasn't sure if anything else would ever live up to it.

But of course, I was wrong a second later, as I shifted and plunged back in, feeling it all over again. Her walls squeezed me, her moans filled my ears as she rutted against me, her hands gripping my arms that held her hips. We moved together, our bodies knowing exactly how to communicate with one another as we chased our release.

Flipping her around, I pulled her back to my chest as I kneeled and banded my arm around her. With small thrusts, I slowed us down, not wanting to come just yet.

"You feel better than I thought possible," I whispered, moving in and out in shallow pumps.

"So. Do. You." She sighed, her body boneless in my arms, her hands gripping me to her. Tilting her head back, she sucked on my neck, leaving a hickey of her own.

I didn't usually like them, not wanting to mess up my skin for anyone. But for her, I did. I wanted people to know she claimed me just as much as I claimed her.

When the pressure had built higher, I couldn't avoid it any longer. Dropping her onto her hands, I gripped her hips as I pulled further out and slammed back in.

"Yes. Fuck me hard, Luke. Slam your cock into me," she urged, making me almost combust at her words.

"Jesus, Slugger. The mouth on you is almost as hot as your pussy."

"Make me feel good, Luke. I want to scream your name. *I need to*," she pleaded, her eyes wide with desire. Her hands gripped the comforter; her back arched as she looked over her shoulder at me. She pressed herself back, and that was it. The last of my control snapped, and I pulled back, slamming into her.

"Luuukkkeee," she belted, making my name sound like the Holy Grail.

My rhythm became sloppy and disjointed as I chased my release, her body melding perfectly to me. Even wearing a condom, she felt incredible, and I knew this wouldn't be the only time we did this tonight. I needed her in all the positions until I could no longer stand. I didn't care that opening day was soon; I'd be willing to be sore for more of her.

"Fuck, I'm coming, Bee," I yelled as she tightened, her body sucking me in and not letting me go. Her muscles tensed as she screamed, her words unintelligible as she released her cry, her body vibrating around me as she came, my own release meeting hers. I pumped into her, my body slowing as everything ignited around me.

I barely managed not to fall on top of her as I pulled out, tying off the condom and tossing it into the trash. I wrapped my arm around her, pulling her to my chest as we both lay there, catching our breath. Our naked bodies felt right against one another, and I smoothed my hand down her side, just wanting to touch her.

"You do have a tattoo," she said, tracing the small dancing baseball I'd gotten during my rookie year on a dare.

"Yup." I chuckled. "Not that cool, though."

"I dunno. It has a certain appeal."

We traced one another's bodies with our fingertips in a lazy haze.

"That's three by the way."

"Hmm, so it is. What number are you trying to get to?" she asked, her voice teasing.

"So many you lose count."

"But first, pizza, then the next round," she said.

Laughing, I nodded, kissing her forehead before I rolled over and grabbed the food. It was cold, but it was some of the best pizza I'd ever had. We ate it naked in bed, in a weird golf room.

"Oh, I got chocolate," she said, getting up and grabbing it out of her bag. I loved watching her ass move as she walked. She grabbed the bar and smiled, shaking her hips as she returned. Her phone vibrated on the table, and she paused, glancing at the name on the screen.

"One second. It's my brother again."

She picked up, giving me a smile with her eyes as she answered. I didn't pay attention to the conversation; I just enjoyed watching her as she talked with him. She was obviously close to her brother, her whole face lighting up as they spoke. She grabbed a pen and the lodge paper, writing down a few things before she hung up.

"Everything okay?" I asked when she returned to bed, ripping open the chocolate.

"Yep. He just wanted to give me some homework for the plane tomorrow. I'm not sure who's more excited, me or him."

"It sounds like he missed you. Do you have any other siblings?" I knew I was entering dangerous territory, asking real questions, but I wanted to learn more.

"Nope. Just us. Well. Technically, I have a half-sibling on the way. My dad remarried last year. His bride is only a few years older than Bry. It's completely ridiculous, but I can't be mad because, of course, she's super nice."

"Was that hard for you when your parents divorced?" I took a piece of chocolate she offered, placing it on my tongue.

"Yes and no. Our family had been through so much before that it was almost a relief. However, I carried the guilt around for a while, believing I was the cause. What about you?"

I wanted to ask more, but could recognize a diversion when I heard it.

"It was just my mom and me mostly. Dad skipped out when I was young, and Mom had a handful of awful boyfriends over the years, never able to keep one for long. Nothing to write home about, though."

I shrugged, my words flat. It was so much more than that, but talking about my childhood was the last thing I wanted right now as I lay naked in a bed with a beautiful girl.

"Hmm, I wonder if your kisses will taste like chocolate now," I said, growling as I pounced on her, bringing the mood back up. She giggled, and I filed the sound away as my second favorite.

Over the next few hours, we explored one another in every way possible. I was amazed my dick managed to rebound that often if I was being honest. After our last round, we decided to shower to rid ourselves of the cum and sweat before finally going to bed.

"Oh, I left my stuff on the dresser. Can you grab it?" she asked, stepping into the steam.

"Yeah, of course."

Walking out into the room, I searched for the bathroom kit when the pad of paper she'd written on caught my eye. I blinked, not believing what I saw.

Three names were on the pad: #13 West, #7 Jameson, and #24 Olson.

Fuck. Why the hell was my name and number on her pad? Why was she doing research on me? Wasn't that what she said?

Too many thoughts exploded in my head as feelings of betrayal rushed me. I couldn't stay here a second longer without making a scene. The urge to drink roared to life to numb it all away, and my hands trembled with the need to make this feeling disappear.

She wasn't any different. Just another woman wanting to use me. To make a fool of me.

Packing all my stuff, I pulled on my pants and shoes, not caring about my shirt, and hurried out of the room.

"Luke?" she called from the bathroom, making me pause as the memories of the night flashed through my mind.

Damn. She'd been a good actress. I'd actually believed her. The lengths people went to amazed me. Though, it really shouldn't shock me as much as it did.

Had the whole thing been orchestrated? The airport? The vomit? The seat?

Everything raced through my head, making me sick, and pushed me to take the last few steps out the door and down the hall. I ran down the stairs, pulling on a shirt and not stopping as I made it to the first floor. Bee could deal with checking out. If that was even her name.

The sun peeked over the horizon; the storm had cleared. I

didn't know which direction the airport was, but I just needed to get away before I opened my heart anymore.

One thing was certain—her nickname still stood.

She'd swung at my heart and hit it full force like the slugger she was.

CHAPTER
SEVEN

BLAKE

Humming to myself, I danced under the water spray as I tried to think of ways to prolong my time with my golden guy. Spotting shampoo and soap in the shower, I decided not to wait for him to return and wash my hair now. That way, I could spend my time ogling him as water ran down his body.

Solid plan.

Lathering it in my hair, sounds of movement filtered through the door, and I moved out from the water as suds ran down my face.

"Luke?"

When there wasn't an answer, I opened my eyes to see if he'd entered the bathroom instead. The steam filled the space, but there wasn't anyone else there. It sounded like the latch of the main door closed. I frowned in confusion. Maybe he needed something?

Soap ran into my open eye, and I cursed, moving backward to rinse it out as it burned. The pain intensified, and I knew I'd have to take out my contact before I'd have any relief.

"Luke? You back? I need help."

With no answer, I quickly rinsed the remainder of the shampoo out of my hair as I blindly turned off the water and stepped out of the shower. I patted around for the towel I'd sat on the counter and wrapped it around my body. Peeking open my eyes, I pulled out my contact as the burning feeling spread. My eyes watered, and I bent at the faucet, cupping cold water to give myself an eyewash.

When it didn't burn as intensely, I turned off the faucet and disposed of the other contact. I had no extras, but at least I had my glasses. Except I'd forgotten how blind I was, the blurriness of an unfamiliar place made navigating it more difficult.

"Luke? Are you hiding? Heads up, I can't see, so no jumping out and scaring me," I joked as I stepped out into the room with my hands out in front of me.

Even with my near-blind state, I couldn't spot another person in the room. Concern filled me, my brow dipping as I stumbled over to my bag. The soap I'd requested still lay next to my things, making my frown deepen. What was going on?

Opening my bag, I dug into my front pocket and pulled out my glasses case. Once I had them on, I could see, but it didn't help the mystery in front of me. All of his things were gone.

His stupid designer bag.

The pile of clothes and shoes he'd tossed to one side of the bed.

Even the charger he'd been using for his phone.

The only trace that he'd been in this room was the condom wrappers and pizza boxes. Tears burned my eyes for an entirely different reason as I stared around the empty space.

He was gone. I'd been ghosted.

It shouldn't hurt this bad. We hadn't promised anything. But it felt so real.

He'd been the first guy I'd felt connected to on a level like

I did with Hawk. And now, once again, I was left alone in a hotel room after a great night of sex, only sore muscles to show for it.

Was that all I'd ever have? One night of fun?

Despite the circumstances being different, the devastation swamped me. I wasn't enough. No one would ever fight for me. It hit me full force in the chest, and I gasped as my knees buckled, and I fell to the floor. Sopping wet in only a towel, I let myself fall apart as I tried to console myself.

It's better this way. I need to focus on what's ahead. We wouldn't have worked long-term.

That might've been true, but it didn't make me feel better. None of it did.

I had no idea how long I sat there with tears running down my face before my phone vibrated and scared the shit out of me. Wiping my face, I stood, my legs wobbly as I grabbed my phone.

> **Bryce:** Any update on the flight?

> **Blake:** I haven't checked yet. One sec.

I opened my email but didn't see anything, so I went to the website and checked my flight status. It still showed me pending, not filling me with hope of getting out of here today.

> **Blake:** Doesn't look like anything today.

> **Bryce:** Okay, I have an idea.

> **Blake:** I'm listening.

> **Bryce:** Hawk's driving back from spring training and can detour to get you.

Bryce: That work? Opening day is soon, and Dad's in town. He wants to meet tonight to discuss something. I'm already stressed I won't get to go through my whole pre-season ritual.

My heart kicked up for another reason. I instantly wanted to say no. The thought of being trapped in a car with Hawk for a few hours while we drove to Wilmington hurt my chest, especially after this. It all felt too raw. But I couldn't say any of that to Bryce. He'd believed me when I told him I didn't have feelings for Hawk, so to say something now would open me up for questions I wasn't ready to address.

Blake: Yeah. That works.

Bryce: Perfect. Send him your address, and he'll tell you when he'll be there.

Bryce: Sorry I won't get to see you first and hug you, but as soon as you're here, I'll give you double.

Blake: I'm holding you to that, big Brother.

And despite my better judgment, I asked Bryce the question I'd been dying to know.

Blake: Why's he driving? He didn't go down with the team?

Bryce: He dropped Roxie at her family's house on the way down to FL and then stopped to see his sister after training ended.

Blake: Ah, cool. So, he's still with her? That's the gf, right?

Bryce: Yep. She's cool.

Bryce: Okay text him. Be nice, and I'll see you in a few.

Blake: I'm always nice.

I took a deep breath and opened the text thread I hadn't used in years.

Blake: Hey. Thanks for the ride. I'll drop a pin.

I sent the pin and rested my head against the dresser, debating if I wanted to go to sleep or try to find food. The phone vibrated in my hand shocked me out of my reverie, and I screamed. Mortification from my blunder coated me, and I prayed no one had heard me.

Hawk: I'll be there in thirty.

Blake: *thumbs up*

Gulping, I jumped up and attempted to run a brush through my hair, but it was a tangled mess between not using conditioner and letting it air dry. And I didn't have any of Luke's magic spray this time.

"Fucking great," I mumbled. "I'm gonna look like a drowned rat."

Even though I knew Hawk had a girlfriend, I still wanted to look my best when seeing him for the first time in three years.

Throwing on the clothes I'd bought last night; I realized I still needed to figure out my luggage. I picked up the room key and pulled a baseball cap on, hoping it would hide my hair until I could get a proper brush through it and not some shitty comb.

Memories of Luke combing my hair smacked me, and I sucked in a breath. Shit. He'd imprinted on me more than I'd realized. An ache opened in my heart, and I rubbed my chest, wishing I knew how to make guys stay. It seemed like the ones I wanted never wanted me in return. My fate would be stuck with mediocre lovers for the rest of my life.

I knew there were worse things, but after the second-best night of my life with amazing sex, it didn't feel like there were.

After a frustrating call with the airline, I managed to get my luggage rerouted to Wilmington and canceled my flight. I gave them Champion Field's address since I didn't know Bryce's off the top of my head. Apparently, it would take a few days to sort everything out, so I'd be basically naked for my first day of work until it arrived. Looked like another shopping trip was in my future. Hopefully, this time, I could find something without platypuses on it.

My phone vibrated again, and I knew it was time to face the music.

Hawk: I'm here.

Blake: I'll be right out.

Glancing around the room, I didn't spot anything left out. I slung my bag over my shoulders, wrapping my hoodie around my waist as I stepped out into the hallway. After turning in the keys, I couldn't help but ask the hotel clerk the question that plagued me despite knowing the answer.

"There wasn't anything left for me, was there? By the guy I'd come in with?"

The woman pretended to look, giving me a sympathetic smile before she shook her head.

"Sorry. Did you want to leave a message?"

"It's fine," I said, stepping away. We both knew there

wasn't anything for me to say, only making myself feel lamer and more desperate if I did.

Sucking in a breath, I let it out slowly as I stepped outside. The sun was bright in the sky, and I shielded my eyes as I glanced around for Hawk. I spotted his black Mustang with the red racing stripes parked off to the side. I started in that direction, my steps faltering at the sight of the man leaning against the hood, his head down, eyes on his phone. I was thankful for that as it gave me time to digest this new version of him.

Hawk had always been muscular, but it seemed since he quit playing baseball, he'd bulked up even more. His tattooed muscular arms were on full display, his shirt straining across his chest. Tight jeans hugged his thick thighs, making me remember what rested between them. An ache in my chest opened as a familiar throbbing between my legs started, gluing my feet to the ground.

How did he look more beautiful now? It wasn't fair.

Someone exited the lodge behind me, forcing me to move out of the way. I stepped off the curb, heading in Hawk's direction, and his head immediately snapped up, the phone he'd been staring at slipping into his tight pocket. The mismatched eyes of my dreams seared into me, more vivid than I recalled. His dark hair was shorter, but a beard adorned his face now. And unfortunately, it made him even more rugged and drool-worthy. So unfucking fair.

I gave a wobbly smile and waved like I was a five year old. "Hey."

He didn't say anything, his throat bobbing as I approached. I knew I had to look ridiculous in the leggings and lodge tee, the hoodie tied around my waist.

"Nice hoodie," he said, his voice even.

I glanced down, immediately regretting putting this one in my bag. But a favorite was a favorite for a reason. And mine had always been his.

"Um, yeah, well, it's comfy." I shrugged, my bag sliding off my shoulder to the ground.

His eyes traced over me, landing on my bookbag.

"That all you got?"

"Yeah. The airline is sending the rest. Something about being unable to release them to me now or something." I shrugged.

The conversation was tame, dull by most people's standards, but my heart beat hard against my chest, my fingers tapping against my leg as I forced myself not to pick my nails.

"Right. Well."

Hawk moved, not saying more, and reached for my bag as I lifted it, our hands making contact. Fireworks lit up my arm, and I held in the moan. His hand stuttered, our palms touching before he seemed to remember he had a girlfriend, and he grabbed the strap instead, breaking our contact.

Hawk deposited my bag in his car, and the engine revved within seconds, breaking me out of my frozen state as I rushed and slid into the passenger seat. He didn't say anything as he pulled out of the parking lot and headed in a direction I didn't know. It was quiet, the music low as he navigated us. Occasionally, I'd glance over, feeling his eyes on me. But I'd find him staring straight out the window each time I did.

I'd expected things to be weird between us, but not like this.

This felt like we were barely strangers, much less two friends who'd had a great night of sex.

The longer we drove with the silence, the angrier I became. I knew it was irrational. Hawk wasn't a talker. He barely spoke to most people.

But until that night, I hadn't been most people.

He'd always made a point to talk and listen to me, giving me his undivided attention. When I'd been sick, he was the one person who hadn't treated me like an invalid and had told me stupid stories to make me smile. We spent summers together, watched movies, and pranked Bryce together. Then, three years ago, he'd rescued me from my wedding as I ran out of the stadium in my wedding dress and hot pink high tops.

We'd stolen my wedding feast, eating it and the wedding cake in his hotel room before swimming in our underwear, where things had shifted. From there, the most unforgettable night of my life unfolded. Hawk showed me how sex could be, taking my virginity and treating me with such care that I felt beautiful and loved.

For a tiny moment, I'd thought we could be more. That he wanted it.

But my brother had ruined it when he stumbled into his best friend's room, looking for me. We'd been able to pretend we hadn't slept together until Bryce spotted the condom wrapper on the floor. Things escalated quickly, and I knew the only way to save their friendship was to sacrifice my own.

That day, I gave my brother my heart, my love for his best friend.

And Hawk had let me. He didn't fight me on it.

I knew he couldn't, but the doe-eyed girl I'd been had wanted him to show some emotion, to give me a sign he felt the same. But Hawk had always been known for the cleat retreat, and I became the next victim, even if mitigated by my own actions.

The hopeless romantic in me had believed I'd been special, that things wouldn't be this awkward between us now. But apparently, I'd been naive about that, too.

Well, screw that. We'd been friends once, and this wasn't how you acted. Sex shouldn't change years of friendship.

Time to use that voice you worked so hard to find, girl.

"This is how it's going to be then?" I asked when I couldn't take it any longer.

"How what's going to be?" he repeated, making my blood boil.

Turning in my seat, I stared at the side of his head, my eyes narrowed as I fueled all the intense emotions I'd felt over the past twenty-four hours. Directing them all at him might be unfair, but he was all I had currently.

"We've seen each other naked, and yet you can't spare more than a few words for me!" I shouted, shocking myself at the volume and anger, but I wouldn't back down. This conversation had needed to happen for over three years. "I didn't even get a hello. Just a few two-word responses and grunts!"

Hawk's jaw dropped briefly before he clenched it, grinding his teeth. His hand tightened on the wheel, his tattoos flexing with the move. But he still said nothing. I was sick of nothing.

"You didn't fight for me. You let me leave. I thought I meant something, but apparently not. How could you do that to me?" I screamed, the words more emotional than I meant, tears gathering in the corner.

Hawk's nostrils flared, but he kept silent, revving my anger even more. Fine. He wanted to stay silent? I'd be loud for both of us.

"Am I just one-night material? Is that all I'm good for? I fucked a guy last night, and he couldn't wait to leave me either. The second I was in the shower, he bolted. Why? What's so wrong with me?"

I slunk into the seat, my energy gone now, and my lip wobbled more than I wanted.

"Nothing. There's nothing wrong with you, Blazy." His voice was soft, and I almost didn't hear it, but I did.

Hawk had finally spoken, but the words didn't heal the damaged part of me. In fact, they only made it hurt worse.

Turning away, I leaned against the window and tugged my hat down. I wanted to burrow into my hoodie, but even that felt tainted now. I'd been holding on to something that hadn't even existed for three years.

Kicking off my high-tops, I pulled my legs into my seat and wrapped my arms around them. Exhaustion coated every inch of me, and I could no longer fight my tiredness. I closed my eyes, letting the tears roll down my cheek.

One day back in America and I already regretted leaving Greece. I might've changed, but it didn't seem like the rest of the world wanted me to. I was still the broken and helpless girl everyone else saw me as.

If this job wasn't the perfect fit for me, I'd grab my luggage and hop back on a plane, never to return again.

But I owed it to my brother and myself to see this through. It was time to be a grown-up and suck it up.

Two guys had ghosted me, but it didn't mean everyone would. Maybe I needed to try the casual hookup thing to avoid getting attached? Yeah, that sounded better. No feelings meant no heartbreak.

My phone vibrated in my pocket, reminding me Hawk and Luke weren't the only two men in the world. With that knowledge, I let myself drift off to sleep and hoped I wouldn't feel so broken inside when I woke.

CHAPTER
EIGHT

HAWK

My hands tightened on my steering wheel as I tried to calm my raging mind. But Blake's words revolved around it, making me crazy.

I fucked a guy last night.

You didn't fight for me.

What's wrong with me?

Pain lanced my heart, and I wanted nothing more than to rescue her. To pull this car over and cradle her in my arms, to soothe away all of her pain, and then kiss her plump lips so she didn't think about the guy from last night.

But I couldn't. I wouldn't.

I wasn't hers, and she wasn't mine.

It didn't matter that it felt like we'd always been that to each other.

Things were different now. I had a girlfriend, for one. However, that was stretching the truth. Knowing it would get back to Blake, I hadn't corrected Bryce when he asked about Roxie.

In reality, the two of us were more of a convenience-with-benefits thing. Neither of us saw anything long-term together, but it was nice to hang out, have sex, and not feel so lonely all the time. We were friends, it was comfortable, and it worked for both of us.

Roxie didn't care that I barely spoke and didn't get mad if I didn't text her throughout the day. I didn't mind that she was allergic to feelings and hated baseball. Those things weren't necessary since we weren't in a relationship. It was the perfect arrangement for someone like me who was closed off and didn't like sleeping with random people.

I didn't know why Roxie chose the arrangement, but I'd never cared to ask. She was an incredible tattoo artist and had been doing my ink for the past two years. Things had transitioned from friends to fuck buddies from there.

Neither of us wanted drama, and we agreed that the second one of us met someone we wanted something serious with, things with one another would end. And we were both okay with that.

Again, no feelings were involved on either side. But I wasn't going to mention that to Blake. I needed a layer of protection for myself. Because I couldn't go down that path again, only to be rejected. I wouldn't survive it.

Blake had always been and always would be my kryptonite. Unfortunately, it just wasn't in the cards for us. I'd foolishly believed after our night together, we could be more, but she shot that down so quickly the following day it had left me broken inside.

The rational part of me knew she'd done it for Bryce. But the soft and vulnerable side I only showed her felt punched in the gut. She was the one person I'd always felt safe with, and then my heart had been discarded to the side like yesterday's trash and left out in the heat too long. It no longer beat the same or looked the same.

So, to hear her shout that I should've fought for her, that she had wanted me to stop her, had my mind buzzing. I didn't know what to do with it.

Because I thought I had fought for her. That I'd shown her I was all in.

But had I been wrong all these years? Should I have ignored her wishes and stood up to Bryce to claim her? Would that have changed anything?

It was too much of a mindfuck to consider.

My phone beeped, and an incoming call came through the Bluetooth. Seeing Bryce's name, I popped in my earbuds so the call wouldn't go through the speakers. It took a second to transfer, bringing his voice loudly into my ears.

"Hawk? Can you hear me?"

"Everyone on the coast heard you, man. I had to connect my earbuds; you don't have to shout, dude."

He laughed, the volume lower, and I merged into the far lane.

"Sorry. You got BB?"

"Yeah. She's asleep. Hence the earbuds."

"Gotcha. How is she? She seemed a little lost last night but wouldn't say much. I'm worried about her. I've wanted her to come home for so long, but now I wonder if I pushed her too much. I don't want her to run away again."

I glanced over at her sleeping frame, the rise and fall of her chest in my hoodie, and I had to drag my eyes back quickly before I popped a boner in the car. Seeing she still had it after all these years did something to my chest—something I didn't want to focus on.

"I think it's the jetlag," I lied, hoping it would quell his fears. Bryce had always been overprotective of Blake, and her illness had forged a bond between them more profound than most siblings. I loved my sister and was protective of her and my nieces, but not like Bryce was with Blake.

He sighed, his breath whooshing out of him. "Good, good. Okay, that's great. I'm meeting my dad for dinner, so I might not be home when you arrive. You can drop her off, or I can pick her up from yours."

"She's staying with you?" I asked, trying not to sound angry or excited. Both emotions warred within, knowing she'd be close.

"Yeah. For now, at least. It's not going to be weird, right? You said you were fine with being around her."

"I am fine. You know Blake's like a sister to me."

Lies. All of it. I wasn't fine. Nothing about this was fine.

The words tasted sour on my tongue, but it was the only thing I could muster up for my best friend.

"Good. Okay, I'll see you both in a few hours then."

"Later."

The call ended, and I stared out the windshield as I drove, lost once again in my thoughts. It was unfair how hot she looked after all these years. She'd filled out more, her body more curvy and supple than before, and it made me want to get my hands on her. To update the memory of how she felt beneath my fingers.

But then the knowledge she'd fucked some random guy last night would enter, and anger and jealousy would take over. I wanted to throttle the guy for making her doubt herself. Didn't he realize how easy he had it?

He could be with her.

Possession over her flared to life, but I knocked it down. I couldn't feel that way about her when I was getting my dick wet. I wouldn't be one of those hypocritical men who wanted the girl to stay faithful to only them when they weren't.

The simple truth was that our love was flawed and never meant to last. We could never be more because of who we were to one another.

The sign for Wilmington came into view, and I sighed in relief, even if my heart fell to my stomach. I wouldn't have a reason to be in her presence once I dropped her off. It was a torture I wanted and fought against simultaneously.

I turned off the interstate, the car slowing as I merged into traffic, and Blake seemed to feel the car shifting as she sat up, wiping her eyes and putting her glasses on. She pulled off her hat, and her hair fell around her shoulders. I sucked in a breath as I spotted the pink on the ends. It suited her.

Visions of gripping it from behind, the pink strands sliding through my fingers, of her head thrown back as it brushed my thighs, flashed across my eyes, and I shifted my hard cock as I turned. Fucking images I didn't need in my mind but were there nonetheless.

"We're here?" she asked, her voice soft with sleep.

"Yep."

I knew it irritated her I wasn't saying more, but if I allowed myself to, I'd only end up hurting us both again. If I opened my mouth, secrets I'd been holding might spill forward, and we couldn't have that.

She pulled out her phone, smiling down at it as she responded to something. The fact she wasn't paying attention to me now made me want to poke her. To have that anger directed at me. Because her indifference was suffocating. I'd rather have her fire, even if it scorched me.

"You know, I have you to thank for introducing me to Roxie." I didn't say, girlfriend, the lie unable to pass from my lips. But I wouldn't correct her assumption. She stilled, her head swiveling to me as she narrowed her eyes.

I watched from the corner of mine, smirking at her response. It pleased me that it made her angry.

Yes, I was a sick fucker, but we already knew this.

"Oh, this I have to hear," she mumbled, crossing her arms over her chest.

"She works at that tattoo shop you went to that morning you ran out on me and left me to pick up the pieces of our night together."

Okay, harsh, dude. But the words were already out, and I couldn't take them back.

"Excuse me?" she huffed, her cheeks turning red. "It wasn't like you stopped me!"

"You decided for both of us, Blazy. What was I supposed to do?"

"Tell me to shut up! Tell my brother how you feel! Anything but walk away!"

I rolled my eyes, my heart thumping loudly in my chest. This was the fight I needed. She'd spend less time around me if I made her hate me. And I desperately needed that. Each second I spent around her, I felt myself slipping.

"Running away is your MO, Blake. You couldn't even call me when…" I shook my head, not wanting to rehash *that* nightmare of a night. The night my career ended.

"I sent you something," she whispered, but I heard it.

Yeah, she had. But it wasn't the same, and she knew it.

"So, this is how it's going to be? Fighting and at odds with one another?" she asked, her words thick with emotion.

I took a deep breath as I made the last turn into Bryce's condo. I pulled into his parking spot and turned to face her. I had to do this now, or every day would be torture.

Okay, more torturous. Living without her was already hell.

"Actually, no." Her eyes lit up, and I hated that I had to squash it. "There's *nothing* between us anymore. I'm not the same man you left behind."

"So, we ignore each other? Pretend like we don't exist?" she asked, her eyes wide and pleading.

"We politely acknowledge one another. We can't erase our history. But as far as friends go, that died that day in my hotel room. I can't be your friend anymore, Blake." I swallowed, the words hard to force out. They were thick in my throat, but I had to. I needed this break. I could already feel my heart crumbling. She made a choice, so I had to respect it. Even if everything in me wanted to rebel.

"I feel nothing for you anymore."

Her face fell, tears streaking down her face, and I hated myself for making her cry. I was two seconds away from caving and hauling her into my arms. But thankfully, she hardened herself and opened the door. Despite her next words being spoken away from me, they landed all the same.

"You're wrong. It was never *nothing*. You were the first guy I loved, but I won't let you be the last."

She stood as her words sent me reeling, my hands flexing on the steering wheel as I wrestled with myself. Was I making the right call?

Blake tossed something into the car and slammed the car door, stalking up to Bryce's condo before I could respond. I glanced over; the black hoodie she'd stolen three years ago now graced my seat.

For some reason, that was the last straw, and I stalked out of the car, unable to stop myself. I needed her to be the villain, the enemy. It was easier when my anger felt righteous.

She stood on the stoop, her fist knocking on the door, and I brushed her aside, halting her.

"Bryce's out with your dad," I grumbled, unlocking it with my keys. I braced my arm across it, pinning her with a look. My heart pounded in my chest; my vision blurred with anger as I stared at the most beautiful woman I'd ever known.

"*You* fucking broke me, Blazy. So, before you get all high and mighty on your white horse, maybe consider you weren't the only one wrecked that day. You chose for both of us, so I'm sorry I didn't have it in me to fight you on it." My nostrils flared, and I clenched my fists, my nails biting into my hand. "I was the one left to pick up the pieces. The one that had to lie to his best friend every fucking day for *you*."

Her blue eyes were glassy, staring at me with so much emotion, I didn't know which one. All it did was make me want to grab her and kiss her until neither of us could breathe.

But I couldn't, and that was the problem.

While I understood her reasoning for the choice she made, I didn't agree with it. And maybe I should've said something, but I hadn't. So here we were, three years later, with the remnants of a perfect night that could never reoccur.

I'd made peace with it... or at least I pretended to.

She opened her mouth and closed it, her jaw clenching as she stared at me. This pain and hurt between us wouldn't be solved today, but I was at my rope's end of how much more I could endure.

"Let's stay away from each other as best as possible. It will be easier for us both."

I hated the words but knew they were the best course of action. Turning on my heels, I stalked to my car and jumped in. I didn't look at her or the hoodie as I pulled out of his parking lot. I just gunned my car and headed to the place that always made me feel better.

CHAPTER
NINE

HAWK

Champion Field came into view, and my body relaxed as I neared it. The lights were dimmed, but I had my coach's pass and could access it after hours. There were still a few cars in the lot, so the odds that a few guys might be here were high. They would try to get in some last-minute practice with the season starting in a few days.

The same feeling of knowing baseball was around the corner still filled me with excitement despite not playing anymore. At first, it had been hard to accept I wasn't a player, but I discovered I loved coaching more over time. I got to do the things I loved without the pressure. I could instill my knowledge and hard work into the players and watch the game surrounded by others who loved it as much as I did.

It had been the perfect transition for me, and I'd shown my value to the team. This year, I'd been promoted to bench coach, along with my pitching coach duties. I was excited to be used for more than just pitching, assisting the head coach on plays, roster, and managing the team. It was the next step to one day being a head coach.

Stepping out of my car, the cool air kissed my cheeks, and

I grabbed my bat bag from my trunk. I had a change of clothes in my locker, so I stopped there first. The halls were empty, but it didn't mean people weren't there.

I made my way to the batting cages, not surprised when I came upon someone. Olson had missed most of spring training for rehab on his shoulder after surgery. He'd been placed with the YellowJackets last season for his rehab assignment. He was expected to return to the Blue Devils any day now. But something had been going on with him. He hadn't been playing the same, but I was the last person he'd talk to about it. We weren't on close terms since he and Bryce were rivals.

I understood why, but most of it seemed petty outside the one incident. But sometimes, Bryce didn't like people. Things had been icy between them from the start, and I didn't think either of them knew why it had begun. It didn't help when Olson took his starting spot on the Blue Devils. Bryce didn't want to admit he was on limited time, but I had a feeling this was his last year.

But no one wanted to hear they'd hit their peak and needed to retire. I'd gladly plead ignorance on this one as long as possible. And being the good friend I was, I'd support him in his career choices and be there to commiserate when it ended.

The whoosh of the ball from the machine greeted me before the crack of the bat as Olson made contact with it. The sound filled me with serenity as I made my way to the cage I liked the most. Olson stopped after a few more, wiping his brow and spotting me.

"Coach." He nodded in my direction, and I assessed him. His face was pale, and he seemed more withdrawn than usual, but since I wasn't a talker, much less friends with the guy, I wouldn't be one to ask him about it.

"Olson." I nodded back, slipping on my batting glove and

helmet. "Your shoulder ready for the physical?" I asked, curiosity getting the better of me.

He stared at me blankly before he blinked, rotating it, and nodded. "Right. My shoulder. Yep. Good as new. Ready for the physical. I'm ready to get back to the Devils."

I snorted, going back to my process. I didn't buy his answer, but I wasn't the general manager, so it didn't matter. I'd do as Coach Phillips said and offer my opinion if he asked.

Getting into the zone, I picked up my bat and turned on the machine, getting into my stance as the first ball whizzed out. Ball after ball, I swung my bat and smacked the balls as hard as possible until my arms felt like jelly, and I could barely hold them up.

Olson was no longer in the cages, so I turned everything off as I cleaned up and closed them down. The two new guys were in the locker room as I entered, their heads snapping as I dropped my bag into my locker. I'd worked extensively with them over spring training and had great hopes for them this season.

"Coach," Jameson said, smiling as he hopped over his chair and trotted over. "What are you doing here?"

I liked the kid, but he was a bit too excited at times. He embodied the energy of a Golden Retriever, always eager to please. He was a helluva pitcher, though, and his connection with West, the catcher, was the type of symbiotic battery-mates teams dreamed of for their catcher and pitcher. They'd been traded to us in the off-season as a package deal.

The team had started to call them that since they spent so much time together. Where there was one, there was the other. I hadn't ever seen them apart. West was the quieter of the two, more reserved and calculated. He seemed to think about things more intensely than his counterpart. In true West fashion, he merely nodded when I glanced over.

Jameson continued bouncing on his feet before me, and I remembered he'd asked a question.

"Just needed to hit some balls."

"Cool. That's cool." He nodded, his head going so fast I worried it would fall off.

"You okay, Jameson?" My brows creased as I stared at him. "The bathroom's back that way."

"Haha, funny. And I'm peachy, thanks for asking." He turned but then spun around so fast he almost fell over. "Just out of curiosity. What are the odds that Bryce would punk us? You're friends with him, so you have the inside knowledge."

"Bryce? Punking *you*?" I asked, trying to filter through the words he'd lobbied at me. My forehead creased as I stared at him, wondering if *I* was the one being punked.

"Told you. It's not him," West said, climbing off the chair he'd been sitting on backward. He grabbed Tucker and pulled him back to their lockers, giving me an apologetic look.

"But she hasn't responded in forever." Jameson pouted, his face falling.

"Then let's send her something," West said like it was the obvious solution.

Jameson scrambled back to him, smiles lighting their faces as they typed out a message, laughing and putting their heads together as they discussed it. They were weird.

Shaking my head, I grabbed my stuff to head home, ready to crawl into bed after the emotional gamut I'd been through today.

My phone lit up with an incoming call when I got into my car. I answered it as I pulled out of the lot, hoping Bryce didn't need anything. I was dead on my feet.

"Hey," I said when he didn't immediately say anything. "Bryce?"

"Yeah, sorry. So, um, I have some news."

"Yeah?" I swallowed, hoping he wouldn't ream me out for how I talked to his sister. He had one of those video door-bells, making our entire conversation available for him to listen to. The knowledge of that hit me square in the gut. Part of me had known, maybe wanting to test the boundaries, make Blake admit it to her brother, and bring it all out into the open.

But now that I was faced with it, I wanted to plead exhaustion and insanity.

"It happened," he said, his voice slightly breathless. "I'm getting moved up. Olson's not ready, so Dad's giving me my shot. My last one."

The information slammed into me; the relief I wasn't caught filled me with happiness, along with a twinge of sadness that he'd be leaving.

"What? Wow! That's so great, Bry. I didn't think they were making the decision yet."

"Yeah, me either. But apparently, I made heads turn at spring training, so they decided to go ahead and make the decision. It still feels so surreal. I've been fighting so hard to get back."

"Yeah. I know. You deserve this. I'm happy for you, man." I paused, the question I wanted to know hanging in the balance. "Does Blake know? Is she going to the Blue Devils, too?"

I didn't know which way I wanted him to answer.

"No. That's the only sucky part. Dad wants her to stay here and do some magic for the team to get more fans at the games. Attendance has been so low that the team is in danger if things don't change."

"Shit."

"Pretend you don't know that part. Fuck." He paused, and I could almost hear him pacing. "The timing sucks, but I'm ready to play in the Majors again."

"You deserve this chance, Bry. You're in great shape and

have been playing your best ball. You're not going to fuck this up."

He sighed, and I could imagine him running his fingers through his hair as he smiled. "Thanks, man. I needed to hear that. I feel awful, but I'm also so fucking excited. I didn't want Blake to feel like I was abandoning her."

"You'll still see each other, just not as much. But she's here, and you got your shot. She'll be happy for you. She knows how these things go."

"Yeah. You're right. I guess I better go tell her."

"Good luck. When do you leave?"

"Tomorrow morning."

"Shit. Okay. Well, anything you need from me?"

"Can you look after Blake? I'm not worried about the guys but about her adjusting."

I didn't want to be the one to tell Bryce he should worry about the guys. Blake was a knockout. She always had been, but she now seemed more confident and sure of herself. It was a dangerous combination. But I knew he didn't need to think about his baby sister having sex with his former teammates. I'd make sure to give them all the talk, though. Purely selfless reasons, of course.

"I don't think she'll like me being around, but I'll look out for her. You know I always will."

"Thanks, man. Okay, I better get off here so I can face the music and then pack. It's such a whirlwind."

"Text me when you're in Columbus."

"Will do. Later, man."

"Bye, Bryce."

The call ended as I pulled into my house. I bought it last year and had been remodeling it during the off-season. It wasn't much, but it was mine, and I was proud of that.

I went through my nightly routine, feeding the hamster I'd gotten for my nieces and heating up food from the fridge. I'd paid someone to water the plants and feed Sunny while

I'd been away at spring training the past month. I also had them stock the fridge so I wouldn't have to worry about it when I returned. I'd never been so happy to spend the money on something useful as I was right now.

Belly full and showered, I crawled into my bed and stared at the ceiling, sleep evading me despite my exhaustion.

Blake was back, *my* Blazy.

No. She wasn't *mine*, and I had to live with that.

CHAPTER
TEN

BLAKE

When I stepped into Bryce's condo, the urge to rage out and destroy things was intense. But since my brother had a nice place and it wasn't mine, I decided not to welcome him home with it wrecked.

So, instead, I called my mom and talked to her while I fixed something to eat, and she promised to send my things from her house in Columbus.

Feeling slightly better after eating, I decided to call my best friend, Emory, in Greece. Technically, we were some form of pseudo-step-cousins since her mom married my aunt. We'd instantly bonded when I arrived and became besties over the last three years. I'd never had a girl best friend before, and Emory had shown me the value of having one. Like now when I wanted to vent about the guys in my life. Hitting the video call button, I hoped it wasn't too late there.

"Yiasoo, Lake!"

My face instantly lifted at her bubbly greeting as she came into view.

"Yiasoo, Em." I lay on my stomach, propping the phone

up on a pillow.

"How's it going?" she asked, squinting as she tried to assess me. "What happened?"

I rolled my eyes, smiling. "How do you always do that?

She shrugged one shoulder, winking. "It's a Greek thing. So, what is it? Tell your bestie your woes, and I'll fix it."

I blew out a breath. "I don't know if you can fix this." I gave her a play-by-play with Luke from the bump to vomit-gate to turbulence orgasm.

"And then, there was only one room left, so he asked me to share it with him."

"Okay, okay, I like where this story is headed. Tell me you said yes, Filia!"

I nodded, hiding my cheeks in my hands as I blushed. "I did, and it was amazing."

"Yes!" She giggled, falling back on her bed and kicking her legs up in the air. "You got some D! Get it, Lake!" She did a dance, moving her arms around.

"It was… as good as the first time. I felt sexy and free, not worried about what my face was doing or how my body looked. It was near perfect. But—" I groaned, pulling myself up as I propped against the headboard, taking the phone with me. "He ghosted me. Literally left while I was in the shower! Then, there were no flights, and I had to ride back with Hawk and listen to him tell me how I meant nothing to him. It's been a day," I rushed out.

"Shit. Yeah, okay, that explains this look." She pressed her lips together, waving her hand at the camera to encompass my face.

"I have a look?"

"Yeah. The 'post-orgasm ghosted' look doubled with the 'stuck in a car with my first love' look."

"That's not a thing."

"Have you seen your face? It's *totally* a thing."

I stuck out my tongue, rolling my eyes. Despite the fact she was calling me out, I already felt better.

"So, what are you going to do?" she asked, her voice softer.

"What Delia taught me to do. I'll keep pushing through. Persevering. Tomorrow, I start my job, and that will give me something new to focus on. Maybe I'll meet a new guy to crush over." I shrugged one shoulder, giving half a smile. "It sucks and hurts, but they're not the only two guys on the planet. In fact, I think I'm going to try the casual thing."

"There's my girl! Get back out there and ride all the dicks, Filia!"

"I don't know about *all* the dicks, but I'll be open to date requests. I've done things wrong in the past, jumping into sex before dates. So maybe I need to do it the traditional way and date all the toads to get my prince." I sighed, a new message coming in that made me smile.

"Oh, oh, what was that? You smiled. The plot thickens."

Rolling my eyes, I laughed as I informed her about being texted accidentally as Bryce and the conversation I'd been having with the two guys.

"They sound fun. You should get between *that*."

"Both?" I gasped, shaking my head, my cheeks heating. .

"Why not?" she asked. "Two is better than one, Filia. Trust me."

"I'm not sure I'm there yet. I just had my first one-night stand, though he was more of a plane stand. Anyway, I think I have a few more steps before a threesome."

"You might be closer than you think," she teased, a yawn following her. "Don't rule it out. Explore with them."

I glanced at the time, realizing the time difference. "Shit. Sorry, I know it's late, so I'll let you go. We'll talk more tomorrow."

"Don't worry about it. You know I always have time for

my girl." She air-kissed the camera, an ache in my chest opening up at missing my best friend.

"Love ya, Emory!"

"Love you too, Lake."

The call ended, and I fell back against the pillows in a daze, the phone vibrating again and reminding me the mystery texters had responded.

Pitcher: I'm not saying I'm worried, but if you're not Bryce, I just wanted to ensure you were okay.

Catcher: Despite his jokes, he does have feelings.

Pitcher: Thanks, bro. I feel things deeply.

Catcher: Ahem. Well.

Pitcher: What did I miss?

Catcher: Nothing.

Blake: Hey. I'm good. Still not Bryce, btw.

Pitcher: I'm starting to believe you. He doesn't seem like someone who has the attention span to carry out a prank this long.

Blake: You'd be correct there.

Catcher: So, you know him well?

Pitcher: Oooo, good catch. Ha, get it?

Catcher: Yes, dude.

Blake: I'm not sure what to think of you two.

Catcher: You wouldn't be the first person.

Blake: Does that bother you?

Pitcher: No. He's my best friend. He's stuck with me.

Pitcher: By the way, it's so hard not to use names. I need a nickname!

Catcher: For yourself?

Pitcher: You, numbnuts. And our secret texter.

Blake: You make a good point. I have you as Pitcher and Catcher.

Catcher: How do you know that?

Blake: Based on your comments. *Shrug*

Pitcher: Well, damn. Our girl's a smart one.

I tried not to get all the warm feelings, but it was too late. These two made me feel comfortable and part of the group. Their care for my safety was also nice. After the crappy day, it was a nice change.

Catcher: I have an idea, just one last test per se. Just give us a few minutes to get home.

Blake: Okay, text me when you're there.

While I waited, I decided to unpack the few things in my bookbag. I pulled out the tattered blue paperback I'd read numerous times and sat it on my nightstand. I plugged in my DSLR camera so the battery would be full for tomorrow, and I checked on my beloved retro film camera Delia had given me. Everything appeared promising, so I slid it back into its case. I set the pad of paper with names on it on the bed with my computer and gathered up my clothes.

I shoved my two outfits into the wash, then stole a shirt and pair of shorts from Bryce. I quickly brushed my teeth and placed my toiletries into my bathroom. I checked my phone, but there still wasn't a message, so I decided to do some of the research Bryce had suggested.

Pulling my laptop into my lap, I first went to the Yellow-Jacket's roster to see what the team had listed. When I came upon the first name, I froze.

#13. Graham West. Catcher. Age 25, recently traded from the Omaha Sluggers.

Could this be one of my mystery texters? My heart sped up, and I typed in the next.

#7 Tucker Jameson. Pitcher. Age 25, recently traded from the Omaha Sluggers.

Bunting hell... I'd found them. This had to be the two guys I'd been talking to. Curiosity made me want to click on the team photo, but my phone vibrated before I could.

Pitcher: Honey, we're home. Did you miss us?

Blake: Loads and loads.

Pitcher: Yes! We're basically married now.

Catcher: Stop saying things that make girls run away.

Pitcher: I'm not. You're just jealous of my game.

Catcher: Speaking of... Ready for my idea?

Catcher: You there? You scared her off, dummy.

Blake: I'm here.

Blake: And what do you have in mind? Because as it stands, I'm the only one who showed the goods.

Catcher: How about we make it a game? And this time, anything goes.

Pitcher: I like games. I'm in.

Blake: Okay. But be warned, you're at an unfair disadvantage because I have a better chance of figuring out who you are first.

I didn't want to admit I already had, worried they'd stop talking to me. I didn't want that. I liked them, and their instant connection made me feel good. It was easy with them, and I needed that right now.

Catcher: I'll take the odds. Besides, as you said, we do owe you.

Pitcher: What's the test then?

Catcher: Let's do a group audio call. No video, only sound. That way, we can hear your voice.

Blake: Okay.

Pitcher: Ooh, solid. Come in here, though, so we're together.

Catcher: So needy. One sec. I need to change.

Pitcher: I never claimed not to be needy, boo.

Catcher: Okay, cutie. Are you ready?

Blake: Yep.

My hands sweated, my heart thumping in my chest as I waited for the phone to ring. I felt like a teenager again, waiting for a boy to call. When it started to ring, I almost dropped it as I waited a few seconds to answer. Hitting the answer button, I inhaled a big breath as I waited to hear them.

"Hello?" a deep and smooth voice asked, making goosebumps break out.

"Hi." I rolled my eyes at myself.

"I'll be damned. She's real." This voice was playful and full of sunshine if that was possible. If I had to guess, this was Pitcher.

"I am," I said, smiling. "So, did I pass?"

"I never doubted you," the deep voice said.

"Catcher?" I asked, needing some form of identification.

"Yup. How did you do that?"

Despite the fact they couldn't see me, I shrugged as I settled back on my bed with my feet crossed at the ankle. "I pay attention. And Pitcher's more flirty, where you're more sweet. So I took a chance."

"You hear that, Gr—I mean, um, shit." I giggled as he floundered. "You laughing at me shouldn't sound so hot, cutie."

"There are worse things, I suppose," I teased.

"I'll be Catcher and you Pitcher, just to keep things easy."

"Fine. But I want it noted that it's Mr. Studly Pitcher."

"Anyways," Catcher said, making me laugh.

"Works for me. What's mine?"

"Future Mrs."

"Sunshine."

They said it at the same time, making me pause. I cleared my throat, my cheeks heating. Why did that make my heart race? Were these butterflies I was feeling?

"Well, hm, okay."

I could hear some rustling and low muttering, but I was

too shocked to listen. He was joking, right? We'd only talked a handful of times, and yes, I'd shown him my cleavage, but most relationships were built on more.

Right? *Right?*

Blinking, I tried to get my brain back online.

"Ignore him. He's a big flirt and doesn't often know the limits," Catcher said, and I exhaled.

"Yeah. Sure. So, what now?" I asked, hoping to move the conversation along. Excitement bubbled low in my belly, helping me to forget the horror of the past twenty-four hours.

"We ask questions and then make guesses? I'm just pulling things from the air if I'm honest."

"You should go first since I already know more about you both."

"What do you know exactly?" Pitcher asked. "Just so we're on the same page."

"Well, you're baseball players. A pitcher and catcher and are on Bryce's team."

"That's all?" Pitcher scoffed, making me smile.

"And your names start with a G and T. So, yeah. More than you." I laughed.

"Fair, cutie pie. Okay then, I'd like to know how you know Bryce."

"Hmm, maybe like a hot and cold thing. It feels like cheating to answer it right out. I want you to work for it."

"She has a point. There's two of us figuring out her identity," Catcher agreed, his smooth voice making my toes curl each time.

"Fine. You're both annoying. Are you an ex of Bryce's?"

"Ew. So cold," I said. "Like frozen."

"Okay. Not a fan of Bryce." He laughed. I wanted to correct him, but that wasn't the point of the game, and I was competitive.

"She didn't say that. Don't jump to conclusions," Catcher said, proving he was the more level-headed one.

"My turn?" I asked, smiling.

"Yeah, go ahead." Pitcher sulked.

"Is this your first year on the team?"

"Hot."

"So, that's a yes?"

"Yeah," Pitcher said. "Come here, Catch. I need cuddles. I'm sad we're losing."

"Needy fucker," Catcher huffed, but you could hear the love and friendship these two had as he moved closer. "My turn. Are you connected to the YellowJackets?"

I froze, his question taking me by surprise. "Hot," I said, swallowing.

"Yes! Okay, we're back in this," Pitcher said. "Are you—"

"My turn," I said, cutting him off.

"Ah, man. Fine. Hit me, Mrs. Sunshine."

"Um, what?" I laughed, then realized I didn't want an answer. "Are you starting this week?"

"Hot," Pitcher grumbled. "You're gonna have us figured out in one more question. We should get two to your one."

I rolled my eyes, finding his sulking kind of cute. "Fine. Ask me two now."

"You're only encouraging him. He's just like a puppy, pushing the limits to see what he can get away with," Catcher warned.

"It's cool. He does have a point."

"See. I'm irresistible," Pitcher said, and I could hear the smile in his voice.

"Are you single?"

I chewed my lip. Technically, yes. But the way my heart felt, I wasn't sure how to respond.

"Hot," I said, going with the truth.

"Score. That means there's a chance."

"For what?" I teased, pushing the conflicting feelings out of the way. Casual dating, remember?

"To make my nickname true, of course."

"My turn," Catcher interrupted, helping take the heat off my face and give me time for my heart to return to normal. I wasn't used to guys flirting that overtly toward me. "Do you like to read?"

"Hot," I said, smiling.

"Why did you ask that one? It doesn't tell us who she is," Pitcher argued.

"Sure it does. Now I know something real about her."

The door to Bryce's condo opened, and I sat up, excited that he was home. "Well, boys, this has been fun, but I gotta go. I'll talk to you tomorrow."

I hung up before they could respond and hopped off the bed, padding out into the loft and peering over the edge. Bryce was on the phone, rubbing the back of his head as he paced.

"Can you look after Blake? I'm not worried about the guys hitting on her but about her adjusting."

His words hit me square in my chest, and I retreated to the bedroom.

Bryce wasn't worried about his teammates hitting on me because I was broken.

Was that what he meant? And what about me adjusting concerned him? A gap in our relationship appeared, and I wondered if things between us were as I always thought or if I'd been fooling myself these past three years.

I didn't get time to think about it as I heard his steps on the stairs and then his knock on the door. He entered before I could say anything, smiling as he spotted me on the bed. He rushed toward me, pulling me into a hug.

I let myself hug him back; it felt too nice for me to ignore. This was my brother, my best friend. I had to have misunderstood him.

"Hey, Blanket. I'm so glad you're here," he said into my hair, holding me tightly for a long time. When he pulled back, he took his time looking me over.

"How was dinner with Dad? I'm shocked he's here and not back with the Blue Devils yet."

"Yeah, about that. Let's sit."

I quirked a brow, taking a seat on the bed with him. He fidgeted, not meeting my eyes. He took a deep breath, then stared back at me.

"I've been called up. Dad wants me to take the open first baseman spot. Olson still isn't ready, so I'm getting my chance."

"That's great, Bry!" I flew across the bed, hugging him again as I smiled. That was until I realized what it meant. "But wait, what about me?" I pulled back, my face falling.

"Dad still wants you here. He's invested in helping the YellowJackets."

"But you'll be in Columbus…"

Bryce nodded ruefully. "Yeah. I'm sorry. I didn't know this would happen."

"I know. It's the nature of the game." I gave him a watery smile, happy for my brother but sad we wouldn't get this time together. I'd missed him and had looked forward to working with him.

"You're welcome to stay here. Don't feel like you have to find another place."

"Duh." I rolled my eyes, making him laugh.

"You'll be okay, right?" he asked, squeezing my hand.

"Yeah. I'll be fine."

He relaxed. "At least Hawk's here."

"Hawk. Right." I nodded, trying to put on a brave face. "This is your chance, Bry. I couldn't be happier for you. You've earned this."

I hugged him again, needing to hide the tears that wanted to fall. It was the way my life worked. Each time something good happened, something painful accompanied it. I couldn't seem to have one without the other.

"When do you leave?" I asked, wiping my face before I pulled back.

"In the morning."

I nodded, figuring as much. "Right, well. I'm beat, and I bet you have some packing to do. I'll make you a farewell breakfast in the morning."

"Thanks, BB. Love you, little Sis."

"Love you more than pumpkin spice lattes," I said.

"Love you more than double chocolate brownies," he replied, giving me one final hug and kiss. He shut the door to my room, and I curled up on the bed, pulling a pillow into my arms as I tried to sort through everything that had happened since I'd arrived back here.

It had been one pitch slap after another.

So far, nothing had gone to plan, and I wasn't sure I was ready to face this without Bryce. But it was too late to back out, so I'd stick with it, even if it meant my heart was smashed to smithereens by the end of the season.

Vibrations had me pulling up my phone. I had a group text and two private ones.

Group Text:

Pitcher: Wear something yellow for me.

Catcher: Those are the team colors, dork.
How will you know it's her?

Pitcher: I just will.

Private Message:

Pitcher: Good night, cutie-pie. Here's your prize.

Pitcher: *image*

I gulped. I hadn't really wanted a dick pic, but staring at his cock, with the bead of precum on it as he squeezed the tip, I couldn't look away. His beautiful abs were also in the shot, and I squirmed as I licked my lips. He had a pretty dick —a really nice one.

Before I could stare at it any longer, a private message popped up.

Catcher: I'm only a few guesses away, and I have a feeling I'll know when I see you.

Blake: You're a bit of a romantic, aren't you?

Catcher: Guilty.

Blake: Good night, Graham.

Catcher: Fuck. I won't tell Tucker you figured it out. It's fun watching him sweat.

Blake: He sent me a pic, you know.

Catcher: Oh? Did you like it?

Blake: Yes.

Catcher: Do you want one from me?

Blake: Only if you want to send one. I'm not an extortionist.

Catcher: So you're not just into him?

Blake: No.

Blake: I like you both. Is that okay?

Catcher: Better than okay.

Blake: Do you like me?

Catcher: I'm starting to. And Tucker's already smitten. You're the first girl to make him work for it. So that right there is a plus in his mind.

> Blake: But neither of you have seen me. How do you know?

Catcher: Not all guys are superficial, sunshine.

Catcher: Your soul speaks of your beauty.

Catcher: Good night.

> Blake: Good night, Graham.

Feeling bold, I sent a picture to the group message of me with my hand down my pants. It was risky, but Bryce's comment about none of the guys being a problem echoed around my head.

In the past, I hadn't cared if any baseball players liked me. I was in a relationship. But something about the casual statement thrown out like it was a given rubbed the rebellious streak in me. And what better way to dip my toe into the casual dating pool than by dating a few baseball players.

CHAPTER
ELEVEN

BLAKE

"You'll take good care of my baby?" Bryce asked, biting his lip nervously. I rolled my eyes but pushed him toward the door.

"Yes. Once I get my updated license. I'll meet you when our schedules overlap. Now, go. You'll miss your flight, and then Dad will be forced to bench his son."

Bryce pulled me into another bear hug, squeezing me tight. "It's hard to be excited when it takes me away from you. I was looking forward to being around you every day. I've missed you, Blanket."

Do not cry. Do not cry.

"I've missed you, too, Bry. At least it will be much easier to see each other now that we're only a few hours away instead of an ocean. I bet you'll be so annoyed with me in a few months."

"Never." He squeezed one more time and then kissed my cheek. "I'll let you know when I land. Good luck, Sis."

"You too, Bry. Try not to be too much of a pain for Dad and Mallory," I teased, waving.

He rolled his eyes, cupping his mouth. "Love you more than seasonal Oreos."

Chuckling, I wiped a tear I hadn't been able to stop. "Love you more than Netflix."

Bryce waved one last time before the door enveloped him, stealing him from view. I wiped my cheeks again, sucking in a breath as I headed to the Uber waiting on the curb. Wiping my tears one more time, I slid into the back seat, and the driver took off, heading for the stadium. The driver stayed quiet, and I relaxed into it as I prepared myself for my first day.

I had several meetings and an orientation I had to go through before the season started tomorrow. Once it did, it was full steam ahead until the end of August when the post-season began.

The life of a baseball player wasn't as glamorous as other professional sports. The seasons were long, the weather was often hot, and the pay wasn't always that great in the Minors. Add in traveling for half of those dates; it was a wonder people did it at all.

But as my dad said, when baseball was in your blood, you kept playing as long as possible because nothing else felt as good.

I'd taken offense to that as a child, feeling like he loved baseball more than me. But eventually, I understood that baseball was more than just a game; it was a lifestyle. It taught you teamwork, patience, and perseverance. In a game of nine innings, anything was possible.

I no longer believed in baseball miracles, but I could accept the power baseball had for people. Maybe one day I would fall in love with the sport again, but for now, I was just happy to have a new way of relating to it.

I directed the driver around to the staff entrance of Champion Field and took a deep breath before climbing out of the car. I hadn't had time to go shopping yet, so I'd borrowed a hoodie from Bryce and paired it with my platypus leggings. I was glad it was mostly staff in the building today since I still looked like I'd dressed myself in the dark with clothes a colorblind monkey picked out.

"Do my eyes deceive me, or is that little BB gracing my stadium?" a deep voice rang out as I approached the side entrance.

Smiling wide, I ran the last few steps to see Clive smiling. "Hey, Clive."

"Well, I'll be damned. Little BB's not so little anymore. How you doin', suga'?" The man I'd known since I was a child braced his hands on his hips, giving me a haughty look. Stepping forward, I pulled his now more diminutive frame into my arms, his familiar scent of licorice and peppermint tickling my nose.

"It's so good to see you, Clive. How's Theresa and the grandkids?"

He smiled wide, launching into a tale about his grandkids and how they love to come and see him at work and thought he had the coolest job. I laughed and smiled, enjoying seeing a familiar face first thing.

Unfortunately, that meant I'd lost track of time reminiscing and stayed outside longer than intended. The rumble of an engine hit my ears first, my body tensing as the familiar sound triggered all of my emotions.

I continued to nod and smile, but my body knew full well who was there. I tried to end the conversation, but Clive wasn't having it, keeping me firmly where I was as Hawk strolled up.

"Coach Anderson. Good to see you."

"Morning, Clive."

"Happy to hear about Bryce, but sad to miss him this season. It would've been like that one summer when you three were here."

Oh, yippee. Clive woke up and chose to be a meddling gossip today.

Way to remind me about my first kiss and the first time Hawk chose my brother over me. Nothing like a kick to the gut first thing in the morning.

"Yes, well, we're not kids anymore. I better get inside. Mira's gonna be waiting on me. Good to see you, Clive."

I hurried off, not even acknowledging Hawk. He'd said we were nothing to each other, so that was what we'd be. I didn't want to spend energy on him if it wouldn't be returned. Plus, it hurt too much to only receive indifference from him.

"Blake, wait," he called after me, but I waved my hand over my shoulder, not turning.

"Sorry, can't."

I jogged off, unsure I was going the right way, but I didn't care as long as it was away from him. Spotting an office up ahead, I took a chance, opened the door, and rushed in. A few heads glanced up at me with curious expressions as they watched me catch my breath against the wall. I waved them off, not needing more people to witness my embarrassment.

Stellar first day, girl.

"Blake, that you?" Mira asked, stepping out of an office.

"Yep. Hi. How's it going?" Geez. I sounded like an idiot.

She gave me a curt smile, her eyes searching my face as she directed me to her office. Peeling myself off the wall, I followed her and sat, determined to do well at this job.

"Sorry to hear about the plane trouble. Were you able to take care of everything you needed?"

"Oh, um, I still need to update my license, and my luggage should be here soon. Which will be nice since I'm stuck wearing Bryce's stuff in the meantime." I pinched the material of the hoodie between my fingers, hoping it was okay that I'd dressed casually.

Her eyes roamed over me, distaste clear in her gaze. "Do

let me know if I can be of any help. I'll be your mom away from home." She grinned, but the effect was lost on me. I'd had too many people trying to mother me in my life. I didn't need another one.

"Thanks." I smiled tightly before I cleared my throat. "The agenda for today is packed full."

Mira's face fell, and she picked up a stack of papers. "Jumping right in. I shouldn't be surprised. You *are* a Baker."

Okay, lady. Way to make it weird two times within thirty seconds. First, you want to be my mom, and then you have a problem with my name?

I gave her a tight smile, hoping she'd take the cue and move on. Thankfully, she seemed to finally get the hint and reviewed the departments I'd be meeting with. Then, she finally covered what she wanted me to focus on for the first home games.

"How do you feel about helping with some in-between inning entertainment?"

I blinked owlishly, hoping I misheard her. "As in what exactly?" My heart thumped loudly in my ears as I tried not to panic. I did not do crowds or anything that put me at the center of attention. I preferred to stay behind my camera for a reason.

"I'll have Rue talk to you about it. Once you set up the account, send me the first couple of drafts before posting so I can sign off on them to ensure they're in line with the Yellow-Jacket brand. We want it to be fun, sexy, and edgy."

I frowned, tilting my head. "I'm not sure sexy is the best idea after the fallout with the hockey community on BookIt. I've been doing some research, and while there's a fanbase for it, the fun videos the Banana Pajamas do are more interactive and garner more traffic to games. Our focus market aligns with theirs and aims to pull in families."

Mira dropped the papers she'd been holding, her eyes narrowing at me as her mouth resembled a puckered anus. It so wasn't pretty. "I know you're new in this role, so I'll let that slide *this* time. I'm sure your"—she waved her hand in the air like my very presence offended her now— "research was backed by data? Well, mine was, and I know what works. It's why they pay *me* to run the department."

Gaping at her, I stopped myself from going full Baker on her. She was in this position because no one else had wanted it, but I didn't think I'd win any friends by spilling *that* bit of info. Taking a moment to pull in air slowly, I let it out as I unclasped the hand that had clenched during her attack.

It was clear to me now what type of woman Mira was. She wanted to use me to get her in with the Baker name but didn't want to hear anything I had to say. My ideas would not be met with openness if they went against hers. Noted.

"Sure. I'll confirm we have proper consent from the players before I proceed so we don't have any backlash. Oh, wait," I snapped my fingers, waggling my finger at her like I was the dumb one, "you've probably already done that as part of your due diligence. Duh. Okay, well, since we have the players' consent, I'll work on some thirst trap videos, lawsuits be damned."

I stood and turned to leave, smiling as I watched her reflection backpedal.

"You know what, you're right. We don't want to be like those other accounts. Send me what you have at the end of each day. Kay?"

"Absolutely. I'll get right on that."

Giving her a finger wave, I rolled my eyes as I left her office. A girl with short black hair and purple highlights in jeans and a YellowJackets polo caught me, laughing into her hand as I turned the corner.

"Um. Hi." My cheeks heated, and I shoved my hands into the hoodie pocket, shifting my camera bag on my shoulder.

"You must be Blake. I'm Rue."

"Oh, yes! Mira told me to talk to you. Though, I honestly

can't remember about what." I cringed, and she grabbed my arm, walking me away as she leaned in to whisper.

"She has that effect on people. I'll introduce you to the cool people and the best places to hide from Mira."

"I like you already."

"Good. I like you, too."

Her smile was friendly, her brown eyes sparkling and carefree, and I was happy to have met her. Yay, I made a work friend!

The rest of the day was busy as I went from department to department, meeting so many people I lost track of their names after the third one. Some of them were like Mira, only wanting to suck up to me because of who my brother and father were, but most were genuinely lovely and willing to give me a chance.

By the time I finished all the paperwork, initiation videos, and reviewed the equipment I had at my disposal, it was dark outside. I ordered another Uber and headed out when they were close. I really needed to get my license renewed. Clive was no longer at his post when I stepped outside, but another man I didn't know was.

"Good evening, Miss. Would you like me to walk you to your car?"

"Oh, I'm good. Thanks, though." My cheeks heated.

"Of course, Miss. Be safe. Just scream loud if you need me." He gave me a friendly wink, and I laughed, waving bye as I walked the two feet to the Uber and conveniently ignored the hulking man leaning against the black Mustang. I'd managed to avoid him all day and not run into him, so I wasn't going to fold now.

My body sagged as I got into the car, exhaustion hitting me like a ton of bricks. I'd planned to run to the store to get some clothes, but at this rate, I didn't have much energy beyond getting home and climbing the steps to bed. I glanced down at the pair of leggings I'd worn for two days and

debated whether I could get away with the extra-large sweatpants tomorrow.

"Looks like it's laundry night."

Sighing, I hoped there was a frozen pizza in the freezer, or
I wouldn't make it through laundry.

CHAPTER
TWELVE

BLAKE

AN HOUR LATER, WITH MY BELLY FULL AND MY CLOTHES DRYING, I climbed into bed, ready to sleep.

Yet, sleep did not come for me.

Ugh. Why was my brain always like this? I replayed through the day's events, Hawk's looming shadow pressing into me the more I thought about it.

Why was he constantly watching me if he didn't feel anything for me? Was it just because Bryce asked him to?

"Boys are the worst!" I yelled, pulling the extra pillow over my head as I screamed into it. Giving up on sleep while my brain was active, I unplugged my phone from charging and rolled over in an attempt to read a book. Instead of opening my e-reader app, a notification caught my eye instead.

New messages.

It flashed at me, and I realized I hadn't looked at it most of the day. I'd been so busy I hadn't had the time. Giddy excitement filled me as I rolled over and opened the text thread from my two guys.

Whoa. Hold up. They weren't *my* guys.

Yet, my brain whispered.

Rolling my eyes at my eager vagina and brain, I scrolled to the top of the messages to catch up.

Pitcher: Do you think dogs dream?

Catcher: Yes. Just not what you think they dream about.

Pitcher: What about cats?

Catcher: Only about scratching your eyes out.

Pitcher: Why would you tell me that!

Catcher: Truth isn't always pretty, my friend.

Pitcher: There's a pop-up sale tomorrow before the game.

Catcher: No.

Pitcher: But...

Catcher: No.

Pitcher: You're so mean.

Catcher: You told me to tell you no. I'm only being a good friend.

Pitcher: Ugh. I hate having to be responsible. What if?

Catcher: No.

Catcher: Quit annoying our mystery girl. Ask her questions so we can guess.

Pitcher: Ooo, right.

Pitcher: Is it weird I'm nervous about seeing you tomorrow?

After laughing at their back and forth, I took pity on them because I was nervous, too.

> Blake: Hey, sorry. Busy day at work.

> Blake: No, it's not weird. I'm nervous, too.

> Catcher: How was your day, Sunshine?

> Blake: Tiring, but now I can't sleep.

> Pitcher: I can't either. First game jitters, and G won't even let me look at new shoes.

> Catcher: Why am I the bad guy? You asked me to.

> Blake: Yeah, don't be mad at him. He's being a good friend.

> Blake: But what are you nervous about?

> Catcher: Thanks, Sunshine.

Warm tingles spread through me, and I smiled at my phone. This felt nice. I'd dated Brandon for so long that I'd forgotten what this part of flirting felt like. Though, to be fair, we'd met at school and were friends first. I didn't think we ever had this flirty back and forth. With Hawk, it was a different type of flirty. One with someone who knew you so well, they had insider information.

I had dated a guy for a few months back in Greece. With him, things had been fun and easy. There had been little tingles like this initially, but they'd fizzled out after a while. The first time I felt anything close to this had been with Luke. The reminder of how he'd ghosted me after sleeping together sent a spiral of sourness over my mood.

What if my curse for leaving Brandon at the altar was to never progress past one-night stands?

I'd been with Brandon for five years, but we'd never had sex together since he'd wanted to wait until the wedding... the wedding I ran away from.

And now, each person I clicked with ran away from me after sex?

Had I reverse-cursed myself?

My phone vibrated in my hand, reminding me I'd been in the middle of a conversation.

Pitcher: It's a new team, and everyone will be looking at me.

Pitcher: Our last team wasn't great, even though we were in the Majors.

Catcher: We've been playing well together, TJ. We've got this.

Pitcher: I know. I... overthink everything.

Blake: I do the same. Just was, in fact.

Pitcher: Oh, what about, fellow overthinker?

Blake: Relationships. I suck at them.

Catcher: I find that unlikely.

Blake: Well, it feels that way at the moment.

Pitcher: I can't say I've had the greatest luck in that department. I'm either too invested or not enough.

Catcher: I'm usually too slow and miss opportunities.

Blake: So, we're three oddballs? Is that what I'm hearing?

Pitcher: Seems so. I like that. We're the proverbial screwballs, which happens to be one of my favorite pitches.

I sucked in a breath, all the baseball knowledge my dad and brother had ever bestowed upon me running through my head. With trembling fingers, I typed out my next message and held my breath.

Blake: Isn't that also known as the reverse curse?

Catcher: Yeah. You know your baseball pitches.

Pitcher: Fuck, that's sexy.

Pitcher: Talk baseball to me, baby.

Pitcher: I just got a chill.

Pitcher: Okay, now I'm excited about tomorrow.

Blake: Yeah? How about we all send a pic for good luck?

Pitcher: Yes, please.

Catcher: Private or group?

Blake: Whichever you prefer.

Pitcher: You're not using us for our bodies, are you?

Blake: And if I was?

Pitcher: Then I consent.

Blake: Honestly, my dating life isn't the only thing I'm bad at.

Blake: It's kind of embarrassing, but what are mysterious texters for, right?

Catcher: We won't judge.

Pitcher: You can trust us.

It was weird since I hadn't met them yet, and we'd only been talking for a few days. But I did. I trusted them both.

Blake: My first time was at the age of 25. I'd done other things but with only one person.

Blake: I've only been with 2 people in the past three years.

Blake: One was the other night.

Blake: So, see… I'm cursed with dating and sex.

Catcher: Believe it or not, my history isn't much better.

Pitcher: I might have volume, but not quantity.

Blake: I find that hard to believe.

Catcher: Not every baseball player is… well, a player.

Blake: Okay, fair.

Pitcher: It was fun in the beginning. But girls always want me to be someone I'm not.

Catcher: And like I said, I tend to say the wrong things or get my foot stuck in my mouth.

Blake: So I'm in good company.

Pitcher: The best.

Catcher: I have a suggestion.

Pitcher: Another?

Blake: I'm not getting the whole 'too slow' thing.

Catcher: I'm great over text.

Catcher: What if we all explore together?

Pitcher: How so?

Blake: Sounds intriguing…

Catcher: It could be fun and less stressful.

Pitcher: Like a sex truth or dare, but all dares?

Blake: That could be fun.

Catcher: So our first task… send a picture. You pick the level of spicy.

Pitcher: I'm so gonna win this game.

Catcher: We all win at this game, dude.

Blake: Right. Goodnight, my fellow screwballs.

Picher: Goodnight, Future Mrs.

Catcher: Goodnight, Sunshine.

Biting my lip, I debated what type of pic to send. I didn't want to show my face, so I rolled onto my arms and braced myself on my elbows. Squeezing my cleavage together, I took a picture before angling the phone against the pillow to give them another tease. My nipples were practically popping out of my shirt, making it just provocative enough. I was rather pleased with the effect, so I sent it before I chickened out.

Shock followed by arousal hit me when their pictures soon followed. Pulling out the bullet vibrator I'd packed in my carry-on, I let myself imagine being with them both simultaneously. I hadn't thought I was ready for a threesome, but maybe Emory was right. They both made me feel things, and their chemistry together was undeniable. They could be precisely what I'd been looking for. A little fun.

Squeezing my nipple, I placed the vibe right over my clit as I rocked back and forth, my breathy moans filling the room. Pitcher had sent another shot of his dick, with his hand wrapped around it, the tip laying against his abs. He already had a drop of precum beading there, and I could imagine him stroking himself. I rocked into my hand, filling my head with how he might sound when he came. My arousal climbed higher, and I stared at Catcher's picture next.

It wasn't as revealing, but the outline of his dick in his boxers made my mouth water. Just how big was he? His muscular thighs were almost as seductive with the dark hair covering them. He said he was the quieter of the two, but I didn't get that yet. He was softer, but he was engaged. Something told me he'd be a generous lover and would surprise me with his silent commands. The way he ordered Pitcher at times was hot as hell, and to imagine that dynamic in the bedroom had me gasping.

I envisioned Catcher watching as he directed Pitcher and me, his desire evident, pushing us all close to our release.

My body tensed, and I let go as I came, my clit pulsing with the vibrations of my orgasm as my cum covered my hand. I lay there for a few minutes as I recovered, hoping they were the answer to my curse—my screwballs.

CHAPTER
THIRTEEN

GRAHAM

My phone fell to the counter as I stared at the racy photos. It was hot as hell, and my cock took notice. Snapping a picture of my hard-on through my boxers, I sent it before I could talk myself out of it. When Tucker's came through right after, I sucked in a breath at his beautiful cock on display. Licking my lips, I was about to pull my cock out when I heard Tucker's groan.

Jolting up, I strolled into the hallway, spotting him through the crack in his door. I knew I shouldn't move closer to see what he was doing. But I was ultimately weak, and my feet took me right up to his door.

I argued that he didn't care if I watched since he left it open like he always did. It sounded lame even to my own ears, but I wasn't one to look too closely at my reasoning regarding my best friend.

I'd been in love with Tucker for so long that I didn't remember a time I hadn't been. There was only friendship initially, but it quickly became more for me in college.

And when I came out as pansexual, he hadn't even

blinked at it. He became my biggest ally and supported me against the guys on our team who had a problem.

I knew I was a cliche, falling in love with my straight best friend. But Tucker Jameson was the best person I knew, man or woman. Only a few people could come into contact with Tucker and not fall under his charm.

"Fuuuck," he groaned, and I inched closer, finding his tall, muscular frame standing at the foot of his bed, completely naked. The muscles in his ass flexed as he gripped his cock and stroked himself. His phone lay on the bed, and I assumed the picture our mystery girl had sent was on the screen.

My cock leaked against my thigh, my heart thumping loudly in my ears as I battled with myself on the right thing to do. Tucker continued to stroke himself, his moans growing louder as he bit his lip, staring at the image. It was pure pornography, and I was weak to the pull he had on me.

Sliding my hand into my boxers, I stroked myself from root to tip, brushing against the pelvic piercing I had. It sent tiny tendrils of pleasure as I rubbed against it at the base of my cock, and I had to bite my lip to stop myself from moaning too loud.

Tucker picked up his pace, and I matched his strokes, eventually pulling my cock out of my pants. I stayed in the shadows, leaning against the wall to keep myself upright as I envisioned myself being the one to touch his dick. Our mystery girl would kiss him while caressing me, and Tucker's fingers would play with her nipples before plunging into her. The three of us worked in tandem in my mind, Tucker's moans filling my ears as he pleasured himself faster and adding to my fantasy.

The image was so intense and mind-blowing that my balls drew up quicker than I thought possible. Before I could stop it, my orgasm crashed over me as my cum spilled onto my hand, my strokes sloppy as I chased the last remnants. I'd managed to cover my mouth with my fist, moaning into it as I watched Tucker explode, his cum shooting out and hitting his bed and phone.

He laughed, shaking his head, and I remembered I wasn't meant to be outside his door creeping. Quickly, I stumbled into the bathroom to wash my hands. Righting my clothes, I stepped out as he appeared. He'd thrown on some boxer briefs that should've been criminal. They were so tight and short they barely covered his ass.

Tucker smirked in my direction as he slid into the bathroom, shutting the door behind him. Had he seen me? What did his smirk mean? Did he think it was weird I hadn't used my bathroom?

The toilet flush had me jolting out of my stupor, and I headed back to the kitchen to finish preparing overnight oats for the morning.

"Night," Tucker hollered as he returned to his room.

"Night," I responded, watching him go, longing sitting heavy in my chest. His door stayed open, his sound machine coming on before he face-planted onto his bed like a starfish.

Shaking myself out of it, I turned off the lights and checked the locks. Once everything was settled for the night, I went into my room and crawled into my bed. I needed to get over my crush on Tucker. It wouldn't go anywhere, and I was only torturing myself by entertaining it.

Despite those words of caution, I couldn't ignore how good it felt when I'd come earlier. Imagining our mystery girl between us made me orgasm so hard that I would've fallen over if I wasn't leaning against the wall.

Determined to figure out who she was before I gave up all hope, I closed my eyes and focused on the game. Opening day was tomorrow, and it was the second-best day of the year after Halloween, and I wanted to do well.

Add in potentially meeting our mystery girl, and it might eclipse my favorite day this year.

Tucker and I arrived at the clubhouse six hours before game time. Despite what people believed, a lot went on beforehand. Our job might be playing baseball, but it was still a job. And that meant there were several things required to do outside of playing.

The two of us had cultivated a foolproof routine over the years that worked best for us. Baseball players were creatures of habit and some of the most superstitious athletes. However, most sports thought that of themselves.

Tucker and I got up and ate our high protein breakfast with just enough carbohydrates and all the other things we'd need for the day. Then, there was silence between us, both running through the pitches and playbook until we got in the car, where we listened to the same '90s pop playlist Tucker had made in college.

We'd do our stretches, batting practice, and warmup pitches from there. If any publicity or marketing was scheduled, we fit that in as well. Once we were ready for the game, there was some downtime where we could relax or fall into our pregame habits. Tucker liked to talk and play cards, whereas I wanted to meditate and zone out by reading. These had worked for the past seven years, but something felt different about this team, this city.

It might be time to find new routines. But was I willing to jinx the season to try?

The last song tapered off as we stepped into the facility, our earbuds going quiet as we walked up the concourse to the clubhouse. Typically, we stayed quiet until we got out onto the field, but Tucker had been fighting the urge to ask me something all morning. Now that the playlist was over, he jumped on the opportunity, proving something was changing.

"Who do you think she is?" he asked, his gaze sweeping

over everyone. Not that there were many people around at this time of day.

A girl hurried by with a tray of coffees; a guy shouted something into his phone as he paced up ahead; the camera girl crouched down in her spot, taking pictures as the players entered the stadium. They were all part of the background, typical roles in the scenery.

Except there was a buzz of something that wasn't typically there.

"I have a few ideas," I said, looking around for the source of the buzzing. "Do you feel that?" I asked, rubbing my arms.

"My skin feels alive, but I assumed it was because of opening day." Tucker shrugged, shaking out his arms as he peered around. He glanced over, his eyes wide. "Do you think it's her? Last night was hot!"

I shrugged as we kept walking, not knowing how to answer him. Last night had been incredible. I'd been shocked they'd both been willing to go along with my game. But I could feel it. The three of us were bordering on something, and I didn't know if they both understood what. *If* Tucker understood it.

As my thoughts tumbled around unsuccessfully, the electrifying feeling intensified in my body, spreading across my chest, and I knew it had to be her. Only one other time I had felt this energy, and I'd been too insecure and nervous to do anything about it. I wouldn't make that same mistake again. But first, I had to locate the source.

"Do you think she'll say anything to us?" he asked. "I want her to like us. I've never felt this sure before about a girl. Plus, those pics were scorching. I got off to them again this morning," he admitted as we passed the photographer. She'd been snapping pictures, glancing up as we passed.

She snorted, covering her mouth as her cheeks pinked at his comment. My eyes met hers, perfect blue ones the shade of the sky and somewhat familiar, stared back at me through round glasses. I felt a zing between us, like a string reached outside me and connected straight to her.

Fuck. I'd been reading too many comic books if I suddenly thought I was having some existential Spiderman moment.

Her eyes burrowed into me, and something in the back of my skull shook loose as I stared. She blinked, breaking the spell as she returned to her camera, snapping pictures of the players behind us.

I took a second to take her in, turning my head to observe every detail I could. A YellowJacket hat covered her head, her hair pulled into a ponytail with blonde and pink strands spilling out the back. The bill obscured most of her face, hiding her features. I couldn't tell much more from her squat on the floor, but the feeling of knowing her, of being *familiar*, was so strong.

Was that her? Was she our mystery texter?

Shaking my head, I kept walking with Tucker as the other players caught up, slapping us in greeting.

"Package deal! You two ready to shine?" Tommy, one of the outfielders, asked.

"You know it," Tucker cheered, smiling wide at the other guys. He was the friendly and outgoing one of our duo. He knew everyone by name and asked questions about their families. It wasn't that I didn't, but I preferred one-on-one versus a large group.

Shane, the other catcher, walked up, giving me a nod. "How you feeling?" he asked, falling into step with me.

"Good. Feel ready for today. Baseball's back, baby."

He smiled, clapping me on the back. "Yeah, it is."

The noise in the clubhouse was boisterous as we entered, as everyone's excitement for opening day spilled out, growing bigger and bigger as the team arrived. Well, except for one player.

Luke Olson slammed his locker, kicking his chair as he

stormed out. The rest of the YellowJackets stopped, looking around for the cause of his outburst.

"What's that about?" Tucker asked two of the older guys. Jack moved closer, attempting to keep his voice low.

"Bryce was traded up in place of him. They're not trusting his recovery," Jack said, pulling everyone's attention.

"Shit," Hector cursed, doing the sign of the cross as he kissed the saint he kept around his neck.

"Bryce's gone?" Tucker asked, his eyes wide.

"Yep. He left yesterday," Shane said, nodding to Coach Anderson as he walked out of the coach's office. It was well-known that they were best friends, and if anyone had the inside scoop on Bryce, it would be him.

"Well, damn. I'd been looking forward to playing with him. I guess he's really not pranking us now," Tucker mumbled, changing into a pair of compression leggings, dri-fit shorts, and a shirt.

The gossip around the clubhouse dwindled as everyone got into the right headspace, changing into our warmup gear and heading out onto the diamond. Champion Field was luxurious, with brick stands and an open backfield that over-looked the water in the distance. The sun would set right there at night, giving the fans a nice view. Me too, if I was honest.

Being the catcher, I got to look out into the field more than most of the players, and a beautiful sunset against the ball-park lights was one of my favorite views.

Halfway through warmups, I felt that buzzing feeling again, and when I spotted the camera girl talking with the head coach, I knew my earlier guess had been correct.

Somehow, the girl with the camera was our mystery girl. I didn't know her name or who she was, but I was confident. Everything fit, including the first picture she'd sent us, "Pho-tographers did it better."

Coach Anderson pulled Tucker and me over to the side to

warm up his pitches, and he caught me staring at her in the stands.

"You know who that is?" I asked, unable to stop myself. Tucker spun around, searching for who I spoke of.

"Yes," Coach said, not elaborating. I typically didn't care since I disliked talking almost as much, but his refusal to say more here felt deliberate.

"Ooh, do you think that's her?" Tucker asked, jumping up and down like a hyperactive kid on candy.

"Yeah. I think so." I watched her, taking in the way she laughed and talked like she knew this place and the people better than I did. "Just who is she?" I asked again, keeping my gaze on Coach Anderson. His jaw clenched, and his hands tightened, giving me more of an answer than he realized.

"No one you need to worry about. I'd drop it if I were you." His eyes narrowed, and typically I'd be scared shitless as this tattooed bear of a man stared me down, but for some reason I wasn't.

"I'm just asking her name, dude. No reason to Hulk out."

"You realize you just made us want to figure out who she is even more, right?" Tucker asked, laughing. He turned to me, his eyes sparkling.

"I bet you dinner. I can find it out before you," I challenged.

"Add in dessert, and you're on." We slapped hands, making it official.

"Fucking hell," Coach Anderson cursed, rubbing his temple. "Get into position before I tell Coach Phillips to bench you."

Dismissing his threat, I crouched down with my gear and helped Tucker warm up before we moved over for batting practice. Once everyone had gone through each rotation, Shane and Austin switched us out so we could get in a few hits. Luke decided to return right then, too, storming onto the field, his face red and angry as he gripped his bat.

"You're not going to hit anything that pissed off," I said, despite knowing better.

"Fuck off, West," he gritted out, swinging too soon and missing the ball. He did it several times, only making contact on the last one. It popped up, going high over the foul line and angering Olson even more.

He tossed his bat against the boards, stomping toward the dugout as he stormed off. Tucker shook his head, his brown locks falling into his eyes as he sighed. Shrugging, I took my turn, hitting two into the outfield and two line drives. It wasn't my best, but it was enough to warm me up for the game in a few hours.

Tucker took his turn, nailing one after the other, disproving the theory that pitchers weren't great hitters. If there was anyone who broke the stereotype, it was Tucker Jameson. The man breathed, slept, and lived baseball more than anyone I knew.

He slung his arm over my shoulders with a big smile, and we headed into the clubhouse. Now, we'd have an hour to goof off before it was time to dress out. Happy vibrations raced through me, knowing opening day was even closer.

Luke scowled at his locker, drinking a water bottle as he stared at the floor like he wished it would open up in front of him. He pulled on his headphones, ignoring the team as we all trickled in from warmups. I only knew him by reputation since he'd missed spring training, but I wasn't getting the vibe he was happy to be here.

And while I got that, everyone wished they were playing in the big leagues instead; we still had a game to play, fans to show up for, and teammates to support. We wouldn't win with poor attitudes.

Somehow, I didn't take Olson as the type to be welcoming of a pep talk, so I'd leave him alone for now. But if it continued, my need for team peace would force me to say something.

Let's just hope it didn't end with a fist to my face.

Sitting in front of my locker, I wiped my brow and gulped down a water bottle before pulling out my book. I'd only read a few pages when the buzzing feeling hit me again. Coach Phillips walked over, his hand on the shoulder of the camera girl as they chatted. He stopped before he went too far, checking everyone was decent.

"Get yourself dressed if you ain't," he shouted. "I have an introduction to make."

I patted Tucker, his head snapping up as he took in the woman. Now that she was standing, I could make out more features. She was medium height, coming right to Coach's shoulder as she stood in neon yellow hightops, black leggings, and a YellowJackets jersey knotted on the side. It almost looked like she'd raided the gift shop decked out in her YellowJackets gear.

I took in her curves, wishing I could see more of her and feel her body against mine. My eyes ran back up, meeting those piercing blue ones, and I noticed how pink her cheeks were. Her gaze strayed to Tucker and then back to me, a twinkle in her eyes as she waited to see if we'd figure it out. I gave her a knowing smirk while my best friend floundered in her presence.

It was cute to see him so flustered.

"Do you think...?" he whispered but was cut off from saying anything else as Olson erupted again. Mystery girl jumped at the shout, and everyone turned to Luke as he stood, seething.

"Are you fucking kidding me?"

I glanced back and forth between them, watching as her face turned hopeful as she spotted him, to pale as he shook with anger.

"Luke?" she asked, her voice small but the same one I'd

heard the other night. Tucker tapped me excitedly, but I was too focused on the drama unfolding.

Holy shit. Was Olson the plane guy?

She'd told us snippets of her night, and I'd pieced together something had happened. The entire room swiveled from one to the next, waiting for the next bite of information like the hungry gossipers we all were.

Luke's jaw clenched, and he shook his head, storming out the other direction as everyone gawked. I wanted to jump up and comfort her, the look of horror on her face making me itch to make it right, but it wasn't my place, and now definitely wasn't the time.

Coach Phillips cleared his throat, bringing everyone back to focus. "Right, not sure what that was, but this is Blake Baker. She's filling in with social media and footage while Rachel is on maternity leave. She'll meet with each of you over the next month to set up some new ideas to get people excited about coming out to see us. Be nice. She's like a daughter to me, and, yes, she is *that* Baker." He narrowed his eyes, his message clear, but what he didn't realize was the target he placed on her instead. Some guys would consider that a challenge, especially since Bryce was gone.

"Yes, *that* Baker." She crossed her arms, her fight returning. "I've been around ball players my whole life. You don't intimidate me. I'm not going to fall all over your feet like a cleat chaser. I take my job seriously and have good ideas. So, trust me to do what I'm here for, and we'll work out great," she said, her voice stronger now, sending the same goosebumps she'd given me the first time across my skin. "And it's Bee. You might be YellowJackets, but don't forget I also know how to sting." She winked at us before turning on her hightops and leaving, the clubhouse eerily silent in her wake.

The buzz in my chest intensified, my skin alive as the puzzle pieces clicked into place—the wrong phone number, how she knew information about us, and teased us about Bryce.

Tucker leaned over, his hand gripping my bicep as he whispered into my ear, his hot breath adding to my goosebumps.

"I think I'm in love. She really will be the future Mrs. Jameson." He sighed wistfully.

A tiny part of me broke at that, knowing he would never be mine, but maybe she could be ours together. A plan formed in my head, and I only had to figure out how to convince them. It felt like we were already halfway there after the past few days. And this time, I wouldn't be too slow or insecure, missing my chance.

The setup was there; I just had to call the right pitch to win her heart.

CHAPTER
FOURTEEN

BLAKE

SOMEHOW, I MADE IT THROUGH THE GAME, FOCUSING ON TAKING pictures and listening to Rue give me a rundown of her plans for entertainment. I nodded along at the correct times and offered up ideas at others, but truth be told, I couldn't remember a damn thing we'd talked about.

Because my entire being was focused on the first baseman, number 24.

I'd been anxious already walking into the stadium, knowing I'd see Tucker and Graham today and wondering if they'd know it was me like they said. Top it off with Hawk's ever-present shadow, and I was on edge with the need to prove myself in this job.

The need to show I was good at something and had value to offer had grown exponentially with Bryce's departure, especially after Mira's attitude. I wanted to be seen as more than a Baker, the owner's daughter—even if I had used that to prove a point.

Baseball players didn't scare me, but love sure did.

But the moment my eyes landed on his green ones, so

reminiscent of a baseball diamond, it felt like all the oxygen had been sucked out of the room.

My Luke was Luke Olson.

It was bad enough that my plane-night-stand was on the YellowJackets where I now worked, but that he also happened to be my brother's biggest rival was staggering. Especially when Bryce had just taken Luke's position with the Blue Devils—the one he'd been working hard to regain for his daughter.

A daughter I now had insider information about.

With the way he glared fire at me every time our eyes met, he hated that I knew his secrets. I wasn't sure if he thought it meant I had the upper hand or if I'd use it against him, but either way, I wouldn't. It wasn't my secret to spill, and I would never do that to a child. I'd been that little girl in the spotlight and wouldn't put anyone in that position.

Outside of the surprise of seeing him and the hurt of his rejection, my traitorous body still wanted him. My heart jumped each time I looked in his direction on the field, butterflies raring to life as I watched him play.

Not that he played great.

I didn't know if it was coming back from an injury or something else, but the Luke Olson on the field was not the player who rivaled my brother. Because this Luke Olson kinda sucked.

He struck out each time at bat, flubbed catches thrown to him, and overthrew others, missing key plays. Coach Phillips pulled him in the fifth inning, not that it mattered. The YellowJackets were down and couldn't rally back, losing the game 4-10.

My fellow screwballs had played well and were two of the runs, getting onto base in the third inning to score. My cheeks pinked at every mention of them by the announcers, wondering what they thought about me now they knew who I was. Or at least I assumed they knew. Graham seemed to have put the pieces together, and based on the big smile on Tucker's face, he'd shared it.

Hawk hadn't tried to talk to me again, but I could feel his stare boring into the side of my head. Yet, his stern gaze was off in the distance each time I looked. The man had the reflexes of a cat, apparently.

Wiping the sweat from my brow, I squinted behind my glasses, hoping my luggage would arrive soon. Wearing glasses in the sun was the worst! My glasses slipped and fogged constantly, making it difficult to see, much less take pictures.

Shifting my camera strap to my other shoulder, I checked my watch to gauge how much longer I needed to stay. The hours weren't listed with this position and were more of a suggestion. I returned to the tunnels to catch players as they left out, hoping it meant I could go home after. It had been a long day, full of—

The door slammed open, and it barely missed smacking me in the face; my hands reached out just in time to stop it, my camera shifting on my shoulder.

"What the hell?" I shouted. Tiny needles raced up my palms, and I rubbed them to soothe the ache.

"Do I need to get a restraining order?" Luke hissed, and I jerked my head up.

My words caught in my throat, his mere presence sending tingles over me as my cheeks heated with embarrassment. The stony look on his face triggered my anger, erasing all of my mortification.

Why did he get to act like the wronged party? He'd left me!

I'd had enough of this douche talking to me like I was the gum on the bottom of his shoe, especially when I had no idea why he hated me.

"Me? You're the one who ghosted me in a room of golf balls!" I moved closer, narrowing my eyes. "I don't do things like *that...*" My cheeks heated at the confession. I swallowed, ignoring his look of disbelief. "I don't sleep with people I just met. So imagine my surprise when I get out of the shower, and poof, you're gone!" The hurt in my voice wasn't as covered as I hoped, nor were the tears glistening.

Luke gritted his teeth, his green eyes shimmering with rage as he stared down at me, not caring. His golden hair was wet, making it darker. The ends curled as they dried, and my finger itched to brush them aside. Luke rolled his eyes, breaking the moment and reminding me of our standoff.

"Like *you* didn't know who I was, Blake Baker. Bee, my ass." He scoffed. He stepped forward, his words freezing me. "You lured me into that room to get whatever story you wanted." He looked me up and down, clear disdain covering all of his features. He crossed his arms, his lip curling in disgust. "What did you tell your dad to keep me here? Did you think you could lock me down if I was closer? Are you just waiting to use..." He swallowed the word. "When's my life going to explode?"

My mouth gaped as I tried to piece together the vitriol he spat at me. He thought I was the reason Bryce was called up?

"What?" I blinked so hard that an eyelash stuck to my glasses. I pulled them off, his face blurry as I wiped them, buying time to formulate words. Once they were back, I glared at him, turning my hurt into hatred.

"I had no idea who you were. I've been in Greece for three years, if you don't remember. Far away from the baseball world!"

He scoffed, clearly not buying my explanation.

"Then why was *my* name written down on your pad of paper, hmm? If you had no idea who I was like you said?"

My nose scrunched up as I recalled what he was talking about. "The pad by my bag?" I asked, making sure I had the correct info.

"Yep. It had my name, Jameson's, and West's. Care to

explain how that doesn't make you a sneak, a reporter, or a cleat chaser, then?" I jolted back like he'd slapped me.

"Wow." I threw up my hands, taking a step backward. "Do you remember anything else from that night? From all the beautiful things we shared?" I shook my head, fighting back my tears as my heart splintered. "Bryce, *my brother*, had called me. He was helping me prep for my new job." I held my camera up. "*This* job. Funny enough, I hadn't made it to your name on my list yet. So, when I walked into the club-house today, it was like I could breathe again for the first time in days. And then I was abruptly reminded how much it hurt to have a heart break."

Spinning quickly, I had to get away. I hadn't meant to share anything that personal, and the tears were no longer willing to stay put. But I stopped a few feet away, tilting my head slightly over my shoulder.

"If you would've asked me, you could've saved us both a lot of heartache. But no, you assumed the worst-case scenario and bolted." I wiped my cheek. "I didn't tell my dad, and I'm not going to. Despite what you seem to believe, I'm a good person. Your secret's safe with me. I wouldn't do that to you or Willow."

Hurrying away, I took the next corner, not caring where I went as long as it was far away from Luke. The pain in my chest wanted to make him hurt, but I didn't have it in me to lob anything at him in this condition. I kept going until I almost caught a door to the face for the second time today.

"Whoa, there!" a masculine voice said, then paused. "You okay?"

I shook my head, wiping my cheeks as I gave a watery smile, lifting my eyes to meet a vaguely familiar guy. He tilted his head, his demeanor changing.

"You're the new camera girl, right? I'm Seth Davis, third baseman." He pointed to himself. He was cute, with that sort of boy-next-door look about him. His brown hair was short, and his brown eyes reminded me of brownies. But most of all, he had a kind smile that I needed right then.

"Hi, yeah, I'm Blake." I wiped my cheeks, then wiped my hands on my leggings. "Nice to meet you. Sorry, I wasn't watching."

I grimaced, my face flaming, and moved to step around him; his hand caught my arm and stopped me. I glanced back, giving him a curious look.

"Hmm?" He paused, licking his lips and moving his eyes over me. I felt nothing, though, and I just wanted to find a place to cry in peace.

"There's a tradition of going to The Dugout after the first game. You should come. Fried food and beer can solve most problems."

It was on the tip of my tongue to say no, but then I spotted Luke out of the corner of my eye as he came around the bend, and the words fell out of my mouth before I could stop them.

"I'd love to. When do we leave?" I asked, looping my arm through his and walking in the opposite direction I'd been going.

"Cool. You can ride with me. A bunch of us are carpooling. Gotta be on the safe side." He winked but didn't make the butterflies dance.

Perhaps I needed a guy cleanser for my soul. Someone I didn't get all the feels for, just to get back up to bat, so to speak. My brain warned me about the last guy I didn't have butterflies for I almost married, but I shoved it away, already too emotional to think rationally.

Seth gave me a smile that probably worked on most girls as we walked, nodding at Luke as we passed. I kept my eyes forward but watched him grit his teeth out of the corner of my eyes. It didn't slip my notice Luke didn't get the invite. Did the others not like him? Based on his surly attitude, I could understand why.

A group of guys waited in the lot, cheering when we neared. The overwhelmingness of what I was doing hit me, and I opened my mouth to back out, but Seth moved his arm around my shoulders, trapping me.

"Look who I found."

I gave a small wave, anxiety creeping up my neck until I spotted Graham and Tucker by another car. Despite not speaking face-to-face with them, I felt better about this outing. But the bond with them was natural, even if it had only been texting back and forth, sharing pictures, and one phone call.

Just staring at them right now motivated the butterflies back to life, and I hoped they didn't think I was with Seth despite having considered using him moments before.

With how they held my eyes, I was hopeful they didn't. My cheeks heated the longer we stared, and my pussy throbbed at the look Tucker gave me as he bit the corner of his lip. My feet moved in his direction, but before I could take two steps, Seth ushered me into a Jeep. I was squashed in the middle between two players quicker than I could blink.

"Oh, hi." I gave a smile and wave. "Bee."

"Noah. You're Baker's sister?"

"Yup." I nodded, his position coming to mind. "Outfielder?"

"You're good." He smiled before looking out the window.

I turned to the other guy, but he had his head bowed. His long, reddish hair was pulled back, his arm muscles bulging as he gripped the upper bar of the Jeep.

"That's Ledger. He doesn't talk to anyone," Noah said, nudging me in the side as the car took off.

Ledger Collins. Short Stop, my mind supplied.

Apparently, osmosis worked when learning team positions.

The cool night air whipped around us, cooling my cheeks, and I held my hat down to keep it in place. Seth had the top and doors off his Jeep. It was early April and still slightly too cold for the wind, but apparently Seth disagreed. I didn't understand guys' love for driving with the wind whipping around them, but I suppose if they didn't have long hair to deal with, they didn't care.

We pulled up to The Dugout a few minutes later, and I was thankful it wasn't too far from Champion Field. I needed to orient myself to Wilmington when I had a chance. While it had been Bryce's team for the past three years, it had been while I'd been away. In some ways, it was nice. There were too many people back home who remembered all of my most embarrassing moments, including bolting from the altar.

The staff there had watched me grow up, get sick, and then subsequently treated me like glass. Plus, there was no mistake about who they answered to—dear old Dad. Nothing I did ever went unnoticed. All those eyes on me, I shuddered just thinking about it.

The triple-A team might not be the Majors, but it was far enough away from my father and mother's prying eyes. And now even my brother's. Only a handful of staff remembered me from the few summers I volunteered, and only one coach knew me from childhood.

And well, the one who wasn't speaking to me because I meant nothing to him, so he didn't count.

"First drink on me," Seth said as we climbed out. He wrapped his arm around my shoulder, leading me into the bar. I guess he wanted me to sit with him. I glanced back, spotting the two people I wished I could talk to, a handful of players between us, and longing filled me.

Use your words and sit with them, I encouraged. But the thought fled when I spotted Hawk in jeans so tight they should be illegal and an equally tight black t-shirt across his frame, those delicious tattoos on display. My mouth drooled, and I forgot my heartache as I drank him in. But when I spotted where his hands were on a girl's ass, I about fell over. It was only Seth's arm that kept me upright.

"Coach Anderson! Now the party's starting," Seth sang out, the patrons of The Dugout whooping and hollering as everyone spilled in. Tables and chairs were pulled together, and I ended up between Seth and the quiet one in a corner, far away from the two I wanted.

Tucker and Graham were at the other end of the table. They both stared; Tucker frowning at the occupied seats next to me. I returned it, feeling more hopeless the longer I was in this bar. Tucker wiggled his phone in my direction, and my eyes lit up.

Yes! We could text.

I patted my pockets but only had my camera around my neck. Shit.

Face falling, I shook my head at the realization. I'd been so annoyed with Luke that I'd left all my stuff in my locker, including my phone and wallet.

I poked Seth. "Um, so this is awkward, but I left my bag back at the stadium. I'm gonna see if I can get a ride back to get it."

"No worries, babe. We got you."

I grimaced. That hadn't been what I meant. It seemed like Seth had made a claim on me, and I didn't like it. Nor did I want to feel like I owed him anything, but if I brushed off his generosity in front of the others, it might come across as a bigger slight. And I definitely didn't want to make a scene on my first day.

"Thanks," I mumbled, deciding I'd try to find a ride back later once he lost interest in me. From past experiences, it wouldn't take long. Most guys got bored within a few minutes. They gave up once they realized I wouldn't help them meet my dad or brother. Add in the fact Seth wasn't even talking to me but to the guy on his other side, and I figured it would be quicker than most.

Drinks and food were placed on the table despite anyone taking our orders. The team dug in, grabbing food and pouring drinks, so I assumed it was the standard protocol. A few girls were mixed in with the players, hanging off some of the guys. I couldn't tell if they were partners or the cleat chasers were already out in force.

A cold glass was placed in my hand, and I smiled in thanks, sipping the beer slowly. I wasn't a huge drinker, and I'd likely be dancing on tables after two if I wasn't careful. Especially since I'd barely had time to eat all day.

However, my beer disappeared quicker than I intended with no one to talk to or a phone to look at. Each time I tried to reach for food, it disappeared before I could get any. I lifted my hand to get someone's attention, but the guys ignored me as they jibed each other.

On the contrary, my beer glass stayed full. Each time it got halfway, it would magically refill. Okay, it wasn't magic per se. I hadn't drunk *that* many beers. At least, I didn't think so. I'd lost count of how many beers it made.

I did manage to keep my eyes away from the end of the table Hawk was at, not wanting to watch him with his *girlfriend*. I wasn't ready for another round of torture today. As the night wore on, girls and guys surrounded my screwballs, so I hadn't even been able to sign for them to rescue me.

I wasn't sure how this was better than wallowing at home. I was trapped with no one to talk to, and I couldn't even eat my feelings. Leaning my head on my hand, I stared out into the crowded bar as my stomach growled, and I wondered how gross it would be to crawl under the table.

It might be worth it. Even if I didn't have any clothes that weren't my brothers.

A plate of wings and nachos appeared in front of me, the quiet man on my left had shoved them at me. When I stared too long at them, worried they'd disappear like everything else, he nudged me. Ledger pointed at the plate and then at me, apparently wanting me to eat. Smiling wide, I wrapped my arms around his big bicep, snuggling my face into him.

Okay, I definitely had more beers than I thought if I snuggled strangers.

"Thank you, Ledge. You're my hero for the day."

He froze, his blue eyes wide as he stared down at me like I'd just told him I was pregnant or something. Someone from across the table laughed, drawing my attention.

"He's gay, sweetie. But I'll be your hero."

I rolled my eyes, ignoring the blurry man across from me. "No, thank you. I've watched you eat. Gag." I picked up the wing, biting into it and moaning around the flavor as it exploded on my tongue. I didn't even care if I had sauce all over my face. I was that hungry. "And he's my hero because he gave me food."

Ledger chuckled, the sound soothing, and I grinned wide at him between bites of wings and nachos. When my plate was empty, I had to remind myself not to lick it. There were just enough brain cells left to remember that I worked with these people. Instead, I sighed, staring at it longingly.

"Shit, I wish a girl looked at my dick the way she's looking at that plate," one of the guys across from me said, causing the others to laugh.

I rolled my eyes, running my finger over the sauce and sticking it in my mouth.

Hey, I stopped the plate licking. Finger-licking was still fair game.

"Have you tried putting barbeque sauce on it?" I asked, squinting at him. The table roared, and I shrugged, not understanding what was so funny.

"Come and dance with me," Seth said, acknowledging me once again.

Before I could answer, he pulled me off my stool and onto the dance floor. My legs wobbled, the beer hitting me harder now that I'd stood up. I didn't know if that was a thing, but vertical drunkenness sounded totally like a thing.

I had absolutely no desire to dance with Seth, but it had gotten me out of the corner I'd been stuck in, so I'd do one dance and then make a break for it.

With a solid plan, I focused on moving my feet and staying upright to avoid falling on my face. Seth wrapped his arms around me, pulling me into his warm body. His shirt was scratchy against my cheek, and his cologne overwhelmed my beer-addled brain.

I lay my head on his chest. Mainly because it was too heavy to hold up; his hand ran up and down my back as we swayed back and forth. I closed my eyes tight. It was easier to pretend he was someone else if I didn't look at him.

"You're so pretty, Blake."

"Oh, um, thanks," I whispered, feeling weird.

"Could you ask your dad to meet with me?"

"My dad?" I asked, confused. Was he still here? I looked around, my vision blurring from the movement, and I gripped his arms tighter.

"Haven't I been so nice to you tonight? I brought you out with the team and covered your dinner and drinks. And now we're dancing. You're having a good time."

"Good. Time." The words fell from my lips, but something felt off. More like a question than a truth statement, one filled with hesitancy. My head swam, and my skin felt flushed. I squeezed my eyes closed to stop the swaying. He laughed, the sound sending a shiver of repulsion over me.

"It wasn't even a hardship to pretend," he said, mistaking my shiver for desire. "We could be something real. Open your eyes, babe."

"Pretend?" I slurred, the world spinning more, and none of his words made sense.

"For the bet."

I tilted my head, his image blurry, and touched my face to

ensure I had my glasses on. He swam in and out of focus, and I tried to recall his appearance. Brown hair? Brown eyes? My stomach tumbled, and I felt bile rise up my throat.

Before I could verify, his lips pressed down on mine, shocking me. When his tongue swirled inside my mouth, it was the last straw. The nausea I'd felt rose up, and I suddenly had my own vomitgate to contend with.

Thankfully, he let go of me, and I closed my eyes, glad I didn't have to deal with him anymore, even if it meant the world swayed more.

"Blake!" someone shouted, but I couldn't tell who, so I lifted my hand in a wave.

I closed my eyes and let my body sway to the music before everything darkened.

CHAPTER
FIFTEEN

TUCKER

ALL NIGHT, I'D BEEN TRYING TO MAKE MY WAY OVER TO BLAKE but kept getting cockblocked in the worst ways. Between my teammates seeming to hog her and trapping her in a corner, the abundance of ball girls hanging around, and fans wanting to reminisce about that time I'd been in the Little League World Series, I hadn't caught a free second. The only solace was Graham hadn't seemed to fare better either.

Usually, I loved the attention, wanting to bask in it and pick a girl to take home. It wasn't a bad life, and I'd enjoyed it after most games. But tonight, I just wanted to talk to one girl—Bee, aka the Future Mrs. Jameson.

I knew she thought I was being silly. Still, something about her had me falling hard and fast, a sensation I hadn't experienced before. I sighed woefully, my eyes watching her from across the bar. Graham snickered at me but had the same look on his face. I didn't know how this would play out between the three of us, but I wasn't worried about it because Graham was involved.

And while he didn't enjoy the attention as much as I did, his preferred nature being more introverted than myself, he was always with me. Where one of us was, the other was near. We were a duo on and off the field. And somehow, I knew that meant we could handle dating the same girl.

"Hey, PD! You guys rocked today," a guy shouted across the bar, using the term the team had given us—Package Deal.

I waved, smiling at him as I tracked Blake finally on the move. I gritted my teeth at Seth's hand on her, but I had no claim. We'd texted and sent sexy photos, and while I felt our connection in my soul, it wasn't a binding contract.

Didn't make me like him touching her though.

"I've never liked him," Graham whispered close to my ear, his breath warm and fanning across my skin. I ignored how good it felt and the tiny goosebumps forming as I focused on our girl. Whoa… our girl.

"Davis? I don't know much about him," I admitted, swirling my water. We had another game tomorrow, so after one beer, I'd stopped.

"He played with Kayce on the Bulldogs. He told me some stories."

"What kind of stories?" I asked, glancing back at him, bringing our noses imperceptibly closer.

"The 'not good' kind." His gray eyes flicked up to mine and then down to my lips before he moved back. I frowned but wasn't sure if it was because of what he said or the move.

"I don't like him dancing with her. After this song, I'm cutting in. Then, we're taking her out of here. She doesn't look too good."

Graham nodded. "I've been watching him and Noah. They'd constantly fed her drinks, and it wasn't until Ledger gave her food that she got any. I don't like it."

"Shit." I jumped off the stool at that and pulled out my wallet. I quickly tossed down some dollar bills onto the table. My bad feeling meter had gone off, and I wanted to be prepared. Graham followed suit, and we nodded to the guys we'd been sitting with that we'd see them tomorrow.

"Oh, fuck! So gross!" a few guys at the other end of the table shouted, the crowd noise growing louder as we neared. "Get it on film, man! That's Baker's sister."

My instincts went into overdrive, and I spun, racing through the group growing around the small dance floor. I stuttered in my steps as I watched Seth, covered in vomit, curse out the girl in front of him. It took me a few seconds to remember that it had been Blake.

"Oh, shit. Did she puke on him?" someone behind me said. "That's nasty."

Blake swayed on her feet, everyone more focused on the jackass than the drunk girl who needed help.

"Bee!" I shouted.

She didn't seem to hear me, her eyes closing as she tilted toward the floor. With quick reflexes, I slid across the floor to catch her, not caring if I got vomit on my pants. They could be washed, but her head might not survive the same fate if it cracked. By some miracle, I caught her right before she fell to the ground, landing in my arms instead of the hard floor.

"That was some kind of heroic shit there," a guy muttered, moving away now that the drama was done.

"Come on, let's get her out of here. Too many people filming this instead of helping," Graham urged, the anger evident in his voice.

"Hawk?" Blake slurred, her head rolling into my chest. She nuzzled me, licking her lips. "You smell good."

"Bee? It's Tucker." I stood and lifted her, smiling at how cute she was, even covered in vomit. I honestly didn't care. She was finally in my arms, and that felt right.

Graham pushed people out of his way, powering through them with his catcher's thighs, and led us to the restroom. He leveled an icy glare at anyone who laughed or had their phones out. A few lowered them, their faces adequately chastised, but most didn't seem to have any decency.

The noise of the bar quieted as we stepped into the unisex

bathroom, and Graham latched the door as I carried her to the sink. Together, we mopped up the vomit with some wet paper towels as best we could.

"I think she got most on Davis," Graham snorted. "Serves him right. I'm gonna go out on a limb and wager the stories are true. We'll need to watch him." He gritted his teeth, his eyes fierce as he stared. Graham was typically easygoing and stayed out of drama, but he had a protective streak a mile long, especially regarding women. Growing up with four older sisters would do that.

"I don't think we can salvage the shirt." I grimaced, pulling her arm free and balling it up to toss into the garbage.

"You just want her to wear yours," Graham teased. But he wasn't wrong.

Even knowing Baker was only her brother, it made me oddly jealous to see her in another man's jersey. Sliding off my zipped sweatshirt, I pulled it around her shoulders.

"Should we take her home with us? She has no phone, and I don't know where Bryce lives."

"And Hawk's gone. Probably the best option. We're not letting Seth take her, that's for damn sure," Graham huffed. "I'll text Hawk since she asked for him, and that way, in case anyone asks, it doesn't seem like we're kidnapping the boss' daughter."

"Good call."

I lifted her back into my arms, the place I quickly believed she belonged. I couldn't help my smile as she snuggled into me. I loved how she looked in my sweatshirt and how it made her smell like me. I wasn't afraid to admit I could be a possessive guy. It just took a lot to trigger it. But once I claimed something, I licked it all over so everyone knew.

Lick. Lick. Lick.

Graham unlocked the door and opened it, coming to an abrupt stop as Ledger peered down at us. The dude was tall, clearing both of our heads, and could bench-press the weight of my car.

Probably. I didn't know for sure, but he seemed like the type.

He'd pulled his long strawberry-blond hair into a low ponytail, and his hard face glared daggers at us. He was one of the league's best shortstops but didn't say much. It didn't typically bother me, but with his glare aimed at me and no words, it set me on edge.

"Edge, Ledge. I get it now." I chuckled, making the man in question narrow his eyes.

"Um, did you need something?" Graham asked, ever the diplomat.

"She okay?" he asked, nodding to the girl in my arms.

"For now. We're gonna take her back to our place, let her sleep it off, and ensure she doesn't choke on her vomit."

"Give me your phone," he said in response, holding his hand out. Graham handed it to him before peering back at me with raised eyebrows. We both watched the quiet giant enter something before returning it. "I'll message randomly and require proof of life that she's not being molested."

"We'd never," Graham hissed. He squared his shoulders, ready to take on Ledger if needed. When his protectiveness was questioned, it became a touchy subject for him. Graham was a big teddy bear, but the bear part roared to life when someone threatened his integrity.

"Down, boy. If I had any doubt, you wouldn't walk out of here with her." He gave something that resembled a smile and patted Graham on the shoulder, squeezing it hard before he turned and walked out the exit door.

"That was weird, right?" Graham asked, his shoulders dropping. He glanced both ways before following Ledger out the back exit. It was the wisest option, allowing us to avoid the crowd in the main area of The Dugout.

"Um, yeah. I thought he would go all Andre the Giant on

your ass, and I'd have to find a new best friend." I snickered as Graham rolled his eyes.

"Good to know I'd be missed."

"Nah. It's more of the hassle of breaking in a new one. Who else will make me delicious breakfasts and snuggle as we watch our favorite shows? You're stuck with me, dude. I'd follow your ass to the grave."

Graham cleared his throat, his cheeks red as he pushed out the door. "Yeah, same."

If I weren't carrying a drunk girl, I would've jumped on his back and given him a noogie until he stopped acting weird. But since I couldn't, I let it go for now. I knew most people thought our relationship was odd and that we were co-dependent or whatever.

Maybe we were. I didn't really care.

No one in my life had ever gotten me quite like Graham, so I'd suction-cup myself to him as long as I could and not care what other people thought.

"Thank fuck we don't have to drive anyone else," he muttered as his car appeared. With his signing bonus, he'd gotten a conservative car, a moderate sedan with excellent gas mileage. In comparison, I'd gotten the flashy sports car. The one with no legroom and sucked more gas than a vacuum cleaner. Meaning most of the time, we drove his car because it actually fit both of our large frames.

I didn't even want my car anymore, but it had been the first thing I'd bought myself, and it felt like a slap to sell it now. I knew it was silly, but growing up poor and never having anything, it was hard to part with things. It was how I'd gotten into collecting sneakers and owned a collection worth thousands of dollars.

But at least it isn't drugs.

Or that was what I told myself each time I bought a new pair, anyway.

The drive to the apartment we rented was short, and I

was thankful we'd gotten something close to Champion Field.

"My turn to carry her," Graham said, getting out of the car before I had my seat belt off.

"Fine," I grumbled, but honestly, I didn't mind. I shared everything with Graham; it felt natural to share her with him, too. Jogging up the stairs, I unlocked the door and held it open for him as he carried her over the threshold.

"Congratulations!" I laughed. He quirked a brow, and I rolled my eyes. "Put her in your bed. We can share mine tonight." I opened his room since it was the closest. Plus, he had his own bathroom, which she might appreciate if she got sick again.

"I'll grab some water and medicine and leave a note. I saw something on LiveIt I want to do," he said, laying her down.

While he cared for that, I tugged off her shoes, admiring her cute feet. I had to admit a part of me liked her because of her kicks. A girl who could rock neon yellow hightops was my kind of woman. I debated leaving her socks on but ultimately took them off. I hated sleeping in socks, so I figured she'd be the same. Tucking them into her shoes, I pulled the ball cap off her head and placed her glasses on the nightstand.

Using my fingers, I combed out her hair, massaging her scalp as I let down the messy bun she had going on. Although she'd upchucked earlier and had been at the ball field all day, she looked beautiful. My fingers traced over her face, brushing her hair behind her ears before I stepped back. I could quickly become addicted to touching her if I wasn't careful. Her skin was so soft, and I wanted to trace her freckles.

Graham walked in, rolling his eyes, and pointed at the phone against his ear. I took the water and medicine from him and placed them on the nightstand.

"Yes. She's fine. I'll send a picture for confirmation. We're putting her to bed now. No. On her own. Jesus, man. I have four older sisters; I respect the shit out of women. We're not going to take advantage of her. She's probably in the safest place she could be."

He sighed again, rubbing his temple as he moved over and pulled out some clothes. While he continued to listen to whoever was on the other end, he propped the phone on the dresser and undressed. First, he shucked his shirt and jeans off, baring his boxer-clad ass to me. Seeing one another naked wasn't new, but something about how his butt muscles flexed as he bent over to pull on his sleep pants had my eyes glued to them. Had they always done that? And those little dots at the top… why were they winking at me?

Graham had thighs of steel and a bubble butt from all the hours of squats he did as a catcher. And dayum. It had paid off.

Blinking out of my stupor, I returned to our Sleeping Beauty as he finished the call.

"Yeah, okay, man. Later." He sighed, tucking the phone into his pocket, and I lifted a brow, wondering who it was. "Hawk. He finally answered my text. Dude was worse than Ledge. Fuck." He took his phone back out and snapped a picture before presumably sending it to Ledger.

"She sure knows how to collect them. I'm suddenly glad her real brother isn't here," I mumbled.

"Yeah. I'm guessing none of this would've flown if he had been. And with the way Hawk yelled, I'm surprised it got as far as it did. It had to be because he left early on. Though, between you and me, he sounded a lot more protective than a big brother."

He slipped the note he'd written under her glasses and grabbed his charger before heading out of the room. I closed the door lightly, leaving the hall light on so she could see if she woke up. I waited as Graham double-checked the lock on the front door then threw my arm over his shoulders, ushering him to my room.

"Come on, Daddy Graham. I'm beat."

"Dude. I told you not to call me that. I'm so not the daddy in this relationship."

"And I am?" I laughed. He snorted, shaking his head.

"No. You're right. We need to find us a sugar daddy." He laughed harder, the sound filling me with happiness. I loved it when Graham laughed. It was the whipped topping on a delicious sundae type of feeling.

"Maybe Hawk will be our Sugar Daddy," I teased. "Is he your type? You never tell me what your type is? Do you know if he swings that way?"

Graham shuddered, but not in a good way.

"Fuck no. That man looks like he'd eat me alive. He scares me, honestly. He's all dark and brooding and has the tattoos and piercings to accompany it."

"Hmm, what about Ledge? He's very manly," I said as I flopped onto the bed like a starfish before Graham kicked my foot to get me to move.

"Undress first, Tuck. You'll be a bear to move if you get too comfortable."

I groaned but rolled over. It was mostly because I still had on my shoes, and I always wiped them clean and placed them back into their sneaker home. Once I had them back in their spot, I stripped off my clothes, opting to keep my boxers on. For some reason, Graham didn't appreciate it when I slept next to him nude.

I quickly brushed my teeth and washed my face, checking out my brows and realizing it was time for another wax. I spent a lot of time grooming myself, taking pride in my appearance. Some girls found it odd, saying I was more high maintenance than them, but it didn't bother me. Feeling good about myself made me feel more secure in who I was. I took joy in my hard work and wasn't afraid to flaunt it.

Once my routine was finished, I plugged in my phone and snuggled in under the covers. Graham was reading on his Kindle, his blue light glasses perched on his nose. He always looked so cute like that, and I smiled as I snuggled up to his side. I was very tactile and affectionate with the people in my life. Call it not receiving enough as a child, or whatever, but I wasn't shy about showing the people I cared about how I felt.

Thankfully, Graham was as big of a snuggler as me, and we often had platonic cuddles with one another. Some of our other teammates had made fun of us over the years, saying we were lovers, especially after Graham came out as pansexual, but it didn't bother me. People would think what they wanted and feared things they didn't understand, so I didn't waste time trying to change them. Plus, it felt too good to care what others thought anyway. And I liked knowing someone I cared for was near.

Besides, hugs were healing, and I could hug the shit out of people. Not really. That would be gross, but you get my point.

"Mm, night," I said with a yawn, throwing my arm over his bare chest. He patted my arm, continuing his reading. His hand started to run up and down my forearm after a while, sending goosebumps over my skin. It felt nice, though, so I didn't say anything.

He chuckled at something he read, then tapped the screen to mark his place. Once he saved it, he placed it and his glasses on the nightstand, turned off the lamp, and moved down into the bed. I shifted, realizing his arm brushes had made my dick hard, and suddenly felt self-conscious about it.

What was happening to me?

"Do you think she'll be here in the morning?" I asked once he was settled.

"Where would she go? She doesn't have a phone or a car."

"True." I bit my lip, the question we hadn't discussed hanging in the air. "You like her," I whispered.

"Yes. So do you."

We both said the words matter of factly and not a question.

"What does that mean then?" I finally asked when he didn't expand.

"Does it have to mean anything? It didn't seem to matter when the three of us were texting."

"True." I bit my lip as I thought.

"We've done everything else together for the past seven years; why not this?"

I felt him shift, his eyes boring into me in the dark. I couldn't look yet; my breath held in my lungs as I thought about his suggestion. Would we sleep with her together?

For some reason, it didn't feel strange. It felt right.

"What would it look like?" I asked after a few minutes.

I felt him shrug, his pillow moving with the motion. "Who knows? We've just been going along with it; why must we define it now?"

"Because she's real."

"She was real before; we just didn't know her face," he teased.

"True. And we all admitted we were terrible at dating. Maybe we could find something in between?"

Graham was quiet, and I worried he fell asleep or didn't like my question.

"I've been reading a new genre. It's called Why Choose. Have you ever heard of it?"

I shook my head. I wasn't a reader unless comic books and laundry instructions counted.

"No. What is it?"

"A girl dates multiple men at the same time. She doesn't have to choose between them."

"And it works?" I asked, hope blossoming in my chest. I

liked Bee not having to choose. Then, I wouldn't be left behind because Graham was the best of the two of us. If it came down to one of us, I'd want them to be happy. Even if it killed me. But maybe this could be the solution. It felt right. Like Graham and I did.

"In fiction, it seems to, but there is a whole community of people living the lifestyle, too. It's called polyamorous."

"How do you know so much?" I whispered. Graham was so smart. I could listen to him tell me about anything.

He chuckled, his breath fanning across my face. "I dunno. Reading, I guess."

"Damn. Welp, I'm out."

We both laughed.

"Do you think that would really work?" I asked after it had been quiet for a while.

"It's worth a try. I know we've just met Blake, but I like her. I want to continue exploring things like we said, and maybe with these boundaries, we could without anyone getting hurt."

"I like her too."

"The idea of dating her together… it's also what I like," he admitted, his voice soft. My face heated, and I nodded.

"Yeah, me too. I'd never want to ruin our friendship. You're my person, G."

"And you're mine, Tuck."

My heart raced as I thought about what he said, and as I fell asleep with Graham next to me, I knew it was the way forward. It sounded like the perfect way to have my best friend and the girl who made me feel more than lust in years.

CHAPTER
SIXTEEN

BLAKE

Things captured my attention in bits and pieces. First, I noticed the sunlight that poured through a window. Then, it was the sound and smell of the place, something unfamiliar yet welcoming, like pine and spice. Next, it was the way the sheets felt against my skin, a smooth and silky texture I wanted to roll around in.

But the most overpowering sensation was how my throat felt like sandpaper, and my mouth tasted like Bryce's baseball bag after a week of away games. My head wasn't much better, the pounding reminiscent of a Britney Spears concert.

Bunting hell. What happened last night?

Stretching my arms, I rolled over in search of the night-stand, praying I'd been conscious enough to place my phone or glasses nearby. My hand smacked a plastic bottle, throwing it to the floor.

Son of a pitch.

Cursing, I sat upright, my hair falling into my eyes and resembling more of a crow's nest than actual hair. Squinting, I patted around the nightstand and found my glasses. Once I put them on, I pulled them away and back, hoping the scene would change.

It did not.

Nothing in my surroundings was familiar. Just how much fun did I have last night? I'd only been at Bryce's house for two nights, but I definitely didn't remember any of this stuff.

The big swivel chair in the corner, the bookcases overflowing with paperbacks, and pictures tacked to a corkboard were all foreign to me. Plus, the colors were different. Whereas Bryce's room was a muted gray and blue, this room was done in forest green and mint. It felt like the inside of a tree, and now that I could see it, the smell of pine and grass made sense.

But the question I still couldn't answer… Why wasn't I at home? Or what was as close to home as I had now since I was a nomad, or a womad. A woman with no home.

Deep thoughts for an early morning in a strange place.

Shaking my head, I searched for my phone, hoping it would provide more answers. When I came up empty, I spotted a piece of paper lying on the nightstand with two Tylenol on top of it.

Score! Make the concert stop!

Reaching for the bottle of water I'd knocked off earlier, I barely kept myself from sprawling out onto the floor. My coordination had not improved while sleeping. Damn.

I quickly took the pills, hoping my head would feel like its normal size soon. I did not want to be one of those Funko Pops.

Picking up the paper, I squinted at the neat handwriting and tried to find some clue as to who'd left it.

HEY BEE,

YOU GOT SICK LAST NIGHT AT THE DUGOUT.

YOU DIDN'T HAVE YOUR PHONE WITH YOU, AND WE DIDN'T KNOW WHERE BRYCE LIVED, SO WE BROUGHT

"Graham," I whispered, my throat feeling marginally better after the water. The sour taste still clung to my breath, and I'd need a good brushing before I spoke to anyone. Wracking my brain, parts of the previous evening came into focus.

I ran into Luke and felt like my heart had been ripped out. *Again.*

Then Seth invited me to The Dugout, where he ignored me.

I'd been fed copious amounts of beer. Until… *Oh god.*

My memory of throwing up all over Seth after he kissed me came rushing back, my face flaming from the embarrassment. I quickly climbed out of bed and ran to the door I hoped was the bathroom, making it just in time. Nothing like a dose of mortification to wake you up.

Kneeling around the porcelain goddess, I emptied the

remainder of my stomach into the water. Crackerjack! Why was my life full of so much vomit recently?

Wiping my mouth, I fell back onto my butt and glanced around the space as I calculated my odds of getting out of this unscathed.

Odds not likely.

Yeah. I didn't think so, either.

Yanking off my nasty clothes, I wasn't even going to try to keep them. They were a lost cause as far as I was concerned. It just meant I'd be stealing everything I could from Graham. It wasn't the worst idea.

Turning on the water in the shower, I climbed in and let it fall over me as I wished the water had miraculous properties that could change the last twenty-four hours.

From the moment I arrived at the stadium, to the time I walked into the clubhouse and came face-to-face with not one, not two, but four people I had somewhat awkward feelings for had been overwhelming.

Awkward feelings weren't the most solid of terms, but it was the best I had. I suddenly felt like I was in middle school, and my friend wanted to know if I "like-liked" a boy.

No. I *like-liked* four of them, two of which I also wanted to punch in the face most of the time. Simple.

Groaning, I rubbed my hand over my face. Unfortunately, it wasn't that simple.

Did I like the way Hawk made me feel in bed? Hell yeah.

Did I like the way that Luke kissed me? Most definitely.

And I one hundred percent liked how Tucker and Graham flirted and pushed boundaries with me, not caring who I was. Mainly because they hadn't known, but it still counted.

What I didn't like... was feeling second best, that I wasn't good enough, and that everything I did ended in failure.

And right now, with the crushing weight of all the events over the past few days, my life felt like a complete shitshow.

Squirting the shampoo into my hand, I let the smell of

eucalyptus invade my nose. As I scrubbed it in my hair, I wondered if I could pretend I was a different person by changing how I smelled.

I didn't really think it worked that way, but hey, I was willing to try anything at this point: desperation and all that.

And perhaps the worst part was wondering what my therapist, Delia, would think of what I'd been doing the past two days. Would she be disappointed in me? I'd worked so hard with her over the past few years to get to a healthy place mentally, and now I felt like all I was doing was fucking it up.

Epic. Fuck. Up. That was me.

Rinsing everything off and scrubbing my body within an inch of its life, I finally turned off the water and stepped out of the shower. I spotted a wrapped toothbrush on the counter and smiled. Damn, these guys were thoughtful.

Brushing my teeth and swishing some mouthwash, I felt like a new person now that the sandpaper feeling and sour taste were gone.

Picking up the brush on the counter, I managed to comb out most of my hair. I'd been taking way too many showers lately with secondhand supplies. I was grateful, but there was something intricately pleasant about using your own products that made you feel more you.

Feeling more aware and ready to face my rescuers, I peeked out the door into the bedroom. It was still empty, so I tiptoed to the dresser and opened a drawer, hoping it was right. Bingo!

I grabbed a pair of boxer briefs and rolled them over at the waist, but they actually fit on my thighs. Next, I found the softest pair of pants I'd ever touched and eagerly pulled them on. The next drawer held t-shirts, and I paused when I held one up, reading what it said on it.

Oh my God! He had shirts as good as mine. Giggling, I grabbed the one that said, "I tried being normal once. Worst two minutes of my life."

"You might not get this shirt back," I whispered, snuggling into it and loving how it smelled. Oh! I could make one myself. Graham seemed like the type of person that would be cool with matching shirts.

With my armor on, I walked through the door, ready to face the music. No time like the present to get the embarrassment out of the way. Besides, I was tired of dwelling on this crap. The only way to deal with it was to push through.

At least I'd learned that part—no cleat retreat this time.

The incredible smell of bacon and eggs invaded my nose when I opened the door. My stomach rumbled in agreement, and I moaned as my feet led me toward the kitchen. I stopped in my tracks as I came around the corner, my body coming alive at the sight in front of me—a bare sexy as fuck back.

Holy muscles, Batman.

My eyes fixated on them as they flexed and moved. Two twin dimples appeared at the dip, just above his waistband, and I couldn't look away. Graham stirred the eggs on the stove, completely unaware of the show he was giving me.

Why was that so sexy? I traveled further down the bare back, my gaze sticking on the snug boxers wrapped around the sexiest butt I'd ever seen.

Seriously! How was that allowed? To be *that* good-looking *and* willing to fix me food? My ovaries were already weeping.

"I think I just got pregnant."

A snort behind me had me spinning, my face flaming as I quickly wiped my mouth for any drool. The view in front of me was just as mouth-watering, with tanned skin and abs on display before me. A baseball diamond tattoo was on his left rib and a lunar cycle on his thigh. My eyes eagerly drank every inch up before my brain came online, and I remembered I was ogling him right before him.

"Um, sorry." I grimaced, my cheeks flaming but not caring at the same time.

"No apologies needed. I like to be admired. Look away." He posed for me, flexing his muscles.

"If you insist." I reached out, his skin jumping at my touch. "Wait, did you say I could touch? Or is this like the museum, and it's viewing only? My brain is fried from last night, and your hotness has short-circuited me. Otherwise, I'm sure I'd be mortified right now, but since I've already seen your dick, I'm weirdly not," I spewed.

Tucker laughed, the sound so carefree and joyful that it made me want to capture it so I could listen to it whenever I wanted. The air felt loaded with dopamine just from the sound. He grabbed my hand, placing it on his body.

"I'm not shy, and I'm a very *touchy* person." The way he said touchy told me precisely what he meant. Oh, to be *that* brave.

But hey, a hot baseball player wanted me to touch his muscles. Who was I to say no?

Walking around him, I trailed my fingers over the defined form, loving how he responded to my touch. It was a bit of a high, and I knew I was in trouble with these two. I just wasn't sure if I cared.

"How you feeling?" a voice from behind asked, and I spun around, remembering there had been a sexy back before I'd begun to caress Tucker.

"Better. My head still feels a few sizes too big, but all in all, it's an improvement. Thanks for taking care of me. I..." I shook my head, then regretted it. The reality of the disaster I'd made crashed down on me and stole all the lust. I lifted my head, meeting his gray eyes with a grimace.

"How bad is it?"

"It could be better. Let's discuss it while we eat. But first..." Graham lifted his phone off the island, and I fought to keep my eyes on him and not check out his tight shorts. It was like they wanted to kill me. He snapped a picture of me before I realized what he was doing, and I blinked, twisting up my lips.

"Um, I'm not sure right now is the best time for a selfie."

Tucker laughed, wrapping his arm around my shoulders and pulling me over to a table where three plates sat filled with food.

"It's not for that, but you're beautiful like this. Though, my favorite was when you wore my sweatshirt last night." He looked me up and down, his eyes heating. "I guess Graham's weird clothes work, too."

"Weird? They're awesome. I make shirts like this all the time. In fact, I'm either stealing this one or making my own. Too soon to wear matching shirts?" I asked.

Graham sputtered, then walked over to cup my face and leaned down. I sucked in a breath. Was he going to kiss me? He smirked, his gray eyes dancing.

"You're perfect, Bee, and I'd gladly match you."

He bopped my nose, the action more cute than sexy, but it woke my butterflies up nonetheless. I gaped after him as he walked off like he hadn't short-circuited my brain, his tight butt muscles flexing with each step.

"Hawk and your new bestie, Ledger, required proof of life," Tucker explained, and I spun around in a daze.

"Hawk. Right." I grimaced, rubbing my forehead. "Shit. He's gonna murder me."

"Sounds like a story there," Tucker said, catching me off guard.

I blew out a breath. "One so big, it required an ocean. Even then, it still wasn't far enough away." I absently rubbed my heart, the pain lancing me as memories surfaced.

"Coffee?" Graham asked, shocking me from behind. He'd pulled on some clothes while I'd been reminiscing, and I frowned. At least I wouldn't combust into a puddle of goo while I ate.

"Pitch, yes!" I groaned, happy to have something to focus on outside the two hot specimens in front of me and my memories. "I will judge you, though, based on your coffee. I've been spoiled the past three years in Greece. Their coffee was top-notch."

"Come and learn, grasshopper!" Tucker teased, ushering me into the kitchen and stopping in front of a coffee addict's mecca. There was a French Press, an espresso machine that rivaled most coffee shops, and even a drip machine. Tucker leaned against the counter, crossing his arms as he gave me a smug look.

"What were you saying about judging?" He walked behind me, resting his head on my shoulder. The touch was comforting, and I grinned up at him.

"I underestimated you. I'm thoroughly impressed. Now, to decide how I want my coffee?" I tapped my chin in thought. "So, which one of you is the coffee snob?"

"The kitchen's my domain. Coffee is *my* addiction, closely followed by ice cream and bubble baths. Tuck's are sneakers, pizza, and zoos."

"But not together." Tucker laughed again, the sound vibrating through me, and I instantly felt lighter. How did he do that? I swear the sound had dopamine in it. His arms were warm around my waist, and I desperately wanted to lean back into him and feel his whole body against me.

"I'm gonna go with the French Press today because I need something strong, but I'll be back to try a latte."

"Sounds like a promise, grasshopper." Tucker squeezed me before letting me go, and my cheeks heated. I spun, needing to even the score.

"That's not a thing, right? Grasshopper? Because I veto it if it is."

"Ugh. Fine. Take away my fun. You only get two vetoes, though. So, be wise with how you use them," he warned, his warm brown eyes dancing.

"Still vetoing grasshopper," I mumbled as I filled the press.

"Damn. I was hoping I'd scare you into accepting." He winked, and I relaxed, deciding to rip the bandage off and share my tale.

"I grew up with Bryce and Hawk and survived a childhood illness; it takes a lot to scare me. Actually, public humiliation, geese, and being late scare me. But teasing is my love language," I rambled as I made the coffee, keeping my back turned.

When the coffee was ready, I spun around to face the guys. They'd gone quiet. Crap. I was so used to everyone knowing my past that I didn't censor myself. At their pitying looks, I rolled my eyes, taking a sip.

"I had, or I guess still do, a bone marrow deficiency. I got a transplant, thank you, big brother, and now, I'm fine. For the most part, at least. We good?" I asked, not waiting for their response, and moved to the table.

"You grew up with Hawk? I guess that explains the long story," Tucker said, changing the subject, his face returning to normal.

"That's part of it. How much of my baggage do you want to know over breakfast? You've seen me upchuck, put me to bed, and know I almost died. So I guess not much more can embarrass me at this point."

I shrugged, but inside, I was scared. What if they ran away? What if they laughed? What if they told everyone? What if they didn't want to send me sexy pics after this?

"You don't have to tell us anything you don't want to, Blomit." Tucker cringed, and before I could open my mouth to veto, he held up his hand. "I hear it. It's off the table."

"Nothing to do with bodily functions. That should be a given, *Tuckgasm!*"

"I mean, you can call me that anytime, baby."

I brushed him off with a smile, knowing he'd done it to

help ease me. Graham was the quieter one, sitting back and observing, while Tucker was a shameless flirt. Their energy together was comforting, two perfect balances of one another.

"Well, if we're gonna be besties, I should give you the scoop." As I ate the delicious egg, bacon, and cheese biscuit, I gave the unabridged version of what happened three years ago that had sent me running across the world. They were patient and listened, letting me share what I needed to.

"So, yeah. That's the gist of it. I cleat retreated, runaway bride style. I lost my virginity to my brother's best friend and then ruined it all in under twenty-four hours. I spent the last three years healing. I learned photography, I make shirts, and I'm trying not to be so hard on myself. Which is easier said than done when I've made mistake after mistake since returning."

"You cleated yourself," Tucker joked, making me smile. "Get it, like yeet? I'm gonna need a shirt that says 'Go cleat yourself' in a large, please."

I laughed, my eyes sparkling at the man as I held my mug of deliciousness up to my mouth, already on my second cup and feeling more human with each sip.

"Sure thing. Once I get my stuff delivered, that is. That's all been a cluster. I don't even have my luggage, so yeah, thanks for the clothes. Hope you didn't need them today because it's this or my brother's."

"Wear his!" Tucker interjected. "*Ours.*"

Graham gave him a side-eye look before facing me. "Will you make me a shirt too?"

"For sure. What do you want?" I asked. His gray eyes ran over me, something in the recess of my mind niggling at me, but I couldn't quite place it.

"What about 'thick thighs and catcher vibes'?" he asked. "And one that says 'Pitch please' both in X-large. Because I don't like my shirts to suffocate me." He narrowed his eyes at Tucker.

"If you got the goods, flaunt it. I like my abs looking like they're trying to jump out of my shirt." He ran his hand down his so-called abs, and I had to stop myself from drooling. Yeah, he so had the goods.

"I'd almost think you were serious, but you're too laid back to be that vain."

"Nah. He is. He's just good at hiding it. The dude's got more hair products than most pharmacies."

"These curls require lots of work. They don't just magically do this perfection on their own. These waves take days," Tucker argued, running his fingers through his hair and making me wish I could.

"I'm glad you accidentally messaged me. Sorry for keeping my identity hidden. It's usually Bry's ball girls trying to get a hold of him, so I like to have a little fun with them for the headache they cause me."

"Best mistake we've ever made," Tucker said, picking up my hand and linking his fingers with it. I was jealous of the ease at which he did everything. He didn't second-guess or question himself. I needed some of that to rub off on myself.

"Elephant in the room time. We both like you." They both stared, and I appreciated they didn't mince words.

My cheeks flamed. "And I like you both."

"Good." Tucker winked, and I relaxed.

"The other night, we'd talked about exploring things."

"We did." Were my cheeks red? My cheeks felt red. Clearly, I was braver behind a screen.

"Now that you've seen us in person, does that change?"

I snorted. "Hell, no." I swallowed, worried maybe it had for them. "Wait. For you?"

"No!" Tucker shouted, almost coming across the table. This time, his cheeks flamed. It was endearing to see the usual flirty guy bashful. "I mean. If anything, it's increased."

"Oh. Good. Good." I stared at my coffee, my cheeks flaming, peeking up every few seconds.

"And we were thinking…" Tucker said, nudging Graham.

"That maybe while we expand our sexual repertoire, we also get to know each other as friends. We'll keep it easy, no demands," Graham finished, making my heart patter.

"But just so we're clear, we want to dick you down and make an honest woman out of you." He paused, tilting his head. "Do people still say that?" Tucker looked between us like he hadn't just said one of the most obscure things ever.

"What?" I spluttered, almost spitting out coffee. "Dick me down? Honest woman?" I couldn't even form a sentence.

Graham slapped his friend. "What did I tell you about saying shit like that to girls?"

Tucker rolled his eyes. "He thinks he's an expert because he reads copious amounts of romance books. But I find it best to put everything out in the open. I don't like things to be unclear. That's my ADHD flaw because I read into them if they're not, and with baseball starting, there's no room for second-guessing myself a million times a day." He rolled his eyes at himself good-naturedly, and I caught Graham giving him a soft look full of affection.

Ohhh. Wait up. Did he?

"That's a good point. Casual fun will allow us to focus on baseball *and* get to know you."

"And that includes sexting?" I asked, looking between them.

"Sexting, mutual masturbation, all the touchy-touchy you want," Tucker said, moving his hands down his body. "I'm down for whatever, honey bee."

I rolled my eyes, but didn't bat it down, making him perk up. Holding my mug, I glanced down, thinking it over. "Actually, that sounds perfect. Between Hawk and Luke—"

"Olson?" Tucker asked, his eyes climbing his forehead.

"Oh. Um. Remember the plane…" I blushed, hiding my eyes.

"He was your plane guy, right?" Graham said, proving he saw way more than people knew.

I nodded. "Yup. We spent the night together after being stranded. It was amazing. Everything I thought sex could be until he ghosted me the next morning. So, yeah." I rolled my lips inward, my leg bouncing. "*That* was hella awkward running into him yesterday. We hadn't exchanged full names, so I had no clue who he was."

"I guess that explains his reaction then. So, do you still have feelings for him?" Tucker asked, something uncertain appearing in his eyes for once.

I shrugged. "It was one night, but we bonded on the plane. I thought it could've been something, but he ripped my heart out. Not sure where we stand or if I could move forward with him."

"But you want to," Tucker said, not making it a question. Before I could respond, Graham asked another doozy.

"And if Hawk were single?" He had a calculating look, and I had no clue what he was thinking about. I sighed loudly, gulping the last of my coffee.

"It wouldn't matter. He's my brother's best friend. *That* hasn't changed."

The two of them exchanged a look, a whole conversation passing between them. I blew out a breath, noticing the time. I needed to get my stuff and deal with the fallout from last night. I could already see the missed calls from my mom, dad, *and* brother.

"So, casual friends with benefits with my screwballs!"

"As your new bestie with perks, let's get you to the clubhouse so we can tackle upchuckety gate before the game tonight."

"We're not going to call it that, right? I'm not a fan." I narrowed my eyes at him.

"Damn, girl. You're not good for my ego," he teased. "But

besties with perks is staying." He smiled at me, and I couldn't deny I liked the perk part.

Graham handed me my shoes, shaking his head at his friend. "I'll drive. We can't fit into Tuck's car unless we surgically remove some body parts."

"Okay, fine!" Tucker threw up his hands, and I had to guess this was a conversation they had a lot. "It might be time to sell it because I'm not getting rid of you, little buddy," he shouted down at his crotch.

I widened my eyes at Graham as we both held in a laugh. Tucker grabbed his shirt and shoes, picked up his bag, and finally noticed our look.

"What?"

"Nothing," we said together, laughing. Tucker narrowed his eyes suspiciously but ignored us, pulling me under his arm.

The three of us headed out together, and I felt better than I expected the morning after embarrassing myself. Meeting these two was just what I needed, especially if drooling over them was allowed.

I loved how easily the three of us had connected. They continued to make me feel included, and I thoroughly enjoyed being around them. I honestly felt better just from their energy alone. They were like an energy drink for the soul with a side of cotton candy.

CHAPTER
SEVENTEEN

LUKE

I KNOCKED ON THE BEDROOM DOOR AND PUSHED IT OPEN TO reveal the young girl sitting on the bed, her back to me.

"Good morning, Willow." I cleared my throat, shuffling on my feet. I might be thirty, but I was terrified of a four-year-old girl.

After escaping Georgia, I rented a car and drove the rest of the distance to meet Jasmine, my ex, and Willow. I didn't know if it was because things with Slugger had gone so horribly, but my introduction with Willow did not go as I'd envisioned.

The smiling girl from all the photos was not to be found. She'd been distant and shy, barely saying a word to me since her mother had left. Visions of her running into my arms and crying tears of happiness did not happen. In fact, the only time she seemed happy was when she was holding her new favorite stuffed animal or talking to her mother.

Because, of course, she'd loved the platypus.

I'd also caved and gotten her an iPad so she could call her mother, hating that the one thing she'd liked was the item Blake had picked out. I'd been jealous of her easy affection with her mom, which led me to consider the iPad. It felt ridiculous for a four year old to have one, but it was the first smile I'd gotten from her, which had felt like a huge win.

"What would you like for breakfast today?" I asked, hoping the more I spoke to her, the more she would adjust. Her little shoulders shrugged, moving her dark brown hair. "We have pop tarts, cereal, donuts, or I can make eggs and toast."

I would never eat half of the things I'd bought at the store, but it seemed like what kids liked. But so far, I hadn't seemed to find anything she loved. The nanny told me it could be worse. She could be screaming and throwing a fit the whole time.

But I disagreed.

This little girl was sad, and it triggered something in me. I'd been that little boy with the mom who couldn't see he was hurting. Who chose something else over his happiness.

My dad had never been around, but the men my mom dated weren't worth the space they took up. Yet, she couldn't perceive being alone and preferred letting them abuse us both instead.

I wanted to be different. I needed to be. I just wasn't sure how.

The urge to drink and numb it all was more present than ever, especially after the shitshow of the past game. I had to get my groove back. Baseball had always been my haven, my escape from the nightmares at home. It was the one thing I'd been good at and had worked my ass off to succeed in. To have it failing me now felt soul-crushing.

I didn't know how to handle the disappointment or feeling like I was failing in every area of my life. I was Luke Olson. I didn't suck at anything.

And yet I was. Epically.

Baseball, being a father, and Bee—a triple I didn't want.

I'd be back on the bottle by next week, proving I was just

like my father. And he wasn't someone I ever wanted to be like.

Even knowing I needed to ignore the urge, the thought of the alcohol made my mouth water; the need to drown out the anxiety and fears and let the burn take them away was intense.

Shit. I needed to try something different before I stumbled too far.

Willow depended on it, and I wouldn't let her down—even if she wasn't talking to me.

Stepping into the room, I sat on the bed but kept space between us. I just had to keep trying.

"I watched that YouTube video on how to do two braids. Would you like me to try it?" I asked, my voice soft and hesitant.

I knew her avoidance wasn't personal, but it hurt all the same. I had to remember I was the adult in this relationship and needed to manage my emotions. Willow would look to me on how to respond, and I couldn't expect her to make me feel good about myself. That wasn't fair.

Parenting was fucking hard, and I'd only been doing it for a few days.

"Sure," she said, her voice soft.

Taking that as a positive sign, I stood up and grabbed the brush off the unicorn dresser I'd bought her. The whole room was a rainbow of color with unicorns. I'd gone out and bought everything I could when I learned I wouldn't be moving back to Columbus, hoping by showing Willow I had a space for her that I was serious. But now I wondered if she even liked it. Was it too much? That would have to be another day's problem.

Brushing her hair, I recalled how I'd done the same thing for Slugger, or Bee as I should call her. Slugger was too intimate, too close to my heart.

Seeing her on Opening Day had been the biggest mindfuck of my life. I didn't know what to think about what she said. She'd been adamant she hadn't known me, and maybe it was egotistical to assume she had, but I called bullshit. The anger I felt each time I thought of her getting one over on me reared back up.

"Ow," Willow cried, and I froze, suddenly remembering I wasn't with Bee but with my daughter.

My daughter… damn, that still packed a punch.

I wanted to rage at Jasmine for keeping it hidden from me for the past four years, but I'd been nowhere ready to be a dad. Still wasn't, if I was honest. But I wouldn't run from my responsibility.

No, just your heart.

"Sorry. I'll be more careful," I whispered, clearing my throat. "Did you have fun at Pre-K yesterday?"

"I guess." She shrugged her shoulders again, and I briefly wondered if I had the oldest four-year-old little girl ever to live. Willow acted like she was four going on sixteen with all her teenage angst.

I parted her hair, deciding to try a new tactic. Maybe the room should be today's problem. It might be a safer topic, after all.

"I was thinking… maybe we should redo your room. I want you to feel like it's your space. But I get the impression you're not a fan of unicorns?"

"They're okay."

"What would you want if you could have anything?" I asked, braiding one side. I concentrated, doing the steps I'd watched a million times last night. Thankfully, it wasn't too difficult, and her hair plaited well.

"Anything?"

"Yep. What's your shoot for the moon idea?"

"I like baseball," she said, so low I stopped braiding to ensure I didn't mishear.

"Baseball?"

"Yeah. I played T-ball. It was fun."

My heart skipped, and a tear came to my eye. She liked baseball. Baseball, I could talk about.

Slow your roll. Don't be too intense and scare her. You're finally getting somewhere.

"What position did you play?"

"All of them."

"Did you like one over the others?" I asked.

"I like pitching." *Stab to my heart, but that was fine.*

"Hmm, well, did you know I play first base?"

"Mommy said it." She paused, her fingers twirling in her lap. "Is it really your job?"

I smiled, finishing the second side and tying the ribbon. "Yep. It's the best job in the world. Would you…" I cleared my throat, realizing how idiotic I sounded. "Maybe you could come and watch me play one day. Would you want to do that?"

"Really?" She spun around and looked up at me with green eyes so familiar it was eerie. Her dark lashes were long, laying on her cheeks as she blinked.

"Of course. You'd get special treatment, too, since you're my daughter."

"Okay… Daddy." She gave me a tentative smile, and I almost burst into tears. This felt huge, and I immediately reached for my phone to tell...

The reality slammed back into me, and I remembered she was a liar.

"So, what about that breakfast?" I asked, hopping off the bed.

"Can you make me cheesy eggs?"

"Can I? I happen to be an expert on cheesy eggs. Want to be my sous chef?"

"What's a sues chief?" she asked, following me out of the room. When she placed her small hand in mine, the tears practically jumped out of my eyes. Shit. I needed to get it together.

"So-oz ch-ef," I pronounced. "It's the person who helps the head chef."

I picked her up, sat her on the counter, and turned to the fridge before I realized what I'd done. Peering over my shoulder, she swung her legs as she watched me, her face not as withdrawn. It had felt so natural, I hadn't thought.

Relaxing, I pulled out the eggs and cheese and grabbed a bowl. "Do you know how to crack an egg?"

She shook her head, the braids swinging with the move. She giggled as they hit, the sound so pure and light it stole some of the darkness around my heart.

Taking her hands, I showed her how to crack the eggs and then whisk them. Her technique was lacking, but she was only four, so I wouldn't hold that against her.

After a breakfast of cheesy eggs and toast for Willow, I felt more confident about things with my daughter. Three days in, I had this in the bag.

That confidence was the first mistake of my day.

"Come on, Willow. These purple pants look just like the others, and they're right here," I begged, waving them in my hand.

She sat on the floor, half-dressed with her arms crossed and a pout so big, you could hang a pail on it.

It broke my heart. But I wouldn't give in. Nope. Not gonna happen.

"No." She shook her head, her braids flying again, but there was no laugh this time.

Sighing, I crouched next to her, rubbing my forehead with my free hand as I tried to find a solution. Usually, I was great at problem-solving. But apparently, four-year-olds were terrorists, and there was no negotiating.

"How about this: wear these pants for me today, and I'll wash the others tonight?"

"No. I want *my* purple pants."

The 'my' was the sticking point. She didn't want anything to do with the clothes I'd bought.

"But they're dirty, sweetie. You only brought a couple outfits, and you've worn them both. Your mom gave me your sizes and told me to get you some things. So, I did. If you don't like them, we'll take them back this weekend and get you what you want. But right now, I need you to dress so you're not late for school."

"No! I don't wanna," she wailed, big fat tears falling down her cheek. The iPad trilled on the corner of her bed, and she dove for it, answering it with tears streaming down her cheeks. "Mommy," she cried as she hit the answer button.

"Just great," I muttered. Standing, I walked over to where she spoke nonsensically to Jasmine.

"Put your daddy on, honey."

Willow shoved the iPad at me, crossing her arms with all the 'tude of a teen.

"Hey, Jas." I sighed and entered the hall. It was one thing to get dressed down by your ex-baby momma, but I didn't need for it to happen in front of my daughter, whom I was trying to build a relationship with.

"You look like shit, Luke." She laughed, rubbing it in even more.

"Thanks. Unfortunately, you don't." She preened, turning her head back and forth as she checked herself out.

"I look good, don't I? It's amazing what a full night of sleep does for a person." I stared blankly, not taking the bait. She could've asked for help years ago but chose not to. She huffed but dropped the attitude. I suddenly saw where Willow got it from.

"I can't get her to wear the clothes I bought," I admitted, rubbing my forehead.

"She's being difficult. She gets that way at times. Let her wear the dirty ones if she won't put the others on." She waved at the camera, dismissing the issue. I frowned. It felt like more than just her being difficult.

"Are you sure it's not something else?" I asked, knowing I had to suck it up and ask for help in this area. I had to, for Willow's sake. That and I couldn't take screaming matches every morning when it came to getting dressed.

"What else? She's just bratty at times. Give her a spanking or time out, and move on. Don't look too deep into it. So, listen, the reason I called was… well, they love what I'm doing and want me to do another campaign."

Jasmine had on her 'I want something smile,' one I knew well. It had worked on me while we'd been dating, and I'd given her everything she wanted. At first, it had been because I enjoyed spoiling her, but later, giving her what she wanted was easier than fighting. She'd eventually gotten bored. Apparently, she thrived off the conflict—the fighting and making up.

So she'd moved on to my other teammates but forgot to tell me we'd broken up until I caught her. From that alone, I hadn't believed her at first that I was the father, despite Willow's eyes saying otherwise. One paternity test later, though, and it was confirmed. I honestly believed she assumed I'd forgive her, continuing the game of back and forth indefinitely.

Realizing I'd been giving in to Willow when it got hard, I vowed to change the dynamics. I didn't want my daughter to become like her mom, using manipulation to get what she wanted. Fuck that.

"What is it that you want, Jas?" I asked.

"I'm not going to be able to return in a month to take her for a week." I opened my mouth to protest, but she cut me off. "And I'm going to be gone longer than we originally discussed. But you're doing great. You'll be fine. Oh, look, they're calling me. Tell Willow I love her. Bye."

She kissed the camera and hung up before I could stop

her. Banging my head against the wall, I closed my eyes. I didn't even care about her changing the dates, but I knew Willow would, and I'd have to deal with that.

"She's not coming back, is she?" a small voice asked, and I realized Willow had heard.

"She is, sweetie. She's doing so well at her job that they want her longer. But it's not forever." At least, I didn't think it was. Willow nodded, dropping her head as she took the pants out of my other hand and returned to her room.

Why did her easy acceptance now break my heart so much? Was she used to Jasmine failing her already at the age of four?

My determination to be a better parent rose, and I straightened myself. I'd figure this out one way or another. Even if I had to return all those clothes and buy fifty pairs of the ones she liked, I would.

Unfortunately, my determination didn't bleed into other areas of my life, leading to my second mistake of the day— assuming if I avoided Blake, I would play better.

Both activities were becoming impossible.

CHAPTER
EIGHTEEN

BLAKE

"Yes, Mom. I'm sure. I'm fine. I don't feel sick or faint." I rubbed the back of my neck, glaring up at the sky as I prayed for patience. I loved my mom, but sometimes she smothered me with her love. Almost like she forgot to turn off the cutthroat sports lawyer side of herself when she wasn't making her players millions in business offices.

"Yeah, okay. I promise. Bye."

Dropping my phone onto my desk, I pulled off my glasses, rubbed my eyes, and hoped that was the last phone call I had to make today. As expected, I received numerous messages from my father, Bryce, my mother, and Emory. Apparently, my upchuckety moment had made it on LiveIt, even all the way in Greece.

Yay, social media.

I'd spent all morning putting out fires with my family and the team and constructed a statement to release to the public per my father's request. I hadn't missed this aspect of baseball while in Greece. No one cared there. Being invisible had perks.

"You ready?" Rue asked, popping her head over the

cubicle wall.

"Um, sure." I nodded but then stopped. "Wait, for what?" I asked when I realized I had no clue. The game had started an hour ago, so after I'd gotten the players' entrances and the opening plays, I'd run away to hide at my desk. Too many fans were pointing and talking about me, so I opted to get ahead on editing and uploading videos instead. Which meant I had no clue what Rue was talking about.

"The unicorn and dinosaur dance off. We discussed it yesterday." She tilted her head, assessing me as I tried to make sense of the words she'd spoken.

Unicorn and dinosaur dance-off. Please don't let that be what it sounds like.

"Right. That." I nodded. "What is it again?"

She laughed and rolled her eyes, coming around the cubicle to take my hand and lift me from my chair. I was too impressed with her ability to do it that I didn't stop her. She chatted away happily in front of me, only every other word reaching me. The horror of what she meant sank in, and I grabbed her hand, stopping her.

"No. I can't." I shook my head, my hair whipping around.

"You agreed to do it yesterday. What's the problem?"

"Um, everything. I don't do well as the center of attention. I freeze up or run into things. Seriously, I'm a disaster."

"No one will know it's you. Plus, it'll be fun." She grabbed my wrist again and pulled me along, her strength surprising me.

"I think we have different ideas of fun," I groaned, dragging my feet.

My armpits leaked sweat, and my heart galloped like a stampede the closer we got to the baseball diamond. The walk-up music swelled as the batter stepped up to the plate, mixing with the buzz of the crowd and the announcers.

The smell of popcorn and hotdogs filled my nostrils, reminding me of a calmness I didn't remotely feel. But the ballpark had always been a sanctuary, a place where the world's worries could disappear for a few hours. So even though I was terrified of making a fool of myself—again—I couldn't find it in me to fight her.

"We're here," she sang, smiling at a guy standing before a door that said employees only. He glanced down, looking us over before nodding and opening the door. It was only out of curiosity that I followed her into the room. I thought I'd been in every room in this stadium.

"What is this place?"

Rue looked over her shoulder, smiling at my astonished expression.

"The fun zone."

"Seriously?" I asked, lifting my eyebrow.

"It should be. It's where the mascots change, and all the supplies for the games and entertainment between innings are held. There's the t-shirt cannon, the bats for dizzy bat races or water balloon tosses, and, oh, my favorite, the bubble guns."

"You're saying words, but they don't compute."

Rue waved me off, laughing as she headed further into the space. "I can tell you've been around the Majors too long. The Minors is baseball at a carnival."

I scrunched up my nose, slightly offended by her comment. I'd just told Mira how we needed to show more fun to pull in families. I wasn't *that* out of touch.

"Sorry, I didn't mean anything by that; it's just that things aren't as strict here, which makes my job so much more fun. And today, yours too, since you volunteered to be my helper." Rue smiled at me, fluttering her eyelashes so innocently.

"I know what you're doing."

"Is it working?" she asked, popping her bottom lip out for an added layer.

"Fine." I sighed. "As long as no one can tell it's me."

"Promise. Here."

I unfolded the plastic costume, revealing a bright pink and white suit. Stepping into it, I zipped it, happy when it did cover my head.

"Now what?" I asked, watching as her dinosaur suit inflated.

"Hit the button to turn on the fan."

Her voice was muffled, but I could understand her enough to do as she said. Once we were both inflated, we waddled our way back to the door when the realization hit me. How were we going to fit through?

"Um?"

"Trying turning sideways, maybe?"

The guy who had been standing there peered back at us, a smirk tilting at the corner of his lips as he spotted our new look.

"Stand back," I warned, trying to suck in as much of the costume as possible. I took off at a run, making it halfway before I got stuck. I hadn't anticipated the horn and tail, making my profile wider.

"Here," the guy said, taking my hand and pulling. His grip was firm, and I flew through the door, barely keeping my footing.

"Eek!"

A few people stopped to watch us, laughing as the dinosaur ran at the door and bounced back. The guy heaved a sigh before reaching in and yanking her free. Though, if I had to compare them, he held onto Rue's hand much longer than mine.

Hmm. I'd have to get the scoop on that later. I could use some distance from my own love life for a change.

Rue pointed to a gate, and I worried we were about to have the same situation as the door, but thankfully, it had two sides that opened, allowing us to fit through.

Note to self: Don't inflate until you're at your intended

destination.

"Now what?" I asked. We stood in a tunnel that connected to the outfield.

"We wait until the end of the inning."

"And then?"

"We dance." Her dinosaur attempted to shrug, but the movement was lost in the giant inflatable.

Music played, and she opened the door. "That's our cue. Give me all you got, Bee!"

With those parting words, she ran out onto the field with a chuckle, leaving me to follow. My legs moved of their own accord, taking me onto Champion Field. The dirt was soft beneath my feet, and despite my heart hammering in my chest, I could feel the excitement of being here race through me. The costume kept me from seeing anything outside of what was directly in front of me, so it helped ease my nerves.

If I couldn't see the people, they didn't exist, right?

The crowd cheered as we came into view, and I peeked to see if it was the YellowJackets or the Golden Spikes on the field. When the number twenty-four appeared close by, I sucked in a breath. Just being this close to Luke again made my body sing. I hated the effect he had over me, considering, in the end, he'd been a jerk.

"Take a moment to look at the field for our first unicorn and dinosaur dance-off. Who do you think has what it takes to win? If you think the dinosaur can out-dance the unicorn, then let me hear it?"

Claps and shouts echoed around the stadium, and I glanced as Rue did the floss in her dino outfit. The crowd grew rowdier as she twerked, her dino butt shaking with her tiny arms. I snorted until I realized I had to do something next. Nerves hit me, and my legs shook as I waited for my fate.

"That was quite a roar, YellowJackets. Now, what about some unicorn love? Give it up for our dancing unicorn!"

To my surprise, there was some fanfare as people clapped despite my frozen state. I waved, hopping back and forth from one foot to the next.

"Oh, oh. I think our unicorn is shy. Come on, YellowJackets, let's make it louder for the unicorn so they show us their moves."

The noise grew, and I sucked in a breath, moving my arms and shaking my butt. I closed my eyes, hoping it would help as I let myself be free, moving and dancing. I did a split leap before spinning around and doing a toe touch. When I landed, I crouched down and did a somersault.

Which was a mistake I soon learned as I couldn't get my big bubble body back up. Lying flat out on my back, I laughed as the crowd cheered. There was no way I could get up inflated.

"How about that? Those were some fancy moves, unicorn. Hey, number 24, how about you help our unicorn out and give them a hand up?"

Panic at his suggestion engulfed me, and I tried harder to get up, attempting to roll back and forth when sitting up didn't work. Unfortunately, I was like a turtle on its back and unable to get up due to my circumference.

"Here," Luke said, reaching down to help me. He smiled at first, his goldenness beaming down at me and blinding. But the second his eyes met mine through the plastic screen, his face hardened, and his green eyes flashed. I expected him to drop my hand and leave me on the field for a brief second, but he didn't, pulling me up and releasing me as soon as possible. I guess the crowd stopped him from showing his true colors. Lucky me.

Rue grabbed my hand and pulled me back toward the door we'd entered the field on. I followed her in a daze; my brain scrambled from that brief interaction with Luke. My hand still tingled from his touch.

Why did he have to be so handsome? That brief second

where he hadn't directed hate at me had been glorious, reminding me how good it had been for those few hours.

"You okay?" Rue asked, pulling me from my daze.

"Yeah. Who won?" I asked, shedding my costume once it deflated.

"You did with those crazy flips. For someone who didn't want to do it, you have a funny way of ensuring the crowd loved you."

I blushed. "I blacked it out and pretended I couldn't see anyone. I even closed my eyes."

"You hate being in the spotlight that much?"

"Yep." I nodded vigorously; glad my hangover was gone now.

"Why'd you volunteer then?" she asked, giving me a quizzical look.

I grimaced. "Was it yesterday?"

She nodded.

"So about that. I was only half listening. I'd just run into a guy I had amazing sex with, only for him to ghost me while I was in the shower. He thinks I lied about who I was, but I honestly had no clue. After running into him, the rest of the day was a bit of a daze."

"Ah, well, that explains so much. Sorry about the guy. Baseball player?"

"Yeah." I sighed.

"Too moody for me," she said, her eyes lighting up as we neared the mascot room.

"Uh-huh. I think I know your type," I teased.

"If you put up my costume, I'll recruit someone else next time."

"Done. Though I have to admit, it wasn't as awful as I expected. I could be persuaded to do it again. Like once every month or something."

"Deal." She laughed, handing me the dino as she stopped to flirt with the security guy.

CHAPTER
NINETEEN

BLAKE

It took me a while to sanitize and fold both costumes to fit back in their packages, but it kept me away from the crowd and the men who confused me. Rue was gone when I left, and the security guy nodded as I stepped out. I checked the scoreboard, noting we were up by one run with one more inning.

Rushing back to the office, I grabbed my camera and headed back to the stands to capture more footage of the fans and plays. Behind my lens, the world disappeared, and I entered the meditative stance I loved so much. With each click of the shutter, I felt more at peace and like myself. The world made sense this way; it was easy for me to manage. I knew it couldn't last forever, but I'd take it while it did.

The game ended thirty minutes later, and I captured the players as they left the field, their faces full of smiles for winning their first game. Tucker and Graham gave me flirty grins and waves, making my insides take flight as they walked by.

Seth was one of the last players on the field, shocking me when he drew near for some reason. My body locked up as I recalled everything he'd said and how he'd attempted to use me to get to my dad. In the aftermath of everything, I'd somehow forgotten his part.

"Bitch." He sneered as he passed, the word hitting me like a blow to the chest.

"Excuse me?" I gasped, dropping my camera down and spinning as I stared at him in shock.

He rolled his eyes, looking me up and down like he found me lacking. "It's no wonder *Daddy* put you here. You're too humiliating to be at the Blue Devils."

I gaped at him. Was this guy for real? It shocked me so much that I didn't know what to say. Unfortunately, that gave him the upper hand.

"Please save yourself the embarrassment, and don't chase me. I was only pretending for the bet, but getting barfed on isn't worth the fifty bucks." He looked me up and down, a sneer on his face. "It's not likely your dad even listens to you, so don't waste my time."

Seth's lip curled up, and my heart raced as I tried to put the guy from last night with this version. With his lip like that, it changed his whole appearance and I had a feeling this was more his true nature. He stalked off, not caring he'd insulted me and done the equivalent of upchucking his hatred and disdain all over me.

"You okay?" a deep voice asked.

I jumped and looked up, and then up some more until I met the pale blue eyes of the quiet guy from last night.

"I'm not sure what I am. That was..." I shook my head. Words could not express the fucked up emotions I had swirling in me.

"I'm sorry," he said, and I frowned.

"Why are you sorry? You didn't fill me with booze and bet someone you could... You know, I don't even know what the bet was for. Fifty bucks, I guess." I shrugged, my hands fidgeting in front of me. "Surely he didn't think he could meet my father after cheap wings and beer?" I rambled, my brain getting ahead of me as panic swirled in my gut. I needed to get out of here. I'd come in early tomorrow and take care of everything, but I'd officially hit my limit of shit for today.

I gave a tight smile and waved, not remembering whether I finished my thought. Regardless, I was in no state to chat anymore. I'd find Ledger tomorrow and apologize.

The walk to my desk was a blur, and I blindly grabbed my bag from my desk. As I headed to the parking lot, I remembered I still didn't have a new driver's license and needed to order a car.

Great balls of fire.

Groaning, I dug out my phone and pulled up the app, staring at it as it loaded. As I neared the exit, a hulking figure stepped out of the shadows, and I jumped back, screaming.

"Ahh! Don't hurt me; I know karate!" I held up my hands and pretended to do a karate chop.

"It's just me." The deep voice settled my nerves but did nothing for my racing heart rate as Hawk stepped into the light. I grasped my chest, trying to calm my breaths as they sawed out of me.

"Is hiding out in the shadows your new hobby?" I spat, moving past him to the door. I had no more energy left to have a Hawk encounter tonight.

"What happened last night?" he demanded, his jaw tensing.

"Nothing. I'm fine."

His hand shot out, and he grabbed my forearm to stop me. "*Blazy*. Tell me."

"It's fine." I narrowed my eyes, grinding my molars as I braced my hands on the door.

"Like hell it is. Tell me. What did he do?" Hawk practically growled at me, and I hated how much it made my pussy throb. If I stayed here a moment longer, I was bound to jump him, which wouldn't solve anything.

"I guess you were too busy with your girlfriend to notice." I lifted my brows, daring him to contradict me. "Why do you even care?" I stepped out of his hold, needing the space, and crossed my arms. His touch did stupid things to me, and I didn't need that clouding my head.

"Because Bryce asked me to look after you. And on your first night with the team, you're puking all over the floor and going home with two guys." He seethed, his jaw tight.

My eyes flicked to his, the mismatched hues vibrant with emotions as the colors swirled. My gaze traveled over his face, hungrily taking in every inch of him. I didn't let myself look at him for this long often. It was too hard. But now that I was, I noticed he'd put his gauges back in, making him look more menacing. Though, not to me. I swallowed, remembering what he said.

"Right. *Bryce*. Well, I've already talked to my brother, and he's good. So, your duty is over." I took a step, and he jerked his arm out, stopping me from opening the door.

"*Please*." The sound was like gravel, and he wouldn't meet my eyes. Exhaustion hit me, and I realized how tired I was of men bossing me around today.

"Seth invited me out. I didn't want to drink, but they kept filling my glass and ignoring me. I was bored, so I drank it. I tried to eat, but it always disappeared. It wasn't until Ledger gave me food that I got any. Then Seth asked me to dance. Which backfired on him when he kissed me, and I threw up in his mouth. There. Are you happy? Can I go now?" I asked, my voice hollow. I stared at his chest, not letting myself look into his eyes again.

"No. I'm not happy. Far from it," he whispered, his body vibrating with tension.

"Too bad."

Ducking under his arm, I pushed the door open and

escaped into the parking lot. I scanned the lot but knew I wouldn't find my Uber. My phone had buzzed in my hand twice, and I knew what it meant.

They'd arrived and then canceled when I didn't respond. Bunting hell.

My breath quickened, and I knew I was so close to falling apart. Tears blurred my vision as I tried to order another Uber.

"Bee?" a soft voice asked, and I spun around, clutching my phone to my chest. Graham stepped closer, taking my hand in his. "What's wrong?"

All the emotions I'd held back fell at his gentle touch, and I readily accepted his embrace. My tears soaked his shirt as he held me, his hand soft as he rubbed it up and down my back. After a while, my tears subsided, replaced by hiccups.

"Let me take you to get some food."

"I'm so pathetic."

"Stop. You're not. Let's get some food and talk. I find it helps." He winked.

"If you throw in a stop at Target, I'd love you forever."

Graham paused, and I realized what I said. His cheeks pinked, and I hoped I hadn't scared him.

"Deal." He took my hand, leading me to his car. I looked around, realizing he was missing part of himself.

"Where's Tucker?"

"He needed to ice his shoulder, but he also had to do an interview. I was going to grab some food and then pick him up after, but now I get to spend it with you." He smiled over at me, and my heart soared. Graham was sweet and comforting, and I felt better just from his hug.

Graham surprised me by opening the door, and I smiled at the gentlemanly gesture. It was quiet in the car as we drove, but it felt soothing. Like I didn't have to be on in his presence.

"How do tacos sound?"

"Like you're reading my mind."

Graham laughed and pulled up to a local place. I climbed out of the car but noticed how he frowned that I'd done it. Why was that so cute?

"How do you know local places to eat already?" I asked as we stood in line.

"Research." He shrugged, laughing. "Plus, I'm a foodie, so I always look up the best places. But this one was actually recommended by your brother."

"Really? Damn. My own brother won't even give me the good food places." I grinned, the weight of the day lifting more and more the longer I was in his presence.

Once we ordered, we took a booth in the back, and I couldn't hide my smile when Graham slid in next to me instead of across.

"This morning feels like weeks ago," I admitted, turning to him. Graham picked up my hand, linking our fingers as he played with it above the table.

"Want to talk about it?"

I blew out a breath, ruffling my hair that had fallen around my face. I'd gone with braids this morning, hoping they'd hold all day, but I wasn't so sure by the state of my hair now. Though, it could've been the unicorn dance that had messed it all up.

"Do you ever feel like you have the weight of the world on your shoulders?"

"All the time." Graham's eyes roamed over my face, and I found a kindred spirit staring back at me in his gray eyes. "Being the youngest of five and the only boy, I felt intense pressure to be everything my father dreamed of in a son. Unfortunately, I tend to disappoint him more than I live up to it."

"I get that." I nodded. "It's why I almost got married. My mom seemed so excited about it. The fear of losing me as a child made her believe it would never happen, and when the opportunity came, she ran with it. She planned my entire wedding and I could never say no to her." I scrunched up my nose at the memories. "It was awful. I worried about disappointing her and my dad more than Brandon."

"That was your ex-fiancé?"

"Yep. Nice guy. Had nothing to do with baseball, which I'll admit is what drew me to him. Kind of boring, but he did have a nice dimple," I mused.

Graham snorted. "Dimples. Romance's siren song."

Laughing, I couldn't deny it. But I wouldn't admit he had ones in his back that could probably get him away with just about anything.

Our food was delivered, and we stopped talking as we ate. I instantly felt better and knew some of my emotions had been from hanger.

"Oh, my. These are delicious. Roscoe's, you're my new favorite place," I said around a mouthful.

Graham nodded in agreement, moaning as much as me around each bite.

"Did my eyes mistake me, or was that you doing a dance on the field?"

My cheeks heated. "It was me."

"You were great."

"Thanks. I don't normally do things like that. It was kind of refreshing."

"You don't like being the center of attention."

"Nope. You?" I asked, licking my fingers clean. His eyes tracked the movement, heating at the action.

"It's not my forte like Tucker, but I got used to it with baseball. Being a catcher means everyone is staring at your butt for half of the game. I can be embarrassed or accept it and focus on the game."

I narrowed my eyes. "So, you're saying all I need to do is embrace the stares, and all my mortifications will disappear?"

"Yup." He nodded, laughing. "I don't think it ever goes away completely, but it feels less important. People are going to do what they're going to do." He shrugged. "I don't have to waste my time being embarrassed by something I can't control."

"Most people tell me to get over it."

"Yeah, well, most people are assholes."

"Ha!" I laughed, a few people turning to look. My cheeks heated, but I tried Graham's approach. I wouldn't feel bad for laughing.

"You're beautiful when you laugh," Graham whispered. He leaned closer, his eyes dropping to my lips.

His hand cupped my cheek and brought his lips down to mine in a soft caress. Once. Twice. Three times before he pulled back, taking my breath with him.

"Let's go get you some clothes, then it might be time to get Tucker."

I nodded, following him out of the booth. And for the first time that I could remember, I didn't think about the other patrons. I didn't wonder what they thought of me or if they were whispering.

With a kiss like that, nothing else seemed to matter.

And it had been a chaste one.

I wasn't sure if I'd survive one with tongue. It could very likely alter my axis, sending me entirely off course.

But at this point, I'd willingly jump in. Feet first.

CHAPTER
TWENTY

BLAKE

Graham held my hand as we neared the Target entrance. Everything with him felt natural and easy, and I loved how calm he made me feel.

"Good evening, folks. Just to let you know, we close in thirty minutes," a red-shirt employee said.

"Race ya?" I turned to Graham, my lips tilting up at the edges.

"What are we racing for exactly? You're the one who needed to come here."

"True. Okay, well, I need to buy bras and panties. Let's go." I took off toward the women's section, snatching a red basket. My cheeks heated as I power-walked, attempting to outrun my embarrassment.

"If you need privacy, you can have it," Graham said, "but I am an excellent shopper. Product of being the baby of four older sisters. They took me everywhere."

"Bryce and I are close, but the thought of him buying me underwear makes my skin crawl." I shuddered, keeping my focus in front of me.

"I don't buy it for them." He laughed, some of my mortification easing. "I've just been with them when they have. Growing up, I also had to do laundry, so women's lingerie doesn't scare me. It fascinates me, actually. Not my sisters'. But in general." He flubbed, making me turn to look at him this time.

"Ah, you're cute." I stopped and faced him.

"And that is why relationships are disasters for me."

"Why?" I asked, honestly confused.

"Because I tend to say things that make girls see me as more of a friend than sexual. Guys are easier in that capacity."

"Their loss then." I kissed his cheek, took his hand, and led him to the section I needed. "Do you mind me asking…" I trailed off, attempting to find the words.

"You can ask me anything, Bee, but if it's about how I identify, I'm pan."

I nodded, already having assumed so. "And do you have feelings for Tucker?" I asked, dropping a package of panties into the basket.

"What?" Graham's eyes widened, and he blinked multiple times.

"Relax." I placed my hand on his arm, feeling his pulse thrum quickly underneath my palm. "I just thought I picked up on a vibe this morning. That's all."

"So, it's not obvious?" he asked, relaxing.

"Not to Tucker."

I moved over to the bras, searching a few for my size. Once I had one, I dropped it in the basket and hoped it was enough to get me through until my luggage arrived.

"Does that bother you?" Graham asked as we moved to the clothing section. I scanned through the leggings section first.

"Not at all." I paused, looking up. "Well, as long as it means you still like me."

Graham smiled, stepped closer to me, and placed his

hands on my hips. "Of course I do." His lips found mine again, the kiss soft and slow, warming my insides like a warm bath.

"Good evening. Target will be closing in fifteen minutes. Please bring all of your purchases to the register at this time. Thank you."

"Crap!" I jumped back, picked out two pairs of leggings, and grabbed two shirts. Graham added some socks, and I smiled in thanks. I rushed to the hygiene section, tossing in a brush, hair ties, detangler, sunscreen, feminine products, deodorant, and face wash. I scanned the aisle, quickly assessing if I needed anything else, and decided it should be enough for now.

The two of us got in line, and I spotted a pack of batteries. My bullet vibrator was getting low, so I casually placed them into the basket. The cashier looked annoyed as I perused the chocolate section and magazines. Feeling anxious, I grabbed a few things, not paying attention, and slid down to the end to pay.

Graham lifted one of the magazines after it had been scanned through. "I didn't take you for a Golf's Digest reader." I snorted, glancing at the magazine and the two others. My smile dropped as I took them in.

Luke Olson on the cover of Men's Health, his beautiful abs on display. Add in the Golf Digest with the heading, "Three Platypus Lodge: the South's hidden golf secret," and the Cosmo with "How to turn that one-night-stand into more," and it was clear my subconscious hated me.

I slid in my debit card, hit the numbers, and took the bags from the cashier in a daze. Graham walked beside me quietly as we left the store, the doors locked behind us.

The drive back to the stadium was quiet, but unlike before, I could feel the questions in his stare. He finally asked once we pulled into the parking lot at Champion Field.

"You okay?"

A combo of a snort and a hysterical cry escaped me, and I

covered my mouth in humiliation, aiming to prevent any further sounds from leaving. Graham rolled his lips inward, holding back his laugh, but as I stared at him with wide eyes, I lost it. Dropping my hands, I let out a sound that sounded more like pigs rutting than a laugh.

"Oh my god. I can't believe that sound came out of me." I placed my hands on my cheeks, cooling the heated skin.

"It was adorable."

I shook my head, wiping the tears. "To answer your question…" I shrugged. "Yes, no. It's been a day."

"You really liked Luke." I appreciated how Graham just put things out there.

"I don't want to. He hurt me, but my brain and body don't seem to get that."

"Have you talked to him since the outburst? Did he explain anything?"

"If yelling at each other is talking, then yes." I chuckled. "He said he saw his name written down on my pad of paper, freaked out that I was a spy who now knew all his secrets and was about to ruin him. So, he ran."

Graham grimaced, his gray eyes soft. "Not to excuse his behavior, but from what I've heard around the league, Luke's had some run-ins with crazy fans. According to clubhouse gossip, one girl took pictures of him while he slept, another collected his toenails, and a few sold stories to tabloids. He shouldn't have hurt you, but his paranoia comes from a real place."

I sighed, rubbing my temple. "Why are you so understanding? Shouldn't you be pushing me away from him?"

"The way I see it, it's not a competition. And like I mentioned, monogamy isn't the only answer. Do you like to read?"

"Yeah." I raised my brows, not understanding the shift in conversation but glad the focus was off Luke and my confusing feelings. I wanted to be mad at him right now, and thinking about his feelings clouded my own.

Graham reached around the seat and unzipped his bag. I heard him dig around in it before he found what he wanted and then turned back around. He handed me a book, his cheeks pink as he stared at me.

"Read that and let me know what you think. I find understanding things from books helps." His smile was boyish, his gray eyes warm, and I had a weird déjà vu feeling.

"Thanks. I will." I placed it in my bag, suddenly feeling awkward. "So, what do we do now?"

"I have an idea…" Graham's eyes dropped to my lips, and I licked them. He groaned, the sound making my pussy throb.

I didn't know who moved first, but one second we were each in our own seats, and the next, I was pulled across the console and straddling his lap. His hands twined through my hair, his lips taking mine in a forceful kiss.

Gone was the slow perusal from before, and it was replaced with full steam. We couldn't seem to kiss each other fast enough, our tongues and teeth battling. I smoothed my hands up his chest, rounding over his shoulders. Had shoulders ever felt this sexy before? They were strong, and I wanted to massage all the muscles in his arms.

My hands ran through his hair, the dark strands tickling my palms. He smelled like his room—spice and pine—and something uniquely him. Graham's hands moved from my face, traveling down my back and cupping my ass. He shifted, dropping one hand, and the seat jerked back.

"Whoa." I giggled at the abrupt movement, but the steering wheel no longer dug into my butt.

"Now I can touch every inch of you," he whispered, wrapping one around my back and the other on my ass. My thighs fell on either side of him, bringing me into direct contact with the bulge between his legs.

Our lips found one another again, and I rocked on his lap, dragging my center across his hardness. We both moaned, the sounds vibrating between us and spurring us to move more.

"Fuck, Bee. You feel so good."

"Mmhmm," I moaned. "More," I gasped.

"Does my sunshine need me to touch her?" His voice was huskier, the need evident as I rocked my lower half.

"Please," I begged, not even caring how needy I sounded. With Graham's hands on me, nothing else mattered.

Graham groaned, his fingers moving to the waistband of his pants and slipping under. When he felt the elastic band of his boxer briefs, he paused, pulling back to look.

"Are you wearing my underwear, Sunshine?" His voice was rough and thick with desire.

"Yes. That okay?"

"Fuck. Yes. Is it bad if I steal your new package and replace them with only mine?"

"Not if it ends in this. But please don't. I'm desperate."

Graham chuckled, his fingers brushing back and forth on my stomach. His lips moved to my neck, and he peppered small kisses as he pushed his fingers lower, brushing over my pussy. I could already feel my wetness, so I wasn't surprised when his fingers easily slid between me.

"So wet." He groaned, the sound vibrating through my neck.

I hummed, rocking to move his finger lower. He took the hint and rubbed his thumb over my clit, setting off the bundle of nerves with each stroke. My fingers gripped his shoulders, my nails biting into him as I held on. The muscles in my body were taut as I rocked myself on his fingers, chasing that high.

"You're so beautiful to watch like this," he cooed.

"More," I demanded, ignoring his compliment.

Graham chuckled but did as I asked and inserted two fingers into my throbbing pussy. My walls clamped around him, finally happy to feel fuller. It still wasn't enough, but it would do for now.

"Yes, yes," I chanted, tilting my head back and rocking with his movements.

His hot breath skimmed my neck as he held me close with one arm, the other deep inside of me. I lost all sense of time, place, and awareness as I chased my orgasm. My walls tightened as it approached, my muscles locking until everything exploded.

"Ahhh! Yes! Graham!" I shouted, my body spasming around his fingers. Tiny pinpricks of light danced behind my eyes as I shuddered and collected my breath.

When I blinked them open, I first landed on Graham's smug face. Once he knew I was watching, he withdrew his fingers, licking them one by one as he held my eyes.

"I can't wait to taste you for real, Sunshine. That was fucking beautiful to partake in." My cheeks reddened, but for once, I didn't care.

"You're something else, Graham West."

He winked, and I smiled, dropping a kiss to his plump lips. A knock on the window had me jumping, and I clutched my heart.

"Hey guys! That was hawt," Tucker said outside the steamed-up window. "Or at least what I could see. Unlock the door and let me in before the boogeyman gets me!"

Graham laughed but hit the button. I hid my face in his neck as Tucker scrambled into the backseat.

"I'm not even mad I missed whatever you two did because I got to see that. I'll do whatever stupid publicity thing I need to if I get that welcome home show."

"This isn't home," Graham said, shifting me back to my seat.

"Home isn't a place, G. It's people. Duh." Tucker leaned between the seats, rolling his eyes. "Did you save me any?"

he asked, snatching Graham's fingers that had just been in me and shoved them into his mouth.

Graham and I stared at one another in shock as Tucker licked his fingers, moaning. "Damn. Don't be so greedy next time, G. That wasn't nearly enough to satisfy." Tucker turned to me, kissing me quickly. He winked and then sat back, buckling his seat belt.

I blinked; the Tucker whirlwind took a moment to process. Graham recovered before I did.

"How was it?" he asked, driving us out of the lot. I gave him directions to Bryce's as we listened to Tucker give us a play-by-play of his night.

"Then she asked me if I ever wanted to play on a team without you." Tucker rolled his eyes. "So, I asked her if penguins have knees." He laughed, apparently finding his question funny. "Reporters are weird."

"That they are," Graham said, winking at me.

"Do we get to sleep over tonight, lambchop?" Tucker asked.

"Nope and nope." I laughed.

"Fine. I'll find you a nickname you'll love, honey bee."

"I'm sure you will." I smiled, feeling ten times better than I had earlier in the evening. I almost didn't want to get out when Graham pulled into Bryce's condo.

"Thanks for the ride. I guess I'll see you tomorrow?"

"You're not getting rid of us yet, Bee!" Tucker hopped out of the car and opened my door.

"Bye," I said to Graham, unsure if I should kiss him. He took the pressure off and leaned across, giving me a sweet kiss.

"See you tomorrow, Sunshine."

Tucker walked me to the door and then pushed me against it, cupping my face as he kissed me thoroughly. His kiss was playful and had me panting within seconds.

"Mmm," he moaned. "It's like I can taste you both."

I blushed despite not being embarrassed. The thought of a kiss with both of their tastes sounded divine, and I wondered if Tucker was as far from liking Graham as Graham thought.

"Night."

Tucker hopped down the stairs, whistling like he had no care in the world. I envied his carefree spirit and vowed to embody it more starting tomorrow.

The condo was eerily quiet as I climbed the stairs, only the ticking of a clock present. I clutched my possessions tightly, happy to have something different to wear for once. As I passed the extra large jacuzzi, I paused. A hot bubble bath sounded exactly what I needed.

Turning on some music, I filled the tub and added some bubbles, climbing in once it was full. With the music playing, it didn't feel so quiet in the house, and I pretended I wasn't alone.

My muscles relaxed as I soaked, and I stared off into space, zoning out and ignoring all my thoughts about the past few days. When my skin was pruned, I climbed out of the tub and dried off. That weird, lonely feeling hit me again, so I set an alarm and crawled under the covers with the book Graham had lent me.

I didn't make it far before my eyelids grew heavy, and I fell asleep, hopeful tomorrow would be better.

Unfortunately, life hadn't pitch-slapped me enough and had decided to up the ante.

Turning off my alarm, I rolled out of bed, my feet meeting wet carpet.

"What the heck?"

The smell of raw sewage hit me, and I gagged, racing to the bathroom. After spewing the contents of my stomach for the second morning straight, I wondered when vomit had become such a focal feature of my life.

Holding my nose this time, I surveyed the damage. Ice-cold water stood at least two inches deep and had the foulest smell known to man. It rivaled Bryce's ball bag after a month at spring training.

"Just great. Wonderful. I'm living the dream here," I groaned, rubbing my face. I so didn't want to deal with this. Couldn't I get one morning without a disaster?

Tears streamed down my face before I could stop them, and I hiccupped as I contemplated what to do.

"When I asked for help, this isn't what I meant, World!" I shook my fists in the air like the world could hear me and cared.

When nothing happened, I picked up my phone and called the one man who'd know what to do.

"Daddy, I need help. Baseball can't fix this one."

CHAPTER
TWENTY-ONE

HAWK

I watched the sun move across the ceiling as the morning light filtered through the window and realized I should invest in blackout curtains.

Yeah, because the sun's why you're not sleeping.

Rubbing my hand over my face, I sighed. I focused on the rough bristles of my beard against my palm, letting the fine hairs calm my frazzled brain. Though, at this rate, it would take more than grounding to help me.

My mind was tired as fuck, but it wouldn't shut off, meaning sleep had been little to none. The less sleep I got, the more neurotic I became. There were moments I wasn't sure if they were real or just lucid dreams… or nightmares might be more accurate.

Sounds of Blake haunted me everywhere I went. Her laugh, her sigh, her scream. The little noises she made when she slept or when she read something funny and snorted. But the worst was the way her moans plagued every available brain cell.

Once I heard her in my mind, I then saw her everywhere. I couldn't escape her—real or imaginary.

For three years, I'd been able to push our night out of my mind. I focused on my friendship with Bryce, cared for my sister and nieces, and played baseball. Despite yelling at her for staying away, it had helped.

Out of sight, out of mind, and all that. Or it was at least easier to pretend.

Then I was injured, and my whole world shifted. Baseball was gone, and all my routines and distractions with it. Jack, my physical therapist, had believed I was extra committed to rehabbing because I wanted to play again. I showed up at dawn every day, pushed my limits to the max, and took everything he gave me. The pain grounded me, and I desperately needed it. When Jack had given me the news that I couldn't return to playing, he'd taken it harder than I had.

Because the truth was, I could live without baseball, but I couldn't live without Blake.

Mr. Baker offering me a coaching job had given me a new focus. Moving to a new area, a place without constant memories of Blake, was also a bonus. Each day, I pushed forward, and something new settled into my life. Eventually, I accepted my future and was happy with it.

I bought a house, put down my own roots, and created something for myself. After becoming friends with Roxie, our dating relationship evolved naturally. It was simple. Friends with benefits with no drama.

Being states away from my family created new dynamics. I relinquished my responsibility of caring for them for the first time in years.

My sister, Wren, met someone who wasn't a dirtbag and got married. I no longer had to take care of her, which allowed me to be the fun uncle instead of an overbearing brother. I got my nieces now for weekend visits and spoiled them because I could, not because I had to. That felt different, and I liked it.

My father got his meds stabilized and started therapy,

finally dealing with my mother's death. He got a job he didn't hate, stopped drinking away his paycheck, and met a lovely woman at the senior center. I had someone check on him weekly, but I no longer felt responsible for his choices.

Letting go of familial guilt and my mother's death had been life-altering, freeing me from a burden I'd carried since I was a child—the seven year old whose parents needed him to be the adult.

My life hadn't been perfect, but it had been good. Easy.

But with one woman waltzing back into my life, she'd turned everything I'd ignored upside down. And now I couldn't find a free moment without thoughts and sounds of her plaguing me.

Deciding I might as well get up since I was unlikely to fall asleep, I kicked my legs out from under the comforter and took a deep breath. My body ached with bone-deep tiredness that I didn't think could be fixed with sleep. Today's game would be brutal.

But at least you'll get to see her. Be near her.

Sadly, I didn't know if it was a blessing or a curse.

Cracking my knuckles, I flexed my hands and stared at the red spots on my right knuckles. There were a few bruises and marks, but I'd gladly endure them, knowing that asshat's jaw would feel it long after mine healed.

Smirking at how shocked his face had been, I felt a little adrenaline pump through me as I stood and stretched. The sight of the partially naked woman in my bed with her purple hair spilling over the pillow did nothing to me. She gave a tiny snore, rubbing her nose before she rolled over, showcasing her ass to me.

It was cute, and Roxie was hot, but my dick didn't even twitch. I was unsure if it was exhaustion or just on strike. It hadn't so much as perked up for Roxie since I'd picked Blake up in Georgia.

So far, Roxie hadn't said anything about my lack of

interest in sex, but I knew it wouldn't last. It was all our relationship was founded on. Without it, it was hard to classify what we had as casual sex. It would just be… casual.

Grabbing my phone, I walked out to the kitchen and got the coffee ready. Reading my reminder on the fridge to feed Sunny, I chopped lettuce and apples and took them to the cage in the princess room, otherwise known as my spare room—the one my nieces had claimed. Sunny ran on his wheel, the little clinking sound soothing in the early morning.

"Hey, turd. Eat your food, little guy." I dumped it in, checking his water and whether his cage needed cleaning before I left in a few days. We had three more home games after today before we went away for six. Thankfully, Roxie checked on him for me while I was away, meaning I wouldn't have to tell my nieces I'd killed their pet.

Satisfied with Sunny's eating and habitat, I returned to the kitchen, opened the fridge, and stared at the contents. Sleep fog made it difficult for me to identify meals, everything seeming like one ingredient that wouldn't work with anything else. Giving up, I grabbed the eggs and set them on the counter.

"Toast," I mumbled, remembering something else I could make. I felt dumb, the lack of sleep finally catching up to me, and the simplest things seemed like complex equations. Just another reminder of how hellish coaching would be today.

Cracking the eggs into a pan, I shoved two pieces of bread into the toaster, glad neither of these were complicated. While the eggs sizzled, I swiped my thumb across the dark screen of my phone to wake it up. There were a couple of notifications from sports apps and social accounts, along with a few texts.

Flipping the eggs, I stepped back and clicked on the ones from Bryce to see how his game went. We had a tradition of sending our stats to one another and talking through the games. Typically, I watched his game and gave feedback after. But lately, I'd fallen behind in my best friend duties. However, he had asked me to watch after Blake, and it seemed my brain had taken the request to the extreme.

I couldn't do anything else but watch her.

> Bryce: Did you find out anything about Davis? He better be glad I'm not there, or I'd make sure he didn't play again.

> Bryce: I could've done better in the 3rd inning, but I got a good hit in the 7th.

> Bryce: Man, the energy of being back in the big leagues is like nothing else.

> Bryce: Not that I didn't enjoy my team with the 'Jacks, but yeah… my heart beats for this game, and I love where I am.

> Bryce: The team's so different than four years ago. That's been an adjustment.

> Bryce: Blanket isn't giving you too much grief, is she?

I rubbed my eyes, debating how to respond, when I remembered my eggs. Dropping my phone, I rescued them from the pan and plated them with toast just before they burned. They were more cooked than I'd intended, but they'd work. Ensuring I turned off the burner, I plopped onto the barstool with my coffee mug and phone.

As I ate, I thumbed out some responses to Bryce, hoping my vague comeback didn't sound off. I'd blame it on the tiredness if he asked, but I knew my short answers stemmed from keeping secrets from him. Not speaking to many people meant I hadn't conquered the art of small talk.

My phone rang halfway through my responses, and I almost dropped it when I spotted the number.

Steven Baker.

Dread sank into my stomach as a million worst-case scenarios ran through my head.

Bryce had been in an accident.

Blake was in the hospital.

I was fired for lusting after his daughter.

"You going to get that?" Roxie asked, stopping my spiral, and I hit the answer button before it went to voicemail.

"Sir?" I asked, the sound coming from deep in my throat and full of dread.

"We've been over this, Hawk. Call me Steven."

"Sure, Steven. What's..." I cleared my throat. "What's going on?"

"My poor daughter seems to have pissed off the baseball gods." He sighed, not helping my anxiety. "I hate to ask this of you, but there's been a situation at Bryce's house. Someone is coming over to handle it, but I don't feel good leaving her alone. I know she's a grown woman, but I can't help but want to protect her."

The instant he'd said there was a situation, I'd jumped off my stool and headed to the bedroom, pulling on a pair of jeans. He was still being vague as fuck, frustrating me, but it didn't matter. If it involved Blake, I'd be there.

"I'll head right over."

"Thanks, Hawk. With Bryce being away, you're the only *brother* she's got around. With everything she's dealt with this week, I don't want her to feel alone in handling this." His voice sounded different, almost like he was teasing, but I couldn't figure out what it could be about. I swallowed, rubbing my hand over my face, feeling sick at the thought of only being seen as Blazy's brother.

You did it to yourself, dumbass.

"For sure. It's not a big deal," I said as I pulled on socks and grabbed my wallet. I headed into the living room, grabbing my shoes. "Just what exactly am I heading into?" I asked.

He chuckled, making me relax marginally. If he was laughing, it couldn't be all that bad.

"There's been a little water leak. From what I can guess, there's a clog, and after she took a bath last night, it overflowed the drain trough."

I paused, trying to put the words together. "You had to Google it, didn't you?" I asked, my heart slowing slightly. It wasn't critical. Everyone was safe.

"Ssh, to my little girl, I'm still the solver of all her problems. I want to hold on to that as long as I can."

"Your secret's safe with me, Steven."

"Good. I knew I could count on you."

He trailed off, talking a little about the Devils and the 'Jacks as I finished getting ready, running my fingers through my hair to flatten it. When he let me off, I jumped when I spotted Roxie drinking coffee in the kitchen. In the chaos of everything, I'd forgotten she was there.

"She's back, isn't she?"

"Who?" I asked, moving over to pick up my keys.

She smiled softly, letting me know my lie hadn't been bought. Draining the last dregs of her mug, she walked closer and patted my cheek, her hand soft and warm. I leaned into her touch for a second, the familiarity and safety of it pleasant.

But that's all it was anymore.

"Yeah. That's what I thought," she whispered. "We both know that display the other night wasn't for my benefit." She gave me a smile, kissing my cheek before stepping back. "This isn't working for me anymore, Hawk. You should tell her how you feel."

"It's not—" I stopped myself, remembering who I was talking to, my shoulders dropping. "But Bryce." I shrugged, knowing I didn't need to say more. Guilt flooded me, but I didn't have time to dwell on it.

I'd initially met Roxie back in Columbus. When Bryce had

mentioned Blake getting a tattoo, I'd gone to the same shop in a desperate attempt to find out what it was. Believing it might be some hidden clue to how she felt. And while Roxie wouldn't tell me, she did become my friend, and later, tattoo artist. When she moved to Wilmington, it felt like fate, and we started our arrangement.

But she knew the tale, the whole sorry saga, and always told me she'd step aside if Blake ever returned. She might not be searching for love but believed it existed and would never stand in its way.

"You know my stand on that, babe. You've let go of all your family shit, finally living your life for you… except in this one area. Bryce's your best friend and wants you to be happy. He might be upset, but he'll get over it."

She rinsed her mug, grabbing a box of granola she kept in the cabinet and a phone charger from a junk drawer. She turned back to me, giving me a soft smile.

"I don't think you will, though. Not from her. You've loved Blake most of your life. Time to stop being so scared and shake off this last burden and choose *you*."

Her words were delivered in a gentle tone, but they smacked me upside the head all the same.

"I'll lock up after I shower. Do you still need me to look after Sunny?"

I nodded, the move stiff. "Yes." I cleared my throat, emotion clogging.

"I'm rooting for you, Hawk Anderson. Go out and get your love story."

I wrapped my arms around her, breathing in her familiar smell one more time. "You've been the best gift I never deserved. I appreciate your friendship, Rox."

"I am great, aren't I?" she teased, stepping back and winking. That was Roxie. Able to give sage advice to everyone else, but when it came to herself, she avoided love with a ten-foot pole.

As I headed to my car, I watched her walk away, feeling lighter than I wanted to admit. The drive to Bryce's went by in a blur, and I blinked in shock when I pulled up, not having realized I was there. Shit. I needed to sleep tonight, or I'd get myself killed. Turning into the lot, I almost plowed into a water restoration van parked in front.

'Little' leak, my ass.

Parking down a few spaces, I entered the house and stepped over the big tube coming out the front door. Plastic covered the floor in places, and huge fans blew air, the noise deafening. No one stopped me as I walked through, just nodding as they went about their business and pulled up the carpet.

I finally noticed Blake, her back to me with her arms crossed as she spoke to an older man. She was only wearing a tank top and a pair of boxers, and I immediately saw red. I caught a few of the guys checking her out, and I snapped.

Blame it on the no sleep, but I couldn't take these assholes looking at her. I might not be able to have her, but I'd be damned if I let them leer.

Stomping to her, I yanked off the flannel shirt I'd put on over my tee and draped it across her shoulder, glaring at the guys. They quickly dropped their eyes, finding something else to stare at as they did their work.

"What?" she gasped, glaring up at me with fire in her eyes.

"You're practically naked in a house full of men, Blake." I seethed, my words harsher than I intended. She instantly bristled, her eyes flashing as she doubled down on her stubbornness.

"So? Last time I checked, I was a single woman and free to do whatever I wanted. So take your 'big brother energy' out of here and leave me alone. I have this handled."

I hated to admit how much her words hurt. I gritted my teeth, grinding my molars as I stared down at her, debating if any of these men would stop me if I threw her over my shoulder and carried her out of here. The only thing that stopped me was not knowing for sure, and I didn't have time to be arrested.

"As I was saying to Ms. Baker, the house needs to be evacuated. She can't stay here for at least a week, probably more, while we remove and restore the damage. It's extensive and requires new drywall in several rooms, carpet and flooring in the affected areas and a new subfloor. But first, everything has to dry out so we can make sure no mold can grow. That will take days. To top it off, the air quality isn't habitable since it's mixed with the sewage."

"She can stay with me," I said automatically.

"Fuck, no. I'll find my own place." She glared at me, and I missed how she used to look at me like she saw the whole world in my eyes.

The man held up his hands, stepping back. "I don't care where, Miss, just that you go somewhere. Grab what you can and move anything you don't want left out in the affected areas." With that, he returned to his team, giving directions on what needed to be done.

"Don't be stubborn, Blake. Your dad called me." Apparently, that was the absolute wrong thing to say.

"My *dad*. My *brother*. Do you ever do something *you* want, Hawk?"

She turned on her heels with an exasperated sigh and entered the guest room as I stewed over her words.

Because they weren't wrong, but I had changed. I had started to... Hadn't I?

Everything else in my life seemed futile compared to this.

"We'll be in touch with your father and let him know when it's ready," the man said later as she stepped out with a bag over her shoulder. She'd at least put on pants, decreasing my heart rate a twinge.

"Fine." She sighed, giving in to the inevitable.

"Just need your signature here and here." He handed her a clipboard, and she signed it, rolling her eyes when she spotted me looming.

"What are you still doing here? I told you I didn't need you."

"Let me give you a ride to the field."

She held my eyes, her arms crossed as she debated. I could see the fight leaving her with every second, the ordeal of the morning taking it out of her.

"Fine. But only because I still don't have my license." She stomped away, tossing more words over her shoulder. "You're stopping for coffee and donuts."

My heart galloped, and lightness entered me. I suddenly felt energized with a renewed sense of purpose.

She hadn't fought me. It was a simple thing, but it was a start.

Even if all we became again was friends, it was better than nothing. I'd been kidding myself, believing I could keep her out of my life when I saw her every day. Now, I just had to remember to guard my heart. If there was even such a thing with my Blazy, but I'd try. Because being on the outside of her life didn't work.

CHAPTER
TWENTY-TWO

BLAKE

My eyes blurred as I stared at the computer screen, the words doubling the longer I stared. Removing my glasses, I rubbed the bridge of my nose and cleared my eyes. *This day.* Would it ever get easier? Or was I doomed to fight tooth and nail each day? Each time something good happened, the world tilted on its axis to remind me not to get too comfortable.

I got the message, World. Could we lighten up a little?

Maybe the baseball gods were mad at me? I stopped believing in them, and now they were smiting me.

All right. I get the point. Baseball is the best!

I sighed. Fine. So I couldn't bullshit baseball, but it had been worth a try. Putting my glasses back on, I picked up the coffee Hawk had bought me and cringed when the cold liquid hit my tongue.

Gross. How long had I been sitting here?

Like the baseball gods could hear my plight, Hawk walked into the media office. I immediately felt his presence, my body so attuned to him like a magnet. I watched as he stalked toward me, the other staff glancing up and jerking back at the sight of him. I got it. Outwardly, Hawk looked like the last person you'd see in an office. And I didn't even think it was the gauges still in his ears or the tattoos decorating his arms. No, it was the resting asshole face he constantly wore that scared most people off.

My defeated heart didn't have it in me today to fight him, so I let myself greedily drink him in. He was like a shot of espresso to my exhausted body, sending my heart racing as he neared. Remembering how his smell had enveloped me in the car this morning, sinking straight to my marrow, I crossed my legs in an attempt to curb the throbbing there.

His mismatched eyes never left mine as he approached; there was something different in them today. I held my breath, not sure I'd be able to hold back today.

Because I was weak as a paper bag when it came to Hawk Anderson.

His presence loomed as he stood before my desk, his eyes boring into mine. Neither of us said anything, just stared. Hawk leaned forward, his sandalwood cologne invading my senses and erasing all logical thought. I closed my eyes, my lips ready for the kiss, accepting defeat when it came to Hawk.

But instead of his lips pressing into mine, only cool air greeted me. I blinked open my eyes, the space before me now empty. I glanced around but didn't spot him, and I vaguely wondered if I'd hallucinated Hawk. Just great. I had a Hawk specter haunting my daytime hours now, too.

Except when I glanced down at my desk, a new coffee cup sat in the middle. Wrapping my hands around it, the heat from the liquid inside warmed me, and the heaviness of it concluded my observation.

He'd brought me a new coffee.

A little bit of the anger I had fell away as I picked it up, savoring the flavor as it exploded over my tongue. Gah, that was good stuff.

With a fresh coffee, I jumped back into work, the weight of the morning slipping away as I focused on editing the pictures and videos I'd taken. There was just something about sports photography that got my blood pumping unlike any other. I'd sold several prints of landscapes and silhouettes in Greece, but I never felt as passionate about them as I did the sports stuff.

I guess it was in my blood, after all.

Hitting send on an email, I slumped into my chair and drank the last of my coffee, enjoying the moment of peace.

"I've sent back my suggestions on the latest uploads. What are you doing for the away games?" Mira asked, startling me. I jumped, fumbling the coffee cup, grateful it was empty. My cheeks heated as I retrieved it from the floor, straightening myself as I looked at my boss.

"Since I have to ride with the team, I'll use the time to do some candid interviews."

"Good luck with that." She scoffed, setting me on edge. She sat on the corner of my desk, picking up the random picture of Bryce, Hawk, and me from when we were kids. Bryce had left it on my desk for me on my first day as a welcome gift. I strategically placed a pen holder in front of Hawk, so I didn't have to look at his face.

I cleared my throat, stopping myself from ripping the picture out of her hands. She sat it down, her eyes meeting mine. "What do you mean?" I asked.

"The players are creatures of habit. They won't be kind to you interrupting their downtime."

"Oh, well, I can ask and see what they think." I shrugged, not worried about the guys. I had ways of making them talk.

"Hmm." She stared at me like she was trying to read my mind. It was a bit creepy. "How are you adjusting? Do you feel like you're getting the hang of the operation?"

I tilted my hand in front of me from side to side. "Eh. I

feel like I've been playing catch up since I got here, but I like it."

Her brow furrowed, a fake frown of concern on her face. "Perhaps you should spend time here and not attend the away games."

"Tempting, but I need to find a routine. I think the away games will give me that. And hopefully, I won't have any more outside issues and will be able to catch my breath."

"Steven told me about Bryce's condo. Do you need a place to stay?" Her brows narrowed, that look of fake concern back on her face. It rubbed me the wrong way, and I'd rather sleep in the outfield than at her place. At least here, I could guarantee I wouldn't wake up with my legs strapped to boards as she screamed, 'See what you made me do!'

Hard pass.

It didn't surprise me that my dad had spilled the beans to her; they had been friends or co-workers for a few years. Dad was very hands-on in running operations, so it shouldn't bother me. But it did. It had that 'seen as a kid instead of the grown-up' feel to it that I loathed.

"I'm good. Thanks." I gave Mira a strained smile, and she nodded.

"Right, well, the offer is open if you need it." *Not in this lifetime, Annie.*

"Thanks." I gritted my teeth as she squeezed my shoulder, finally leaving me. I sank back into my chair, the earlier energy now gone as I debated what to do. I should get up and prepare for the players to arrive. But I didn't feel like doing the things I should do today.

My phone vibrated on the desk, and I picked it up, spotting a text from Graham and Tucker. My grin widened, my heart flipping over as the butterflies woke up at seeing their names.

Graham: How's your morning? You've been eerily quiet, Sunshine.

Graham: I had to stop Tucker from staging an intervention three times already.

Tucker: Besties with perks text, sugar bear.

Graham: I will go out on a limb and say no for Blake. She still keeps her veto.

Tucker: You're right. You're more my sugar bear. My Teddy Graham.

Tucker: Oh. My. God. Why haven't I realized that before now?

Graham: Because you value your life?

Tucker: Sure, Teddy Graham.

Graham: Try it to my face and see what happens.

Tucker: Oh, I love it when you go all Dom on me.

Tucker: I'm a bad boy, Teddy Graham. Teach me a lesson.

Graham: Blake, rescue me from his ridiculousness.

Tucker: Clearly, you didn't read the fine print. There's no return policy.

Graham: I should've turned around and walked out freshman year.

Tucker: You love me, Teddy Graham. Quit fighting it.

Graham: Only because I need to save my energy for the game.

Blake: Hey, screwballs. Thanks for the laugh. It's been a morning.

Tucker: Do you need help?

I smiled at his immediate response. Tucker might be a goof most of the time, but he was genuine and sincere when it came to it. Their easy banter had also eased the tension in my chest, making me excited for the game, something I'd vaguely considered skipping for about two seconds. But the thought had been there.

I didn't know where I stood with Luke or Hawk. Most of our interactions were full of animosity and tension, but at least with GT, things were easy to figure out. Tucker had a point. Straightforward communication might be uncomfortable to start, but it kept things clear.

Blake: Not now, but thanks.

Graham: Can we hang out later?

Tucker: Good idea. Another sleepover, but this one without clothes!

Graham: Tucker, do you listen to the things you say?

Tucker: It's texting, how can I listen?

Blake: He's got a point, Grahamable.

Blake: But not tonight. I have to find a place to stay.

Graham: Not you, too.

Graham: What happened to Bryce's?

Blake: Eh, something to do with water not having a place to go, and it flooded the house.

Tucker: That sounds serious, pudding.

Blake: Say that out loud.

Graham: Stay with us.

Tucker: Yes. Perfect idea, Teddy Graham.

Blake: That's sweet, but I don't want to put you guys out. I'll take care of it.

Graham: Offer stands. Indefinitely.

Tucker: Yes. Plus, the coffee machine. Don't forget about the coffee machine, love bug!

Blake: You know how to tempt me. And no.

Tucker: Wahoo! Did I win, turtledove?

Blake: I want to find my own place. It feels important.

Graham: Okay, we'll respect that, Sunshine.

Blake: Good luck today.

Tucker: See you in a few, Honey Bee.

Smiling at my phone, I felt ten times better. GT were quickly becoming my favorite type of medicine. And with how my body craved their touch and heart yearned for their easy acceptance, I rapidly fell under their spell. They effortlessly supported me, respected my wants, and helped me explore how to ask for things I wanted instead of going along with others.

They called to that part of me that always felt invisible.

Which was odd to say, but I wasn't viewed as my own person but as an extension of others.

Steven and Candi Baker's daughter.

Bryce's little sister.

And then just titles, erasing my entire identity and narrowing it down to one aspect.

The sick girl.

But perhaps the worst one… *the embarrassment.*

Graham and Tucker erased all of that and saw me as Blake. *Just Blake.* And that made me confident in who I was, all on my own.

The game ended an hour ago, with the YellowJackets hanging on to their lead in the 7th inning to win, bringing them to 2-1. There were still three more home games before the team headed for their road series.

A baseball player's schedule could be brutal with a six-game home and six-game away rotation. But I was intimately familiar with it, having grown up with it. Away games had their own energy, and the aspect of being stuck with my screwballs felt exciting. It would be a good chance to get to know them more with less distractions.

On the flip side, I was extremely nervous about the forced proximity with Hawk and Luke. At Champion Field, I could find ways to ignore or avoid them, but it would be different on the road. I'd be stuck with the 'Jacks more, my access limited to areas that weren't open to visiting teams.

This meant that to avoid Hawk and Luke, I'd also have to avoid Graham and Tucker, which felt unfair to all three of us. But I guess in the war of my heart and vagina, they were casualties, where Hawk and Luke had weapons capable of decimation.

"You did not just call your hoo-haw a weapon of destruction," Emory crowed, laughing at me on the video call.

I ducked behind a potted plant, peering through the branches to see if the coast was clear. She kept laughing at me, so I rolled my eyes.

"No, I said their penises were weapons capable of decimating my va-jay-jay."

"And that's better how?" she asked, barely holding in her laugh.

"Um, Bee?" a deep voice behind me questioned. My eyes widened on camera, and I spun around and came face-to-face with Ledger, dropping the hand that held the phone.

"Hey, Ledge. How's it hanging?" I asked, my voice cracking on the last part.

He cringed, rubbing his head as he rocked back and forth on the balls of his feet. I'd never seen him look so nervous, which eased my own. His cheeks pinked, and I felt terrible for embarrassing him because odds were, it was my fault.

"Sorry, I, uh, didn't mean to overhear your conversation."

I blinked, staring at the giant bumbling man in front of me. It was the most words I'd heard him say in one go, and it took me a minute to process them.

"Eep. Sorry about that. I have a big mouth." This time, my cheeks flamed, and we stood staring at one another awkwardly.

"Things better since, you know?" he probed, stuffing his hands into his pockets.

"Ah, yes. I didn't get a chance to tell you thanks. Bad Blake." I slapped my hand, laughing at myself. His eyes narrowed, and he glanced at the hand I'd slapped, drying up my laugh.

"Do you do that a lot?"

"What?" I asked, wrinkling my brow. This was the weirdest conversation I ever had.

"Harm or diminish yourself."

His words struck me, and I jerked backward as I thought them over. *Did I do that?* I didn't think so, but being back home had opened up a lot of old wounds. Bunting hell, I needed to get a grip.

"Sorry, nervous habit."

He nodded, accepting my answer, and my shoulders relaxed. The nervous man had evaporated, the no-nonsense now in his place.

"Seth hasn't said anything to you, has he?"

I cringed. "Um, well…"

"What did he say?" His voice boomed, and my head jerked back in response.

"A lot of shit, mostly about a bet and that I'm worthless," I rambled on. I was suddenly so glad Ledger was on my side. Fuck, he could be scary.

"I'll have a word with him."

"Oh, thanks. It's not needed." He narrowed his eyes, and I backtracked. "But I appreciate it. I'm grateful to have befriended you, Ledge."

He smiled for the first time, softening his face. "You too, Bumblebee." He patted my head like he was scared to touch me, and I didn't know if that was because I was a girl or he didn't touch much, to begin with.

Ledger walked off, stopping a few feet away, and turned back. He rubbed the back of his head, his cheeks matching the color of his hair again. "Um, if you need help with anything else, like, the ones with the, um, weapons. Just… you know." He cleared his throat and stalked off.

I stood there in shock, attempting to process the entire interaction. Ledger had apparently become protective of me and got embarrassed talking about dicks. I smiled, some devious ideas entering my head. Oh, I'd have fun with this.

"Hello, Lake? You still there?"

"Shit, sorry, Emory." I lifted the phone, finding her still filling the screen.

"Who was that, and are they single?" she asked, wiggling her eyebrows.

"That was Ledger, and I'm not sure. He's very private. Doesn't talk to most of the team and sticks to himself."

"He sounds hot. Is he?"

I thought about it and shrugged. He hadn't given me the tingles, but I couldn't deny he was good-looking. "Yeah. I think so. He's a ginger, and his hair is long. He's very tall and muscular." Something else about him tickled the back of my mind.

"Yum. Introduce me when I come to visit," she said, dropping her eyes to her nails like she hadn't dropped a bomb.

"Wait!" I stopped, my mouth hanging open. "You're coming to visit? When? How? Why?" I ran in place, the camera shaking with my movements.

"Not if you make me sick!"

"Sorry, sorry. Details, woman!"

"Well, my bestie is there, and I decided it was time to visit. Do I need another reason?"

"Of course not. It's just expensive."

She rolled her eyes. "I have miles saved up, and just to ease your mind, I have a few interviews with possible pâtisserie openings." She said it so blandly you'd almost believe she didn't care how big of a deal it was.

But I knew Emory and anything she made *not* into a big deal was the biggest. The girl was the most dramatic person I'd ever met, even more than Tucker, and used every possible second to celebrate the minor things. So when she didn't, you knew it was important.

"Shut up! That's amazing! I'm so happy for you."

"Thanks, Lake. I'll send you the details of my flight. Lola coordinated your schedule with your mom. Baseball doesn't make sense to me, so I don't try to understand it." She waved me off, knowing I'd launch into an explanation otherwise.

"Okay, babe. I can't believe I get to see you soon. Keep me updated!"

"Loves you, boo!" She blew me kisses before exiting the call, and I slunk back against the wall, smiling. Emory was coming to visit.

BLAKE

I CONTINUED TOWARD THE PARKING LOT, PULLING OUT MY PHONE to order a rideshare when his frame came into view. I'd been dreading this fight since he brought me that second coffee. It was harder to be mad when he was nice.

"You're coming with me, Blake," Hawk said, turning toward his car without waiting.

"I'm not, actually."

He stalled, spinning and glaring at me like I was the biggest nuisance known to man. Well, too bad, buddy.

Hawk rubbed his beard, his lips moving slightly like he was counting. "You can't go back to Bryce's. There's work to be done."

"I know. I wasn't planning on it."

He threw up his arms like I was purposefully making this difficult.

"Perfect, then we're on the same page. Let's go."

"Still not going with you. I made other plans." I waved my phone.

"What do you mean other plans? How?" He narrowed his eyes, not buying my plans.

"There's this thing called the internet, and I searched for someone needing a roommate. Problem solved. You can take your big brother hat off. Your responsibility to my dad *and* brother is fulfilled."

I walked past him to stand at the curb when his arm reached out and spun me. His face was hard, the one most people ran from, but it only made my blood pump harder. *Perfect.* I could use his anger to fuel my own.

"No." One word. No explanation, just an order.

Fuck that. I jerked out of his hold.

"*No?*" I scoffed. "Newsflash. You have no say in my life. We're not even friends, remember? *We're nothing.* You're the one who said it."

"I'm sorry. I was wrong." His jaw twitched, his hands clenching as he held himself back. Whether it was tossing me over his shoulder or hauling me into his arms to kiss me was anyone's guess.

Because same damn energy.

"Bringing me coffee and donuts doesn't erase the hurt. I'm not gonna fall in line and do whatever you say like a robot. *Words hurt, Hawk.* I know because everything I said three years ago still haunts me." I gripped my chest, the ache spreading as he opened this wound. Angry tears pricked my eyes. "I wish I could change them, but I can't. You were right when you said we shouldn't be friends."

This time, he looked like my words had physically struck him as he jolted back. He shook his head, taking one step forward. His hands reached slightly out in front of him toward me. My body leaned forward until I realized, rocking back on my balls.

"I was wrong, Blazy. So fucking wrong. I can't be around you and not be your friend." His words were heavy and full of emotion, and I didn't have the capacity to understand what it meant.

I stepped back, his face falling and almost making me step forward.

"Problem solved then. Don't be around me." I swiped the tear that had the guts to fall.

Hawk's face twisted, and he groaned, throwing up his hands. "You're so frustrating! Just forgive me already so we can move forward."

"Doesn't work that way, big guy." I took another step backward. Hawk's eyes narrowed, tracking the movement. His jaw ticked, and he took a breath.

"If you don't think I won't toss you over my shoulder and carry you to my car, then you clearly don't remember how stubborn *I* can be." He seethed through his teeth. His face turned red, the anger dripping off of him. "We're not talking about this any further today. We're both tired and need sleep. Come back to my place, and then we can continue."

"No can do." I shook my head, needing to clear it of visions of us sleeping.

He took a step forward, his intention clear to follow through on his words, but thankfully, my guardian angel in the form of Ledger Collins stepped in.

"Problem here, Coach?" he asked, glaring at Hawk. When he didn't answer, he turned to me, placing his back to Hawk. Not many men were brave enough to do that. "You need a ride, Bee?"

"Yes, thank you. That would be lovely." I nodded quickly, worried Hawk would tackle Ledger before I could escape. My ginger angel nodded to a truck up ahead. I followed, noticing Graham and Tucker had stopped at Graham's car, their eyes on me.

Son of a pitch! I had another audience to my humiliation. They waved when they caught my eyes, and I nodded to let them know I was okay. Climbing into Ledger's truck, I sighed in relief as he pulled away. I spotted other players who had also stopped in the parking lot to watch our show-down. Lovely.

Ledger was quiet as he drove to the address I'd given him, and I appreciated it. I stared out the window as I calmed my racing heart, my fingers tapping on my knee as I replayed everything. One step forward, two steps back. Would Hawk and I ever get out of this dance? We seemed destined to hurt one another now.

The truck stopped at a house a few minutes later, and I hesitated as I stared, debating getting out. The pictures had shown a quaint cottage, but this place looked like it hadn't been 'quaint' for years. Peeled paint, an overgrown lawn, and trash stacked in one corner littered the yard like it had been meant to go out to the curb but never made it the last few feet.

"You sure about this, bumblebee?" Ledger asked, startling me.

The honest answer, no. But it felt imperative to see it through, so I nodded.

"Yeah. Thanks for the rescue. See you tomorrow."

He nodded as I climbed out, waiting as I walked up to the door and knocked. When it swung open, I heard his loud truck pull away from the curb. The person on the other side stared, not saying anything.

"Hi, I'm Blake." Silence. Okay, then. "Your new roommate."

"Fucking hell," she groaned, rubbing her temple. "That would be Brenda." She sighed like the biggest grievance known to man had just been completed. "I'm Renea." She opened the door, gesturing me inside. "She's always doing things like that and then leaving me to pick up the pieces. Come on, and I'll show you the room."

I followed her inside, my eyes trying to take in every-thing. The inside of the house wasn't much better, but it smelled nice. I followed Renea through tunnels of boxes and considered that maybe being independent wasn't all it was cracked up to be. Maybe I overreacted to Hawk's suggestion. What was a little discomfort compared to tetanus?

The house was dark, and boxes marked with several stores took up every inch of free space. Had I accidentally answered the ad for the next home on Hoarders? Who needed all this stuff?

Renea stopped before a door, pushing it open as she crossed her arms and leaned against the jamb. I peered around the other side, my eyes bulging as I looked at the space. Though calling it space was considerate.

The room was barely bigger than my closet. A dirty mattress lay on the floor with a chair and nightstand next to it. They took up the entire space. A lone light came from a flickering bulb hanging from a string that had seen better days.

Actually, this was a closet.

I gulped, stepping backward and wondering if it was too late to flag down Ledger. If I made a run for it, would she chase me? Was that a chainsaw I heard in the background? The *Children of the Corn* music? Gulp.

"Have you signed anything?" Renea asked, looking me over with a critical eye.

"Um, not yet. We were gonna take care of it today."

"Hmph." She moved off the wall. "Well, I just got off a double shift at the hospital, so I'm headed to bed. Just lock the door if you happen to leave."

With that, she turned and headed further down the maze, opening and closing a door before I could ask anything else. Anxiety ramped up inside me, and I knew I couldn't stay here. I'd rather swallow my pride and ask Hawk than prove I could do it alone in this place.

There was dumb, and then there was stupid, and I didn't want to be the latter and end up on the news as a missing person.

"She moved in with a hoarder, and they never saw her again. Rumors state that a box of dildos fell over and suffocated her, but it will be days until someone can make it back to her closet to check."

Yeah, double nope.

I walked back to the front door as fast as possible, only getting lost in the maze of boxes once. When the door appeared, I flung it open in relief and stepped out into the air, gulping it down as best I could. Locking it as Renea asked, I pulled it shut and sank onto the step as all the adrenaline leached out of me.

Now that I was out of there, I could think clearly about what to do. I pulled out my phone, but a horn honking startled me, and I almost dropped it.

Lights flashed from a car parked at the corner, and I stood, recognizing it immediately. My shoulders sagged in relief, and I wasn't even mad he'd followed us. I hurried to the Mustang and climbed into the passenger seat without hesitation.

Hawk opened his mouth, turning, and I held up a hand, stopping him.

"Let's just not. You're getting your way. Do we need to rub it in?"

He chuckled, the sound bringing a smile to my face despite myself.

"I was only going to ask if you've gotten your tetanus shots recently?"

My mouth fell open as I gaped at him before turning and looking out the window.

"What are you doing?" he asked, the laugh still there.

"Searching for flying pigs. Hawk Anderson told a joke."

Hawk smirked, laughing as he pulled away, and I smacked him playfully but couldn't deny it had been funny. The laughter helped relieve the tension from the nightmare house and our earlier fight.

"You hungry?"

"Always." He snorted, turning.

"Pizza?"

"Duh." I leaned my head against the window, allowing myself the comfort of him. I needed to remember he had a girlfriend and hoped I hadn't made a giant mistake.

Must resist temptation. Must resist.

"I am sorry, Blake. For the way I acted when I picked you up," Hawk said, breaking the silence. He swallowed, like he had more to say, but couldn't get the words out.

"Thanks." The word felt inadequate and not like the right one, but what else was I supposed to say? *No problem. Thanks for breaking my heart?* "Um, me too," I added, figuring I owed him just as much for what I said.

"I would like to find our way back to being friends. If that's possible," he said so quietly I almost missed it.

"No promises," I teased, earning myself a Hawk smile. One with the corner of his mouth lifted up only slightly. It might be small, but it was powerful, and it punched me in the gut all the same.

This was a dangerous game I was playing, and I might lose more than my heart this time.

The rest of the drive was quiet, and when he turned down a long drive, I did a double take. Hawk's house wasn't what I expected. At all.

Bryce had a modern condo with all the bells and whistles with sleek designs and angles, and all the ease and luxury I pictured a professional baseball player desiring.

Hawk's house, on the other hand, was none of that.

First, it was cute. It had a farmhouse look with slanted beams in white contrasting with a dark blue exterior. Second, the porch was wide, with a bench on one end and a swing on the other. And lastly, the front yard had two flower beds beginning to bud. There were three picturesque windows with the telltale sign of a couch just beyond them.

I stared at it briefly, wondering why it shocked me so

much. Because if I really thought about it, it was precisely the type of place I pictured Hawk having.

Maybe that was the part tripping me up. I hadn't imagined Hawk having a life beyond our night in the hotel. Conceptually, I knew he had a girlfriend, a house, and a new career.

But I hadn't allowed myself to picture what it would be like. Now that I could see the proof before me, it hit me hard.

Because while I'd been licking my wounds in Greece, Hawk had made himself a life—one without me.

"It's nice," I finally said, ignoring how my voice croaked. I grabbed my bag, climbed out of the Mustang, and walked to the front door.

"You sound like you expected me to live in a spooky mansion or something."

Snorting, I turned my face toward his and shrugged. "I wouldn't put it past you to have an all-black house. It does seem to be your favorite color." I motioned to his clothes—all black—and to his car—black with a red racing stripe. That corner of his mouth ticked up again. Not a smile, but close, and once again stealing my breath.

"Glad to see I can still surprise you after all these years, Blazy."

My cheeks heated as I followed him up the steps and waited for him to unlock the door. It gave me the time to force myself to ask the question I was dying to know.

"So, um, did Roxie help you decorate?"

This time, he snorted, shaking his head as he turned on the entryway light, kicking his boots off at the same time.

"If Roxie had helped, it would be black and hot pink. She's as bad as me with colors."

"Right." I nodded, untying my shoes and leaving them next to his. There was also an old pair of tennis shoes and a small pair of rain boots that had to belong to his nieces.

Sitting next to his black boots, they were so cute that I instantly wanted to capture them with my camera.

It didn't escape my notice there weren't any feminine shoes. Maybe she didn't stay over that much? That would be a relief. I didn't know if I could handle seeing them all loved up. Hawk walked into more rooms and turned on lights, illuminating the place bit by bit, stunning me with each new detail of his life that was revealed.

"Are you hungry now or want to wait?" he asked.

Right on cue, my stomach growled. My cheeks flushed at the noise, and I covered my stomach like I could keep it contained by sheer force. Hawk chuckled, the sound traveling through me and making me feel light-headed.

Dear Babe Ruth,

Please have Bryce's place fixed ASAP. I don't know how long I'd last here. I was already crumbling.

Your reluctant baseball fan

"Come on. I'll give you a tour once I get the pizza in the oven," Hawk said, breaking me from my silent prayer to the baseball heavens.

I nodded, following him through the living room. The couch I spotted through the window turned out to be an overstuffed navy blue one in the shape of an L. It faced a large television and had an enlarged photo of a baseball stadium hung over it. On another wall were pictures of whom I assumed were his nieces. The couch had a soft throw on the end of the lounge with coordinating pillows in yellow, tying the room together.

The whole space was clean and tidy and more decorated than I expected from a man. I knew that was horribly cliché of me, but in all the years I'd known Hawk, he'd never had his own place, so it wasn't like I had anything to base his style on.

Noises traveled to me from further in the house, so I followed, passing two doors. One looked like a bedroom, and the other a bathroom. The kitchen came into view next and had a modern feel, with an island in the middle and a couple of barstools. Taking a seat in one, I glanced around the gray and white tiled kitchen while Hawk pulled pizzas out of the freezer.

A large window sat over the kitchen sink, showing the backyard, but it was dark, so I couldn't see anything. A small breakfast nook sat to the left of the island with a bench recessed into the wall. It was cozy and quaint, and an image of mornings there with his nieces hit me harder than I'd imagined. Two doors sat along the back wall, presumably a pantry and a mystery. To the side of the table, a pair of sliding doors led out to a screened-in porch. The light from the kitchen illuminated a fire pit and a colorful wicker couch from this angle. Turning the other way, I eyed the double-wide fridge and oven before spotting a hallway.

My gaze landed back on Hawk, who leaned against the counter, his silhouette outlined in the window. His eyes were directed on me, watching me as I observed my surroundings. We held eyes for a moment, one that had the weight of so many unspoken words. The oven beeped, breaking the stare off, and Hawk moved, setting the timer and placing the pizzas in the oven.

He crossed his arms, making his tattoos stand out in the kitchen's bright white and oddly bringing him more into focus.

"Pizza will be ready in fifteen. Um…" He paused, his cheeks heating slightly as he rubbed the back of his head. "My spare room is set up for the girls. We can get a different bed once we're back."

"I'm sure it's fine, and Bryce's place should be done by then. Or I can stay with GT."

He didn't say anything; only nodded and moved to the hallway.

"My room," he said, pointing down the dark path, then

turned and headed back toward the living room. He stopped at the room on the right, flipping the light on. "Guest bathroom. Towels and extra shampoo are under the sink."

"Thanks. I finally heard from the airline that my bags will be here tomorrow. Mom's supposed to send some stuff to Bryce's, too, so we might need to check it before we leave if they arrive."

"Sure." He paused, flipped on the light across the hallway, and cleared his throat. "I let them decorate it."

Curious about his statement, I stepped into the room and stopped. Again, I hadn't expected this room to exist in Hawk's house. It was the girliest little girls' room I'd ever seen. Princess stuff decorated the walls and a castle canopy over the bunk beds. There was a small table with a tea party set up, a castle made out of blocks in a corner, and a pile of pillows and stuffed animals so large I worried for a second they might come alive and suffocate me.

Scratching noises pulled my attention to the right, and I spotted the cutest hamster as he sniffed at the glass.

"Oh my god, he's adorable. What's his name? Can I hold him?" I rushed out, running over.

"That's Sunny, and yeah, though he might pee on you."

"It's fine," I said, already lifting the lid. I smiled as I cupped my hands around him. It was official. I was in love. I stroked his head, smiling down at the cute little guy.

"Oh, Sunny, you're my new best friend." I snuggled him up to my cheek, his soft fur against my skin.

Hawk chuckled behind me, but I didn't care. I'd always wanted a hamster, but my mom and dad never let me get one.

"I hope the bunk beds are okay for a few nights."

"It's fine. Promise." I turned, meeting his mismatched eyes. "I know I wasn't the easiest to convince, but thank you for letting me stay. I thought I needed to do it on my own, but that house was one wrong move from being mincemeat." I shuddered, and Hawk smirked but had the good sense not to affirm anything.

"I'll let you get settled while the pizza finishes."

I nodded, walking to the princess bed and ducking under the canopy. The bottom bunk was a full-size bed, making it larger than the twin above. Lying down on the pink comforter, I sat Sunny on my chest while I petted him. He roamed around, spinning in circles until he found a spot he liked, right between my boobs.

A knock on the door had me sitting up abruptly, hitting my head on the bunk above.

"Ow." I rubbed the spot and climbed out, forgetting Sunny was in my cleavage.

"What the fuck," Hawk hissed, making me stop.

"What?" I looked around, searching for the danger.

"Is he…" His eyes bulged as he stared at my chest, and I remembered my passenger. I blushed, then shrugged.

"He likes it there."

Hawk swallowed, nodding, but didn't once take his eyes off my boob guest.

"Right. Um, pizza's ready."

He turned on his feet and hurried out of the room, leaving me chuckling after him. At least I could still fluster the man.

TWENTY-FOUR

LUKE

TODAY WAS THE LAST HOME GAME FOR A WEEK, AND I HADN'T had any improvement. The suffocating weight of failure squeezed like a vice around my chest. I pulled down my cap to block the rays and took a deep breath as I stared at the batter. But it did nothing to diminish that feeling in my chest.

Sweat ran down my face, smearing the eye black as I tried to focus, but just like every other game this season, this one wasn't off to a great start. Coach Phillips had started me, but the scowl on his face told me he regretted that decision.

So far, I'd missed a throw to first and allowed the other team to advance. Then I'd overthrown to Davis at third, and they'd scored, giving them the lead. I'd already struck out twice, swinging for pitches I knew were bad. But it was like my body had a mind of its own and didn't listen to anything my head said.

Nothing felt right anymore.

Anxiety had become my constant companion, making my limbs tight. And no matter how much I tried to take a breath, I couldn't. I kicked the dirt, trying to distract my brain and focus, but it was pointless. I needed to find the reason—the cause—for my awful gameplay.

There had to be something because I'd done everything else like usual. My routine was flawless and had worked perfectly for years. I ate the same meal, listened to the same songs, and even showered in a specific order using the products I only used during the season. Even all my usual lucky charms weren't helping.

So, what was the difference?

I wasn't back with the Blue Devils like I'd planned.

I had Willow to care for.

I had shoulder surgery.

I wasn't drinking.

And...

My eyes snagged on the beautiful girl behind the camera, the pink ends of her hair catching my attention. She snapped photos of the team, moving gracefully through the stands like she belonged there. And I supposed she did, considering her dad owned the team.

Anger surged through me at that, remembering how I'd trusted her. *She* was my problem. Blake Baker. My slugger.

Bee was the cause of my messed-up juju. Everything awful that had occurred started with her crashing into my life.

Her brother had taken my spot on the Blue Devils, leaving me in this town. I had to cancel everything I had in Columbus and find a new place to rent. In addition, Willow had to change schools, making her transition with me even more complex and our relationship rockier. To top it off, Bee had gotten into my head and messed up my focus. I was a sexual guy, but I hadn't felt like it in a week. Not since her.

That had to be it. I wasn't drinking, and sex was my go-to outlet. I typically would go out and get laid after games, but for some reason, it hadn't worked this season. I hadn't even masturbated in days.

Fuck. She was more problematic than I'd realized.

Rage replaced the fear, the failure disappearing as I stared at her. My lungs expanded, and I breathed my first deep breath in hours.

I wouldn't be having these problems if I'd never met her. She'd given me the yips, so it was her responsibility to fix them.

Eyes narrowed, and venom burning in my veins, I stalked toward the dugout when the inning was over, a new mission in place.

Find Bee and make her fix this.

"Olson! Where are you going?" Coach Anderson shouted.

"To shit!" I didn't stop, tossing my glove and cap onto the bench and stormed down the steps.

A few guys jeered, but no one stopped me. I was playing so poorly that my presence wouldn't be missed. If anything, they were happy to see me go.

My steel cleats snapped loudly against the concrete as I wound through the tunnels. Anger and rage radiated from me with each step. This had to end now. I couldn't afford to lose anything else, especially not Willow. She counted on me.

Yeah, because you're getting your dick wet for Willow.

Fuck off, brain. If you had it together, I wouldn't need to do this.

Geez. Now, I argued with myself. Fucking yips.

"You," I hissed when I came to the area she'd been.

A few fans turned, their gazes bouncing between me and the woman I stared daggers at. She didn't immediately look over, irritating me more. Someone patted her arm, and she smiled at them, following their finger.

Her eyes narrowed when they landed on me.

"Aren't you supposed to be playing?" she asked.

"I wouldn't call what he's doing playing," one of the spectators said, causing others to laugh around him.

"That!" I said, pointing at the dude. I wasn't even mad.

He was right. I had one job, and it was to play ball well. And right now, I sucked at that.

I didn't fail when it came to baseball.

"I don't understand," she said, scrunching up her nose in the cutest way.

"*You* need to fix it." I seethed, grabbing her arm and dragging her with me. I wasn't getting anywhere having this conversation around a crowd of people.

"Let go of me," she hissed.

"Fine. But I need you to follow me. We need to talk."

"I'm not going anywhere with you."

"Blake, so help me." I stopped, my nostrils flaring as I stared at her. "I'll throw you over my shoulder and carry you kicking and screaming from here if you don't come with me right now," I shouted at her, my face red and spit flying. Her eyes grew wide, and she swallowed.

My cock, the fucker that hadn't so much as twitched in days, perked up.

Yes. This would work.

Holding her chin between my fingers, I stepped forward and tilted her head to look at me. I leaned down and whispered in her ear, pressing my body heat into hers so she could feel me. All of me.

"What's it going to be, Slugger?" The term slipped off my tongue before I could stop it. My breath was hot against her, goosebumps flaring up in its wake.

She gasped, her tongue darting out to lick her parted lips. Her eyes dilated, and I watched as her breathing hitched. She might hate me, but she wanted me too.

Good. I didn't need her to like me for my plan. I just needed her to agree.

"You have five minutes," she said, attempting to put some bite into it. It fell flat, but I'd let her keep up her delusion.

For once, I would use my partner to meet *my* needs

instead of vice versa. It was time I turned the tables, and I wouldn't even need to lie.

Grasping her wrist, I pulled her down the tunnel with me and ducked into the player's quarters. There was a free weight room that would work for what I needed. I'd find something better for next time.

Next time. Already planning ahead.

"Four minutes and counting," she huffed, dropping my hand and crossing her arms over her chest as the door shut. I smiled, brushing my thumb over my lip as I watched her. She wanted me to believe her stance was from annoyance, but I knew it wasn't. Her nipples peeking through her shirt confirmed that.

Oh, baby. This is going to be fun.

"You broke my game, so it's your responsibility to fix it," I finally said, her blue eyes flashing.

"Fuck you," she cursed, rolling her eyes. "That all?"

I jumped forward, trapping her against the door. "I'm not joking, Bee. I can't afford not to play well. And since I can't drink," I gritted out, "then sex is the next option."

"Excuse me?" she spluttered. "You expect *me* to have sex with *you*?" Her voice grew louder as her eyes widened. But her breath hitched, her pupils blown wide as a blush colored her cheeks. She could act like she hated me all she wanted, but her body told a different story.

"You heard me. I want to fuck *you*."

"Fuck. You," she gritted.

"That's what I'm trying to do, Slugger. Did you hit your head? Heat stroke?" I glared; my smile not friendly.

She blinked rapidly, her breasts rising with her breathing. "Is this a joke? Are you pranking me?"

"Nope. Dead serious." My eyes dropped to her lips, my cock as hard as marble now. It pressed against my cup, the need to release it intense.

"But I hate you," she said it matter-of-factly, but like she almost didn't believe it. Her body hummed beneath mine, her pulse thrumming against my fingers.

"Feeling's mutual, baby," I growled. "But for some reason, my dick doesn't agree. So the way I see it, since you broke my game, this is how you fix it. Tit for tat."

She rolled her eyes, and I almost lost it. Why did her bratting so hard turn me on?

"Grow up, Luke. I didn't break anything, and you're responsible for yourself."

"Bullshit. You pretended to—"

"I didn't pretend anything!" she roared, cutting me off.

"Fine. So *you* say." This time, I rolled my eyes. "But regardless, your actions have messed with me whether you agree or not. You grew up with baseball players; you know how superstitious we are. There are only three things different this season, and you're the one I can do something about." I clenched my jaw, not wanting her to see how desperate I was.

If she said no, I didn't know what I would do. I'd lose everything. Fear knocked into me, and my legs gave out. Thankfully, I had her against the door, so I fell into her, my cock brushing against my cup. I rocked it into her core, using the hardness of it to hit her just right. She tried to stifle the moan, but I heard it all the same.

"What's it gonna be, Bee. Can I fuck you?" I gritted out, trying not to sound like I wanted to murder her.

"Funny. My father never fucked someone he hated just to play a game." She sneered, lifting her chin. But her lower half rocked forward slightly, shifting the cup and hitting my cock.

"Good for him. But I don't have a lot of options. Things with Willow—" I stopped, shaking my head. I didn't want to get into it with her. But Bee softened, her body relaxing. I blew out a breath, my eyes searing into hers.

"I *need* to play better. I'm out of options. This is all I got." I paused, my eyes searching hers, looking for a clue, and taking one last shot, changing it up slightly. "I'm not going to beg, so last time I'm asking, Slugger. Will. You. Fuck. Me?"

The air between us sizzled, our gazes locked on one another, neither of us breathing as the precarious balance between us rested on the next few seconds.

CHAPTER
TWENTY-FIVE

BLAKE

MY HEART BEAT WILDLY AGAINST MY CHEST, AND I VAGUELY wondered if I was hallucinating. But the smell of Luke's cologne mixed with dirt and sweat was too unique to have made up. His green eyes shimmered, and even with the smeared eye black on his face, he still was one of the most gorgeous guys I'd ever seen.

His goldenness encapsulated us, providing us a small bubble where everything outside of it didn't exist. I knew I shouldn't care that he was playing horribly. That there was no logical explanation that I'd given him the yips.

Yet, like most things with Luke, the words tumbled from me before I thought them through.

"You better have a fucking condom." The words were harsh, yet full of lust.

"Why do you think I brought you to this room?" he countered, his body sagging into mine, and I felt how much he needed this to work.

I caught amusement and light entering his green eyes seconds before they were replaced with pure heat, his lips crashing into mine with desperation.

We bit and nipped at one another, not caring about technique or skill, as we tried to fuse our lips together. Our tongues fought for dominance in a kiss that was more teeth than anything. A whimper escaped him, his hands squeezing my ass as he pulled me impossibly close.

That sound alone was enough to disintegrate my panties right on the spot. My mind shouted at me. To stop and think about what I was doing. I was giving in to this guy who'd ghosted me and flung words like weapons. Passion outweighed critical thought, pushing me to see this through.

Because my body craved his touch and wanted to feel him against me again. And when he sounded like *that*, it made me feel powerful. This was my chance to change my one-night stand status, and I would take it.

Because even if it only ended in disaster, I had an excuse to be around him right now, to feel the pleasure he brought me.

And oh, what pleasure it was.

"I still hate you," I hissed, his hands moving across my body as I melded into him.

"Likewise," he groaned, barely breaking the kiss to speak.

We rutted against one another with my back pressed to the door, our bodies moving to the rhythm they knew well.

"Fuck," he cursed, plunging his hand into my leggings and instantly spearing me. My knees buckled at the invasion, my pussy eagerly accepting him as I clamped around his finger.

"Oh god." My head hit the door, my hips moving with him.

"You might hate me, Slugger, but you want me." He gave me a cocky smirk, and I hardened my eyes, wanting to wipe it off his face. He needed to stop talking.

"Like you have room to talk. You ghost me, but come begging me to fuck you so you can play better," I threw back, feeling validated when his smile dropped.

"You know what," he said, withdrawing his hand, and I panicked for a second, thinking he was stopping this. "It will work better if I don't have to look at your face."

He stepped back, the coolness of the space hitting me before he grabbed me and spun me around, my back now against his front.

"Hands on the bench and spread your legs," he ordered. I did what he said, surprising us when I didn't fight back. "Already so much better," he crooned, snapping me out of my trance as he gripped my ass.

"Likewise," I tossed over my shoulder, not meeting his eyes. His hands moved up to my hips, and he squeezed. He leaned down, his body heat pressing into me.

"I hope you brought extra pants," he whispered before he ripped my leggings at the seam, exposing my backside to him. Cool air hit my cheeks, and I yelped, my eyes growing large as I jumped. What. The. Hell.

"Luke!" I shrieked, but the asshole pushed me down in response.

"Stay, or I'll destroy all of your clothes, and you'll have to walk out of here completely naked. Have fun taking your pictures without clothes."

"You fucking twatwaffle. These are the only pants I have here, dumbass." Because, of course, my luggage hadn't shown up today.

He snorted, his fingers brushing my hair over my shoulder. It was soft and contradicted his harsh words. "Too bad. Looks like you're gonna have to wear this asshole's hoodie around your waist all day or buy some new ones then."

"You did that on purpose." I glared. I had Tucker's hoodie, which I'd stolen from him the other night.

To my surprise, Luke chuckled. "Hell yeah, I did. I might not like you, but I'm still possessive, and I don't want to see another man's name on your back."

His warmth left me, his steps moving away, and I gritted

my teeth as I clenched my fingers against the bench. My mind came back online, and I debated with myself about staying and letting him get away with his attitude. I argued I didn't deserve his hatred and should leave because no orgasm was worth this.

I'd just convinced myself to go when he returned, grabbing my hips and slamming his cock into me in one fell swoop.

"Ahh," I screamed. My arms gave out, and I fell to my elbows, inadvertently giving him a deeper angle as my ass tilted more. Thankfully, he'd stayed still after his entrance, giving us time to adjust. I breathed loudly, my pants the only sound I could hear.

"You good?" he asked, his voice softer than I expected after that intrusion.

"Mmhmm," I mumbled, nodding my head. If I opened my mouth, things like praises and affirmations might fall from them, and I was done giving him compliments.

He chuckled, apparently still able to read me better than I wanted. Slowly, he pulled back and pushed in, his cock sliding deliciously against my walls. My eyes rolled back with his slow rocking, my legs trembling as I held myself up by my forearms. It was too much and not enough, and I was already so close to combusting.

I hated that this felt so good. That my body craved his touch. That I hadn't been strong enough to tell him no.

Before I was ready, my orgasm crashed into me, and my legs gave out. Luke caught me before my head smacked into the bench, bracing his arm around my waist and holding me up.

Both of us breathed hard as my body spasmed, his cock twitching in response. Tingles spread through me, and I let myself enjoy his embrace as he held me, his mouth pressing warm kisses on my neck. In the golden bubble of the two of us, we could ignore our hate and pretend things were still like they were back at the lodge.

Like we were lovers and not enemies. Like we could be something beautiful. Like he was just a boy, and I was just a girl, nothing else mattered.

"You okay?" he whispered, his thumbs soothing circles on my hips.

"Yeah." He pressed one last kiss on my neck before the bubble popped.

And just like that, the world rushed back.

He lifted me onto my feet and raised me up. I hadn't even noticed he'd come, my orgasm overtaking my entire focus. I stood on shaking legs as I turned, my hand falling to the hole in the back of my pants.

"You owe me a pair of pants." I seethed, finding it easier to focus on them than the world-shattering orgasm and everything it meant. I wrapped the hoodie around my waist, Jameson now on my ass. His eyes dropped, and he smirked, but then he saw the name, and his jaw ticked.

I smugly crossed my arms, liking that it had backfired on him.

Luke tucked his cock back into his jockstrap and put his cup back in. He'd kept all his clothes on, his steel cleats still on his feet, and I hated how sexy it was.

"Next time, wear a skirt and not another man's name on you."

I gaped at him, regretting having him talk me into this. "Next time? You're delusional. This was a one-time thing. You gave me an orgasm on a plane, and I gave you one in…" I paused, looking around the room. "In a free weight room." I scrunched up my brows, not knowing what to call this room. It wasn't the sexiest of places, but I guess that hadn't mattered.

"Whatever you need to tell yourself, babe." He stalked over, looming over me. I glared up, not afraid of him. He gripped my chin, but his hold was softer now. Luke stared at me like he wanted to say something else, his thumb ghosting over my lips. I wondered if it was intentional or reflexive.

"Give me your phone."

"No."

I pulled out of his hold and crossed my arms, my stubbornness in full force. Luke rolled his eyes and reached around me, removing it from the pocket I'd put it in after learning my lesson. Upchuckety gate had blown chunks everywhere, and I was not a fan. He flashed it in front of my face before I could react, typing something into it.

"There. I'll text you before the game next time."

He returned it to my pocket, his hand brushing my ass and squeezing before he stood back up to his full height with a satisfied look. One I desperately wanted to wipe off with my fist.

"I already said it's not happening."

Luke snorted, turning toward the door, but stopped and spun back around. He cupped my cheek, his face softer.

"Willow loved the platypus," Luke said, shocking me. His green eyes searched mine for a brief moment before he made up his mind and dropped a kiss on my lips. He quickly spun, not stopping this time as he left. The door shut behind him, the silence deafening now that I was alone.

"I'm so screwed," I muttered, dropping my head into my hands.

After a few self-wallowing moments, I'd collected myself and double-checked my butt wasn't waving hello at everyone. As I left the room and neared the clubhouse, an idea popped into my head. If Luke thought he could rip my pants and not have me retaliate, he had another thing coming to him.

"Let's see how he likes it when he doesn't have pants," I mumbled, going to his locker. I checked over my shoulder.

No one was there, but everyone was out on the field. How he'd left mid-game was a mystery, but I'd explore that later.

A tiny amount of guilt crept up my spine as I unzipped his bag. Thankfully, a cool breeze hit my exposed backside as the sweatshirt fell off me, reminding me he'd started it.

Grabbing his black joggers, I quickly pulled off the leggings I'd just bought and wadded them up, placing them where his pants had been. Feeling better now that my ass wasn't hanging out, another idea hit me.

I ran to the supply closet and pulled out the medical tape, IcyHot, and gauze rolls. Chuckling to myself, I momentarily wondered if I'd gone crazy. My actions were pretty out of the norm for me. I squirted IcyHot into a few of Luke's jockstraps, then used the medical tape to partition it off, covering the whole front.

"Good luck getting into your mummy locker, 4A!"

For good measure, I filled Tucker's locker with gauze rolls and tied all of Graham's shoes to one another. If I also happened to squirt IcyHot over Seth's clothes, well, I'd never tell.

Hiding my supplies, I left the clubhouse full of giddiness as I hurried away. I pulled out my phone and sent Emory a quick text. I wasn't surprised when she immediately responded, laughing at her response.

> Blake: I just had hate sex and then stole his pants.

> Emory: I'm gonna need more context, babe.

> Blake: Golden guy. Scorching hate sex. He ripped my pants in the process. So, I stole his.

> Emory: Yaasss, Queen! Get it!

> Blake: Am I being crazy?

Emory: Did you have fun?

Blake: I think I blacked out.

Emory: Then yes. Lots of fun.

Blake: I might've also filled his locker and pranked him.

Emory: I'm loving this side of you, bestie. Tell me more.

Blake: I was thinking of changing his password for the pro shop and buying more clothes. Too far?

Emory: OMG! That's gold. Do it, and then post pics and tag him on Instagram.

Blake: You're cold. Maybe I shouldn't have used you as my too-far meter.

Emory: Or you knew I'd say yes, and you really want to do it.

Blake: Maybe.

Emory: If anything, it will just be fodder for the next round of hate sex.

Blake: Nope. No more.

Emory: Sure.

Blake: I hate you.

Emory: Sure.

Blake: *sticking tongue out emoji*

Emory: * heart face emoji*

Laughing, I continued on my mission and headed to the business offices. Perk of being the boss's daughter… I had the password for the system. If Dad knew I used it for this reason, he'd ban me. So I just needed to make sure he never found out.

After a quick change-a-roo in the system, I spun in the chair and let out a maniacal laugh, feeling very villainous as I hurried to the pro shop.

I'd planned only to buy a new pair of leggings to replace the ones he'd torn, but another idea struck me when I remembered how mad he got at Tucker's name. It had to be a fugue state as I picked shirts off the hangers, socks, under-wear, and pants. I even ended up with a bathrobe with the team logo on it.

Like I said, I wasn't cognizant as I grabbed things around the shop.

Sure, sure.

Tossing it onto the counter, I huffed as I let go of the bundle, pulling my arms out from under it. The cashier gave me an odd look but scanned it all and bagged it for me.

"The total's $450 after your discount," she said, recognizing me. I guessed buying your wardrobe from the pro shop two days in a row wasn't a good look.

"This is actually going on Luke Olson's account."

"Okay." She eyed me, popping her bubble gum. "Do you have the password?" she asked in a bored tone, her long nails tapping against the keyboard.

"Yup, it's 'I'm a dick because mine is small,'" I said, somehow managing to get through it with a straight face.

Her eyes jumped to mine, and her mouth fell open, gaping at me, some expression finally covering her face. "I'm sorry, what?" She glanced around, clearly thinking I was pranking her. I leaned forward like it was a secret.

"I know. A bit too on the nose, but I guess it's easy to

remember." I shrugged. "Go ahead and type it in; I promise you it's right."

"Um, okay. Any capital letters?" she asked, not believing me.

"Nope. All lowercase, no spaces." I grinned wide as she repeated it out loud with each word she typed. When the screen flashed that it had gone through, her cheeks pinked.

"Well, okay then. You hear something new every day. At least he's playing better," she said, waiting for the receipt to print and tucking it into the bag.

"Wait, who?" I asked the one confused this time.

"Olson. Your boyfriend?" she asked, looking me up and down with more interest.

"Not my boyfriend," I huffed, rolling my eyes. "Just someone who owed me." I picked up the bag, remembering the part that had stumped me. "Wait, you said he's playing better?"

"Yeah." She nodded. "He returned late in the inning after sitting out the third and hit a grand slam to take the lead. Then, he made a double play. It's like a switch flipped."

I'll be damned. It had worked.

A smug smile spread across my face. My pussy had yip healing powers. As quickly as it had formed, the smile dropped when I realized what it meant. He wouldn't let this go.

"Crackerjack. I should've sprung for the shoes, too," I grumbled, stomping off with my bag in tow.

I'd decided not to post my purchases, but after hearing that, it felt like I had to. Ducking into the staff bathroom, I changed my clothes, took a cute selfie, and uploaded it to Instagram with the caption, "I woke up in my villain era today. Thanks, @lukeolson24 for the new threads." #baseballisforever #catchersdoitbetter.

Feeling better, I shoved the rest into my bookbag and returned to the game. I ignored the cheers for Olson as he made it onto first base. The cocky smile on his face made me angry, and I had that same urge to push him into the dirt again.

Knowing what he'd find when the game was over was the only thing that got me through the rest of the innings as he continued to have one of the best games of his life.

Son of a glove.

Not having it in me to stick around tonight, I sent a message to Hawk that I'd taken a car to his house. I emailed Mira to let her know I'd be in early tomorrow to finalize the press kits before the road games.

And lastly, I sent a message to my screwballs, GT—as I was now calling Graham and Tucker—stating I'd talk to them later tonight.

BLAKE

Hawk peeked into the princess room when he returned, fighting back a smile as he took me in.

"It's been a day," I said, not making any attempt to move from my spot. Under all of the stuffed animals and pillows, I'd discovered a gigantic bean bag. Which I immediately claimed. Piling all the stuffed animals around me, I propped myself up with them, looking like I floated on a sea of animals.

I'd taken a shower and decided to touch up my pink ends with blue, so my hair was wrapped in a towel, and I wore the YellowJacket robe I had Luke buy me. At that thought, I smirked, debating if I should send a picture of me lounging in it. Sunny was perched between my boobs, and I had the book Graham had given me in my lap.

Hawk's eyes scanned up my bare legs, his eyes heating far too much for a man with a girlfriend. I wanted to yell at him, but I liked how his attention made me feel. My cheeks pinked, and I recrossed my legs in the other direction. When his eyes took in Sunny, he snorted and shook his head.

"That damn hamster."

"Don't be jealous," I teased, petting Sunny's head.

"Hard not to be," he whispered so low, I almost missed it. I jerked my head up, his face a neutral mask, and I decided I must've misheard him. "Need anything?"

I shook my head. "I just need time to recharge." I lifted the book, and he nodded in understanding.

He tapped the door like he wanted to say something, but didn't, before he stepped out of the princess room. Part of me was curious, but I was too tired tonight, so I dived back into my book. It was good, and the whole multiple dating partners didn't seem so far-fetched when reading a story.

I'd just gotten to the first steamy scene when my phone vibrated, and I did a full-body shudder when I saw it was Bryce.

"Hey," I said, clearing my throat and tossing the book away like he'd somehow know I was reading porn.

"Um, you okay there, BB?"

"Yep. Yep. *All good.* How's you?" *How's you? Did smut make your brain melt?*

Bryce chuckled, and I smacked my forehead. He couldn't see what I was doing through the phone. Get a grip.

"I'm good, BB. How are you doing with Hawk?"

"Um, fine. Why? Did he say something?" I swear I could hear Bryce rolling his eyes.

"No. He's Hawk. He doesn't say much in general."

"Right. Right." I nodded. "How's the team?" I asked, deciding to divert that line of questions.

"Uh…" This time, it was Bryce's turn to sound like a drunk two year old. "Good. It's good."

"Great." Silence fell between us, an awkwardness settling that didn't usually exist with Bryce. "Um, was there a reason for your call? Not that I'm not excited to hear from you," I rushed out.

"Oh, just missing my baby sister."

"I'm your only sister," I deadpanned.

"Same diff."

"Dork." I laughed, feeling a little lighter.

"Takes one to know one," Bryce shot back.

"Wow. Are we five?"

"I'm glad you're settling in well," he said, softness in his voice that made me feel bad for lying.

"Yeah. It's, um, great." I yawned exaggeratedly. "Speaking of, I should go to bed. We leave for our road game tomorrow."

"Right. Okay. Good night, Blanket. I'll talk to you soon."

"Night, Bry. Love you more than clean sheets."

He chuckled, and I wrapped the sound around me. "Love you more than rainy days."

The call ended, and I rubbed my chest, an ache spreading in my heart I wasn't used to feeling with Bryce. It made my earlier activities with Luke feel even more reckless.

Yet despite knowing that, I couldn't deny how much I craved Luke. I needed to avoid him, but I wasn't sure if I could. At least for now, I had my pillow pile, a cute burrowing hamster, and a smutty book to occupy my time.

Seeing the airport van outside the stadium this morning made me hopeful for the away games. I'd be heading into them with my full armor. Which I would need if I got trapped on a bus with four men I had dirty thoughts about. Gird your loins!

I wasn't sure what that meant, but it felt like it might fit there. Probably not, but I was going with it all the same.

The office was quiet this early in the morning, allowing me to focus on my list and finish all of the press kits. The long work days were draining and something I hadn't adjusted to yet, but I loved everything else about this job.

It was fun and exciting while allowing me to think

outside the box. Each day was different and challenged me to find new ways for people to fall in love with baseball. My history with the sport had always seemed like a burden growing up, but now it felt like a gift.

Signing off my computer, I loaded it into my backpack with an extra charger before pulling out the suitcases. I'd stuffed them under my desk earlier since I'd taken an Uber in and had nowhere else to keep them for the next week since I wasn't taking them both with me. I could just imagine the comments from the team if I rolled up with two huge suitcases.

Diva. High Maintenance. Princess.

No, thank you. I was still finding my footing among the team. I didn't need to create a larger gap, especially after the Seth debacle.

"Time to rearrange," I muttered, opening my suitcases and peering inside. The amount of clothes before me now seemed outlandish after having three options for a week.

"All my pretties." I petted my shoe collection, sighing as I found them all intact.

The realization I would get to wear an outfit that wasn't YellowJacket paraphernalia or covered in platypuses was exhilarating, and I eagerly pulled out some new options for a week away. I picked out something for today, zipping the rest up and stuffing it under my desk.

A zing of happiness zipped through me, and I wondered what my screwballs would think of my new attire. The fact they'd liked me in leggings and baseball tees said a lot about Graham and Tucker. Smiling, I suddenly couldn't wait to show them something different.

"You're playing with fire," I warned myself, but it didn't stop me.

With my suitcase and backpack sorted, I snuck into my dad's private suite and used his bathroom to change. After sleeping on my hair wet, it was a disaster. But at least the ends were bright blue. Braiding it in pigtails, I liked how the blue looked plaited. Yay, team spirit!

Pocketing my glasses, I put in my contacts, blinking as my eyes adjusted. I didn't like to wear them for long periods, but being in the sun made it easier with contacts. This time, I ensured I had extras in my backpack in case my luggage got lost again.

Turning in the mirror, I smiled at my reflection. I had on my 'Calm your mitts' shirt, a pair of cut-off shorts, and my black and red Converse. I tied Hawk's flannel I'd stolen this morning around my waist, pleased with my appearance.

Now to keep Luke's dick out of my vagina, and everything would be perfect. Though recalling his texts from last night made me chuckle all over again. I just had to keep tapping into my violence arc, and I'd be okay. Simple.

Luke: You're not funny.

Luke: What the hell! What did you do?

Luke: Dammit, Blake. What's my password?

Luke: I'm going to get you back for this.

Luke: We'll see how funny you think you are when I shove my dick down your throat. You thought those leggings were bad? I'm going to turn you inside out so your cunt has my cock imprint.

Luke: Ignore me all you want, but we both know we're good together.

Luke: I'll fuck you later.

Blake: New phone. Who dis?

Snorting at my cleverness, I decided the easiest way to keep myself in check was to avoid him. Because there was no way I wanted to test him and see if he really could imprint his dick in me. Yeah, bad idea. Bad. Bad. Bad. Idea.

Great balls of fire! Why was his hate just as sexy?

There was something wrong with me. So, to counteract giving in to Luke, I replied to the messages I'd missed last night from my screwballs.

> Graham: You've officially checked off all of Tucker's boxes.

> Tucker: Prank war activated!

> Graham: Damn, whatever Olson did to deserve that, please let me know if I ever get close to pissing you off that hard.

> Tucker: I didn't know his face could get that red.

> Tucker: He looked like one of those blowy things at car lots.

> Graham: Oh my god, you're so right. Dead.

> Tucker: I'm just mad I didn't rec it.

> Graham: Especially with how loud Davis screamed.

> Tucker: Well deserved. Round of applause was had for that one.

> Graham: Hope you're okay.

> Tucker: Sweet dreams of me. Actually, no, dirty dreams of me.

Laughing, I knew the perfect way to avoid temptation.

> Blake: I have no clue what you're referring to.

> Blake: Someone was pranked?

Graham: *wink wink* Your secret is safe.

Tucker: Smart. Don't incriminate yourself.

Tucker: Even your brain is sexy. Did you have any dreams of me?

Blake: I'll never tell.

Tucker: Damn.

Blake: Could I sit near you guys on the bus?

Graham: You're riding with us?

Tucker: Dude, the correct answer was yes. No questions.

Graham: Yes. Sorry, I thought that was implied.

Blake: Yeah. It's part of my punishment. My dad wants me to get to know the team better.

Blake: But basically, it's his way of keeping a babysitter on me and ensuring the other players get the message.

Graham: Which is?

Blake: Don't mess with me. *Shrug* It was Bryce's idea, and Dad agreed.

Blake: 'Course, he framed it as good team building and a way for me to get behind-the-scenes footage.

Blake: But it's the kind of stuff he's done my whole life. Sics his pet bulldog on me.

Tucker: OMG, I won't be able to unsee that now—Hawk as an English Bulldog. I want to buy him a bandana.

Graham: You'll be lucky to pitch again if you do.

Tucker: Might be worth it.

Graham: Your funeral. He scares me.

Blake: Thanks, guys.

Graham: I'm picking up lunch. Want anything?

Blake: You're my favorite person today. I'm not picky.

Tucker: No, fair. I want to be your favorite person.

Blake: There's still daylight to change my mind.

Tucker: You hear that, Teddy Graham? Your time is limited. I'm gonna win!

Graham: Enjoy getting your own lunch, then.

Tucker: Wait. I take it back. You're my favorite person every day.

Blake: I see how it is.

Tucker: Wait. *Crying emoji* I can have two favorites! You're both my favorites.

Graham: I get the window seat.

Tucker: So, Bee, how do you feel about being besties?

Graham: You're so spoiled, punk.

Tucker: Never said I wasn't a princess. I own my high-maintenance ass.

Graham: Punk princess, then.

> Blake: Thanks for the laughs. I'll see you in a few.

Smiling, I grabbed my bags and headed outside. The weather was warming up as summer grew closer, and I tilted my head to feel the sun on my face. Letting out an exhale, I headed over to the pickup area. I waved at Clive as I walked by, smiling when he gave me one back.

The huge charter buses idled at the curb decked out in the YellowJackets logo. Dad had upgraded them a few years ago, making them the nicer of the buses for Minor League teams. I didn't know for sure, but I think he got tired of listening to Bryce complain about the terrible traveling conditions. While the Major League teams had private charter flights, the Minor League teams were left with charter buses and commercial flights, depending on how well the club did.

However, I had to agree with Bryce; the old buses were horrible, and I was secretly glad I got to ride in these now that I was here. But I'd never let Bryce know. His ego was already big enough. Now, to somehow convince GT to be on a different bus from Luke and Hawk. I didn't know if I would be that lucky.

Handing my bag to the travel director—yes, that was their title and not a job I'd want to handle for a group of fifty people—I located a shady spot that put me at an excellent angle to snap the players' pictures. Fiddling with my camera settings and checking my lens, I missed him walking up to me, his shadow blocking the sun.

But the energy coursing between us was palpable, alerting me to his presence before he even spoke.

CHAPTER
TWENTY-SEVEN

BLAKE

"What's my password? I need it changed back. Today."

"Hi, Bee. How are you doing today? I'm glad you got some pants since I ripped yours," I replied, focusing on my camera.

Luke crouched down, blocking the sun and making it impossible to ignore him. Especially when his hand gripped my chin. Shivers raced through me, that fire emerging at his touch.

"Go away, Luke. I'm working." I pulled out of his hold, needing the distance so I didn't accidentally tackle him and do something dumb like kiss his stupid face. I leaned back on my hands, giving me more breathing space. The grass was rough against my palms, a comforting reassurance as it grounded me. My heart thumped in my chest and I slowly took in breaths.

Luke rolled his eyes, crossing his arms, but stayed level with me. I tried not to notice how nice he looked in his jeans and t-shirt, his forearms on display, or how his thighs looked from this angle. His blond hair was slightly disheveled, and he had some stubble on his face, giving him a more rugged look. I gulped, reminding myself not to be distracted by his charisma.

Do not fall for it. Do not fall for it. No dick, no entry.

"Password?" he growled, the sound making my nipples pebble.

I dropped my eyes from his, the green searing into me and stealing my words. I picked up blades of grass to distract myself, but of course, they were a similar color of green that only made me think of his eyes.

"I don't remember you being this much of a dick before. I mean, you were a little snobbish, but I didn't want to actively scratch your eyes out."

"Believe me, the sentiment is mutual."

I jerked back, his words striking me hard in the chest. I'd never had someone actively hate me before. A people pleaser's MO was to be liked by everyone, so this was new territory for me. I opened my mouth but was saved by my surrogate big brother.

English bulldog has been activated.

"Olson! Get on the bus. This isn't social hour." Hawk stomped over, his eyes hard as he glanced between us.

"Yeah, *Olson*. This isn't social hour. Some of us are working." I picked up my camera and snapped a picture, not even looking through the viewfinder.

"This isn't finished," Luke hissed, standing and walking away.

My eyes followed him, falling to his butt and I sighed at the beautifulness that man was. Hawk growled, and I jumped back.

Crackerjack! I'd forgotten he was there. What was with all the growls today?

I rolled my eyes, attempting to brush off my embarrassment at getting caught ogling the enemy. Ignoring him too, I went to work, focusing on the players as they arrived. Hawk stood there glowering, making the silence uncomfortable for once.

"If you have something to say, say it," I said, snapping pictures. I smiled when I spotted Graham and Tucker. They both waved, smiling wide when they spotted me, but left me alone. It could've been because they respected that I was working, but more likely, it was my Hawk shadow. If only he'd been here earlier to stave off Luke.

"Is there something going on with you and Olson?"

"Nope." I popped the 'p' and avoided eye contact.

"Hmm."

"Hmm," I mocked. I smiled, unable to stop myself.

"I like the blue. It brings out your eyes," he said before stomping off in the other direction.

I froze, not sure how to handle that. Hawk continued to turn me upside down with his back-and-forth behavior. One minute, he was friendly, giving me coffee and complimenting my hair. Then, the next, he was in full big brother mode, metaphorically peeing on me to scare off others.

"He has a girlfriend. We're just semi-friends," I repeated it until I believed it.

After a few breaths, I focused on my camera, and like the first time I picked one up, I fell into the routine and comfort of capturing a moment.

Snap, snap, snap. Check settings. Adjust if needed. *Snap, snap, snap.*

It was a straightforward cycle that allowed me to go offline and fall into the simplicity of photography. When everyone had exited the clubhouse, I stood and dusted off the dirt. Stretching my back and arms, I threw my bag over my shoulder and headed to the bus. I'd watched GT climb onto the first bus, so I headed toward that one.

It wasn't until I'd climbed aboard that I remembered this was the luxury one reserved for the fifteen players who were part of the Blue Devil's forty-man roster. Which meant Luke,

Graham, and Tucker were all on the same bus. So much for luck.

Thankfully, Seth was on the other bus. His jaw had seemed bruised earlier, but I couldn't tell precisely from my angle. It made me wonder what had happened, though I had a sneaking suspicion based on the red splotches I spotted on Hawk's knuckles.

I didn't want to like that he'd done that, but I did. Damn him and his sweet sentiments at times.

Hawk lifted his bag as I neared, motioning for me to sit next to him. I couldn't imagine anything more uncomfortable than sitting beside Hawk, except for Luke. So I kept walking, watching out of the corner of my eye as Hawk's hand twitched, almost like he wanted to reach out and pull me into his seat. Thankfully, we were on a bus full of players, meaning he'd avoid making a scene in front of them.

A few others watched me as I neared the back, where Graham and Tucker had taken their seats. Luke ignored me as I passed, glaring out the window with his headphones, but I preferred it that way—less chance of giving in to him and his crazy demands.

I made it to the back, the middle seat between the both of them open. "That for me?" I asked.

"Yep." Tucker beamed at me, patting the seat as he waited for me to take it. "Nice shirt."

"Thanks. My luggage finally arrived." I took the seat, looking around. There were still a few empty ahead of us. "Why you'd pick the back? It's next to the bathroom." I scrunched up my nose as the door opened, and Levi exited, gesturing to air it out.

Gross. Shaking my head.

"True," Graham said, pinching his nose, "but it has three seats. We couldn't decide who got to sit next to you, so this was a compromise." He pulled out a bottle of air freshener and sprayed it, making it smell slightly better. "Don't worry. I came prepared." Graham gave me a big grin, the corners of his mouth tilting so far that a small dimple formed on the left side. We held one another's eyes, something passing between us.

"Dimple smile! Hold that pose. I need to capture this," Tucker shouted behind me, breaking the spell. "Ah. I said hold it." Tucker pouted.

"Too bad. Can't have that on film," Graham said, smirking at his friend. He reached into his bag and pulled out sandwich boxes, handing Tucker and me one before taking his own. We pulled down the trays on the back of the seats as the buses pulled away, the journey beginning.

"So, shortstop, what's the deal-e-o?"

"Ew. No. Doesn't Levi play shortstop?"

"And?"

I pointed to the bathroom and held my nose. Tucker snorted and Graham almost choked on the bite he'd taken.

"Fair. No shortstop." Tucker held up his hands.

"I forgot you guys got the nicer bus. Thank god Pukey isn't on it."

"Pukey?" Graham asked around another bite.

"Yeah, the guy from The Dugout." I shuddered. I knew his name, but saying it gave him power. Or maybe that was demons, but eh. Worked the same.

"I'm so gonna call him Pukey," Tucker teased, taking a bite of his sandwich and making my mouth water.

The sandwich looked amazing, so I picked mine up and barely held back a moan as flavor exploded in my mouth. As we ate our food, I disclosed my indiscretion of the day before with Luke.

"That's why he played better when he returned?" Graham asked, his face inquisitive. "Huh. He told everyone he was taking a shit."

I snorted but shook my head, biting my lip. "Bunting hell. I'm not sure that's better."

"Is it me, or does that sound hot? The hate sex, not the taking a shit part," Tucker said, wiping his mouth as he finished eating.

"That's because you're an exhibitionist *and* a voyeur," Graham prattled off without skipping a beat, wadding up his trash.

"He's not wrong," Tucker agreed, shrugging and owning his kink as he winked at me.

"Wow, that's…" I cleared my throat, trying not to picture what those words brought to mind. "I'm honestly shocked you're not calling me a slut and asking me to move." I fiddled with my watch, fighting the urge to pick my nails.

Graham took one hand and Tucker the other, and my cheeks heated at their attention on me simultaneously. Okay, this was nice.

"No slut shaming here," Tucker said, drawing my chin up with his free hand. He shrugged. "Remember, neither of us is going to ridicule you for enjoying sex. That's kind of the purpose of sex."

My cheeks flamed, my insides warming at his words. But then I dropped my eyes, revealing a little more truth.

"I feel a little ashamed. *I hate him*. He hurt my feelings and ghosted me." I picked at my nails. "But I couldn't make myself leave that room if I'd tried. I told him it wasn't happening again, but I'm not sure either of us believe that."

"Not to make it sound like your vagina is a genie lamp, and when he rubs it, he gets three wishes, but…" Tucker grimaced. "Would it be so horrible to do it again?"

"You want me to have sex with another man?" I asked, blinking my eyes.

"Kinda." He cringed, and I whipped my head to Graham, my braids whipping around with the move. He had a faraway look on his face like he was watching something unfold in his mind.

"Graham, do you feel the same way?" I asked. He blinked, his gray eyes focusing on me.

"Hmm." He looked between me and Tucker. "Oh. Um. I don't disagree."

"Unbelievable," I muttered. "Hawk's trying to piss on me so he can clam jam my vagina, and you two want to rent it out."

"Not like that," Tucker hissed, his eyes laughing. "For Luke only. Here's how I see it. We can all agree he's an asshole." He lifted a finger before continuing. "But you said he wasn't in the beginning." Another finger. "Having sex with you makes him play better." And another one. "You like him despite your best efforts." Now, a fourth. "The sex was hot." Now, all five were up. "Any of that untrue?" he asked.

"No." I chewed my lip, suddenly not as sure about my hostility.

"Baseball players are notoriously superstitious, and I can't say I wouldn't do the same thing if I were playing as shit as he was during those first three games. He wasn't wrong to freak out. Being one of the fifteen means we always need to perform. We could move from the 40-man roster at any second and lose our shot at the big leagues. It's cutthroat in the minors. The conditions aren't the greatest, and most make pennies compared to the MLB contracts." Tucker gave me a look, one that said my privilege might've been showing.

Properly chastised, I pressed my lips together, stopping myself from speaking. He was right, and Minor League baseball players had it the roughest. Luke just became a dad, and I knew he wanted to provide a good life for Willow. With his schedule, that meant hiring someone to take care of her while he was at away games.

Most players couldn't afford to live off their minor league salary alone, so if they hadn't received huge signing bonuses from the major league affiliate team, then they were more than likely barely making ends meet and working random jobs in the off-season. I shouldn't judge their drive, their need to prove they belonged in the majors.

It didn't make me want to bend over and let him have his way with me, but it melted some of the rage and hurt I felt.

"He's not saying you need to be a vagina ATM and be available whenever he wants," Graham added quickly. "Consent is very much needed, and you shouldn't do anything that makes you feel bad. Instead, he's saying the opposite. *Don't* feel bad for doing this *if* it feels good. That is if you didn't hate it and *wanted* to do it again. Shame has no place in the minor leagues."

I bit the corner of my lip, feeling some relief and acceptance of myself from their words. "Does that mean you're no longer interested in our pact then?" I asked.

"Don't get the wrong idea, glove genie." I lifted my brows at Tucker, daring him to use that one again. He smirked, ignoring my look. "We still want to explore things with you. *Promise.* We're just saying it doesn't have to exclude him, either." He shrugged, his cheeks slightly pink. It was the first time I'd seen the mega-flirt blush, and it endeared me.

I looked at Graham, his eyes calculating.

"Like the book."

"You've been reading?"

I nodded. "Yeah. It's um, good." I cleared my throat, shifting my legs.

"If a book makes you feel that, then I need to read it," Tucker said, drawing my attention.

"Feel what?" I asked, playing dumb.

He leaned close, his breath warm on my neck, and his lips brushed my skin. "If I touched you right now, how wet would you be?"

I gulped, the pulsing increasing between my legs.

Tucker pulled back, a cocky grin on his face as he licked his lips. "I'm ready for my one-on-one time, honey bee."

"Huh?"

"Graham got his, so now I want mine."

"Okay."

"Before Tucker melts your brain, just know we're open to Luke. You met him before us and have a connection, even if it's mostly aggression. Just keep talking to us about this. That's what we all wanted."

"You're right. Thank you, Graham." I looked between the two of them. "I'm really glad I met you both. You make me feel safe."

"Tell me how else I make you feel," Tucker purred, and I laughed.

"I'll think about Luke. He'll need to work for it, though. I'm not going to make it easy on him or follow him at the snap of his fingers." I straightened my spine, feeling the honesty of the words to my bones.

"That's fair, and the chase might be what he needs to get out of his head," Graham agreed.

"I can't believe you changed his password and bought our jerseys. Do we get to see you in said jerseys, perhaps with nothing else on?" Tucker asked, wiggling his eyebrows comically.

"Maybe." I winked, looking between them both. "You're not what I expected at all."

"We get that a lot," Tucker said, pushing up his tray and settling back into his seat. "Now, come and cuddle me. It's my pre-game necessity," he teased.

Grinning, I pushed up my tray and settled back against his chest, his arms wrapping around me. Graham left his tray down and placed his iPad on it. He queued up something and handed me an earbud, leaning back in his seat. His leg pressed into mine, making me a cozy filling in the GT sandwich.

I should get up and do some interviews, but as I glanced around, I had to admit Mira was right. Everyone was doing their own thing. Tucker already had his eyes closed, his head on a pillow against the window as Graham and I watched a documentary on theme parks.

I knew from experience this calm wouldn't last forever, but I'd enjoy it while it did. I needed to learn from my screwballs and quit trying to control everything, letting them play out how they would for once.

Surely, that option included less vomit.

Pulling out my phone, I sent a text, hoping the olive branch would garner me some goodwill.

Okay, baseball gods, I'm being good. Time to reverse the curse.

GRAHAM

THE RICHMOND ROYALS WERE PROVING TO BE MORE DIFFICULT than expected. That or we didn't play well on the road. Which wasn't a good stat to have with 150 games to play in a season with half of those on the road.

I shifted my feet, my thighs burning from the crouched position. It was a burn I'd grown used to and weirdly craved. My eyes bore into Tuck's, and I threw down a hand signal for him. We changed them every season, so players couldn't familiarize themselves with our calls. It was bad form to steal call signs, but it didn't mean players didn't do it. Nonetheless, we went out of our way to make them so confusing that anyone other than us wouldn't understand them.

It was part of what made us so good together. We could read each other so well.

Tucker shook his head, then lifted it, telling me he wanted to throw a screwball. I debated it for a second, considering the outcome and odds.

"Tell your boyfriend to throw the ball already," the batter hissed, settling his feet in the dirt.

I rolled my eyes, not bothering to get into it with him.

This dude had a chip on his shoulder the size of Texas. Giving Tucker the go-ahead for the screwball, I held my glove in position as I watched the runner behind him on second, all while categorizing every shift Tuck made.

The second the pitch left his hand, I knew it was good.

Bracing for the catch, I tightened my muscles to launch up and throw the ball to third once I caught it. The batter swung too high, the ball breaking in the opposite direction he'd anticipated and earning his third strike. The ball smacked into my glove, and I barely missed the bat swinging back as I stood and fired it to Emmett Michaels on third.

Thankfully, he'd been ready, having eyed the runner on second, too. I held my breath as it flew through the air, and the Royals player advanced. It would be close.

Come on, come on.

Michaels wrapped his glove around the ball and turned, tagging the runner just as they touched base. It felt like time stood still as we all waited to hear what the third base umpire would call. Had he tagged him first?

"Out!"

The YellowJackets cheered, jumping up in celebration like we'd just won the game. We hadn't. But it was the first play that had been successful, ending the bottom of the fourth and sending us into the fifth. I tugged off my catcher's helmet, jogging toward the dugout with the rest of the team, a smile on my face for Tucker.

"Fucking amazing, G!" he shouted, slapping me on the back.

"Me? You're the one who remembered he wasn't patient enough for the screwball."

Tucker beamed, sighing as he climbed down the steps into the dugout. "Ah, the reverse curse. My favorite secret weapon."

"Jameson, West, good partnership," Coach Phillips said as we took our spots on the bench.

As the team passed, a few patted us and Michaels on the back. Luke slumped in the back of the dugout, a cloud of darkness practically swirling around him. He'd missed a big play in that inning, letting the Royals gain two runs. They were up 4-1, but there was still plenty of game left to play. Tucker nudged me as he prepared to go up to bat, his eyes shifting down to Luke.

I knew what he wanted me to do but didn't know what to say.

So, Blake told us about your hate sex? No, too weird.

Go take another shit? Might think I was hitting on him.

After a few back and forths with Tucker, where we both widened our eyes and lifted our brows in a silent convo, I sighed and stood. He smacked my butt as he grabbed his bat and helmet, blowing me a kiss as he left the dugout.

"I swear they're gay together," someone said as I passed. It wasn't the first comment we'd gotten, and I knew it wouldn't be the last, so I ignored it. It only hurt because I wished it were true, but I knew it never would be.

Luke glared as I approached, crunching on sunflower seeds like they held all the secrets to his game. He narrowed his eyes as I sat beside him.

"Go away," he grumbled, spitting out the seeds.

"Sorry, can't." I took a breath, then pushed the words out. "Have you talked to, um, Blake?" I asked, fidgeting as I tugged at the material of my pants. The material stuck to my sweaty skin as I shifted on the bench.

"I'm not talking to you about this," he hissed, spitting out more seeds. Thankfully, away from me, or I'd have to hurt him.

"Too bad, Olson." I turned, hitting him with my full glare. "I'm your only option and you know it. You haven't exactly made friends."

He snorted, shaking his head. "This isn't my team. I was

here to recover. I did. But now, I'm stuck here while Baker steals what was mine."

I held up my hands, the venom in his words shocking me. "Hey. I get it. We were on a shitty team, but it was still the Majors. Moving down to the Minors wasn't exactly the career path we envisioned, but it's not all bad." I held my breath and then let it out. "It could be worse, man."

"How?" he asked, glaring at me. His green eyes were bright as he stared, daring me to be positive. I could tell he wasn't in the mood to look on the brighter side, so I didn't waste my breath. Change of tactic.

"Did you, um, not take a shit before the game?" I asked, cringing at myself.

"Why the fuck do you care?" he snapped.

I shrugged, stopping to watch Tucker make contact with the ball and hit it deep into the infield. I jumped up, clapping as he made it to first safe.

"Hell, yeah! Go, Tuck!" I shouted, smiling. I turned, deciding I was done with Luke. I was all about team spirit, but only if he wanted to be a team player. I crossed my arms and leaned back against the fence. Hard truth time.

"I care because this game is my livelihood. And a winning team brings in more fans, has better morale, and feels good to be on. Maybe try being a team player for once."

"I did," he hissed. "She told me no. I might be a lot of things, but I'm not a rapist."

"Then try harder. You didn't give up the first time you struck out in baseball, did you? The hit you get after a whiff always feels better."

I walked away and took my seat, paying attention to the game and Tuck as he ran to third. I'd missed him getting on second in my rant. Coach Phillips stomped by, approaching the sulking man I'd just left. The older coach glared at him, his hands on his hips. Since it wasn't directed at me, I found it comical. I hid a smile in my hands as I openly watched. Coach Anderson glared from the front but didn't interfere.

"Do you need to take a shit again, Olson?" Coach Phillips asked when his glare didn't work."

Luke spluttered, sitting up and almost choking on the sunflower seeds he'd been chewing. "Um, what?"

"You're sitting the next inning until you get your head in the game. You might as well go and do whatever you did last game to change your attitude. I'm not putting you back in until you quit sulking like a baby who had their favorite toy stolen."

"But Coach, you don't understand," he started, sitting up.

"Get out of my sight. I can't bear to look at you," he muttered, dismissing him with a turn and stalking back toward the front of the dugout.

Coach Anderson hid a smirk in his hand, his gaze returning to the field as he updated Phillips on the game. Tucker jogged down into the dugout, smiling wide as he took his seat, and I gave him a fist bump.

"So, how did it go?" he asked, nudging his head toward Olson.

"Awful. The dude is stubborn and cranky."

"Hmph. Well, whatever you said must've worked because he's gone."

I whipped my head around, finding the spot he'd been brewing empty. Chuckling, I shook my head.

"Nah. That was coach. Told him to get out of his sight and take a shit."

Tucker grimaced, looking at a few of the other people near us. "If Bee discovers her 'contributions' are known to the team, she'll kill him."

"Better him than us." I chuckled, gulping my sports drink.

"I'm confused." Tucker's brow furrowed and he scuffed his cleat.

"About?"

"Shouldn't we be helping him? Get that happy family thing?" Tucker lifted his brown eyes, the orbs warm and open. A lot of people thought Tucker was too clingy, but he had the biggest heart I knew of. He cared for people and just wanted the same in return.

"I'm not against him, and I do believe there's a way to make things work with us and Blake. But I'm not going to do all the work for him. If he doesn't treat her right or make her feel good about herself, then he's not worth inviting in."

Tucker nodded, rubbing his chin. "That's a good point. What do you think about the bulldog?" he asked, flicking his eyes up to Coach Anderson. "Is he a contender?"

I shrugged, looking over the scary man. "Not sure. Blake wants him to be even if she denies it right now, but he's harder to read."

"Yeah. Outside of you, he's the best catcher I've watched play."

"Aw, you do love me," I ribbed, poking his side.

Tucker let out a high-pitched giggle, jumping away from me. His cheeks blushed, and I wondered what that was about. He cleared his throat, kicking at something on the ground as he answered. It took me a second to remember what it was in response to.

"Yeah, I do, G."

Turning back to the game, I rolled those words around, letting myself hope for a microsecond he meant them the way I wanted.

I love you, too.

By the top of the seventh inning, Luke had returned. He stood in the dugout with his gear ready, his cheeks rosy and his eyes vibrant. I guess he got to rub the Blake genie again.

"Hit a homer," Tucker shouted, cupping his hands around his mouth so it echoed.

"No way." Seth sneered, spitting onto the floor. I screwed up my nose at the puddle. I hated how barbaric some guys could be in the dugout. We might be outside playing the best sport known to man, but I didn't want to walk through someone's loogie. There were limits.

The thwack of the wooden bat hitting the ball had everyone standing and looking out into the field, watching Luke's ball soar across the outfield.

"Go, go, go!" we all shouted, encouraging him and the ball. The ball kept soaring, hitting the sign in the back and earning Luke his first home run for the game. He jogged the bases with a big smile as he rounded third.

"Dude looks like he got laid," Levi murmured.

"That's one helluva shit," Wyatt commented.

"Damn. I want a good luck shit." Sal sighed, crossing his arms.

"Nah. Yours is just shitting," Dalton retorted, ducking in time to miss Sal's slap.

Luke returned to the dugout, receiving slaps and cheers for his efforts. His entire demeanor changed now that he'd found his rhythm.

"Looks like you found a reason to win," I challenged, slapping him harder than necessary. I leaned in, whispering only for him, "Fuck it up, and you'll have us to answer to."

He rolled his eyes, but I watched as he swallowed and took his seat. His leg bounced, but the dark cloud was gone, and he focused on the game. I got ready for my at-bat, pushing everything out of my mind as I placed my helmet on and latched the Velcro of my glove. Picking up my bat, I jogged up the steps into the on-deck position and took a few swings to warm up my arms.

The crowd's noise faded into the background as I approached the batter's box. I spent so much time behind it that being in it always felt surreal, the height difference taking me a moment to adjust to.

Taking a deep breath, I let it out slowly as I positioned my feet, keeping them straight as I lifted my arms into the air. My elbow tilted up, and I gripped my bat as I watched the mound and waited for the pitch.

Tucker and I examined so much film together that I could almost anticipate which pitches the Royals' pitcher would throw. Daniels wasn't very dynamic, but he was consistent. His favorite was the cutter, and since I was batting left-handed, it meant it would cut toward me instead of away like he was used to.

Smirking, I assessed him as he wound up, clocking the position of his fingers on the stitches, how he held the ball, and how it left his hand, confirming what I'd expected. The ball flew fast toward me, but I waited, knowing it would cut soon toward me, and I needed to be ready to swing when it did.

The second it was near, I swung, twisting my body around as I propelled it forward, using all of my momentum to build up power and smack the ball at the exact moment. Hearing the sound of it hitting the bat, I jumped into action.

Tossing my bat, I broke off toward first base, my leg muscles working overtime as my cleats bit into the dirt and I pumped my arms. My breathing was choppy as I ate up the distance, my sprint bringing me closer to first.

My foot landed on the base a second before the baseman caught it, and I flew past it, slowing as I regained my breath.

"Safe!" the ump called, the crowd booing my run as I collected myself.

I heard, "Go, Graham!" from the stands, rising above all the other chatter and zinging to my heart. *Blake.*

Smiling, I took a few steps off the base and watched Sal, feeling invincible when I played this game. Out on the diamond, I felt completely confident and sure of myself.

Outside of an injury, the worst thing that could happen was to lose, and when you played so many games, even that wasn't all that bad. It always sucked, but odds were, there was another game the next night to try again.

Baseball was my happy place, and I loved playing this game.

Out here on this diamond, the game didn't care what your sexual orientation was. It didn't care if you were great in bed, or if you could hold a press conference. The only thing baseball cared about was heart, skill, and the love of the game.

Baseball was my safe place to be, and I relished it.

Sal got a walk to first, sending me to second, and I made it to third after Ledger's hit. But Dalton and Wyatt struck out, ending the inning. Trudging back to the dugout, I redressed in my catcher's gear, feeling hopeful despite not getting a run. There were still two innings to bat, and we were only down by one now.

It was anyone's game, and that was exhilarating.

With a pat on my back, I ran to home plate and did a few warmup pitches with Tuck before crouching down to start the inning. I could feel the energy in my blood, the shift in the air as throw after throw, Tucker struck out the batters at the plate.

"Three up and three down, easy peasy," he sang as we jogged back to the dugout for the new inning.

"I'm beginning to think Blake does have a genie lamp vagina," I whispered, making Tucker bend over, clutching his stomach as he laughed.

"I dare you to tell her that," he said once he recovered and wiped his eyes.

"I'm not stupid." Smiling, I sat, ready to get my chance at bat again which came in the ninth inning.

And just like that, we won the game, finishing 10-4.

I didn't like to brag, but I'd gotten a home run in the ninth. Feeling high on the comeback win, even the press interviews didn't seem as annoying, and the entire team showered and headed back to the bus. We had five more games here this week, meaning we'd stay in a hotel for the next few nights. Tradition was to go out and celebrate together, but for once, I just wanted to head back to our room and chat with Blake.

"Is it me, or does staying back and eating room service sound like the most amazing idea ever?" Tucker whispered.

"It's scary how you read my thoughts sometimes."

Tucker wiggled his eyebrows, making me wonder what else he knew I thought. Assessing him, I let myself look at his body as he settled into the seat. His chocolate brown hair was still damp, the ends curling up. His stubble was thick, and I dreamed about feeling it over my body. Licking my lips, I forgot I wasn't supposed to be checking out my best friend.

"Thinking about that burger?" Tuck asked, tilting his head to observe me.

"Yep. You know it."

My cheeks heated as I fiddled with my phone, sending Blake a message and seeing if she could come and hang with us.

Graham: We're skipping the bar and getting room service. Want to join?

Blake: Wish I could, but I have a dinner I can't get out of.

Blake: Non perk of being a former baseball princess. Everyone knows you through your dad and wants to catch up.

Blake: I regret saying yes already.

Graham: Former princess? I think you still are one, babe.

Blake: Ew, gross, take that back. I'm making my own path.

Graham: Retracted. *laughing emoji*

Blake: Better.

Graham: How did it go with Olson?

Blake: *face palm emoji* I caved.

Blake: You guys got in my head, and his game was sucking. I felt bad.

Graham: It seemed to work. He got two home runs.

Blake: Why do I have to be so good at sex?

Graham: Way to flex.

Blake: I immediately regretted it. I'm sure I'll be reminded not to get too cocky later.

Graham: That's my line.

Blake: You have every reason to be cocky.

Graham: Speaking of, you're making mine hard.

Blake: Sorry not sorry. *kissy face*

Graham: Be good. Text when you're back.

Blake: Will do. *smiling face*

"Blake coming?" Tucker asked.

"Nah. Has dinner plans."

"Bummer. I guess you'll have to entertain me." Tucker nuzzled his head between my neck and shoulder, falling asleep instantly. I let out a slow breath, the contact making my body sing. Between Blake's teasing and Tucker's contact, my cock was suddenly very awake.

When we pulled into the hotel, my cock had remembered Tuck was our friend and not our next meal. Grabbing our bags, we headed to our room and waved off the invites. I heard a few grumbles and another homophobic comment, but it didn't seem to penetrate Tucker. That, or he just didn't care. It was always hard to tell with him.

"Order my favorites; I need to drop off some kids at the pool," he said as he stepped into the bathroom and shut the door.

Shaking my head, I called the restaurant and ordered what we could eat from our meal plan, not what Tucker wanted. He'd be mad at me, but he'd thank me for it tomorrow when he wasn't sluggish.

"Ah, man," he groaned twenty minutes later when he opened his box.

"Did you expect anything else?" I teased, taking a bite of my plain chicken breast.

"Just once." He sighed but ate his food.

We sat next to one another on the bed, a movie playing as we ate. It was comfortable, and I was glad we hadn't gone out. The energy to maintain my social persona and play always wore me out, and I needed my alone time to recharge.

Tucker was the opposite. He loved to be around people and would force me out of my hole most of the time. Tonight, I was glad he seemed to need his downtime, too.

"Do you think she's being honest and likes us still? I'm worried she might grow closer to Luke," Tucker said, biting his thumb. He'd been quiet for a while, leaning back against the pillows as we absently watched the movie.

"If she only wanted to date him, she wouldn't spend time with or talk to us."

"But," he started, turning his head to me, "what if?"

"What if what?" I shrugged. "You said to keep it clear so you wouldn't do this. So, listen to yourself, sage one, and trust her."

He nodded, taking a deep breath. "Yeah. You're right."

"Ooh, can you say that again? I need to record it." I picked up my phone, and Tucker shoved me, laughing. It vibrated in my hand, so I glanced down, practically swallowing my tongue at the picture.

"Did you?" I wheezed, the only words I could get out.

"What?" he asked, grabbing his from under a pile of blankets and pillows. "Fuck. Is that?"

"Her ass." My eyes bugged out at the picture, my cock taking notice as I stared. Two photos of Blake's ass lifted in the air with my name and then Tucker's emblazoned across the back of her panties, claiming her ass.

"Best piece of merch ever," Tucker groaned, biting his knuckles. I nodded, my words dry on my tongue. It wasn't even that racy, but fuck, it was sexy as hell.

> Blake: Sorry I couldn't hang out, but here's your reward for playing so well.
>
> Blake: Night, GT. *Kiss emoji*

"Does that calm your mind?" I asked, shifting my cock as it thickened against my leg.

"Uh-huh. Fuck, I want to jack off," he groaned, then looked at me with a challenge in his eyes. I swallowed, not knowing what he'd do.

"What?"

He didn't answer right away, his eyes traveling over me as he gripped his cock.

"Bathroom's right there," I said, my voice cracking. I couldn't move, too worried my dick would take a dive out of my pants and weep for Tucker, making it obvious I wanted him.

"If we're gonna be with her together, we gotta get used to seeing one another's O face. And if I don't touch myself right now, I'll die." Tucker's voice was strained, and I swallowed.

"Dramatic much." I rolled my eyes, but inside, my heart beating a mile a minute.

"Maybe." He smiled sweetly before it turned wicked, and he yanked his joggers down, his cock springing free. Nothing could have stopped my eyes from looking. I'd seen it before. You couldn't walk in a clubhouse without seeing dick swing, but I never let myself look-look.

I swallowed as I took in the bead of precum already at the tip. The picture he'd sent drastically lacked from the real thing. He was long with dark veins, his tip already red and swollen.

"Besides, you know how much I like to perform and be watched. This is so doing it for me," he purred, gripping himself. Tucker stroked himself up and down before swiping his thumb across the tip and spreading his pre-cum.

I froze with my heart in my throat. I couldn't tear my eyes away, captivated by his movements. My fingers twitched to touch myself, to touch him. I licked my lips, and he groaned, making my cock twitch.

If I joined in, what would that mean? Would he know I was thinking of him? Did he know I'd watched him before? I always thought he might; why else would he leave the door open? Was this his way of telling me he liked it?

"Quit thinking and get your dick out, G," he rasped. I finally broke the trance with his cock and looked up, swallowing as I took in his blown pupils and rapt expression. He looked utterly blissed out as he stroked himself, his eyes half-lidded as he watched me.

Nodding, I slowly tugged down my joggers and boxers, pulling my cock free. I couldn't bear to see if he watched me, so I focused on stroking myself and watching his movements. He tapped his phone, bringing the picture back to life and groaning again. He sat it between us, his shoulder bumping into mine. That small action almost sent me over. I squeezed my shaft, stopping myself from coming first.

"I can't wait to paint her tits with my cum," he groaned.

"Mm-hmm," I rasped, worried I'd say too much if I allowed myself to. I hadn't anticipated him wanting to chat. Was that a thing? Did guys circle jerk and dirty talk? Have a wank with a side of praise kink?

"Tell me what you want to do. Make it real, G."

I groaned, my breathing quickening as I allowed myself to look up and found him staring at me. I licked my lips, my mind blank because all I wanted to say was how I wanted to suck his cock while he ate her out. That was the fantasy on repeat in my head.

"Um, well, I'd kiss her."

"Where?" he teased, giving me that soft smile again. Damn him.

"Her pussy. I like oral sex and making my partner scream with pleasure."

He slid his hand up, squeezing his tip as more precum emerged and groaned. "Yeah. I could see you taking the time to please your partner," he gasped. "Keep going. I'm so close."

"If she were riding you, I'd feed her my cock and touch her all over, wanting everything to feel a million times more when she came."

"What will she feel like with your piercing?" he asked, his eyes dropping to my dick. It twitched in response, my tip leaking so much I didn't need anything else to stroke myself.

Him watching me, licking his lips, the dirty talk… it was already too much.

"It would hit her clit and send her over," I moaned just as my orgasm crashed into me. Tingles ran up my spine, my balls drew up sharp, and cum exploded as it ran over my hand and hit my abs, arm, and joggers. It sprayed in multiple directions as I chased it through, moaning loudly at the most powerful orgasm I'd ever given myself.

"Holy shit," Tucker whispered, and I opened my eyes,

watching as he squeezed his tip and then let go, his cock erupting with cum as he stroked it. His hips jerked up slowly, his abs and hand slick with his release. I barely stopped myself from reaching out and scooping it up.

I was playing a dangerous game, balancing on a tightrope with one too many secrets. I was destined to topple over, but I didn't know if I'd fall flat on my face or right into his arms. The second option didn't seem as unlikely as before. Each step we drew closer to Blake brought us together, too.

"Damn, that was hot. We'll have to do that again and see if it was just the novelty of it or if jerking off with your bestie is a secret level we unlocked that no one told us about." He chuckled as he climbed off the bed and stepped into the bathroom. My brain was too fuddled to formulate words, so I jumped when he dropped a warm cloth into my hands, not expecting it.

"See, I can wait on you, too, Teddy Graham." He winked, heading back to the bathroom.

Cleaning myself up, I picked up our trash and returned our room to rights while Tucker went through his twenty-step nighttime routine.

"Night," he said, climbing into the other bed, turning off the light on his side, and casting the room into darkness. We might have to skip bar nights if it ended that way.

CHAPTER
TWENTY-NINE

BLAKE

I STAYED BUSY THROUGHOUT THE NEXT FOUR GAMES AND AVOIDED being alone with Hawk and Luke as best as possible. My feelings had grown too complicated, and I needed clarity before moving forward. I didn't know what direction that entailed but knew I couldn't keep this up. The constant state of apprehension was exhausting, and my physical and mental well-being were suffering.

Hawk had apologized and wanted to be friends again. But my heart couldn't decipher the difference with Hawk. We'd always been friends but more, even if only in my heart. I didn't trust myself not to fall back into old patterns where I loved him completely, so I kept my guard up, trying to remember he had a girlfriend.

Friendly, but not too friendly, that was all we could be.

But Hawk didn't make it easy. I could feel his penetrating stare as I worked, always warm on my skin. No matter how much I hid from him, he found me. I half expected he'd inserted a tracker with the way he could locate me. Hawk had crashed a couple of my dinners out, inserting himself into the invite from old acquaintances on the Royals. And while I knew he'd known them in the same capacity as me, he'd never been interested in schmoozing or networking.

When he wasn't crashing boring dinners, or asking me about my day, he'd surprise me with coffee before games, cheesecake, cookies, and a cinnamon roll after. Each time, he'd hand it to me, or place it next to my belongings, and then walk off. No words or conversation. Just a delivery of goods and he'd be gone. He was slowly thawing my heart with food and I hated him for knowing my weakness.

Girlfriend. He has a girlfriend.

Which was easier to remember when he'd forward me pictures of Sunny from Roxie. I wanted to hate her, but so far there wasn't any reason I found other than she got to fuck Hawk.

Luke proved just as tricky to sidestep, and I might've ducked into the restroom or hid behind the Royals' mascot once or twice to avoid him. My heart had become too entangled in the hate sex and if I kept it up, I wouldn't be able to decipher the sex from my feelings. He'd still played well in the second and third game but slowly deteriorated in the fourth. By today's game, he had flagged early and was pulled out. He'd sent me another text asking for help, but I held firm, proving that I could avoid trouble if I avoided everyone.

Which wasn't all that enjoyable, really.

With only Hawk's shadow for company, I'd never felt more alone than I did on this away series. It was all taking a toll on me, and from the past, I knew I was on the verge of a breakdown if I didn't do something.

I'd kept texting Graham and Tucker, but as the week wore on, the exhaustion wore on us all, and even those conversations had been limited. A few quick hugs, and one night of sexy pictures weren't enough to sustain. I missed our easy friendship just as much as the sexy exploration.

"Time to suck it up, buttercup." With my pockets full of

snacks and two sodas in hand, I walked to the elevator. Nerves rattled me with each step, but I knew it was time. I had to do something. I couldn't stay in this limbo.

After today's game, I'd overheard Luke talking to Willow on the phone, and something in me shifted. He'd looked so sad when he hung up and a feeling of wanting to make it better had rushed over me.

Taking a deep breath, I fortified myself and hit the button for his floor. My knee bounced the whole way up, and I debated hitting the emergency stop button a few times, but the hotel wasn't that big, and the doors were already opening onto floor twelve before I could.

Tomorrow was the last away game, making it eight in a row for the YellowJackets. After winning four games at home, they'd won three in Virginia, bringing their season record to 7-4.

Spirits were high, and the odds for tomorrow's game were in the YellowJackets' favor for the first time in years. The dynamic duo of Graham and Tucker were a huge cause, but Luke had also been batting his personal best. Outside of today's game at least.

Tucker had divulged how he and Graham had masturbated to the pictures I'd sent and teased that Luke might be right with his theory. Not the yips part, but that sex with me makes people play better.

I'd denied it, pointing out I hadn't since the first away game, and Luke still played well four out of five games. Tucker argued that there must be a residual period of performance-based enhancement. Graham smacked him for me, but it didn't stop the smug smile on his face when he said he'd used my pic every night to jack off to, and had thrown the last five innings with no hits in today's game.

Graham had looked so stunned at his admission that I knew Tucker wasn't lying.

It still didn't mean I wanted to pimp my vagina out as

some miracle juju. I'd been around baseball long enough to know that all lucky charms stopped working at some point, and the fallout from being the cause of a loss was too heavy for me to bear. Nor was it fair.

I was a person, not a lucky charm.

It was way too close to falling back into that spot where I did things to make others happy and ended up running away from a wedding.

Since I'd already covered the runaway bride square on my bingo card, I needed to change the trajectory of my path.

Which meant I needed to quit running from Luke.

Knocking on his door, I took a deep breath and hoped he wouldn't shut it in my face. Things were still icy between us when we weren't in the throes of scorching hot sex. One extreme to the next, and it gave me whiplash. I didn't want to avoid him every game.

The door opened slowly, and he appeared shirtless, his golden skin on display and a pair of athletic shorts low on his hips highlighting his delicious V. I gulped, snapping my eyes back up to his.

"Ah, look, you do exist. With how you've avoided me, I worried I'd imagined you."

His dig made me grimace, knowing he wasn't wrong. Luke crossed his arms, attempting to put some space between us, but his eyes gave him away. The green swirled with uncertainty, hope, and desire.

"I once ate a cricket on a dare, didn't learn to swim until I was sixteen, and I like you even if I shouldn't." I sucked in a breath, keeping contact with his eyes. "Spot the lie, Luke."

He swallowed, the sound audible in the quiet hallway. His eyes searched mine, looking for something. I held his gaze steady despite the urge to run away and hide. I hated being vulnerable, especially if it could be thrown in my face. But I had to risk it. Neither of us could continue doing the hate-sex thing, no matter how much we convinced ourselves we could.

"Willow hates me, I think about drinking to numb it all, and I don't want to like you, but I do. Spot *my* lie, Slugger."

I sucked in a breath, unsure if his not answering my question was good or not. He seemed to read something on my face and took my hand.

"Your lie was the swimming one, wasn't it?" I nodded as he stepped back into the room, pulling me with him. "Well? What's your guess?" he asked when I still hadn't responded. He sat on the bed, dragging me down with him. I dropped my candy and sodas, wiping the condensation onto my leggings.

"The father one. I don't believe Willow could hate you," I whispered.

His shoulders dropped, and I worried I'd said the wrong thing, but then I realized how all the tension in his body had drained. Luke finally resembled the man I met on the plane. Gone was the hatred and anger.

"What are you doing here?" he asked when I said nothing.

I picked up the candy and soda. "I brought a peace offering."

He snorted, taking the bag of M&M's. "Okay. What else?" He opened the package and dumped some into his hand, tossing them back into his mouth. The movement was far too distracting, so I cleared my throat and opened the gummy worms, biting into one as I thought.

"I can't be your hate-fuck buddy or lucky-charm sex," I blurted

His head dropped and he picked up the package and nodded. "I understand."

"But," I added, his head snapping back up, his green eyes piercing mine.

"But?" he asked, swallowing.

"I'd like to amend our agreement."

"I'm listening." He stole a gummy worm from my hand, biting into it with a smile.

"Being used to make you play better makes me feel dirty, and I don't like that. Not to mention the stress of worrying it won't help."

"I'm sorry, I didn't—"

I held up my hand, stopping him.

"I know. You might've been angry at me, even if I didn't deserve your hate, but even during those times, I never felt you pressured me or forced me. It's just." I paused, shrugging one shoulder. "I thought I could have sex without feelings, but I can't. And each time we're together, it hurts when it's over to think you might actually hate me. Especially when…"

I shook my head, dropping it so my hair covered my face, and focused on the blue pieces. I bit into another gummy worm until his hand reached through, lifting my chin.

"Especially when what, Bee?" he asked softly.

I shook my head, a tear falling down my cheek.

"Fuck," he cursed, reaching forward and pulling me into his lap. He cradled my head against his chest and squeezed me tight.

"I'm sorry. I don't mean to cry."

"It's okay. Don't apologize for crying." Which only made me cry more. Everyone always made me feel bad for my emotions. Luke didn't. He held me, rubbing my back as I cried.

"I'm the one who should be apologizing. I made a mess of things. We shared the best night I've ever had. It was perfect, Bee. You should know that. Or at least until I let fear take control."

"You thought it was perfect?"

"You didn't?" he asked, pulling back so he could peer into

my eyes again. He brushed my hair back, wiping my wet tears off my cheeks.

"No, I did. I'm just surprised you did because you're, well, you."

He grinned, giving me one of those cocky boy smiles that made my knees weak. "Please, say more."

Giggling, I slapped his shoulder. "You're insufferable."

"I know. I'm not the easiest person to be around."

"Hey, now. Don't be talking bad about yourself." I glared, not liking how defeated he'd sounded.

"Do you disagree?" he challenged, lifting an eyebrow.

"Absolutely. Now, Seth, he's not easy to be around." I shuddered.

At the mention of his name, Luke's face hardened. "I heard what he did; the jackass better be glad Coach got to him first."

"Wait, so it's true? Hawk did something?" I asked, biting my lip.

He nodded, searching my face. "Is there something between you two? He's always watching you."

"That's more complicated than Graham's call signs and not something I want to get into tonight."

"Speaking of Graham." He took a deep breath. "Are you with him?"

I shook my head. "No. I'm single. I wouldn't have, you know, if I weren't."

"So there's nothing between you and him or even Tucker?" he countered, holding his breath.

I knew my answer would hurt him. I just hoped it wouldn't be the end of finding a middle ground between hate and lust.

"I didn't say that. I said I was single, not that there wasn't anything there."

His body tensed, and he breathed slowly through his

nose, the nostrils flaring as he narrowed his eyes. "I didn't peg you for a jersey whore."

I slapped his cheek before I thought, shocking us both. I stared at my hand, then the red imprint on his cheek.

"Shit. I'm sorry."

He shook his head, deflating. His fingers flexed on my hips. Luke hadn't let me go.

"Don't be. I deserved that." He cracked his jaw. "I'm sorry, Slugger. That was uncalled for. Not that this excuses it, but I don't know how to handle this feeling. I'm so out of my league here."

"What feeling?" I asked, holding my breath.

He tilted his head, quirking one eyebrow. "Really, you're gonna make me say it?"

I nodded, still not breathing until he did.

"Jealousy," he gritted out like the word tasted bitter. "Happy?"

I let the air go, and it rushed out of me in a puff. "I wouldn't say happy, but it makes me feel better."

"Am I competing for you then? Where do I stand?" His eyes searched mine.

"How about we start over before we go there? We had a night of perfect bliss followed by heartache, betrayal, and then hate sex. Let's do something boring like getting to know one another as friends first."

"Friends with benefits?" he teased, leaning closer. His breath ghosted over my lips and I ached to lean and taste his.

"Nope." I placed a finger on his lips. "You haven't earned a kiss. Kissing leads to more, and I'm not strong enough right now," I admitted.

"Fine," he groaned. "But I'm gonna need you to get off my lap then."

Climbing off, I sat next to him on the bed. "I'm not saying never, Luke. In fact, benefits could be negotiated. Later. As I see it, you still have some groveling to do." I tried to smile, to let him know I wasn't angry.

He nodded. "Yeah. Okay. That's fair. I've never been friends with a woman before. Especially one I've slept with first and want to continue doing that with."

I handed him the soda and candy, picking my own up.

"Okay?" he asked, giving me an odd look.

"Welcome to the alternative to sex and drinking."

"Sugar?" he asked skeptically.

"Yep." I smiled, biting another gummy worm.

"Yeah, the trainer won't like that." He ate more M&M's, popping the tab to the diet soda.

I rolled my eyes. "I know they factor alcohol into your plans, and since you're not partaking, you have extra to use. So, enjoy your M&M's and quit complaining."

"Yes, ma'am." He chuckled, giving me one of his rare smiles. He tossed another handful into his mouth, making a big show of eating them.

"Good boy," I teased, his eyes heating at the word. I gulped, the look close to making me give in. I reached over and grabbed the remote, and flipped on the TV.

"Don't you have a TV in your room?" he grumbled but slid down on the pillow closer to me.

"Yep, but it doesn't have you." I watched as he smiled, his cheeks pinking.

"Fair point. So, we watch TV together? Is that what friends do?"

"Yep. And chat. We gotta get to know one another outside of the naked department. You mentioned Willow. How is that?" I turned on my side to look at him, the side of our bodies lining up.

"I'm pretty sure she hates me. I don't know why I expected her to automatically love me, but I did. I envisioned her running toward me, her arms wide as she yelled 'Daddy,' leaping into my arms as I hugged her and swung her around.

Instead, she barely peeked out from behind Jasmine's legs. She barely talks to me, and for some reason, the purple pants I bought her are the wrong kind, and she refuses to wear them," he rambled. It was so cute, and I enjoyed just listening to him talk.

"You're a new person. Just give it time. Who's watching her while you're at away games?" I assumed he'd hired a nanny, but I wasn't sure.

"Matilda. She's the nanny I hired. I don't think she likes me either."

"Wow, two women who didn't fall for Luke Olson's charm right off the bat. What has the world come to," I teased.

"Three," he said, his eyes flicking up to mine. "You didn't either. I had to win you over."

"There you go. You gotta keep trying." My cheeks flamed, and my insides warmed. I had to be careful with him, but falling back into our easy banter filled my soul with happiness.

"Okay, something real about me. I'm a closeted nerd and love anime. I was watching this before you came."

Luke clicked it over to a different channel and explained the characters and plot to me.

"Hmm, so what's that one's deal?"

"Part fox, so cunning magical powers, but he's still a kid, so they're tame."

"They're cute. I like them."

He laughed but smiled, and I think he liked that I hadn't laughed at his interest.

It grew quiet as we watched another episode, the comfortableness between us returning. At some point, my eyes drooped. Luke pushed my hair back, his thumb caressing my cheek.

"You're falling asleep."

"I've been working eighteen-hour days. It's exhausting dealing with baseball players," I groaned.

He chuckled. "I bet. We're bigger divas than people know."

"Especially the superstitious ones." I looked up into his eyes at that. He didn't look mad; he just accepted the truth.

"Want another truth? Let's call it a freebie. I convinced myself my poor playing was your fault so I could see you. I was as mad as I was because it hurt. I really liked you." He stopped, shaking his head like an etch-a-sketch, erasing the word he'd said. "No, *like* you. And that scared me. No one has ever picked me. I've always been a means to an end. My mother, my high school girlfriend, all the ball girls. They didn't like *me*, but what Luke Olson could bring them."

"I didn't even know who you were," I whispered.

"I know. I knew that, too, but I let myself believe you were undercover and lying. It seemed safer to break my heart before I got in deeper. It was dumb. But once I stepped down that path, I had to keep going. Admitting I was wrong and terrified didn't feel good. You didn't give me the yips, Bee; I gave them to myself. Being with you made me feel confident and hopeful. I'm sorry you felt used. I never meant for you to feel that way."

"I believe you." I cupped his cheek, his stubble sharp against my palm.

"I'm worried I'm gonna fuck this up again. You should choose one of the others. They're better guys than me."

"It breaks my heart you don't see how amazing you are. But it doesn't have to be a choice thing. You should talk to Graham." I shrugged my shoulders. "Thank you for opening the door. I'm excited about getting to know you more, Luke Olson. Good night." I leaned forward and placed a soft kiss on his lips. He kept it brief, resting his forehead against mine as he searched my eyes.

"Good night, Slugger." He pecked my lips and sat up,

helping me climb off the bed. His hand held mine as he led me to the door and it felt like it had the first time—natural.

Waving, I smiled as I returned to my room. I felt proud of myself for taking a stand and healing something that had the power to break me. Now, I just had to pray his game didn't falter tomorrow, ruining everything before it started.

Don't fail me now, baseball.

BLAKE

Baseball didn't fail me.

Luke went into game six of the away series with a new attitude. Or at least toward the game. From what I could tell from the stands, he still didn't interact with his teammates. But he played a great game, proving to himself—and thankfully, my vagina—that the magic had been in him all along.

I spent the bus ride back to Wilmington, completing my interviews and learning about the YellowJackets.

Levi was the youngest of five and loved cornbread.

Sal hated the color pink but had three little girls at home, where he was surrounded by it.

Dalton liked country music, and played the guitar.

Every single guy on the yellow bus spent time talking to me, sharing parts of their lives with me, and endearing themselves to me forever.

And while I was sad I hadn't gotten to sit next to Graham or Tucker for the whole ride, I was happy with my progress in cementing myself as part of the team.

Even Ledger had talked to me, surprising the rest of the guys. From what I gathered, everyone on the team respected him—well, most of the team. There were a few jerks on the blue bus, but the yellow bus had a good group—but no one really took the time to talk to him. He was quiet, a bit broody at times, maybe, but he was sweet to his core.

Plus, I secretly loved how he called me Bumblebee. He was my first true friend in Wilmington, and I had no romantic interest in him. Granted, he was gay, but I hadn't remembered that from the first night since I'd been so drunk, so I could've totally caught feelings.

Sure. Sure. You're too wrapped up in four guys. Even you have your limits.

Reprimanding voice aside, I felt accomplished and like I'd proved Mira wrong. Something I wanted to do more of.

Once we returned to Wilmington, we had a day off before we jumped back into six home games. And while things were better with Hawk and me, I chose to spend the day at the movies with Graham and Tucker. Mostly because I figured he'd want to spend his day off with Roxie, and no amount of truce between us would heal the pain of hearing his sex noises with another woman.

When the home game series started, I regretted not going home with Graham and Tucker the night before. Because my victory over Mira was short-lived. She used it to keep me busy non-stop over the six games. Early mornings, meetings during lunch, and late nights editing left me with little to no energy to do much of anything else.

I barely saw any of the guys outside of them playing. Even Hawk, I didn't see all that much. After finally getting my license renewed on our day off, I'd been driving myself in Bryce's car to Champion Field, missing Hawk in the mornings. Then, I would be asleep when he returned in the evenings. We were roommates, but it felt more like ships passing in the night.

The positive—the YellowJackets were playing amazing baseball, and I felt as if I'd finally discovered my role within the organization. My dad had been pleased as attendance increased and the team's overall morale improved.

The negative—every other area of my life suffered. There was no balance, and I was miserable. Mira kept demanding more and more of my time, and I didn't know how much more of myself I could give. I needed time to unwind, to recharge my battery, and to have something outside of the baseball diamond that made me happy.

Right now, there was only time for sleep, work, and eating. All work mode Blake made me cranky.

Graham, Tucker, and I still texted daily, but it was often check-ins and funny memes. I appreciated their attempts to help me destress and not get upset that my time had been stolen. Because that was what had happened. Mira capitalized on my positive changes and desire to do well, pushing me to give her my all.

I kept fighting it, trying to squeeze in a few video sessions together, but even those hadn't lasted long with me falling asleep midway through. Graham and Tucker were wonderful, constantly reassuring me they were interested in me and not just the sexual stuff. It filled me with confidence and reinforced their earlier claims. They were my constant, my foundation in an ever-changing background.

The most significant shift was with Luke. He'd taken our peace talk to heart and actively worked on being my friend and earning some benefits. He would send me two truths and a lie every morning, and I would send one in return. However, I'd come to believe all his facts were true, making me like him even more, knowing he wasn't lying even in a game.

So far, I'd learned he loved to cosplay and went to conventions where he had a group of people he met up with. His middle name was Oliver, making his initials LOO, which made me laugh so hard that every time I looked at him that day, I broke out into peals of laughter. He also feared clowns, enjoyed showing off his pecs—no duh—and his first endorsement deal was for a shaving cream company. He still had a storage locker full of the product and wondered if he'd ever get through it all.

Seeing him around the stadium now and earning a smile instead of his scowl was nice. I looked forward to those texts each day, coveting them like a dragon with their gold.

While I didn't see much of Hawk, he continued to bring me coffee each day. I'd also find my favorite foods in the fridge when I'd get home, making dinner easy. I had a sneaky suspicion he did it on purpose, knowing I'd end up eating cereal otherwise.

I kept looking for signs of Roxie in the house, but I'd yet to see any. And since it was easier to pretend she didn't exist if I didn't see her, I also didn't ask.

Denial was an excellent coping tool.

Heading into the second away game series, the Yellow-Jackets were 13-5, feeling confident about playing the Tallahassee Strikers. I was hopeful I'd have more time to myself, but of course, Mira joined us on this leg to observe me, occupying even more of my time than back in Wilmington.

The stalker metaphor appeared more likely each day or she wanted to clam jam me. Either theory was about to end with me locking her in a closet and throwing away the key.

The worst part was that it felt like a weird test. To see if I would tattle to my father to make it stop or if I was capable of enduring her torture. It was the people-pleaser Olympics, and I had a gold medal—even if I was reformed now. Sorta. I was working on it.

So endure I shall for the time being. I wasn't giving in just yet. Even if I was sick of my own hand and had replaced the batteries in my bullet vibrator two times already.

Yawning, I climbed onto the yellow bus and headed to the seat in the back. Game six against the Strikers had run over into extra innings, ending after 11 pm. By the time the team showered, met with the press, and grabbed dinner, it was close to one in the morning. At least we got a day and a half off after this series, even if we had to deal with a bus ride home first. I couldn't believe I'd been doing this job for over a month.

Nodding to the guys still awake as I passed, I noticed the various travel pillows and blankets covering their large frames. I felt terrible as I watched them attempt to find a comfortable position. It was like the ultimate version of Tetris.

Luke's head popped up as I approached, and he gave me a soft smile that I returned. This morning's three truths—let's just call it what it was—involved a disastrous school trip, which superhero he'd be if he had a choice, and his favorite baseball players. The shocking part… Bryce had been part of that list.

It made me curious about their past, but I wasn't brave enough to ask either of them.

"Hey," I whispered, conscious of the sleeping and nosey players. "Good game."

"Thanks. Crazy how that believing in yourself thing works." He gave a sheepish shrug that was cuter than it should be on a professional baseball player.

"For what it's worth, I believed in you. Even when I didn't know you were who you are."

"It's worth more than you realize," he whispered, his green eyes brimming with an emotion I couldn't explain.

I cleared my throat, unsure what to say next. Luke reached into his bag, the same designer bag he had on the plane, and pulled out a bag of candy.

"I got you these for the ride home."

Grinning, I took the candy. "Thanks. My grumbling stomach thanks you, too. I'll, uh, talk to you tomorrow?"

"Yeah, sounds good."

"Okay, goodbye." I waved, feeling dumb, but hurried on

to the back. We'd shared a few kisses briefly, but surrounded by a busload of guys wasn't the time. As I approached, Tucker gave me a flirty look, clearly having watched the entire interaction.

"Nope. Not talking about it right now," I said as I hiked one leg over Graham's lap and wobbled. His hands shot out, landing on my hips to steady me. When his thumbs grazed my bare skin, it sent heat through me, and my tired body suddenly woke up. I froze, my legs bracketing him as I glanced down. My hair fell forward, creating a bubble of only our heads.

I licked my lips, and his eyes tracked the movement, his hands flexing unconsciously. This was the most I'd been touched in weeks, and my body sang from the contact. We held one another's gaze, the tension heavy between us. Before I could say anything, or do more precisely, Tucker popped his head through my curtain of hair, bringing his face uber close to both of our mouths.

"What are we doing? Is this the new clubhouse?" he asked, his brown eyes sparkling.

Graham rolled his, dropping one hand from my waist to push Tucker away. With the spell broken, I continued to the space they'd saved for me in the middle and plopped down. This seat had unofficially become theirs and mine when I had time to use it. I'd been forced to ride with Mira on the way here, but thankfully, she'd left earlier today, leaving me on my own for the first time in weeks.

Tucker slid my bag under the seat, then covered my legs with a blanket I hadn't noticed. Graham pulled down the tray in front of me and placed a water bottle and a food container on it. God, I loved how they took care of me. It wasn't like with my mom, where it felt more obligatory, but with GT, it was how they showed they cared. It was nurturing and completely them.

"You got me food?" I asked, my mouth watering.

"It's just a baked potato, but I figured it was better than nothing. I didn't think you got to eat when we did." Graham shrugged his shoulders, his cheeks heating.

Tucker leaned into my side. "He went through ten until he picked that one and then had to fight half the team from trying to steal it from him," he whispered.

Smiling, I placed a kiss on Graham's cheek. "Thank you, Teddy Graham." I giggled as he rolled his eyes, Tucker cheering behind me.

"You're stuck with it now," Tucker taunted, doing a dance with his arms.

Graham huffed and rolled his eyes like he was put out by it, but I could tell he secretly liked it. The bus pulled away from the Striker's stadium a few minutes later, and our journey back to North Carolina began. I opened the baked potato, my stomach growling as the smell hit me. The next few minutes were a blur as I devoured the thing, not even caring who watched.

Fluffy potato with butter and sour cream, a hint of cheese, and bacon. It was perfect, and I wasn't ashamed to lick up every drop. Sitting back when I was done, I remembered the two men beside me and glanced at them.

Tucker's eyes were wide, his pupils blown, and his mouth slightly open as he stared at me with a bit of awe. Graham's face was more subdued, but I could see the pleased expression in his eyes, the smug smile on his lips as it tipped at the corner.

"Dude. I've never been turned on by a potato before. It gives a whole new meaning to *Hot Potato*," Tucker groaned, shifting something hard in his pants. I blinked, realizing what it was.

"Oh. Um. Sorry?" I cringed.

Tucker's face snapped to mine; his brows creased as he stared at me. "Why? I'm only sorry I can't do anything about it right now. Though…" he trailed off, his scheming face on as he tapped his lip in thought and glanced around.

Almost like the bus agreed with him, the overhead lights blinked out, leaving only the runway ones lit. The bus was pitch black since the other guys had their overhead lights off. The bus was quiet, just the occasional conversation happening as men slept, watched a movie, or talked with their families. Being so late, most of them opted to sleep.

But there was no doubt that everyone was distracted or occupied, not paying a lick of attention to the three of us in the back. Graham and Tucker stared at me, the hunger evident in their eyes, waiting to see what I'd do.

My breath caught in my throat as I looked between the two guys. My heart thumped hard in my chest, and I swallowed. I'd been horny for weeks with no opportunities to explore things. I didn't know what Tucker had in mind, but I knew it would be risky. After the way the past twelve days had gone, it made me not want to waste this moment regardless of the risk. Before I could overthink it, I nodded and cleared my throat.

"What did you have in mind?" I whispered.

As soon as Tucker had the green light, his whole face changed, and the confident lover I believed him to be emerged. His fingers grazed my ear as he pushed my hair behind it, his lips brushing against the lobe as he lowered his mouth.

"Did you know that Graham is a great storyteller? It's all those books he reads, you see."

"Yeah?" I glanced over at Graham; his body turned toward me as he stared intently at me.

"Do you want to hear one?" Graham asked, his voice low and husky.

I nodded, biting my lip as my body responded, anticipating what was to come. "Yes. Please, tell me a story, G."

His eyes lit up for a second at the shortened name, the

corners of his mouth tilting in happiness as he stared at me. Then, like a switch, he went into business mode, telling Tucker and me exactly what to do.

"Tuck, give me your pillow, and keep the trays down. Bee, lean back and place your legs over ours under the blanket, and whatever you do, don't make a sound."

"Bossy Graham is hot," Tuck whispered in my ear, tossing the pillow to Graham and tugging my leg over his thigh.

My leg nudged up against his erection, and I gasped, waiting for him to pull away. But Tucker wasn't embarrassed, and if anything, he smirked bigger, pressing it harder into my thigh, letting me know how much he wanted this. His large hand rubbed up and down my leg, sending tiny shivers through me, and goosebumps littered my skin.

"Fuck, I've missed you. I think about you constantly." He trailed his nose up the column of my neck, hitching my breath. "The things I want to do to you, honey bee." Tucker placed an open-mouthed kiss on my throat, his tongue hot on my skin as he licked me. I shivered, fighting hard to hold in my gasp. "It's been pure torture these past few weeks. Seeing you, wanting you, but unable to touch you." My hands clutched their forearms, my fingernails biting into their skin.

"I love how responsive you are. I can't wait until we can hear how loud you'll get," Tucker hummed. "Do you agree, Graham?"

"I think I could come just from the sounds she's making now," Graham purred. My body involuntarily responded, shuddering and soaking my panties.

"Holy fuck, Bee, my cock is practically weeping already. If you keep making sounds like that, I'll pull you onto my lap and fuck you right here, not caring who hears you," Tucker warned.

My eyes widened, and I licked my lips, not wholly opposed to the idea despite knowing it wasn't a good one.

"She likes that idea, Tuck. We'll have to table that for

another day, though. This bus ride isn't merely long enough to get away with it," Graham whispered, nearly making me wish it was happening right now.

Tucker squeezed his cock through his joggers, the blanket hanging off his legs as he rubbed himself, his head thrown back. A small wet patch had developed, and I felt relieved to know I wasn't the only one making a mess of their pants.

"Fine. Tell us that story, G," Tuck whispered, letting out a lungful of air.

"Anything you're not okay with?" Graham asked me.

I snorted, shaking my head. "You're asking that the wrong way, remember? Disaster of sex. I'm pretty inexperienced in the grand scheme of things."

Graham smirked, taking my chin between his fingers. "I'll take care of you, Sunshine. Do we have your consent?"

"Yes," I breathed, the sound barely capable of escaping as he sealed his lips with mine. It was soft, full of want and longing, promising me much more than the back of the bus could give.

"My turn," Tucker said when Graham pulled back. My face was turned to him, his mouth taking over mine before I could process it. Tucker gave me his trademark kiss, making it playful, as he peppered me with little pecks before swiping his tongue inside my mouth and then pulling back.

It amazed me how much their kisses were like them—Graham, sweet and steady, and Tucker, fun and playful.

"If we had all the time in the world, we'd lay you out and show you how being with two guys simultaneously would be," Graham promised, his voice wrapping around me like warm butter on a hot pancake. His hand on my thigh moved up and down, making me antsy as I waited to see what he'd do or say next. I needed him to do something.

"Have you done that before? Been with the same woman?" I asked, unable to help myself. I suddenly needed to know.

"Nope. You'd be the first," Tucker answered, nuzzling his nose in my neck some more. "You smell so fucking good. Like sunshine, Crackerjacks, and baseball."

"Do you like knowing you'd be the first girl we've been willing to share?" Graham asked.

"Yes," I said, licking my lips. "Tell me more."

Graham's eyes sizzled as he turned his body more toward me. As it was, they'd created a barrier so no one could see past him if they walked back this far. Well, as long as they weren't giants and didn't happen to lean over the seat in front of us. Even then, the tray and blanket provided a barrier. They might guess, but there wouldn't be any evidence, at least, making me feel beautifully brazen.

"Tucker would undress you, revealing your body to us inch by inch. He'd lick and lave at your nipples until they were hard peaks and glistening from his mouth."

My nipples pebbled at the mention of the treatment, and I kept my hands on their thighs, tightening my grip. *That sounded good. Yes, let's do that.*

"While he showered your tits with love, I'd do the same to your pussy, licking you right up the center and flicking my tongue on your clit. Once we had you good and edged, I'd tease you with the tip of my finger."

Tucker's hand ran up my thigh, dipping into my shorts and grazing my soaked panties. He groaned into my neck when he felt how wet they were, nudging my hand to stroke him. As I rubbed the outside of his joggers, he hooked his finger into my panties and ran it up the center, coating it in my wetness.

"She's soaking wet, G. Just as I thought she'd be that first bus ride," he murmured. "Keep going, Teddy Graham. Our girl is craving it."

"*Please*," I begged, not even caring how needy I sounded.

Graham's hand moved between my legs, his fingers joining Tucker's as they worked together, stroking me. He nibbled at my neck lightly with his teeth, and I had to bite my cheek to keep my moan in.

"I can smell your arousal, Blake. It makes me wish I could drop to my knees and taste you right fucking now."

He pushed in next to Tucker, and they moved in tandem, pressing in deep. Feeling brave, I pulled down Tucker's pants and stroked his cock. It was hot against my hand, my palm sliding smoothly up and down. I spread the pre-cum with my thumb, Tucker's head falling back against the chair as I touched him. His finger kept a rhythm with Graham's, and I nearly toppled over.

"We'd bring you to orgasm after orgasm until your legs shook and you couldn't hold yourself up. Then we'd take turns fucking you, watching each other as you got close, stopping and switching, and not letting you come again until you were out of your mind with need."

I whimpered, clamping my lips shut to keep the rest in. Graham's thumb flicked against my clit, their joined fingers pumping in and out in perfect precision, and I watched Graham lick his lips as I stroked his best friend, his eyes glued to my hand around Tucker's dick. Tucker still seemed oblivious, but I saw how he watched Graham and wondered if he even understood their connection.

Squeezing Tucker's cock, I pulled Graham's mouth to mine as I came, screaming my release into the kiss. He eagerly kissed me back, his fingers not stopping until my body quit quaking. It wasn't until I broke it that I realized Tucker had also come, my hand coated in his release.

Tucker pulled out his fingers covered in my cum, licking them as he stared at me. His eyes rolled back, a muffled moan emanating from him.

"Fuck, you taste good. I should call you Blakeberry—my new favorite fruit. What do you think, G?" he asked, glancing over at his friend.

"He should try this instead." I lifted my hand covered in

Tucker's cum and placed it on Graham's lips. His tongue darted out, tasting the liquid, his eyes bouncing to his friend. Tucker was frozen as he watched us, his brown eyes so blown, they were almost black as he watched his best friend clean off his cum.

"Shit." We both froze at his words, only relaxing when he continued. "That's hot. Here, try this too." I didn't know what he meant until he pulled Graham's hand from my still sensitive pussy and placed them next to mine on Graham's lips. Even though it was his hand, Graham let Tucker control him, keeping us connected in this moment.

Tucker moaned, the sound deep and heady, and sent a new jolt of desire to my aching pussy. Graham looked like he was two seconds away from shoving Tucker's hand into his mouth when the door to the bathroom opened, jolting us all back to reality. Thankfully, whoever it was didn't glance backward and continued to their seat. Hopefully, they hadn't seen anything on their way in since the three of us had forgotten.

"Here, let me clean you up," Graham said, pulling out some wet wipes from his bag and cleaning me. It was tender and soft, making me feel cared for in a way I'd never experienced. He even took each finger and wiped it clean, too.

"What about me?" Tucker dared, pointing to his stomach. His soft cock laid against his abs. Graham halted, his eyes glancing up to his friend's.

"Such a princess," he teased, before shrugging and following through, wiping Tucker's abs and around his dick before tossing them all into a trash bag. Tucker had frozen, his face shocked that he'd gone through with it and perhaps a little turned on by the act if the twitch in his dick was anything to go by.

Yeah, I didn't think Tucker being into Graham was as big of a stretch as Graham imagined, and I'd gladly help these two open up about their feelings. It was the least I could do with how much they'd helped me.

The bus rolled into Champion Field in the early hours of the morning, the sun rising as it came to a stop. After our busgasm—as Tucker called it—we cuddled up and slept for the remaining hours. My eyes were heavy as I descended the stairs, and I couldn't wait to go to bed.

"You coming with me, Blazy?" Hawk asked, taking me by surprise. It was the first time he hadn't demanded it.

I nodded and followed him to his car after grabbing my bags. Unfortunately, Bryce's place was still being worked on, according to my dad, which meant I was stuck at Hawk's for the time being. However, I didn't hate it as much as I expected. Even though we hadn't seen much of each other, it was nice knowing I wasn't alone. That had been harder to adjust to than I'd expected those few nights at Bryce's without him.

"So, how's Roxie?" I asked, knowing I needed to get over this hurdle. If we were going to be friends, I needed to support his relationship—even if it killed me.

"I assume she's good. We didn't text much outside of her sending me pictures of Sunny."

"Oh." *Because you had phone sex every night?*

It was a weird answer, and I didn't have the brainpower to deal with it. So I turned my head against the window, wondering how long it took to get over a broken heart. Surely, it would be any day now. Right?

Okay, baseball. Help a girl out.

HAWK

BLAKE WAS QUIET THE REST OF THE WAY TO MY HOUSE, HER HEAD against the window. I knew I should've told her the truth about Roxie, but I felt myself clamming up every time I opened my mouth. The more time she spent with Olson, Jameson, and West, the more I worried I no longer had a chance. So, I'd selfishly kept the truth to myself, hiding the Roxie information to keep that thin shield of protection.

Because what if I told her and she didn't care?

I wouldn't survive her rejection.

As usual, a million questions, like how she spent the past three years, would emerge when I was around her. But each time I opened my mouth to ask, nerves hit me, and nothing came out. I was used to feeling that way with others, but never with Blake.

So, instead of learning about her life and rebuilding our connection, I just kept leaving her coffee and food because I couldn't find the words to talk to her.

By the time we pulled into the driveway, I itched to get out of the car, the anxiety pressing tight against my chest with another failed moment. The air was tense with all the words we hadn't said as we went inside. Blake kept her gaze focused ahead, not looking at me once.

My body was heavy with guilt and fear as I unlocked the door, shoving it open for Blake to enter. Her intoxicating scent of sunflowers and apples wafted up to me as she passed, and I clenched my jaw, my hand itching to reach out and haul her into my arms.

I'd thought having her back as a friend was what I needed. But now I wasn't sure if it was any better. I wanted more each moment I spent in her presence, and the crumbs I was given weren't enough to sustain me anymore.

Because knowing what she felt like beneath me, how she sounded when she came, and what she tasted like was its own level of torture. Knowing those things made it impossible to accept scraps. The urge to kiss her was always there, my feelings roaring back to life like nothing had transpired between us. Like three years and distance hadn't existed.

I'd been deluding myself with Roxie. Blake's distance had been a false sense of security, diluting my love for her. But now that she'd returned to my stratosphere, I knew she was the only one for me.

And where before I could distract myself with casual sex, I knew it wouldn't work anymore. The scary part was I didn't know where that left me. Was I destined to live in this perpetual purgatory where everything I wanted was just out of reach, and every replacement was only a cruel substitute?

I knew I should either find the courage and tell her how I felt or put distance between us so I could try to recover. But the uncertainty of both left me in this weird limbo where I wanted to show her I cared without scaring her off.

It would have to be enough for now.

Blake dropped her bag in the princess room, immediately opening Sunny's cage and scooping him out. She cooed at him, cradling his furry body to her face as she rocked back and forth. A warmth bloomed in my chest, knowing I'd given her that.

I always told everyone I got Sunny for the girls, but really, I knew how much my Blazy had wanted a hamster growing up. But with her illness and baseball's long schedule, her parents had never gotten her one. It had been a way for me to have something for her, a little piece of Blake with me.

I also liked having that secret piece of her without anyone knowing. Watching her with him now—the hamster named after her—my heart wanted to burst out of my chest. It was too perfect, too overwhelming, almost like that good burn in your muscles after an intense workout.

The pain hurt, but it felt good and worth it at the same time.

I was intimately aware of how empty it felt to be out of her life, so I would gladly take this feeling instead, even if it never became more. I guess I'd just accepted my fate.

Leaning against the doorframe, I soaked her in, needing my Blake fix for the day. Her eyes glanced up but then dropped down as she moved toward her bag.

"I was going to make breakfast for dinner. Want anything?"

Her blue eyes captured mine like they always did, the whole world stopping while I was held in their grips. Blake blinked, the moment disrupted as she dropped my gaze.

"Yeah, sure."

"Cool." I cleared my throat, trying not to be offended by her standoffish behavior. "Do you want your usual?"

Blake gave me a soft smile, one corner ticking crookedly as her cheeks pinked.

"You still remember?"

"Of course." I nodded, shifting my arms and not dropping her eyes. I remembered everything about her. Hadn't she noticed?

"Yeah, pancakes sound perfect," she said, giving me

another smile before returning to her bag. She paused as her hands wrapped around something before dropping it back into the bag and pulling out her dirty clothes.

Stomping to my room, I tossed my bag onto my bed, kicked off my shoes and jeans, and pulled on athletic shorts. Feeling a little reckless, I pulled off my shirt and kept my chest bare, smirking at my tactic.

I'd accepted my fate as her friend only, but it didn't mean I couldn't push her buttons. Because at least when I tested them, I got a bigger response from her. I knew it was dangerous territory. But it was better than the polite indifference I'd come to know lately.

I grabbed my phone and called Roxie to tell her I was home and thank her again for feeding Sunny. Once that was done, I opened the pantry and pulled out everything to make her favorite campfire pancakes. It shouldn't have surprised me to notice I had everything in stock. Even when she was away, she was still with me.

I could try to convince myself I wasn't still in love with her, but it was hopeless. Once I had everything, I started on the batter, mixing it and heating the griddle. Blake headed into the bathroom just as my phone rang. Seeing she was occupied, I hit the speaker button when I spotted Bryce's name.

"Hey man, what's up?" I asked, trying to keep my voice even.

"Ah! You do exist. I was starting to wonder if you'd been arrested or something." He chuckled, but the sound was strained. "It's been almost a week since I've heard from you."

"Sorry, man. Things have been crazy on the road, and I've been working extra hours with West and Jameson," I explained, hoping it didn't sound as weak as it felt. He hummed the sound heavily.

"They've been playing well. I can tell you've been

working with them," Bryce said, letting my lie rest between us. "How's BB?"

I cleared my throat. "She's good. Things are good." My voice cracked on the second sentence, and I anxiously cleared it.

"She's not giving you any trouble?"

Far from it.

"Nothing I can't handle."

"Any more issues with Davis?"

"Nope. Nothing since I reminded him of his place."

"Good." Bryce growled, the sound menacing. But it worked to give us a neutral thing to focus on. "If I ever see him, he better watch out. The shit stain doesn't deserve to keep playing."

"Yeah, well, I think he'll be running the other direction for a while. His face took a while to heal."

Silence hung between us, and I flipped the pancake, stacking it onto the plate. I hated this distance between us but wasn't sure how to fix it. There was so much I wanted to tell Bryce, but I didn't know where or how to start. Words didn't seem adequate enough.

Oddly, it seemed he felt the same. Or maybe there was something he was hiding himself. Whatever the reason, something had disrupted my friendship with Bryce for the first time.

"Your stats are looking great, Bry."

"Yeah, I've been playing well," he answered, clearing his throat. "It's good to be back."

"The team's dynamics better?"

"Of course," he answered too quickly, making me wonder if there was more to that story. "So, um, I messaged Roxie when I hadn't heard from you, and she mentioned that you guys were no longer together."

I looked up, wondering if Blake had heard that. Spotting

the bathroom door still closed, I cleared my throat. "Yeah. We decided we were better as friends."

He started to ask me something else, but I didn't know how much time I had before Blake exited.

"Hey, Bry, can I call you later? I'm making pancakes and don't want to burn them."

"Campfire pancakes?" he asked with a groan.

"Yep."

"Man, I miss those."

"Come back to the minors, and I'll make you some," I teased.

"Nah. I'm good." He laughed. "Give BB my love and tell her to call me later. She's been as bad as you with touching base."

"Sure thing," I said, holding back what I wanted to say.

The only love I want to give her is mine.

"Later."

I hung up and finished the pancakes, stacking them high on the plate. I quickly diced up the strawberries and heated the fudge while I scrambled some eggs. When everything was ready, I called out to Blake as I set the island.

"Food's ready."

The bathroom door opened, and I heard her approach as I finished making her coffee. Her feet stuttered, and I glanced up, wondering what the problem was. Her eyes were fixed on my bare chest, tracking over all my tattoos.

I'd forgotten my ploy during my talk with Bryce. Triumph over her response was temporary, though, as I noticed her outfit and wondered who really had the upper hand here.

Blake wore tight spandex shorts that barely covered her ass, along with a long tank shirt with large holes on the side showcasing her bra underneath.

It wasn't anything scandalous. Yet she looked sexy as hell.

I gulped and forced my gaze back to the coffee, finishing it and setting it on the island beside her plate. I suddenly felt very uncomfortable sitting next to her; another awkward silence on the horizon.

"Do you want to watch something while we eat?" I asked, motioning toward the living room.

Blake glanced over where I'd motioned, her eyes roaming over the sofa before she nodded. "Yeah. Sounds good."

"Fix your pancakes, and I'll take over the coffees."

She followed my instructions, making me happy we'd moved past her denying everything I asked. Blake followed me to the living room once she had marshmallow, fudge, and pancakes on her plate and sat on the couch. I placed TV trays in front of us, making eating easier.

We settled into a comfortable silence as I searched for something to watch. When I came upon a movie we'd watched together one summer when Bryce and I had been ball boys, I paused and looked at her.

"Do you remember when we first saw this?" I asked.

She laughed, covering her mouth as she took a big bite. I watched her intently as she swallowed. "Oh, yeah. Was this the one where you kissed me and then ran away?" she teased, pushing my shoulder.

I snorted, taking a bite of plain pancakes and giving myself time to think, the place she'd touched my shoulder still tingling.

"Teenage Hawk was a bit of a coward."

"Just teenage Hawk?" I heard her whisper, halting the words in my throat. I picked up my fork and shoved eggs into my mouth this time, hoping I wouldn't have to answer.

Because, yeah, Adult Hawk was also a coward.

I'd done the right thing my whole life toward Blake; the only time I'd given in had been on her wedding night. And then that had blown up epically in my face the following day.

But did I still need to keep living that motto? What was the right thing anymore?

Bryce wasn't here, and Blake was.

Was Roxie right? Would he eventually get over it? Only wanting us to be happy in the end? But was that even what would make her happy now?

I spaced out the rest of the movie, shoveling food into my mouth as my thoughts swirled and I debated with myself. When the credits rolled, I realized how in my head I'd been.

"Thanks for the pancakes. I'm gonna"—she yawned—"catch some sleep."

"It's been a long day," I agreed, nodding.

"Yeah. I'm so looking forward to our day off." She smiled one of her genuine smiles, stalling my breath as she took our plates and placed them in the sink.

"Sleep well," I called out, remembering to use my words as she entered her room. Blake waved, shutting the door behind her with a click.

Standing, I returned to my bed, all the thoughts and feelings clamoring in my head. I needed to talk it out with her. Being a coward wasn't who I wanted to be. We'd repaired things somewhat already, so I had to trust we could be open and honest with one another, too.

When I couldn't handle the uncertainty, I climbed out of bed and marched to her door. My hand froze in the air as a light moan escaped beneath the door.

Bracing my hands on the doorframe, I tried to decipher if what I heard was real or my imagination. Resting my forehead against the door, my cock thickened in my shorts as her breathy moans filtered out the bottom of the door.

I lifted my head, pressing it more into the door, stopping myself from barging in when the minimal contact pushed the door open. The latch clicked open, releasing the door, and I remembered it didn't work. I'd meant to fix it but hadn't gotten around to it yet. In this second, I was suddenly very glad I hadn't.

The view that presented itself trapped me, locking me in

place. I gripped the overhead doorframe, my eyes locked on her.

Blake was on the floor, a pillow behind her head as she plunged a dildo between her legs. Her free hand gripped her breast as the other continued to move in and out of her pussy. Her skin was flushed pink, and her orgasm was near as she writhed on the floor.

I was caught in a trance of her, my dick fully involved now as I watched. Need pounded in my veins; my shorts tented as my cock throbbed, the tip leaking.

An unbridled moan escaped me before I could stop it, and Blake's eyes snapped open and spotted me in the doorway.

I expected her to stop or roll over in embarrassment, but instead, she kept going, her blue eyes never leaving mine.

A second later, she shuddered around the dildo, her orgasm taking her as she came. It was ravishing, and it was only with tremendous effort that I remained standing, my legs threatening to give out.

Blake sat up slowly as she was done, pulling what I could now see was an odd-looking dildo from her pussy. She kept watching me, waiting for something.

"Why are you masturbating on the floor?" I asked when I couldn't take her stare.

She smirked, standing. "That's what you want to ask?"

Her confidence was sexy as she stared at me, almost daring me. No longer was she nervous or shy about her body. She embraced her sexuality, making me want her even more. My eyes raked over her, noticing where her curves had filled in since I last saw her naked. Her hips and butt were rounder. Perfect for me to grab onto.

My eyes refused to leave her, wanting to memorize every new detail about her. When she spoke, I tried to remember what I'd asked.

"It had felt wrong to do that in your niece's bed," she said, pulling me from my inventory.

"Right." I licked my lips, continuing to stare.

"Did you need something?" she asked, quirking an eyebrow like I hadn't just watched her orgasm.

All thought had left my brain as I stared, my dick hard and leaking, tenting my shorts and not hiding how much she turned me on.

"Bryce called earlier. I forgot to tell you to call him. He wanted to know how you were doing."

The instant the words were out of my mouth, I knew they were the wrong thing to say as the sexual tension between us instantly shriveled up, and her mask fell back into place. Blake grabbed the closest item of clothing and pulled it on.

"Right, okay, thanks. Close the door behind you," Blake said as she grabbed her phone and the strange-looking dildo, brushing past me to head to the bathroom. It shut forcibly, leaving me with a curse on my lips.

As I returned to my room, I fell onto my bed and shoved my shorts down as I gripped my cock in my hand, stroking it root to tip. New images of her swirled with my memory of our night together, merging together. I stared down at my hand, wishing it was her pussy.

"Looks like it's just you and me, bud."

Stroking myself faster, I recalled how it felt to be inside her. How tight she'd been, her warmth and wetness wrapping around my dick. Quicker than I'd come in a long time, I spurted out thick ropes of cum. They landed on my abs as my balls emptied themselves, everything in me spilling out. I quickly cleaned myself up before passing out, promising to try again later.

Because if one thing was certain, I was done denying myself. I had to trust in my relationship with Bryce that we'd survive this. Because I didn't know if I could anymore without her.

BLAKE

My cheeks heated as I washed the rainbow and glittery unicorn dildo I'd discovered in my bag with a note from Graham and Tucker to have fun. I'd almost fainted when my hands wrapped around it, worried Hawk would see it.

Welp, the joke was on me. He saw it all right. And in use!

Shaking my head, I cleaned the toy and left it to dry on the counter. There was no use in hiding it now. Throughout dinner, I'd debated what to do with it. After the tension between myself and Hawk had become too much, I'd hurried back to my room to do just what the note said… have fun.

I'd even planned to send them a video of me using it as a little thank you. What I hadn't expected was Hawk's interruption. The thing I couldn't make heads or tails of was what confused me the most: how he'd responded.

He'd been turned on.

Not only had Hawk stayed after stumbling into the room, but the tent in his pants gave away exactly what he thought about my unintentional show.

But he had a girlfriend.

Feeling tied up in knots over everything, I knew standing

in the bathroom wouldn't solve anything. Peeking out the bathroom door, I was relieved—and slightly disappointed—when he was no longer standing there. Pulling on a shirt I'd stolen from Graham and a pair of borrowed boxer shorts, I sat cross-legged on the bed and dialed my brother's number, who answered on the first ring.

"Baby Sis!"

"Hey, Bry. How are you?"

"I'm good, good. I feel like I haven't spoken to you in ages. What's going on?" he asked, his voice lined with concern. Another unintentional side effect of working so much was that my calls with Bryce, Emory, and my parents suffered. However, I'd unintentionally ignored Bryce more as I processed my feelings for his nemesis.

"I'm finally feeling like I fit with the team. It's been exhausting, though. Mira has me working eighteen-hour days." I gave a dry laugh. "You settled into your new place yet?"

My mind drifted as Bryce talked about his new place and the batting regimen he'd started, and I replayed everything that had happened in the past month.

"How are you doing with Hawk?" he asked, returning me to the conversation.

"Oh, we're fine. Sorry, I caused so much damage." I grimaced. While I'd called Dad, I hadn't had the guts to face Bryce yet. I picked at the comforter as I listened.

"Not your fault, BB. I'm sorry you're having to deal with it alone."

"Dad's been doing most of it, and I guess he delegated *me* to Hawk."

"Yeah, but I'm glad you're at his place. I worry about you." I could hear the love in his voice, and I softened. Bryce had always been my biggest protector.

"No need to worry about me. I'm doing great."

"Uh-huh. Like that thing with Davis?"

I groaned, dropping my head into my hands. I was so over Pukey. "I took care of Pukey. I handled it."

"Not what I heard." The steel in his voice was unmistakable.

"It's done and over with. There's nothing else to do, Bry."

"You realize if I ever see him—"

"Stop, Bryce. I'm not fifteen anymore. You can't bully guys into fearing you. I'm gonna make mistakes. I'm gonna have flings. I'll date some winners and some losers. That's part of it. I don't question you about your love life, so please, just let me manage my own. It's hard enough as it is without having an overbearing brother threatening to hurt someone because I'd stupidly trusted them."

I sucked in a breath, holding it for a few seconds before letting it out, calming my heart that had sped up. I'd never disagreed with Bryce before. This was big for me.

"So I shouldn't bring up the other players you've been chummy with?" he questioned, but his tone was lighter this time.

"Definitely not," I grumbled. "I never knew baseball players were so gossipy."

"Ha! What else do you think they have to do on those long bus rides?"

"Mm-hmm. Sure."

"But seriously, BB, I'm not judging, and you're right. You don't pester me about mine, so I'll try to be better. It's just hard when you're my little sister. I don't want anyone to take advantage or hurt you."

"I know you mean well, and I love you for that. If I need advice, I promise to come to you first."

"Not Emory?" he teased.

"Well." I laughed, the lightness returning between us.

"How's Hawk doing?" he asked, blessedly changing the subject. "I was shocked Roxie and he broke up."

"What! He broke up with Roxie?" I screeched.

"Actually, he said she did a couple of weeks ago, before the first away series, I believe."

"What the actual fuck!" I hissed.

"Something you need to tell me, Sis?" he asked, his tone suspicious.

"No. It's just, y-you know," I stuttered, "I've been living here for over three weeks, yet he said nothing. I thought we were friends. That's all," I backpedaled, attempting to calm my racing heart. My hands shook, and my vision spun. There was no way…

"Don't take it personally. Hawk doesn't share his feelings willingly. I only found out because Roxie spilled the beans after I hadn't heard from either of you."

"Oh." My mind spun with this information—they had broken up almost a month ago.

So, did that mean? Was he? Was I?

I couldn't think about any of that with my brother on my phone. So, I quickly wrapped up the call.

Well, I tried to, but Bryce had other ideas. But finally, I used my voice and asked for what I wanted.

"It's been a long road series. Talk to you later?"

"Yeah, sure. Oh, wait. Mom said you'll be in Charleston in a few weeks?"

"Uh-huh. It's not far from Columbus. Are you home that week? Emory's visiting, so I won't have time to travel to you, but maybe you could come to me."

"Emory?" His voice went high as he choked on the word.

"Yep. She's coming over."

"Cool. That's cool."

Smiling, I remembered I never followed up with either of them about what happened between them. Maybe it would distract him from focusing on my love life for once.

"Yeah, she's interviewing. She might get a job here. Just think, she could be here more permanently."

"Wow, really, that's, um, yeah. Well, I need to go."

"Bye, Bry!" I giggled, loving that I could torment my brother so easily. I fell back onto the bed, my mind racing with everything he'd told me about Hawk. My mind kept rolling around thoughts I couldn't make heads or tails of.

Crackerjack. I needed to talk to somebody and process it. Texting Graham and Tucker about another guy seemed weird, and Luke and I were nowhere near that yet. It was too late to call Emory, and I wasn't all that close to Rue yet. And while Ledger was my friend, he didn't seem like the type to appreciate me sharing my confusing emotional entanglements.

Graham and Tucker, it was!

At the last second, I clicked on Graham's message thread and sent a single message.

> **Blake:** My brother told me that Hawk and his girlfriend are no longer together. In fact, they haven't been together since we left for the first away series.

> **Graham:** How does that make you feel?

> **Blake:** Wow. I didn't realize you became a therapist overnight.

> **Graham:** *laughing emoji*

> **Graham:** Don't avoid the question. It's a valid one.

> **Blake:** Fine. I'm confused. A little angry he hasn't said anything. Nervous he doesn't want me. Scared he'll reject me. Afraid it will mess up everything.

> **Graham:** That's all?

> **Graham:** It seems natural to feel all of that. What's the issue?

Blake: It feels selfish. Or like I'm cheating by hoping he wants more.

Graham: Did I miss a conversation where we put a label on things?

Blake: No. *pouty face*

Graham: I thought the entire purpose was to allow you to explore without judgment? Besties with benefits, remember?

Blake: It feels too good to be true. Like I'm using you both.

Graham: You're not. We're all being open. That's the key.

Graham: Do you still like us?

Blake: Yes.

Graham: Then we're still on the same page. And we're not making you choose. We just want to be included.

Blake: I need to finish that book.

Graham: If you want, we can talk about it as you're reading.

Blake: Yeah, that'd be great.

Graham: Perfect. Let me know what you think so far.

Blake: Okay, I will. It does make it sound more fun.

Blake: You're really great. I know this is probably weird.

Graham: It's not weird at all. In fact, we should be able to talk about these things, especially if we're going to be more.

Blake: Thank you for making it so easy.

Graham: You're worth it, Sunshine.

Blake: Night, Teddy Graham. I have something to send to both of you.

Before I could talk myself out of it, I closed out the message and sent the video from earlier to the group thread.

Blake: Thank you for my present. Enjoy. *Kissy face*

Turning off all the lights, I lay under the covers as I attempted to fall asleep, but my mind wasn't having it. So I pulled out the book I hadn't picked up in weeks and read. When I finished it, my mind seemed even busier as it raced with possibilities, the new information filtering through. The later it got, the more anger and hurt fueled me, and I concocted a plan.

I'd stayed away once I returned because I believed he'd moved on. But if he was available and still wanted nothing to do with me? That was something completely different.

So, I would make sure he knew what he was missing out on.

Yes, it was petty. But I'd never been rational when it came to matters of the heart with Hawk.

When my alarm went off, I jumped out of bed despite only getting a few hours of sleep last night. Today was a full day off, and I had a new goal in mind.

Operation Break Hawk Anderson.

Throwing on a pair of underwear that showcased my butt cheeks, I kept on Graham's shirt and pulled my hair up into a bun. Spritzing a little body spray, I donned deodorant and brushed my teeth. Good hygiene was sexy.

Grabbing my new best friend out of his cage, I petted Sunny's head as I let him perch himself between my boobs and sauntered into the kitchen. Opening the fridge, it didn't surprise me when I found it fully stocked. Hawk would've used the same service as Bryce did.

Grabbing the ingredients I needed, I turned on some music as I danced around the kitchen with Sunny nestled between my breasts and beat eggs into a bowl, Operation Break Hawk Anderson underway.

"What's this?" a sleepy-eyed Hawk asked as he stumbled into the kitchen.

"Most people refer to it as breakfast," I retorted, my sassy side in full force. I peeked over my shoulder. "I wanted to thank you for letting me stay here," I said innocently.

"By trying to kill me?"

"Ha ha. I can make breakfast." I rolled my eyes, my cheeks heating a little at the insinuation. Culinary skills were not my forte.

He rubbed his eyes, blinking at me with a scrutinizing gaze. "Really though, it's unnecessary. You know I'll always be there for you."

"Right. Because you're like my *brother*," I said with a little more bite than I meant.

Hawk grimaced as he walked over to the coffeepot, hitting buttons and filling mugs as I continued flipping French toast in the skillet. I could feel his eyes on me the whole time. The more he woke up, the more he realized what I wore. His jaw tightened the longer he stared.

Smirking, I reached up to the top cabinet, and my shirt lifted. I heard him groan a moment before a body pressed against me, an arm on either side of the counter, effectively trapping me in a Hawk bubble. His hot breath fanned across my neck, sending shivers through me.

"What do you need, Blazy?" he asked, his voice husky and dark.

I didn't answer with words, purposely rubbing my ass against his front. Hawk's hands moved from the counter, stilling me as he placed them on my hips to stop me.

"Plates," I huffed, turning around and watching him swallow as he stared down at me. When he spotted Sunny, his eyes lit up briefly before he smirked.

"He has the best seat in the house."

Shocked, my mouth dropped open, and my body naturally leaned into his. His fingers flexed against my hips, almost like he'd forgotten he was touching me as we stared at one another. The air between us heated, sparking that familiar inferno between us back to life.

"Why didn't you tell me about Roxie?" I blurted, unable to stop myself.

Hawk didn't respond immediately, his mismatched eyes fixed on my lips. When he lifted them to my eyes, he still didn't give me a straight answer.

"Bryce?" he asked, and I nodded.

His eyes returned to my lips again, and I licked them, his gaze tracking the movement. I wondered for a moment if he told his best friend, my brother, so it would get back to me. Unfortunately for him, he wouldn't get off the hook that easily.

"So? Why didn't you?" I urged.

"I don't know. I didn't even tell him. Not really." He swallowed, his Adam's apple bobbing with the force. "It seemed if I kept it to myself, then I wouldn't have to…"

"Have to what?" I whispered when he stopped.

"It kept you further from me," he admitted, his eyes swirling with something.

"Do you ever think about that day? About telling him?" I whispered, the words falling from my lips before I could stop them. It hadn't been what I'd meant to ask, but I couldn't take them back now.

"Every damn day." His eyes were intense as they seared into me, dropping to my lips for the millionth time. He leaned forward, and my breath caught in my throat right as a sizzling sounded, followed by the beeping of the smoke alarm, interrupting us.

"Crap!" I jumped out of his arms and grabbed a spatula, flipping a very crispy piece of French toast. Oh well, at least all the others were fine. I laughed at the burned masterpiece, dropping it into the trash as Hawk got the smoke alarm to stop.

His mouth tilted up at the corner as he handed me the plates, the energy between us somehow easier now. I plated the food and set it on the island, noticing two mugs of coffee. One made perfectly how I liked it, just like he always did.

I'd been worried he didn't feel anything for me since he hadn't told me. But the more I thought about it, he'd been showing me all along. It wasn't with words, but in the ways he showed me, big and small, how well he knew me. Hawk paid attention to the details—all of them.

Some women might consider a guy noticing their haircut or their outfit sexy, but for me, it was this. And Hawk had been doing it for weeks. I'd just been too stubborn to see it.

"Thanks."

I smiled softly as I took a sip, moaning as the first burst of coffee hit my lips. It was quiet after that as we ate in silence. But it differed from yesterday. This quiet felt more anticipatory... like it balanced on a hairspring trigger between one moment and the next.

When we finished eating, we moved easily to the sink and rinsed the dishes as we cleaned up together. I kept him in my peripheral vision as we worked together, his shoulders more relaxed. I knew I needed to up the tension for my plan to work. Time to activate the next phase of Operation Break Hawk Anderson. It was button-pushing time.

I turned the nozzle toward him and sprayed him with the water. Hawk froze as the cool liquid dripped down his chest, and I instantly realized my mistake. My eyes tracked each little bead of water as it moved over his tattoos, urging me to move forward and lick it from his chest. Because, of course, he hadn't worn a shirt again.

"Are you sure you want to start this war, Blazy?" Hawk growled the sound, and it rumbled out, touching me straight on my clit.

I didn't respond or give him time to retaliate as I resprayed him. Hawk launched forward, trapping the nozzle between us and spraying us both. Thankfully, I'd returned Sunny to his cage before eating breakfast; otherwise, he would be one wet hamster. My giggles ricocheted off the walls as we wrestled for the hose, becoming soaked in the process.

"I concede." I giggled, letting go.

As he pulled it away from both of us, our panting breaths echoed around us as we took in our plastered bodies. All the emotions from earlier roared back to life as we stared, the tension heating the space between us. Hawk glanced back to my lips, licking his own before scorching me with his mismatched gaze, the emotions swirling.

"I won't walk away this time, Blazy. So, if we're doing this, we're doing this."

"I don't want you to walk away," I whispered, my breath catching. "But I can't ignore my feelings for other people either." I swallowed. "Graham believes he has a solution." He shook his head, and my heart dropped. Well, fuck.

"I don't care about any of that right now. I just need to know if you're mine."

"Always. I've always been yours."

Hawk sealed his lips to mine with those words in a punishing kiss full of three years of longing. Three years of anger. Three years of regret.

He kissed me until it turned into joy; into happiness that we'd found our way back here.

Each swipe of his tongue erased the tension between us, bringing us right back to the last place we'd been together. He pulled my wet shirt over my head, the material clinging to me and making a *thawp* sound as it landed on the floor. Laughing, I pulled back as he drew my panties down my legs, watching him as his fingers trailed over my skin. He added them to the pile, lifting me to the counter as my legs wrapped around his waist.

My nipples pebbled from the cold air, and I dug the heels of my feet into his waistband, pushing down his shorts as he sucked on my breast, his beard rough against my skin. I carded my fingers through his hair, ecstatic when I pushed his shorts down. Hawk stepped back, his cock standing at attention as he stroked it once.

My mouth hung open as I stared, the metal jewelry reflecting in the sunlight that filtered through the window.

"That's new," I gasped.

"Just wait," he teased, moving back toward me and dragging me closer. His teeth nipped at my nipple, pain and pleasure exploding as I moaned. My head hit the cabinet, and I clung to him, trying to bring him closer.

"More," I demanded, praying he had a condom close. I didn't think I'd make it if we had to move or wait a second longer.

The sound of a drawer opening and things being flung

out as he searched had me opening my eyes. Hawk reached behind himself; his face triumphant as his fingers closed around a condom wrapper.

Magnum.

It had once sent us spiraling apart when Bryce discovered it on the floor. And now it was getting its redemption arc as it brought us back together.

Hawk sheathed himself in a matter of seconds, gripping my hips and pulling my ass to the edge of the counter, tilting my hips up as he draped my legs over his forearms. He gave me a second to stop him, notching his cock at my entrance.

"Yes," I hissed, needing him more than anything else right then.

He slid in, the stretch familiar but the rubbing of his Jacob's ladder new. My eyes rolled back as I clung to his shoulder, one hand braced behind me as he thrust in deep.

Time seemed to disappear as we fell into a rhythm, everything feeling more intense and overwhelming as we found our way back to this place. I knew we still needed to discuss things, but they didn't seem to matter right now.

Because Hawk was all in, and I was too. There wouldn't be a cleat retreat this time.

The knowledge this wouldn't be one time sent me careening over the edge as I let go of the fear and embraced everything good between us.

"Yes, Hawk, *fuck*," I moaned, my pussy clasping him inside me as my muscles tensed and trembled.

Hawk moaned into my neck, stilling as he jerked in me, his breath hot on my neck.

"Hot damn, I missed that," I gasped.

Hawk pulled back, his eyes light and shiny as he stared at me, an emotion I recognized within myself swirling.

"That's just the warm-up, Blazy. I hope you didn't have plans today because you're not going anywhere."

CHAPTER
THIRTY-THREE

TUCKER

I stared at my phone, urging it to send me a message or some sort of reply. I'd even take a meme or gif at this point. Hours had passed since Blake sent us the best video known to man and then had gone radio silent.

I couldn't even remember how many times I'd jacked off to the sight of her last night. Though if the emptiness in my balls and cum coated sheets could attest, it had been a lot. I wasn't even embarrassed about it. Blake was sexy in a way I'd never encountered before. She was sweet and strong, sassy yet vulnerable, and didn't fall over me just because I was a baseball player. I had to work at it with her, and the challenge-loving part of my brain found that invigorating.

When the black screen stayed dark, I dropped it back to the counter with a groan. It made a thud as it landed, echoing how my heart felt. Graham walked out of his bedroom, shaking his head at my vigil as he filled his cup with more coffee. Once it was full, he leaned against the counter, sipping it as he watched me.

I stared back, my cheeks heating for an entirely different reason as I took in his bare chest and the peppering of chest hair. His joggers hung low on his hips, and I could make out the faintest outline.

Jerking my head back up, I grabbed my glass of water, surprised when it was empty. Graham chuckled, taking it out of my hand and refilling it for me.

"Thanks," I mumbled, not meeting his eyes as my cheeks heated.

"You're welcome, Punk Princess."

My blush grew at the words, and my lips tilted in a satisfied smile. Ever since we started down this path with Blake, my feelings and sexual desires for my best friend had changed. I didn't know if it was because of the journey we were taking together with Blake or something more. Graham kept watching me, sipping his coffee like he didn't have a care in the world.

"What?" I asked when I couldn't take his gaze anymore.

"Nothing." He smirked as he took another sip.

"Yeah, I don't believe that. Go ahead. Say it." I waved my hand in the air in front of me, hoping to get him to say whatever he held in.

"You really like her."

My brows creased at that. It wasn't what I expected him to say. "I thought we already had this conversation," I answered, sighing as I stared down at my hands. "I'm worried she's, I don't know, changing her mind after the bus. What if I pushed her too far?"

"A girl doesn't send a video like that and then change her mind a few seconds later. She was into it, Tuck. Blake has never been dishonest, so trust in that. Besides, she's probably busy talking with Hawk."

I perked up, my eyes snapping to his, which wouldn't meet mine now.

"What do you know?" I asked, practically leaning across the counter like our proximity would force him to answer.

Graham sighed, draining the last of his cup before he

placed it in the sink. He braced his hands on the back of the counter, making his muscles flex in an entirely new way. My eyes trailed over him, unable to stop myself from ogling his half-naked frame, cataloging every twitch of muscle.

"She messaged that her brother told her Hawk and his girlfriend had broken up weeks ago, and she was confused."

My eyes immediately jerked back up. "Wait, what? Does that—"

Graham shook his head, stopping my spiral of thoughts. "It changes nothing, Tuck. She still likes us. We knew she had feelings for Luke and Hawk when we talked with her. Things with Luke have shifted, and now it seems Hawk is finally making his play. We didn't label this because we wanted her to figure things out. So... we have to let her do that." His voice was soft and reassuring, but it did nothing for the panic brewing in my chest.

"I know, but—"

"No buts." He narrowed his eyes at me, his bossy side emerging and spiking my heart rate for an entirely different reason. *Shit, get it together, dude.*

I blew out the air between my lips, making a noise to distract from the fact I needed to slow my pulse. Hanging my head, I ran my finger distractedly across the dark screen of my phone as I admitted my fear.

"It seemed easier when it was just us."

"Don't let your fear of being abandoned ruin this. Trust her, Tuck."

"Sometimes it feels easier not to care," I admitted, picking at the non-existent dust on the counter.

"You don't really believe that," Graham said, moving closer and knocking his shoulder into mine. His body warmed mine, grounding the flighty feelings inside. This was why I was so clingy to him. Graham always made things feel more stable. I pressed back into him, letting his presence remind me people didn't always leave.

"I know." I sighed, closing my eyes and counting.

"How about we check out that new store and see what their sneaker selection's like?"

My head perked up, my eyes wide. Graham spoke my love language now.

"Really? You'd go with me?" He usually tried to get out of sneaker excursions.

Graham rolled his eyes, but his lips tilted up. "Yeah, yeah. Come on. Maybe if we're lucky, I can pick up a new book for Blake."

"You do love me, Teddy Graham!" I cheered, hopping off the stool and almost face-planting into his chest. Graham righted me, his warm hands sending goosebumps over my body. He ignored the nickname, but I swear he smiled. I slapped his butt, my hand stinging at the action.

"That's what you get for touching these buns of steel." Graham flexed the muscles in his ass, making them bounce, and I had to forcibly pull my eyes away. Shaking my head to clear it, I stumbled into my bathroom, my face flaming at the erection in my pants.

I needed to figure out whatever confusing things I felt for him out of the way. I didn't want to ruin our friendship. But as my hand wrapped around my cock in the shower, Graham's voice filled my head from the bus as he dictated what he would do to both me and Blake. Combined with the visual of her squirming on the ground as she fucked herself, I shot my load so quickly that my legs shook and almost gave out under me.

Fuck. I had the hots for my best friend.

Two hours and one pair of new shoes later, I followed Graham around the bookstore as he picked up books, read the blurb, and then placed them back on the shelf. After the tenth one in a row of hot, shirtless guy covers, I'd had enough.

"Can't you just pick one already?" I whined.

"It's a process. I'll know it when I see it."

"Is that a real thing?" I picked one up and flipped it open, my eyes widening at the words on the page. "These are the kind of books you like?"

"What?" he asked, looking over his shoulder, smirking as he read the passage I pointed to. "Yep. You got a problem with smut?"

Graham raised his eyebrow, his gray eyes piercing mine. Gulping, I shook my head and returned the book like it might tell my secret.

"Nope. I just never knew that was what you were reading. Maybe I should give it another try," I admitted, glancing at a cover of two shirtless guys wrapped around one another.

"You can borrow one of mine at home."

"Or," I said, an idea coming to me. "I get the same one you get Blake and we do a read-along. That could be hot."

Graham paused, his hand frozen on a spine. "We'd actually talked about doing something similar last night. You'd want to join?"

"Hell, yes. You had me at smut." Graham snorted, and I smiled, feeling proud of myself. However, it only lasted a minute as he continued his endless search.

"Teddy Graham," I whined, pushing out my lip.

"Go get a pretzel or something. You're hangry." He shooed me off toward the snack bar.

"Fine," I mumbled, stomping off, hating how right he was. Plus, I wasn't being fair to him. I'd taken longer at the shoe store, trying on ten different pairs before I committed to the ones I bought, and Graham hadn't complained once.

Walking up to the counter, I didn't even pay attention to the people around me; I was entirely focused on food and how I could get Graham to give me more attention. Ordering two pretzels, water, and a muffin for Graham, I paid and moved over to the pickup area.

"Hey, sexy, you're Tucker Jameson, right?" a girl asked, sidling up to me.

Shocked at her presence, I whipped my head around, barely registering.

"Yeah." My voice was devoid of emotion, my usual flirty tone gone. I wasn't unused to girls approaching me. It happened a lot. But today, it felt annoying. I just wanted to eat my pretzel and wait for my best friend to pick the perfect book for the girl we both wanted to date.

Scanning over her, I didn't even see her features, my eyes doing it out of reflex. But apparently, she took it for interest and moved closer, placing her hand on my arm. An unwanted feeling coursed through me, and I shifted back, making her hand fall off me.

"My friend and I are both free. Want to take us back to your place?" she cooed, her voice raspy. She stepped closer, pressing her breasts against my arm. Revulsion filled me, and I grabbed my items quickly as they were placed down and jumped away from her like she had cooties.

"No. Sorry. Can't."

Words with girls had always been easy, but suddenly, I couldn't find myself able to say more than one- or two-word answers. Darting off with my goodies, I hurried to the registers, where Graham stood with a bag in his hand.

Of course, he'd seen the whole thing!

He chuckled, his body moving up and down as he held in his laughter.

"Shut up." I stalked off, laughing with him as we exited the store and approached the car.

"Did she ask you to be her sperm donor or something? You looked like she was about to take you back to her place and dissect you!"

Cheeks flaming, I handed him the muffin and water after

checking on my shoes in the back seat where I'd buckled them in. You could never be too careful.

"Worse," I said, biting into my pretzel and chewing. "She invited herself and a friend over."

"For you or both of us?" He snorted.

"Honestly, I don't even remember. All I could think about was getting out of there." I bit more into the pretzel, the salty bread soothing the hungry pit inside me. Damn. I had been hangry.

"Wow, that's a big step for you, Tuck," Graham said, unwrapping his muffin, a tiny smile on his face as he bit into it. Warmth and pride that I'd done something he liked whirled in me. "I don't think you've ever turned down sex before," he added after taking a bite.

I'd been so busy watching him eat that it took a minute for his words to filter through. I froze, realizing how true they were.

"Wow. I guess you're right. It didn't even cross my mind."

"Does this mean our flirty pitcher has finally found a girl he likes enough to settle down?" Graham chuckled, but he wasn't far off from the truth. Add in found a boy, and he'd know my entire truth.

"Yeah, I guess it does."

We finished our snacks in comfortable silence as we processed this revelation.

"What book did you get?" I asked right as our phones went off. We both grabbed them, reading the message.

Blake: I'm glad you liked the video.

Blake: Sorry it's taken me so long to respond.

Graham: You were a sight to behold, sunshine. Sexiest thing I've ever seen.

Tucker: I nutted so many times, I lost count.

"Dude," Graham groaned, rubbing his face. I shrugged. I wouldn't start censoring myself now.

Blake: I'll take that as a compliment.

Tucker: It was.

Tucker: What's your day been like? It's weird not seeing you.

Graham: Don't let him fool you. He's been staring at the phone, waiting.

I punched Graham in the shoulder but couldn't deny he wasn't being truthful. The fucker didn't even flinch, just stuck his tongue out at me.

Blake: I was wondering if you wanted to come over for dinner?

Graham: We've got no plans.

Tucker: Even if we did, I'd drop them for you.

Blake: You sure know how to make a girl feel good.

Tucker: You have no idea, honey bee.

Blake: Things with Hawk have changed, and I think we should hang out.

Graham: He's not going to punch us, is he?

Blake: No.

Blake: I don't think so.

Blake: I'll tell him he's not allowed to.

Tucker: Is this a date?

Blake: Maybe? Or just a hang? I dunno how any of this works.

Graham: I got you a new book, and Tucker wants to join our read-along.

Blake: Really? That's a great idea.

Tucker: I'm full of them.

Graham: You're full of something.

Blake: So, you'll come over?

Graham: Send us the address and time, and we'll be there.

Blake: Hawk says to bring some sides.

Graham: Done.

Blake: I've missed you guys. See you soon.

She sent over the address with a heart, the one in my chest galloping at the thought of getting to see her. I glanced down, debating if what I wore was good enough.

"Don't overthink it," Graham said, punching the address into his GPS and starting it.

"On a scale of 1 to 10, though, how fuckable do I look?" I asked.

"Those girls at the bookstore thought you were," he said, not answering, but it wasn't what I wanted to hear. I needed to know what he thought.

"I don't care about them. I care what you think. So? Would you fuck me?" I asked, my breath hitching at the question.

Graham's eyes snapped over to me, his car idling at the end of the line in the parking lot. I held his gaze before he lowered it, taking in every aspect of me. It was weird, but I could practically feel his eyes as they trailed over me, taking in my body. My cock twitched, chubbing in my jeans from the perusal. I held my breath, my heart thundering in my ears as I waited for his response.

A horn honked behind us, and he broke his assessment, clearing his throat as he checked both ways and pulled out of the parking lot. It was quiet as he followed the GPS. My brain stuck on how it had felt to have him check me out.

That was what it had been, right?

"Ten," Graham said later, clearing his throat as he pulled into the driveway, effectively sending a horde of butterflies free.

BLAKE

"What did they say?" Hawk asked, grabbing my hand and pulling me next to the tub. His thumb ran back and forth across my palm, the tenderness melting me from the inside out. It was late afternoon now, and we'd spent the past eight hours naked.

I wasn't complaining about it, but my vagina, on the other hand, needed a little TLC after my five-hundredth orgasm—I'd honestly lost count at this point.

Hawk finally took mercy on me and suggested we take a bath to soak. But what really surprised me was when he suggested I invite GT over for dinner. He stated if I insisted on being 'besties with benefits' with Package Deal, he wanted to get to know them personally, too. He even offered to grill steaks if they brought the sides.

It wasn't a hard decision for me. I instantly said yes and texted them while he ran the bath water.

"Tucker was Tucker, and Graham said he'd bring some food." I stepped into the tub, using his hand to keep my balance. The water sloshed as I adjusted myself between his legs, leaning back against his chest. His arms wrapped around me, trailing his fingers up and down my body.

We'd spent time reacquainting our bodies with one another, touching and feeling without the fear of being caught. And if possible, the sex had been even better.

Hawk hummed, his beard scratching against my shoulder. "Did you ask Olson?" His voice was tight as he cupped water and rained it over my skin.

"I did." While Hawk had been more accepting of Graham and Tucker and thought the mistaken text conversations were funny, it wasn't the same with Luke.

I wasn't sure if it was because he was the most recent guy I'd had sex with—one who'd given me multiple orgasms and stole Hawk's crown—or if it had more to do with Bryce and his loyalty to my brother.

"He couldn't find a sitter for Willow on short notice."

Hawk's body relaxed. "Bummer."

"Yeah." I laughed. "I can tell you're real torn up about it." I turned my head, tilting it up and catching his eyes. "What's Bryce and Luke's beef, anyway?"

Hawk's beard rubbed against my shoulder. "That's something you'll have to ask your brother."

Sighing, I turned my head forward, not expecting him to answer it. "Fine." I took a breath, running my fingers up his arm hair. "You're sure you'll be okay with Package Deal?" I giggled at the term. "Yeah, I can't call them that."

I understood why the team coined the term. They were two peas in a pod. But they were GT to me, my screwballs. Hawk blew out a breath, kissing my shoulder as his arms tightened.

"I'm going to try to be."

"Thank you for trying."

"I meant what I said, Blazy." The emotion in the air thickened, and I had a weird inclination of what the next words out of his mouth were about to be. As much as I wanted to hear them, I wasn't ready for those words. "I—"

"The next words you're about to say better be, 'I like my steaks juicy,'" I teased.

Hawk chuckled, his body vibrating against my back, the water moving with the action. He dropped another kiss on my shoulder. He hadn't stopped all day, and I secretly loved it.

"Fine. I like juicy steaks. But I also like you, and while it's not the story I envisioned for us, I wasn't lying when I said I wouldn't leave this time." He sucked in another breath like he kept using all of his allotted breath up with all the words he was sharing. "I'll hear Graham out. What can I expect?"

"From the book I read, it's really lovely. The girl is loved by them all and doesn't have to choose. I don't know how it works in real life, and it sounds a little too good to be true," I admitted, letting water filter between my fingers.

"Take it one step at a time, baby," Hawk said, filling me with warmth and butterflies that were immediately swallowed by anxiety as all the outside forces against us pressed in.

"Not to mention we still have to tell—"

"Not today," Hawk said, cutting me off. "We will. But let's take time to figure us out before we bring your brother in. I think that's the mistake we made last time. We let him decide how we felt about each other."

My body relaxed, loving how well he knew me. Hawk knew when I needed him to take charge, showing me I wasn't alone.

"Okay, you're right. Patience."

We grew quiet, comfortable being in each other's arms. Animosity and anger were no longer between us, just acceptance and peace.

"So… you weren't serious with Roxie?" I asked, needing to hear it.

"No, Blazy. We were just a means to an end for one another. I'm sorry if I hurt your feelings by not being honest."

I shook my head. "You didn't owe me anything. I was overseas, licking my wounds. I dated someone, too. It's water under the proverbial bridge and all that."

"I know, but I didn't tell you the truth, and I let you believe I'd moved on. She's a good friend, and I do care for her, but we were never in love with one another. Will it be weird for you to see her?"

"No, I trust you." And as weird as it might be at first, to think she knew what Hawk looked like naked, I meant it. She might have had his body, but he'd never given her his heart, and that I could accept.

"Good, because I don't think she'd let me ghost her." He chuckled, and I tried to imagine the tattoo artist I met three years ago.

"If you can get on board with the other people I like, then I can get on board with your ex-bed buddy."

"Ew. That sounds like bed bugs."

I snorted and tilted my head, finding his scowl in place. I rolled my eyes at him, and he tickled me, sloshing water around us.

"Do you think she'd give me another tattoo?" I asked once he stopped tickling me.

"Maybe. Speaking of…" Hawk picked my thigh up out of the water, his fingers grazing over the hawk and bite mark. "I can't believe you did this."

"I can't believe you didn't notice until about round four." I laughed.

"Yeah, well, there were a lot of other parts to reacquaint myself with." He bit the skin between my shoulder and neck where he'd been kissing me.

"Ow! You can't go around biting me and hoping I'll get it tattooed."

"Why not? Then you'll have my mark all over you forever."

Gasping, I turned my head to stare into his eyes. His mismatched hues were dark, filled with lust and longing.

The doorbell rang, breaking the connection, and he groaned. Tightening his arms around me momentarily, Hawk tilted my head back and kissed me deeply.

I could feel the tightness in his arms before he let me go, and I climbed out and quickly dried off. I snagged one of Hawk's shirts out of a drawer as I ran to the door, excitement and adrenaline pumping. I still couldn't believe this was happening.

With Hawk, I had butterflies made of first love. They'd grown and blossomed into full-grown butterflies, their wings beating heavy against my chest each time I looked at him.

Graham and Tucker gave me an entirely unique feeling. To them, I'd always only been Blake, and the energy between us was electric. They were more like fireflies buzzing bright and constant, lighting me up on the inside and filling me with giddiness.

I threw open the door to their smiling faces, returning their grins.

"Hey," I said immediately, wanting to hit my head for my lame opening.

"Hey, yourself," Tucker said, all smiles as he stepped forward and wrapped his arms around me, lifting me into the air.

My legs naturally wrapped around his waist, forgetting I didn't have on underwear. His hands landed on my butt to hold me up, his eyes widening when he came into contact with bare skin.

"Hot damn, gummy bear, you're gonna make me embarrass myself on my coach's front door."

"Sorry." I cringed, my cheeks heating. "But if anyone is a gummy bear, it's Graham."

The man in question raised a brow, staring at me over his best friend's shoulder, his face confused.

"Can I call you gummy bear?" I asked, and he laughed, shaking his head.

"Not happening."

"Duh, because he's Teddy Graham. It's canon now," Tucker said, but Graham ignored him, lasering me with his eyes.

"What did Tucker mean?"

"Oh, you heard that part too?" He smirked, waiting for me to answer. "Well, you see, I'm not wearing any panties. I just got out of the bathtub."

His eyes widened, his pupils dilating and making his gray eyes more silver as he took in Tucker's hands on my backside, his mouth on my neck.

"On that note," he said, pushing us through the door and shutting it. "Let's not give anyone a show. Thankfully, Hawk's far off the road, but that doesn't mean there aren't nosey people."

"Good point," I said, kissing Tucker's cheek and motioning for him to put me down.

He groaned into my neck, releasing his grip as I slid down, his moan louder as I brushed against his erection. His hands tightened on my arms as he held me close to him, and I panted. Our bodies vibrated against one another, and I was this close to rocking against his cock—

Hawk cleared his throat behind us, reminding us he was there. I turned, hoping he wasn't too uncomfortable. His eyes were cast down as he rubbed the back of his head.

"Coach," Graham said, breaking the ice.

"West. Jameson. How do you like your steaks?"

"We like them medium, and I bought stuff for baked potatoes and a salad." Graham held up his bag.

"Cool," Hawk said, nodding. He glanced up, meeting my

eyes and then the other two, letting his shoulders drop. "I'll start grilling soon in case you need more time."

"That sounds perfect," Graham said, moving toward the kitchen.

Hawk paused, glancing at my bare legs and then my eyes. "Maybe put on some pants, Blazy? It's hard enough as it is," he groaned.

"Yeah, okay." I smiled, nodding. At least it seemed his awkwardness was about wanting to touch me and not the other two guys also touching me.

I went into the princess room, Tucker following me. He really was like a puppy as he peeked into all the rooms and looked at everything as I rifled through my suitcase.

"Never took Coach for the princess type," he joked as I pulled on panties. "Don't let Graham see this room; he'll say it's perfect for me."

I laughed. "He made it up for his nieces. I think it's cute."

"Man," he groaned, "you had to say something to make me like him more."

Chuckling, I slid on a pair of leggings when Tucker noticed Sunny's cage. His eyes lit up, and he ran over to him.

"Oh my god, can I hold him? Her?"

"Go ahead. His name is Sunny." I walked over to the cage and helped him remove the furry hamster. Tucker did the same as me, rubbing his head against his fur.

"He's my new friend." He kissed his twitching nose, laughing. "Oh my goodness. Aren't you the cutest thing?" he cooed.

While he was distracted, I finished dressing, even adding socks and tying an oversized shirt into a knot on the side, hoping all the extra layers would keep tonight on the casual side.

Emory might joke I needed a foursome, but I'd barely gotten used to a threesome, so I didn't want to jump in too quickly before I was ready. When I was done, I put Sunny back in his cage and took Tucker's hand, dragging him into the kitchen where Graham had already made himself at home. We both washed our hands, and Graham gave us directions.

The three of us fell into an easy arrangement as we made the salad and baked potatoes. Hawk stayed outside at the grill the whole time. I didn't know if it was intentional or if he really was that serious about steaks. It gave everyone time to adjust to being in his home. So, by the time we were sitting around the table with our plates full of food, my cheeks were no longer red, and Tucker and Graham were more relaxed.

The four of us stayed on safe topics, focusing on the food, Hawk's house, and the last away games. When the plates were clear, Graham pushed his away and cleared his throat.

"I take it things have shifted between you two?"

I didn't know when or how Graham had become the unofficial spokesperson for my relationship drama, but somehow, he had. He was the most introspective of everybody, always watching and monitoring feelings. Which gave him good insight into us, I supposed. Plus, the man knew exactly how to put things into words that made them easier to understand. He was articulate, thoughtful, and took his time. I guess it did make sense.

I glanced at Hawk, wanting him to answer this one. He cleared his throat, pushing his plate away, too.

"They have," he said, crossing his tattooed arms. It looked like a power move, but I knew it was his way of protecting himself.

"And you're cool with Blake being with us?" Tucker asked, his voice anxious. Hawk looked between the three of us, his gaze assessing.

"I'm not going anywhere. I don't know how I feel about this, but I will try for Blazy."

"Well, that's a start," Graham said, clearing his throat. It had to be hard to stand up to someone he respected, especially considering he was his coach. "The most important thing is talking about what we're comfortable with and what we're not."

"How about right now, we just chill and hang out?" I interrupted, the anxiety getting to me. "I don't want to put too much pressure on everyone when I'm still figuring it out myself."

"Sounds good to me," Tucker said, squeezing my hand under the table.

"How about we play Mario Kart or something?" I suggested.

"Sure." Hawk gave me a soft smile, letting me know he was okay. The four of us cleaned dinner and headed into the living room. I debated where to sit but ended up sitting next to Hawk since Graham and Tucker were next to one another on the other side of the couch.

It was tense at first as we played; no one was talking. But by the second race, Graham and Tucker were fighting with each other, pushing and shoving, and it added fun to the room.

"They bicker back and forth like an old married couple," Hawk whispered, relaxing beside me.

By the third race, even Hawk grinned and laughed. Apparently, my sucking at racing cars bonded the three men as they jibed me.

"Another?" Tucker asked at the end of the round. Hawk tossed his remote down, rubbing the back of his head.

I yawned, and everyone zeroed in on me. It was intense under the stare of three men.

"We should go," Graham said. "Tomorrow's game will be tough."

"I'll walk you out."

Hawk squeezed my leg, and I stood, leading GT to the door. We stepped outside, the night quiet as we walked to the car.

"I'm glad you guys came. It was fun."

"Coach isn't too bad," Tucker said. "But now I need my kiss."

He pulled me into him, sealing his lips to mine before I could protest. Not that I would. Tucker kissed me thoroughly until I lost my breath and then spun me around to Graham. I loved how seamlessly they worked together, their friendship and battery mate connection apparent in everything they did.

Graham's lips sealed over mine slower, but his kiss was as hot and thorough. When my thoughts were fuzzy and my head dizzy, he let me go.

"See you tomorrow." I touched my lips.

"Night, Honey Bee," Tucker said, adjusting himself as he climbed into the car.

"Sweet dreams, Sunshine." Graham winked, walking around to the driver's door. I waited outside until I could no longer see their rearview lights, heading back in as I walked on a bed of clouds.

BLAKE

"W‌HAT ARE YOU DOING?" R‌UE ASKED, SPOOKING ME. I‌ JUMPED and spun, a guilty look on my face.

"Hiding from Mira," I admitted. It was the third home game of the series, and Mira hadn't relented on her goal to apparently undo me. Based on the last tasks she'd given me, I had to believe that she was creating busy work for me at this point.

Because I couldn't reconcile how going through old team photos was related to the current team. I went home yesterday covered in dust and five papercuts. So today, I'd come into work with the intention of doing my normal tasks and avoiding Mira at all costs.

It was midway through the game, and I'd been successful so far. There might've been a few duck-and-go's behind fans and one costume change—but neither Jack, the mascot, nor I were speaking of that.

"She does seem to be targeting you more than most," Rue said, looking around the stands. I'd retreated to the top of the stadium.

"Yeah, I can't decide if it's because of my last name or something else," I admitted.

Rue nodded, taking a seat and patting it. She picked up a box of discarded popcorn and opened it. When she noticed it was still full, she took a handful.

"Gross."

"What? It's fine," she said, waving me off. "I think she had a hard-on for your brother."

"Is your intention to make me puke? I've gone several weeks now without a vomit incident, and I'd like to keep it that way."

She snorted, munching on her popcorn. "Your brother is hot. Takes after your dad." Rue fanned herself like the mere idea of my dad and brother got her hot and bothered.

I gagged, and she only laughed. "I don't think I want to be your friend anymore."

"Why? I'm an awesome friend."

"If awesome means annoying, then maybe," I teased. "Besides, my dad is remarried and about to have a baby. Well, he's not, but Mallory is."

"Is that weird?"

"What do you mean?" I asked, turning to her and shielding my eyes.

"Your dad being married to someone only a few years older than you and having a sibling who's young enough to be your own."

I shrugged. "Nothing in my life has ever been normal from what the movies portray. I knew what the paparazzi were before I turned six. We lived half of our year on the road, and my first friends were grumpy baseball players. I knew how to tie cleats before shoes. Things slowed when Bryce started to play ball, and my mom took on more clients. Then, I got sick a few years after that. People I didn't even know would ask me questions on the street about my family like they had a right to know."

I took in a breath, then released it. I hadn't thought about the media in years. Being in Greece, I'd been sheltered from their interest and had worked hard before my runaway bride moment to stay off their radar. I hadn't done anything interesting enough to warrant their interest. Yet.

Was I ready for all of that to return? Yes. Maybe. I dunno.

"Most people have the wrong image of who my dad is. They see his pennant wins, his sprawling mansion, and winning baseball clubs and believe his life has been easy."

"I didn't mean—"

"I know. If you had, I wouldn't be sharing this with you. After the divorce, I didn't think my dad would ever love again. Yeah, he's fifty, and Mallory's thirty-five, but she makes him happy, so it's enough for me."

I could only hope my family would accept my... whatever we were-ships when it came out.

It was quiet as we watched the game, so Rue's next question took me a while to parse out.

"So, what are you going to do?"

"About?" I asked.

"Mira."

"Oh. Hiding seems to be working out." I cringed, knowing it wouldn't last.

"Except it didn't. She sent me to find you."

"Well, damn." We both chuckled. "I can't keep this up, that's for sure. I'm exhausted, and I have no time for..." I paused, realizing I almost said the guys' names. "Anything else."

"Why haven't you used your name?"

"I wanted to prove I got this job on my own merit, and it felt like a test."

"That's honorable but also stupid." She tossed a piece of popcorn at me.

"Excuse me? Again, I thought you were nice!"

"I am nice, but it doesn't mean I'll feed you lies." Rue

leveled me with a knowing look, her eyes slanted, and her mouth quirked on one side.

"Fine. What do you suggest?"

"If you don't stand up to Mira, she'll think she owns you and that's not good for anyone. Whether you go to your dad to step in or use your name, the one you've built for yourself is up to you."

"What do you mean?" I asked, my heart thumping. She eyed me, searching my face.

"You have no idea, do you?"

I swallowed, shaking my head, and she placed her hand on my arm, squeezing.

"Do you know why Mira sent me to find you?"

"Because I'm awesome at hiding?" She laughed, shaking her head.

"No. Sorry to break it to you, but you're kind of bad at hide and seek."

"Then how did you find me?"

"It's not that I found you; it's that Mira hasn't."

I scrunched up my nose. "What's the difference?"

"The difference is that every single staff person in this stadium loves you. You've shown them all kindness, from the janitor to the concession stand to security. When Mira asked them if they'd seen you, they all said no. The stadium has been hiding you all day. They respect your father, but they love you. Think about that, Baker. But either way, you gotta do something."

I stared in shock, her words bringing tears to my eyes. Rue squeezed my arm, picking up the trash around her and standing.

"Thanks, Rue."

"Nothing to thank me for. I was never here." She winked, walking to the end of the aisle before she stopped. "I don't want to know what you did to Jack, but a bouquet of his favorite cookies might go a long way. He looked stressed."

Snorting, I covered my mouth to contain my laugh. Yeah. He could have two bouquets.

Glancing around the stadium, I took in the people who ran this place, seeing them with new eyes. I'd earned their respect by being myself, so why was I killing myself to prove something I didn't need to? Mira didn't deserve my dedication. She was either capitalizing on it or punishing me for something I had no part in. Either way, I'd never get from her what I'd effortlessly earned from the people that actually mattered.

Decision made, I stood up and held my head high. It was time to hang up the people-pleaser medals and fully embrace retirement.

First step—knock a bitch off her pedestal.

I seemed to float on my way to her office, my body weightless from all the guilt I let go. Damn. I needed to have done this weeks ago.

I didn't knock or stop at her door; I strolled through it like I fucking owned it. Because the truth was, I kinda did. I'd worked so hard to not be seen that way that I let her use it against me. Well, not anymore, sister.

"Blake! There you are. I've been looking for you all day." She stood, bracing her hands on the desk, narrowing her eyes at me. "It's not very professional to slack off on the job. I need you to go through another whole room of boxes."

"No."

"No?" Mira jerked back like I'd struck her.

"No. My job description lists me interacting with the fans and team. I'm to photograph the players' arrival, build up community spirit, and team camaraderie. Which I did. Really fucking well, I might add. My job is not to do whatever the fuck you want."

"Excuse me—"

"I'm not done talking. Second, my hours are flexible. Typically, this position is held by two people. Two people to alternate morning and evening games, and split the away games. No more eighteen-hour days. I will work hard and stay until my tasks are done, but I will no longer be doing anything outside of my description. If you need someone to do those things, hire an intern."

Her face was red, her hands gripping the edge of the desk. "Your father—" she started, but I cut her off again.

"My father is your boss, and if I was to tell him even a sliver of what you had me do, it would be you in the hot seat, not me. He is not the threat you think he is. Not to me, at least."

"You can't—"

"Actually, I can. Because I'm Blake Baker."

"But—" Mira spluttered, but I couldn't help myself and cut her off again.

"I haven't asked for any special treatment, but you've gone the other direction, treating me worse than any other employee. And I let you! I thought I had to prove myself. But I don't. Especially not to you. So, the nonsense stops right now. In fact, I'm leaving. I've put in enough hours today already."

I turned, letting out a deep breath as the adrenaline receded.

"Your last name won't save you forever. There will come a day when it will be your downfall, and I hope I'm there to witness it," she whispered so no one outside her office could hear.

"You misunderstood." I paused, looking over my shoulder. "It isn't my last name I'm betting on. It's my first."

I tapped the door and walked to my desk, barely stopping to grab my bag and camera before heading out. The few people in the office gave me a nod and smile, helping the anxiety that wanted to rise disappear.

"*Badass*," Rue mouthed as I passed her.

Giddy and high on adrenaline, I felt like I could conquer anything. But first, I'd start with dinner.

Three hours later, I regretted my earlier confidence as Tucker and Graham stared at the burned remains of my roasted chicken.

"Um, I think you overcooked it," Tucker said.

"No shit." I laughed.

"The salad looks good," Graham said, looking at the bowl on the table.

"It's the one you made the other night."

"Oh." His cheeks pinked, and I let out a hysterical laugh.

"Let's hope you weren't with me for my culinary skills. Apparently, it's limited to breakfast."

Hawk walked into the kitchen, halting as he took in the three of us. His eyes traced over me, taking in every inch he could see. It was such a natural thing he did now, constantly checking to see how I was. It was warm and full of the emotion I didn't want to open yet.

"Honey, I made dinner." I lifted the burned chicken so he could see it.

"You know what? I told Roxie I'd meet her for pizza, and I gotta run by the stadium to view some film." Hawk backed up, barely hiding the scared expression.

"It's not that bad!" I yelled, laughing.

"I think you had the stove on Celsius instead of Fahrenheit," Graham said, looking at it.

"I'll be back in a few hours. Don't do anything *too* vigorous." His eyes heated, his joy apparent at teasing me as he stared. My cheeks stained red at the implication. Lots of sex with Hawk had left my vagina a tad sore.

"Uh-huh," I said, trying to hide from him as I dumped the

chicken in the trash. "Tell Roxie I said hi, and I want a tattoo."

Because I had my face down, I didn't notice he'd returned to the kitchen until he was right before me. He tilted my chin up before placing the pan on the counter. In the next second, he lifted me into his arms and planted a kiss to rival all kisses on my lips.

It wasn't a simple goodbye kiss. No, this was a claiming kiss.

Whether to show me he appreciated I trusted him when it came to Roxie or to communicate—very loudly—to Tucker and Graham where he stood, I wasn't sure.

I swayed a little as he returned me to my feet, my breath stolen and my heart racing. Hawk winked as he picked up his keys.

Tucker fanned his face, leaning into me. "Damn, girl. That was hot. I'm half in love with him, too."

"Not happening," Hawk barked, rolling his eyes.

"That's what you say now," Tucker teased, blowing Hawk a kiss. Graham laughed, his shoulders shaking. He'd moved over to the fridge, peeking in.

"I think I can throw together something."

"Thank you!"

Hawk gave me one last look before he walked out of the kitchen. Tucker and I followed Graham's instructions, and I relayed how I'd stood up to Mira through dinner. When the last bite was eaten, we all stared at one another, and Hawk's words echoed around my brain as the tension crept higher.

My pussy throbbed in time with my heartbeat, and I felt my body coming alive with each lingering gaze.

"Now what?" I asked, swallowing as I glanced between them.

Never before had a question felt so loaded.

CHAPTER
THIRTY-SIX

BLAKE

Tucker didn't answer; he just leaned in and captured my lips, showing me exactly what he wanted. As usual, his kiss was playful as he swept his tongue inside my mouth, his fingers tangling in my hair as he moved closer to me, pressing his big body into mine. The heat of his skin was electrifying as he kissed me, and I soon lost myself in Tucker's kiss.

When he stood, I followed, letting him direct us. I didn't care where we went as long as the three of us were together. Almost as if in response, hands skimmed my back, running up and over my shoulders, showing me Graham was there.

Soft cushions met my legs as we tumbled onto the couch, none of us breaking apart as we settled. Graham shifted my hair and peppered kisses on my neck, his hands locked on my hips. The two of them worked together, lifting me onto their laps, with my legs wrapped around Tucker's waist and my ass colliding with Graham's abs. Their knees pressed into one another, making us one twisted pretzel.

Panting, I broke the kiss, my body buzzing with sensations as hard body parts rocked into me from every direction.

It was mind-blowing and overwhelming as I tried to follow where everything was coming from. Tucker kissed down my throat, pulling my shirt to kiss me lower. Graham's hand cupped my breasts as he gently squeezed them from behind.

"I've watched your video every night since you sent it, Bee. It's the sexiest thing ever. Far better than porn," Tucker said, his tongue sweeping out to wet my skin. His hands gripped my thighs, spreading them as he rocked his hard length up into me.

It was too much and not enough, yet I needed more.

"I was worried Tucker would make himself raw with as many times as he's jacked off to it. I'm surprised we haven't gotten noise complaints with how he moans," Graham added, sneaking his hands under my shirt. The minute his hot skin hit mine, I reared back into him, giving him more access.

"He's not wrong, honey bee." Tucker chuckled, not at all embarrassed. It was one of the things I loved about him. He grazed his fingers over the outside of my leggings, and I melted.

"I never asked you how you got it into my bag." I moaned as he increased the pressure. "When did you put it in there?"

"When I placed your bag under the seat. It was easy to transfer it from my bag to yours when you were watching something with Tucker," Graham admitted, his voice smug.

"Very clever, G." My voice hitched as his fingers found my nipples, palming them in his hands.

"How far do you want this to go?" he asked, sucking on my neck.

I bit my lip, my body screaming to go all the way, but the slight twinge in my pussy reminded me of Hawk's words. "I'm good with everything but sex. My vagina needs a minor break."

"Get it, Coach," Tucker cheered, leaning back to pull off my socks.

"Works for us." Graham's voice was smooth as he lifted my shirt over my head.

"What if I gave your pussy some attention but kept it gentle?" Tucker asked, licking his lips as he trailed his hands up my thighs. His touch alone sent shivers racing up my body, and I really wanted to know what else he could do.

"Yes," I moaned, nodding so fast I almost head-butted Graham.

"Easy, Sunshine." He chuckled, lifting me so Tucker could pull my leggings off.

I loved it when I got to watch them work together. It was beautiful and so effortless. When they combined their forces, using their connection to bring me pleasure, it truly was mind-blowing.

Tucker stared at my naked body, blinking as his hands reached out to touch me. His fingers skimmed over my pale skin, tracing invisible lines from my hip to my navel and then up to my breasts.

"So pretty," he whispered. "I know I've seen these before…" His voice was awed as he traced my breasts with his fingers, creating goosebumps with each swipe. "But they're so much better in person."

"Lie down, Tucker," Graham commanded, the mood instantly changing.

"Yes, Teddy Graham," he said, winking as he dropped his hands and pulled off his shirt and shorts without a care in the world.

His cock bounced free, and I licked my lips as I stared at it. He was right. Seeing it on my tiny phone was nothing compared to in person. Even on the bus, I hadn't gotten a good look at it. Now that it was right before me, I observed it, wanting to commit it to memory.

It was a good length that tilted at the end, curving up. He had a thick vein that ran along his length, making me want to trace it with my tongue. It was slightly lighter than his skin, the tip a deep red with a bead of pre-cum. I was desperate for it, and I must have mewled as I watched because Graham chuckled in my ear, sending vibrations over me.

"Patience, Sunshine. You'll get your taste."

Leaning back, I took his lips and wrapped my arm around his head. Graham kissed me in his Graham way—slow and sensual. His kisses were full of warmth and seduction, making my toes curl as I tried to pull him into me more. If I could envelop myself in a full-body Graham wrap, I'd never leave.

However, it seemed Tucker had a different idea and was as impatient as me. He leaned forward and pulled me onto his body, breaking the kiss. Shrieking, I braced my hands out, stopping myself from face-planting into his dick and balls.

"Tucker!"

He chuckled, gripping me firmer and moving me the rest of the way up his body slower until I was straddling his head.

"Sit on my face, Honey Bee."

"You sure? I don't want to suffocate you." I bit my lip, debating whether this was a good idea. I could see myself having to tell my dad why his star pitcher died… death by cunnilingus.

"Impossible, but if you do, then it will be the best moment of my life. Please, Bee. I've been thinking about it all week."

"Do it, Sunshine. But turn this direction," Graham ordered.

Turning around, I perched over Tucker's face as I placed my knees beside his head on the couch. "Like this?" I asked, feeling a little self-conscious.

Tucker pulled me down onto his face without further comment. He erased all feelings of insecurity as he locked his arms around my thighs to hold me in place. The instant his tongue hit my clit, I melted into him, forgetting to worry about my weight. His tongue skillfully flicked against my nub before lapping up my folds, diving into my core.

I moaned, rocking on his face, lost in the moment. When I remembered Graham was in front of me, I opened my eyes and was met with a slow striptease as he pulled off his clothes. His muscles flexed and bunched with each movement, highlighting his golden skin. He had an intersecting arrow tattoo on his pec and something on his hip, but I was too distracted by his cock to look at it.

Graham was shorter than Tucker but thicker. The girth on his cock promised delicious things. The pelvic piercing twinkled at me, and I had the sudden urge to forgo my no-sex rule and test it out. My distraction allowed Tucker to pull me closer, his tongue plunging into me deeper, making me squirm.

Falling forward, I braced my hands beside his hips on the couch until his cock bobbed, and I moved to stroke it. Now that it was in front of me, I didn't know what to do first. Sticking out my tongue, I touched the tip to the bead of pre-cum, the salty and tangy taste exploding in my mouth. Graham groaned as he watched me, stroking himself.

Wrapping my hand around Tucker's base, I looked up at Graham from beneath my lashes. He smiled, grazing his thumb across my cheek and barely brushing Tucker's cock. Graham gulped when he realized, his pupils dilating as he watched me suck his best friend's dick.

Swirling my tongue around the tip, I sucked him down as I fondled his balls. I focused on taking him as far as I could. Graham brushed my hair back, giving him a better view.

"I'm not sure which is hotter. You with Tuck's cock in your mouth, or his mouth on your pussy, eating you like he's a starved man."

"Mmmeee," Tucker moaned, sending the vibrations through my body. Graham smiled, stroking himself slowly as he kept my cheek in his hand, every so often brushing his thumb across my lips and Tucker's cock.

While Graham seemed content to do that, it didn't feel right. I wanted him to be part of this as we pushed our boundaries further.

Letting go of Tucker, I took a deep breath and looked back at the man in question. "Tucker, you trust me?" I asked.

Tucker mumbled into my pussy, not breaking away to answer. I took it as a yes, curling my fingers around the base. "Graham, straddle Tuck's legs. I need you closer."

He swallowed, hesitant. I narrowed my eyes at him, telling him to trust me. Graham dropped his shoulders, relaxing as he nodded. I watched with bated breath as he moved, straddling Tucker's thighs and bringing their cocks closer to one another.

Reaching out, I stroked his cock, letting my finger run over the piercing. He groaned, his head falling back at my touch. I'd been watching Tucker for weeks and suspected he had stronger feelings than he even realized. But since our moment together on the bus, Tucker gave Graham the same covert looks his bestie did.

Something had shifted, and with a little push, they might finally be brave enough to open that door. Considering how much they'd helped me explore and open up sexually, I wanted to do the same for them. And at least this way, if it wasn't what I thought I saw between them, they could blame it on me and the moment—minimizing the risk.

I rotated between stroking and sucking their cocks, and then wrapped my hands around the base of both of their cocks. Graham's eyes snapped open, but he didn't stop me as I stroked them together. His eyes rolled back as his dick rubbed against Tucker's. With slow strokes and kisses, I let them get used to it. Graham's abs flexed with each stroke, his breathing quickening as he watched.

I jutted out my tongue and took both of their cock heads

into my mouth. My lips stretched around them, and I stroked their silky bases at the same time. Graham's moans were husky and deep, increasing in volume as I continued. Like he couldn't believe this was happening, like he wanted Tucker to be fully aware that their dicks were touching.

Tucker's hands flexed on my thighs, his tongue never stopping as he licked and sucked me. My pussy wept, soaking his face, and I could feel the hint of his stubble rubbing against my inner thighs. I loved how his moans vibrated my clit each time I stroked and licked their dicks, sending shivers through me.

"Oh, fuck," Graham cursed, rocking forward, no longer hesitant. He was all in.

"I think you should help me," I whispered, taking his hand and putting it on the other side of mine. Graham tentatively stroked their two cocks together, watching behind me for a sign of some sort. When Tucker didn't tell him to stop, he became bolder.

By the way Tuck moaned, rocking his hips up into our joint hands, he was definitely into it, too. A gasp escaped me when he plunged a finger softly into my core, sending me spiraling after having edged me for so long. One flick to my clit, and I fell over, coming all over his face.

From there, it was a domino effect, Tucker's release covering our hands as he came. Hot ropes of cum spurted up, barely missing my eye as I moved back. Graham soon followed, gripping his friend's thighs as he braced himself through the orgasm. I wouldn't be surprised if he left his own fingerprints. His head was thrown back, his abs tight as he surrendered to the pleasure. He sagged as he came down, sweat beading along his brow.

"That was fucking hot!" Tucker exclaimed, lifting my sopping wet pussy off his face and sending me into a round of giggles.

"Yeah, it was," I agreed.

"Uh-huh," Graham mumbled, his eyes closed as he leaned against the couch.

"We gotta do more of that," Tucker said, making me confident he was all about this.

Graham smiled softly, nodding. "Yeah, we do."

"I'm game. That was incredible," I said, shifting so Tucker could sit up. He didn't act differently, and I wondered if it even fazed him. They were so close as it was; it might not be as big of a stretch as Graham or I made it. But if they needed me to be the conductor as we rode this train of sexual self-discovery, then I would. Choo-Choo.

"We might have time to shower before Hawk returns. Unless you want to be sitting in your own cum when he does."

"A shower sounds great. More playtime," Tucker said, jumping up. Graham and I laughed but followed. Tucker started down a hallway, confident despite not knowing where he was going.

"Wrong way!" I called, racing in the right direction with Graham and Tucker hot on our tails. The three of us laughed as we fell into the bathroom, playfully tickling and slapping one another as I turned on the water. Somehow, we made it out within thirty minutes with only a small amount of touching, kissing, and groping.

Okay, there was a whole other orgasm. But hey, Hawk said not to make bad choices. He didn't say I couldn't have orgasms. Now that I knew what they were like, it seemed I couldn't get enough.

"When can we do that again?" Tucker asked as we dried off, pulling our clothes on in the princess bedroom. Once they were dressed, it made it a little easier to focus. But not much. They were too stinking hot.

My phone chirped, stopping me from answering him. "One sec." Grabbing it as I dried my hair, I read the message.

Luke: I miss you.

Luke: Is it weird to say that?

Blake: Not at all. I miss you too.

Luke: Would you want to do something with Willow and me on our next day off?

Blake: You sure about that? Introducing me to your daughter is a big deal.

Luke: Even if we only stay friends, you're a big deal to me, Bee.

My cheeks heated, warmth spreading through me. I felt a tad guilty feeling this way with Tucker and Graham here, but since they were aware, I brushed them away. Things with Luke had been slowly building over the past month, and I loved where we were headed.

Blake: I'd love to, then.

Luke: Great. I'll make the plans.

Blake: Perfect. I can't wait to meet Willow.

Luke: Me too, but I am a little nervous.

Blake: Worried she'll like me better?

Luke: Yeah, actually.

Blake: Well, I am awesome.

Luke: And so humble.

Blake: That's me. *laughing emoji*

Luke: Right, it's story time. I'm being summoned. I'll see you tomorrow.

Blake: Goodnight, Luke.

Luke: Sweet dreams, Slugger.

Smiling, I closed my phone, placed it on the dresser, and jumped when Tucker spoke. I'd momentarily forgotten they were in the room.

"Oh, what's that smile about?" Tucker asked, reaching for my phone.

"I'm going on a date with Luke." I grinned, looking up to meet their eyes.

Tucker's mouth dropped open, and I worried I'd read them all wrong this whole time.

"Shut up. We can go on dates?" he asked, looking at Graham with wide eyes, his mouth slightly open. Graham shrugged, observing.

"Yes. Dates are allowed. Besties with benefits doesn't mean we can't do things."

His shock evaporated, and he went into planning mode, wrapping his arm around Graham. "That's it. We gotta think of the best date ever, Teddy Graham!"

"We? I already took Bee out on a date," Graham said, lifting the corner of his lips into a smug expression. Tucker rolled his eyes, ignoring him as he listed off things we could do.

"We're a package deal. Teddy Graham and Mr. Studly Pitcher. Duh." Graham snorted, shaking his head.

"I'm not even going to touch that nickname. How about you take Blake out first, and then we'll do a group one."

Tucker snapped his fingers, nodding. "Two dates. I like it. You're brilliant."

"You have to ask me first, Tucker," I teased, placing my hands on my hips.

He paused in his planning, turning, and grinned.

Marching over to me with swagger, he dropped onto his knees and took my hands in his.

"Will you go on a date with me, Honey Bee?"

With an offer like that, how could I say no? I grinned. "I'd love to."

"And then with both of us? I want my date requests recorded now," Tucker added, making me laugh.

"Yes, absolutely. Then the three of us." I nodded.

Graham met my eyes, watching me. "Okay. But we're not shopping. She doesn't need to witness your obsessive sneaker personality this early on."

"Good call," Tucker said, nodding as he stood. "How do you feel about skydiving?"

"Not a fan."

"Noted. I'll put it on the no list," he said, whipping out his phone to make said list. We left the bedroom, and Tucker plopped onto the couch like he owned it. "Damn, this couch is nice. And it's not even because my favorite thing happened on it," he said, sprawling out. "Why isn't our couch this nice?" he asked.

Graham shoved his feet, taking his own seat. "We just moved here, and it came with furniture."

"Oh yeah, that." Tucker sat up and snuggled into Graham's side, resting his head on his shoulder before throwing his leg over his friend's. Graham ran his hands through Tucker's hair as he peered at Tucker's phone, making comments here and there as they worked on a list.

They were so cute together that I wanted to take a picture. It amazed me they'd never crossed the lines before with how close they were. It was obvious to me how much they cared for each other. And it was mutual on both sides.

Tucker's phone dropped a few minutes later into his lap, his eyes closing as he snuggled into Graham more. Graham sighed and patted his leg.

"Don't fall asleep. I'm not carrying your ass all the way up the stairs."

"Fine," Tucker whined. "Let's go so I have more time tomorrow to plan the best date ever."

Graham rolled his eyes, but helped Tucker untangle himself

"Oh, wait! I finished the book." I raced back to the princess room, pulling out the first book he'd let me borrow. I handed it to him, our hands meeting on the cover and giving me a strange déjà vu moment.

"Have you started the new one?"

"I have. It's good," I said, my cheeks heating.

"I think the word you're looking for is smutty, Bee." Tucker laughed, crossing his arms over his chest proudly. "Oh, I got this for Coach." He couldn't hold in his laugh as he pulled out a bandana with baseballs on it.

"Your funeral," Graham mumbled, leaning in to kiss me goodbye.

After several kisses from Tucker, I pushed them out the door, promising him a date.

As I crawled into Hawk's bed, he returned home and joined me. He wrapped his arms around me and kissed my cheek.

"I can't believe I'm going to ask this, but how was your evening?"

"Good." I smiled, loving that he was trying. "How was yours with Roxie?"

"It was nice, actually. She said to call her, and she'll schedule you for a tattoo."

"Eek! Okay, now I gotta find something I want. Did you go to work after?"

"Yes, Blazy. I didn't hook up with Roxie."

"I know. I trust you. You're just surprising me with all of this. I didn't think we'd ever get back here, but I definitely didn't see you willingly sharing me as an option."

Hawk blew out a breath, his arms relaxing. "It's not easy, but I'm trying. I want you to have everything you need." He paused, his fingers twitching. "Watching you with them wasn't as hard as I expected."

I rolled over to face him, tracing his beard with my fingers. "You sure?"

He kissed my nose in response. "As long as I get time with you, I'm good."

I kissed him softly, relishing the fact I got to. "You're really not going anywhere this time, are you?" I asked.

"Never, Blazy. And I promise I'll tell Bryce. I just want time with you first. Okay?"

"Okay," I said, closing my eyes. "Oh, I'm going on a date with Luke."

His body tensed for a second before he let out a breath. "If you're serious about him, I'll work on my shit. But I'm not promising family dinners or bro shakes."

"I wouldn't expect you, too," I admitted, leaning forward to kiss him. "Thank you."

Quiet enveloped us, my eyes closing as I listened to the steady rhythm of his heart. "What's with the bandana on the table?" he asked, pulling me from sleep.

"You'll have to ask Tucker." I laughed.

"I'd rather not." He grimaced, then sighed. "Those two are gonna be the death of me."

With a laugh, I snuggled in, a hopeful smile on my face. For once, I felt as if I was ahead in the count, with all the possibilities of a great game before me.

Don't fail me now, baseball.

THIRTY-SEVEN

LUKE

THE NEXT THREE GAMES DRAGGED ON, MY DATE WITH BLAKE looming at the end of them. Nerves and excitement warred within me each day, and I almost canceled it twice. But then I would see her, and all my doubt would vanish, replaced with longing. Especially when I watched her interact with Graham, Tucker, and Hawk.

She'd told me about her 'no label' relationship with Package Deal and her past with Hawk. The scared part of me wanted to bail and run for the hills to avoid getting hurt. But each time I thought about it, my game would suffer, and I knew running away wasn't the answer.

My heart was already invested, whether I wanted it to be or not.

So, I'd keep taking what she gave me and pray that there was room in her heart for me, too.

Because no matter how I sliced it, having Bee in my life made me better. If I only ever had her as a friend, then I would be the best damn friend she ever had.

Checking the list Matilda had made one more time, I double-checked that I had everything we needed for the beach. I'd first balked at Matilda's offer, thinking I could care for a four-year-old alone. But after spending the first day off with her alone, I conceded I was out of my league regarding little girls. And that included what to pack for the beach.

"All right, kiddo. Do you think we have everything now?" I asked, glancing at her.

Willow and I were still figuring one another out, but she'd thawed since Jasmine extended her trip. I'd been attempting to do something with her each day, even if it was only brushing her hair or fixing something to eat. It felt important with my schedule to have these small moments when I was home.

Plus, cooking allowed us to share something without using words, something I discovered we both had in common.

With away games, I video-called her when it wasn't too late, still attempting to read her a book before bed. But mornings were the best, so I called and had breakfast with her before she got ready for school.

Willow still seemed sad sometimes, but she'd made a friend at school, which had done wonders. I'd even worked my parent magic and scheduled playdates during my away games. Matilda had helped return the clothes Willow didn't like, and we'd picked out new ones together—including several pairs of purple pants.

I'd also restarted on her room, exchanging the unicorn furniture and decor with a baseball theme that she selected. I needed to assemble a few more pieces of furniture, but it was almost completed, and I found her softening more each day. By the time it was finished, I hoped Willow would feel like this was her home, too.

"Can I get a puppy?" she asked, ignoring my question. She blinked those long eyelashes at me, waiting for my answer. Once I recovered from the shock, I chuckled and shook my head.

"Nice try, kiddo, but I don't think we're ready for a puppy yet. Maybe start with something smaller and less maintenance."

"Like a kitten?" she asked with hope, and I wondered if I'd just been played.

"I'll think about it." Cats were easier to manage and wouldn't require as much attention as a puppy, but it was still more than I was prepared to handle.

"It looks like we have everything. Our swimsuits are on, and towels are in the bag, along with sunscreen, snacks, water bottles, beach toys, a blanket, and an umbrella. Anything else you want to bring?" I asked as I checked them off.

Willow tilted her head to the side in thought, tapping her finger to her lips. "Nope!"

"Then, let's go!" I smiled as she hopped off the barstool and raced toward the garage. She'd been excited about going to the beach, waking up at five this morning and asking if we could leave already. My one day to sleep in, and I was up earlier than ever.

I picked up the last bag and the cooler and followed her to the car. Once I had everything loaded, I checked her booster seat and started the car, inputting Blake's address.

"I'm excited for you to meet my friend," I said as I backed out.

"Is she your girlfriend?" Willow asked, her eyes down.

"She's a girl who is a friend," I answered.

"Each time I met Mommy's friend, they brought me a toy. But then I had to stay in my room until Mommy made a new friend. She had a lot of friends, but they always left and never visited me again."

Her soft words saddened me, and I wish I'd been there. That I'd known about her from the start. The amount of people that had come and gone in this little girl's life was already too many.

"Willow, I can't promise you that Blake will always be here. I can't control her actions. But she's important to me, and you're important to me, so I wanted you to meet, but if that's too hard, I won't force you." I pulled off into a deserted gas station, this conversation feeling important. Unbuckling my seat belt, I opened my door and climbed into the back seat next to her.

"No matter what, I promise you I'm not going anywhere. I'm new to this whole dad thing, but I'm working my hardest to get better at it because you deserve a great dad. There might've been other men in your mom's life who disappeared, but that won't be me. I don't know what the future holds. That's for your mom and me to figure out, but I don't want you to worry about me leaving. I will always tell you good night or good morning so that each day you know how much I love you and think about you, even if I'm not with you. That's something you can count on."

Her eyes searched mine, far too mature for her age. When she seemed satisfied with what she saw, she nodded, squeezing her tiny arms around my neck.

"Okay, Daddy."

It took everything in me not to fold right then and there and get her a puppy. Kissing the side of her head, I wiped the wetness from my face as I climbed out of the back seat and back into the driver's. The rest of the drive was quiet, both of us in our thoughts, surprising me when I turned down a driveway fifteen minutes later.

Perhaps the most shocking thing was spotting Coach Anderson outside the quaint house, the hood of a black car up. He gave me a look but didn't stop working. I vaguely remembered Blake mentioning something about having to stay with him because of a water issue, but in the chaos of everything in the past month, I'd forgotten. I was about to get out of the car and knock on the door when Blake rushed out, a big smile on her face.

Horses stampede, their hooves beating hard in my chest at the sight of her. No matter how much I tried to ignore the pull she had on me—how my pulse raced or my palms sweated at the sight of her—I couldn't.

She wasn't my girlfriend, but I wanted her to be. She was pure light that I didn't deserve. I'd fucked up majorly with Bee. I'd run away scared instead of talking to her. Then, when she'd magically appeared in my life, I treated her like a ball girl. Worse, actually. I made her feel like the only thing she was good for was her pussy, because I was too scared to admit I had real feelings for her.

And the sad part was, I would've continued on with the arrangement, hurting her each time because it worked for me. Having her stand up to me only proved how much I didn't deserve her.

But I was too selfish and greedy not to have her in my life. So, if she was willing to give me another chance, even if only as her friend, then I'd take it and do it right for once.

With all the new things already in my life, it was probably the most mature decision I'd ever made. Mainly because I didn't know if I could handle more commitment outside of baseball and Willow.

But my body craved her.

My heart longed for her.

And the small amount of willpower I had to keep her at arm's length had rapidly evaporated.

Only knowing I had to be responsible for Willow kept it intact. Slow was good. But fuck, it was hard.

Blake walked over to Hawk, saying something as she touched his arm. I watched in amazement as the grumpy coach I knew gave her a megawatt smile, something I didn't know his face was capable of. She kissed his cheek before skipping to the car, motioning to the trunk with her bag.

In a daze, I nodded, popping it for her.

When the door opened, I jolted, having lost myself in my thoughts and everything Blake.

"Hi," she chirped, kissing my cheek before turning to smile at my daughter. "You must be Willow. Your dad has talked nonstop about you. It's so lovely to meet you." She reached her hand through the seats. "I'm Blake."

My daughter assessed her, taking her hand cautiously. "You have a boy's name."

Blake laughed, the sound so pure and magical I forgot to scold Willow.

"Yeah, it can be. It makes a cool girl's name, though, and I like having something unique. There weren't any other Blakes in school, so I always knew when the teacher called for me."

"No one has my name," Willow said, giving Blake a shy smile.

"Cool name club!" She held her hand up for a high-five, and Willow eagerly slapped it. "Lots of people call me different things, though. My brother calls me Blanket when he wants something," she whispered, making Willow giggle. "My parents call me BB, as does anyone who knew me when I was younger. Lots of my friends call me Bee, and my best friend calls me Lake."

"What does my dad call you?" Willow asked, glancing between us.

"Slugger," I answered, giving Blake a small smile.

"He just had to be different," Blake teased, rolling her eyes.

"Can I choose one?" Willow asked, her eyes lighting up.

"Of course, but only if that means I can make up a cool nickname for you, too?"

Willow nodded, her cheeks pink. Blake held out her pinky finger, motioning for Willow to do the same.

"It's a done deal, then."

Blake turned back into her seat, buckling herself in as I pulled out of the driveway, the GPS telling me where to turn.

"Thanks for letting me tag along today. I haven't been to the ocean yet. Have you?"

Willow shook her head. "No. I've never been to the ocean." Her eyes were big, and I was glad I'd decided to do this. To experience a first in my daughter's life, even four years after the fact, felt significant.

"Cool, we can explore it together. Where are you originally from?" Blake asked, keeping Willow engaged in conversation the whole drive. Sadly, I learned more about my daughter in that twenty-minute car ride than I had in the month I'd had her.

She was so different with Blake—more eager and excited. But I guess it was hard not to be. Blake had a way of making me open up and share things. Willow told her about how she had lived with her mom in Indiana, the home of my first baseball team. That her favorite food was spaghetti, and that she loved to color. She talked about her mom and how she was so beautiful that all these people wanted to take pictures of her.

But what gobsmacked me was how Willow spoke about loving baseball and wanting to be just like her dad.

My eyes teared up as I pulled into the parking lot, overcome by her confession. Not only had she easily called me her dad to Blake, but she wanted to be like me. It made my heart swell, and I had to stop myself from pulling her into a hug and weeping all over her.

Blake squeezed my arm, and I smiled softly in thanks as I turned off the car, hoping she understood it was for engaging Willow.

"All right, Willow, let's have fun at the beach!" Blake cheered, hopping out of the car and opening the door for my daughter, who was all smiles.

As I pulled all the gear out, Blake looked like she was holding back a laugh.

"Either you're a pro at the beach, or someone helped you," she teased.

"Matilda," Willow and I said at the same time, laughing at her own joke.

"The woman might be a stickler for things, but she's been a lifesaver," I admitted, locking the car once I had everything out.

It took us a few minutes to find the perfect spot, and the three of us worked together to set it up. With the beach blanket down and the umbrella behind it, we used the cooler and bags to keep it all stationary. Blake helped Willow put on sunscreen as we debated what beach activity to do first.

"What if we look for shells while there aren't that many people?" I suggested, happy when they both eagerly agreed.

Willow skipped ahead with her beach pail, stopping and picking up shells, running back to show us when it was a good one. Blake would casually snap pictures as we walked. I loved how at ease she was with her camera. It was like seeing a new version of her.

I knocked Blake's shoulder with my own, getting her attention. Her hair whipped around her face, and she brushed it out of the way, looking effortlessly beautiful.

"Thank you for joining me. As much as I love having a full day with her, I also freak out about it."

"I think you're harder on yourself than you need to be, Luke. She adores you."

"You think?" I asked, curious.

"Definitely. Did you hear how she talked about her mom? It was like she was reciting the things she'd been told, but then when she brought you up, it was so sweet. I almost melted when she said she wanted to be like you."

"Yeah, me too. That shocked me." I rubbed the back of my

neck, my cheeks heating as I watched my little girl sift through the sand.

"It wasn't to me. It's clear to anyone around you how smitten she is. She might be shy, but she's comfortable with you. She looks to you for reassurance. Like a lot of little girls, she just wants to make her dad proud."

"Really?" I asked, my throat clogged with emotion.

Blake squeezed my hand, linking her fingers with mine. It had felt so natural to hold her hand like this from the first time I did it. And now, I never wanted to stop.

"I'm glad I'm here, too," she whispered, her body leaning against mine.

"Me too. It's nice to spend time with you outside of airplanes and baseball stadiums. Though we've had some fun in those."

Her face pinked, and I worried I'd gone too far, pushing us past this friend balance we had, but she didn't correct me.

"Look at this one!" Willow shouted, running back to us with a giant shell. Blake dropped my hand, kneeling to peer at it, gushing over it with my daughter. After Willow's bucket was full, we returned to our spot, where we had a sandcastle competition. Then I watched them run in and out of the cold water, shrieking when it touched their legs.

After a lunch of sandwiches and fruit, Willow was invited to play tag with other kids, leaving Blake and me under the umbrella to observe. Blake snapped some more photos, and I needed to remember to ask her to send me some of Willow. A while later, she sat her camera down and leaned against me, allowing me to talk to her more.

"I'd forgotten you were staying with Coach. Um, how's that going?" I asked awkwardly, clearing my throat.

"Better than I expected."

"What do you mean?" I raised my eyebrow in confusion. She sat up, turning toward me.

"Right. When Bryce found us that morning, he freaked

out. So, I gave my brother back the one thing he needed—his best friend, breaking my heart in the process."

"Wow. That's intense." I gulped. I knew she had feelings for him, but I hadn't realized they were that deep.

"Don't look at me like that," she whispered. "It's not a competition where the odds need to be in your favor."

"What do you mean?" I asked, confused. "I know you said you hadn't labeled things, but I don't take Coach for someone who is okay with that."

"Good thing I get to decide then who I spend my time with," Blake said, her voice stern.

"I didn't mean it like that," I said quickly. She blew out a breath before her eyes met mine again.

"Graham had me read this book, or books since I'm on a new one, but in these books, they're called why choose. Like, why choose one when I have all these amazing people? And the most beautiful thing about it is how the group becomes a family and supports each other. The burdens aren't placed on one person. Instead, they're shared. I know it sounds too good, but I think it might be an option."

As Blake spoke, I watched Willow, thinking about how nice that sounded. *To not be in this life alone, to have someone there to help figure it out. To not mess this up.*

"So, Graham's idea, huh?" I asked.

"You should talk to him. He's a great listener and could be a good sounding board."

"He did help convince me to talk to you that second time," I admitted.

"Really? I didn't know that." She smiled, a faraway look in her eyes. It was the type of look that I knew I'd do just about anything to always have.

"I know it's not conventional, but playing professional baseball isn't either."

She had a point. Before I could ask any more questions, Willow returned, sandy and sweaty. Blake noticed she was turning pink, so she applied more sunscreen and suggested we pack up and grab ice cream since the beach had gotten more crowded.

Willow eagerly agreed, holding her hand the whole time as they licked their ice cream cones, walking side by side.

Watching them, I realized a lie I'd been telling myself. One I'd let fear make me believe. Deep down, I'd believed I had to choose between a relationship and Willow, that one would take away from the other.

But what if it didn't? Blake was right. My life hadn't been conventional for a long time. So why start now?

Watching them together, something in my chest opened, a pulse beating strong as I envisioned a future outside of baseball. One where I was happy, loved, and accepted for who I was and not for what I did or brought to the equation.

It was absolutely terrifying, but I'd also wanted nothing more desperately in my whole life.

CHAPTER
THIRTY-EIGHT

BLAKE

LUKE BUCKLED WILLOW INTO THE BACKSEAT, KISSING HER HEAD before he shut the door. I never thought watching a man be a good dad could be so sexy. He didn't believe he was pulling off being a father, but from my standpoint, he was nailing it. Willow was crazy about him. She wasn't the only one.

When Luke let down his walls, he was a force to be reckoned with.

He caught me staring, lifting his eyebrow in question as he opened my door, motioning for me to get in.

"I wasn't waiting for you to open my door."

"I know." He smirked, leaning in like he was going to kiss me, but froze a millimeter away, seeming to remember himself. "I can be a gentleman," he said, stepping back. I immediately hated it.

"I'm beginning to see that." I smiled and could feel it transforming my whole face. It was easy to smile this big around him. He quirked a brow, crossing his arms like he had to stop himself from reaching out to touch me. My smile only grew bigger.

"You going to tell me what that look's for or make me beg?"

"I enjoy hearing you beg," I teased.

"I've noticed." His smile tilted at the edges, his eyes wrinkling slightly. A piece of hair shifted across his forehead and I reached up, brushing it without pause. My hand lingered across his forehead as I realized how easily I'd done that.

"It seems we both struggle with being friends," he teased.

"Seems so." I grinned again, loving this flirty side of Luke.

The window next to me rolled down, Willow sticking her head out. "Are you going to kiss her?" she asked, eyes wide and excited.

"Called out by a child," Luke grunted, stepping back.

"Ahh, poo." Willow pouted, making me laugh hard.

"Nice to see you're rooting for me, Kiddo." Luke huffed.

"I like Lake," she said, surprising me.

"Lake, huh?" I asked, turning to look at her. She nodded, grinning.

"It's like the ocean, and I love the ocean. It's my favorite thing after baseball."

I didn't think my heart could burst, but it threatened to do just that, as a little girl called me her next favorite thing. Pulling myself together, I squeezed her arm.

"I love it, Lolo."

She grinned, her teeth white as she heard my nickname for her. I brushed her hair across her forehead, knowing I was already in love with this little girl. It was impossible not to be. Spending any amount of time in her presence was to fall in love with her. Regardless of what happened with me and Luke, I was committed to being her friend.

"Okay, I guess we should get Bee home," Luke said, moving to his door. I slid into mine, sad that the day was over.

"Does she have to?" Willow asked, pouting. "What if I

take back wanting a kitten? Could Lake come over then?" Willow asked her dad. Luke froze his hands midway in the air to the steering wheel. He turned to me, his eyes wide. I didn't know what he was shocked about.

"What do you have in mind? What are your evening plans?" I asked, shifting the conversation forward as he stared.

Willow shrugged her little shoulders. "I could show you my room."

Luke seemed to gather himself, clearing his throat as he pushed the button to start the car. "We're just making dinner; then I was going to work on building things for her room. Then bath, storytime, and bed."

"You could read me a story!" Willow said, her eyes so big with excitement.

"I am great at reading stories." I nodded. "Dinner wouldn't happen to be spaghetti, would it?"

She nodded her head, smiling. "Daddy and I cook together."

"Well, then. How could I go home now? I can't miss that!"

"Will you be able to get a ride?" Luke asked.

"Yeah. I can ask Hawk to pick me up." I smiled, pulling out my phone and finding a few messages.

Graham: Hope you're having a great day, Sunshine.

Tucker: I miss you. Don't have too much fun.

Graham: She can have fun and miss you. They're not mutually exclusive.

Tucker: Fine. But don't stop liking me, please.

Graham: Such a needy punk. Quit bothering her.

> Graham: See you on the bus tomorrow.
> XOXO.

I sent them back some kissy emojis and a picture of the beach.

> Hawk: Sunny is sad without you here. I think he misses your boobs.

Snorting, I asked if he could pick me up later and that my boobs missed him, too. I glanced at the ones from my family but decided to reply to them later, not able to respond to them with a quick reply.

> Bryce: Hey, Blanket! The condo should be ready in a few days.

> Mom: Hey, BB. Call me when you have a free moment.

> Dad: How's the job going? Mira giving you any trouble?

How did I tell my brother I didn't want to return to his condo anymore? That was a landmine I didn't have the energy for right now. There was no telling what my mom wanted. She swung from concerned to bulldozer so quickly that sometimes I never knew which version I was getting. But the text from my dad made me feel more nervous than I expected.

Had Mira said something? She'd been conveniently absent the last three home games when I peeked into the office. It let me do the job I wanted, so I hadn't questioned it too much. But now I wondered…

Hawk's reply popped up before I could think more, making my cheeks heat in return.

Hawk: I can, but I expect you to scream my name at least two times before we leave tomorrow.

Hawk: When that occurs is up to you, Blazy.

"All good," I said, my voice huskier than intended. I crossed my legs, pushed my phone back into my bag, and smiled at Willow. "I have a crucial question. Do you make garlic bread with your spaghetti?"

Her eyes grew big, and she shook her head. "Do you know how to?" she asked hopefully.

"Hmm, well, I happen to have a friend who's a superb cook, and I bet if I ask him, he will give me his recipe. Apparently, it's the best in nine states."

"Wow. Dad! We gotta try it."

"Who?" Luke asked, peering over at me.

"Graham."

"Ah." He swallowed with chagrin.

"It's never too late to make friends," I whispered, reminding him of our earlier conversation. He nodded, smiling over at me. I patted his leg, hoping he'd take the chance to change that now.

"So, Lolo, what's in your baseball room?"

As she went into detail about her baseball sheets, the rack that looked like a bat where she hung her backpack on, and the bean bag shaped like a glove. I was impressed at the lengths Luke had gone.

"What about your walls? Got anything on them yet?"

"No. I'm still thinking," she said, tapping her lip.

"Willow has strong opinions on her room decor."

"Smart. You gotta live there, so you need to love it." I turned around, meeting her eyes. "I take pictures for the YellowJackets. I bet I could get you some good ones of your dad in action. Would you like that?"

"Really? That would be awesome!" Her eyes grew wide, her mouth open.

Luke groaned, but I could see the smile on his lips that she wanted a picture of him. We pulled into the driveway of an updated colonial home with white siding and black shutters and trim. The garage sat off to the side, the front of the house wrapping around with a porch and extending to the backyard.

"This is gorgeous." I climbed out of the car, taking in the flowers sprouting in the dark mulch.

"It's a rental. I wasn't expecting to be in Wilmington this long," Luke admitted, reminding me my brother had taken his spot back on the Blue Devils.

"Speaking of rivalries. What's the beef with you and my brother?"

Luke grimaced as he pulled out the bags. "That's a hornet's nest I'm not ready to step in yet. I'm not sure why he hated me at first, but yeah, once it was there…" He shook his head self-deprecatingly. "I didn't help matters, and when I was traded to the Blue Devils, I guess it was the last straw."

I nodded, vaguely remembering Bryce talking about him over the years.

"Do you think he's gonna have a problem with us being… friends?"

"Probably, though he might not speak to me once he learns about Hawk, so you got that in your favor!" I joked.

"Lake! Come see my room," Willow shouted, running into the kitchen where we'd stopped to drop off the bags. She tugged on my hand, dragging me with her.

"To be continued," Luke said, waving me off.

Over the next few hours, I assisted Willow in picking out her clothes for the next day, made dinner with her and Luke, and participated in bath time. Luke built a bookcase while Willow and I supervised, offering support he didn't quite need.

"One more book, Lolo."

"Okay." She pouted.

Luke smirked at me, having told me how she would try to sucker me into reading over three. We were currently on book five, and I couldn't say I hated it. But her eyes were drooping, and it was getting late, and I didn't want to keep Hawk waiting too long.

She snuggled into my side, and I combed my fingers through her hair as I read. Luke's phone vibrated, and he motioned he was going to step out, kissing Willow on her forehead before leaving. I kept reading for a few more minutes, but when she didn't move, I carefully shut the book and crawled out from under her. Tucking in the covers, I turned off the overhead light, leaving on the baseball-shaped nightlight before closing the door.

My feet padded down the hallway as I took in the different rooms. It was a big house with more rooms than they needed. Outside of Willow's, there wasn't any personality, and it reminded me of the reality of Luke's situation, of all the guys, really.

Baseball teams weren't permanent.

Trades, injuries, and retirement happen every day in the sport. I'd lived it most of my life, and now I was knowingly signing up for it by falling for not one but three baseball players and a coach.

Babe Ruth, help me.

Turning a corner, I spotted Luke sitting on an enormous bed through the door. His hands were in his hair as he stared at the ground. I knocked on the doorframe, not wanting to startle him by entering.

"Hey," he said, glancing up and motioning for me to enter.

"Everything okay?" I asked, sitting on the bed next to him.

"It was Willow's mom again. She keeps extending her

stay, but this time, she's gonna miss Willow's birthday." He blew out a breath, some of his blonde hair lifting. "Jas wouldn't tell her, making me the bad guy."

"That sucks, Luke. I'm sorry."

"I hate seeing her so sad." He fidgeted and then met my eyes. "I got in touch with a lawyer, and I'm thinking of filing for full custody. I don't want Willow to think I'm going away, too."

"That's a big step."

He nodded, his eyes searching mine. "I know it's a lot, and everything here is new and…"

"Complicated," I said for him.

"Yeah. It didn't help that I initially acted like a tool." He grimaced.

"Yeah, there is that." I smiled, knocking his shoulder with mine. I took his hand in mine, linking our fingers and taking a deep breath. "Your daughter is amazing, Luke. She's so bright and kind. Being with you both today was a gift."

"I feel like a but is coming," he said.

I shook my head, meeting his head. "No buts. It reminded me of what I've been working on these past three years."

"Which is?" he asked, his voice hopeful.

"Living a life for me. Not being scared in the shadows. Knowing that life isn't guaranteed, and not letting opportunities pass me by."

"So I still have a chance?" he asked with so much hope it broke me.

"The only worthless chocolate is tootsie rolls. I tricked my brother when he was twelve that he was shrinking. And I like you. I really like you. Spot the lie, Luke."

Luke smiled, cupping my face. "How did I never see it before? You're a terrible liar."

Gaping, I only held it for a few seconds before I laughed.

"I really want to kiss you. Is that allowed?" he asked,

moving closer, our lips a breath apart. All the heat and tension returned, my body recalling how well we fit together.

"I'm open to negotiations," I whispered.

His lips pressed into mine, and my heart flipped over in my chest as his thumb swept across my cheek. Each time I kissed Luke, I forgot how magnetic it was. It was probably because, if I remembered, I'd never stop.

"Just don't hurt me again," I murmured, breaking the kiss.

"I don't want to, Slugger. I hate that I made you doubt me." His eyes searched mine, sincerity ringing through. "I know I haven't been consistent or shown you my actions can be trusted. And while I'm still unsure about the whole group dating thing you have with my teammates, I know I want you in my life, and I won't run this time. I promise to figure it out with you."

Hope bloomed in my chest, my heart skipping like a rock across a pond. I held my breath as I asked the next question. "Are we jumping in too soon?"

"Like you said, nothing in life is guaranteed. Especially in baseball. We gotta play the inning we're in and hope we've set ourselves up well for the next." He rested his forehead against mine, his thumbs caressing my face. Damn him and his baseball logic!

"I've lived most of my life planning for a future that was stripped away from me in the blink of an eye. One injury and my career was derailed. But then I was given something new. Something I thought would wreck me. And as angry as I was to be stuck in this town, it's given me time to fall in love with a little girl."

He swallowed, his eyes searching mine, his body trembling next to me as his hands held me.

"You reminded me what I loved about baseball and to believe in myself. That my skills weren't wrapped up in superstitions or dependent on what color uniform I wore.

I've gotten closer to you and the magic you possess. While I don't like these other guys wanting you, I can understand it. You're the sun that draws us in, Slugger."

My heart raced, lightning crackling over my skin as I listened, afraid to breathe.

"None of those were things I planned. None of them were on my agenda. I don't think I really even knew what I wanted. So, maybe it's time I try batting left-handed."

Goosebumps spread across my skin, and my pulse jumped all over the place.

This man. He had my heart in his hands, and I was helpless to take it back.

Stopping myself from jumping on him and showing how much his words affected me, I wrinkled my nose.

"I can't believe you just used a baseball metaphor."

Luke laughed, easing some of the seriousness of the moment.

"Habit of the trade." He shrugged, his cheeks pinking.

"Those were beautiful words, Luke."

"Spot the lie?" he asked, and I shook my head.

"I can feel them all the way to my marrow," I whispered.

His hand smoothed over my hair, cupping the back of my neck. "You're the part of my day I look forward to most. Seeing you, even when I thought I hated you, was the best part of being on the YellowJackets. I need you in my life more than I knew possible. I thought I was saving you on that plane, but you've been saving me all along, Slugger. You knocked my heart out of the park, and it's never been the same since. So kiss me. Don't kiss me. But know that I'm here when you're ready. For whatever capacity that entails— friends or more. But I secretly hope it's more."

I thought he'd slayed me earlier, but my heart jumped clear out of my body, beating frantically as he poured out his heart to me. His words were everything I wanted to hear but hadn't known.

I didn't need to think about it anymore. There was protecting oneself, and then there was sabotage. I wouldn't stand in my way any longer.

Slamming my lips to his, I felt my soul join his, as our bodies pressed into one another. Climbing onto his lap, I claimed his lips with mine, needing to feel every inch of him. My hands raked through his hair, tugging at the strands to gain even a centimeter more. His hands ran over my body urgently, the need surging in us as passion and need exploded. Time ceased to exist outside of our kiss.

My phone vibrated in my pocket, jerking us both apart in surprise. Our pants were loud as we surveyed one another. His lips were red and swollen, and his hair tousled from my hands. Glancing in the mirror, my state wasn't far off.

Laughing, I patted my hair down and shifted my shirt where it had exposed my boob. As my pulse returned to normal, I was grateful for Hawk disturbing us before we forgot a young child slept down the hall.

"Thanks for today." I peppered his lips with tiny kisses, barely dragging myself off his lap.

His face was pained as he shifted his erection, clearing his throat. "Um, so, what's next?"

I stopped, spinning on my heels, laughing. "Whatever we want."

"I like the sound of that."

He stood, his erection still tenting his shorts. I bit my lip, debating if I had time, when my phone buzzed again, reminding me Hawk was waiting.

"See you tomorrow."

"I'll walk you out."

It was a quick stroll to his front door, and I shifted on my feet, debating on what to say. In the end, I hugged him, kissing him softly before stepping out of the door. He watched me as I walked down the steps to the Mustang.

Climbing in, I assessed Hawk to see if he was upset about waiting or picking me up from another guy's house.

Hawk peered out the window, nodding as I shut the door. Luke waved before stepping back inside. Hawk was quiet as he pulled out of the drive, the radio the only noise for a few blocks.

"Thanks for picking me up. Willow had wanted me to spend more time."

"He has a daughter?" Hawk asked, his tone soft.

"Yeah. He didn't know until January. He has her while her mom is on a modeling job. She's the cutest."

"How was the date?" he asked, shocking me.

"The ocean was cold, but the day was good. What about yours?" I asked, trying to figure out if he was upset or okay with everything.

I knew right then that I needed everyone on board to some degree. I didn't want to feel like I was cheating when I was with the others or that I had to hide what I did in my time. I might not be able to shout to the world who I was dating, but I wouldn't hide it from the ones I was.

"Is this weird?" I asked, interrupting him.

"A little."

"Too much to handle?" I asked, glancing over.

"No, Blazy. It's just different. It's gonna take some time to adjust to."

"Okay, I get that. Maybe we need to figure out the boundaries and everything. I don't want to hurt anyone, but I can't hide or pretend like someone else doesn't exist."

"That's fair. And despite my discomfort, it doesn't change how I feel about you."

I smiled, pulling out my phone and entering all their names into a group message.

> Blake: I know I said no labels, but I need some boundaries.

Blake: When we return from the away games, let's all sit down and talk.

Blake: It gives everyone a week to think about things and bring any questions.

Blake: I'll make sure to spend time away with everyone this week so we can all see how it works.

Blake: Graham, I've been telling everyone to talk to you. Even though I've read about it, you explain it much better. You're our relationship guru.

Blake: Good night.

CHAPTER
THIRTY-NINE

GRAHAM

I stared at the text message from Blake, exhilaration and fear encompassing me as I read it. I loved that she had that much confidence in me, but the truth was, I felt so out of my league here.

Yes, I read a lot of books. They were my comfort and how I related to the world. But it didn't mean I knew everything about relationships. As much as I wanted to be the relationship guru and loved that she saw me that way, I felt wholly unprepared.

I'd never even had a girlfriend before, or a boyfriend, for that matter.

I would screw this up.

I was the last person who needed to be giving relationship advice. The longest relationship in my life was with Tucker, and it wasn't anything I'd explicitly done to make him stay. It was just the way it was. Like two black holes that had merged, peanut butter on the roof of your mouth, or gum on the bottom of your shoe—impossible to separate from.

"Huh. Who knew?" Tucker said, snorting as he strolled into my bedroom, eating a muffin as he read something on his phone. He plopped down on my bed, rolling into me as he settled himself, licking his fingers.

His bare chest brushed against my arm, sending shivers through me. We hadn't specifically spoken about the things from the other night, adding a layer of apprehension to my skin.

Was he aware of the lines we'd crossed?

Had he liked it?

Was it only because of the heat of the moment?

My mind had been spiraling for days with thoughts, waiting for the moment he told me how disgusted he'd been and how our friendship was ruined.

"How much do you think someone gets paid to write '101 ways to play with a stick?'" he asked, leaning closer to show me his phone screen.

His chocolate-scented breath hit me, warming my skin as he waited for me to answer. His body pressed against my entire left side, making it impossible to concentrate.

"Hmm?" I asked, blinking. I dropped my phone and turned my head, our faces millimeters apart. Tucker froze, his eyes dropping to my lips for a second before meeting my eyes again. His pupils dilated, and he licked his lips as he stared back.

"Playing... with... sticks," he exclaimed, confusing me even more.

"Sticks?" I asked, my voice hoarse.

Tucker swallowed, his Adam's apple bobbing and pulling my attention as I watched it move.

"Yeah. There's an article," he said, softer like being closer made it a secret.

"About?" I asked, lifting an eyebrow.

Tucker smiled, showing his teeth as he stared at me. When he dropped his head back to his phone, I felt like my air was gone.

"101 ways to play with a stick. Can you imagine having to

come up with these ideas? Listen to this: Hold a stick in each hand and pretend to go over a tightrope. Throw them in the air and try to pick them up before your friends. Pretend to conduct an orchestra." He chuckled, and the vibrations leaked into my body from our proximity. "Do you think this person loves or hates their job? But also, I have a weird desire to go outside and do all of them now."

I smiled and shook my head. He'd glanced back up when he finished, bringing our faces close again. Something I'd forgotten until our noses brushed together in an Eskimo kiss. I froze, my eyes locked on his, worried again he'd push me off and tell me to get myself together.

But Tucker did none of that. He smiled, then did it again, brushing our noses and sending electric currents through me. "That tickles. But it also feels nice."

I swallowed, my throat dry as I tried to contain my heart that wanted to jump out of my throat. "Yeah. It does."

He continued to read more, scrolling through the list as he chuckled, shaking his head in disbelief. I stared at him, looking for any sign things were different.

But it felt the same. We felt the same.

When he reached the end, he blackened his screen and laid his phone aside, resting his head on his arms as he stared at me.

"I'm excited," he whispered.

Mimicking his position, I rested my head on my arms as well, our faces a few inches apart still.

"Yeah? Because of Blake?"

He scoffed, like me asking was dumb, and rolled his eyes. "Duh. But also that we're headed to more official things. To being a unit, a group. You had your sisters growing up, but I've never had that… the family thing. My mom worked multiple jobs to make ends meet, so I spent most of my time alone."

Tucker licked his lips, his eyes moving back and forth

quickly as he thought. "Baseball was the only time I felt included, but the season always ended, and my teammates returned home to their families, and I'd be back in our empty apartment with only myself to talk to. No one ever invited me over because I annoyed most of them. I was so starved for attention, I never shut up."

"And you do now?" I teased, making him stick out his tongue, the tip touching my arm.

"Hush, Teddy Graham. I'm having a moment," he admonished.

"You're right. Carry on, Princess."

"Finally, some recognition for my title!" He grinned, his brown eyes sparkling.

Some of his curls were falling into his eyes and I had the urge to brush them aside. I barely contained myself, curling my fingers inward to stop the urge.

"By high school, my baseball skills made me popular, and I'd learned to dial back my enthusiasm. I became the funny guy, the one that made everyone laugh. If you saw me back then, you never would've thought I was lonely, but I remembered how those same kids had treated me. It was nice to pretend at school they were really my friends, that girls wanted me." He shook his head, sadness leaking into his eyes. His hair brushed even more across his eyes, brown orbs scorching me from the inside out. "But I knew the truth deep down, and at the end of the school day, the facade would end, and I returned to that lonely apartment."

"I never knew that," I offered, seeing a new side of Tucker. "You make it seem so easy to make friends that you're always your true self. I've always been jealous of that skill."

"Really?" Tucker asked, his brows lifting in astonishment. "Honestly, it's only easy now because I have your friendship. I'd decided when I got to college, I was tired of pretending. Being roomed with you was the best thing. I instantly had a friend, someone who couldn't escape me." He laughed, knocking my arms.

"Like I would've tried," I teased, rolling my eyes.

"I'm glad you didn't," he admitted, his eyes dropping. "You gave me the confidence to not water down myself and that if other people didn't like me, oh well, because you did. As long as I had your friendship, then life was okay." He shrugged, the motion rocking him into me in this position.

I cleared my throat, emotion clogging it. "I never thought about it that way. I thought you took pity on me, the extrovert collecting the introvert friend out of pity. Then, when we had this connection playing, I felt I at least offered you something of value in return, and that was why you stuck around."

Tucker's mouth dropped open as he stared at me. "You thought I was your friend out of pity? All this time?"

My cheeks heated. "Well, not anymore. But in the beginning. Yeah."

Tucker sighed, rolling his eyes. "Wow. We're both so lame. Let's not tell Blake."

"Deal." I grinned, feeling lighter in a way. "So, you're excited about having more friends?" I asked, wanting to ensure I understood.

"Not just friends, but family." He paused. "Would that make us boyfriends?" He tilted his head in thought, my breath freezing in my throat. "Boyfriend-in-laws? Paramours? Is there a word, guru?" he asked, turning his eyes to mine.

"Um, well, hmm. Boyfriends would only be if you were with one of the guys in addition to Blake. Is that what you're thinking?" I asked, not able to stop myself.

"With the others?" he asked, wrinkling his nose.

I nodded, not trusting my words. It felt like everything hinged on this next second.

"No. Not with the others."

His eyes dropped to my lips again, and I wondered if he knew he was doing it. I licked my lips, his nostrils flaring at the action.

"What… What about me?" I whispered, my breath stalling in my chest.

Tucker's eyes flicked back up, and I had it on the tip of my tongue to retract my words.

"I…" He stopped, swallowed, leaving me on tenterhooks. "I think that's something I'm open to."

The words hung in the air, and I wasn't sure if I heard them correctly or had merely dreamed them. I blinked, the air still.

"But I thought you were straight?" I asked, finding it the easiest way to ask.

"I thought so, too. But lately… I dunno." He shrugged, his arm brushing mine again and bringing more goosebumps. "I've been feeling different things."

"Things… for *me*?"

Tucker nodded, his pupils blown, making his brown eyes molten. He swallowed, licking his lips, his tongue so enticing I almost groaned.

"Do you… have feelings for me like that?" Tucker asked.

"Yeah." I nodded, not believing I was admitting this. "It's how I realized I was pan."

Tucker's eyes widened, his mouth making an 'o' shape as he digested that information.

"But that's been since…"

"Sophomore year," I said, giving a sheepish grin and dropping my eyes as embarrassment heated my cheeks. My whole face flamed.

Tucker grunted, the sound drawing my eyes back up just in time to see him move forward, touching his lips with mine. His eyes were closed, allowing me to watch his face as I processed what was happening.

My best friend was kissing me.

My best friend admitted to feeling things for me.

My best friend hadn't run out of the room screaming when I told him how I felt.

Apparently, I'd taken too long to process it; my body stuck still as his lips pressed into mine. And since my eyes were open, I watched as his brows creased, and he moved to pull back, sending panic through me. No! I wouldn't miss my chance.

Pushing my lips into his, I closed my eyes and gave in to the feeling of his lips on mine. Using my momentum, I rolled into his body, lifting my arms to brace my hands on his face. At the pressure, he melted into me, sighing into my lips.

I'd kissed a few guys since coming out as pansexual, but they'd never felt like this. Tucker's lips were soft and pliable, giving way to mine as I pressed into him. Emotion surged inside me, my heart beating like a herd of wild horses. It hurtled forward, galloping off without me as I stopped thinking and followed my body's wishes.

Slanting my mouth over his, passion erupted as our lips moved together, like they knew perfectly how to fit together. Desire raced down my spine, my cock hardening as my balls drew heavy. Running my fingers up in his hair, I brushed it aside like I'd been dying to. I felt his purr deep in my chest, and I smiled, liking that I could evoke that sound from him.

Pushing more of my body weight into him, I hovered as I led the kiss. Licking the seam of his lips, I snuck my tongue in when he gasped, swirling it around with his as gravity fell away. Everything outside of this moment felt far away, unable to touch us. I deepened the kiss, my tongue and mouth hungry for everything he had to give me. His stubble rubbed against mine, eliciting a zing as I imagined the stubble burn tomorrow.

His hands moved down my back, his fingers tentative but hungry as he explored my muscles. I had the urge to rock into him, but I broke the kiss, panting, worried I'd push him too far into something before he was ready.

Tucker whined, chasing my lips as I drew back, making me chuckle. I stared down at him, brushing my thumbs over his cheeks as I held his hand.

"Shh, Princess. I'm not leaving, I just wanted to ensure you were good. That this was real."

Tucker's eyes opened, full of desire and need, and something I didn't want to misinterpret. His chest heaved up and down, his heart hammering as fast as mine against my chest.

"I'm great, especially if there's more kisses to come. Damn. I've been missing out all these years not sharing my lips with guys."

I growled before I could stop myself, frowning at him. "Hell, no. These lips," I said, dropping a kiss on them, reminding him how good it felt, "are mine, Tucker Jameson. They always have been. You're just now catching up. No other man gets to taste them. Understand?"

Tucker nodded, his eyes so blown that I could no longer see any brown. "All yours, Teddy Graham." He leveled me with a shit-eating grin, his eyes sparkling.

I rocked into him, our erections brushing against one another, and his eyes rolled back at the contact. "You can call me whatever you want, Princess, as long as you know who you belong to."

"Fuck, that's hot," he groaned, rocking back up into me. "Shit, this feels good."

I dropped my head into his neck, sucking on the skin as he rubbed our cocks together beneath our clothes. I was dangerously close to exploding at that simple contact. When Tucker gripped my ass in his hands, squeezing, I couldn't hold myself back any longer.

"Shit," I cursed, "I'm coming, Tuck."

"Aah, Graham," he hissed, squeezing my butt as he shook in my arms, our bodies trembling together. "Wow."

I chuckled, lifting my head to search his eyes. There was still a part of me worried this was just a phase, something he was curious about and he'd freak out and push me away any second now.

"Cuddle time," Tucker said, snuggling into me and wrapping his legs around me.

"We should clean up first. No one wants to go to sleep with dried cum on their balls."

"But I get to cuddle after, right?" he asked hesitantly. Usually, Tucker demanded his affection and never worried about overstepping. This little hesitation erased all my fear. He was just as scared, just as nervous. He wouldn't have risked us for curiosity.

"Yeah, punk, you can. Come on," I said, pecking his lips before rolling off and stepping into my bathroom. I decided to quit overthinking things, stripping off my joggers, and turning on the tap. We'd been us for so long, I had to believe this was just a new addition and not a complete rewrite.

Tucker joined me, doing the same, not at all embarrassed about us both standing with our dicks out. Thank god. I didn't think I could take it if our comfortableness with each other changed.

After cleaning up, I pulled out two pairs of boxers, tossing one to him. Tucker shrugged, pulling them on without a second glance. Part of me had known he'd be too lazy to return to his room, but I also wanted to see him in my clothes. That primal part of me was more prominent with him than Blake. I knew it wasn't because I liked her less, just how I related to each gender.

I plugged both of our phones in and checked our alarms, happy when they were set. Pulling the covers back, we climbed into my bed, and I turned off the light as Tucker snuggled into my side.

He yawned, nuzzling himself into me like always.

"Does this make us boyfriends now?" he asked.

I froze, my heart racing again. "Do you want to be?" I asked, then changed my mind. "Actually, let's just wait until we talk with Blake."

"Okay. But for the record, I'd be your boyfriend if you asked."

"Noted," I said, smiling as I closed my eyes. My eagerness for what was to come surged, and the fear that I wasn't the right person was utterly gone. Tucker had done that, and I planned to show him how amazing he was.

**CHAPTER
FORTY**

BLAKE

Climbing the bus the next morning, I wondered if I was a glutton for punishment. Why had I suggested waiting a week?

Oh, right, to give them time.

But now, I worried if they had time to think about it, they'd decide they didn't want to be part of this crazy relationship *I* suggested.

Because it *was* my idea.

I could say Graham had come up with it until I was blue in the face, but it was only because I wanted to be with all of them that he'd mentioned it.

Fuck. I was greedy.

Why would four hot guys want to be with a woman they had to share?

"You're thinking too hard," Levi said, narrowing his eyes at me. "Stop it."

"Um, what?" I asked, turning my head to peer at him.

"I don't know what you're overthinking, but I can see that you are. Baseball is 90% mental—"

"The other half physical," I finished. "Yeah, I know that one. My dad loves to quote Yogi Berra."

"Regardless, it's true." He smirked but narrowed his eyes, and I couldn't deny he wasn't wrong.

"Fair." I held up my hands, smiling and letting go of my worry.

Tucker and Graham motioned for me to join them in the back, and I exhaled all the anxiety as I took my place between them. Luke smiled at me as he climbed onto the bus, sitting closer to us.

"Good morning," he said, nodding to the guys.

"Olson!" Tucker cheered. "So, clear this up for me. Who would win in a battle between Snoopy and Scooby Doo."

"Um, what?" he asked, freezing with his bag partially under the seat like he was debating not putting it there. "Did you tell my secret?" he whispered.

"Nope." I shook my head, snorting. "But you just did."

"Oh, what secret?" Tucker asked, leaning over the back of the seat in front of us.

They spent half the trip debating every superhero and anime character Tucker could recall and asking Luke his opinion on who would win in a battle. Graham had spaced out hours ago, his earbuds in as he watched a new documentary, and I read the latest book he'd gotten me.

It was oddly nice, and I only wished Hawk could have joined us, too. By the longing glances he shot me from the front, he wasn't opposed to that idea.

Maybe this wasn't so far-fetched, after all.

The YellowJackets were on a hot streak, but I was cognizant enough not to say anything. They'd won the last ten games and only appeared to improve with each win. We were only six weeks into the season, early, really, but the team felt solid.

It was the best starting record at 31-5 the YellowJackets had in years, making it more and more likely we'd be in a good position at the end of the first half.

The excitement had spread among the team, too, and the camaraderie had grown exponentially. And somewhere in all of that, Tucker had declared dugout prank wars.

The first was hot feet, where one person attempted to place a bubblegum match to the bottom of a cleat and set it off. Only two players had successfully pulled it off—Dalton and Hector. Tucker got caught by Levi, who retaliated by ambushing him with silly string when he exited the stadium. Thankfully, I got it on camera and uploaded it, and the fans loved it.

The next prank was bubblegum hat, where they attempted to place a gum bubble on top of someone's hat without them knowing. In this, Tucker shined and had almost successfully 'bubblegumed' the whole team. The few left walked around, constantly looking over their shoulders, which was comical all on its own.

There had also been taping players to the bench, bubble guns when you entered the dugout and pickle-flavored sunflower seed swaps. All the pranks had been harmless, part of the dugout culture, and had worked to unite the team weirdly.

It helped the away games pass by quicker as I spent time with each of the guys, but it brought something I hadn't expected—a sense of longing.

Each time I was with Luke, I wondered what Hawk thought. When I was with Hawk, I worried about Graham and Tucker. When I was with them, I anxiously checked my phone, curious about Luke's perspective.

Basically, I was a hot mess express with enough nervous energy to fuel a power plant.

The casual, no-label thing had been refreshing initially, but now I needed boundaries to know where I stood with people. The ambiguity made me question every action and feeling, putting me back into that space where I did things for everyone else, not myself.

We were finally back in Wilmington and were all planning on having a conversation today after the game. It had been a long, tortuous week, but it had brought me a lot of clarity, so I hoped it had done the same for the guys.

Stepping out of Hawk's Mustang, I tried to hide the permanent grin I now had. Hiking my bag and camera onto my shoulder, I met Hawk at the front of his car. My free hand itched to take his, but I knew it wasn't a smart move to make out in the open, yet.

"It feels like we've been away for months," I admitted, my nerves making me fidgety. My thumb went to my cuticles, picking at the skin as I realized it would be the first time I was with them together.

"Hmm," Hawk said, rubbing his beard. He inhaled deeply, and I frowned, wondering if he was okay.

"I can still smell you in my beard," Hawk mumbled twenty feet from the front gate.

My mouth dropped open, and I stumbled; my face turned red as he continued to rub his coarse hair, smirking.

"One of these days, I'm going to learn how to make black holes appear so I can disappear into them," I grumbled, causing him to burst out laughing.

"Good morning, BB. Coach. It's a good day for some baseball," Clive said as we ambled closer.

"Hey, Clive. How's it going today?" I asked, stopping to talk to him for a minute. Hawk nodded, indicating he would see me inside, continuing on his way as he clapped Clive on the back.

Twenty minutes later, with a promise to stop by his seats during the game to say hello to his wife and grandkids, I made it to my desk. Mira was actually in her office, the first time I'd seen her since my confrontation. That had been eleven days ago. I felt even more confident and stronger in my conviction as I unpacked my bag and got to work.

I had a few hours before I had to engage with the players, and I needed every second of them. Reviewing footage, editing pictures, and uploading them to the various social media pages took forever, and I often grew bored as I waited.

At least today, I had pictures from the last week away and the beach trip to sort through. Willow and Luke were adorable together, and I flagged a few to send to him. Once the accounts were good, I filed the new consent forms I'd gotten and reviewed the interviews I'd done last week before making a list of the players I still needed.

Ugh, Seth. Maybe I'd skip him. That was professional, right?

Sighing, I picked up my bag and camera to head to the tunnel. Getting into position, I snapped pictures as the players arrived. Now that we were starting week seven, most of the players knew what to expect. Most were friendly, waving, and smiling when they spotted me.

I'd ask them about their families or random questions like I decided to do today.

"So, Sal, how many unread messages do you have on your phone?"

He stopped, frowning as he pulled out his phone. "Um, 43. Why?"

"Just curious." I laughed, and he continued by.

"How many unread messages do you have, Austin?"

He cringed but stopped and flashed it toward me. My eyes bugged out.

"1,234! How? Why?" I gaped, and he chuckled.

"I forget." I shook my head, asking the next person who'd stopped.

"What about you, Dalton? I'm scared to ask."

He grinned wide, flipping his phone over. "Zero."

"You're officially my favorite person." I laughed as they

shoved and ribbed one another as they continued. My smile fell as I spotted the next player.

Because while most were friendly, others didn't acknowledge me, either too in the zone, or like Seth, who deemed me beneath them.

He walked by, his eyes on his phone, and pretended I didn't exist.

Did I purposely get a bad angle of him? Well, I'd never tell.

But if all of his pictures suddenly looked heinous, maybe he should be nicer to those he worked with.

A rare few, like Levi, would stop and talk to me, asking how my brother was doing at the Blue Devils. I felt marginally guilty each time, especially since I avoided his texts and calls. I'd only sent a few one-word responses over the past week, and each one made the guilt larger.

Keeping my relationships from him was difficult, and I knew I needed to have that conversation with him soon. Bryce and I had always been transparent with one another, so not sharing something was out of character, and I didn't like it.

An electric energy raced up my arms a second later, alerting me to their arrival before I saw Tucker and Graham. It was the same charge I felt in their presence, wrapping around me like a strand of Christmas bulbs, their light dazzling when our eyes connected.

The grin I'd worn the first half of the day returned, and I fought the urge to run and jump into their arms, hiking my legs around their waists and kissing them both.

My legs twitched with the need to move, but I stayed squatting, snapping pictures like I was paid to do.

Tucker, however, did not have the same reservations.

Running forward, he practically tackled me to the ground when he spotted me.

"Hey, Honey Bee. I missed you." His bright smile made me feel light and airy, like cotton candy.

I laughed. "I missed you too, but be careful. Don't hurt my camera, Tuck. I'm quite attached to it."

He pouted, glancing down at the object blocking us. "I'll buy you a new one."

"It probably cost a couple grand," Graham responded, stopping next to our pile of limbs.

Tucker groaned, sitting up. "Fine. I'll sell my car. Finally, a worthy cause!"

Graham laughed as Tucker hugged me, nosing his head into my neck.

"You smell so good, Bee."

"Thanks, Tuck. You're good for one's ego." I patted his back, not sure what would look the least innocent. Most people were familiar with his touchy ways, but it was also how rumors started.

"Anytime, Honey Bee," he said, finally standing. He wrapped his arm around Graham. Over the past week, I'd noticed a slight shift between them. But with all of my own emotions taking front and center, I hadn't asked.

Well, that was changing right now!

I lifted my eyebrow at Graham; Tucker was too oblivious to the other people walking by as he waved and chatted to notice. Graham delivered a soft smile, holding my eyes, and I interpreted it to mean he would tell me later.

"So, when are we having this chat?" Tucker asked, turning back to us and bouncing on his feet.

"After the game," I said, thinking that was the end of it.

"Or," Tucker said, rubbing his hands together. "We have a break today after practice."

"The four of you will be free?"

Graham nodded, watching me in his Graham way—observing every nuance and emotion.

"Yes. Can you get away?" Tucker pleaded, his enthusiasm the only thing keeping the mania at bay.

"Are you sure you want this talk before a game?" I asked, anxiety blossoming in my chest.

"Yeah, I don't think I can wait any longer. It's already been hell this past week. I want to know beforehand. I promise I'll play better."

"*Or worse,*" I countered. "I can't handle that pressure." I crossed my arms, missing a few players as they walked in, too focused on the two in front of me.

"Please, Bee," he whined, pushing out his lip. "We already know you've got a—"

Graham elbowed him in the stomach, stopping his words.

"I told you to stop saying that."

"I was gonna say good luck," he breathed, rubbing his abs.

"It didn't hurt your six-pack, Princess." Graham rolled his eyes, making me laugh. I loved being around them. I sighed and pulled up my big girl pants.

"I can see if the other two are interested if that's what you prefer." I gulped.

While I wanted this conversation, the other part of me was still terrified. But really, I knew how they felt; I just needed to trust in the relationships I'd been building.

Trust. Communication. Acceptance.

I repeated the words, letting them soak through my anxiety.

Relationships in the past hadn't been my strong suit, and until I returned to the States two months ago, my love life had been sporadic and lackluster.

But now, I had four amazing men vying for my attention. It sometimes felt too good to be true, and I worried I'd strike out. Again.

Destined to never be with someone I loved—my very own curse.

I snapped pictures of players as I debated, knowing it was occurring no matter when we had this conversation, so the time of day didn't matter. I pulled out my phone and sent a message to the group chat.

Blake: GT suggested we chat before the game.

Hawk: Okay.

It didn't surprise me that Hawk's response was short and to the point. It was just how he was. I waited a few more seconds, but Luke didn't respond. Considering he hadn't shown up yet, I figured he was driving and would wait until he arrived.

"Hawk's in. I'll catch Luke when he enters," I said as another text came in. Excitement built, and I glanced down, expecting to see Luke's, but it was Hawk again.

Hawk: Tell those two to quit flirting and get their asses to the cages.

Tucker made a chirping sound, straightening like he expected Hawk to come around the corner and catch him. Graham rolled his eyes, giving me a squeeze on my shoulder, his eyes holding so many things. It was the thing I held on to as they left.

There were only a few more players to enter, and worry built in my gut when Luke didn't appear. Where was he? Did something happen? I checked my watch, wondering what was taking him so long.

Usually, he was one of the first players here. Most days, I didn't even get his picture because he came early to practice. Nerves crescendoed inside me as a million worst-case scenarios ran through my mind.

Willow was sick.

There was a wreck.

He hadn't woken up.

Someone broke into his house.

Jasmine returned and took her away.

He decided he wanted to be with Jasmine.

My heart raced, and I prayed I was wrong because, at some point, I'd gone and fallen for the moody player.

CHAPTER
FORTY-ONE

BLAKE

As if my thoughts conjured them, Luke *and* Willow appeared around the corner, the little girl's hand clutched in his. Willow's eyes were wide as she glanced from side to side, her head swiveling back and forth as she took everything in.

Luke's face was lined with worry, the stress palpable as he neared. I stood, wanting to make it better.

"Hey, everything okay?" I asked, glancing down at Willow. She gave me a little wave, hiding in his side.

"There's no school today, and Matilda had a family emergency. She can't get Willow until later. The other two backups I called weren't available. I didn't know what else to do." His voice was hurried, fear and worry heavy in each word. I stepped forward, placing my hand on his arm.

"It's going to be okay, Luke. You did the right thing," I said, hoping to reassure him. His eyes were wide, his breathing unsteady, and I noticed his hand trembled.

Taking it, I squeezed it as I breathed in and out, getting him to breathe with me. When he appeared more grounded and relaxed, I gave him a confident smile.

"I have an idea," I whispered, dropping to Willow's

height. She didn't make eye contact, hiding her face in her hair, her hand gripping Luke's. Damn, a week without seeing her had made her shyer.

"Want to be my assistant today and help me take pictures?" I asked.

Her head snapped up, her eyes big as she processed my words.

"Pictures? Like yours?" she asked, and I nodded. "Can I, Daddy?" She glanced up at Luke, her eyes owlish, and I didn't know how he'd be able to say no if he wanted to. The girl had skills.

Luke looked over at me, biting his lip. "I don't want to put you out. You're working."

"I promise it's fine. I used to come to work with my dad all the time when he played. Baseball's all about families. That's why it's the best job in the world," I said, ruffling her hair. She smiled shyly, the excitement giving her more confidence.

"If you're sure, it would help me a lot." I squeezed his hand, smiling.

"I promise it's fine. Give me Matilda's number, and I'll message her to text me when she's here," I said as an idea popped into my head. Willow had been talking about wanting to watch her dad play; it just hadn't occurred yet.

"In fact, how about we get Matilda and Willow tickets so they can watch the game? I think it's time for your daughter to watch you play."

"Yes! Yes! Yes! Yes!" Willow chanted, jumping up and down and smiling so brightly.

Luke stood there dazed, watching his daughter be so happy to watch him. It made my heart melt for him even more. He had no idea the effect he had on people when he tried. He cleared his throat, emotion clogging it.

"Yeah, of course. I'll check if Matilda's okay with it. You

won't be able to stay for the entire game since you have school tomorrow, sweetie."

Willow swung her hand in his, dancing. "I don't care. I just want to watch baseball."

"Okay," Luke said, happiness radiating off him. It was such a change from the guy I met at the first game. He dug out his phone, airdropping me Matilda's contact.

"Thank you, Slugger. You're a lifesaver." Luke's eyes sparkled, dropping to my lips, and I licked them.

"It's no problem." My voice was breathy, so I swallowed, hoping to clear it.

"I better get to practice before I'm late."

"Oh wait," I said, stopping him as he turned to leave. "The others wanted to meet after practice, before the game. Are you okay with that?" I bit my lip, nervous.

"For sure. That's cool." He winked, making butterfly wings beat faster.

"Great. I guess I'll see you later." I turned, then shouted, "Wait!"

Luke spun; his eyes wide at my tone.

"Any allergies I should know about?"

Luke's face paled, and he looked down at Willow, making me chuckle.

"Anything you're allergic to?" I asked.

"Nope!" she said, popping her 'p', and Luke's body relaxed.

"Okay, go. I promise we're good. I got her," I said, pushing him off. He walked off backward, watching us, turning when I didn't stop him for a third time. Glancing in the other direction, I saw no other players, so I kneeled beside my little charge.

"All right, Lolo. Let's go find my assistant a camera."

"Yay!" She clapped her hands, smiling big at me. I took her hand in mine as we walked through the baseball arena.

She looked at everything again, asking me questions along the way.

A few people stopped to talk to me, asking who my adorable companion was. I introduced her as Luke's daughter. I didn't know if he was sharing it, but it felt wrong to hide her. Plus, each time she got to say who her dad was, she grinned big, melting my heart.

Finally making it to my office, I dug around a drawer until I found the small digital camera I had, showing her the buttons to push.

"I can take pictures?" she asked in amazement.

"Yep. Go practice. I need to finish up work. Just stay in this area, okay?"

She nodded as she took off, snapping pictures of the ground and walls. I'd need to review a million photos on the memory card later, but it would be worth it.

Once I finished, I realized how quiet it had become, and I stood up as anxiety crept up. I jogged around the office, halting when I spotted her sneakers swinging back and forth in Mira's office.

My anxiety spiked higher as I rushed in. "I'm so sorry, Mira."

She said nothing, giving me a forced smile. "This little girl told me she's *Luke Olson's* daughter."

I didn't know why she was asking me that. Why would a little girl lie about that?

"Um, yeah. She is. Come on, Willow. It's time to go to the field for pictures." She hopped off the chair, practically running to me, her little camera in her hand. Mira's eyes narrowed on our joined hands.

"Hmm. I didn't realize we offered childcare. I hope it isn't cutting into *your* work." Her words chilled me, and I lifted my head and gave a curt smile to my boss.

"This isn't childcare. Willow's working," I said with steel in my voice. She could try to fight me on this all she wanted, but it was one she'd lose. My dad was very pro-family. "She's my assistant today, and we have a shoot to do. Excuse us."

I didn't wait for a response, turning Willow and ushering her out of the office, not stopping as I grabbed my camera and bag.

"I'm sorry, Lake."

"It's okay, sweetie, you did nothing wrong."

She nodded, but I could see how nervous she was.

"She asked me a lot of questions. I didn't like it," she whispered.

"Oh, Lolo, I'm sorry, I didn't realize. I should've watched you better. I won't let anyone else talk to you unless you want to. Okay?"

"Okay." She nodded, putting her arms around my neck.

"You know what? I almost forgot. You need a work shirt," I said, spotting the team store.

Pulling her into the store, we picked out a jersey with her dad's number, a new hat, and a pair of YellowJacket socks. And since I still knew Luke's password—though I had changed it back—we put it on his account.

"Now you look like a legit YellowJacket!"

Willow grinned, wearing her new clothes with pride. I introduced her to Jack, the mascot, and Rue.

I took her picture with Jack and of the guys practicing, showing her how to take some wide shots. She was a fast learner and paid attention to the tips I gave her. She took a bunch of her dad, and I hoped one of them was good so we could use it for her room. I also took a few of each of my guys, smiling to myself as I snapped them.

When the guys cleared off the field, it was about an hour until game time. Matilda texted she was there, so Willow and I met her at the gate, where she talked with Clive.

The older woman instantly scooped up Willow, listening to her intently as she told her about working and watching her dad. It was sweet, and I was glad Willow had someone she felt comfortable with.

"Thank you for hanging out with her," Matilda said as we walked to the suite.

"We had a blast. Lolo's a brilliant assistant."

Willow smiled at me, her cheeks rosy.

"I'm glad Luke and Willow have you in their lives," she whispered, squeezing my arm as I let them into the box.

"I'm the one who's lucky," I admitted. She gave me a knowing smile before returning to Willow as they picked out food to eat.

"All right, Lolo. I appreciate your help today. Can you take some more pictures for me during the game?"

"Yes," she said, nodding thoughtfully.

"Great. Then maybe one day this week, we can look at them?" I asked.

"You could come over for dinner again," she said.

"I'd love to." I hugged her, squeezing her tight. She surprised me when she kissed me on the cheek.

"Bye, Lake."

My heart melted, and I couldn't deny falling in love with the little girl. Waving bye, I checked the time, spotting a text telling me which room to come to.

Nervous butterflies beat their wings against my ribs, and I hastily checked my hair in the window reflection. With all the confidence I could muster, I stepped into the room as four sets of eyes turned to look at me, and I hoped I knew what I was doing.

There was so much at stake here, but it felt worth it, and I knew I couldn't stay on the sidelines in my life any longer.

It was finally my turn at bat. If I struck out, so be it; at least I'd gone down swinging for the fences.

CHAPTER
FORTY-TWO

BLAKE

Gulping, I took in four distinctive stares, each varying with heat, longing, and hope. It baffled me that after all these years of avoiding baseball players, I'd somehow liked four of them enough to date.

But these weren't just any baseball players.

They were men I couldn't stop thinking about all hours of the day. They were men my heart beat for, and my pussy throbbed at the sight of. They made my fingers twitch with the need to touch them, and I constantly wanted to talk and spend time with them. And considering my sex life hadn't been all that active or adventurous until a few months ago, I knew it was only for them.

Luckily, with how they watched me, the feelings appeared mutual. And I supposed they would have to be even to consider trying this unconventional relationship.

Smiling, I gave an awkward wave. "Hey."

They each gave their own form of greeting, ranging from Tucker's sugary sweet hello to Hawk's grunt, as they watched my every move. It was intimidating, but I tried to ignore it as I took in their stances.

Hawk leaned against the wall, his feet propped out in front of him, looking like the bad boy he was in his baseball pants and jersey, his eyes dark as he assessed me. Luke sat upright in a chair, separating himself from the others with a table. His hands were braced on his knees as he bounced the left one. His face was blank, his green eyes the only thing that showed any emotion. Graham and Tucker were together on the couch, the most relaxed out of the bunch. Tucker leaned into Graham; their legs stretched out comfortably as they watched.

All their stares at once were overwhelming, and I swallowed my nerves. I sat at the table with Luke, putting me between him and Hawk, deciding they were the most likely candidates to bolt. No one said anything as I settled, and I felt the immense weight of their gazes. Glancing at Luke, I smiled as I patted his arm.

"I left Willow with Matilda in the suite. She seemed to have a lot of fun today. Oh, and I used your password to buy her some merch." I winked, and he smiled, chuckling as he relaxed.

"Thanks for watching her. I owe you a favor."

"Not necessary," I said, waving him off.

"Who's Willow?" Tuck asked, scrunching his brow as he leaned forward.

I sat back, letting Luke take this one. He turned to the duo on the couch, assessing them before answering.

"She's my daughter."

"You have a daughter?" Tuck asked, his eyes bright. I laughed at the question, considering Luke had literally just said that. He jolted forward, barely keeping his butt on the cushion. Luke eyed him and nodded, making Tucker's smile widen.

"Oh, this is great. I love kids. Can I meet her? I'll be the coolest Uncle Tuck." Tucker's face was so pure as he gushed that it brightened the entire room.

"Who said you get to be Uncle Tuck?" Luke asked, scowling. Tucker wasn't one to be dismayed, though, and rolled his eyes as he returned to his seat, leaning on Graham. I watched as he went to put his hand on Graham's thigh, stopping himself at the last second.

"Uh, because we're going to be bro-in-laws or lovers-plus. I coined that word, but feel free to use it." Tucker grinned wide, proud of himself, as the rest of us stared. His smile dropped the longer no one said anything, too shocked. "Damn. I should've gone with Courtesans' Coup or Concubine Five. Though, paramour galore does have a nice ring to it."

"Tucker, I told you not to call it that," Graham mumbled, rubbing his forehead.

"Hold up," I said, fighting back a laugh. Tucker was too cute sometimes. "Maybe we should discuss what this is before we name it."

Everyone quieted, the spotlight on me, and I swallowed, realizing they were waiting for me to speak.

"Right. Okay. Um, I didn't consider public speaking when I thought about dating four guys." I rubbed my hands on my shorts, taking a deep breath. "I didn't think it was possible to like more than one person at a time. But I do; I like all four of you, making it difficult. I don't want to choose or pick only one of you. Honestly, I don't even think I could," I admitted, dropping my eyes.

Nobody said anything for a moment, the silence heavy in the room as my thoughts spiraled.

Great. This is it. My ridiculous dating life will now return to dull loneliness.

"I was the one who told Blake about why choose, or as people in the community call it, polyamorous."

I lifted my head, giving Graham a grateful smile. He watched me, placing his hands in his lap.

"I'm not an expert, but I can share what I know." When no

one interrupted him, he continued, "First, there's the understanding that love isn't limited. That it's possible to love multiple people at once. Loving one person doesn't take it away from another. It just grows." Graham paused, but when no one interrupted, he continued, "Second, it's founded on commitment to the group. It's not cheating because everyone is on board and agrees on who is involved and who isn't. It's not a revolving door of one-night stands. There's a relationship of love and trust at the core. Third, communication is key. Everyone has to be open, express what they're comfortable with, and diligently work out grievances. We can't expect Blake to fix the relationship between us. That's not her responsibility."

"What do you mean by relationship?" Hawk asked, narrowing his eyes.

"Not like that," Graham said, sighing. "But whether or not you like it, you can't just have your relationship with Blake and pretend *we* don't exist. It's just as important for us to connect, even if it's only regarding Blake. Being vulnerable and sharing the relationship stress creates a union, a family. Most people in this lifestyle say that it's the most important thing, not the sex, though that is second. The companionship and support, the bonding together against the societal norm and loving one another, whether romantically or platonically."

"It sounds beautiful," I admitted.

"It's like being on a baseball team, but everyone sees your dick," Tucker added.

"What the fuck?" Hawk cursed, narrowing his eyes. Tucker ignored him, continuing his bizarre analogy.

"We all have a role to play, and if we work together, then we get a home run with Blake." Tucker grinned, sitting back, looking smug.

Graham groaned as I chuckled, unable to stop it. Even

Hawk snorted, shaking his head at the nonsense, the mood lifting a smidge.

"I don't know if I want to get my dick out with you there," Luke said, pulling everyone's attention. "But." He sighed, meeting everyone's eyes. "It sounds nice. I discovered I was a father at the beginning of the year, and the learning curve has been steep. Today was a prime example of feeling out of my league. I think just having people to talk to about it would be nice."

"You could have that even without Blake," Graham argued, raising his eyebrow at Luke. I sat back, intrigued by their dynamic, as I hadn't seen the four of them interact much. Luke shrugged, picking at his pants. "Yeah, maybe, but it's hard for me to trust people."

"I get that," Tucker said, surprising me. "But not to sound redundant, you trust us on the field. Right?"

Right then, I saw the leader Tucker was on the baseball diamond. As a pitcher, he set the tone and dynamics for the other players. He'd always been the fun, laid-back guy in our interactions, but watching him command the conversation and force the others to think about their feelings was sexy. I shifted my legs, my pussy slick with arousal as I watched.

"Yes," Luke admitted, nodding.

"Then why is it different *off* the field?"

Luke shrugged, biting his lip as he debated. "I dunno. If I think about it, I do trust the people in this room, and by putting a term on it, it's more authentic and solid. Like you're invested in me as much as I am in you."

"Wow, that's deep, Olson. Knuckles," Tucker said, lifting his hand across the floor to him.

Luke snorted, but his shoulders dropped, and he relaxed as he extended his hand to Tucker.

"Solid." Tucker nodded, sitting back like his job was done.

"I like how that sounds, too, Luke. It feels like we're

equally taking a risk and sharing the benefits. It's not on one person to make it work," I said.

"Exactly," Graham said, grinning at me.

"And you don't have to be with each other. It's only what you're comfortable with when it comes to things behind closed doors. I just don't want to hide my time with each of you or feel I can't kiss or hold hands with one person when we're together. Hiding it makes it feel shameful." I ducked my head, my cheeks heating.

"We're totally down for the group dynamics," Tucker said, pointing between him and Graham.

Hawk snorted, letting everyone know he was still in the room and listening despite having not contributed anything.

"Yeah, we figured, Package Deal," Luke said, smiling.

Tucker shrugged, not caring as he casually played with the tiny hairs on Graham's neck. I didn't even think he knew he did it, but with how Graham froze, it was new.

"We don't have to determine everything right now," I said, pulling the focus back to me. "I'm tired of living my life in the shadows; for never taking a chance. I thought I wanted something casual and label-free, but it turns out, I don't. I just want the freedom to follow my heart." I paused, taking in a breath. Time to put it all out there. "Is this something you're willing to try?"

"I'm in," Tucker said instantly.

"Me too," Graham followed.

I glanced at Luke and Hawk, waiting for their responses. Hawk rolled his eyes before heaving a long sigh and marching over to me. How he made baseball cleats appear menacing, I didn't know, but it worked for him.

He gripped my chin, filling my entire view as he stared at me. "I told you I wasn't leaving, Blazy. I meant it. If this is what you need, then I'm on board. This is me showing you I'm fighting for us this time. I'm not letting go."

Hawk kissed me deep, stealing my words as his thumb

brushed against my chin. When he pulled back, he didn't return to the wall but leaned against the cabinet, his hands resting on my shoulder. Feeling rejuvenated by his kiss, I faced the last man. The one I knew who struggled the most with commitment and also had the most to lose.

"I want to try, Slugger. I tried to run from you. I tried to blame you for my bad games. I even tried to hate you. None of it worked, so I'm going to lean into my feelings and quit being so damn scared."

I reached out and took his hand, smiling softly at him. "It's okay to be scared. We can just hold each other's hand while we jump."

"Not to break up that beautiful moment, but what are the rules?" Tucker asked.

"What do you mean?" I asked, turning to the duo on the couch.

"What are the boundaries? Can we post on Instagram that we're dating? Or are we all just friends in a group setting? If it's just the five of us, is it okay for PDA? That type of thing," Graham answered.

"We need to set up a sleepover schedule," Tucker said, raising his hand. "Hawk can't claim you every night."

Hawk growled, an inaudible sound rumbling in his chest. Tucker pretended to ignore him, but I saw him shift behind Graham.

"I don't want to bed hop, though. But I could move back to Bryce's."

"No," Hawk demanded, his voice hoarse and deep.

"I'm tired of living out of a suitcase. It's the simplest solution."

"How about home games you alternate, and away games, we figure out once we're there since we'll all be at the hotel?" Graham offered.

"Maybe. It feels very isolating and exhausting like I'd

never know where my stuff was. I've been a womad for the past three years already."

"Unless we all live together, I don't see how it's possible for you to have your own space regularly and spend time with all of us," Graham added.

I realized he was right, but I didn't like it. Maybe if I had one night to myself at Bryce's, that would feel like I had my space. I chewed on my lip in thought.

"We can talk about it," Hawk said, though I could tell he wasn't happy.

"Um…" I grimaced as I peered around again, realizing how complicated my life was about to be. As much as I wanted to date them all, I hadn't anticipated any of this, and I hoped I was ready for everything else that would come with it.

"No secrets," Hawk said, surprising me. "Nothing official on social media until we've been able to tell the important people in our lives, especially Blake's family. Her dad is our boss, so we must prepare for that."

"I don't have anyone outside this room," Tucker admitted.

"I have my family," Graham said.

"No one for me," Luke added.

Hawk nodded, falling back into the quiet shadow he'd become.

"Equal time. That includes alone and group," Graham interjected.

I nodded, agreeing as a million things raced through my head. It was all suddenly too overwhelming, and I was two seconds away from having information paralysis.

"It's obvious this won't be our only conversation, so how about we leave everything else for later? Maybe we can have weekly dinners together or something?"

I nodded, my head moving quickly. "Yes. I'd like that."

"Great, so we're all on the same page. We're all dating Blake," Graham said, finalizing the merging of my heart.

"But just the five of us," Tucker said. "Lovers-plus!"

I hadn't wanted to be the one to say it, feeling like I had no right, so I was happy he brought it up. The mere thought of them dating other girls made me want to punch the imaginary person in the ladyballs.

"I'm not interested in anyone else," Hawk said.

"Same," Luke added.

Graham's eyes moved to Tucker, then back. He cleared his throat. "There's no other girl I want to date."

It made me smile, knowing I needed to check in with them. Something had developed. I was sure of it.

"Okay, so we're officially boyfriend-girlfriend."

"Personally, I like the term paramour galore," Luke said, making Tucker's eyes widen.

"Aw, my paramour!" Tucker sang.

Hawk rolled his eyes, but I caught his smirk before he lifted me, grabbed my face, and delivered a scorching, passionate kiss that left me breathless.

He turned without any further words, stomping out of the room, the sound of his cleats the only noise. Luke cleared his throat, and I couldn't tell if he was uncomfortable or turned on. Tucker and Graham were both watching, their eyes dilated and their cheeks rosy. They weren't the ones I was worried about, though.

It was my two Grumpy Guses with their alpha-hole tendencies I worried would have the most challenging time with this arrangement. Hawk had just done the equivalent of peeing on me in front of the others, marking his claim, and testing how the others would respond. So I waited to see what they would do.

"Game time," Tucker said, bouncing up and kissing me on the cheek before patting me on the butt.

Graham hugged me tight. "Stay with us tonight?" he whispered, and I nodded.

"I'd love to."

"See you after the game, then." He gave me a quick kiss, still full of passion, before he sauntered out after Tucker, leaving me with Luke.

Okay, that hadn't been awful.

Luke stood, pulling me into his chest, and took his turn, reminding me just how good he kissed.

"Thanks again for taking care of Willow. Every night on the road, she kept asking me when you could come over to read to her again." He rolled his eyes, but I could tell it made him happy. I smiled, clutching his uniform between my fingers.

"Anytime. She's the sweetest." I searched his eyes, needing more reassurance. "You're sure you're okay with everything?"

"Yeah." His smile quirked up, settling me.

"Are you worried about the game?" I asked, my hands running up and down his chest.

"A little," he admitted. "But I'm gonna believe in myself and hit a homer for my daughter."

"I have no doubt."

Luke took my face, delivering another kiss, taking my breath away and made the room spin.

"Wow." I blinked, making sure I was still awake.

"Bye, Slugger." Luke smirked, strolling out like he hadn't just rocked my world with his mouth. By the time he left, my panties were done for.

"Son of a glove! Now, I gotta go to work with soaked panties."

I guess it was the cost of having four hot boyfriends. I'd have to keep a spare change of clothes in my bag from now on.

TUCKER

As the sun descended in the sky, the colors painted the field in pinks and purples. But my only focus was on the man squatting behind the plate—Graham. I didn't even concentrate on the batter, knowing my battery mate would tell me what to do.

Together, we studied each batter and worked with Coach Anderson to create the best pitching strategies. It made the player become only a number, losing any distractions during the game.

I focused on the pitch, trusting Graham to decipher which one to throw. It was a system few pitchers/catchers had, but we weren't just any combo—we were us.

And today, the two of us were on fire.

It was the top of the ninth with two outs, and we were up. I rarely pitched this long into a game but was on the verge of something great. The thing you didn't mention out loud while it was happening. I couldn't even think it in my thoughts without fear of ruining it.

So, I stared down the center, ignoring the shifting of the batter as Graham gave me the call sign for a sweeper.

Nodding, I gripped the ball with a two-seam grip as I took a breath, exhaling as I lifted my leg and released the ball.

Time stood still, and the only sound I heard was my heart beating in my ears. The moment between the ball flying—breaking the strike zone about fifteen inches as it swept across the home plate—and the batter squaring up to swing felt like an eternity, but it was only one beat. The stadium fell silent, my heart pounding in my ears as the umpire drew in his breath.

"Strike."

I stood in shock as the team surged around me, jumping on my back and clapping my shoulder in celebration. I'd done it.

Not only had we just won, but I'd had a no-hitter.

My first for the YellowJackets. It had been so long since I had a perfect game I almost didn't believe it. I wanted to say it was because of my skill, practice, and determination, but that had always been there.

My game was different today because of how my heart beat for two people. Two people who made me feel genuinely accepted and cherished for the person I was. Their belief and faith pushed all the other nonsense and noise aside, allowing me to fall back on my skill.

And what I really wanted to do right now was kiss the man smiling across from me.

But considering our teammates and the 10,000 fans surrounding us, I knew it wasn't wise. And while I rarely cared about making smart choices, I knew this was too important to be reckless. It wasn't just me it concerned, and I'd never be foolish with Graham or Blake's heart.

So, instead of kissing his face off—a new obsession I was eager to explore more—I threw my arms around him, squeezing him tight when the crowd thinned. I kissed his neck softly, enjoying how his body trembled at the touch of my lips. I breathed him in, my muscles relaxing with each second I held him.

"You did it, man."

"We did it," I corrected, squeezing him one more time before letting him go.

Graham smiled, and I wondered how I had never seen it before. *He was breathtaking.* Even with sweat and grime on his face, his eye black smeared, and a catcher's face mask on top of his head, I couldn't take my eyes off him. He blushed, making me curious about what he was thinking.

"Come on, let's get this inning over with so we can spend some time with our girl."

"Best day ever." The urge to kiss him grew stronger, but I tossed my arm over his shoulders instead and headed to the dugout. The inning went quickly, and soon the game was over.

A few more players and Coach Phillips congratulated us as we made our way to the club house. The entire game had been exhilarating in a new way. Knowing we were starting this new adventure and feeling connected to more people than just Graham made my insides buzz. Add in spotting Blake in the stands taking pictures at times; it made my heart flutter. Something I was completely out of my league with.

I'd been attracted to girls before and had slept with plenty of them, but they never made me feel this.

"Great partnership," Coach Anderson said, clapping me on the back. He gave me and Graham a nod of respect, warming those pieces inside me that had never felt good enough.

I'd never had a dad or mom at my games, and while coaches and teammates had told me 'good game,' it had always felt conditional. Like the moment I didn't play well, those affirmations would go away.

But hearing Hawk say it, it was more than just empty words. One, he didn't give them, and two, his words held emotion. It felt like he was proud of me for real, making me feel warm and gooey inside.

"Don't," he warned, his eyes narrowing as I moved to hug him. "Besides, you're pulled for the media." He gave me an evil smile as my arms dropped in defeat.

"Ah, man," I groaned, sulking, as I finished walking to the locker room.

The next hour was the most excruciating sixty minutes of my life. After I showered, I completed my interviews, did my post-game stretches, and sat with an ice wrap on my shoulder. My leg bounced as I waited to be cleared by the trainer, practically bolting out the door when given the go-ahead.

Graham stood in the hallway, his hair still wet from his shower, with both of our bags over his shoulder. I nearly skipped to him, knowing our time with Blake was here. Neither of us said anything as we marched out together, our focus entirely on our girl. The one who'd fallen into our life with a mistaken text and had turned it upside down in the best possible way.

"Thanks for being my rock. I wouldn't have." I paused, lowering my voice. "This 'you know what' without you," I blurted, disturbing the quiet between us.

Graham eyed me, his brow creased. "I just tell you what I think to throw. You're the one who does it perfectly."

"Bullshit. You let me focus on the pitch because you're catching everything else. I wouldn't have *this* without you. So, congratulations to you, too, G."

"That's a lie, and you know it." He rolled his eyes, and I was about to punch him for dismissing my compliment when he smiled, shocking me. "But I'll accept the congratulations all the same."

Graham could believe what he wanted, but I knew the truth. I played well with other catchers, but I played my best with him.

I didn't know if it was just his presence, our connection

and trust, or his uncanny ability to read the players and pitches. I honestly had no clue. Perhaps it was all three of them or none. It didn't matter because Graham West made me a better pitcher, and at this point in my career, I didn't know how to be me without him.

As we turned the last corner down the tunnel, Blake came into sight. Now that fewer people were around, I didn't stop myself from doing what I wanted. I took off running toward her, my excitement palpable; I could feel it.

Blake had her back to us as she talked with someone, so she didn't notice as I approached, lifting her off her feet. She squeaked, her hands grasping my forearms as I spun.

"Ack! Oh my god!" She laughed when she realized it was me, and I nuzzled into her neck.

"You ready, Honey Bee?"

"Yes, but I can walk." She giggled, waving bye to who she'd been talking to. Now that I had my hands on her, I didn't want to let her go.

"I like this better," I protested, placing a kiss similar to the one I'd given Graham earlier.

"At least turn me around or give me a piggyback ride. It feels weird being held from the front."

"Fine," I grumbled, setting her down and turning so she could jump on my back. She did it without hesitation, making me grin as I walked with her and Graham out to his car.

"Amazing game. I was on the edge of my seat that last inning, and I wasn't even sitting!" She laughed, filling me up with pride.

"Thanks, Honey Bee."

"Did you guys eat?" she asked.

"Just something small to tide us over. We can still eat," Graham said.

"Good, I'm starving," Blake groaned, making my cock take notice.

"I got stuff to make homemade pizza. How does that sound?" Graham turned to look at us, his profile so beautiful I almost stumbled.

"Yass. I love pizza," she moaned, making the blood rush to my lower regions more. Thankfully, there weren't many cars left in the lot, or they'd all see my erection. I scanned it but didn't know what Luke drove, and Hawk's Mustang was already gone.

"Did you get to say goodbye to your paramours?" I teased, bending down so she could slide off.

"I did." Her cheeks blushed at my words, giving her an air of innocence that I loved. She was a constant contrast, keeping me on my toes.

"Your chariot awaits, milady," I said, opening her door.

"You don't have to give me the front seat. I've got short legs. I'm fine in the back." She placed her hands on her hips, giving me a stern look.

"Oh, I insist." I helped her into the seat, even buckling her in so she didn't get any ideas about being stubborn. I climbed into the back, spreading my legs wide as I took the middle seat.

"This way, I can see you both."

"Speaking of..." Blake looked between us as Graham started the car. "Did I imagine something shifting here? I've been meaning to ask all week."

"What do you mean?" I asked, smirking.

Blake turned, holding my eyes. She said nothing, just leaned on the console, focusing entirely on me. "I can outlast you, Tucker Jameson."

"Oh really, Blake Baker."

"Yes, sir. You forget I grew up with Bryce *and* Hawk."

"She has a point," Graham said, but I ignored him.

"I like it when you call me sir," I teased, licking my lips. Her eyes twitched, but she kept my gaze to the apartment.

When she made no move to get out of the car, I gave in.

Rolling my eyes, I sighed heavily as she cheered. Hearing her happiness was a gift in itself.

"Fine. I admitted I had the hots for G, and then he kissed me." I shrugged my shoulders, my cheeks heating this time. It still felt weird to say it out loud, even though nothing had ever felt truer to me.

"Eek!" Blake clapped her hands. "That makes me so happy!"

"You're not weirded out?" Graham asked, turning off the car and peering at the two of us.

Her forehead crinkled. "Why would I be?"

"I don't know. Some girls wouldn't like it. I guess they want all the attention."

She shrugged, turning and unlatching her seat belt. "Well, I've never been like other girls, so why start now?"

"You are one of a kind, Blake Baker." I grinned at her as we got out of the car.

"So are you, Tucker Jameson."

Graham laughed at us, shaking his head as we climbed the steps to our apartment. Man, I hated this place. It was so dull and utilitarian. It only reinforced the idea I had earlier.

"Really, though. I'm excited. I think you guys are gonna be amazing together, and I'm just happy to be part of it." She smiled, taking my hand.

"I don't know what we are yet. But I like where it's going," I admitted, eyeing Graham.

He'd been quiet the past week, and part of me worried he regretted what had happened between us. His gray eyes met mine, softening around the edges as the corner of his mouth tilted up, sending shivers and reassuring me. He was on board. The three of us walked into the apartment, and that feeling it wasn't ours hit me. Just another reason for us to move.

"Dude, we need to convince Hawk to let us move in. That way, we can see Blake all the time. Because you know he's not gonna let her move back to Bryce's," I said to Graham. Blake huffed, crossing her arms.

"He's not the boss of me."

I lifted my brow, making her roll her eyes.

"I've been thinking about that too," Graham said, turning on the lights as we walked further into our place. I loved how in sync we were on this.

"He doesn't always get his way," Blake tried again, pouting.

"Uh-huh." I scoffed, tossing my bag down. Blake's brow furrowed before she smiled.

"Though you guys moving in would be fun. Watching Hawk be tortured all the time might be worth him getting his way. Though, I'd worry Luke would feel left out."

"What's his place like?" Graham asked, pulling ingredients from the fridge to set on the island.

"It's huge, but it's a rental. There would be space for all of us, but it's not long-term. Plus, I doubt Hawk will want to leave his house. He's been renovating it and likes his privacy."

"It is a sweet place and private," Graham said.

"Yeah, I do like that. Plus, the backyard is nice," I added, my brain throwing out solutions. "Maybe we just need to get a house together."

"Whoa. Slow down, Tucker." Blake held her hands up. Her face caught between excitement and fear. Shit. This was what I did. I scared people off by jumping in too fast. I needed to slow down a smidge.

"Let's figure out how to date one another before we move in and get joint bank accounts," Graham interjected, eyeing Blake.

I walked over to her, taking her hands. "I already told you that you're the future, Mrs. Jameson. You don't think I'm serious? We can go to the courthouse tomorrow, and I'll prove it."

Okay, so that was a miss for slowing down. I cringed, hating my out-of-control mouth. Blake softened, squeezing my hands.

"I don't need you to prove it. I'm just not ready for that yet. I can't be a Runaway Bride for a second time."

"One thing to know about Tucker," Graham said, spreading pizza sauce. "He jumps in with both feet. But he never expects you to do it as well. So, you can appreciate it about him and join him when you're ready. No rush."

There that man goes, putting into words what I felt. Gah, he was the best.

Blake took a deep breath, grinning. "Okay. Yeah. Spending time with no interruptions with you both would be exciting."

I grinned, tossing a piece of cheese at her. She laughed, her body relaxing the rest of the way.

"Don't waste it," Graham admonished, picking up the cheese bag. He turned to Blake. "What toppings do you like?" He gave me his stern face that I suddenly found very hot. Shit. Bossy Graham did it for me.

Once Graham had the pizzas ready, he put them in the oven and set the timer. I took Blake to my room since she hadn't seen it the last time she was here.

"And this is my sneaker collection," I said, turning on the LED lights I'd installed on the shelves. They lit up in blue.

"Wow. When you said you collected them, I had no clue it was like this. I have five pairs, and I thought that was excessive."

I grinned as she walked around them, petting the leather now and then when they drew her eyes. I loved watching her admire my shoes. Was that weird? Too bad if it was.

"I don't know what it is about sneakers. Maybe because I didn't have a lot as a kid and felt on the outside of those who did. So when I got some, I took care of them and felt more confident in them. They made me happy. And then people would notice and comment, and it seemed like the cooler my shoes, the more people noticed me."

My cheeks heated at my unintentional vulnerability. I shrugged, moving away from the wall I'd been leaning on. Her gaze was focused on me, and I preened beneath her stare.

"That's not a good reason to do a hobby. But it's where it started. It did grow into more." I picked up a pair, turning it over. "I genuinely like the style. They're awesome to look at, fun to shop for, and give me all that fun dopamine." I sat it back down, turning to her. "There's an entire community of sneakerheads that share pop-ups. The hunt for them makes it seem like a true challenge."

"I didn't mean any shade, Tucker. I think it's great." She took my hand, brushing her thumb across my palm.

"I know." I gave her a smile, squeezing her hand back. "I honestly hadn't thought much about it. Sometimes, I tend to stay on the surface with life, but you make me look deeper."

"I get that. For so long, I let everyone tell me how to live my life. I was so afraid to disappoint them that I never made any choice for myself. It got to the point I was so scared that I sacrificed years of my life, worried they'd regret helping me."

"How could anybody regret helping you?"

"Didn't say it made sense." She laughed, her cheeks a pretty rose color. "It wasn't until I was in a wedding dress I hated and getting ready to marry a man whose best features were his consistency and a dimple that I knew I couldn't keep living that life."

"You were going to marry a man because of a dimple?"

"It was a good dimple." She laughed. "But yeah, not my best decision. That's the day that everything changed. I ran away, made a choice for myself, and slept with Hawk." She grimaced. "Only to sacrifice it the next day for Bryce and move to Greece for three years."

She let out a big breath of air, her shoulders relaxing. I

wished I'd known her then. I would've told her how awesome she was.

"Being away from everything, I could breathe. It let me find myself. I fell in love with photography and made choices I wanted. I met my best friend, Emory, my sorta cousin—Oh." She paused, her eyes lighting up. "Emory's coming to an away game. I can't wait for you to meet her."

"I get to meet the family already?"

"'Course. You'll love her."

I already think I love you.

"I can't wait." We smiled at one another, our hands clasped together.

"What was I saying?" she whispered as we moved closer.

"I have no idea."

My lips landed on hers, my hands moving to pull her closer.

"Pizza is done!" Graham shouted, breaking us apart. Blake and I laughed, panting with swollen lips as we entered the kitchen.

"Yum. It smells great, Graham."

"I think you mean Teddy Graham."

"Or Gummy bear."

"Ah, yes."

"I hate you both," Graham muttered, cutting the pizza. "Why do I feed you again?"

"You love us." I smacked a kiss on his cheek as I took my plate, making him blush. It was quiet as we ate, my focus entirely on Blake.

She fit in with Graham and me so well. No other woman had ever slotted in so easily. It was like they saw the other person as competition, trying to pull me away from Graham or him away from me. Not that either of us dated anyone, but even girls we were friends with or had arrangements with did it.

It was probably why I quit trying to date someone. If they

couldn't accept Graham in my life, I didn't want to be in theirs.

But Blake had been different from the start. We instantly liked her, and she liked both of us. It worked with the three of us; our time together was comfortable, easy, and fun. When we were apart, I couldn't stop thinking about her or how happy she made me. Every interaction felt exciting, and I never knew where it would lead.

I recognized that it was too early to feel deep emotions. But considering I never made it this far with a girl, I knew this connection was special.

I would keep my feelings to myself for now. I didn't want to scare her off any more than I already had, considering she'd already turned down my proposal.

It just meant I'd have to be sneakier next time.

"Should we watch a movie?" Graham asked, putting the food away.

"Sure," Blake said, though I think we all knew we wouldn't watch the movie.

"Let's watch it in my room," I offered. At least we'd have a bed this way. As I walked in, I pulled off my shirt, tossing it into the hamper. Next, I pushed off my sweats, climbing onto the bed in only my boxers. Blake stopped as she entered, her mouth dropping open as she took me in.

"I feel suddenly overdressed." Her voice was husky, making my dick twitch.

"Then get underdressed," I challenged, lifting my brow.

Blake's smile simmered at my challenge as she unbuttoned her shorts, lifted her shirt over her head, and crawled on the bed in only her underwear and bra.

"You were saying?"

My mind blanked. She was one of the hottest things I'd ever seen and my dick swelled, filling up and thickening, as I tried not to stare.

Graham sauntered in, pausing as he took in the scene of us staring at each other half-naked on the bed.

"I see this movie has a dress code." He chuckled, raising his shirt over his head, my eyes now drawn to his abs. I licked my lips, my balls throbbing.

"How about we skip the movie?" Blake asked.

"Brilliant idea," I said as Graham's pants hit the floor. He held our gazes as he kneeled on the bed, the three of us watching one another, debating who would start things off.

It truly was the best day ever.

CHAPTER
FORTY-FOUR

BLAKE

THE TENSION THAT HAD BEEN BUILDING BETWEEN THE THREE OF us swelled as our gazes collided. My body felt weightless as the energy surged around me. The electrical current between us intensified, lighting me up from the inside. The minor shocks I'd felt in their presence now felt like live wires waiting to zap me into oblivion.

Somehow, I knew Graham would be the one to move first. He had the sweetest demeanor, always watching, observing, and waiting to anticipate needs. That same intensity translated to a sexy dominance behind closed doors. He unleashed his hold, allowing himself to be free in a new way. He used his knowledge of what someone needed by bringing them to new heights.

Graham West was a man of quiet determination who made you trust him unequivocally.

Holding both of our gazes, he slid his boxers down, his cock heavy as it appeared. The pubic piercing twinkled, and I licked my lips, eager to feel it. Tucker sucked in a breath, his hand reaching out to my bare shoulder, almost as if to ground himself as he eyed his best friend up and down in a new light.

I watched as Tucker's eyes dilated, his dick twitching in his boxers as he tracked Graham's movements, biting his lip. Lust was evident on his face, making the slickness between my legs gush more. I didn't know if I was more eager to watch them or to finally know where our chemistry took us.

Who was I kidding? All the above.

The moment I'd received their text, an undeniable bond had been building between us. Their connection was a big part of it, and seeing them embrace this new dynamic with me had my heart beating triple. It felt like a cherished honor to be included.

Tucker's free hand rubbed the outside of his boxers, and I already felt ready to combust. The sexual exploration with them had given me the confidence to embrace my body and desires and to test out new experiences without fear or embarrassment. They'd given me time to work up to this point, finally having a sexual relationship that progressed naturally instead of dropping in head first like my others had been.

But fuck, I was ready for the main course.

Everything up until now had been foreplay, and I was eager to have the rest.

"Tuck, go to my room and grab condoms, lube, and the black box in my top drawer."

Tucker bolted off the bed, my body swaying from his movement as he raced to do Graham's bidding. I wasn't the only one who trusted Graham unequivocally.

Graham knee-walked his way to me on the bed. I was still on my knees, giving me a perfect view to watch him. His hands cupped my face as he tilted it to him, his thumbs stroking me casually. I could feel his cock pressing into my belly, the tip trailing pre-cum.

"I don't want to assume things, so I want to hear your words, Sunshine. What are your limits?"

I thought about it and realized when it came to Graham and Tucker, I was ready for it all.

"When I'm with you, I trust you to know my limits. I started this journey to expand my horizons. I'm guessing we've just brushed the tip of things, but I'm ready. I promise to speak up if something doesn't feel right or if I don't like it." I shrugged. "But otherwise, I'm open to you showing me new things. I like giving you my control."

His eyes dilated, and his nostrils flared at my words. Graham's throat bobbed. "Words have never been sexier. Are you familiar with the stoplight method?"

I shook my head. "No, what is it?"

"Let's wait—"

Before he could finish, Tucker zoomed back into the room, panting as he dropped the items onto the corner of the bed behind Graham.

"Now what?" he asked, his body vibrating as he stared at me in Graham's hold.

"Boxers off and get behind Blake," Graham ordered, not even turning his head to look. Tucker stripped, his cock hard and leaking as he closed the space between us. He climbed behind me, his hands landing on my hips. His cock nestled between my ass cheeks, rubbing gently as he placed kisses on my neck.

"I can't stop touching you when you're near," Tucker whispered.

"I was about to go over the stoplight method with Blake. Are you familiar, Tuck?"

He shook his head, the hair brushing against my back before he met Graham's eyes.

"It's a way to know consent by using a traffic light. Red means stop, yellow means slow down and proceed cautiously, and green means full mutual consent. That you're okay with what is happening."

"That's easy enough," Tucker said, squeezing my hips.

"Do you have any limits?" Graham asked him.

"Um…" I could feel his hesitation as he debated.

"I promise to be gentle and not push you too far if you're willing to trust me," Graham added.

"Of course I trust you."

Graham smiled, his body relaxing at those words. I could feel Tucker's body trembling with anticipation. He wanted this but wasn't sure what it was.

"Undress Blake and show her your skills aren't only baseball."

Tucker's fingers unsnapped my bra, the straps falling down my arms as he peppered kisses down my back. I sucked in a breath as the air hit my nipples, watching Graham as he settled down to watch. Tucker pressed me forward, my hands falling to the bed as he lowered his hands to my panties, sliding them down my legs. He lifted my knees one at a time to remove them altogether.

"Make her feel good, Tucker, and you'll be rewarded," Graham encouraged, stroking himself once.

Tucker didn't let me up, placing his mouth on my pussy from behind. Sucking my clit into his mouth, he had me gasping in seconds as his tongue speared me. His hands spread my ass cheeks, kneading the flesh as he ate me out from behind, reminding me how good he was at this. My legs shook as I pressed myself back on his face more. My eyes rolled back as an orgasm built inside of me.

Remembering Graham in front of me, I opened my eyes to meet his. He watched with a hungry gaze, his hand stroking in slow movements. I beckoned him forward, and he shook his head.

"I want to watch first," he said.

I didn't have time to pout as Tucker's arm lifted me and

wrapped around my middle, a hand enveloping around my neck as he tilted my head back to kiss me deeply. His cock slid between my ass and pussy, coating himself in my cum, and I lost myself in the movement. There was a shift on the bed and something cold at my opening.

"Color?" Graham asked.

"Green."

He smiled, pushing something in me as he locked with me. From the feel, I could make out a shape similar to a dildo, but the cold and smooth texture had me curious to what it was. But I didn't have time to think about it as my body trembled, the orgasm overtaking me from both of their ministrations. Tucker rolled my nipples between his fingers, his mouth sucking on my neck as he rocked, showing me how good he'd feel inside.

As Graham fucked me from the front with the strange dildo, I threaded my hand in his hair, pulling him closer. Tucker lifted his head, noticing Graham's closeness. I nudged Graham closer, and he took Tucker's mouth, pinning me between them as they locked lips.

It was better than I thought. Not only being between them, but watching as they explored this together. Graham's hand continued to move, shocking me when he rolled a condom on Tucker beneath me. Tucker groaned, his eyes rolling back as he braced himself against me.

"Fuck, G."

"Not yet," Graham teased. "Now, show Blake what your perfect dick can do."

Graham pulled out the dildo, and Tucker thrust up, taking its place. He was bigger than the dildo and warmer, making my nerve endings tingle with the change.

"Oh, shit," I moaned.

Graham moved away, and I whimpered, missing his warmth. But I had little time to think about it as Tucker slid in deep, his cock hitting me just right. We groaned together, adjusting to one another before he unleashed himself.

Tucker withdrew and then slammed back in, his fingers gripping my hips, probably leaving fingerprints, as we found a rhythm together.

The sound of our skin slapping increased as he showed me how much endurance he had. My body was quickly primed again as tingles zipped up inside me, and I fell forward, no longer able to keep myself upright. The new angle gave Tucker more room to thrust, and he used every inch as he bent over me, breathing heavily into my ear.

"Goddam, Honey Bee. Your pussy is the caviar of pussies. I might never leave. Oh, fuck," he cursed, and I glanced up, spotting what made him swear in the mirror. Graham had moved behind him, spreading his ass checks and stroking his finger around Tucker's rim. His thrusts stuttered as Graham teased him, his breathing labored from whatever Graham was doing.

"I didn't say you could stop," Graham reminded Tucker, stopping his movements. This time, it was Tucker's turn to whimper. He flicked his hips forward, pressing his cock nice and slow into me now as he adjusted to Graham's fingers. My body felt suspended in the air as the three of us chased euphoria.

"Let's shift positions," Graham said, stopping and moving away. "Tucker, on your back. Blake, straddle him."

We both did as he said, and I braced my hands on his chest as I sank onto his cock. My eyes rolled back as I felt him all the way. "Holy cow."

Bending down, I kissed Tucker, losing myself in him as we rocked together. Graham came behind us both, running his hands over the two of us.

"You're an erotic sight together," he murmured before I heard the snap of a lid opening. "Breathe," he whispered.

I didn't know if it was for me or Tucker, but when I felt his body tense up at the same time as mine, I realized it was both. I tried to keep rocking, letting Tucker's dick soothe me as Graham rubbed a smaller item over my backdoor entrance, something similar to the dildo from earlier. The coldness and smooth texture were the same, but it had more of a bulbous shape to it.

Soon, Tucker and I were both moaning as we rocked into each other and Graham's attention.

"I'm coming," I screamed as it snuck up on me. The pressure of something in my ass and pussy was too much, and I detonated.

"Fuck," Tucker moaned. "Your pussy is gripping me so tight, Blake. I can't... sta-ll..." he stuttered before I felt him tighten, his muscles clenching as he came.

My body vibrated with tingles as Graham pulled me off, laying me on my side. He pressed small kisses all over my body, letting me relax in the afterglow, massaging my muscles and caressing me with soft touches.

"You ready for more?" he asked, kissing my neck.

"Mm-hmm," I moaned, moving with him. He slid in with ease; my leg hitched over him as we rocked together on our sides. It was comforting and kept that orgasm suspended as he hit my clit with his piercing.

"Geez, that feels good," I moaned.

"So do you," he breathed, kissing me again. When he stuttered, I opened my eyes to find him looking over his shoulder at Tucker, who had moved behind him. His voice cracked as he looked at his friend.

"What are you doing?"

"It's my turn. I want to try," Tucker said, lifting his brow. "I'm still green, are you?"

Graham swallowed, his throat bobbing as he nodded. "Yeah. Green."

Tucker smiled, pressing a soft kiss to Graham's shoulder

before he settled behind him on the bed. I couldn't see what he was doing, but I had an idea as Graham's eyes rolled back.

I cupped his cheek, pulling his face to mine as we rocked together. When I felt Tucker's hand rubbing Graham's cock as it entered me, his finger pressing in along it. I whimpered at the fullness, the stretch driving me wild with need.

Graham flicked his hips harder as he held my thigh up, hitting me deeper and rubbing my clit perfectly; our bodies slapped together in a disjointed rhythm as we chased our release.

"Fuck, Tuck," Graham groaned, then laughed before his head fell back. Tucker bent down, kissing Graham this time, and it was all I needed as I flew over the edge; my walls spasming around his cock as I came again.

"You come so beautifully, Blake," Graham moaned. "Give me all your cream, baby."

His words were salacious and dirty as he speared me one last time, stalling as he filled the condom, his cock twitching. Tucker's hands wrapped around us, holding the three of us together.

"Three is way better than two," he groaned satisfactorily.

"And that's just the beginning," Graham teased.

"What was the thing you used on me?" I asked once I had brain cells again.

"A double-ended glass dildo. Did you like it?"

"Uh-huh. It was interesting."

"I'm going to get you ready to take us both simultaneously, and next time, I'm introducing Tucker to the short end."

Well, hot damn. I blinked as images raced across my mind. Yep, I was here for that. I didn't even hate that Emory had been right.

"That was the best sex of my life," Tucker breathed as he snuggled further into Graham's back.

"Eh, top five," Graham said, making Tucker and I lift our heads. Graham smirked, laughing at our reaction. "Kidding."

"Nope. Let's get him, Tuck," I said as I bounced. The three of us rolled around as Tucker and I wrestled Graham, tickling him until he admitted we were the best he'd ever had.

Spread out on the bed naked, we finally turned on the movie, only making it halfway before round two started. I might regret it in the morning, but I didn't think I would. Great sex trumped sleep every time.

BLAKE

"Do we have time to stop at Hawk's on the way?" I yawned. Graham placed a coffee cup in my hand, my face perking up as I eyed the perfectly layered foam. "You are a god among mortals," I moaned as I inhaled the liquid, everything else fading away.

"Of course, and you're welcome, Sunshine." Graham chuckled, then kissed my forehead before returning to the stove, a spatula in his hand.

As I sipped my perfect latte, I watched him cook us breakfast. Graham was a total stud in his baseball uniform, but my favorite look was this one right here.

Mussed hair, low-slung sweatpants, bare feet and torso, and a spatula.

I sighed as I continued to sip, entranced at the view before me. His back muscles flexed as he shifted, utterly unaware of my ogling.

"I'd be angry you didn't look at me that way if I didn't get it," Tucker whispered, brushing his lips against my neck. I turned my head, bringing our lips closer.

"Oh, I look at you that way, too. Just not in front of a

stove." I lifted my mug, hiding my smug smile as his mouth dropped open. His cheeks pinked for a second before the cocky boy returned.

"Do tell, Honey Bee. I'm all ears." He braced his chin in his hands, fluttering his eyelashes.

"Nope. You gotta catch me, cuddle bug."

His lip protruded as he pouted, his hands dropping to my thighs as he pulled me between his legs.

"I have ways of making you talk, Bee." He licked the column of my neck, nipping my earlobe between his teeth. I sucked in a breath, my eyes closing on their own as I leaned into him. My coffee was forgotten as I focused on staying upright. Tucker's hands wrapped around it, placing it on the counter, his lips trailing to the other side.

"Not to interrupt, but you should eat first." Graham placed plates on the counter, forcing my eyes open as I turned to look. He gave me a knowing smile, licking his lips.

"I know what I'd rather eat," Tucker teased, sucking on the skin under my collarbone.

My stomach growled, breaking the sexual tension as I remembered how hungry I was.

"Food," I moaned, hopping onto the barstool.

Tucker sighed but let me go, his fingers trailing over me and leaving goosebumps in their wake.

"Who are you staying with tonight?" Graham asked, stuffing a bite into his mouth.

"Not sure. Probably Luke, if he's open to that. It's a little more complicated with Willow." I shrugged, holding back my moan as I ate the bacon.

"I can't wait to meet her. I should get her a present!" Tucker exclaimed, doing a happy dance in his chair.

"She's shy but the sweetest. Her birthday is in June, and her mom isn't coming in like she promised. I feel so sad for her."

"We should throw her a party!" Tucker's eyes brightened as he turned to me.

"I love your enthusiasm, Tuck, but check with Luke. He's still trying to figure out his whole role with her."

"Every kid loves a party. It will be great," he said. I wasn't sure if he was purposely ignoring me or just that optimistic.

"Graham, can I grab a shirt to wear? Oh! I made you guys something." I jumped off my stool and raced to my bag, pulling out the two shirts I'd made the other day. "One for you," I said, handing Tucker his. "And one for you."

They both smiled, laughing at the shirts as they pulled them on.

"I love it. Thanks, Sunshine." Graham kissed my lips, lingering before he pulled back. "And you can borrow whatever you want. You can look at my books while you're there, too. You're reading quickly. At this rate, you'll be through all of mine."

"Ha! Unlikely, but it has been a nice way to unwind in the evening."

I slid off the stool, stopping when I encountered Tucker posing with his phone camera, puckering his lips funnily as he took a picture, holding up his shirt.

"This is baller, Bee. Too bad I can't say my girlfriend made it. I'd love to see the trolls' faces then." He laughed, missing the panic on my face, but Graham saw it. He squeezed my shoulder and nudged me to his room, giving me a few seconds to reorientate myself.

I walked in a daze, opening the drawer I remembered held his shirts, holding it to my nose as I breathed him in. The smell of spice and earth helped to ground me, and I wandered over to his bookcases. He had three of them, and they were all overflowing with books. I couldn't tell what his system was, either. Some were on their sides, and others stacked high.

Picking one up, I glanced at the cover and flipped it over

as I read the blurb, but my brain wasn't comprehending anything. All I could think about was Tucker's words. Why were they freaking me out so much? I'd been someone's girlfriend before. And we'd just had a semi-define-the-relationship talk. I'd wanted this.

He's not Brandon. This would be different.

There had to be more to it than that. Surely...

My brain stayed quiet as his words and the other guys tumbled over one another.

We want to be with you.

We want... a relationship... to date... move in together... Marriage.

Was I panicking because of the word? That had to be it.

In a daze, I picked up books and glanced at their covers, hoping to be inspired by one of them. I didn't know what I felt, but I was decidedly overwhelmed as the insurgent thoughts and the guys' desires and wants exploded in my head.

It's too much. I'll never be enough. I won't measure up to the girlfriend they want.

This time, I'll be left at the altar.

Squeezing my eyes closed, I sucked in a breath and slowed down my heart. When I was calmer, I resumed my search. My hands brushed against a familiar blue cover, one I'd read so many times I could identify all the elements; mine more faded and worn from all the love.

I'd first read it on the plane ride to Greece after a cute boy had recommended it to me. That feeling of déjà vu I'd gotten a few times intensified. Was Graham him?

I recalled that day, my memory hazy, as I bumped into a guy with a backward cap, gray eyes, a soft smile, and a kind spirit. If I was to make Graham's face a few years younger...

Great balls of fire.

I'd met Graham way before the YellowJackets!

In fact... the memory of the magnetic boy concerned

about his tennis shoes slammed into my mind next, and I knew I'd met Tucker that day, too! I'd been so lost back then, overwhelmed with guilt, that fear had ruled me. They'd both given me a small drop of sunshine, reminding me the world was bigger than my little pocket.

The question was, did they remember me? Had they even noticed me back then?

Carrying it out of the room, I held it aloft as I stepped into the kitchen. Graham's head perked up, his smile widening as he took in the cover.

"That's one of my favorites, but it's not why choose."

"I know. I've already read this one," I said, my tongue dry and sticking to the roof of my mouth.

"Okay." He tilted his head to the side, observing me as we stood in a weird standoff. Tucker stumbled out of his room, rubbing his wet hair with a towel. He glanced up, looking between us.

"Is this our next read for book club?" he asked, bounding over. He peered at the cover. "It doesn't look very spicy. I need the spice, Bee, or why bother?"

"I was telling Graham I've already read it."

"Okay…" he drew out, peering back and forth. "What am I missing?"

"I read it based on the suggestion of a cute guy I met at the airport."

Graham's chair squeaked as he stood, his eyes wide as he glanced from the book to my face. "No way."

"It was you?" I asked, swallowing around the clog in my throat. Why was I getting emotional? It was just a book.

Graham nodded, stepping forward and cupping my face. "I always thought you looked familiar, but I chalked it up to your family. I thought about you so many times, wondering if you liked it or if it made you smile. You seemed so sad that day."

I nodded, a tear falling. "I was. That was the day I ran away."

"Wait a minute," Tucker said, interrupting and stepping between us. He assessed me from head to toe, his eyes owlish as he put two and two together. "That guy bumped into us, scuffing my shoe and spilling your bag. You told me to use baking soda, and then I touched your vibrator."

Snorting, I nodded. "Though, still not a vibrator. It was a massager."

"Call it whatever you want, babe." He winked.

"She's the girl you couldn't quit obsessing over?" Graham asked, and Tucker nodded.

"Yup. Seems even the first time we met her, we were both hooked."

Hearing him express his attraction and desire this time wasn't as frightening. If the three of us felt it back then, it had to mean something. Like me running into Luke multiple times, unable to escape him, Hawk and I always found our way back to one another.

Maybe I needed to stop questioning things for once and believe in fate.

I opened the door to the supply closet, my arms full of t-shirts, and stopped dead when I came upon Rue and the guard. He had her bent over; her hands braced on the shelves that held the mascot costume as he drilled into her from behind. I blinked, frozen to the spot as my mind processed the scene. They glanced up, staring at me, their eyes wide, when I realized I didn't have to keep staring like a loon.

"Sorry!" I backed up, slammed the door as I laughed, and wondered how I'd ever meet that guard's eyes again after this.

Placing the shirts next to the door, Rue could take care of

them after she dressed. At least I knew now why Mira couldn't locate her. Chuckling to myself, I headed back to the stands for the beginning of the game.

The morning had gone by fast, my good mood not unnoticed by my coworkers. I hadn't thought I'd been in a bad mood the past two months, but based on how many people commented on how I glowed today, it made me question my judgment.

Checking the time, I pulled out my phone to send a few texts. I'd been avoiding my family, and if I put it off much longer, they'd fly down here to check on me, and I didn't need that. Opening the text thread to my mom, I sent her one first, hoping she'd be busy at work and unable to respond immediately. It was mean, but I didn't have the energy to lie through a whole interrogation.

> Blake: Hey, Mom. Thanks for the package! It's so great to have my stuff.
>
> Blake: How are you? Any new clients?
>
> Blake: Let's go shopping soon.

Next, I opened my dad's texts. He was easier to appease and less likely to dig too deep into my response. Plus, he was occupied with Mallory's pregnancy.

> Blake: Hey, Dad! Did you see Tucker's no-hitter yesterday? Amazing, right?
>
> Blake: I'm loving the job. Thanks for giving me a chance.
>
> Blake: How's Mallory and the baby doing?

Blowing out a breath, I opened the last thread I'd been avoiding… my brother's. I hated hiding so much from him. It wasn't how we worked. But I didn't know how to tell him about any of this. Bryce was protective of me on a good day.

If he discovered I was dating not only Hawk but also Luke and two other teammates, he might end up in jail. I had to protect him as much as I did myself with this topic.

Sure, protection. That's why you're not telling him.

Ignoring my thoughts, I started typing so I wouldn't talk myself out of it. When in doubt, activate his inner diva and keep the conversation on him.

> Blake: Hey, Bry! Sorry I keep missing your call. This job is amazing, but so many hours.

> Blake: Great game yesterday. You're playing so well.

> Blake: Any funny ball girl stories?

> Blake: Looking forward to seeing you soon. Miss you, bro.

When no one responded, I sighed in relief, feeling triumphant that I'd pulled it off for another day. Pocketing my phone, I headed to the clubhouse, hoping to capture the team before they hit the field. In the beginning, I'd avoided the area so I wouldn't run into Hawk and Luke, but now that things had changed, there was no reason to. Plus, I wanted to see all four of them before the game, and this was the easiest way.

Before I reached the clubhouse, I spotted Ledger sitting off to the side with his hands in his hair. I slowed, debating if I should interrupt. I hadn't talked to him as much this past week, and I suddenly felt bad for ignoring him when my dating life increased.

"Hey, Ledge. Everything okay?"

His head snapped up, the ginger strands falling over his shoulders. He had the prettiest hair—long, curly, and luxurious. I needed to find out what hair products he used because his curls were on point.

"Oh, hey, bumblebee." He swallowed, his eyes glancing behind me before returning to me. "Did you ask something?"

"Just if you were okay. Which you don't seem to be. Anything I can do?"

He shook his head but stopped, looking at me again. "I… have anxiety." His eyes widened in alarm, his throat bobbing. "I'm not sure why I just told you that." He dropped his head, tugging at his hair. "Usually, I can control it, but none of my usual techniques are working today."

I walked over and sat beside him, not saying anything as I kicked my feet, showcasing my rainbow high-tops.

"I struggle with anxiety, too. I'm not going to judge you." I kept my eyes on the wall but felt his shoulders relax. "One thing I learned in therapy was that you can't compare yourself, well, to yourself." I chuckled at myself, continuing to kick my feet. "I used to beat myself up when I didn't measure up to the same standards each day. Saying to myself, 'I did it yesterday, last week, a year ago, etc. I should be able to do it.' I was harder on myself than anyone in my life. I had to learn that there isn't a single day that is exactly the same. One day, I might get enough sleep, but the next, I'm stressed and miss my double dose of coffee, and my whole day is a cluster. Expecting the same outcome was setting myself up to fail from the start."

I took a chance to turn my head, finding him watching me, so I gave him a smile.

"I don't know if any of that rings true for you, but if it does, then I just wanted you to know you're not alone, and it's okay to not always have your shit together. It took me running away from my own wedding to accept that. So, don't do what I did."

"I dunno, I could rock a wedding dress." He smiled, shocking me. It changed his entire face.

Snorting, I bumped his shoulder. "I bet you would, actually."

"Thanks, bumblebee. This oddly helped."

"You're welcome. Besides, we're friends, and I kinda owed you one."

"No, you didn't. Common decency shouldn't be a favor."

"You might be a man of few words, but I like the ones you say."

He blushed, his cheeks slightly pink, and cleared his throat.

"I'm headed to the clubhouse. You?"

"In a bit. Thanks again."

"Anytime, Ledge. You're stuck with me." I laughed at his expression before it softened.

"I guess I can deal with that. I'll see you in a few."

Bumping his shoulder one more time, I stood and walked out, figuring he might need a few minutes to recenter his thoughts. With a skip in my step, I stepped into the clubhouse as all eyes turned to me.

LUKE

I NOTICED BLAKE'S PRESENCE INSTANTLY AS SHE STEPPED INSIDE the clubhouse. My body had become so attuned to her, like she was my sundial, showing me where the sun was. My freaky new skill allowed me to observe her before everyone else noticed. While it had only been a little over a day since our meeting, it had felt longer, and I wasn't ready to look at that too closely yet.

Her hair was pulled back into her signature ponytail, a ball cap on her head. Her black leggings wrapped perfectly around her thighs, and I wish I had time to lose myself between them. I didn't want to think of Blake as an addiction, but there was no doubt I was hooked on her.

But it wasn't love… Nope, not going there.

Her shirt was yellow, but instead of the YellowJackets, it said "Crop Top" and had a picture of corn. I laughed before I could stop myself, loving her humor. Everyone turned at the sound, noticing her.

The atmosphere shifted, bringing all the chatter to a stop as twenty guys stared. It wasn't uncommon for women to be in the clubhouse or for other staff to pop in and out, but Blake had an energy about her that made you want to watch.

She smiled, giving an awkward wave as she entered the locker room more. Clearly, this didn't faze her; her upbringing had desensitized her to baseball players.

"Pretend I'm not here. Just need to get some footage," she said, lifting her camera, not realizing she was asking the impossible.

There wasn't any way to pretend Blake Baker didn't exist. Believe me, I'd tried. And now, there wasn't a multiverse I wanted to be in where she didn't. I didn't even care if it made me sound like the closeted geek I was. My life was better by knowing my slugger, no matter where our paths took us.

Again, I wasn't ready to look too closely at my thoughts. *So, I'm gonna shove those right back into the jack-in-the-box.*

I watched as Tucker waved back, a massive smile on his face. Graham shook his head at his friend, his eyes tracking her movements despite his pretense. It was plain as day to me how they felt about her. I didn't know how they expected to keep this hidden for long. It was apparent to anyone who watched them how they felt about her. Even Hawk couldn't keep his gaze off Blake as she walked around the room snapping pictures.

Most of the guys returned to what they were doing: playing cards, listening to music, or chatting with the person next to them. This was our rare downtime before the game; everybody had their routines, superstitions, and lucky rituals.

It was one thing I'd been missing this season. My methods hadn't been the greatest with the Blue Devils, something I hadn't noticed until this season. Discovering I was a father had changed my perspective, shining a light on the man I was and whether it was someone I wanted my daughter to know.

Short answer—no.

Which meant the pre-game shots and sips from a hidden flask or the quickies with ball girls had to go. I hated myself now for how I'd treated Blake in the beginning, blaming my insecurities and performance on her. I'd been hiding behind my crutches for so long that I hadn't known what to do when they were gone.

Despite my poor behavior, Blake gave me a chance, proving she was far better than I deserved. Her demand I stopped treating her like I didn't care about her was the proverbial slap to the face I'd needed. It showed me how precious and rare Blake truly was.

She'd been amazing with Willow and understood me below surface level stuff. I'd been so wrong in that creepy golf hotel room, assuming she'd been playing an angle and using me to get a story. Blake didn't care that I was a baseball player. In fact, I was pretty confident if I asked her, it was her least favorite thing about me. She liked me despite it. She had no expectations for Luke Olson—badass first baseman. But instead, only wanted to know Luke—moderate father to Willow.

Shit. I was going to fuck this up.

If I was only me, what did I have to offer someone like her?

Anxiety raced up my spine, stealing my breath as my heart took off. Wild horses barreled across my chest as my heart thumped loudly.

I'd fuck up Willow. I'd fuck up my career.

All I was consistent with in my life was disappointing people.

The room spun, and I fell back into my locker, gripping the sides as everything blurred in my vision. What was I thinking? Fuck. I was an idiot.

My breaths left me in pants, the chatter booming louder and then fading in my ears as thought after thought catapulted at me.

I needed a drink or an orgasm to calm my thoughts and numb my mind. And despite my realization that I was a screwup and Blake was too good for me, I had no desire to hurt her by finding a random hookup. My tongue drew heavy as I thought about drinking, my throat parched now that I'd given credence to the craving.

I was too weak to say no, to avoid this forever. I'd been deluding myself that I could stop.

"You okay?" A hand touched my arm, jolting me as I blinked, unaware of my surroundings. Blake stared at me, concern heavy in her beautiful eyes as I tried to pull myself back from the dark hole my thoughts had taken me to.

"Not really," I admitted. Despite knowing I was a piece of shit, I couldn't lie to her. I took in a deep breath, trying to pretend it helped. "I will be. Don't worry about it."

Blake bit her lip between her teeth, her eyes roving over me as she studied me. "How much time until the game starts?"

Confused by her question, I glanced at the clock on the wall, counting down until we had to be on the field. "Um, about forty minutes. Why?"

"Do you know where the meditation room is?" she asked, her eyes sparkling.

"Yeah. It's a few doors down. I don't think that's going to help, Slugger."

"Just meet me there in five minutes."

I wanted to argue, but she took off, returning to snapping pictures as she walked around the locker room. Everyone had returned to their routines now, her presence no longer interesting as they got their heads ready for the game.

It seemed the quieter she was, people forgot she was there. I didn't know how it was possible since her beauty and spirit were the most magnetic things I'd ever experienced, but I wouldn't point it out to everyone else how wrong they were. I already had to share her with three guys; I didn't need any more.

I lost track of time and stood up, leaving the clubhouse and walking down the hallway to the meditation room. I'd never been in here before, so it surprised me when I stepped into the dark, dimly lit space. The walls were painted a dark green, and the carpet was the same. Small lights hung around the room, giving it a soft glow. A faint track of what I suspected were harps played through the speakers. Several beanbags, ottomans, and soft chairs spread around the room.

Blake stepped in a second later, smiling as she approached me and pulled my lips down to hers. The kiss had been unexpected, but I eagerly followed her mouth as she kissed me, stealing my doubt and insecurities with each slip of her tongue.

"Are you questioning things?" she asked, moving to my jaw.

"No. I'm good. I promise, Slugger."

"You seemed overwhelmed in the clubhouse."

"I'm better now." I kissed her but then stopped, words spilling out of my mouth in a confession. "I still feel out of place with this team. I didn't take the time at the end of last season to get to know them, assuming I wouldn't be here long. And now I have Willow, limiting my time to bond. It's always more obvious right before a game starts and without any vices or routines…"

"It feels suffocating?"

"Yeah." I licked my lips, nodding. She knew. I wasn't surprised. Blake got that part of me.

Her lips found mine again, her tongue swirling with mine as time melted away. I already felt better just by being in her presence. The kissing and confession had also unburdened me.

"Did you just bring me in here to make out?" I asked when I pulled away, smiling.

"Let me show you a trick." Her grin turned wicked, and lust shot through me.

She walked to the far side and picked up a remote, pointing it at something in the wall. A soft whirring sounded as a partition slid from the wall, cutting the room into thirds.

"Whoa. That's some trick."

"Let me show you another one." She winked before pulling me by my belt loop, shoving me onto an ottoman, and dropping to her knees. My brain struggled to register what was happening, convinced I was hallucinating.

Blake unhooked my belt, pushing my cup aside as she pulled me free. My cock had been straining against the device, and I sighed in relief as her hands stroked me. The thrill of being semi-out in the open, combined with the immense pleasure she delivered, had my head dropping back as she wrapped her lips around me.

My dick pulsed with arousal, my tip leaking with pre-cum as she sucked and stroked me, completely erasing all the thoughts from earlier. They should call them gone-jobs because everything in my head was just gone.

"Olson, you in here?" a booming voice asked, freezing me to the spot. Blake stopped her movements, her eyes wide as she stared at me. Despite the fact we were about to be caught, I couldn't help but groan at how hot she looked with my dick in her mouth, her pink lips stretched around me.

"Uh, yeah," I remembered to say when the feet shuffled.

"What are you doing in here?" they asked, and I realized who it was. Coach Anderson. AKA Hawk.

I knew the second Blake realized it, too, her eyes sparkling with a challenge as she resumed sucking me down her throat.

"Um, it's a meditation room. I'm *meditating*," I said, barely keeping my moan at bay. I wanted to tell her to stop, but it was also hot as hell.

"I've never seen you *meditate* before."

"Well, um, ahh, meditation's a private thing." I bit my fist, barely keeping a groan of pleasure back this time. "And that's what this room is… the meditation room. It's to meditate. So, I'm… um… meditating." Blake looked at me, her eyes laughing as I tried to understand what I said, fumbling over my words and repeating myself. I bet no one in the history of the world had ever said meditate that many times in a sentence without, in fact, meditating.

"Hmm." He grunted, his steps stopping at the front. I sucked in a breath, my hands landing on Blake's head to stop her. I didn't want her to bite off my dick if he stormed over here, ready to deck me. When he didn't move any further, I let out a breath.

"How are you feeling about the game?" he asked.

Maybe it was the pre-game blow job Blake appeared insistent on giving me, but I couldn't understand why Coach Anderson was asking me this. We didn't chat, especially not this long. I never knew if it was because of his friendship with Bryce or if the dude just didn't like me.

"Um, yep. All good," I muttered, my eyes threatening to roll back in my head. I couldn't watch what she was doing now, or I'd lose it, and there was no way I'd hold in the sound from orgasming.

Coach Anderson continued to ask me questions about plays and players; my mind fuddled with the information as Blake threatened to suck my soul out with her mouth. I replied with a few "Uh-huhs" and "Yeps," but I still didn't know if he bought it.

"Well, um, I'd like to be alone to, um, meditate now," I said when I couldn't take it any longer as Blake deep-throated me.

"So that's what we're calling Blake sucking you off instead of taking a shit now?"

I froze, my whole body rigid as I debated how to get out of this without losing my dick or getting a black eye. Blake pulled off me, not being quiet now as she let go of my cock with a loud pop. She giggled, apparently not afraid of the big bad wolf.

Coach Anderson walked the rest of the way around the partition, leaning against the wall as he eyed her.

"You knew I was here the whole time, didn't you?" she asked, turning her head back to him.

I didn't know if I should move or tuck myself back in, but considering Blake still had her hand around it, I couldn't do a damn thing. Hawk kept his focus on her, but it didn't ease any of the awkwardness I felt with my dick out.

"Yup. You're not messing with my players, are you?"

"Of course not. If anything, I'm *helping*. Apparently, I have a genie lamp vagina," she teased.

"Better than a magical dump."

"About that," she asked, turning her head to me, her eyes narrowing.

"I…" I stuttered, my brain empty of thoughts, frozen in fear.

"Finish what you started, Blazy."

"You want to watch?" she asked, looking at him again.

"If we're doing this thing, then I need to try to watch. I don't want to miss time with you because I can't."

"Not sure I enjoy being the test subject if you can't," I muttered.

Blake rolled her eyes, sucking the tip of my cock into her mouth, and I soon forgot my reservations. With my eyes closed, I could ignore Hawk being there. Well, almost. The smallest part knew he was, which wouldn't allow me to fully let go.

"Blazy, stand up."

"I don't remember inviting you to boss me around," she challenged but did as he asked. She stood with her hands on her hips, blocking my view.

"Take off your pants and straddle him," Coach said.

"Why?"

"Because my dick's apparently okay with this, so I want to test it some more, and Olson isn't going to cum with me here unless you use that magical pussy."

"What about his comfort level?" she asked, her voice husky, shifting so I could see him.

"He's about to get his 'lucky shit,' so I think he's fine." He lifted his brow in a challenge, but I couldn't deny he wasn't right.

"There's no condoms," Blake said, crossing her arms in a challenge.

Hawk rolled his eyes while he unbuckled his baseball pants and reached into his pocket, tossing a condom at her. She caught it, watching him as he pulled out his dick and stroked himself.

My eyes widened as I took in the monster dick he had, my mind almost exploding when I caught the piercings. I'd never really looked at another man's dick this closely before, and I didn't know how I felt about it. The longer I stared, the more scared I became. Was it a snake charmer and hypnotizing me? Why couldn't I look away?

"Eyes off my dick, Olson."

I blinked, nodding as I closed my eyes and tried to scrub that memory from my mind. I did not need to feel insecure about my cock. Hell, no.

Blake quickly pulled off her leggings and returned to me, giving me a few strokes and kisses to bring my semi-soft dick back to life. Once she had me hard again, she rolled on the condom and then straddled me, facing outward with her back to me. Holding her close, I thrust up into her, my head dropping back as I gave into the sensation of her pussy wrapped around me.

Her mouth was great, but nothing beat her wet cunt.

"Fuck, Slugger. You feel so good."

"Mm-hmm," she moaned, pushing herself up and down.

When she tilted, I opened my eyes, watching as she took Hawk into her mouth. I gripped her hips, focusing on how my dick slipped in and out of her, the sounds of our activities echoed around the room, drowning out the harps as skin slapped and grunts replaced them.

My balls drew up quickly this time, and I didn't fight it as I let go, my orgasm crashing over me as I unloaded into the condom.

"Fuck, fuck," I cursed, my sperm spewed out as tingles rushed over me. I felt Blake tense, her body trembling in my hands as she flexed her walls around me, her orgasm taking over. As the world returned, I held her for a few minutes, and all the doubt and fear vanished.

Once we all came down, the three of us returned our clothes to their proper state and then fixed the room. Hawk unlocked the meditation room door, giving us a knowing smirk as he led the way. At least one of us had been aware of the risks.

As I hurried to grab my glove and hat, only a minute before I needed to be on the field, I realized how natural the whole thing had been once I let myself quit panicking.

And while I didn't think I could convince them both to do that before each game, it made me hope we at least had a shot at making this paramour galore thing work.

BLAKE

The next few weeks soared by in a flurry of sex, dividing my time with my four boyfriends, and, of course, lots of baseball. I still hadn't returned to Bryce's condo despite it being done. I tried one night, and it had been too quiet. I only lasted two hours before I jumped in Bryce's car and zoomed back to Hawk's.

It was now the beginning of June, and summer was in full force in Wilmington. The stadium was packed, and the account on LiveIt was doing so well. Mira left me alone for the most part, but she did give me a lot of passive-aggressive side-eye. I almost couldn't believe this was my life. I was even enjoying the baseball part of my life again.

Wake up. Have sex. Go to work.

Take pictures. Secret sex. Watch baseball.

Go home. Have *more* sex. And Cuddle.

Wash. Rinse. Repeat.

While I was having a lot of great sex, it was the companionship, laughter, and intimacy that had me addicted. Maybe that was a by-product of a lot of orgasms, but I didn't think it was. And as much as the guys might not want to admit it, they were growing on each other, too.

Though, maybe they still needed some time.

"Blake, you better retrieve your puppy before I have him neutered!" Hawk grumbled from the kitchen.

I leaned back to look at Graham. We were cozy on the couch, his arms around me. I gave him a puzzled look because I didn't have a dog.

"Tucker," we both said at the same time, laughing. Scrambling up, I skipped into the kitchen with a smile on my face.

"Are you being annoying, Tuck-Tuck?" I teased, wrapping my arms around him from behind.

"Me? Annoying? Never." He chuckled, turning to kiss my forehead. Hawk and Tucker had been discussing pitching styles, which ultimately bored me after five minutes, so I'd retreated to read with Graham.

"All I'm saying, Hawkster, is that we could take the bunk beds apart and squish them up against your mattress to make a gigantic mattress. See, I've even drawn it out." He slid a piece of paper across the island where Hawk stood, his coffee mug in his hand and a scowl on his face. "Then we can make the spare room into a closet and a darkroom for Blake."

I giggled into Tucker's side. He'd been trying to convince Hawk to let him and Graham move in for weeks now. They practically spent all their free time here when they could, anyway. This wasn't the first sketch Tucker had given Hawk, but it was definitely the most outlandish.

While Hawk had come around to accepting multiple parties during sexy times, he was not a fan of sleeping with more than one person. He needed his space, and GT was crowding it.

"No." Hawk sipped his coffee; his eyes narrowed at Tucker before moving to me.

"But he's so cute and cuddly," I teased, leaning into the puppy comment. "I'm sure he's housebroken."

Tucker nodded vigorously, making his curls sweep into his eyes. "I'm the best roommate ever. Just ask Graham."

"I dunno. He can be pretty demanding with his need for cuddles and food, and he's always jumping on the furniture and sheds like crazy." Graham smiled from where he'd stopped in the kitchen, leaning against the table.

"You're one to talk!" Tucker said, jumping off the stool to chase after Graham. I stumbled back as they took off, racing out the back door into the yard. Hawk sighed and rubbed his forehead.

"Regretting your decision?" I asked, walking over to him and leaned against his chest. Since we couldn't be touchy-feely around the team, I found myself constantly in their arms the second we could be. Keeping our relationship a secret had been more challenging than I'd expected.

And it wasn't just the sneaking off to have sex in random places part. It was not talking about it with my coworkers or mentioning it to my family, which had become more difficult by the minute. It had been almost a week since I'd spoken to Bryce, which was strange for us. Fortunately for me, he seemed to be just as busy, so I didn't think he suspected anything, but I hated keeping secrets.

In a weird counteraction to keeping it hidden, the five of us had become stuck to one another like glue during our off hours, wanting to spend as much time as we could together without questioning every interaction and lying to people. Luke missed the most time since he had Willow, but that should also change after today. He'd decided he was ready to introduce her to the others, expanding our bubble.

I ran my hands up Hawk's chest, loving how solid and muscular he was. He stared at me, his mismatched eyes roving over me before he spoke.

"As much as they annoy me, I don't hate them being here. It makes you happy, and I love seeing that."

"Yeah?"

"Yeah, Blazy. If you haven't figured it out yet, you're it for me. Always have been. I just never believed I deserved you."

"And now?" I asked, my heart racing.

"I still don't know if I do, but I realized it wasn't up to me. I'm never going to stop fighting for you. I never want you to doubt my feelings."

"Even if it costs you everything? Your job? Your friendship with Bryce?" I asked. They were everything I'd wanted to hear, but I didn't know if I was worth that much of a sacrifice despite the swooniness of his words.

So far, everything had been easy and safe as we figured out how to be a five-person couple. But I knew the honeymoon phase wouldn't last, and when the pressure came, where would everyone fall?

"What's a job worth if you don't have someone to share your life with? Not that I believe for one second I would lose it. But I would sacrifice a million jobs to be with you."

"And Bryce?" It was the elephant in the room these days.

"I made plans to grab a drink with him when we're in Charleston."

"You did?" My eyes went wide. I'd been dreading driving to Charleston tomorrow and seeing Bryce face-to-face this week. But I knew I couldn't put it off forever. And now it seemed like my luck had run out. Bryce would know in a few days.

"Yeah. It's time, Blazy."

I nodded. I knew he was right, but it didn't make it less scary. I'd wanted to tell him from the start, but the more comfortable I became in our relationship without telling him, the more the fear I'd lose everything grew.

But we owed it to my brother to be honest, and I'd trust Hawk he was in this. Everything he'd done up until this point proved it, so I had to believe in that.

The doorbell rang, interrupting our conversation, and I wasn't sure if I was upset or relieved about it. Kissing

Hawk's cheek, I hurried to the front, excited to see Willow and Luke.

Throwing open the door, I smiled widely as I greeted the two.

"Hey guys!" I leaned in and kissed Luke's cheek without thinking, and he froze, his eyes wide. To cover my mishap, I dropped to Willow's height and gave her one too. "Hey, Lolo. Are you ready to meet Sunny?"

Her eyes lit up, and she nodded. I took her hand and led her to the guest room. Her eyes grew comically large as she took in the bunk beds, the tea party set, and a pile of toys in the corner.

"These are yours?" she asked.

"No. They're my friend Hawk's nieces. I believe one of them is around your age. It's a cool room but not as cool as yours."

She beamed at that. We'd spent most of the week picking out photos for her to place around her room. Some she'd taken with me, and others were ones I'd shot over the past few months. Willow put one next to her bed of her and Jack, and slept in the jersey she'd gotten every night. She was one hardcore YellowJackets fan now.

I walked over to the cage and pulled out the fluffy hamster. "This is Sunny. Would you like to hold him? He's really friendly."

She nodded shyly but moved closer. I showed her how, and she sat on the ground, petting his little head in her hands. We talked for a little bit as she stroked his fur, and she became more animated the longer she adjusted to being in a new setting. This was something I'd learned about her. She did better the more time she had to adjust.

"Would you like to go outside and play with my other friends? My friend Tucker brought over some baseball stuff—"

"Really?" she blurted, cutting me off and shoving Sunny into my hands.

Laughing, I stood and placed Sunny back in his cage.

"I'll take that as a yes, but first, let's wash our hands. We don't want to spread any hamster germs."

Willow nodded and followed me into the bathroom. At the sight of the unicorn dildo on the counter, I froze, having forgotten it was out. Willow bumped into me from behind, and I grabbed the brightly colored dildo and tossed it into the shower, pulling the curtain close before she entered all the way.

"Um, gigantic spider," I lied.

Willow's eyes became owlish as she stared at the curtain, clutching my shirt in her hand.

"Let's wash our hands," I reminded, stepping up to the sink. Together, we soaped up our hands and scrubbed them under the water, giving my face time to return to its normal color. "Ready?" I asked, handing her the towel to dry. She nodded, her braids moving. "Did your daddy do your hair?"

"Yep." She smiled, her cheeks rosy as she peered up at me. "You should ask him to do yours."

I laughed, hoping that wasn't a knock on my hair skills. "I'll keep that in mind, Lolo."

She preened and took my hand as we walked out to the backyard. Hawk and Luke had joined Tucker and Graham, setting up some makeshift bases and a little bat and tee. However, Tucker wanted to pitch to her first, believing it was his magic skill. Luke was worried Tucker would overwhelm her, but I had faith in my Golden Retriever boyfriend. He was too hard not to love.

"Wow," she whispered, taking in the backyard baseball diamond.

"You and I get to be captains. Let me introduce you to my friends, and then we can pick teams. Okay?"

She nodded, huddling into my side as we drew near the guys.

"This is Graham. He plays catcher." Graham waved, and I pointed to Tucker. "That's Tucker, he's a pitcher. The guy with a beard is Hawk. He used to be a catcher, but now is your dad's coach, and then your dad."

"Hey, Willow," Tucker said, jogging over to us and squatting. "I'm so glad you're here. We need some help, and your dad and Blake said you loved baseball."

"I do," she whispered, blinking up at him.

"Perfect. So, which position do you want to play?"

She pointed to first base, making Luke blush. Tucker sighed, holding his heart as he fell back onto the grass. "Say it ain't so."

Willow laughed, and Luke settled, finally seeing the beauty of Tucker.

"Now that you know everyone. Pick your first player."

"Daddy," she whispered, pointing to Luke. He pointed to himself like he hadn't expected her to choose him. Seeing their relationship grow closer was so special. I loved how much they were trusting one another as they navigated it.

"Then, I'll take Graham," I said. "Pick your last player."

She bit her fingernail as she looked between Tucker and Hawk, finally pointing to Hawk. "Will you be our catcher?" she asked, and he nodded, smiling.

Tucker jumped up and ran to Graham, tackling him to the ground. "Yay, we're still on the same team, bestie."

Willow giggled, the sound so light and precious it had everyone in good spirits.

"You want to bat first?" I asked, and she nodded. Putting on a batting helmet, I helped her pick a bat before picking up a glove and hat and heading to first base.

Luke showed Willow where to stand and perfected her stance, giving her some tips. She nodded, concentrating as he spoke, and lifted her bat when she was ready.

"Let's go, Willow!" Tucker chanted, bending low as he lofted the ball to her. She swung, missing, but it didn't deter her as she redid her hold. Tucker threw a few more, none of us counting as we watched her try. When the bat cracked the ball, we all rejoiced with her as her mouth hung open before she remembered to run. Graham pretended to fall on the ball, kicking it out of the way so she made it.

Luke batted next and hit it on the first try, shouting for Willow to run for it. Ignoring her, I caught the ball and tackled him.

"Um, Blake. This is baseball. It's no contact."

"Not today. You're out, hot stuff."

He laughed, smiling as he shook his head and dusted off his shorts. "Fine. But I'll remember this."

Hawk hit the ball next, sending it sailing out into the backyard. I took one look at it and shook my head. Yeah, so not sweating for that. "Nope. That's all yours, Tucker."

He cursed, but took off running while Hawk causally jogged around the bases, stopping to pick up Willow and setting her on his shoulder as he ran home.

We switched sides after that, with Willow pitching us the balls until Tucker almost took one in the groin, and then Hawk stepped in. I was the weak link on our team, taking five swings of my own before I made contact. Luke didn't even go after the ball but picked me up and tossed me over his shoulder, keeping me from getting to the base.

Willow laughed so hard at it; she had tears in her eyes and called me out.

We all played a few more innings, laughing and enjoying our made-up rules as we fell in love with Willow.

"So, LoLo, what does a five-year-old want for their birthday?" I asked as we sat around the back porch drinking lemonade.

"A pony!"

"Nice try. What else?" Luke said, arching an eyebrow.

"Hmm," she said, tapping her chin in thought. It was so similar to Luke's mannerisms that I laughed. Eventually, she shrugged her shoulders and hid her face. "I dunno."

"What kind of cake do you like?" Graham asked, bringing her back to the conversation.

"Strawberry."

"Oh, good choice," I said. "And ice cream?"

"Oreo!"

"Now you're talking," Tucker said. "You know, I always wanted to go to one of those trampoline places."

"Yeah, good luck during the season," Hawk retorted.

"Ah, yeah. Dam—I mean, dang." Tucker cringed, his face pink.

"It's okay. I don't have any friends to invite," Willow said, her voice small.

"What about Samantha? I thought she was your friend?" Luke asked, his brow furrowing.

"Not anymore."

"What happened?"

"She stole Brittney's crayons and then blamed me, so now Brittney hates me, too."

"Little girls are ruthless," Tucker muttered.

"What if we invited your class to Champion Field for a game?" I asked, an idea sparking.

"Could we do that?" she asked, her eyes big.

"That's a big ask, Slugger," Luke said. He looked concerned, and I couldn't tell if it was too big or if he was worried I couldn't pull it off.

"I know some people." I winked at him. "If Willow wants her birthday there, we can make it happen."

"Yes! Yes! Then I can introduce my class to my new friends," Willow said, looking at the guys.

After that, it was hard to deny her.

Luke and Willow stayed for a few more hours, eating dinner and playing a round of Mario Kart before Luke called it time to go. Willow hugged everyone, officially earning the love and support of Tucker, Graham, and Hawk.

I walked them out to the car, wanting a few moments alone with Luke. After securing her in the booster seat, he pressed me against the trunk, out of sight of little eyes.

"Thank you for today. It was good for both of us. To see that there are people in our lives."

"I'm glad. I had a lot of fun, and I know the guys did, too. I hate that you have to leave." I pulled him close, needing to feel his body.

"I know, me too." His eyes searched mine, and I didn't know what he was looking for.

"Will you sit with me on the bus tomorrow?"

"I'd love to." I smiled, then remembered I was driving Bryce's car. "Oh, shoot. I'm not riding the bus in the morning. Hawk and I are driving up in Bryce's car." I grimaced, hating how it always felt like Luke missed out. "I could ask if you could ride with me instead?"

He shook his head, his eyes sad. "No, it's fine. Might bring up more questions if I did, and we're not ready for that."

Doubt swirled in my gut and I wondered for the first time if maybe it wasn't me at all, but Luke keeping his distance.

"I'll be your seat buddy on the way back."

"Deal. Good night, Slugger."

"Good night, Luke."

He pressed his lips to mine, stealing my breath and making me wish for the millionth time he could stay. It never seemed fair, but I knew today was the first big step in introducing Willow to the guys. We needed to take it slow for her benefit so that one day, we could all be a family.

The thought scared me, but under it was a more prominent feeling of rightness and hope.

Basically… I needed to get out of my own way—story of my life.

HAWK

I headed to the kitchen, picking up the dishes and trash, the need to clean and organize riding me. This was one reason I didn't like people in my space—they messed with my order. I knew it was unreasonable to expect people to hold my standards and that they should be allowed to touch things. But it made me twitchy when things weren't right.

"Need any help?" Graham asked, following me into the kitchen.

"No." I didn't look up, wiping the counters and putting things back.

"You don't like us here, do you?" he asked, halting my movements. I lifted my eyes, catching him watching me.

"It's not you. It's the touching of my things."

"Blake touches things," he countered.

I paused because he wasn't wrong. I *liked* seeing her things mixed in with mine. Loved it, actually. It was evidence she was here. Something I never believed possible.

"Blake's not everyone."

"No, she's not."

He said nothing else as he stared. It was something I'd

noticed more and more about Graham. While Tucker was gregarious and an attention whore, Graham was more reserved and only got pulled into things because of Tucker. Most of the time, he sat back and watched. It made him a great catcher and more like me than I wanted to admit. His friendship with Tucker made little sense, but neither had mine with Bryce, so I wasn't one to judge.

"What are you getting at?" I asked when I couldn't take the silence anymore.

He shrugged his shoulders, dropping his crossed arms, and placed them against the counter. "Nothing. Maybe everything."

I narrowed my eyes, not liking what he was insinuating. "Spit it out, West. Don't hold back now."

His eyes sparkled, and the corner of his mouth tilted up like he was trying not to laugh at me. His response only made me angrier.

"We're not going away. If you're waiting for us to bow out so you can have Blake all to yourself, then you'll be waiting a long time. I don't know what the future holds, but I know that Blake is it for both of us."

Grinding my teeth, my nostrils flared as I bit back my response. He was completely off base. Tucker and Blake walked into the kitchen then, laughing with their heads together, so they didn't notice the tension right away. However, as soon as I spotted her, I relaxed. Having her near me made me breathe easier.

"What's going on?" Blake asked, cluing into the tension. She glanced between Graham and me, frowning.

"Graham thinks I'm waiting for him and Tucker to get bored because I don't like people in my space."

"Oh." Blake's shoulders relaxed, and her smile returned. Graham was the one to frown now as he watched her, realizing he'd missed something. Tucker wrapped his arms around Blake, snuggling into her neck.

"I'm not going anywhere. I'll superglue myself to you if I have to. I'll even learn to pitch with you there. The bathroom might be tricky, but we'll figure it out," Tucker blurted, his words so idiotic it halted my train of thought.

"What the fuck?" I shook my head in disbelief, hoping what the hell he said would make more sense.

Blake laughed, the sound clearing some of the rage. I rubbed my brow, squeezing the bridge of my nose.

"That's not it. Impatient Gen Z'ers," I mumbled. Dipping my head back, I looked up at the ceiling and took a few deep breaths. When I calmed down, I met Blake's eyes, finding my comfort. Her eyes danced with mischief and love, reminding me the irritation would be worth it.

"Do you want to tell them?" I asked her, ignoring the other two. I didn't have an issue with them being here. Not really. I just liked my things a certain way. But that was my issue to work on. Plus, maybe if they had a designated space, all of their crap wouldn't spill into mine.

I could only hope. Tucker seemed like a messy one.

Blake did a little dance, all three of us watching her with a smile. "Follow me," she said, spinning on her heels and heading in the opposite direction of my bedroom.

"Um, are you showing us the murder room?" Tucker teased. "Or is it a shed? I feel like Hawk would have a murder shed." Tucker glanced back at me, his eyes wide.

"If you think I need a shed to kill you, then you haven't been paying enough attention."

He jumped, clinging to Graham. "Protect me, Teddy Graham. The English bulldog is bulldogging."

I blinked. "Do you even listen to half the shit that leaves your mouth? Wait, is this why you left me a bandana?" I turned to Blake. "I've changed my mind."

"No take backs." She giggled, pulling Graham's hand and, by proxy, Tucker's. "It's not a murder room or sex dungeon. But I guess that could be up for debate since it's yours."

She pushed open the door to the basement and flipped on the light, showing it off with her arms like a gameshow host. "Ta-da!"

Despite having finished the basement, I spent little time down there outside of laundry. Bryce said it was because I was an old man, and it hurt my knees. I didn't want to admit he was partially correct. The knee injury kept me from wanting to go up and down the stairs a million times.

"You sure you're not trying to kill us?" Graham asked, peeking down the steps.

"Scaredy cat," Blake said, rolling her eyes. She huffed, offended they hadn't responded as excitedly as expected. To be fair, she hadn't come out and said what it was yet. Blake stomped down the stairs, and the guys followed, giving me nervous glances. I followed behind them, lifting my eyebrow each time they peered back.

When they came to the end of the steps and turned the corner, they both stopped, and I almost crashed into them.

"Can you take your jaws off the floor long enough to move?"

"I don't understand," Graham said.

"You pick up your feet and move forward," I retorted, pushing them apart and moving through them when they didn't go.

"You can move in if you want," Blake said, her voice shyer than I expected. "There's a couple of bedrooms through there and a bathroom."

The guys had stopped in the main room. Over the years, I'd fashioned the perfect man cave with all my baseball paraphernalia. It held a billiard table, dart board, and an old Ms. Pacman tabletop game for two players. A large sofa and TV sat off to the other side, the walls covered in my jerseys and pictures of players I'd met over the years. Then, there were the two glass cases of signed baseballs and trophies. It felt a little narcissistic to keep them, but I'd worked hard for them and, in the end, decided out of sight wasn't that narcissistic.

"This place is sick, man," Tucker finally said, taking off as he ran around the room, taking in everything. He shouted out player names as he peered at the pictures and signed baseballs. "Holy shit. I feel like I see you in a whole new way," he murmured, staring at me as he tilted his head.

"I think Tucker has an idol crush," Blake whispered, wrapping her arm in mine. I rolled my eyes, but the part of me that had worked so hard to be respected preened.

Graham and Tucker checked out the rooms, both empty outside of a queen bed in one. Blake slapped me, narrowing her eyes.

"I'm still mad you made me sleep in that bunk bed."

I shrugged. "I didn't want you too far away. Plus, I never would've walked in on you."

Blake rolled her eyes, but her cheeks heated. I didn't know how she kept up with all of us, but her appetite for any of us never seemed to dwindle.

The two stooges talked a little longer about when they could pack and get out of their lease, officially agreeing to move in after we returned from our next away game series. They left soon after, needing to pack for tomorrow. The bus left early, but I didn't have to be on it for once since I was riding with Blake in Bryce's car.

Verifying everything I would need over the next six days was packed in my suitcase, I shucked off my clothes and climbed into bed naked. I leaned back against the headboard with my arms braced behind my head, crossing my ankles over one another, feeling smug. Blake stopped when she exited the bathroom, her toothbrush in her hand. I frowned at the object like it had personally offended me.

"You don't have to put your stuff away after each use."

"Oh, um, well." She glanced down at the toothbrush. "I'm packing it tonight, but I didn't want to assume anything."

A weight pressed down onto my chest, and I shot up before I could think about it too much. Unfortunately, I momentarily forgot I was naked, and my cock slapped against my leg, the piercing stinging as I yanked her into my arms.

"Oof."

"Sorry, I..." I shook my head, my body trembling, and I didn't know why.

Yeah, you do. Just admit your feelings for once and quit beating around the bush.

"Hey, what's wrong?" she asked, smoothing her hand up and down my back. I picked her up, and her legs wrapped around my waist as I stumbled backward to the bed, holding her to me. I breathed in her hair, letting her vanilla and honey scent soothe me.

"I had a sudden flash of you leaving like you're not really here. Your bags packed, and at any second, you could get up and leave. I didn't like it," I admitted.

It was quiet for a minute as her warm hands brushed up and down my back. When her lips pressed softly into my skin, I relaxed.

"I know you like your space, so I was trying to respect that. But I do also feel displaced. I've lived out of suitcases forever and never feel like I have a place just to be."

Blake had been saying that from the beginning, but I'd been too pigheaded to hear. I thought she didn't want to be with me, pushing against my requests, but it was about belonging.

I drew back, moving my hands to cup her face, my eyes searching back and forth. I thought I'd been transparent about my intentions, but maybe she needed me to say them.

Too much time had already been lost between half-truths

and good intentions. It was time to put it all on the line and deal with the consequences.

I'd rather swing and miss than not swing at all.

"I'm such a fucking fool, Blazy. I thought I was telling you how I felt, but I realize now that I haven't been as clear as I needed. My fear kept me from saying it out loud, wanting to keep that small ounce of safety, but what's the point when all it's doing is stealing something for you? From us?"

I shook my head, taking a deep breath. My thumbs grazed against her cheeks, my eyes never leaving hers. Memories of the first time I kissed her and then chickened out, of the first time she became mine, and then I bailed resurfaced, pushing me to finally do what I kept saying I would.

Fight. Be upfront. Be bold.

"I've been in love with you for so long; I don't know how not to be. I thought I could live a life without you, pretending it was fine, but the second you returned, I knew that had been the biggest crock of shit I'd ever sold myself. I always believed it was Bryce keeping me from saying anything, but that's a cop out too. Do you know why I always take care of everyone else?"

She swallowed, clearing her throat. "Because you have a good heart."

I gave her a crooked smile. "Nah. Because if I'm needed, then people can't leave me. I resented my family for so long for making me take care of them when, really, I was the one afraid of letting go. It took one year without you in my life to realize that, and I stepped back, letting them live their lives and watching them flourish in the process. *I* held them back."

"I think you're being harder on yourself than you need to be."

"I never fought for you because I never believed I was worth it. It wasn't just about Bryce being upset, but that your family wouldn't approve, either. That you'd realize one day how mediocre I was."

"Oh, Hawk. No."

"Let me finish, *please*," I begged, knowing I needed to say it. If she showed me kindness, I'd wimp out.

She nodded, kissing my nose, her eyes glassy. "Fine, but don't talk down about yourself. My heart can't take it." I dropped my right hand, squeezing her hip.

"Having you return, seeing the fire in you, I couldn't ignore how empty my life had become. It brought me back to life. "

"I don't have that much power," she whispered. "Don't give me that much. I'll fail."

"Oh, Blazy, you could never fail at being yourself. Don't you see how enigmatic you are? Everyone loves you, not just because you're a people pleaser. You've been yourself; even when you tumble, you don't let it stop you. You keep on persisting. It's never affected the way people view you. If anything, it makes them adore you more."

"I guess we both need to see ourselves better than we do."

"Yeah. I think so." I swallowed, my mouth dry. "I'm tired of standing in my way. I've said you're it for me, but I'm not sure you believe it. But you are. Unless you tell me to go away, I'm gonna be here. I'm sorry I didn't clarify, making you feel you didn't belong. This is your home now, too. If you want it."

Her eyes glistened, searching mine for something. I dropped all my walls, willing to show her exactly how I felt. I'd rather have my heart smashed to smithereens than have her doubt for one more second. I'd already lost her twice for being a coward; I wouldn't do it again.

"Are you asking me to move in with you?"

"I kind of thought you already had."

"Oh." Her cheeks heated, and I rubbed my hand over them.

"I don't want to live with the two knuckleheads without you. Then it's just some weird bro club. I need my Blazy.

Don't make Sunny a single-parent hamster." I tried to smile as I held my breath, waiting for her to respond.

"Hawk Anderson, I've loved you for longer than I haven't. I don't know how to be me without loving you. I guess we're both dumb for being so scared, but maybe we would've screwed it up back then. I'm just glad we're here now."

"So, is that a yes?"

Her mouth covered mine in a crushing kiss, her tongue sweeping in and stealing my breath. My hands wrapped around her body, bringing her as close as possible to me. We hungrily kissed one another until we had to break apart to breathe. She kept kissing me, smiling as she peppered my face with "yeses."

"In that case," I said, smiling as I stood and placed her on the bed. I stalked over to my closet and threw it open, shoving a bunch of clothes over and then yanking open a drawer and pulling everything out. I didn't know what was in it, but I'd find another spot. I needed her to have her things next to mine, to feel like she belonged here.

"You're giving me closet space?"

"You can have the whole damn thing. I'll make do with the one in the princess room if you need more space." I stalked back over, the reminder I was naked hitting me again as her eyes roved over my body. Smirking, I kneeled on the bed, caging her in. "I want you here, Blazy. I'll deal with the mess."

"You say the sweetest things," she teased.

I tackled her to the bed, kissing her through our laughter as we tickled, fought, and wrestled. Eventually, it turned more heated, and I shoved her shirt over her head, sucking her nipple into my mouth. I desperately needed to taste every inch of her. I loved watching her respond to my touch, to see her writhe beneath me as she moaned. Blake might have been an inexperienced lover our first time together, but she'd always been responsive and vocal. Add in her confidence now and she regularly blew my mind.

Her hands tangled in my hair, tugging the perfect amount as I moved down her body. I yanked off her shorts, baring her lower half to me. No matter how often I got to see and taste her, it never seemed enough. I didn't think I'd ever get bored with Blake Baker.

Lifting her, she wrapped her legs around my waist, with my cock nestled between us. Our bodies aligned as we kissed, rocking into one another. I stumbled over to the side of the bed, grabbing a condom. The need to be inside of her was almost insurmountable.

Her head fell back as I sheathed myself inside her warmth, lifting her hips as I thrust. It was slow and languid, our bodies moving together in a perfect rhythm.

"Yes, oh god, Hawk," Blake purred, her voice husky and raw as she clung to me. My beard scratched against her neck as I sucked and kissed, moving her body in small bouts as we groaned.

"You feel so good, Blazy," I crooned, sucking on her neck.

"You, too. Gah. It's so good."

My cock agreed, twitching as her pussy gripped me. The piercing sent tingles through me as it rubbed against her, my toes curling. Sex had never felt this good.

But this wasn't just sex. This was lovemaking.

Our eyes held our movements in complete synchronization as I plunged into her, my cock deep inside. My balls drew up, and my muscles tightened as my orgasm approached.

"I'm coming, baby," I breathed, unable to stop it. It was like a freight train, and once it was on the track, there was no holding it back.

Blake's mouth fell open, her hair tickling my thighs as her fingernails dug into my shoulders. "Yes, yes, yes," she screamed, bouncing on my dick. Her eyes connected with mine one more time, and I was done. My cock twitched, and everything inside of me exploded as it rushed forward, no longer okay with waiting. Fireworks simmered against my body, lighting every inch of me on fire.

We held one another as we came back down, our breaths syncing as we stared.

"I love you, Blake."

"I love you, Hawk."

I kissed her, no longer scared of the future. No matter what, I'd have her, which gave me the courage to admit it to the one person I loved as much as her.

I was ready to tell Bryce.

GRAHAM

AFTER PACKING LATE INTO THE NIGHT, MY SLUGGISH BRAIN protested waking up. In retrospect, staying up so late with a game today had been unwise, especially with traveling there. But the prospect of being with Blake full-time had been too exciting to contain. Tucker and I had spent hours packing our clothes and things we couldn't live without—which for Tucker was about fifty pairs of tennis shoes and books for me.

We'd left the rest for a moving company to pack while we were gone, moving them before we returned. It wasn't ideal to move during the season, but again... Blake. Which was why I didn't understand why my body wanted to wake up before my alarm went off.

Hot hands. Hot breath. A hot member pressed against my ass.

Oh right. That's why my body was awake. But wait...

"Tuck," I whispered, my voice needy and desperate. I held my body taut, worried if I moved even a millimeter, it would be too much.

His cock rubbed against my ass, sliding deliciously between my cheeks as he rocked forward. I had to assume he was asleep, as this wasn't the typical wake-up protocol with us.

While things had changed and grown between us, we hadn't explored anything other than kissing and dry humping without Blake, and I didn't know if he was ready for more.

Or if I was, to be honest.

I kept waiting for him to freak out about everything and break my heart. Tucker was one of the few people I'd bared my soul to; losing him would be something I'd never recover from.

"Tuck," I gasped, my body shaking.

"Mm-hm," he mumbled, his fingers flexing on my stomach. "Feels good, G."

Squeezing my eyes closed, I held my breath and tried to convince my body to calm the fuck down.

Lips pressed against my neck, and the breath I'd been holding rushed out of me in a loud exhale.

"You're shaking," Tucker whispered, leaning over me. "Am I doing it wrong?"

"No." I tried to shake my head but turned my mouth to his in the process. I froze as our lips met, electricity zipping from him to me.

My control snapped, and I pressed back into him. The kiss quickly became sloppy, our tongues moving faster than we could feel. Tucker's body pushed into mine, his cock hard and thick against my backside. My head became dizzy with lust, and I gasped as I sucked in oxygen.

"We should slow down. We need to talk about this."

"What's there to talk about?" Tucker asked, kissing down my neck. His hands moved over my pecs, the hard calluses sending shivers through me. He brushed against my sensitive nipple, creating sparks. He continued to move forward, my breathing more erratic as he grew closer to my cock. All the while, he rocked into me, sending white-hot desire to my dick.

"God, you feel so good, G. I've been missing out."

His hand wrapped around me, and I dropped my head back against him, surrendering to his will. My free hand gripped his ass from behind, squeezing the flesh and pushing him forward. We rocked together as he pumped my cock up and down, his movements sure and strong.

"You're good at that," I wheezed, my voice broken.

"I should be. I've been beating my own salami for a while."

I snorted, smiling at the idiotic things he said. "Gah, you're the best."

"Ah, thanks, Teddy Graham. I think so, too. Does that mean you'll give me a treat if I'm a good boy?" he purred, nipping my ear.

My brain was mush, all thought processes offline as I chased the pleasure ramping up in my body. I could understand how good of a lover Tucker was just by how he touched me. Full of confidence with a single focus on me.

"What do you need, G? Tell me. I want it to be good," he said, proving my point.

"It already is, Tuck. So, good."

"Then I want it to be mind-blowing, otherworldly. I want to erase every other guy from your memory so all you know is me. You're mine now, Graham West. I want to own your body, heart, and soul."

Jesus fuck, his mouth.

I whimpered, my mind doing precisely as he said, exploding. The fantasy I had for years hadn't even come close to this. His cock rubbed up against my hole, hard and leaking. His hand was tight on me, stroking me slowly, swiping his thumb over the tip as he dragged the pre-cum. His breath was hot on my neck, his lips grazing against the sensitive skin.

It was a tilt-a-whirl of sensations as my body and heart attempted to connect. Cotton candy and pop rocks. Cashmere and lace. Baseball and ballet. The two extremes shouldn't work, but as I rocked my ass back on his dick, his hand fucking my front, it somehow did.

It was him and me. Graham and Tucker. Package Deal.

The orgasm smacked into me, my balls drawing up as everything came to a head and exploded. Fireworks sparked all around me, my body on fire as I came so hard I couldn't see. Every muscle tensed up, my hand gripping Tucker's ass; it was guaranteed to leave fingerprints. Something sharp bit into my shoulder as wetness spread from my front to my back.

My chest heaved, and my heart pounded in my ears. It felt like I'd left my body as the world slowly returned.

"I want to wake up like this every morning," Tucker hummed into my ear. As I felt the weight of his arms encircling me, his head nestled against my shoulder, I realized the depth of his affection. Our relationship meant the world to Tucker, just as it did to me. He wouldn't have said anything if he wasn't absolutely certain. I had to trust him. My doubts were mine, and it was unfair to cast them onto him.

"I think that can be arranged."

"What are you thinking, G?"

"Right now? Nothing. The blood hasn't returned to my head." I laughed, shaking us both.

"Then before? Was it not good?" He asked, his voice hesitant. I turned over, wrapping my arms around him this time.

"Hey, no. It was exactly as you said. The best. Nothing else compares outside of our time with Blake. The two of you are what fantasies are made of."

"Then what is it? It feels like there's a block between us."

"I'm sorry. That's on me. I've been worried you'll wake up and be like, 'Okay, my bi-curious experiment is over, and it's not for me. Toodles.' Leaving me crushed."

Tucker's mouth gaped as he stared at me. "I would never say 'toodles.' Seriously." He rolled his eyes, and I pinched his side, narrowing my eyes. I'd let him have control this morning, but I could easily take it back.

"Watch it, Tuck. Instead of your reward, I'll punish you instead." He shivered, his eyes dilating, and I suddenly wanted him to back talk so I could.

"I wouldn't do that, G. I might be impulsive at times, but I wouldn't have crossed any lines if I wasn't sure."

"I know, Tuck." I ran my fingers through his hair, his eyes fluttering at my touch. "It's what I realized after that; what did you say, 'otherworldly' orgasm."

"Yeah? It was good?"

"Fucking amazing. I can understand why your fuck buddies never wanted to leave now."

"Well," he said, blushing.

"You're a giver, Tuck. You like to see your partner experience pleasure, don't you? It's not just about the watching, but you love it when they enjoy themselves."

He tilted his head. "I never thought about it that way, but I guess you're right. I always chalked it up to the voyeur thing, but that makes sense. When my partner is more vocal and responsive, it sets me off from their moans alone. Like today. I came just from watching you take what I was giving you."

I kissed him, taking my time to map out his lips and how he felt pressed against me. My alarm went off a few minutes later, and we both groaned but pulled apart.

"At least we get to see Blake in a few hours," Tucker said, sighing happily.

"This bus ride will suck without her."

"Let's send her texts to annoy Hawk."

"He's gonna get you one of these days," I warned.

"I'd like to see him try! It's time to prank his grumpy ass. He's the last one left. You want in?" He wiggled his eyebrows as he grabbed his stuff for the shower. I pulled the sheets off, sticky from our combined cum, and tossed them into the laundry.

"I should say no, but when have I ever backed down from a prank?"

"Yes!" Tucker pumped his arm in the air, and I followed him into the shower. "Joint showers?" he asked as he watched me.

I shrugged, turning on the water. "Unless you'd prefer not to. It might save us some time."

"What if I need to drop the browns off at the Super Bowl?"

I rolled my eyes. "Now you're a shy shitter? Remember how in junior year, you sent me daily pics of your poop. I think we're good. Go use your bathroom if you need to, then."

He cringed. "Not my finest moment. I've really grown over the years." He laughed, putting his clothes on the counter. "But no, we weren't dating then. We are now. Feels like something we should keep separate to keep the romance alive."

"You're a dork."

"Maybe. But I'm not wrong." He stepped into the shower, the steam billowing around us.

I pulled him to me, our bodies slick against each other. He gasped, his cock growing hard against our bellies.

"Are you wanting romance, Tuck?"

He blushed, shrugging one shoulder. "I mean. Maybe. I kind of like it."

I kissed his chin. "Okay. I'll give you romance."

His smile reached his eyes, a giddiness taking over and filling my heart with all the warmth it could contain.

Shockingly, we made it through the shower, dressed, and ate in record time. Loading the car with our bags, I looked at the boxes and furniture, knowing the next time we returned, it would be somewhere we could put down roots.

We'd come to the YellowJackets hopeful that we'd get to play the game we loved, and yet we'd found so much more. Friends. Acceptance. Love.

There were still battles to wage, and games to win, but I felt optimistic. Even the prospect of telling my family I was part of an unconventional relationship felt doable. As long as we were together, we could fight anything.

"Check it out. I sent Blake a selfie, and she sent this back."

He flashed his phone screen toward me, and I gulped as I took in the beautiful girl staring back, her hair mussed and blue eyes sparkling as she smiled at the camera. She only had a sheet around her, highlighting her cleavage. It was tamer than most pictures she'd sent before, but it felt more natural. She wasn't trying to be sexy, and yet she was. Her honest personality shone through, giving you a real glimpse of who she was.

"She's beautiful," I whispered. "Send it to me?" I asked, turning on the car.

"Already done. Come here." He pulled me toward him, our cheeks smushed together. Tucker lifted his phone, taking a picture of us both on the screen. Then he turned his head, kissing my cheek with his eyes closed. I did the same, wanting to kiss his cheek this time, but his lips were still there, so I slanted my mouth over them, kissing him as we lost track of time. My elbow hit the horn as I shifted, breaking us apart as we jumped.

"Whoops." I cringed, my face flaming as we both laughed.

"Send them to me, too?"

"Duh." Tucker winked, typing away on his phone as I drove us to Champion Field. For the first time in my baseball career, I didn't care about the game today or how I played. I was more excited about the people in my life and when I would get to spend time with them. Ideas of how I could romance Tucker flooded my mind, making me eager to get on the bus so I could get started.

Now that I knew Tucker was all in, it was time to give him and Blake the Graham West experience.

CHAPTER
FIFTY

BLAKE

Despite driving six hours to the game today, I felt energized. Hawk and I had fun on the drive, jamming out to old-school music and asking each other ridiculous questions. Such as "Would you rather always have a mullet haircut or a ponytail haircut?" And my personal favorite, "Would you rather your only mode of transportation be a donkey or a giraffe?"

Ponytail and giraffe, obviously.

It felt like old times, the ease and comfort so effortlessly given. I wanted every day to be like this.

"You nervous about seeing Bryce?" I asked as we walked into the Charleston Grizzlies' Stadium. I'd avoided the subject on the drive, but it tumbled out now that we were only a few hours away from him.

He snorted, glancing over at me. "How long have you been sitting on that?"

I cringed. "All day. Don't change the subject."

"No, Blazy. I'm not nervous. It's time to be honest with my best friend. It's gonna be fine. I promise."

I bit my lip, nodding as doubt swirled in my gut. I didn't

want to lose my brother, but I needed Hawk in my life. I loved him.

"Bryce will be confused and perhaps hurt, but he won't abandon us. I know that now," Hawk said, his voice soft and reassuring.

I released a breath, shaking out my arms and letting it flow out of me. I wouldn't freak out about this.

"You're right. I can't manage his emotions or avoid things because he might not like them. This is my life, and I want to be with you."

"There's my girl."

Oh, how those words warmed my heart and sent shivers straight to my clit.

The urge to reach out and grab his hand as we walked was strong, so I shoved it into my pocket. My bag slapped against me as we walked and kept me grounded.

"I'm glad you know where you're going," I muttered, following him without thought.

Hawk smirked, his eyes twinkling as we stepped into a room, and I glanced around, confused as to why we were in there.

"Are you going to murder me now? Sell my organs on the black market? Spoiler alert, they're defunct."

Hawk snorted, shaking his head. A door pushed open on the other side, and I spun around, expecting my potential killers/organ collectors.

Tucker's smiling face beamed at me, his legs cutting up into the space between us. He lifted me in his arms, burrowing his head in my neck.

"Honey Bee," he breathed, his voice low and raspy. His grip was firm, and I settled into his hold.

"Hey, Tuck-Tuck." I kissed his neck, and he shivered. I glanced over his shoulder, spotting Luke and Graham. I smiled and waved at them, suddenly so happy.

"Quit hogging her, Jameson," Luke grumbled, elbowing

his way between us and pulling me to his chest. Tucker tightened his grip for a second before letting go.

"Hey, Slugger," Luke whispered, not caring that the others were there as he claimed my lips, and I fell into his kiss.

"That sentiment goes for you too, Olson," Graham said, breaking us apart. I panted, my eyes a little crossed as I caught my breath. Luke growled, the sound doing strange things to my lower half. He kissed me one last time before dropping me back to the ground.

"Stay with me tonight?" he asked before letting go.

"Yes."

At my answer, he smiled, spinning on his cleats and heading back to the door he'd come through. I watched his butt in his baseball pants sway, licking my lips as he disappeared. Hot breath fanned over my neck from behind, arms wrapping around my waist as goosebumps broke out.

"If you didn't look at me the same way, I'd be jealous."

My cheeks heated, and I spun around, clutching Graham's chest before I stumbled. "How was your trip?" I asked.

"Lonely without you. This one wouldn't shut up," he said, tilting his head back. Tucker placed his head on Graham's shoulder.

"Who me?" he gasped, making me laugh.

Graham rolled his eyes but leaned back into his friend's touch. "Is it too early to claim you for tomorrow night?"

"Claim?" I raised my eyebrows.

"He meant, ask you on a date," Tucker interjected.

"I'd love to." I swallowed. "My brother's visiting, so it will be a good distraction."

"We can definitely fulfill that request."

"Good." I smiled, feeling more confident about tomorrow. These two did that, always helping me feel at ease. I cleared my throat.

"Have a good game."

I kissed them both, leaving out the door I'd come in while they headed to the other, suddenly feeling energized and thankful. Hawk ensured I got to hug and kiss my other boyfriends before the game. He really was in this, even if it was five of us.

The game ended late, with the YellowJackets losing by one in the last inning. It was a tough loss, making it their eighth this season and bringing their record to 47-8.

I'd left once I was done, heading back to the hotel to grab dinner and shower, knowing the team would be arriving later. Luke texted me he'd let me know when he was back so I could sneak out to join him. He had a private room; I hadn't figured out how he'd swung that. For all I knew, he paid the difference. I hadn't cared enough to ask since it came in handy for away games when I was roomed with Rue.

She'd already been passed out when I returned from grabbing food, so I'd done my best to not wake her. If I didn't have to answer questions about where I was going, the easier it was to sneak out. Now freshly showered and in my pajamas, I scrolled through LiveIt, not paying attention to the posts as I blindly liked them. So I nearly shouted when his text came in, jerking me out of my daze.

Luke: Room 1834

Blake: OMW.

Quietly, I slipped on my shoes and grabbed my room key as I slid out the door. I let it close softly to not wake her, though I had a feeling Rue was a deep sleeper. Regardless, I hated lying, which made it safer in the bubble.

The elevator was a quick ride up, and I peeked onto the

floor, checking that no one was out in the hall. When it was clear, I hurried down to room 1834. It opened after one knock, and I slipped in.

My back was pressed against the door the second I entered, Luke's mouth crashing into mine. He lifted my legs, and I wrapped them around his waist. His cock hit me exactly where I wanted, and I moaned into his mouth.

"God, I've missed you," he moaned.

Luke rocked harder into me, sending shivers racing. My clit pulsed, and I needed more friction.

"I missed you, too. I thought you'd never get back here."

He spun us around, carrying me to the bed and laying me down as urgency enveloped us. His body covered mine, pressing into me as he continued to ravish my mouth. My hands ran up his back, pulling his shirt over his head, feeling his warm skin beneath my touch. He broke the kiss briefly, and I tossed it away, and my hands greedily returned to him. Luke's mouth was hot and incessant on my neck, sucking as he lifted my shirt, exposing my stomach.

We worked together to remove the rest of our clothes, falling back to the bed in a heap of tangled limbs. His length rubbed against my leg hard as steel, and I reached down to stroke him. He tensed, his body taut as he breathed through his nose.

"Shit, I'm too close already. You make me come undone with the simplest touch."

"Same," I moaned, but didn't stop stroking him.

Luke wrenched my hands above my head, pulling his cock free as his eyes heated. His chest heaved as he caught his breath. His eyes were so dark they resembled emeralds more than grass, the orbs twinkling with lust as he scorched me with his gaze.

"Fuck, I forgot to grab the condom."

I swallowed, my heart beating hard against my chest. "We

don't have to anymore if you don't want to. You're all tested, and I got mine back this morning."

He gulped, his eyes searching mine. "I..." He stopped, shaking his head.

"I'm covered for birth control. No surprise pregnancies here." My mouth tilted up on the side as my heart hammered in my chest.

"Yeah, well, I thought I was last time, too." He squeezed his eyes closed, and my heart plummeted. Shit. I'd gone too far.

"You don't have to. It was just a thought. Where are the condoms?" I asked, attempting to sit up. My face felt hot, and I needed to get out of his line of sight before I cried or something.

"Shit. Sorry. I didn't mean it that way, Slugger. It's taking everything in me not to slam into you. Are you sure? The others?"

"Yes." I licked my lips. "Yes."

We'd all talked about it, but I'd wanted to get tested too. The guys hadn't needed it, but it felt fair.

Luke's fingers flexed against my wrists where he still held them, his eyes searching me as he inched forward. I spread my legs wider, lifting my hips to meet him. The tip of his cock slid against my clit, and my eyes rolled back. I sucked in a breath as Luke pushed in slowly, the pace agonizing.

"If I knew you were going to go this slow, I wouldn't have mentioned it," I taunted, tilting my hips more. He slipped in further, a moan leaving me.

Luke's eyes heated, and he grinned, shifting his weight below as he slammed the rest of the way. He didn't stop moving this time, pushing in and out of me so powerfully that I lost track of his thrusts. Our bodies rolled together; our breaths seesawing out as we chased our orgasms. Luke dropped one hand down between me, rubbing my clit and sending me spiraling over the edge.

"Ah, yes, Luuukee!" I gasped as my body locked up, sensations tingling all over my limbs. Luke picked up his pace, gripping me harder as he slammed home, his hips stalling and losing his rhythm as he came.

"Blake, fuck," he groaned, his eyes blazing as they stared down at me.

For a moment, we stared at one another, our breaths hot pants between us as we relished in this moment. When he slipped out, he moved, letting go of my wrists and climbing off the bed. Feeling returned to my arms as I watched him walk into the bathroom, his butt flexing with each step.

When he returned with a washcloth, I sighed in relief as he handed it to me. I hadn't thought about how messy sex would be without a condom.

Once we were both clean, he pulled me into his arms, kissing my temple before turning out the lights. I fell asleep to his heartbeat and hoped this feeling would never end.

Luke's alarm sounded way too early, but I rolled over, nudging him awake. I needed to make it back to my room before anyone saw me.

"Get up," I mumbled.

"And here I thought you were a morning person," he teased, kissing me.

"Not at this hour," I whined.

Luke chuckled, his hands roaming over my body. "I can't quit touching you. It's becoming a problem."

"Not from my standpoint."

"I want to do it in the open, but I know I can't."

"Hmm." My heart stuttered.

"Do you think we'll ever get to that point?" he whispered.

"I hope so." The words fell from my lips, but they didn't sound true.

I wanted to be out of the bubble, but I wasn't ready for the attention it would bring. First, I needed to tell the people closest to me, and then maybe I'd be prepared for more.

Luke kissed me against the door, leaving me breathless, before he opened it and checked that the coast was clear. Patting me on the ass, he winked as he sent me on my way. I was almost to the elevator when a door further down the hallway opened, jolting me. I ducked into the ice machine room and peeked around the corner. When I spotted Mira, I was confused.

She hadn't attended any away games since the ones where she shadowed me. But she especially shouldn't be here since Rue and I both were. The team only ever sent two of us. The rest of the department's jobs revolved around Champion Field, so they stayed to manage things from that end. Plus, traveling wasn't the most glamorous of benefits, and anyone who could, got out of them.

So why was she here? Was she checking up on us?

But the better question was, whose room was she leaving?

I didn't waste time debating with myself when I could get caught, so I ducked around the corner and hoofed it down the stairs. I didn't need to answer my own questions from my boss about what *I* was doing on the baseball floor this time of the morning.

Wait… Baseball floor.

Which begged the question, who was Mira visiting?

CHAPTER
FIFTY-ONE

BLAKE

I walked in a daze down to the lobby, trying to collect my thoughts. It was still early, and most people were still asleep. I hadn't been able to go to my room yet, too worried Rue would ask me questions I didn't have answers for. I looked around the lobby, unsure why I'd come down here.

Coffee and sugar.

I needed coffee and sugar to get through this day.

The smell of coffee beans hit me, drawing me like a siren song in their direction. The sound of the espresso machine soothed me, and I stepped up to the counter, already feeling better.

"Your biggest vanilla latte and sugariest pastry, please," I begged, making the barista laugh.

"Coming right up!"

I paid for my treats and moved to the side to wait, falling back into that dazed place as I tried to ignore the nagging feeling in my gut that said something wasn't right. Which was probably why I didn't notice him until he was right on me.

"Honey Bee! You're the best thing to see this early in the

morning." Tucker wrapped his arms around me, kissing my cheek. I snuggled back into his hold and then remembered we were in public.

"Hey, Tuck-Tuck." I turned so his arms dropped. "What are you doing up this early?"

He rubbed his hands together, excitement filling his eyes. "Actually, I could use your help. What time do you have to be at the stadium?"

I tilted my head, trying to remember my schedule. "I could probably get away with noon. There's not as much pre-game preparation here. Why?"

"Perfect. How soon can you be ready?"

Before I could respond, my name was called, and I turned to take my coffee and a massive sugary treat.

"I want that!" Tucker exclaimed, making the barista laugh.

I sipped my coffee while he ordered and paid, the caffeine and sugar making their way through my veins and waking me up. I closed my eyes and savored the flavor, the smoothness of the espresso hitting my taste buds and rejoicing.

Oh, coffee. You are so good.

"You good, or do you need a moment with your coffee?"

"Actually, I could use a moment," I teased, opening my eyes and smiling.

"Ha ha! I guess I deserve that one." He chuckled, then turned, his face serious. "So, how soon can you be ready?"

"It won't take too long. I need a shower but don't have to wash my hair. Twenty minutes?"

"In that case, you need to go."

"Pardon?" I asked, my heart dropping. Was Tucker telling me to go?

"Shower, get dressed, and meet me back here. Try to make it fifteen minutes if you can." He grimaced, and my heart returned.

"Oh, okay. I'll, um, be right back then."

I picked up my pastry, eating it as I walked to the elevator, savoring it as I drank my coffee. By the time I reached my floor, my breakfast was gone, the crumbs and my sticky fingers the only evidence.

Rue stepped out of the bathroom, a towel wrapped around her as I walked in. I lifted the coffee and smiled as I walked to my bed. Thankfully, it looked as if I'd slept in it, and considering I was still in my pajamas, I could play it off that I'd just gone to get coffee.

"Morning," she grumbled.

"Hey. Sleep okay?" I asked as I pulled out some clothes.

"Mmm," she mumbled, and I laughed. Rue was not a morning person.

I ducked into the bathroom, changing into shorts and a yellow tee with a sunflower that said, 'Be wild and free.' It felt aptly appropriate for anything with Tucker. After a quick of my teeth and hair, I spritzed myself with my body spray and applied extra deodorant before exiting the bathroom.

Rue was on the phone, so I waved goodbye and grabbed my bag. I finished my coffee as I walked, grimacing as the taste changed after brushing my teeth. Gross. Sighing in disappointment, I dropped it into the trash can as I walked into the lobby.

Tucker whistled and brushed his nose in a move resembling one of Graham's catcher calls. He headed out the door, so I followed, figuring he was making it look like we weren't together.

He jumped out from behind a plant when I stepped outside, and I screamed.

"Tucker!"

He bent over, laughing so hard, he clutched his stomach, gasping for breath.

"Oh. My. God. That. Was. Great."

"I hate you," I mumbled, stomping away from him.

"I'm sorry. I couldn't help it," he said around a wheeze,

collecting himself and catching up with me. He draped his arm around my shoulder. "Sorry, Honey Bee. Honestly."

His arm was warm around my shoulders, and I leaned into him, enjoying how nice he felt.

"So, what are we doing?" I asked after we'd walked a little way.

"You'll see," he teased, leading me to a car. I hadn't noticed it, but I guess this was why I had a time limit—he'd ordered an Uber.

"I'm regretting saying yes to you," I mumbled, but Tucker didn't cave. He laughed, pulling me into his side, and placed his head on top of mine.

"It's nice getting to spend some time with you."

I knew what he meant. We both loved being with Graham, and the three of us were great together. But it was also nice to have this time with Tucker. I'd had it with Graham, but Tucker and I hadn't been able to yet.

"Me too," I whispered. He kissed my forehead, keeping it tame in the Uber in case the driver recognized either of us. It was unlikely in this city, but not impossible.

The rest of the trip was quiet, and when we pulled up to the Grizzlies' Stadium, I turned, narrowing my eyes at him.

"When you asked me out, I didn't think you meant coming to work early," I grumbled.

"Just wait, Bee." He laughed, flashing his smile at the guard and showing his visitor ID. I did the same, surprised when the guy let us through.

I frowned, crossing my arms over my chest as we walked, making Tucker laugh even more.

"Never took you to be so impatient."

"Usually, people are more forthcoming," I countered.

Tucker sighed, then stopped, taking my hands. "I just wanted to do something fun with you, but I'll tell you if you really need to know. It's not worth making you upset."

Cool water rushed over me, and I realized I was being a

brat. The uncertainty with Mira had put me on edge, but it wasn't Tucker's fault.

"I'm sorry. It's been a weird morning."

"Well, this should make it better." He glanced around, and when he didn't see anyone, he kissed me quickly before dragging my hand and pulling me with him.

I was even more confused when he stopped at the side of a concession stand. He knocked three times quickly and then two slow ones before he stepped back. The door opened a second later, a guy stepping out and looking both ways like we were about to exchange drugs or something.

When the employee saw me, he froze. "I said no witnesses."

"She's cool. You got it?" Tucker asked, bouncing on his feet.

"It's gonna cost you more."

Tucker rolled his eyes. "Fine. I'll drop it off after the game. Now, do you have it? I don't have much time."

"One second," the guy grumbled, shutting the door and leaving us in silence.

"Tucker," I whispered, and he turned, grinning wide.

"Almost there, Honey Bee."

Before I could ask if it was drugs, the door opened, and the guy shoved a large trash bag full of popcorn at Tucker before shutting the door.

"Popcorn?" I asked, now more confused.

"Follow me, and it will all make sense."

I did as he asked, glancing around the stadium, but nobody else was here this early. When we stepped into the clubhouse, I was even more confused.

"It's prank o'clock!" Tucker grinned, spreading his arms wide.

"Um, what?"

"You heard me."

"And why do you need me?"

"Because you love it, duh," he teased. "You started it this season with your IcyHot jockstraps."

Okay, he had a point.

"Fine, but what are we doing exactly?"

"Filling lockers with popcorn, obviously." He rolled his eyes at me, his excitement catching.

I didn't know why I expected a date with Tucker to include anything other than pure mayhem. *Dinner and a movie? Nah. Let's vandalize a clubhouse.*

Tucker pointed out a few lockers, shocking me even more when he picked Graham's.

"You sure about this?"

"He doesn't get a free pass just because he makes my dick hard now," he teased.

"Now that's a line for a greeting card."

"Second career option, then." Tucker smiled, taking my breath away. He was so beautiful and pure. My heart thumped, and I swallowed around the emotion.

"Okay, take a picture with me in front of Graham's locker."

"You're a glutton for punishment," I teased but did as he asked.

"Oh, you have no idea." The heat in his words had me stumbling, and I gripped his arm as I caught myself. Lifting my phone, I took a selfie with our hard work in the background.

"Now what?" I asked, turning, our lips millimeters apart. Tucker's eyes dilated before dropping down to my lips.

"There's a fantasy I'd like you to help me with."

"Oh?" I asked, sucking in a breath.

Tucker didn't hesitate, sealing his lips to mine before pulling me into his lap. I went willingly, trusting Tucker to guide us.

He stood, his hands under my ass, and I wrapped my legs

around him. Our kiss didn't break as he walked, stopping in front of a locker and sitting me down.

"We have to be quick. Someone could come in here any minute," he whispered, stepping back to push down his shorts and kick off his shoes. The fact he hadn't taken extra special care with them only proved how much he wanted this. I'd never seen Tucker not give his sneakers the ultimate treatment.

I lifted my shirt over my head quickly, pushing my shorts down, too. Tucker watched me with hungry eyes, the brown so dark it was practically black. He stroked himself once before stepping forward and reaching for me.

"Turn around, Bee. Brace your hands on my locker. I want to fuck you so hard that the only thing I think of every time I look at my uniform is your perfect pussy."

I had never spun around so fast in my entire life.

I gripped the edges of the locker and pushed my ass out, Tucker's hands gripping me as he squeezed my globes, running one finger up my center and finding me drenched.

"Fuck, Bee. You undo me."

I watched as he sucked on his finger, his eyes rolling back as he groaned. His pupils were blown when he released his finger, and he moved forward, a man clearly on a mission. He reached over me, searching for something.

"It's not needed. I got my results. We're good," I breathed, my body vibrating with need. The location, the urgency, and the possibility of being found were too much, and I needed Tucker now.

"Oh, hell. I'm never gonna survive this," Tucker said, gripping me and notching himself. One second, I was trembling as I waited; the next, I was full and shaking as Tucker plunged inside.

We moaned together, our bodies pressed against one another as we let ourselves adjust. But once Tucker did, he moved, thrusting into me so hard I gasped.

"I didn't think anything could feel better than being inside of you, but damn, Honey Bee. Your pussy bare is a dream. It fits like a glove. The best pair of shoes. I never want to leave."

"Yes. Yes. Tuck," I groaned as I held onto the locker, my knuckles white from the effort.

"I'm so close already," Tucker said, his voice strained.

"Me too," I gasped.

My legs shook, the muscles burning as I lifted on my toes to give him more of an angle. He slipped further in, his cock hitting my G-spot perfectly, and I lost it.

"Right there! I'm coming. Tucker!" I shouted as everything inside me exploded; pleasure filled every available space within me.

"Fuck, fuck, Bee!" Tucker's thrusts became sloppy as he chased his release, stuttering as he gripped me to him, his cock twitching inside.

Sound returned to my ears, a ringing of silence as our moans quieted. Only our breaths could be heard as we clung to one another. Tucker's entire body pressed into me, and I barely held myself up. His jersey pressed into me, along with some other odds and ends, my upper body more inside the locker than out.

"Holy fuck, Honey Bee." Tucker laughed, kissing my neck before pulling out and helping me to stand. "That surpassed the fantasy."

"Yeah?" I asked, surprisingly shy.

"Grand slam, baby. I'm gonna be hard the whole game."

Laughing, I let him lead me to the showers, where we both quickly rinsed and redressed.

"So, how was your first Tucker date?" he asked as we headed out of the clubhouse. As we walked, we spotted a few more people, and I knew our time had been limited.

"It was exactly as I expected. Fun. Hot. And one will never be enough."

"I'm stealing that for my second greeting card."

Grinning, we headed out of the stadium and back to the hotel, pretending an hour later that we hadn't already been there when we climbed onto the bus. It wasn't until later that I remembered I hadn't told Tucker about spotting Mira.

BLAKE

FOLLOWING THE GUYS TO THE CLUBHOUSE, I TRIED TO KEEP MY face neutral so I wouldn't give away what I knew. Tucker kept sending me flirty looks that Graham had picked up, and he eyed us curiously.

"Where did you run off to this morning, Tucker?" he asked.

"Nowhere. Just went for a walk."

"You do things without Papa G?" Levi heckled, earning him a punch from Tucker and a scowl from Graham.

"Don't call me that," Graham muttered.

"You can't deny you're the daddy of the clubhouse," Sal said, wrapping his arm around Graham's shoulders.

"We do things on our own," Tucker argued.

The guys laughed, shaking their heads.

"I wouldn't be surprised if you shit together," Dalton said, laughing.

"We have boundaries," Tucker grumbled, losing some of his spark.

"I pity the girl that ever tries to come between the two of you," Hector said, laughing. "Can you imagine the scandal the team would have on their hands? 'Flirty Blonde tries to break up the YellowJackets' power duo.' Yeah, the fans would rake her through the coals."

Ice filled my veins, and I wondered if that was true. Would people care that much?

"Don't be an asshole. It could be a guy. Papa G's pan," Shane said, giving his fellow catcher a shoulder squeeze.

The team stepped into the clubhouse a minute later, and I forgot about wanting to film it after the topic of conversation. I knew that most of it was just chatter. But was there truth to it, too?

Laughs and jeers rang out, and I lifted my camera to take shots, but the joy was gone.

"I'm gonna kill you, Tucker!" Levi shouted, jumping over his chair and chasing the pitcher around the clubhouse. "I'm gonna smell like stale old butter. I hate popcorn."

As the guys laughed and picked on the players who had been pranked, I felt myself dissociate from them for the first time all season.

"You okay?" Graham asked, his face full of concern.

"Totally." I nodded and pretended to check the time. "Look at that! I need to go before I'm late. Have a great game. See you later," I called, zipping out of the clubhouse so quickly that I probably left skid marks.

I wandered aimlessly around the stadium, a weird buzzing and numbness coating me. I didn't know what I was doing, and I kept looking for someone, hoping if I saw them, then I'd know. But so far, people were just blobs of blur.

When I spotted Rue talking with someone in a Grizzlies' polo, I felt relief.

"Rue!" I shouted, getting her attention. She turned, nodding, when she spotted me and ended her conversation.

"Hey, Bee. How was your morning?" she teased.

"It was great. I went for a run."

Ew, gross. Why would I say that? I hated running and sweating unless an orgasm was involved.

She snorted, giving me a look like she didn't believe me. "So, about what you saw with me and Ted—"

"I saw nothing." I winked, happy for the distraction. We hadn't talked about it yet, but I wasn't one to gossip. Her shoulders relaxed, and she sighed happily.

"Great. Awesome. It's still so new, and I haven't told Mira." She cringed.

"Why do you have to tell her?" I asked, my heart skipping a beat. Freaking Mira.

"Her policy. While it's not forbidden to fraternize, she wants to be informed of all relationships. She pretends she can prepare any PR statements, but she's not even the PR director. She's media. But she didn't let that stop her last year and fired one of the assistants. Honestly, the cow's just nosey and lonely and likes the control since no one will touch her frigid body with a ten-foot pole."

"Tell me how you really feel." I grinned at her but couldn't help but think that wasn't true. Not based on what I saw this morning.

Should I tell Rue? No. Not until I knew something. Harmless gossip was one thing, but a scandal was completely different.

"Sorry. It's just, she's so critical and never says anything nice. She's been marginally better since you told her off, but it still gives me hardcore middle school flashbacks." She shuddered, shaking her whole body. "How did it go when you told her about you and..." she trailed off, raising her eyebrows.

"Me and?" I asked, not falling for her line of questioning. Unlike her, I'd been media-trained my whole life. It had never been about my love life, but the skills still applied. And this question I'd been prepared for.

Never give more than they ask for.

Stick to the truth as closely as possible.

Trust no one asking questions.

"Oh, come on! I know you're dating someone. I just can't figure out who." She stopped, turning to me so I couldn't avoid her eyes. "Is it the sexy coach? He's so hot but secretive. I've never seen him with anyone."

"I've known him since I was six," I said, sticking to the truth. I raised an eyebrow, letting her infer what she wanted.

"Fine. The broody first baseman? He watches you a lot. And that man is fire. I bought so many copies of his magazine cover last fall." She fanned her face, and I recalled the shirtless shoot Luke had done.

And now I needed to find a copy, stat.

"He is hot, and his ego matches. He and my brother hate one another." Again, the truth.

"But weren't you watching his daughter?" She hedged, proving she'd been watching me more than I'd realized. Was she a spy for Mira?

"It's not her fault who her father is." I laughed.

"Fine. Then it must be the duo, Package Deal. Oh, to be the meat in that sandwich."

My face heated. This one was hard to dodge. Her eyes lit up, and I knew I had to give her something. I spun, walking away. I couldn't say this with direct eye contact.

The need to people-please and ensure she liked me flared to life, begging me to give her what she wanted. To spill all of my secrets.

"They might've accidentally texted me, assuming I was Bryce before the season started, leading to some… NSFW text messages."

There. Hopefully, that would appease her curiosity. I liked Rue and wanted to trust her. Plus, talking to someone about everything outside our bubble would be nice. But I couldn't forget they weren't just my secrets. This didn't affect only me;

telling people was a decision the five of us had to make together.

There were real-world consequences of that knowledge.

"Whoa! No way!" Her eyes grew big, and panic rose up my throat. "Holy cow. I never would've guessed it. You definitely can't tell Mira this! She'd go ballistic!"

My heart stopped, and my vision blurred, and it felt like I was back in that flash mob with everyone around me, waiting, looking, watching.

What had I done?

Suddenly, I realized how my wants might screw up the guys' lives. I'd been so focused on my heart being broken, on being the center of attention, that I hadn't thought about the consequences for them. Not in a tangible way.

It wasn't just hearts on the line, but careers.

Was it worth taking this big of a risk?

Hawk believed so. I knew that.

But could Luke? I had strong feelings for him and believed his mirrored my own, but there was so much more to consider. Like how he wanted back on the Blue Devils. What then? Would we do long distance?

He already felt out of the loop, living a few miles away. How would that affect our connection if he was in a different state from April to October?

And Graham and Tucker were still young in their careers. This was only their third season in the league. Would they stay on the YellowJackets? They were too good to not dream about the Majors. Could they risk their potential stardom and sponsorships to share me?

I stalled, my heart falling out of the bottom of me.

Bunting Hell.

I'd focused so much on choosing what I wanted and not letting others determine my decisions that I'd lost sight of the ball. While I'd been focused on one play, another slipped under my nose, and now I was in danger of striking out... or worse, losing the game completely.

"So, how is it? Those two seem like fun," she teased, continuing to talk and not noticing my panic attack.

"Um, it's great," I mumbled.

Had I fallen under the great sex illusion? Allowing it to delude me into thinking my biggest problem was which bed to sleep in? How did I think this would work long-term? Would anything be real if I was too embarrassed to tell people? If I had to keep them hidden?

Luke already wanted more. What if I could never give him the freedom to hold my hand or kiss me in public? How long would the four of them stay if we never moved out of the bubble? And was it even fair to ask them to hide for the rest of their lives?

I'd stepped out of one shadow right into a different one.

The bubble had felt safe, but it was only an illusion. One quickly dissolving right before my eyes.

"You okay?" Rue asked, her hand gentle on my arm. I jumped, having gotten lost in my head that I hadn't even noticed we'd stopped walking. My mouth felt like cotton, my head fuzzy with sand as I gave her my best-practiced smile.

"Being fake is the only thing you're good at," my brain whispered.

"Yeah. I'm fine. Just need to get started on the footage," I blurted, my words coming out so fast I didn't know if she understood them.

I stepped into the door, tossing my bag and fumbling with my camera. I yanked out the straps, my hands shaking as I pulled it over my shoulder. Pulling on a hat, I rushed out, not waiting to hear what else she had to say.

I'd started today feeling hopeful and like everything was headed in the right direction. That I was maybe even falling in love with all of them. I'd been optimistic we could make this relationship work.

But I could see now how I'd forced them into this—to a future of being a laughingstock when the media found out and jeopardizing the trajectory of their careers.

I'd gone from being a people-pleaser to a selfish bitch.

I snapped pictures aimlessly, not paying attention to anything I captured as the bubble I'd been in the past few months popped. Reality was a cruel bitch, but she was honest.

The longevity of this was too hard to maintain. Even without the media circus we'd become, it merely wasn't sustainable. Players were traded all the time. Injuries happened at any moment. We wouldn't all be together forever. It wasn't logical.

It was such a cruel joke to find one thing I loved only to sacrifice another—relationships, careers, children.

And I'd been around this game long enough to know that baseball always won out. My mom had learned it the hard way, and I refused to be another casualty of the game. Whether for me or them.

There were no extra innings.

I swung, and I missed.

It was time I accepted fate and called it... for all of us. I wouldn't be the reason they lost everything.

I might be a reformed people-pleaser, but I wouldn't become the entitled princess everyone expected me to be, either.

I wasn't sure where that left me, but there was no doubt—*Blake Baker had just struck out.*

CHAPTER
FIFTY-THREE

TUCKER

Riding the high from a successful popcorn locker, I set out to conquer my last target—Coach Anderson.

Very slowly, I lifted my hand and placed the bubblegum on Coach's cap while Graham asked him about pitches. There was no way I'd be able to keep a straight face, meaning Graham had gotten voted in as the distraction. After this, I'd officially be crowned the dugout prank king.

In a lot of ways, dugout culture was like returning to high school, where we all became immature boys, burping, farting, and spitting at any given second. Oddly, pranks built team spirit and bonded the team. And as the newbies, Graham and I had been responsible for kicking off the war. Something I took great pride in.

It was a rite of passage, and no one in YellowJacket history had ever gotten one over on Coach Anderson. Which made him the perfect target for me, especially since I figured he'd be distracted by thoughts of Blake. Or, more likely, he'd assume we didn't have the balls to do it.

Wrong, Hawkster. I had huge balls.

Brain cells were debatable, but balls, I had.

And I was about to prove it. Letting go of the bubblegum, I backed away slowly as it stayed, finally remembering to breathe.

"Thanks, I'll try that," Graham said as I pretended to walk by Coach, all natural-like.

"Hold it," Hawk said, throwing his arm out and halting me. I gulped, my heart galloping as I peered into his mismatched eyes.

Do not look up. Do not look up.

"Yes, Coach?" My voice came out high-pitched.

"How prepared are you to throw a slurve?"

His question threw me, and I froze as I digested it. It wasn't my best pitch, combining a curveball and a slider and needing to be horizontal and vertical, but it wasn't my worst.

"Um..." I tilted my head, confused by the question. Apparently, that wasn't the correct response, and Coach rolled his eyes.

"Go to the bullpen and throw a few," he ordered, sending me off in the other direction. I barely contained my laugh as I spun, my eyes wanting to peek at the bubblegum.

"Got it, Coach." I sped away, pulling Graham with me. We made it a few feet past the dugout before bursting into laughter.

"Damn, I wish I'd gotten that on film." Graham laughed, tears running down his cheeks as he held his sides. "I can't wait until Blake hears. She'll appreciate it. How did you get her to help you?"

"I have no idea what you're talking about," I said, grinning too much to keep up the ruse.

"Uh-huh. Based on the hickey I spotted on her neck, I highly doubt that."

Snickering, I zipped my lips as we got into formation, and I grabbed balls from the bucket. Falling into the rhythm, I lifted my arm and gripped the ball as I focused on Graham's glove before letting the ball fly. I threw several until I felt comfortable with the slurve. Stretching out my shoulder, I nodded to Graham that I was good, and we huddled together as we returned to the dugout.

"If you prank Blake with me, I'll forget about the popcorn locker," Graham said.

"Deal. We should do the shaving cream pie or shoestring tie. Both would be funny but shouldn't make her too mad at us."

"Why not both?" Graham chuckled, smiling widely as we clomped down the steps into the dugout. Hawk glared at me, his arms crossed. The rest of the dugout silenced as they watched the show.

"All set, Coach," I chirped, keeping my eyes on his instead of looking at his hat.

"Payback's a bitch, Jameson."

"I have no idea what you're referring to, *Coach*. You sure you're not imagining things? Losing your memory? I hear that happens to guys your age."

I knew I was skating on thin ice, but I couldn't seem to make my mouth shut up. Thankfully, it was our turn to head out to the diamond, Shane and Austin staying in the dugout this inning. They nodded, patting us as we walked by; the respect between the pitchers and catchers was solid on this team. There had been a few battery pairs in college we'd gotten along with, too. Yet, our last team had concentrated on competing rather than playing as a team.

It was always hard balancing those two things. I got it was a team sport with individual players fighting for their own goals at times, but I'd never been the jealous type. I wanted to hype up my fellow pitcher and wish him good luck while playing my best. The lifespan of a pitcher wasn't long, and injuries happened all the time. So, I wouldn't waste time feeling petty or insecure about someone else succeeding.

Instead, I'd cheer them on and focus on my skills. Friends

lasted longer than seasons, and if you were lucky, your team-mates became your family.

"Three up, three down," Graham said, tapping his glove on my ass as he jogged to home plate. The umpire glanced over Graham's equipment, giving a nod of approval. I centered myself on the mound, going to that place in my mind where nothing but me and home plate existed.

I didn't know how I'd been able to ignore the connection between Graham and me this long. It sizzled to life between us, like a wire connecting me to him as our eyes met. We both took a breath, our exhales in sync. I tuned out the batters, the crowd, and the players behind me. I focused only on the calls Graham gave me, completely trusting him as the inning started.

My focus became laser-sharp, and I threw three strikes, getting the first batter out quickly. I did it again, adrenaline pumping as I centered on the man behind home plate.

Three more strikes and another out. Two down.

Graham smiled, making my heart flip over itself, and I returned one to him. This season had been everything I'd always wanted, and I knew my future would be just as incredible. Baseball. My best friend. And the family we were building with the girl we both had feelings for.

Staring at him behind the plate, my heart stuttered. This man.

Graham threw down the call for the slurve, and I nodded, centering myself as I called on my muscle memory, letting the ball fly.

"Strike!" the umpire called, my heart thumping a solid rhythm in time with his shouts.

Time seemed to slow as I pulled back my arm and released the second throw. It sailed forward, and the batter swung. But it was too low, and the umpire said that beautiful word.

"Strike!"

One more pitch. I had this.

Meeting Graham's eyes again, we breathed together, and he flashed his call sign for a knuckleball. Smiling, I nodded and got into position. I threw the ball and felt the strike before it was called, the ball soaring through the air in a perfect flutter dance. He hesitated a second, and it cost him, the ball changing direction as he swung too late.

Yes!

My glee turned to panic as I watched the ball bounce behind the plate instead of into Graham's mitt, hitting him on the inside of his thigh. I watched in horror as his hands flew to the spot, and he fell over with a curse. I froze, my feet unable to move as I waited in suspended disbelief. The umpire bent down to check on Graham, but he waved him off, standing a second later and returning the air to my lungs.

"Oh, thank fuck," I whispered. I took off, wrapping him in a tight hug as we walked off the field. "I'm so sorry, G."

"Not your fault, Tuck. It's how they break sometimes. Knuckleballs are the hardest to catch for a reason." I nodded. It wasn't the first time he'd taken a ball, but it was the first time since he became mine.

"You sure you're okay?" I asked, worry swirling in my gut.

"Yeah. It'll be a nasty bruise. Missed the crown jewels, at least. Stung like a bitch." He gave a dry chuckle.

"That's good." I nodded, letting out a deep breath, and then smirked as I glanced at him. "I've grown attached to those jewels." Graham sputtered, his cheeks heating as we neared the dugout.

The moment was broken when someone shouted from the stands, "Faggots."

I stumbled, the slur taking me by surprise, and I stood there in shock. While it wasn't the first time someone had called us a gay couple, it was the first time it was true, and the first time I identified as something else, even if I didn't know what it was yet.

The words sliced through me, cutting me to my core. I suddenly had a new appreciation for queer people and the battles they faced.

"Ignore him," Graham said, pulling me. I let him, too shaken to reply, and sat on the bench. Graham left me to get checked over by the medic, and I sat there feeling numb.

Why did that man think it was his place to comment on my love life? Why did the world see anything different as a threat?

"You good?" Luke asked, stopping in front of me.

"Uh. Yeah."

He held out a water bottle, and I took it, squeezing some into my mouth. The cold liquid helped to restore my sense of awareness.

"Thanks."

"No prob. I know we're not really friends, but, uh, you can talk to me if you, um, need to."

I snorted, a smile returning to my face. I knocked his shoulder with mine. "Damn, Olson. You hitting on me?" I teased.

He scowled, crossing his arms. "Forget it."

"I'm just teasing. How hard was that for you to say?"

"The hardest," he grumbled, but his lips tilted up on the corner, belying his words.

"How's my niece?" I asked, leaning back with a smile. If I talked to him, it would make my worries about Graham disappear and push away the rage I felt for the ignorant asshole in the stands. Luke rolled his eyes, crossing his arms, but played along.

"She's not going to call you Uncle Tuck."

"So you say. Me and the Wills bonded. We're tight now."

"Wills? Really?"

"Yup. She agreed." I nodded, loving his uncomfortableness. "Would it be weird if I got her a birthday gift?" I asked, seriously this time.

Luke stalled, turning to look at me. "You want to?"

"Of course. She's the sweetest and deserves an awesome birthday."

"Not to sound like an asshole, but why? You don't know her, and we're barely friends." I rolled my eyes, scoffing at him.

"I let you get away with it the first time, but if you say we're not really friends one more time, I'm going to feel offended, Olson. We're closer, actually. Paramour bros. Lovers-plus." I shrugged, being serious. "But even if we weren't, I adore kids. Not in a creepy way," I hurried to say, lifting my hands. "I didn't have anyone who cared about me growing up, and I would never want her to experience that."

He searched my face, his green eyes softening as he came to some conclusion. "You're not how I expected you to be."

"I'm awesomer, right?" I winked, nudging him.

"And I take it back." We laughed together, tension leaving. A few minutes later, he surprised me by continuing the conversation. "If you want to get her something, she'd like that. Just don't go *too* crazy."

"Not too crazy. Got it. I'll keep it to a small amount of crazy."

"I think I'm going to regret this," he murmured before standing to bat. Graham returned to the dugout as he did, giving me a questioning look.

"I got hit by one ball, and you already replaced me," he whined.

"Nah. There's no replacing you, Teddy Graham. But he needs friends. The dude doesn't have any. I never see him talking to the other players."

"Ugh, socializing. Gross," Graham teased.

"You'd be lost without me, Teddy Graham." I held my heart, batting my eyelashes.

"I didn't think you two could get gayer." Seth sneered as he walked to his spot on the bench.

"Why do you care, Davis? Jealous?" I snapped. Graham's hand landed on my leg, cautioning me to keep my cool.

"Whatever, homos."

"Hey!" Hawk belted, making the whole bench jump. "There's no room for hate speech here, Davis. You can spend the rest of the game in the clubhouse."

The dugout was silent as everyone watched Seth, his jaw twitching as he gritted his teeth, clenching his fists at his side. Hawk stood coolly at the entrance, his tattooed arms crossed as he stared Seth down.

The game continued on outside of the dugout, but for once, no one watched, too busy waiting to see what Seth would do. It felt ages before he picked up his glove and spat out a wad of tobacco, barely missing Graham's cleats as he stomped toward the stairs. He pushed over the water container, spilling it over the floor as he disappeared.

"Fucking asshole," I mumbled, brushing off the water where it had splashed. Luke jogged back into the dugout, his bat on his shoulder, giving us all a questioning look.

"Anyone playing? That was third out," he said, breaking us all from the mind-fuck Seth Davis was. The team moved, but our movements were sluggish. Luke stopped me, pressing his hand into my arm, a question in his eyes.

"Davis made a homosexual slur, and Coach sent him to the clubhouse," I answered when he wouldn't let me go.

"Good. Now, push it out of your head." His tone was no-nonsense, but I could hear the care there, which settled the anger.

I nodded, letting out a breath, but I couldn't shake the last two comments, and they niggled their way under my skull. Was that what Graham put up with? Would it be worse when people found out about us? How tiring it must be to constantly be on edge, waiting for that one asshole to make a comment and ruin a perfectly good day.

I shook my head, knowing Luke was right. As if that thought wasn't sobering enough, I glanced around the stadium, searching for Blake. I needed some of her sunshine. Worry creased my brow when I couldn't find her, and I returned to the game. I threw a few pitches, but the earlier fire was gone.

Graham motioned for me to stop, that he was coming to the mound. I nodded and kicked the dirt, rolling the top of my cleat in it as I waited for him to jog over.

"What's going on?" he asked.

"You know what's going on," I mumbled.

"You mean the part where we're in the middle of a game, and you're on your way to pitch another… awesome one."

I glared, annoyed he almost mentioned the dirty word—no-hitter. But I knew he was right. I needed to use my super-power and push everything else away.

"You're right. I'll focus."

Graham gripped my shoulder, squeezing. He leaned in, his lips brushing against my earlobe. "Three out again, and I'll wrap my lips around your cock in the shower."

My eyes bulged, and my dick twitched against the cup.

"Not fair," I groaned.

He smirked, jogging back to the plate. I crushed my eyes closed, sucking in deep breaths and thinking about nothing but clouds.

Clouds. Clouds. Clouds. Graham's mouth. Shit.

Shaking out my body, I zeroed in on my prize, a new determination in my blood.

And then it happened. Three pitches, three strikes. One batter down.

Everything felt like it was coming together, the baseball gods aligning as I threw three more, getting three more strikes. Second batter down.

A flash of yellow caught my attention, and I glanced over, finally spotting Blake. She stared out onto the field, a solemn look on her face, so different from her typical smile. I couldn't read her eyes, but I knew something was wrong. Frowning, I looked at Graham, ready to throw three more so we could head to the dugout. Then we could make a plan.

Yes. That was a good idea.

Centering myself, I threw a changeup. Then a sinker. Both times, the batter swung hard, determination on his face to make contact. His bat went wide, and Graham dodged it twice, moving quicker than a spider monkey. My heart thumped loudly in my chest as he ducked.

One more pitch. I just needed one more pitch.

The call for the reverse curve made me smile. That feeling I got sometimes settled over me as confidence surged in my blood. I moved my body perfectly, and the ball flew toward the batter. I glanced at him, taking my eyes off Graham for once to watch. He sneered, swinging his bat hard at the pitch. His body turned, the bat flying behind him, and I watched in disbelief as he let it fly. The bat flew back toward Graham at high velocity, and yet, Graham stayed stationary.

His focus was on catching the ball, his glove closing over it as the bat smacked him hard. It smashed into his helmet on the backswing, pushing his mask down with the force. As the recoil came forward, it struck his temple, and Graham went down, splayed out behind the plate.

The world blurred, and I forgot about the rules. I forgot about the game. I ignored everything around me as I ran to the man I loved. I didn't care if people found out about me. It seemed so small compared to losing my best friend.

I dropped into the dirt, the dust flying around with my arrival. My hands shook out in front of me as I noticed the blood. Shouts echoed around me, but I was numb. I was oblivious until Hawk pulled me out of the way as the trainers wheeled in a gurney, strapping him to it.

"*Focus*, Tucker. He needs you to focus right now."

I nodded, letting him walk me to the dugout, realizing it was the first time he'd used my first name. "I want to go with him," I mumbled.

"You can't. I'm sorry, but you have to stay." His face was pained, but it only made me angry.

"Fuck you. I'm going." He gripped my shoulder, stalling me as I spun around by the force, and he ducked down to stare into my eyes.

"Listen to me. You can't, Tuck. Not right now." He shook his head, his eyes swirling. "But I promise I'll have them give me updates every five minutes, and as soon as the game is over, I'll drive you there myself."

Hawk's face was a mix of hardness and sympathy, and I knew I'd never make it past him. My shoulders dropped, and I nodded.

"Fine. After the game."

He nodded, releasing me, but I'd lost all my drive.

When it was my turn at bat, I walked with purpose, pissed at the other team, and ready to get back at them. Unfortunately, anger did not make a good batting companion, and I struck out. Stomping back to the dugout, I danced on the balls of my feet as I waited to return to the mound.

It took a few more innings, but I knew what I had to do once the batter that struck Graham reappeared.

With a deep breath, I framed up and threw my fastest pitch right at his leg.

Take that bean ball, asshole.

He threw down his bat, stalking toward me, and the dugouts cleared. Every player rushed to join the fight, and I stood back and smiled, glaring at Hawk. He shook his head, sighing. But I caught the look of pride in his eyes and knew he approved, even if he couldn't say it.

"You're benched," he said when I returned, and I shrugged, not caring. Sighing, he hung his head. "Go find

Blake. You can take Bryce's car." He handed me a set of keys, and exhilaration flooded me.

"I'd kiss you right now if I didn't think you'd punch me."

Hawk's brow raised, and I took that to mean not to even try it. Grabbing my stuff, I raced to change my shoes and to find Blake, hoping she was still here. If not, I'd take an Uber.

I was getting to that hospital one way or another.

I had a man to tell I loved him.

CHAPTER
FIFTY-FOUR

BLAKE

I'd barely been able to watch the game after my relationship epiphany. I snapped pictures and talked to the staff, but it was like a pod person had taken over, and I wasn't really there. At the crowd's gasp, I glanced at the field, seeing the guys for the first time.

I hadn't let myself look earlier, too afraid my emotions would be broadcasted on my face. I needed to get myself together before I faced them. I had to know what I would say before the swooniness and sex haze clouded my judgment.

There had to be a medium between people-pleasing and feeling entitled and selfish. Pulling out my phone, I dialed the one number I'd been putting off for far too long.

"Bee?" an accented voice asked, my heart slowing already at the sound of her voice.

"Hey, Delia. I'm sorry, I know it's past your business hours—"

"I told you anytime. What's going on? I'm assuming something big, or you wouldn't have used your 'break in case of emergency' card."

I gave a wry chuckle. "Yeah. You could say that. I seemed

to have gone from one extreme to the next."

"What do you mean?" Delia asked softly.

Before I knew it, I was spilling my guts, telling her about all the ups and downs I'd felt since landing back in America, from the plane ride to the accidental text to even the vomit-induced kiss. I told her how I'd been striving to make choices for myself and how great it had felt.

"It sounds like you've had a lot of obstacles but that you've overcome them gracefully. I'm not sure I understand what the problem is."

"By choosing what I want, I'm not considering how it affects them. They won't want all of this stress. It's too much." I sucked in a breath, hating how desperate I felt.

"Bee, I need you to take a deep breath." I did as she asked several times, my heart slowing. "Better. Did I miss part of the story where you forced your relationship onto these men?"

"I mean, no. But—"

"And they've all told you that they want to date you, but you're the one who shied away from the term girlfriend?" she asked. I furrowed my brow. I could tell where she was going, but didn't she understand?

"Yes, but—"

"No buts. You know the rule," she lightly chastised, and I let out an annoyed breath and smiled.

"Fine, fine," I grumbled.

"Yes, I know, I'm super annoying," she teased, and I laughed. "I just have one more question for you, Bee."

"Okay, I'm listening." I chewed my lip as I waited, nerves swirling in my gut.

"Could it be that you're actually scared of them sacrificing so much for you and placing you back in those gratitude shackles?"

I sucked in a breath. Was that it? I hadn't considered that.

"I… I don't know."

"Have they asked you to be anything other than yourself? To do anything outside of a relationship?"

"Of course not!" I practically shouted.

"Hmm." I could hear her smile, and my heart slowed as I waited.

"Did you think you're the first person in the world to be in an unconventional relationship?"

"Absolutely not." My cheeks flamed, her insinuation clear. The world didn't revolve around me, even if I thought it did.

"It's scary to step into a new relationship, but you're doing it beautifully. Nothing will ever be perfect, but the five of you are talking about things. Your one guy was right; communication and boundaries are vital. That's how you know this isn't an entitled choice. Self-love isn't selfish; it's healthy, freeing, and allows you to share your authenticity with others. That's the most attractive thing in the world, and it's no wonder four men were drawn to it."

I gulped, her words bringing tears to my eyes. They were exactly what I needed to hear. "So, I'm not being entitled and selfish?" I asked, needing to hear it.

"Do you love them?" she asked instead.

"I love Hawk, and my feelings for the other three are strong. I think I'm headed there," I admitted, my heart flipping in my chest at the confirmation.

"Then you have your answer, Bee. You've had a few stumbles, but what did you tell me about baseball uniforms?"

I sighed, smiling. "The best games have the dirtiest uniforms."

"Ah, yes, that one." I could practically hear her smile through her voice.

"Why do most of my questions get answered with another question?" I teased.

"Do they?" She laughed. "You know that one, too."

I nodded despite her not seeing me. "Yeah, yeah. Something about having the answer within me the whole time." I rolled my eyes but didn't feel the annoyance. If anything, I loved how Delia made me work for it.

"Wow, that's a brilliant thing to say. You must have very wise people in your life." She giggled, and the sound lit up my insides.

"Thank you, Delia."

"Anytime, Bee. Now, can I return to my true crime podcast? They're about to figure out who the killer is."

"Ha! Have fun. Bye," I said, hanging up the phone, already feeling better.

The facts of my relationship hadn't changed; there were still a lot of consequences. But removing myself from the equation wasn't the only option. I wouldn't continue to be foolish with their hearts. So, I needed to either be all in or all out. There was no middle ground. No five years pretending everything was fine. They were worth knowing where I stood, alone and with them. Now, I had to figure out what that was and if I was brave enough to go after it.

"What's with the face?"

I spun around, my mouth dropping open as I took in my brother, smiling at me. My eyes traveled over him, trying to recognize that he was here in this setting. His hair was a little longer on top, his stubble a little more pronounced, but otherwise, he outwardly looked the same. Same blond hair, same blue eyes.

But something had changed. I just couldn't put my finger on it. Nonetheless, I could feel it. There was a gap between us that I'd never felt before, even with an ocean between us. Had my secrets created this?

"You okay, Blanket?" he asked, his voice serious now. His smile dropped as he stepped forward, taking my hand. The familiar touch undid me, and I threw myself into his arms, my tears falling before I could stop them.

All the emotions poured out as Bryce wrapped his arms

around me, moving us out of the way. He uttered soothing words, letting me cling to him.

God, I'd missed my brother. He'd been my best friend and protector most of my life, and I hated feeling this way.

"Ssh, it's okay. Tell me what's wrong?"

I shook my head. I couldn't, and that was the problem.

"I can't." I hiccupped, wiping my eyes. Bryce stepped back, assessing me.

"You can tell me anything, BB. I promise."

My lip wobbled. I wanted to, so badly. The thought of blurting it out and being done with it was alluring. I could let Bryce take care of it—consequences be damned.

But that wouldn't fix the problem. This wasn't something Bryce could do for me.

"You're scaring me, BB. Tell me. Something."

"I… I'm dating someone." There, that part was true.

Bryce's face screwed up, then turned stony. "Did they do something? Tell me who."

"No. They didn't. They're perfect." I dropped my eyes, latching on to the neutral pronoun he'd used.

"Then what's the problem? Why are you in tears?"

"I'm worried about what people will think. If I can go through being in the spotlight again."

"First of all, fuck them. Who cares what people think. Anyone—guy or girl, I don't want to make assumptions here —you decide to date, I know will be special. If other people can't see that, then that's their problem. But if they hurt your feelings, let me at them, and I'll make it clear."

I snorted, wiping my nose, then cringing at my hand. Bryce laughed, grabbing a napkin off the concession stand and handing it to me. It was then I realized where we were. He'd moved us into the inner part, out of the view of the main arena. It gave at least a semblance of privacy.

"Thanks, Bry." I blew my nose, and my brother shifted.

"I'm gonna guess that if you're worried about the spotlight, you're dating a player?"

I bit my lip but nodded.

"It's not Davis, is it?" Bryce's eyes went hard. "Because if so, I take it back. He doesn't deserve you."

"Davis?" I asked, trying to put the name with the player.

"Seth."

"Oh. Fuck, no. He's left me alone since Hawk punched him."

"Good." Bryce smiled a toothy grin, apparently pleased his best friend had stood up for my honor. "Then who?"

I shook my head. "I can't say. Not yet."

Bryce let out a long breath, his fists clenching at his sides as he opened and closed them.

"Fine. You don't have to tell me their name, but you can still talk to me. Come on, let's go find some seats in the nosebleeds. The fresh air, the sound of balls smacking the bats, and the crowd will be good for the soul."

I rolled my eyes but let Bryce pull me up the stairs to the top level. "Trying to use Dad's 'baseball fixes everything' remedy?"

"Duh. It works," he teased, sitting in an empty row with no one else around. Midweek afternoon games didn't tend to sell out. Sucked for the Grizzlies, but worked for us right now to have a private conversation.

We sat in silence as we watched the game. My eyes didn't really focus on the players; I just watched their movement as they proceeded around the diamond. I felt weightless like I was floating above, watching without being present. Bryce nudged me a while later; my time to avoid everything was over.

"Spill, Blanket. What's *really* troubling you?"

I sighed, blinking as I let myself return to my body.

"You know how people always know who you are and want your autograph when we go out in public? To talk to you about baseball and rehash all the plays?"

Bryce nodded, his face turned toward mine. "Well, I hate that part of our life. People only want to talk to me because of who Dad is or who you are, or worse, my illness. Being invisible was a blessing. I never knew if people liked me for me or for what I could do for them."

"Is someone trying to use you?" he questioned, his voice harsh.

"No. It's not like that. I'm not explaining this well." I gripped my thighs, trying to find the words I needed to say. I stared out at the field, not seeing it.

"Do you remember when we were young, and you'd dance during the innings? You were always the first one to want to be part of the entertainment."

"I don't remember that," I whispered. Bryce turned away from me, his knee bouncing as he stared out on the field.

"I'm not an expert, but it seems to me that you started hating the spotlight after the diagnosis. Mom became hyperfocused on you, not giving you any space. Every person who used to give you smiles and laughs now looked at you with sadness or pity. Dad didn't know how to deal with it, so he stayed busy, letting Mom run the show. In her need to control, Mom went overboard. Every minute of every day became about how you were doing."

"What are you saying?" I asked, swallowing. My throat was suddenly parched.

"You shone so bright as a child. Even when you were sick, you didn't dim. Not at first. Things weren't good with Mom and Dad for a while, long before they got divorced, but I don't think you knew that."

I shook my head, staring at my brother.

"I didn't understand it then, but I think about that time a lot. I watched my effervescent sister dull right before my eyes, and I hated it. I'm not blaming Mom, but I think her need to control the situation sucked the life out of you. That she saw you as a way to save her marriage. Maybe I'm wrong." He shrugged one shoulder, one side of his mouth tilting up. "Maybe it was the bone marrow deficiency, but to me, it seemed like the more you weren't allowed to be you, the more you withdrew."

He let out a harsh chuckle, shaking his head and rubbing his hand over his face. I wanted to reach out to him, but his words had me frozen. My illness and everything that came afterward with the divorce was a period in our lives we pretended didn't exist.

"That sounds idiotic and probably like an oxymoron, but you've always been intuitive, Blake. You sense people's emotions better than they do themselves. I think it got twisted somehow that if you were the person Mom wanted, it would make everything okay. Like you had the power to save them… her… you. I dunno. I'm probably talking out of my ass, and like I said, I'm not an expert, and this is a really long-winded way to say that I don't think you hate the spot-light. At least not for the reasons you assume."

Bryce's words were heavy and a lot to digest. Some of it paired with the things I'd discussed with Delia—my grati-tude shackles and people-pleasing ways.

"I'm not sure that helps my situation."

He shrugged, turning back to me. "Maybe not. But the sister I know is a badass. She's not afraid of anything. Not a chronic illness, not pretentious people who think they know better, and especially not love."

"Love?" My heart stalled. How did he know that? I still wasn't even sure. I shook my head, trying to dismiss his comment and the fear it drew up. "I'm not a badass, Bry. Far from it."

"I've been following your account." He leaned back, shielding his eyes from the sun.

"Okay." I blinked, the sudden direction change throwing me.

"And some of the other players have been filming you when you're doing your thing."

"They have?" My brows jumped at this.

"Yep. The account's entertaining and engaging. It's great stuff, Blake. You're doing exactly what you wanted, and it shows. If Dad doesn't offer you a full-time position after this season, any other team will. You're getting the players noticed and reviving the fandom. But what I love is seeing their clips. It's obvious the team respects you and admires what you've done."

My breath hitched, worried he'd seen more than I realized. Had it been obvious? Did he already know? But there was also an element of truth that settled. That feeling I had when I realized who I was and stood up to Mira. People had accepted me, and I felt it.

"I do feel like I'm at home with the team."

"I'll admit I was jealous at first. I hated missing out on witnessing this real side of my sister again." He laughed, lighting up the moment. "The unicorn dance-off was my favorite. Seeing you smile and hearing you laugh was the best medicine." He paused, staring straight into my eyes. "You might not like to be in the spotlight, BB, but there's no denying you shine. It naturally follows you."

His words stunned me, and the urge to tell him everything, to unload my doubts and concerns at his feet, was strong.

"What if I do something to ruin someone's career?" I asked hesitantly.

"Not possible. If dating ruins a career, then that person's career wasn't strong to begin with."

Could that be true? My dating relationship wouldn't be that exciting?

"I'd like to think that if I liked a person enough to seriously date them, we'd both be willing to do whatever it took to be together. I'd move mountains, fight any battle, and burn the world down for the right person. Baseball is my job, and I love it, but it's not my everything. If I'm willing to choose it over a person…then either I'm a scared dipshit and undeserving, or they're not the right person."

Bryce made it sound so simple. So, maybe I was overthinking this. When I realized I was more worried about the fallout they'd face versus my own, I knew I was. Fear they didn't feel the same way, that this was a phase if they were willing to share me, had made me doubt their feelings.

I couldn't make choices for them any more than they could for me.

But we could fight and stand together.

"Thanks, Bry. That actually helps." I knocked his shoulder, leaning my head on him. He kissed my forehead, wrapping his arm around me, and I felt that distance thin.

I needed to tell him the truth. I didn't want to keep anything from my brother anymore. But Hawk deserved the right to tell him first.

We continued to watch the game, sitting next to one another, that familiar comfort settling between us. With my fear and guilt out of the way, a niggling that something was going on with Bryce resurfaced.

"Are things going okay with the Blue Devils?" I asked, turning to look at him. His eyes widened, and he opened his mouth, then closed it. "Bry?"

The crowd gasped, and Bryce's face paled as he shot up. I stood with him, not understanding what was happening until the sight at home froze me. The crumpled form of Graham with Tucker kneeling over him stopped my heart.

I trembled as I watched in fear, and my face paled at the sight of the gurney. I gripped Bryce's arm, clutching onto him, and I was pretty sure he was the only thing keeping me standing.

I could use a baseball miracle right now. Please, baseball, let Graham be okay.

BLAKE

I didn't realize I was hyperventilating until Bryce sat me down, pressing my head between my legs. He spoke softly, telling me to breathe. His presence grounded me, and I found my air, slowing down my breaths.

"Are you okay?"

"No. I need to go see if he's okay."

Bryce searched my eyes, probably guessing Graham was special to me.

"Okay. Let's go see what we can find out."

We walked slowly down the steps, my balance still off-kilter from the panic attack. It felt like it took forever to get to the clubhouse. But no one was there when we entered. We checked the medical room but still struck out.

"Let me see if Dad knows," Bryce said, pulling out his phone.

The door to the clubhouse crashed open, and I jumped. Tucker stumbled through, his uniform a complete mess, his face probably as ashen as mine. He held his glove and hat in his hand, his balance off as he raced in.

"Blake! Graham. Hospital. Shoes." His words came out tangled, but I got the gist.

"Here, I'll help." I rushed over and helped Tucker change out of his cleats into his sneakers. He grabbed his bag and Graham's, looping them over his shoulder. I wish I had mine, but I wasn't wasting time to go get it. I'd text Rue later and have her bring it to the room.

I took Tucker's hand without thinking. We needed each other.

"Bry," I said, turning to him. "Can you—"

"Take you to the hospital? Yeah. Do you have my keys?"

"I do!" Tucker shouted, pulling out the key with a baseball keychain. Bryce practically purred as the keys landed in his hand.

"Let's go."

His eyes bounced between me and Tucker, but he didn't ask. That was what I loved about my brother. He trusted wholeheartedly. Which made me feel even worse for keeping things from him.

The drive to the hospital was quick, and we were allowed up to the private floor but not to his room. Bryce was on the phone with someone, trying to get us clearance. He motioned he'd be back, taking his phone out to the area reserved for calls.

Tucker spent his time pacing or dejected in his seat. He'd bounce his knee, lean forward, and tug on his hair before slumping back in it. He would then get up and pace, leaping at everyone who came through the door, hoping they had an update.

Finally, when a doctor came, he took pity on Tucker and allowed him back, saying Graham had called out his name. I slouched in the chair then, my heart still racing. We hadn't heard anything yet, and it felt like the longer we were kept out, the more my mind grew with worst-case scenarios.

The emotional roller coaster of today was not my friend.

High from my time with Tucker, to panic as I realized the future consequences, to relief from talking to Delia, to guilt from hiding things from Bryce, back to panic as Graham got injured.

It was too much, and I was ready to get off.

I pulled out my phone, but I couldn't find anything on Google, and nothing else distracted me enough to help. Slumping down in the chair, I tapped my foot as I took over Tucker's vigil.

The elevator dinged, and I glanced up; when I spotted Hawk, my heart slowed. He was here. His face softened as he spotted me, making his way over to me.

I stood as he neared, needing to tell him Bryce was here. I opened my mouth, but Hawk didn't stop his approach. He gripped my face with his hands, kissing me hard before I could say anything. All my thoughts fled, and I sank into the safety and comfort only Hawk could give me. In the back of my mind, I knew this was a bad idea, but the comfort outweighed the fear and eased my worried heart.

We would get through this together. My earlier revelation seemed to be coming true. That had to be good, right?

Hawk finally eased back, our breaths coming out hard from the kiss. He dropped his forehead to mine, his eyes searing into me. His thumbs rubbed my cheeks, where they still clutched me.

"I'm glad Tucker found you. How's Graham?"

"I don't—"

"He has a concussion and a laceration over his eye. They're not sure if he needs surgery yet. They have to wait for the swelling to go down," Bryce said behind Hawk.

Hawk's body tensed, eyes wide as he dropped my face and turned, keeping me behind him. My heart stalled and my stomach dropped through the floor. This was it. The moment I'd been fearing. Hawk took my hand and pulled me beside him as he faced his best friend—my brother.

"Bry, I was going to tell you."

"Funny, I remember you saying you didn't have feelings for one another." Bryce's words were hard, his eyes shiny as he stared at the two of us before landing on me. "I thought you were with Jameson or even West… But Hawk? Have you both been lying to my face for years?"

"Bryce," I said shakily, stepping forward. Tears ran down my face as the guilt poured out of me. I couldn't lie. Not anymore. My brother's face fell, my tears apparently confirming his suspicions. "It's not like that," I said, hating my own words. Would I ever be brave enough to say them? Why did it have to be one or the other?

"Yes, it is," Hawk said, refusing to hide. I loved him for it, but it wasn't helping when Bryce thought we'd been hiding this for longer than we had.

"No. I mean, yes. I mean, no," I said, shaking my head.

"So what, you fuck my sister, and you couldn't even tell me like a man?"

"Bry, it's—" I tried again.

"Stop. I don't want to hear any more lies, Blake. I spent all afternoon consoling you, and for what? To discover you're screwing my best friend. I need space. I assume you can find your own way back? Great. Don't follow me."

He spun on his heels, not waiting for a response before taking the stairs. Hawk turned to me, his eyes pleading with mine. I pulled his face down and kissed him once.

"Go talk to him. I'll be here. I'm not ending this. I promise."

"I love you, Blazy."

"I love you, too. Now go let my brother know he's not losing you either."

He gave me one more kiss and then hightailed it out of there. I tried to ignore how eerily similar it felt—Hawk kissing me before chasing after my brother.

It was a pitch slap to the gut, but this time, I would trust in love, believing it wouldn't end in a cleat retreat.

I didn't know how long I waited until Tucker returned. I'd been staring into space, wondering how I'd gotten into this mess. It wasn't until Tucker crouched down, his hands landing on my thighs, that it stirred me. With a soft smile, he took my hand and nodded for me to follow him.

"He's okay for now," he said as we walked down the hall.

I nodded, swallowing. My throat felt thick like cotton.

"Bryce managed to get someone on the phone and gave me an update."

Tucker glanced down, frowning. "Where did he go?"

"Hawk showed up, so yeah, that happened."

"Oh shit. Are you okay?" He grimaced.

I shrugged my shoulders. "I don't know anymore. I'm trying to trust in my relationship with both of them that it will be."

Tucker gave my shoulder a sympathetic squeeze, then opened the door to Graham's room. Graham sat on the bed, his baseball pants and cleats on his lower half, a hospital gown over his top. He grinned when he spotted us, and I ran to him, throwing my arms around him.

"I was so worried."

"I'm sorry. It was pretty scary."

"Don't apologize. Besides, it sounds like Tucker beaned him."

"Tuck," Graham sighed, letting me go. I shifted to sit next to him, needing to feel his body beside mine.

"What? He touched what was mine. He deserved it."

"I should be mad at you, but I really enjoy hearing you say I'm yours. The possessiveness is hot."

"Agreed." I fanned my face, making them laugh.

Tucker joined us around the bed as we waited for the

doctors to hear if they would discharge Graham or keep him overnight. We talked about dumb things to keep it light, all our emotions too strained to do much more. I responded to a few messages from my dad, Coach Phillips, and even my mother.

Rue replied she'd drop my bag off in our room before returning to Wilmington. She didn't give any other details as to why she was leaving early, and I didn't feel like I was at the place in our friendship to ask. At least it meant I'd have the room to myself.

The worst part of waiting was no messages from Hawk or Bryce. I tried not to worry about it, knowing my brother could be stubborn at the best of times, but particularly when he felt betrayed. He had a right to feel upset; I just wanted to talk to him about it so I could make it right. It was like an itch I could feel under my skin, and it wouldn't go away until I did. But all I could do was let them work it out.

Emory had also texted what time she'd be arriving tomorrow, making me instantly feel guilty that I'd forgotten about her visit. Her first round of interviews was done, and she had a break in between the next set.

When the doctor finally stopped by, I felt as if I'd run a marathon.

"You'll need to check the stitches in a week to see how they're healing. Once the swelling goes down, we can tell more if surgery is required. You need to sit out the next few games, too, until you're cleared of the concussion," the doctor ordered before finally releasing Graham into our care.

Tucker morphed into responsible mode and went downstairs to grab Graham's pain meds while I helped him change into his regular clothes.

"I like it better when you take my clothes off," Graham grumbled, leaning on me. I smiled but knew he didn't like feeling helpless.

"Me too, but you heard the doc. Gotta take it easy."

"All I heard was him setting a challenge. How to get sexy with Blake without messing up my stitches."

I giggled, slapping his shoulder. But it was nice to hear him joke. It eased some of the overwhelming fear from earlier. Once we reached the lobby, Tucker awaited us, a relieved smile spreading as he spotted us.

The three of us grabbed an Uber back to the hotel, the lateness of the evening hitting us as we trudged to their room. When Tucker tried to carry Graham, he got swatted away.

"I cut my head. I can walk, Tuck."

"Fine. But don't come to me when you need someone to wipe your butt!" Tucker huffed, stalking off down the hallway to their door.

"Um, no worries. I don't think I ever need our relationship to go there." Graham grimaced, treading slowly with me. Apparently, I'd missed him getting hit in the leg earlier, the bruise now large on his leg and making it difficult to walk.

"Ah, the romance is already gone," I teased, easing some tension as they laughed. "I think we're all hangry. I'll go across the street and get some food. Text me what you want."

I headed to my room, exhaustion filling every fiber of my being as I changed out of my clothes and pulled on a pair of leggings and a hoodie. Tomorrow would suck, and I suddenly wished I could call in sick. But this wasn't a job that made being sick all that easy.

When I opened my door, I stumbled forward into Luke, who had his arm up, preparing to knock. He wrapped his arms around my waist, catching me.

"Whoa."

"Thanks. What are you doing here?" I asked, righting myself.

"I was coming to check on you. You didn't answer your phone, and I wanted to see how everyone was."

"Oh, sorry." I grimaced, pulling my door shut and heading to the elevator. "Things went a little bat-shit crazy. My brother showed up on top of everything going on with Graham."

"Damn. I'm sorry, Slugger. That had to be hard. How's Graham?" Luke asked.

"He's good for now. It doesn't seem to be anything too serious, thankfully."

"That's good, that's good," he said, letting out a breath of relief.

"You were actually worried about him." I smiled at that. I loved that they were developing their own connection. I'd hoped they would, but Luke had been the most resistant. He snorted, hip-checking me as we stepped into the elevator.

"Believe it or not, I tolerate those two, and well, I'd miss them if they were gone. They're good for the team."

I chuckled, already feeling better being around him. "Sure. For the team. That's all it is."

Luke winked, his hand going to the small of my back as we stepped off the elevator. "You headed somewhere?"

"Yeah, I was going to get some food and bring it to them."

"Need some help?"

"Always." I smiled, happy to see him. It felt weird when I didn't get my dosage of them each day.

We walked across the street to a sandwich place, and I was immediately glad Luke had joined me as I read off the list of things the guys had sent. Sometimes, I forgot I hung out mostly with athletes.

"Damn. I would've needed a wheelbarrow to get all this back."

Luke chuckled, our arms full as we carried it back to the hotel.

"Dinner!" I shouted, knocking on their door.

"Lukey!" Tucker called, pulling the broody first baseman

into his arms and sharing the first genuine smile I'd seen in hours. "How's my niece doing?"

Luke rolled his eyes, but I caught the corner of his lips tilting up. "I just got her to bed. Had to read three stories tonight, but she told me to tell Graham to get well soon."

"Ah, thanks, man." Graham smiled, a little loopy on the pain meds. He attempted some kind of awkward bro, clap, hug combo before giving up, and we settled down to eat. Luke and I took one bed, Tucker sitting near Graham on the other.

"How did the rest of the game go?" Tucker asked after he inhaled a few sandwiches.

"Shitty. After the benches cleared—"

"Wait, you cleared the benches?" Graham asked, kicking Tucker in the thigh.

"Oh, did I forget to mention that part? My bad." His expression did not match his words, though. He didn't feel one ounce of sorry.

"Damn. I can't believe everyone did that," Graham said, something coming over his face.

"Well, yeah. You're a YellowJacket. We stick together," Luke said. "Even if that incurs a fine."

"Shit." Tucker cringed. "I didn't think about that part."

"No one cared. In fact, it seemed to unite everyone oddly. However, Austin and Shane are nowhere near your level, so we lost by one."

"Ah, fuck. I just realized I'm gonna have to play without you." Tucker groaned, his head falling into his hands.

"You'll survive," Graham teased, his eyelids growing heavy.

"We should go so you can sleep. Call me if you need anything. I'll take a rain check on our date."

"Damn. Getting hit in the head really messed up my night."

"I'll make you feel better," Tucker teased.

"Sleep," I warned, pointing my finger. Tucker rolled his eyes but smiled, and I knew he was only saying that to help ease Graham's worry.

I kissed them both, leaving with Luke after he did a different version of their earlier hello. It was a bit clumsy still, but it gave me hope they were becoming friends—a family.

And I really wanted that. The realization, in combination with the fear of Graham being hurt, had made my feelings crystal clear.

CHAPTER
FIFTY-SIX

BLAKE

"Do you want to stay?" I asked Luke as we stepped into the elevator.

"Is that all right? I know I had you last night."

"It's more than all right. I don't want to be alone, and Tucker needs to stay with Graham. While I could've stayed there, they needed some time to talk. I assume Hawk's still dealing with my brother. So, yeah, I'm all yours if you're free," I rambled, realizing I sounded like a spoiled princess who couldn't be alone.

Luke gave me a big smile as he pulled me into his arms, kissing my temple and making me feel coveted.

"Then it's my lucky night." He grinned, and it oddly eased some of the anxiety in my chest from not hearing from Hawk or Bryce yet.

We both fell into bed once we returned to my room, exhaustion from the day catching up to me. While we didn't have sex, it still felt nice to wake up in his arms, knowing I wasn't alone. It replaced the doubt with assurance, and I felt more confident than ever that we could do this.

But first, I needed to fix things with Bryce.

With the dawn of a new day, I felt refreshed and determined to fix things with my brother. He might not understand or accept my relationship right now, but I believed we could find a solution. We'd been through too much already together. It had been dumb to think that this would be any different.

Yet the anxiety kept rising the longer I didn't hear from Hawk or Bryce, and I worried it meant things were irreparable. Trying to ease some of my worry, I sent them both a message again and then opened Emory's.

"Crap. Emory's headed here."

"Who?" Luke asked, rolling over. His blond hair was ruffled, and he looked so goldenly gorgeous. I smiled, leaning forward to kiss him.

"My best friend. She's here from Greece."

"Ah, cool. Does she…?"

"Know about us? Yeah. She's very much on board for the Blake express train, as she calls it."

Luke snorted as I quickly climbed out of bed, hoping to have enough time to shower before she arrived. I stripped off my clothes and turned on the shower just as a knock sounded.

"I got it," Luke said.

"I guess today is a sink bath day." I turned off the shower and pulled out my toothbrush. I placed toothpaste on it and moved closer to the door to listen. I'd left it open in case Luke wanted to join. I was envious that I wouldn't see Emory's reaction to Luke.

"Oh, sorry, I must have the wrong room," a very familiar voice said, one that wasn't Emory.

"Um…" Luke mumbled, and I could imagine the shock on his face as he faced off with my brother.

"Wait… Olson! What are you doing…"

Panic climbed up my throat as he trailed off, undoubtedly putting the pieces together.

Shit, shit, shit, shit, shit.

Was my brother going to discover all my relationships in the worst way possible? I guess this was the price to pay when you kept secrets.

"Where is she?" Bryce barked, slapping his hands against the doorframe. I jumped, hurrying to pull on clothes. I did not need to add nakedness to my humiliation for today.

"Who?" Luke asked, apparently pretending not to know and save me.

I could take it and stay hidden in the bathroom, but that wasn't fair to either of them. Plus, I was determined not to be that girl anymore.

Opening the bathroom door, I touched Luke's lower back to move him. He tensed, his jaw tight, but he eventually moved back and revealed my brother. Bryce's eyes landed on me, his face full of anger. I'd never seen that look directed at me before, and it was unsettling.

"First Hawk, and now *him*? Are you, what? Fucking the whole team?" His face screwed up with a look of disgust under the anger.

"Whoa, Bry!" I shouted, holding up my hands to ward him off. My face flamed as the hurt his words inflicted eviscerated my heart. Tears gathered at the corners of my eyes, and I shook my head to clear the emotion in my throat. "That's too far. I know finding out this way wasn't the best, but you can't talk to me *or* him that way."

This time, Bryce stepped back like my words had physically slapped him. He grabbed his chest, and I worried things would never be repaired from here.

"I've been walking around this damn city all night, trying to make sense of you and Hawk. When I finally calm down enough to talk to you about it and apologize for storming off, I find *him*. How did you expect me to react? My best friend *and* my rival." He shook his head like the very image of me before him was too much. His blue eyes were cold as ice as he stared at me. "I got you this job as a favor, and this is how you repay me? By making a fool of me? Who are you? Because you're not *my* sister."

His words stung, and I wanted to deny and cover to make things right. Desperation clawed at me, my heart cracking as I watched the one person I always counted on splintered. Maybe I deserved this pain for lying. His hurt was the price I had to pay, even if his words broke something inside me.

Tears fell freely, and I had to blink to clear my vision. My whole body trembled, and my breath came out in choppy gasps.

"It's not what it looks like," I tried, but the words fell flat.

Bryce sneered his upper lip lifting. "It looks like you are cheating on my best friend. I expect it from him, but not you."

I shook my head. "No. It's not like that. I don't know what your deal with Luke is—"

"*Luke.*" He scoffed, shattering all hope that Bryce would ever accept him. There was nothing but venom in his voice.

"Listen, Baker," Luke started from behind me, but it only fanned the flames.

"You can shut the fuck up, Olson." Bryce glared at the man behind me, pointing his finger as he vibrated on the spot with rage.

They glared at one another, neither willing to back down. I'd always known Bryce didn't like Luke, but I had no clue why. It had to be more than just a rivalry. Bryce didn't hold grudges, so for him to hate Luke violently meant it had to be something serious. Knowing the man Luke was, I had no clue what it could be about.

It had to be a misunderstanding. A very big one.

Before I could ask any questions, Bryce's rage bubbled over, and he shoved Luke, who'd stepped slightly in front of me at some point in my mental battle. The power of his push knocked Luke back into me, slamming me into the doorknob.

"Ow!" I cried out, falling to the ground as I clutched my back. I think I just bruised a kidney. I heard Luke fall behind me, but the pain hurt too much to check. I squeezed my eyes shut tight as I tried to breathe through it so I didn't throw up. There had already been too much vomit in my life.

"Fuck. Shit. Dammit, Blanket! I'm so sorry. I didn't mean to," Bryce called out, his face full of shock as he bent down toward me. His hands gripped me for a microsecond before everything went apeshit.

"Get your fucking hands off her!"

In an instant, whatever it was between Luke and Bryce bubbled over at the sight of me on the ground in pain. Luke charged forward, tackling Bryce, and I lost visual as they wrestled on the ground, something crashing behind me.

Clutching my side, I rolled over to spot Luke on the ground, blood trickling down his face. With everything that had happened yesterday, it was too much too soon, and tears poured from my eyes.

"Stop. Please. Just stop," I cried, but my voice could barely be heard over their insults.

"What in the world?" an accented feminine voice asked. I glanced out into the hall, finding Emory. Unfortunately, she wasn't the only one. Apparently, the sounds of our fight had drawn others as they stared at the three of us.

We were a fucking spectacle.

Bryce and Luke stopped, and my brother tried to reach for me, but I jerked back, shaking my head. I couldn't do this right now. There were too many people watching. Too much anger. And I didn't have it in me to pick sides or solve anything with an audience.

"Bry, *please*. Just go," I cried, near hysterics.

Bryce's eyes bore into me, now filled with sadness and devastation instead of anger, as his silent tears fell down his cheek. He swallowed once, stepped out the door, and didn't look back.

It broke my heart as he left, despite my request for him to go, and my sobs became louder as I lay on the floor in the fetal position, feeling like everything was falling apart around me.

Emory instantly jumped into crisis mode, stepping into the room and shutting the door, cutting off the attention from outside. She kneeled beside me, cradling me in her arms, letting me break down.

Everything was a complete mess, and I didn't know how to fix it. Or if it was even possible anymore.

I hadn't wanted to choose between the guys, but it didn't seem like what I wanted mattered. The world would make me choose.

Either them, or my family.

Them, or normalcy.

Them, or peace.

Why did it feel like in order to keep people, I had to sacrifice what I wanted? I didn't know any set of boundaries that would fix this.

CHAPTER
FIFTY-SEVEN

HAWK

My eyes struggled to stay open as exhaustion settled deep in my bones like I'd never felt. I ran my hands over my head and my beard, attempting to stimulate my brain into thinking I was awake.

I'd been all over the city but hadn't found Bryce. It didn't help that Charleston was unknown to me, but I'd checked all the spots I assumed he would go. And when that didn't work, I'd camped out in the hotel lobby, hoping he'd return here at some point. I wasn't sure if he'd booked a room, but since the team was staying here, it was my best guess of where he might end up.

Out of all the ways I imagined him responding, that had been the worst.

Considering he'd punched me the first time, I'd expected something similar. But for him to run away and ignore me, to give the silent treatment all night, it felt harsher than any punch he could've given. It was the pitch slap I'd never seen coming.

The fact I had to clarify 'the first time' made my own brain scream at me. I couldn't even be mad because I'd brought this on myself. I'd selfishly put it off, telling Bryce. The insecure part of me desired to keep her to myself as long as I could, knowing everything would blow up at some point. But now, the choice had been taken away, leaving me with only the crumbles.

The difference was, this time, I would fight for Blake.

I didn't want to lose my best friend, but I could no longer sacrifice the love of my life to avoid it.

My phone rang in my hand, jolting me in my chair, and I scrambled to answer it. I hoped it was Bryce, but my stomach sank when I saw it was Blake. Not because I didn't want to talk to her but because I didn't have any news to share. I'd been putting it off until I had something, but I wouldn't leave her hanging. Before it could go to voicemail, I hit answer.

"Hey, Blazy."

"Hawk." Her voice was tired and sad, and I instantly hated myself for not checking in sooner. "Thank god. I hadn't heard from you, and—" Her voice hitched, and my heart broke. I might be the oldest in this relationship, but I was an idiot. I'd never had a girlfriend before, and I kept messing up.

"I'm sorry, Blazy. I really am. I haven't found Bryce, but I didn't mean to worry you." I sucked in a deep breath, closing my eyes as I scrubbed my hand over the back of my head. "I'm not giving up. I'm fighting, baby."

"I know," she said softly. "He, um, was actually just here."

"Here as in your hotel room?"

"Yep, and Luke answered the door."

"Shit."

"Yep. As you can guess, it didn't go well."

"Where is he now?"

"I don't know. He took off when Emory showed up. Um, he pushed Luke, and I fell into the door. Then they sorta fought/wrestled and Luke ended up with a cut. Thankfully, Emory patched him up."

"Fuck, fuck. I'm sorry I wasn't there." I tugged at the ends of my hair, desperation and panic warring within.

"This isn't all on you, Hawk. Don't be a martyr. We both knew what we were doing."

The corners of my mouth twitched. God, I loved this woman.

"You're right, baby. I'm still sorry I wasn't there." I glanced around but didn't see him. "I'm in the lobby, so I'll try to catch him."

"Give me an update when you can so I don't worry. I'm not sure what to do about the game yet. Luke should be fine to play, but god, I wish we got sick days. I could use a mental health one."

"You're so fucking right." I sighed, the exhaustion heavy in the sound. "I'll call you back in a little."

"Okay. I love you," she whispered, her voice so small. I wanted to run up to her room and pull her into my arms.

"I love you, too, Blazy."

The call ended, and I hung my head. Overwhelming paralysis sank into my bones as I tried to find a solution. Getting Bryce was the number one priority. Hitting his number one more time, I prayed he'd answer. When the phone behind me rang, I jumped and spun around, coming face to face with my best friend.

Bryce looked wrecked. His eyes were bloodshot, his face tired, and his hair a ruffled mess. His clothes were wrinkled, and he looked like I felt... like he could drop at any second. We stared at one another for a moment, holding each other's gaze, communicating in the way we often did. But this time, I had no clue what my best friend was thinking.

"Hey," I said, the word croaking. I cleared my throat, my words thick and gravelly. "I've been looking all over the city for you."

Bryce crossed his arms, scoffing. "Well, you found me."

Witnessing Bryce's stubborn side gave me hope. If he was mad at me, it meant he cared.

"I'm an asshole," I said, deciding to start there.

He laughed, but the sound wasn't happy. It was full of derision and smacked me in the heart.

"Can we go somewhere and talk?"

"I don't want to be anywhere you are right now."

"Fair." I lifted my hands, trying to appear non-threatening. "I'll say my piece here and then leave you alone."

Bryce made a gesture to carry on, so I took a few steps closer, not wanting to shout my business for all to see and hear in the lobby.

"How long?" he asked before I could start.

"As long as I can remember," I said, despite knowing that wasn't the question he asked. He reared back like my words slapped him.

"You've been fucking my sister for years?"

"No." Bryce's body relaxed at that. "I've *been in love* with your sister for years."

All the fight had left him, and he sagged on the spot. "Why didn't you tell me?"

"Because I'm an idiot. I didn't know how to. I didn't want to break bro code." I shrugged. "Which answer do you want? Because I've had them all over the years."

"The truth. I'm sick of lies."

I nodded, knowing I needed to just say it. "I was too scared."

"Of me?" His eyes were teary, his face falling as he stared. I stepped forward, closing the distance between us.

"No. No." I shook my head emphatically. "I was afraid I wasn't good enough. That she would see right through me and tell me to go to hell. That you'd find out and laugh or tell me to go away. Or I'd be alone for the rest of my life."

Bryce stared at me like I'd just spoken Greek.

"The torture felt easier. At least then, I had my two best

friends. So, I kept my secret and pined for the one girl I loved but would never have."

"I wouldn't have stopped being your friend."

I raised my eyes, challenging him. Bryce laughed, the tension dissolving more between us.

"I wouldn't have," he said earnestly. "It's hard to wrap my brain around, and the selfish part of me wants to keep you both to myself, but there's this other part that is ecstatic for my best friend and sister to find such amazing people to love. And bonus, to have you as a brother-in-law is a dream come true." He wrinkled his nose, shaking his head. "As long as I don't think about what you guys do in your spare time." Bryce gave me a wry smile, easing the fear of abandonment.

"I went to your room first, you know. When you weren't there, I went to Blake's, hoping I'd find you both. I wanted to apologize and listen so I could be cool with you guys together. I realized that as long as you both didn't push me out, I'd be okay." He took a deep breath, his eyes searching mine. I wanted to reassure him, but it felt like he needed to get out more first.

"I think I've always noticed the connection between you two, plus the fact I've never seen you with anyone serious made me wonder. Even with Roxie, I could tell it wasn't anything serious. I love the way Blake is with you. She's her most comfortable, and I love seeing her like that."

"I feel like there's a but coming."

Bryce's lips lifted in a small smile. He shoved his hands into his pockets.

"But then her bedroom door opened, and I found *Luke Olson* there." He peered up at me like he was afraid I would go on a rampage.

"And?" I questioned. Bryce jerked, not having expected my response.

"You're not mad?" He looked at me curiously, his eyes seeking an answer he didn't understand.

"I know about Luke. Blake isn't cheating."

"Then I don't understand." Bryce's brow furrowed, and I'd laugh at having perplexed my best friend so much if I wasn't so tired.

"Can we go talk about it somewhere more private now? Then I can try to explain the whole situation." The lobby was filling with people, coming and going as the world woke up. Bryce shuffled on his feet but finally nodded yes.

"There's a diner around the corner. How about we go there?"

"Sounds good."

I took the lead and headed out of the hotel. I didn't look to see if he followed, but my body relaxed when I heard his measured footsteps in line with mine. We walked in silence, not talking, while we ordered our food and were given coffee. We stared at one another for a long while, waiting for someone to start. Guess that would be me.

"Have you ever heard of polyamorous?" I asked, figuring I should start there.

Bryce lifted his brows and swallowed. I could've sworn a flicker of recognition or perhaps surprise flitted through his eyes first. He cleared his throat when I said nothing else as I tried to figure out what he was hiding. My silence made him talk, only proving my assumption. He was hiding something.

"Is that like when everybody's together, and it's a huge orgy or something?" His face morphed into abject horror. "Please tell me that you're not having an orgy with Olson. Oh god, I need brain bleach." He shuddered. "Nope, I need whole body bleach."

I chuckled, taking a sip of my coffee. I could've put him out of his misery sooner, but I enjoyed torturing him for a second.

"No, I mean yes, but no." Bryce cringed, his face going pale. "I'm not sleeping with any of the guys."

"Wait, wait… *guys*? Fuck, I need something stronger than coffee."

"I shouldn't be the one to tell you this." I blew out a breath. "But I know Blake's tired of secrets, so I think she'll forgive me. Just, don't be mad at her, because I asked her to wait."

"Why did you want to wait?" Bryce asked, his voice full of hurt, and I hated I was the cause.

"It felt like this was a conversation that deserved to be face-to-face. If I wasn't brave enough to tell you I'm in love with your sister and wanted to spend the rest of my life with her, then I didn't deserve to be with her, to begin with." I sucked in a breath and held his eyes as I admitted the next part. "I was also afraid you wouldn't accept it, and I'd lose her again. I couldn't go through that again."

Bryce drank his coffee, digesting the information, his eyes far away. "That still doesn't explain Olson."

"Do you remember Blake telling you about the person she met on the plane?"

"Yeah. Didn't they share a room?" Bryce's brows furrowed, and I waited for him to connect the dots.

"Yup. It was Olson."

"Fucking asshole. I'm gonna kill him." His face morphed, and I knew I'd gone about this entire thing completely wrong.

"Bry!" I reached over and grasped his arm. "Before you jump to conclusions, neither of them knew who the other was, and while it sounds weird for me to say this, they do have a real connection."

Bryce paused, opening his mouth and then shutting it before tilting his head to stare at me. I let go of his arm and sat back. "So, you're not going to date my sister?"

I blew out a breath. "That's where the polyamorous thing comes in. Since it took me so long to get my head out of my ass and realize no matter what I did, I would never stop loving Blake; she had time to connect with the others." I swallowed, taking a big gulp of the hot coffee to calm my nerves.

"I watched her joy return as she shed layers of doubt, emerging as our Blake, the one with no fear." I chuckled. "Hell, I witnessed her tell an entire baseball team what to do without missing a beat. Everyone who gets to know Blake falls for her, and I couldn't be the one to tell her she couldn't have everything she wanted. Not when she finally allowed me to be part of her heart."

"But isn't that weird? Don't you want to kill them?" he asked softly, more curious than disgusted. I finally felt like I was getting somewhere. I nodded.

"There are moments when I have to rein in my jealousy and possessiveness. But mostly, I see how carefree she's become and the love she oozes. She's a sunflower, and we're all helpless to her pull."

"But *Olson*?" He grimaced, his face screwing up like he'd tasted something sour.

"And… West and Jameson."

Bryce hung his head. "I knew there was something between one of them and her. I just hadn't expected… Shit." He shuddered right as our food was served, so I gave him a second to gather himself. But if he had issues, I wouldn't let him off the hook.

"What?" I asked once the waitress left.

"I just pictured my sister in bed with four dudes." His face paled, and he dropped his fork like he couldn't eat. He took a few deep breaths, hanging his head in his hands. "Fuck. I'm an asshole."

"From one asshole to the other, the best thing to do is to apologize. I hear they go a long way." I took a deep breath, meeting my best friend's eyes. Hoping he saw the sincerity and regret. "Bryce, I'm sorry. I should've had the courage years ago and told you how I felt about her. But especially when things changed with us. I owe you that. I would never gamble our friendship, yet I treated you like you didn't matter. That you're not one of the most important people in my life."

My eyes glistened, and I grabbed my mug, taking a big gulp as I tried to corral my emotions. Damn tears. It had to be because I was exhausted. I didn't do weeping.

It was quiet at the table as we pretended to eat and not notice the emotion swirling around us.

"Thanks, man. You're my brother and just as important to me." Bryce paused, placing his mug down. "I wish you had told me, but I understand how hard these conversations are." He cleared his throat, picking at something on the table as he avoided eye contact.

The busboy came by once we finished eating and took our plates, placing the bill face down. Once they were gone, Bryce met my eyes. Something about his comment nagged me, but the relief he didn't hate me or say I wasn't good enough for his sister won out.

"So, you guys are all dating?" He asked more curiously this time instead of being angered.

"Yup, well." I grimaced. "We're all dating Blake. Only West and Jameson are kind of together, but that's not common knowledge."

"How does that work? Not Package Deal, the four of you dating my sister, and not like the ew things, but the dating stuff," he rushed out, his cheeks heating. I chuckled, feeling more relief.

"We've been spending time together as a group and time individually. We go on dates and hang out. Kinda like normal dating, really. West is really committed to making sure we all talk about shit, which you can guess I love." We both chuckled. "Before I left, I invited West and Jameson to move into the basement."

"No shit." He sat back, his face awed, staring at me like he didn't recognize me. "You, my grumpy friend who likes his space and everything just so… you invited people into your space?"

"Yep." I felt smug as I smiled.

"Fuck. *This is* a big deal."

I tossed a wad of napkins at him. "No shit, asshole."

Bryce chuckled, but the tension between us left, the familiar bond between us returning.

"I wouldn't have kept something a secret if it wasn't the real deal. I love your sister, but I think they do, too."

"Why Olson, though?" he asked, his voice hardening.

"You know he's not as bad—"

Bryce held up his hands, his face stony. "Don't. Don't defend him. I can't take you being with my sister and friends with my nemesis on the same day."

"Fair. But I think you should consider that Blake doesn't spend time with people she doesn't deem worthy, and considering he just found out he has a four-year-old daughter, his whole world has shifted. He's changed."

"Fuck. Seriously?"

I nodded, and he hung his head, his fist hitting the table.

"But it's *Olson*," he whined. I gave a dry laugh.

"I know, and despite what happened between you guys, I can't help but wonder if there was a misunderstanding."

"Hard to misunderstand—"

I stopped him, cutting him off this time. "You don't have to explain it to me, but you will have to tell your sister. Because I don't think he's going anywhere," Bryce grumbled, leaning back and crossing his arms, acting more like a toddler than a thirty-one-year-old. "You don't have to be best friends with him, but you do need to deal with your shit and figure out a way to be around him. Something tells me he might not be the same guy he used to be."

"It still doesn't justify…" he grumbled.

I held up my hands. "I know, but maybe if you give him the opportunity, he'll show you he's changed."

"Unless there are genies or angels involved, I doubt that."

I held back a laugh at the genie part. No way I was telling Bryce that Blake had a magic lamp vagina. There were some things you didn't need to tell your best friend.

"Are we good?" I asked, pulling out cash and tossing it on the table.

"I'm still pissed at you," he mumbled.

"I expected as much."

Bryce sighed, meeting my eyes. "But you're my best friend, and I love you. If you can make my sister happy, then I'll give you my blessing if that's what you need."

We stepped out of the diner, walking side by side as we headed back to the hotel. "I was going to choose her, whether or not you did," I admitted.

"And for some reason, despite being the one *not* chosen, it shows me how serious you are and gives me reassurance you're not messing around with her."

"I would never." My voice was gruff, my words loud.

"I know." Bryce nodded, and I accepted it. The cord that connected our friendship in my heart snapped back in place, and I felt whole again. I still needed to make amends to him, but knowing we'd be okay felt good.

"How long are you here for?" I asked as we neared the hotel.

He shook his head, wiping his face. "Honestly… I was supposed to head back this morning, but I need to stick around and make things right with BB. I don't know if she told you what happened in her room." He cringed, glancing at me. "I feel awful. So, yeah, I'll pay a fine for missing the game, not that it matters much anyway," he mumbled, but I caught it.

"What's going on, Bryce?"

He sighed and gave another wry chuckle. "I never could

get anything past you. I'm guessing the only reason I've gotten away with it this long is that you've been too consumed with Blake."

Shit. I'd been a lousy friend in more than one way. Hiding my relationship with Blake hadn't done either of us any favors and only ended up hurting all the people I cared about.

As we made our way into the hotel, Bryce caught me up on the struggles he'd been having with the team. I listened, letting him vent. It reminded me nothing in life was guaranteed. Even when it looked like someone had a perfect life, everyone had something going on underneath.

We stopped at the elevator bay. Bryce looked even more exhausted after spilling his demons. He rubbed his head, glancing at me. "You wouldn't happen to have two queens in your room, would you?"

"Yeah, do you wanna crash in it?"

"Thank god, I don't think I've ever been this dead on my feet. I'll text Blake and see if I can catch up with her later."

I nodded, opening my phone and debating whether to skip the game. I still had a few hours before I needed to be at the field. I decided to take a nap first and see if that helped.

I gave Blake a brief update, checked in on West, and reported it to Coach Phillips, while also adding I wasn't feeling well in case I needed an out.

Bryce and I didn't talk the rest of the way to my room, both of us barely able to get our shoes off before we crashed onto the beds.

BLAKE

RELIEVED I'D FINALLY BEEN ABLE TO GET A HOLD OF HAWK rushed through me, and I sank on the bed. Now, I just had to hope he found Bryce.

I could feel Emory's stare on the back of my head as the door closed, Luke leaving now that she'd cleaned him up. Thankfully, his injury didn't appear serious, and he could play later. I felt horrible that Bryce had attacked him, but Luke had brushed it off, stating he was owed it.

I didn't like it, but I didn't want to get in the middle of them. I had enough of my own drama.

"So…" she drawled when I didn't immediately jump up to explain. "That looked like fun." Emory gave me a big grin as she plopped onto the bed, shifting me. I groaned, falling back, hoping it would be easier if I wasn't looking at her head on.

"I think we have different definitions of fun, Em."

"Eh. To each their own." She poked me in the side, and I rolled over, narrowing my eyes at her.

"How was the interview? I didn't get to ask you much about it yesterday."

"Nope. We're not skipping what all that was about." She twirled her finger, grinning. I sighed, dropping back to the bed.

"It was worth a try. Could we get sugar and caffeine? I can't deal with this day without a bunch of calories."

"You're speaking my love language, Filia."

I quickly threw on a pair of leggings, a bra, and a hoodie. I tossed my hair into a ponytail and pulled a hat over it.

"God, I want to call in sick. But Rue left, so I doubt that's likely," I moaned as we headed out.

"I'll help you. Just tell me which baseball player to touch. I'll take one for the team." She winked, bumping my hip with hers.

"I don't touch the players." I frowned.

"Could've fooled me."

I stuck my tongue out at her, laughing despite myself. We entered a coffee shop and bakery a few minutes later, and the smell of sugar and caffeine instantly healed my nerves. I took a deep breath, feeling myself already being energized. I needed one of these in my home.

"Ah, yes," Emory moaned, the sound practically pornographic. "That's the good stuff." She inhaled, her whole body shaking.

"I worry about you, boo." My face heated as people stared. Emory shrugged, not caring, as she perused the bakery cabinet and picked out a few things for us both. Once our order was up, we went to a small table in the corner, giving us a semblance of privacy.

"So..." she said before biting her chocolate croissant. Rolling her eyes, she moaned again. "Oh, that's heaven."

As I drank my latte and ate my sugary carbs, I updated Emory on everything that had occurred yesterday.

My fears. Graham's injury. My realization.

"People might not understand my choices, and my

parents might be disappointed, but it's my life, and I want to be happy." I shrugged. "They make me happy."

"I'm so proud of you, Lake. But what was that scene I walked in on? I've never seen Bryce so upset before."

I sighed, filling her in on the whole Bryce ordeal—first with Hawk and then Luke.

"Yikes." She grimaced.

"Yep." I nodded, wrapping my hands around my latte. "I still don't know what the beef between them is. But I don't even know if I care because unless it's about me, it shouldn't matter. They need to deal with their own relationship or lack thereof."

"What now?"

I shrugged. "What can I do but wait."

She gave me a sympathetic smile as we walked back to the hotel. "How about you introduce me to your other two boyfriends?"

"I can do that. I want to check on Graham anyway."

I glanced around the hotel lobby but didn't spot Bryce or Hawk. I hoped it meant they were talking. We rode the elevator up to Tucker and Graham's floor, and I didn't spot anyone from the team. It was odd, but I'd take the reprieve.

Tucker opened the door shirtless, his sweats hanging low on his hips, and I stalled, taking him in. He smiled, pulling me into a hug. I loved that he never hesitated. Tucker didn't know how to hide things, and I loved that about him. His arms felt so good that I had to remind myself not to break down in tears, but apparently, I wasn't that great at hiding it.

"What's wrong, Honey Bee?" he whispered into my neck.

"Bryce."

"You guys will work it out."

"I hope so, but he found Luke in my room this morning, and before I had a chance to explain things, he pushed him."

"Yikes," Tucker grimaced.

"Hey! That's what I said." Emory chuckled behind me,

reminding me she was there. I kind of loved that Tucker hadn't even noticed. Emory was gorgeous, and it was only because she was so sweet that I didn't wish her horrible things.

Tucker pulled back and smiled but kept his arm around me. "You must be Emory."

"Perfect; I love it when my reputation precedes me." They both laughed, and I glanced between them, suddenly scared of what they'd get up to together.

"Oh, no, you two together… I'm in trouble! Graham! Where are you? Save me," I hollered, shaking my head at the other two.

They both laughed, but I was being serious. It wasn't until that moment I realized how similar Tucker and Emory were.

"Well, since our lovely guest didn't introduce me, I'm Tucker, and Graham is the hideous old man."

"I heard that!" the man in question yelled. I walked into the room and spotted Graham sitting up on the bed. He wore the nerdy shirt I'd made him—'thick thighs and catcher vibes.'

"Love the shirt."

"Some hottie made it. Though, I think she got the size wrong."

It was a little snug, but I wasn't complaining.

"Maybe blame the man who does your laundry?" I teased. I sat down next to him, checking out his stitches. I didn't know what for, but I hoped if it was infected, I'd be able to tell. I kissed his cheek, leaning my head against his shoulder. Graham wrapped his arm around me.

"How are you feeling?"

"Much better now."

"You're still not playing," Tucker said, and I jolted up, turning to Graham and narrowing my eyes.

"Don't worry, Tuck. The doctor won't clear him. I'll make sure of it," I said, my eyes narrowed.

"I wasn't going to," Graham insisted. But I had a feeling he had a little, but realized it was a losing battle.

"Graham, this is Emory, my sorta cousin/best friend."

"Nice to meet you, Emory."

"You too, cutie. So, tell me everything about how you met Blake," she said, lying across the spare bed. I rolled my eyes but settled in between Tucker and Graham as they shared their side of the mistake texts.

Graham and Tucker asked Emory about her stay so far in America and how her interviews went. Throughout the whole conversation, they both touched me in little ways. A hand on my shoulder, my thighs, or ankle. An arm around my shoulders, a hand linked with mine, brushing fingers through my hair. It was constant like they couldn't help themselves.

I loved it, relishing how easily they showed affection in front of others. I might even love them, but since that emotion felt too big, I shoved it down for now.

My first priority was to fix things with Bryce. I kept staring at my phone, slightly relieved when Hawk messaged.

> Hawk: We talked. We're grabbing some sleep. Bryce said he'll catch you at the game or for dinner. He's missing his game.

> Blake: Okay. I'll be at the game. I didn't figure out a way to call in. Find me if you can. I need to see you to ensure everything's all right.

He didn't respond, but I figured he was already asleep. I sent a message to Luke next, hoping he was okay.

> Blake: Hey, just wanted to check in with you. You good?

> Luke: I'm fine, Slugger. Promise.

Blake: If I don't see you before, find me after.

Luke: Will do.

Feeling slightly better, I put my phone in my hoodie. When I realized the time, I knew I needed to get ready and head to the stadium.

"What are you doing during the game?" I asked Graham, tilting my head to him.

"What do you mean?"

"Since you can't play, are you staying back here?" He frowned.

"I might not be playing, but I'm still going to the game."

"Oh." My eyes widened. I hadn't expected that answer. He smiled, soothing the line between my brows.

"I was going to see if you needed an assistant. I'm injured, not an invalid."

I grinned wide. "Looks like I get two assistants today. Oh, I can't wait to be your boss!"

Emory and Graham glanced at each other. "Maybe—"

"Nope," I cut them off, laughing maniacally. "You're all mine."

"That sounds creepy, but I'm kind of turned on," Tucker said.

Shoving him on the bed as he laughed, I grabbed Emory and hurried out of the room, my cheeks on fire.

"We'll meet you in the lobby!"

I instantly regretted having them follow me around. Not that they weren't fun to have, but they both kept asking questions, and I had to stop every two seconds to explain something. Because of that, I missed out on seeing Hawk and Luke before the game started. I wasn't sure if Bryce was here, but we hadn't seen him yet as we walked around the stadium. I had to keep moving since I was behind on obtaining new footage and would be here all night splicing the few things I did get at this rate.

"Not to sound like an asshole, but I never thought about how much went into all this," Graham said.

"You're not the first to assume that," I said, looking at the digital screen on my camera.

"I'm bored," Emory said for the tenth time.

"Go get food and annoy someone else, then."

"Cool. I'll find someone for my bingo card. I'll text ya later." She flounced off, and my shoulders sagged. I loved her, but I was drained. I hadn't realized it until thoughts of pushing someone I loved down a flight of stairs popped up. Oops.

"Bingo card?" Graham asked.

"You don't want to know." I smiled, but it didn't reach all the way.

"You okay?" His brows furrowed. Of course, he didn't miss it. I met his eyes, and he wrapped an arm around me.

"Not really. I'm emotionally exhausted, physically tired, and feel unsettled. I just want things to be right with my brother."

"You're just getting footage of the plays? Both batting and field?" He asked, changing the subject.

"Uh yeah. I need some dugout, too; I just haven't gotten up the courage to head down there yet. I'm not sure I can see Hawk, much less Luke, and not want to kiss either of them."

"And I just need to press here?" he asked, pointing to something.

"I mean, there's more to it, but ultimately, yes."

"Cool. Give me your camera. I'll go to the dugout."

"Why?" I furrowed my brow this time. I was tired but didn't need him to do my job.

"Because you're going to go talk to your brother."

"My brother?" Graham placed his hands on my shoulders, spun me, and pointed.

"Hey, Blanket." My brother stood a few feet away, a shy smile I wasn't used to seeing on his face. But most of all, it was the look of remorse and regret.

I pulled the strap over my shoulder and placed it in Graham's hands. "This is my baby. Please don't break her."

"I won't." He said it seriously, and I knew he would take care of her. I glanced around and decided to go for it, kissing his cheek.

Once I was free of my duties, I ran to my brother, practically tackling him in a hug. He didn't hesitate, wrapping his arms around me, too.

"I'm so sorry," we both said simultaneously. Tears fell down my cheeks, and I pulled back, laughing with Bryce. I was tired of crying, but these were more in relief.

"Come on, I know a place." I pulled my brother to the office where I kept my stuff. I was overdone with the emotional heart to hearts, but I knew this needed to occur. I wouldn't be able to rest until it did.

"I should've told you the truth about Hawk years ago," I started, but Bryce held up his hands.

"Let me, please." His words were full of anguish, so I nodded. "Hawk explained, um, your situation."

My cheeks heated. Fuck. Who knew your brother knowing you were getting regularly railed by four guys would be embarrassing? Huh!

"And while it shocked me initially, I just wanted you to know I'll support you."

Shocked, I wrapped my arms around him, smelling his detergent and soap, the fragrance comforting me. If Bryce was on board, I could fight any battle.

"Thank you."

"I do have one favor."

I nodded. "I'm willing to listen, but if it's not to date Luke, I can't do that."

His jaw tensed, his nostrils flaring slightly, but he nodded. "It's not Luke. I…" He shook his head. "That's a story for later. Hawk said I need to deal with my shit with him first and not pull you into it, and while I hate it. He's right."

"Then what's the favor?"

"Promise to let me be there when you tell Mom and Dad." He grinned, giving me one of his shit-eating ones. I slapped his forearm playfully.

"Ass."

"Come on! It will be great fun. I want to record it and use it for our Christmas card."

"Why do I love you?" I asked, fighting a smile.

"Because I'm awesome, duh." He rolled his eyes but smiled.

"Ugh. Fine. I'll try to include you when I tell them, but I can't promise anything. The first chance I get to, I'm taking it. I don't want another situation like the one at the hospital."

"Fair point. But in all seriousness, if you need support, I'll be there for that, too."

"Thanks, Bry. Love you more than fully charged batteries."

"Oh, snap. Well, I love you more than perfectly brewed coffee."

My shoulders dropped, and my heart returned to my chest. Finally, it felt like things were slotting into place. I'd been so scared that Bryce wouldn't listen to us and push me away. To have him supporting me and accepting me was everything and such a Bryce move that I felt dumb for questioning him in the first place.

"Where'd Emory go?" he asked, wrapping his arm around my shoulder as we returned to the game. He tried to act nonchalant, but his voice had risen slightly higher than usual.

"Why?" I eyed him out of the side.

"I didn't get to say hi earlier. That's all."

"Mm-hmm. She went to get food and fill a bingo square."

"Bingo?" Bryce frowned.

"Um, yeah." I hesitated. It felt weird sharing this with Bryce for some reason. "Something she found online. A travel challenge."

"What kind of challenge?"

"Like the kind that tells you certain things to find."

We stopped, and Bryce grasped my shoulders, giving me his big brother look.

"Blake, quit beating around the bush and just tell me already."

I sighed. "It's a sex challenge. So, like, finding someone with a mullet, having sex in a public place, someone with tattoos or a motorcycle. That kind of thing."

"Oh." Bryce blinked, and I almost swore I saw jealousy flash in his eyes. But it was gone as quick as it came. "Thank you for telling me. Do you have plans after?"

Hello, abrupt subject change.

"Nothing solid. Would you like to have dinner with my… lovers-plus?" I cringed. We really needed a better name.

"What the fuck?" Bryce laughed while also grimacing.

"Tucker," I said, shrugging. "He also suggested para-mours galore."

"God, no. Please don't ever say any of that again. My ears can't take it."

"Lovers-plus. Lovers-plus. Lovers-plus," I taunted like a little sister should.

Bryce ran from me, covering his ears as I laughed, trailing behind him. We both slowed when we got back to the public side, my face hurting from laughing. I still felt physically tired, but my heart was on the path to being restored.

We walked through the stands, and I glanced at the dugout. Graham was down there talking to Tucker and

Hawk, and I even spotted Luke close by. I relaxed at the sight of the four of them. The game was in the top of the eighth inning, and the YellowJackets were up by two runs.

"Want to watch the last bit of the game?" I asked Bryce. He nodded, so we took some empty seats and settled in as we watched his old teammates bat. Midway through the inning, a whispered chatter started around us, but it stopped each time I turned to see what it was about.

At the bottom of the ninth, Bryce and I stood so we could make our way to the clubhouse. The chatter and looks continued, making me more paranoid.

Emory waved us down, running full force to us with her phone in her hand. She almost knocked us both down when she stopped, and Bryce righted her before she did. She bent over, her hands on her knees, and gulped in big breaths.

"Hi… Bryce… Nice… to… see… you…while… not… in… a fight." She smiled at my brother, then appeared to remember why she'd run to us. "Lake!" She took a big gulp of air. "I've been trying to find you."

"What's wrong?" Bryce asked, gripping her arms.

"Not me." She looked at me, and that was when I noticed the pity. She thrust her phone under Bryce's face, and he took it from her. I watched as he read whatever was on the screen, his face transforming from concern to hatred and then fear.

"What is it?" I asked, my heart sinking to the floor. Had someone died? "Is it Mom? Dad? Mallory's baby?" Still couldn't say sibling.

"No. As far as I know, they're all okay." He swallowed, meeting my eyes. "Someone leaked a story. A story about you dating four baseball players."

My heart pounded, and I tried to find words. "But… but… there's no way to prove it. It's just gossip," I tried, my voice high-pitched as some of the media training sputtered out. *Spin. Spin. Spin.*

"There are pictures," Emory said, her voice soft. "And it

says it's from a reliable source. Someone in your department."

There was no way this was Rue. Which meant… fucking fuckface fucker.

Graham's injury and my brother's arrival had been all the misdirection my life's proverbial pitcher needed. I'd taken my eyes off the ball, and now I was being beaned with it. I didn't know if it was the reverse curse—the screwball—but there was no doubt I'd been screwed.

It was the pitch slap heard across the world.

LUKE

My leg bounced as I sat on the bench watching the game, but my mind wasn't present. The ache in my face kept reminding me of what a complete dipshit I was. I'd somehow convinced myself that since Blake had deceived me, I didn't need to worry about my past coming back to haunt me.

Yet despite my perception changing on our whole encounter, I clung to that erroneous belief, ignoring the fact that one day, I would have to face her brother and his hatred of me.

I'd done a lot of stupid shit in my life, but probably the dumbest was what I'd done to Bryce Baker. The worst part was, I hadn't even intended to be a thorn in his side—well, at least not at first.

The first two things were out of my control. Honestly.

During my rookie year, I'd been selected to be part of an "Up and Coming in Major League Baseball" article. The magazine selected five first- and second-year players across the league. Which, of course, included Bryce Baker and Hawk Anderson.

I'd always looked up to Baker and had followed his

career, hoping to emulate his success one day. I told the reporter the same, but they spun it that I believed myself better than Baker and would soon beat his records. I liked to hope they hadn't intended for a rivalry to be born, but because of that article and the events after, one was.

For the rest of my rookie year and the next, it was all any reporter asked me about. Announcers would comment on our 'rivalry' during each game, and sports analysts would compare our stats side-by-side, effectively reinforcing a rivalry that had never existed.

I tried to correct it, saying I admired Baker, but that somehow made me the humble one and him the arrogant one. Our roles were cast in the media, and we were forced to play them. Next, I tried to talk to him to explain my side. But Bryce wanted nothing to do with me. Not that I blamed him. The focus had shifted from what we were doing on the field to what the other was, and it was a heavy shadow to play under.

The second time I slighted him was when I'd been offered a sponsorship over Baker. Again, I didn't know we were both being considered, but to him, it was something else I took from him. The rivalry grew, and a feud was born.

So, every time our teams played against one another, it became an all-out war. Oh, yeah, did I forget to mention we were also division rivals?

The media ate it up, increasing the animosity between our two ball clubs. The year I got the winning out in the Division Series was, you guessed it, against Bryce. It didn't matter that we lost in the next round and didn't go on to the World Series; I'd tagged Baker out at first in the bottom of the ninth during game five, and that was all anyone talked about.

By my fourth year, our rivalry had solidified into a living, breathing thing all of its own. I stopped any attempts to talk to him so I could explain. Considering they'd gone unanswered for years, his avoidance created the perfect storm of emotions within me: the constant rejection from the player I admired, the stress of being pitted against one another, and the minimization of my own success whittled down to only a mere byproduct of Baker's hatred boiled over.

So, I leaned into it and became the cocky asshole everyone wanted me to be. I upped the party lifestyle, hopping from bed to bed and drinking nonstop. The people I surrounded myself with weren't any better, and the instant my success dimmed, they were gone. It reinforced everything I'd always believed—I wasn't good enough on my own. I needed success to have friends, money to have women, and winning games to have fans.

Without it, I was nothing—just a sad, drunken loser.

This led to the third reason Bake hated me, the one grievance he legitimately could have against me. It was my second to last year playing for the Denver Rockets, and our team was shit. I'd been hearing for weeks already how the Blue Devils had been doing, inciting my own self-hatred and worthlessness. I needed someone to blame, and the media had given me a target years ago—Baker.

It was petty, but I was beyond caring at that point. Focusing on Baker gave me something to think about instead of my miserable life. So, while we were visiting for our first away series, I led an attack on Bryce.

I had his car towed, bribed someone to change his walk-up song, and posted anonymously on social media that Baker loved when fans hugged him but was too shy to ask. I wanted a fight, a proper reason to hate him, but Bryce ignored it all and laughed it off like a pro. It only incensed my rage, and I felt desperate when we lost that week of games.

I was so desperate that I hooked up with his girlfriend at the time on purpose.

I later learned from a mutual friend that Baker had

planned to propose that night but walked in on me fucking his girlfriend from behind instead.

Like I said, I was a dumbass.

He didn't rage at me or go to the press and drag me through the mud. He did nothing, and that made me feel even worse.

I'd wanted the world to know how much of an asshole I was, to give credence to the feelings I held inside, but I couldn't even do that right.

Later that season, he got injured and moved to the Yellow-Jackets for rehab, ending our rivalry and feud. If we weren't playing in the same league, the media didn't care. That was until before spring training three years ago when the Rockets traded me to the Blue Devils.

And I took Baker's position on the team.

Again, I had no part in it, but it didn't matter. It had to be some cosmic justice that he took first baseman back this season, inadvertently giving me time to fall for Blake.

Not that it mattered since the name Luke Olson meant shit to him. There was no world where he'd ever allow me to date his sister. My time with Blake was officially over.

"Olson! You're on deck."

I jolted, the sudden slap back to reality hitting me in the face, and I swayed as I stood, my vision blurring slightly. I grabbed my batting glove, bat, and helmet and stumbled up the steps, blinking myself back to the game.

The voice in my head told me to give up that I'd known all along that my time with Blake was limited. That was why I agreed to date her with three other guys, because there was no long-term for us and I'd been stupid to hope for more.

But the part of me falling in love remembered how it felt to be on a date with her and Willow. How wonderful it had been to play ball in the backyard with the other guys. Or how they wanted to invite her class to the game for her birthday.

It was the first time since I went pro that I felt like I had genuine friends. Not guys who wanted to be around me because I was playing well, but men who valued me for the messed up person I was, and it had nothing to do with baseball.

And my Slugger... She was everything.

Discovering I was a father had been the slap in the face I needed to get my life on track. To stop drinking and focus on a future outside of baseball one day. Not being sent back to the majors was a reality check, forcing me to open my eyes and appreciate where I was instead of wishing to be somewhere else.

But neither of those was the reckoning Blake had been.

When I thought she'd lied to me, I'd been wrecked. I couldn't play, and the need to drink had never been stronger. If I hadn't had Willow at home, I would've succumbed and drank myself stupid.

Being with Blake showed me the man I could be. And if I didn't fight for her now, I deserved to lose her.

My music faded out, and I took my stance at the plate. The noise of the crowd became muted as I lifted my bat up and zeroed in on the pitcher. He eyed me, watching the catcher for the call as I cataloged as much about him as possible. After playing so many games against the same team back-to-back, you picked up on tells. And Jacobs had a big one.

He shifted his foot, sliding the ball between his fingers as he gripped it. I took a breath, holding it for a second before letting it out. My heart slowed, my mind focused, and I found my zone. As soon as the ball left his fingers, my muscles bunched, preparing to strike. The ball flew toward me, and I waited, not giving in to the need to swing early.

Now!

Swinging through, I felt the ball hit the wood, the sound of the contact music to my ears as it flew. Throwing my bat back, I took off for first base, looking to the coach for my cue.

Reading the motion, I rounded toward second and pumped my arms as hard as possible. I caught sight of the outfielder throwing the ball infield, and I dove, sliding on my knee toward the base.

My hand slapped against it just as the second baseman reached down to tag me. I held my breath as I waited to hear the call.

"Safe!"

Jumping up, my heart thumped against my chest, and tingles raced through my body as that alive feeling rushed me.

This was baseball. This was how I wanted to play.

I rounded home plate two plays later, giving us the lead, and my teammates slapped me on the butt and back with congratulations as I entered the dugout. The feeling of camaraderie and achievement swarmed me, giving me that high I loved.

Yet, I knew despite loving this game, I could live without it.

But Blake… I didn't know if I could anymore.

Which left me with one goal in mind—I had to find a way for Bryce to forgive me. And this time, I wouldn't let him brush me off. My heart—and I was expecting Willow's, too—was on the line.

It was rally cap time.

**CHAPTER
SIXTY**

TUCKER

Luke entered the dugout amid celebration, his smile genuine for once as he acknowledged his teammates. It was then that I finally saw the man he was away from the team— the man Blake had feelings for.

"Good job," I said as he sat next to me. "I thought for sure Samuels was gonna tag your old ass out."

He chuckled, nodding. "My muscles agree with you."

"Something changed," I said, leaving it as a statement rather than a question. He glanced over out of the side of his eyes before facing front.

"People don't give you enough credit."

"You're not wrong." I grinned, knocking his shoulder. "But flattery won't get you out of answering. Come on, we're bros who hose—"

"I'd leave it at that if I were you," Graham said from my left.

I turned at his voice, that buzzy feeling I always had with him more potent. I gave him a smile and had to restrain myself from pulling his delectable lips to my own. His eyes heated as we stared at one another until he shifted on the bench, picked up Blake's camera, and resumed shooting.

"Well?" I asked, clearing my throat and returning to Luke.

"Believe it or not, I had an epiphany."

"Ooh, do tell!" I placed my head on my fist and stared at him, giving him owlish eyes.

Luke shook his head, laughing. "I'm kind of an asshole."

"That's the epiphany? I thought they were supposed to be new information."

Luke laughed. "And I haven't always made decisions I'm proud of—"

"Like the rumor you slept with three porn stars, or that you paid someone to make your enemy's clothes smell like shellfish. Or, or, or, the one you trashed a hotel bar because they refused to let you start a jello-wrestling ring—"

Luke held up his hand to stop me, his eyes huge. "None of those are true, and if you're gonna guess everything I'm saying beforehand, then I'll never get this out."

"Sorry." I mimed zipping my lips and tossing the key. Graham snorted next to me, though he pretended to be looking at something on the screen.

"But yes, I was reckless and idiotic, playing a part I didn't want but then didn't know how to stop. Because of that, Baker hates me, some of it for good reason."

"And now you're wondering if that's gonna mess up your chance with Blake," I said, feeling the weight of his sadness.

"That's just it… I was until I realized I'd choose Blake over baseball," he whispered, holding my eyes.

"Whoa." My eyes widened, and my own heart skipped a beat.

Luke nodded, and I could see the determination and resolution in his eyes. He meant it. Fuck. He loved her. I wonder if he even realized it.

"I'm gonna make things right with Baker. Do you think Hawk will help?"

I chewed my bottom lip in thought. "I dunno. That might go against best friend code, and he's already on thin ice with hiding his relationship."

Luke slumped down. "Well, I'm not giving up." He crossed his arms, his eyes far away as he thought.

I nudged him, and he looked up at me. "Good. But you don't need Hawk to make up with Baker."

"I've tried over the years, and he didn't want to hear anything I had to say."

Aw, was Olson pouting? Why was that so adorable? I bit back a smile.

"I bet he will now," Graham offered. "He loves Blake, so he'll do it for her. Even if it's just to say he did. But it means you have an opportunity."

"And we'll help," I said.

"Thanks, but I don't want to put this mess on you two."

"We're friends, teammates, and dating the same girl. That makes us family, Olson. Plus, don't forget I'm Willow's favorite uncle," I whispered. "Your mess is our mess. That's how it works. You don't have to accept our help, but it's there."

Luke stared at me like I'd grown a second head, and I carefully lifted my hand onto my hat, checking for bubblegum. When I didn't come into contact with anything, I sighed in relief. Graham snickered next to me before leaning over me and making my 'do not touch Graham while in the dugout' rule even more challenging to keep.

"You said it yourself. He's smarter than people give him credit for. Don't be one of the dumb ones." Graham lifted his brow in a challenge, and I had to fight myself not to maul the man. Stupid rules were stupid.

Luke debated Graham's words while I listed the stats of pitches in my head, willing my cock to soften. By the time I got to knuckleball, Luke agreed with Graham.

"You're right. It's time to bring in the outfield. I need all the help I can get."

I snorted, patting Luke's leg. "It's cute you think I'm outfield, my friend." Luke rolled his eyes but accepted my words, his shoulders relaxing.

For the rest of the inning, the three of us brainstormed ideas, and it gave me something to focus on outside of not having Graham behind the plate with me.

Not that I pitched awfully, but it wasn't my best, either. It helped once he entered the dugout and talked me through some pitches, but it wasn't the same. Coach pulled me for the closer in the eighth, and I didn't even care. Pitching without Graham sucked. It made me thankful I didn't have to do it often, and I viewed Luke differently. Not having a good friend on the team would be so lonely. No wonder he was a broody loner most days.

Thankfully, the rest of the team held it together, and we won by two runs. I'd continued to toss out ideas to Graham and Luke when he was present, and by the time we headed into the clubhouse, we had a solid plan in place.

Graham left to find Blake and, hopefully, Bryce, enacting step one of our plan. There was no time like the present to fix this, especially since Bryce would head back to Columbus tonight.

"We have a problem," Hawk gritted, his face stony and red. I glanced at Luke, finding him just as confused. Had Bryce refused already?

"What?" I asked, stripping out of my uniform.

Hawk shook his head. "Hurry and change."

Luke and I nodded, speeding through our routines as we showered, cooled down, and redressed. I expected Luke would get called to press, but when no one called his name, we headed out of the locker room together.

"What do you think it is?" I asked.

He swallowed but shook his head. "No clue."

Hawk waited for us outside the locker room, leaning against the wall, his face still as stoic and shut down as ever. He said nothing as he turned and walked off, apparently wanting us to follow.

Luke and I exchanged anxious glances before we followed Hawk through the tunnels, heading toward the stadium. The air felt heavier with each step, and I worried something awful had happened. My anxiety climbed up my throat to the point of choking me, and I couldn't take it any longer.

Grabbing Hawk's shoulder, I pulled him to a stop. He narrowed his eyes at me, giving me a look that would make most people piss their pants. But my panic was immune to angry faces.

"Tell us something! I can't take this! Is Blake okay? Did someone die? Is it *Willow*?"

"Oh, shit. Willow. You think it could be *Willow*?" Luke asked, his voice more panicked now.

"It's not Willow," Hawk said, glaring at me harder. I held my hands up, stepping back.

"Sorry, but I'm not someone who can be told we have a problem and to hurry with that face without jumping to the worst conclusions. I need information," I huffed.

Hawk gritted his teeth, his jaw jumping as he clenched it. "Someone leaked to the press that Blake is dating the four of us."

I rolled my eyes. "So? It's not like they have proof."

Hawk didn't budge, his fists opening and closing. "Do you really think I'd be this angry if it wasn't serious? Now, will you follow me so we can comfort our girlfriend and figure out how to deal with this, or should I tell you my entire life story?" he deadpanned.

"I mean, I wouldn't mind hearing it one day but now's not the time, Hawk. Geesh. Pick your moments," I joked, trying to lighten the mood in an attempt to avoid my freakout. It didn't work.

Hawk rolled his eyes but turned and continued walking, though it was more stomping than walking. I glanced over at Luke; his earlier confidence about confronting Bryce was gone, and nothing but fear lined his features.

"Hey, we'll figure this out. Team, remember?"

"But Willow," he mumbled. He swallowed, his eyes meeting mine. "I can't lose her." His words were guttural and brought tears to my eyes.

No, he couldn't lose her.

"You won't," I promised, though I didn't know how I'd keep this one. I clasped him on the shoulder, instilling all the hope I could.

That doubt that I would lose them all surfaced, and I struggled to knock it away. Maybe I'd been kidding myself the whole time, believing we could be a family? The world didn't like anything different, and not only was I in an unconventional relationship, but my sexuality had changed.

I had no clue if I was bi, pan, or even fluid. I tried to look it up the other night, but all the terms and definitions had overwhelmed me, and I'd exited out, assuming I had time to come to grips with it before people knew.

Time was now up, and I didn't know if they only leaked Blake and us or if it was all out there. And if it wasn't, then it was only a matter of time before it was.

The reality was... I didn't care if people knew I loved Graham and was in a relationship with him and Blake, plus two others. But the questions that would come, the answers I needed to have but didn't yet, and the stress it would put on our relationship *that* terrified me.

I could lose everything I've ever wanted.

I turned to Luke, determination and resolve shining in my eyes. I refused to allow other people to decide my future.

"We might be behind in the count, but we're not out. We're gonna catch them sleeping and remind them of our crackerjack skills. Forget the single; we needed a grand slam. Are you with me?"

Hawk stared at us from a door he held open, glaring like he was mad we were taking too long, but I knew this was important. If we didn't walk in there united, we'd drop the ball, and Blake would be the casualty.

Luke swallowed but slowly nodded. His fear receded slightly, and he pushed his shoulders back, some of his earlier confidence returning.

"I'm with you." Luke gripped my forearm, the action pushing my fear away.

Hawk stopped us before we entered, his shoulders relaxing as he glanced between us. "I'm with you, too."

Then he turned, continuing to stomp forward while I tried to pick up my jaw before the door shut in my face.

"There's our first home run, only three more to get our grand slam."

"You think Blake would let us—" I asked.

"Nope." Luke chuckled, shoving me through the door. The question had been worth it for that smile.

GRAHAM

I RAN MY EYES OVER TUCKER AS HE ENTERED THE ROOM, MY NEED to ensure he wasn't freaking out riding me hard. He gave me a crooked smile, easing some of my nerves as he bounded into the room with Luke. None of the fear I expected was present on his face, only determination.

My heart settled, and I took my first full breath since Emory had tracked me down, bringing me to this room and filling me in on what had occurred. I wanted to feel guilty for leaving Blake to go to the dugout, but I knew that wasn't helpful, so I brushed it off and focused on what I could do to make this right.

Tucker walked over to Blake, pulling her from Hawk's arms and planting a kiss on her lips. Bryce turned his head, his jaw ticking. I wasn't sure if it was the display of affection or Luke.

Luke had stalled when he entered beside Tucker, his eyes wide when he took in the people present, including the guy we'd just worked on a plan to win over—Bryce Baker. I half expected Luke to flee, but in a shocking turn of events, he swallowed once and then marched over to Blake.

Now it was his turn to take her from Tucker, smoothing her hair back as he whispered something. Blake hugged him, nodding into his chest as he continued to soothe her. Bryce's nostrils flared, and he crossed his arms but kept his mouth shut. It seemed he was willing to put their beef aside for the moment.

"What do we know?" Hawk asked now that we were all here.

Blake turned in Luke's arms, wiping her face. "There are pictures of me with all of you. Some of them are innocent, others more suggestive."

"But nothing outright sexual?" Tucker asked, grimacing as he glanced back at Bryce and Emory.

"No." Blake shook her head.

"Do we know who?" I asked.

"I'm guessing Mira."

"Wait… as in the director?" Bryce asked, his face turning molten.

"Yeah. From the start, she's been weird with me, like she had something to prove. I finally stood up to her a month ago, and since then, she'd backed off. It was still awkward, especially that day I had Willow with me." She swallowed, glancing around the room like she was choosing her words. "Rue told me yesterday she has a weird rule about dating and that she might've been a little obsessed with, um, you." Blake's cheeks heated. "Add in the fact I spotted her leaving a room early in the morning on the baseball floor… Yeah, I think it's her."

"Which room?" Luke asked, saving her from having to say she was with him. Though, by the way Bryce gritted his teeth, he'd figured it out.

Blake tilted her head. "I hid, so I don't know the number, but it was on the left, a few from the elevator."

"Do you know who?" Bryce asked Luke, shocking us all.

"It's either Davis or Ledger."

"It's not Ledger," Hawk said, surprising us all.

"Ledger, as in the ginger hottie?" Emory asked, swinging her legs back and forth on the table she sat on. Bryce's focus switched to her, and I watched as he clenched his jaw but said nothing. *Interesting.*

"Yes. As in the very *gay* ginger hottie," I added. Tucker and Luke turned, their mouths falling open, but I noticed Hawk and Blake didn't seem surprised.

"Bummer," Emory said, shrugging her shoulders.

"How?" Hawk narrowed his eyes. "That's not common knowledge. He's only out to a few people on the team."

"Wait! Does this mean I get a built-in gaydar now?" Tucker asked, raising his hand.

"Sorry, it doesn't work that way." I chuckled, loving Tucker's enthusiasm. I met Hawk's eyes, remembering he'd asked a question. "I'm one of the few. There's sort of a queer club in the league. Some are out, and others aren't." I shrugged.

"A club! How do I join?" Tucker asked. "That sounds awesome. Is there an initiation? A cool handshake? Are there elected positions? Can I be treasurer?" I laughed as he rambled off questions.

"It's—" I started.

"Not to be an ass, but maybe we can discuss the ins and outs of this club *after* we deal with this fiasco?" Bryce interjected.

"Right. Still not Ledger." I nodded, suddenly feeling like I'd been called out in school by the principal. My face heated, and I dropped my head, crossing my arms over my chest in a protective stance.

"Bry! Not cool." Blake walked over, wrapping her arms around me and resting her head on my chest.

"Ledge told me too, and he might not be as closeted as you believe. One of the guys I was with that first night said it too; I just didn't remember until later because, yeah, beer and puke-face." She grimaced, and I loved her for taking some of the heat off me.

I clung to her, needing the feel of her love to ground me so I didn't spin off into my head, my rejection sensitivity being triggered. When Tucker wrapped his arm around me from behind, they both surrounded me, and my heart slowed, my breathing evened, and I felt as if I returned to my body. I hadn't even noticed I'd had a moment of derealization until I returned. I'd blocked everything else out and floated above my body, separating myself from the yucky feelings I didn't know how to deal with.

"Sorry." Bryce sighed, rubbing his head. "I didn't mean to be rude. I'm just trying to get ahead of this, and every second we don't, feels like quicksand is pulling me under harder."

Bryce appeared contrite, and I knew what it was like to be a brother. Even if I was younger than my sisters, I always wanted to protect them. I swallowed down the cotton in my throat and nodded.

"Yeah. I get it."

Bryce's eyes held mine, and I could see his concern, helping me know he hadn't rejected my contribution out of spite. No, Bryce worried about his sister, which overrode everything else.

With a deep breath, I settled and squeezed the two people who'd become my anchors. "Thanks, I'm good. So, do you have a plan?" I asked Bryce.

He scrubbed a hand over his head, his tired eyes landing on Blake as he debated. Sighing, he placed his hands on his hips, his face soft yet serious as he addressed his sister.

"We need to call in the big guns, Sis. The runner's already on the base, so the only way to save this is to force an out."

"Mom and Dad..." she breathed, her voice hitching.

Bryce nodded, his face morphing to concern. There was no doubt he loved his sister and would do anything to take away her pain.

"If this goes back to Mira and Davis," he gritted, "it stems further than a rumor. There are other things at play here. Sabotage, NDAs, and club policy at the breach. It's not coming from one front, but all of them. It's not just an attack; it's an all-out war." He paced, running his hands through his hair. "I'll be honest, I'm way out of my depth. We need someone who knows how to fight this, whichever you decide."

Blake peered around at the four of us, picking at her fingernails as she struggled to find the words. I took her hand, rubbing my palm over it to soothe her. She gave me a grateful smile, sucked in a breath, and asked what she was nervous about.

"Is this what you guys want? Because it doesn't just affect me. It's your careers. Your lives. I can step down, and no one will care—"

"Not happening," Hawk said, not letting her continue. He stalked forward, crowding her space and cupping her jaw. "I meant it when I said I wasn't going anywhere, Blazy. If this is the fight we have to take, then let me fight beside you. No running this time."

Blake closed her eyes, her body shaking as she leaned into his touch. With a deep breath, she pulled away and faced the three of us. Her eyes were glassy, her face pale, and I worried she was about to say something that would break my heart.

"I'm not running. I just can't make this decision for each of you. You should talk to your agents and maybe the team PR rep and figure out your options. I can't be the reason you lose something. I wouldn't be able to live with myself, and it would ruin our relationship."

She wiped her cheeks, her hand trembling, and she glanced back at Emory and Bryce before returning to us. My heart raced, and I knew it didn't matter what my agent said. I wouldn't walk away from her, from this.

I wanted to talk to my family first so they could hear it

from me, but otherwise, I didn't care. I was tired of hiding parts of myself to make it easier for society to accept me. I'd spent most of my life conforming without considering what made me happy.

Blake and Tucker made me happy, and I liked the bonds I was building with Luke and Hawk. We could be something real—a family. I knew it wouldn't be easy, but I was ready to fight, too. If Blake needed us to take time to think about it so she didn't doubt our affection, then I would. But it didn't change the answer.

No one said anything, the room eerily quiet as Blake's words hung in the air. Luke stared at the ground, his body slumped and defeated. Tucker had his head tilted, more than likely trying to solve this, and Hawk had gone full stubborn. His jaw was tight, his arms crossed like he dared her to get by him. He looked more like a linebacker than a baseball coach. I seemed to be the only one who wasn't freaking out for once.

"If that's what you need, then we'll do it," I said. The others opened their mouths to protest, but I ignored them. "But it changes nothing for me, Sunshine. I want to be with you, and if I have to answer that question for the next fifty years, I will do it with a smile. Because no matter what other people believe about our relationship, I get to come home to you and hold you in my arms. Nothing they do will ever make me want to step away from that."

"Damn, G. Now I really can't wait to be romanced by you if that's a taste of what is to come," Tucker said. He leaned over and wrapped his arm around my shoulders, pressing a kiss to my cheek.

"What he said, Honey Bee. I'll coach Little League and work at the car wash if I have to. Other people don't get to determine how I live my life. Not anymore, at least. You showed me that, actually."

"I did?" she asked, wiping tears from her cheeks.

"Yeah, Bee. You're the bravest person I know." Tuck

smiled at her, and she held it for a second before shaking her head.

"I don't want you to give up your dream, your career."

"Dreams can change," Luke whispered, his head lifted, his eyes landing on her.

"But Willow—" Blake said.

"Isn't going anywhere." He swallowed. "I'll talk to my agent, but I agree with Package Deal. It doesn't change how I feel."

"Welcome to the club!" Tucker cheered. "What's a word for a trio? We could get shirts! Triple Crown? Three Musketeers? Ice cream?" Tucker tilted his head as he thought.

"More like the three stooges," Hawk mumbled, shaking his head as he sighed. Bryce leaned over to his friend.

"You still sure about that? You'll be coaching a little league team at home," Bryce teased, showing his first smile since we walked in.

Luke looked between me and Tucker, frowning. "I changed my mind… I disagree with—"

"Nope, Lukey-booky. You're stuck with me now." Tucker ran at him, throwing his arms around him in a bear hug, and made loud kissy noises as Luke struggled to escape.

"Now, take off your shirt!" Emory chanted.

"Em! Seriously? Now is not the time," Blake groaned, her head falling to her hands.

"What? It was worth a shot." She shrugged and then leaned back, her smile mischievous. "At least get me some popcorn. This is superb entertainment."

Everyone laughed, the tension leaving the room.

"Not to be the adult in the room, but we should head out soon." Bryce looked at us, his shoulders relaxing. "The longer you delay a response, the more speculation you'll gain. I don't want to tell you what to do, but I agree with BB. Talk to your agents and get them up to speed, and then everyone reconvene before any statements are given. I'll call Mom and

Dad and fill them in. I'm sure they'll have lots to say on the matter." He sighed, rubbing his temple. He lifted his eyes, meeting everyone before landing on his sister. "If you're choosing not to deny the story, then you'll need to be united, and you might pull it off."

Everyone nodded, the earlier fear erased as strength and resolution took its place. It might be dumb, but we'd be brave together, which counted for something.

We'd either succeed together or not at all. Just like a team.

CHAPTER
SIXTY-TWO

BLAKE

MY HEAD POUNDED WITH THE INTENSITY OF A THOUSAND DRUMS against my skull, and I swayed a little as we exited the room. I hadn't expected the guys to respond the way they had, easing my heart that they were in this as much as I was. This had been the ultimate test, and they hadn't faltered.

"Your guys are all pretty great," Emory whispered, pulling me close. She linked our arms as we walked.

"Yeah, they are." I nodded, smiling at her, but it didn't reach my eyes. My vision swam, and I swayed, swallowing down the bile that had risen.

"Hey, you okay?"

I nodded, but that only worsened things as the corners of my vision blackened. Great balls of fire!

"Bryce!" Emory shouted, piercing my eardrum.

"Ow," I mumbled, raising my arm to my ear. "Too loud, Em. Ssh."

"Shit."

Warm hands bracketed my face, and I leaned into their warmth. My body felt weightless a moment later, and I sighed in relief. It was much easier to move when I didn't feel so heavy.

"When was the last time you ate, Slugger?"

"She had coffee and a pastry this morning," Emory said next to me. I tried to open my mouth, but it felt glued shut. I attempted to lift my arm instead. However, the thing was heavy and didn't follow my instructions.

"Anything since?" I heard my brother ask, but it sounded far away. "Her blood sugar might've crashed with the added stress. Any other signs or symptoms?"

"I don't know," Emory whispered, her voice shaking. I wanted to reach out to soothe her, but I didn't feel like I had control of my body.

My weight was shifted, and I felt someone lift my arms, proving they still worked. Good, I hadn't become a weighted blob of goo like I felt.

"Anything?"

"No bruises that I can see."

Light pierced my vision, and I pulled away, curling into the darkness. "No," I managed to mumble.

"Pupils seem okay. Her pulse is a little sporadic but doesn't seem too fast," someone mumbled.

"I'm fine," I whined, attempting to swat the hands on me.

"Here, drink this."

Something wet and cold was placed on my lips, and I opened them, allowing the juice to enter my mouth.

"Wait!" Bryce yelled, making me jump. "She's allergic—"

"To mango, I know," Luke said, his voice soothing. "I checked it. It's okay."

"Oh. Um. Good."

The liquid returned, and I drank more, my energy returning slightly as the sugar entered my body. I was shifted again, my body curling into one I recognized as the smell of his expensive cologne reached me. Eventually, I opened my eyes, the light shining too brightly, and I immediately closed them.

"Here, Slugger." A hat was placed on my head, shielding my eyes. "Can you stand now? I think your blood sugar dropped from not eating and stress. You'll feel better once you drink more fluids and eat something."

I nodded, and the world didn't spin this time. Luke stood, taking his smell and heat, and I missed it instantly. He reached out a hand and helped me up. Thankfully, I only wobbled a little before I stabilized. I took the rest of the juice and drank it, some energy returning.

"You good, Blanket?" Bryce asked, worry etched over his features.

"Yeah. Sorry. I didn't mean to worry you." I dropped my eyes, that familiar guilt reemerging.

He stepped forward, ignoring the man behind me as he clasped my hands. "I'm your big brother. I'll always worry about you, BB." He sucked in a breath, lifting his eyes over my shoulder, presumably meeting Luke's eyes. "But I must admit you seem to have some good people looking out for you." I watched my brother swallow, letting some of his rage go as his shoulders dropped. "It's obvious you care about my sister, so I'm willing to put the shit between us in the past if you are?"

Hands landed on my hips, squeezing me. "I'd like that. I never wanted the rivalry to begin with. The media twisted my hero worship of you into a sensational story. After fighting it for so long, I gave into the role they wanted me to play." Luke took a deep breath, letting it out slowly. It seemed like he'd been holding in those words for years and finally had gotten the chance to share them.

"I'm sorry, Baker. I owe you a few of those for the things I did. You might not believe me, but I'm not the same guy I was. I have a daughter now and want to be worthy of Blake. I still have a long way to go, but I'm working on it."

Luke's words shifted something in Bryce, and I watched as my brother let years of hatred go. He was doing what I asked, and I loved him even more for that.

"Thank you for saying that. I know I didn't make it easy, and perhaps we can start fresh and create a new dynamic between us."

"I'd like that." Luke sagged behind me.

"But when it comes to Blake, she gets to decide who she deems worthy, not me." Bryce looked at me, reaching out to take my hand. "And if you weren't to start with, you wouldn't be here now." He dropped my gaze and lifted his back to Luke. He narrowed his eyes, pure menace in his eyes. "I have no problem kicking your ass if you forget and pull any crap. Messing with baseball is one thing, but hurt my sister, and you won't be able to score on or off the field. Got it?"

I heard Luke's swallow behind me, and I wanted to admonish Bryce, but I knew I couldn't. They had to work out their own baggage without me.

"Yep. I got it. I'd even let you."

Bryce nodded once, his face morphing back to one of friendly ease. "Good. Can you get Blake back to the hotel?"

"Yeah. I can do that."

"I'll call the parents and get some food. I'll meet you back in your room," Bryce said before kissing my cheek and squeezing my hand.

"I'll come with you," Emory said, skipping over to him. Bryce stiffened for a millisecond but then relaxed as they headed off, Emory talking a mile a minute. I glanced around, not noticing any of the others.

"Where are…?"

"The guys?" Luke asked.

"Yeah."

"They went separate ways to throw off the press and get a ride. We're to meet them."

"Oh. Cool. Wait, press?" I grimaced. It was already starting. At least now I knew why people had been looking at me during the end of the game.

Luke chuckled as he shifted me, keeping his arm around my waist as we walked. I felt much better now and could walk on my own, but for the first time, I liked someone pampering me.

"I can't believe Bryce is cool with me," Luke muttered.

"He loves me at his core. I knew if he took the time, he'd see what I do."

"But I—" Luke shook his head. "I did some messed up stuff. He should hate me. *You* should hate me."

"Maybe, but that's between you two. I'm not delusional to believe my brother's a saint or that he didn't have a justified reason for hating you, but I realized it didn't matter. It didn't change my feelings for you."

Luke shook his head, his protest on his tongue. I stopped, pressing my finger to his lips.

"If you need to tell me, you can. But it won't change how I feel. I know who you are now, and that's the person I'm falling for. So, tell me if you think it will absolve you, but you don't need it from me."

"You really are amazing, Blake Baker. You say I don't have to prove I deserve you, but you make me want to be better every day."

"You do the same for me, Luke Olson. So how about we agree to keep pushing each other to be our best?"

"I can get behind that." He smiled, his green eyes sparkling and warming my insides.

I pulled him down, taking my time as we kissed. For the first time since I saw the article, I felt calm. Things would be chaotic and a mess, but I wasn't worried about it for once because I had them and didn't have to hide anymore.

"Come on. I'm suddenly *starving*."

Luke chuckled but did not up the pace despite my desire.

He kept us at a steady walk, not letting me pull him when I tried. Thankfully, there were barely any people around as we exited, and I relaxed as we neared the gate.

Unfortunately, relief was short-lived when we came upon the exit, and I spotted reporters around the other guys.

"Shit. Okay, Plan B."

Luke pulled out his phone and sent a text to Hawk. I watched as he ignored the reporter and pulled out his phone. His jaw clenched, but he looked up and nodded. I didn't think he could see us in the dark, but Hawk always seemed to have some sixth sense with me.

He typed something and shoved his phone into his pocket as Luke's and Graham's phones went off. Graham read his and then tugged Tucker away with no further comment to the reporters, heading in the opposite direction of Hawk.

"This way," Luke said, steering me away and headed for a separate door. He tucked my hat down lower and placed my bag over his shoulder. "You feel okay to run?"

"Yeah."

"Good. When I say go, run to Hawk. I'll meet you back at the hotel."

Before I could ask any further questions, he kissed me and pushed me out a side door. A motorcycle turned the corner, and I sucked in a breath.

"Go, Slugger," Luke urged, and I hoped he meant toward the motorcycle and not away from it because I was in no shape to outrun it.

The bike slowed but didn't stop. An arm I recognized as Hawk's reached out and wrapped around my waist, pulling me onto the bike.

"Eek!" I shrieked, the sudden movement disorienting. I shifted my legs over the bike and clung to Hawk's body as he drove. Every part of me was wrapped around Hawk, and I tucked my head into his neck. He slowed once we were out of the ballpark, pulling over in a parking lot.

Once the engine was off, I leaned back as he lifted his visor. "Not bad, Blazy." His smirk was dangerous, and the heat hit me.

"Bunting hell." I laughed. I climbed off on shaky legs, noticing a rough and tumbled man standing in the lot.

"This your girl?" he asked, eyes locked on Hawk.

"Yep. Thanks for letting me borrow it." Hawk handed him the keys and helmet, grasping his forearm. "Tell Tiny I'll stop by before we leave and sign some merch."

"Will do. Be safe, and let us know if you need any more backup. Tornadoes for life." The guy knocked his fist against his chest before strapping on his helmet and climbing onto the bike. He waved over his shoulder before he took off, leaving us standing in the lot.

"KC Tornadoes?" I asked. They'd been Hawk's team before he was injured.

"Yep. I still have some fans out there." He winked.

"That you do, Hawk Anderson." His eyes heated as he stared down at me, drawing me into his arms with possession.

"I love the shit out of you, Blake Baker, never forget that. Nothing will keep me from you again. Not Bryce. Not the team. Not your parents. *Nothing*. I'll tell you every day until you get sick of hearing it."

"I never will."

Hawk slammed his lips down to mine, stealing my breath and setting my heart flying. The sound of a car pulling into the lot was the only thing that drew me away, remembering I didn't need to give the media more cannon fodder.

"That's our lift."

I turned and spotted the guys in a black SUV, and relief they were safe flooded my veins. Hawk and I climbed into the back, and I took the middle seat with Luke on the other side of me.

"I'm so jealous, Honey Bee. I wanted to be the one on the motorcycle, but Daddy Hawk said no." Tucker pouted.

"Daddy," I coughed, my face flaming.

"Not your daddy, Jameson. Call me that again and see what happens."

"Promise?" Tucker teased, turning to lift his eyebrows.

"West, you're benched for the next week," Hawk said, his voice no-nonsense.

"What? That's not fair!"

"Neither is Tucker propositioning me. If you can't keep your battery mate in line, then I will." He lifted a brow like he dared Graham to argue.

"Ugh, fine. You're no fun." Tucker pouted but pulled out of the lot. It was weird seeing him drive. "For someone who claims not to be a daddy, you sure act like one," he mumbled. I snorted, unable to hold it in.

"And this is why I only have sex with Luke." Hawk sighed, rubbing his forehead.

"What?" Tucker screeched, slamming on the brakes and turning.

"Watch the road!" Graham yelled, and Tucker turned back around.

"And not like that," Luke said, his cheeks burning.

"Fucking hell," Hawk grumbled.

Laughter overtook me, and I held my stomach as giggles erupted. Tears leaked out of the corner of my eyes for an entirely different reason. When I controlled myself, I leaned closer to his side and kissed his cheek.

"You said nothing, remember?"

"I take it back." He frowned, crossing his arms over his chest. I pulled it away from his chest, linking mine through his, and leaned on his bicep.

"Nope. You're stuck in my heart forever. No escape." I blinked up at him until he dropped the frown, bending down to kiss my lips.

"I wanna have sex with Luke and Hawk," Tucker pouted.

"Do you even hear yourself?" Graham muttered.

I reached over and took Luke's hand, his face still flaming. Thankfully, he took my offer, linking our fingers together.

Thankfully, we pulled into the hotel a minute later. After a few laps around the parking lot, there didn't seem to be any reporters hiding in wait.

We left in different groups, and I changed my hat and pulled on Hawk's hoodie. One group took the stairs, and we took the elevator. When the five of us made it to my floor, I sighed in relief. All the cloak-and-dagger stuff was fun, but it was also exhausting.

Opening my door, I was hit with a waft of rose water and chamomile I hadn't smelled in at least a year. Stepping in, I came face-to-face with Candi Baker.

"Mom?"

"Blake Baker, you have some explaining to do."

She stood, her pink pantsuit immaculate and commanding as she waited for me to explain. The guys halted behind me, and I didn't blame them. Candi Baker had that effect on people.

"Looks like the gang's all here. You might as well come in and get comfortable since this involves everyone screwing my daughter."

"Mother!"

"Is it not true?" she dared, lifting her eyebrow.

I opened and closed my mouth as words left me.

"You might want to work on your poker faces and get your stories straight before your father shows up."

Humiliation swamped me, and I debated turning and running. But then I felt them behind me, touching me slightly to remind me they were there. Right. Shut off the flight response. Time to fight.

While having my mother air out my sex life was embarrassing, I wasn't embarrassed about them. And that was something I would stand up for.

"Actually, Mom, meet my boyfriends. Hawk, Luke, Graham, and Tucker. We don't need to work on our story because there's only one that matters. The truth."

My mother froze, her mouth hanging open this time as she gaped at me. For the first time, I smiled triumphantly at my mom because I'd just shocked *the* Candi Baker.

Looked like my pinch hitter was here to play. I wouldn't count us out just yet.

BLAKE

The door to my room opened again, breaking the tense silence, and I spun, wondering what attack I would face now. Seriously, it had not been my day for hotel room intruders.

"We got a ton of food, Blanket, so you better eat up. I can't have you passing out—" Bryce stopped as he turned the corner, his head lifting and taking in the occupants of the room. His eyes widened, and he smashed his lips together, realizing his mistake immediately.

I rubbed my temple. "Just how many people have access to my room?" I grumbled.

My mom instantly shifted from badass lawyer Candi Baker to overprotective mom in two seconds flat.

"You passed out? When was the last time you talked to Dr. Middleton? What's your blood pressure?" She pushed the guys aside as she hovered over me, checking my temperature with her hands and scanning my body.

"You what? *When*?" Hawk asked, his face stony.

I rolled my eyes. "I'm fine. Just a little dehydrated and low blood sugar from not eating." I turned to my brother and glared, reaching my hand out to the bags of food. Bryce grimaced and pulled out a sandwich, placing it in my hand. He mouthed "sorry" and then shifted the bags of food into Tucker's arms, instantly going into brother mode, making me forgive him.

"Mom! What are you doing here?" He guided her away from me, giving me some air, and I sat on the edge of the bed and ignored everyone as I ate my sandwich.

"Me? What are *you* doing here? Didn't you have a game today?" She asked, bracing her hands on her hips and switching straight back into lawyer mode.

The whiplash from Mom sometimes could make my head spin. As I ate, I tuned out the room, debating if I could slip out the door before anyone noticed. All this attention directed at me was overwhelming.

But no, I wasn't running. Sighing, I finished my sandwich and crumpled the paper in my fist. A bottle of water appeared under my nose. Glancing up, I found it attached to Hawk's arm. He lifted his brow but said nothing, and I knew I'd be in trouble later with him.

Oh, well. Bring it, Mr. Grumpy pants.

"Okay, Mom, unless you're here to help with the mess Mira's created, I can't deal with anything else right now."

"Mira?" Candi asked, rearing back. "What does Mira have to do with this?"

Groaning, I covered my eyes and fell back on the bed. "Can someone else explain?"

"Um, hi, Mrs. Baker," I heard Emory say, making me feel guilty for not being more attentive to my best friend. Thank goodness she was an extrovert and didn't know a stranger. "Mira's a *skila*, um, what's the word, oh, yes, bitch!" I heard her snap her fingers, triumph in her voice.

"But what does that have to do with BB?" my mom asked.

"Just your basic jealousy and revenge scheme," Emory said. "When she couldn't get the male Baker, she went after Lake."

"Male Baker? What? I need to take a seat," my mom mumbled, moving to the other bed.

"Welcome to my day." I groaned. "We believe she's been sleeping with Davis—" Luke offered.

"The player?"

"Yep. The one who asked me out as a bet and then tried to get me drunk, but I inevitably puked on," I mumbled beneath my hands. They couldn't see me if I couldn't see them, right?

The bed dipped, and someone turned me, pulling my legs into their lap. Peeking beneath my fingers, I wasn't surprised when it was Tucker. The guy hadn't lied when he said he was touchy-feely, and I wouldn't complain about it. He untied my shoes, placed them lovingly on the ground, and pulled off my socks. I was worried my feet might stink, but he started to rub them, and all thoughts left my head.

"What in the world has been going on here? Is your father aware?" My mom's voice grew higher, but it didn't penetrate me this time. Graham sat behind me, so I set up and leaned into him, letting my screwballs manage my weight. The comfort of their presence was heaven.

"Dunno." I tried to shrug, but my shoulders barely lifted.

"We assume they teamed up to get back at BB," Bryce finished.

"About what?" my mom questioned.

"Again. Dunno. I guess Seth is mad Hawk beat him up and the whole vomit thing, but Mira, I have no clue other than being a Baker. She tried—"

"You beat him up?"

"Mom, I love you, but this is going to take forever if you keep questioning everything we're saying," Bryce interjected, saving me from screaming at my mother.

"It's just…" she muttered before I felt the bed dip on my other side; her perfume wafted over me again, comforting me with just her smell. Gently, she took my hand, stopping me from annihilating my cuticles, and held it in hers. I met her eyes, the emotion present shocking me.

"I had no idea any of this was going on." Her voice was small and sad, and I regretted keeping her out of the loop so much now.

"I know, and that's on me, but I wanted to show you I could handle things. That I didn't need my mommy stepping in."

"Oh, honey. It's not like that." She wrapped her arm around me, not caring Graham was there.

"It is, but it's fine because clearly I do." I rested my head on her shoulder. "We're in over our heads here, Mom. Will you help us?"

"Are you sure you need it? Because despite what you believe, it sounds like you *have* been handling things. You've built up a group of people around you that care about you, and that's all I've ever wanted for you, honey."

"So you're not mad?"

"No. I'm still trying to process the four-boyfriend thing, but I'm not mad. You're an adult, despite my attempts to still mother you." She ran her fingers over my hair, smoothing back the flyaway pieces. "You're gonna have to tell your father, though. You're dating three of his players and a coach. He needs to be brought into the loop. Especially if the director of media is the one leaking things."

"I know," I groaned. "Bryce?" I glanced up, meeting his eyes.

"Left a message. Same as Mom's. So, he might be showing up here soon, too."

"Great," I grumbled, my cheeks heating.

"Before he does that and scares off all your boyfriends, I'd like to get to know them."

In a surprising turn of events, my mom chatted to Graham, Tucker, and Luke, asking them questions about their lives, not just things about baseball. I eventually turned and cuddled between GT, eating some brownies that Luke handed me. In the grand scheme of things, it wasn't as bad as I imagined my mother meeting the men in my life. In fact, it was kinda nice.

"Do you have a lawyer for that?" Mom asked after Luke shared he was going to file for full custody of Willow.

"I do. David Jones."

"That's who I'd recommend, so you're in excellent hands." She turned her gaze, narrowing her eyes on Hawk. He'd been leaning against the dresser listening, and I had a feeling he thought he'd escaped the parental inquisition.

"Don't think you're off the hook just because I've known you since you were this tall," she said, moving her hand to her hips.

I watched with fascination as he gulped, and I saw my big, scary boyfriend, afraid of my mom. Laughing, I kicked my mother in the thigh with my foot.

"Mom, be nice. It's been a tough couple of days. Besides, you already knew about Hawk, so don't pretend you didn't."

"Oh, fine." She waved, chuckling. "I doubt Steven will take it as easy, though. So, prepare for that."

Hawk relaxed marginally, his muscles flexing as he digested my mother's words, giving her a nod.

"Ugh, I need to get back to Columbus, or you won't be the only one flayed by the great Steven Baker," Bryce said, tossing his trash away. "Love you, Mom." He kissed our mom on the cheek, hugging her. He nodded to Luke, Graham, and Tucker, saying some type of man message with his eyes before hugging Hawk.

I climbed off the bed for my own hug. "Actually, can I talk to you in the hall?" he asked.

"Sure."

"What about me? Do I not get a hug?" Emory asked, and Bryce froze, his eyes wide.

"Um, you want one?" he asked, his voice squeaking.

"Give your cousin a hug," Emory said, mischief in her eyes.

"Not my cousin," Bryce mumbled, giving her the most awkward hug I'd ever watched as he tried not to touch any part of his body to hers. Okay, that was weird.

"Really, Bryce! She doesn't have cooties," Mom said, sighing. She picked up her purse, turning while Bryce reattempted to hug Emory with all of us watching.

"I should head back too, dear. I'll plan a trip to Wilmington in the next few weeks so we can hang out, and I'll be in touch with you after I speak to James and Steven about Mira."

"Thanks, Mom." I hugged and kissed her cheek, momentarily letting her comforting presence sink into me.

"Oh, I almost forgot. I have some of your boxes in the trunk of my car. Perhaps some of your boyfriends can retrieve them for me?"

"We'll help!" Tucker said, bouncing off the bed and pulling on his shoes. Graham and Luke followed, the room clearing out quickly.

"I guess there are several perks to multiple boyfriends," my mom whispered. "Maybe I'll have to try it out." She winked.

"Just keep it PG. I don't need to think about that." I groaned.

She chuckled as she kissed me one more time, patting my cheek fondly. "You've become so strong, dear. It's beautiful to watch."

With that, she departed, leaving me wordless as she sauntered out the door, only Emory, Hawk, and Bryce remaining.

"Wow, I never thought Mom would accept all this so easily," Bryce said.

"Same. Sorry, maybe Dad will be more embarrassing, and you can get your Christmas card photo," I teased.

"Brat." He wrapped his arm around my shoulder, tugging

me with him as we headed out of the room. When the door closed, he stopped, turning toward me. "I'm sorry all this shit is happening, BB."

"Not your fault," I said.

"I know. But it's not fair." He took a breath. "I'm also sorry for how I responded and the things I said. I've been struggling with the change, but it's no reason to take it out on you when you're brave enough to live your life and go after the things you want."

"You think I'm brave?" I blinked up at my brother.

"You've always been the bravest person I know, Blanket."

Tears welled in my eyes, and I sniffled. "It's not fair if you make me cry because then I can't be mad at you."

"I hope you won't be mad at me anymore in general. I truly am sorry, and I'll be your biggest defender on this."

"Even Luke?"

He took in a breath and let it out, nodding. "Even Olson. I can tell he cares about you, which goes a long way in my book. I'm willing to start fresh, but if he steps out of line, I'll be the first to punch him."

"No punching needed, Baker," Luke said, carrying a box.

"Hope not. I have a mean right hook. Just ask Hawk."

"Noted." Luke smiled, knocking on the door and leaving us again.

"Keep me in the loop. I don't want to be on the outskirts of your life."

"I won't. I promise to resume normal texting." I gave him a smile so he knew I was serious.

"Good. Otherwise, I might have to get injured or something just to return to the YellowJackets so I can be part of your life," he teased. Still, I could hear the hint of vulnerability and an ounce of truth. Bryce was struggling, and my keeping secrets hadn't helped. I vowed to follow up more with him.

"Love you more than chocolate chip cheesecake," I said, giving him a big hug.

"Love you more than baseball," he whispered.

I sucked in a breath, pulling back from the hug.

"Bryce."

"Blake." He lifted his eyebrows, daring me to challenge him. "I know you always felt like Dad picked baseball over us, but I'm not him. I love baseball, but it's not my entire life. If I ever had to pick between it and helping you, I'd choose you. Every time. You're my baby sister, and I'll always protect you. That's never going to change no matter how old we get."

"And if I don't need protection anymore?"

"I'll still be by your side. It's you and me. Big brother and little sister. Always." He hooked his finger in mine, giving me a smile.

"Okay, Big Brother."

Graham and Tucker stepped off the elevator just then, and Bryce squeezed me tight one more time before jogging to catch the elevator.

"You guys good?" Graham asked, his eyes roaming over my face, tracking the tears.

"Yeah. We are. I always underestimate my brother's love for me."

"You guys are lucky. I love my sisters, but we don't have that close of a bond."

"You're right." I nodded. "Going through a childhood illness together bonded us for life."

We stepped into the room, only the five of us plus Emory, and exhaustion weighed on me. I just wanted to go to bed with my boyfriends but needed to be a good friend.

"What do you want to do tonight, Em?" I glanced at the alarm clock. It was a little past eight in the evening, but it felt closer to midnight to my body.

"I think one of your boyfriends is going to let you stay

with them so I can have the room to myself," she said, leaning back on her elbows on the bed and wiggling her eyebrows.

All four of them raised their hands, and a laugh bubbled out. I might have to tell the world tomorrow that I was dating four guys, but tonight, I got to relish in the perks of having four hot boyfriends pamper me.

"I'll bow out since I got last night," Luke said, dropping his hand.

"Rock, paper, scissors?" Tucker asked Hawk.

"No." Hawk glared at them, and Tucker stepped back into Graham with a squeak.

"You know, Graham's still on observation, so we'll call dibs on tomorrow night."

After kissing all the guys goodnight and making plans with Emory for the morning, I walked with Hawk to his room, hand in hand. Being out in public and showing affection had felt nice, so there was one good thing about this mess.

"You can't always use intimidation to get what you want."

"Until they learn not to fear me, I can," he teased.

We both got ready for bed, and I borrowed a shirt of his to wear, plugging in my phone on the nightstand. There was a missed call from my dad, but I'd deal with it in the morning. He could talk to Bryce or Mom at this point, but I was done.

Curling into Hawk's muscular arms, I let the world disappear, and happiness settled in my bones. I hated how my family discovered my relationship, but it felt nice to no longer have that shadow hanging over me. I fell asleep, confident in my relationships and knowing we could fight anything together.

CHAPTER
SIXTY-FOUR

HAWK

I woke up feeling at peace, something I hadn't noticed I'd been missing until I had it. For ten years, I'd felt conflicted over my desire for Blake. Guilt, shame, and regret were familiar emotions to wake up to.

Guilt for not telling Bryce the truth. Shame for wanting her even when I was with other people. Regret that I hadn't fought harder.

And now, all of that was gone.

There was no more guilt. No more shame. Only regret I'd waited as long as I did to go after what I wanted. This morning felt like the best morning in the world. The start of my true future.

"Why are you awake so early?" Blake grumbled into my chest, pouting with her eyes closed.

"Because you're in my bed, and there's no longer any secrets between Bryce and me."

She blinked, opening her eyes slowly, the blue orbs bright. Her smile spread slowly as she took in my face. "Even though you're all blurry, I have to agree with you despite the time."

"And to think a month ago you were the one being obnoxiously cheerful in the morning," I teased.

"Hmm, are you sure it was me? Cheerful and morning don't sound like things I'd do."

"Yup." I smiled, the action so easy around her.

"Must've been at a reasonable time then, like *after* nine."

Chuckling, I kissed her hairline as my hand smoothed across her back. "Perhaps, but that's because back then, I didn't need to have my fill of you before my morning coffee."

"Oh." Her eyes blinked owlishly, filling with heat as my words permeated her sleep haze. Blake licked her lips, her fingertips flexing against my chest as I palmed her ass cheek. The moan she let out had my cock harder than granite as arousal engulfed me.

"Crawl up my body, Blazy."

"Why?" she asked, but already moved to do as I asked.

"Do you know what goes great with coffee?"

"What?" she rasped, her voice husky.

"Your cream. Sit on my face, Blazy."

"Fuck. Your mouth."

"That's what I want you to do. *Now*."

Her eyes widened, but she quit delaying, crawling up my chest and placing her thighs on the side of my face. I gripped the globes of her ass, running my palms up the back of her thighs. She held onto the headboard, peering down at me with want and a little indecisiveness. That wouldn't do.

"Sit, Blazy. Grip my head with these thighs I love so much."

"Oh, god."

"Hawk will do," I teased, pulling her to where I wanted. Her pussy already glistened with her arousal, the smell intoxicating as I trailed the tip of my nose up. With my hands directing, she finally lowered herself completely, spearing herself on my tongue.

"Eek." Her hands tensed, her thighs locking around me at

the sudden intrusion. I didn't stop, licking her like my favorite treat. Her body relaxed into me, her surprise turning to moans as she quit fighting me.

"Son-of-a-pitch. God, that's good."

Licking up her center, I flicked my tongue over her clit as my beard rubbed against her lower half. Blake rocked her hips up, hitting just right on my tongue with each rock. Her thighs trembled already, and I moaned as she soaked me.

Moving one of my hands from her ass, I covered my finger in her wetness and plunged it in as I continued to assault her bundle of nerves with my tongue.

"Oh, god, Hawk. Yes, fuck, right there!" she screamed, her moans shaky and urgent.

One of her hands moved to my hair, tugging on the short strands as she rode me, urging me on. My finger slid in and out of her with ease, and I knew I'd gladly do this every morning for the rest of my life.

I loved everything about it. The way her smooth skin felt against my beard, the smell of her around me, and the tight pressure of her thighs as she quit thinking and took her pleasure.

My cock throbbed with need, the piercings tingling as my dick twitched in anticipation. My balls were heavy, and it wouldn't take me long to unload once I felt her around me. I knew sex with Blake was better than anything else I'd ever had, but knowing she loved me and Bryce wouldn't murder me now made this even sweeter.

Blake's legs tensed, her hips slowed as she trembled, her pussy fluttering around my digit and tongue. Her hand tightened on my hair as she came, filling my mouth with her cum. I licked her clean, relishing in her taste.

"Hot damn. I could get used to waking up like that." She sighed, her voice spent and heady.

"That's just the opener, Blazy."

With my arms under her legs, I lifted her as I sat upright.

Blake shrieked, her arms tightening around my head as I shifted her lower. Holding her eyes, I thrust upward, impaling her in one go as I dropped her down onto my cock.

"Jesus, Fuck."

"I know you have a lot of boyfriends, babe, but you really need to learn my name," I teased. Blake opened her mouth to argue, her eyes narrowing at me, but instead of letting her, I lifted her with my arms, smirking as she scrambled to hold on to my shoulders.

"Dear G—*Hawk*," she said, moaning around my name. It had never sounded better, and I vowed to make her say it that way every day from here on out.

Moving my legs to the side of the bed, I placed my feet on the ground and used the floor for resistance. I alternated between thrusting and lifting her on my cock; her walls were tight and hot with each slide. The metal piercings rubbed with each thrust, lighting up my nerve endings and sending jolts of pleasure.

"Hold on," I ordered, knowing I didn't have much longer in me.

Blake wrapped her arms around me, her breasts in my face, and I cursed myself that I hadn't taken the time to enjoy them.

"Fuck, fuck, fuck, I'm coming. Hawk!" Blake screamed, her moans taking the last of my restraint.

My movements stalled as I jerked, holding her tight to me as I unraveled. My cock jerked, and I was done as I came. Our bodies were slick with sweat, and we panted together, attempting to catch our breaths. The muscles in my arms ached, and I couldn't wait to feel it all day and remember how fucking amazing this had been.

Letting go of her leg, I smoothed her hair back as I stared at my girlfriend. "Love you, Blazy," I whispered, kissing her softly.

"Love you, Hawk." She sighed sweetly.

"Feel up for a shower?" I asked, in no hurry to move just yet.

"Hm, yeah. That sounds good. I'm not ready to check my phone yet."

I kissed her temple, pulling her body snug to me as I stood. Her legs wrapped around my waist and my cock twitched at the proximity of its favorite place.

By the time I had the water on and Blake in the shower, my cock stood at full height, throbbing and needy again.

"Damn." She licked her lips as she stared at me.

"Against the wall," I rasped. The water ran over her naked body, and my control was slipping.

"How?" she asked.

"Hands against it," I ordered, tilting her hips up as I rubbed my cock over her entrance. Bending my knees slightly, I sank into her as the steam rolled around us. With more patience than before, I slid in and out of her slowly, cherishing the feel of her as I fucked her. Our wet bodies slapped against one another, barely heard over the running water as our moans filled the space, echoing off the walls.

"More, Hawk. I need more," she said, squirming backward.

"Then brace yourself."

Wrapping my arm under her, I lifted her higher, putting her hips right where I needed them. In one move, I pulled out before slamming back in, hitting her deeper than before. Over and over, I did the same until my balls drew up, the familiar tingle racing along my spine.

Pulling her closer to my body, I moved one hand around the front and stroked her swollen nub, her legs shaking as she pressed back on me, her head falling to my shoulder. Together, we chased our release, moving our bodies in a rhythm I loved.

By the time we got out of the shower, there was a knock at my door, and I knew my solo time with her was over. As much as I assumed I'd hate sharing her, I didn't. Blake did well dividing her time and sharing her affection. I didn't feel like I lacked anything, and seeing her happy with the others was a bonus.

And weirdly enough, like Bryce said, I liked the guys and enjoyed their company. But I wouldn't let Tucker know that anytime soon. It was too fun messing with the happy-go-lucky man.

"Good morning, Honey Bee. I see you've already had your world properly rocked." Tucker kissed her as he moved into the room carrying a tray of coffees. "High five, Hawk!" He lifted his hand as he neared, and I glared at it, tugging my shirt over my head.

"Tough crowd." He set the coffees down as Graham and Luke entered.

"We brought breakfast. There're a few reporters mingling in the lobby already," Graham sighed.

"Lovely," Blake muttered, accepting the coffee from Tucker. "This is nice, though," she said, sitting cross-legged on the bed as she sipped her coffee.

"Cream?" Tucker asked, and I glanced at Blake. Her cheeks heated as I accepted the cup.

"None needed," I said, sipping it as I licked my lips. She wiggled and sucked in a breath, dropping my eyes as she focused on the donuts. Damn, that was hot.

Chuckling, I sat in the chair and spread my legs out as I unplugged my phone and scrolled through it as Blake chatted with the guys.

Bryce: Spoke with my dad. He's headed there, FYI.

Bryce: He won't be as easily won over as Mom. Good luck.

Perfect.

Hawk: Thanks for the heads up.

Hawk: Good luck today. Let's review schedules later and see when we can meet again.

Bryce didn't respond, but I wasn't surprised. He'd sleep until the last second. I scrubbed my hands over my face, sighing. Steven Baker wasn't an unreasonable man, but this was his daughter. I didn't know many fathers that would be okay with their little girl dating four guys. I was prepared to step down from the team if he wanted. I'd been serious when I told Blake she was more important than baseball to me. I could find another job, but there was only one Blake Baker.

"Crap," Blake cursed. "My dad's here and wants to meet with me."

"Us too?" Graham asked.

"It only says me." Blake bit her bottom lip as she thought.

"What do you want, Blazy?" I asked.

"I want you all there, but I'm trying to decide if it might go over easier if you're not."

"And?"

"I can't decide. Talk to me about something else. I need time to ponder it."

"Hm, well, my mom called me," Tucker said, cringing.

"How did that go?"

He shrugged. "About the same as always. She pretends to be interested in my life until she asks for something, and when I don't give in, she attacks. Said I was going to Hell because I was with Graham and that I wasn't much of a man anyway since I was willing to share a girl."

"Fucking hell, that's brutal, man," Luke said. He patted Tucker on the leg, and I snorted. "What?"

"Just glad to see I'm not the only one emotionally stunted. Watching you try to console him is like watching a baby deer walk. Hella awkward."

Luke flipped me off, but the others laughed. Graham rubbed the back of his neck, some anxiety showing as he peered at us.

"My family called, too. They were mostly accepting. About what I expected."

"Then why the anxiety?" I asked, picking up on that not being the complete answer.

"Oh. My agent dropped me, so I'm on the market for someone new."

"Shit. I'm sorry, Graham."

"Not your fault," he started, and Blake moved to argue. "No, really, it's not. He'd never been on board with me being out in the league. I'd wanted to switch for a while but hated confrontation, so I hadn't yet." He blushed. "Now, I can without guilt. I'm still not convinced he hasn't quietly been sabotaging my sponsorships for years. I didn't know it, but he has strong opinions on queers."

"I can put you into contact with some good ones," I offered.

"Thanks. I'd appreciate it."

"Oh, me too! My agent told me to say Blake was a slut and had dated us all with no one knowing to save my career."

"What?" Blake gasped, her cheeks heating.

"What's their name?" I demanded, a growl escaping my throat.

"Oh, I fired them and then texted Candi. Your mom's a badass," Tucker said, smiling.

"I'd still like their name."

"Sure thing, bulldog."

"That's not becoming a thing," I said, narrowing my eyes.

"Okay, bulldog." Tucker grinned, his brown eyes shining bright.

I rolled my eyes, knowing the best way to stop it was to ignore it. Tucker acted like my nieces ninety percent of the time, so I needed to implement some of the same techniques.

"I'm scared to ask you, Luke," Blake said, picking at her fingernails.

"My agent was shockingly cool and said to defer to whatever the team agreed on. And my lawyer said it showed I was in a committed relationship with a support system and would go a long way for the custody agreement."

"Well, at least some good news," Blake said, relaxing.

"I consider mine good, too. I got rid of dead weight," Graham added.

"I love the way you see things." Blake smiled, leaning into his touch.

The little jealousy that had been there in the beginning no longer existed. My heart warmed as I watched Blake accept and receive love from them. There was no doubt my life was fuller; even if Tucker and Graham annoyed the shit out of me, I liked having people in my life to do it.

"I think I'll meet my dad alone, but if you could walk me up there and not go far, that would be great."

"Of course," we all agreed, cleaning up our mess. Blake finished getting ready, pulling her hair into braids and accepting Luke's hat. I could already anticipate the war each morning to have her wear our belongings. Still, instead of dread filling me, it was the anticipation of a new challenge. Things would never be boring, and the excitement of what was to come intrigued me. It was life with Blake wrapped in a joy sandwich.

"All right, let's do this," Blake said, holding her head high and making me fall in love with her more.

BLAKE

Nerves rattled me as I walked toward the suite. I pressed my hand flat against my stomach, trying to settle the pit. Blowing out a breath, I raised my hand and knocked. Scenarios of what might occur played out in my mind in the expanse of one heartbeat to the next, and I prayed to all the baseball gods that my dad understood.

Standing up to my mom had been easier. I knew deep down she'd accept me. Candi Baker had two settings: ball buster and fluffy bunny. And while she primarily operated as the arduous bulldozer the world knew, I had the blueprint to her off switch.

But Dad...he hid his emotions unless it was about baseball. It was easier for him to show his players, the fans, and his workers he cared than it was his own children. Sometimes, I wondered if his brain only worked in baseball plays and phrases, and anything outside of it made him nervous.

The door opened, and I kept my gaze forward. It was too tempting to steal comfort from the four guys who meant the world to me. But this, I needed to do on my own.

"Hey, Dad."

"Hey, sweetie."

He pulled me into a hug, kissing the top of my head. I sank into his embrace, tears pricking my eyes. God, I'd missed his hugs. I never remembered how good they were until I got one. It must've been some safety measure my brain built in so I wouldn't always be homesick.

"There's not much time to talk before the others arrive, so why don't you tell me what's going on. I spoke with Bryce, but I want to know where you stand," he said, leading me over to the couch.

I blew out a breath. "The simplest way to explain it is that my heart chose four guys. Each one of them gives me something different, and together, we're a unit, a family. Mira's trying to make it into something gross and scandalous, but it's not. We're adults. We're committed to one another, and we're happy. I'm not sure how much more loving or boring we could get." It all rushed out, my face red as I realized the truth of my words.

That was what annoyed me the most. Her uncomfortableness, or even jealousy, was sullying something beautiful.

"And you're committed to this relationship? There's nothing I could do to sway you?"

"No." I pushed my shoulders back, my head lifted as I stared my father in the eyes, so similar to my own. The nerves I felt earlier dissipated, and I wrapped the confidence I had in their feelings for me and my own together, strengthening my resolve. There had been so many decisions in my life where I'd buckled under the pressure and gone with the one of least resistance. But not this time.

I wouldn't let other people tell me how to live—even if that was my father.

I'd stepped fully out of the shadows into the sun, and it felt fucking marvelous. I smiled as the warmth of their affection spread through me. I was in love with Hawk, and my feelings for the others were headed there, too. I was confident in our future and the life we'd build together, regardless of all the obstacles.

No matter what, we'd face them together.

"Good." My father smiled, shocking me.

"Um, what?" I blinked, looking around. "Is this a dugout prank? Is Bryce hiding around the corner to dump something on me?"

My dad chuckled, patting my leg. "No, honey. Though, I can't say I love the idea of you dating four guys, all of whom I employ." He paused, lifting his brows before continuing. "But if you can stand up to me, then I know you'll be able to handle the attention that will come from this."

"Oh." My cheeks pinked. "Sorry about that."

My dad sighed, a smile gracing his lips. "I can't complain too hard. All these years, I secretly wanted you to fall for a player. I honestly thought Hawk would've tried after Brandon was out of the picture."

"You did?" I blinked.

"I know baseball can be hard for you at times. It was your first love. But then it let you down, and it was like you tried to put as much distance as possible between it and you."

"And inadvertently, you and me," I said, seeing my dad in a new light. "Hawk did try," I said, licking my lips. "After the wedding, I mean. But then Bryce found us, and he didn't take it well. So I gave up Hawk for Bryce."

"You felt you owed him for saving your life." He said it as a statement instead of a question. My dad perceived more than I gave him credit for.

"Yeah." His eyes searched mine, looking for something.

"Did you know that when you got sick, Bryce stopped playing baseball? He said it didn't matter if you weren't in the stands to cheer him on."

I gaped, positive I misheard him. Because that didn't make sense. My dad only smiled, squeezing my leg.

"Your brother didn't do well as an only child. He

followed Candi around like a lost puppy. It drove her crazy." He chuckled. "When you were born, it was like his entire world shifted. Everything he did from that point on, he included you in. It was the sweetest thing to watch. He'd talk to you like you understood, and sometimes it seemed like you did."

"I didn't know that," I said, smiling at the image of a tiny Bryce carting around a baby Blake.

"I think you had it wrong. He didn't need you to sacrifice something for him. Bryce just wanted to be included."

I nodded, my heart mending itself. "I get that now. The fact he pushed aside his hatred for Luke proved it."

"Yeah, that one surprised me, too."

"I'm impressed you've gotten through all of this without one baseball reference," I teased.

"I must admit, it came at me from left field. But I'm ready to play hardball and bring in the big hitters."

We both broke out into peals of laughter, tears running down my cheeks, this time for a much different reason. *There's my cheesy dad.*

"So, what now?" I asked once we gathered ourselves.

A knock sounded at the door, and I stiffened. "Just follow my lead, honey. I support you in this and promise to make it right. Okay?"

"Of course, Dad."

He squeezed me to him, kissing my cheek before standing and walking to the door. I wanted to peek out and see if the guys were there, but I knew they weren't. They'd waited a few minutes and then headed to the room, giving me time with my dad. So, when I saw the two people that did walk through the door, I froze.

"James, Mira. Thank you both for *rushing* to get here so quickly," my dad said. I couldn't be sure, but his words sounded full of sarcasm. I trusted my father so I'd see where this went before throwing coffee on Mira.

"Of course, Steven. All hands on deck," James said.

"I'm just appalled at this news, Steven. I had no idea Blake was behaving in this way," Mira said, her voice so saccharine I wanted to barf.

"It's Mr. Baker," my dad said, causing Mira to falter.

"Apologies, Mr. Baker."

"This way."

The moment Mira spotted me, her facade fell away, and she delivered me a scathing look. I crossed my arms and held my ground. I couldn't wait to see what my father had in store for her.

Steven Baker hadn't won a World Series both as a player *and* a coach by being meek, and I had a feeling he was about to wipe the floor with Mira.

"Hello, Blake. It's good to see you," James said, hugging me. The man was one of baseball's most ruthless PR directors, but he'd always been a teddy bear to me. He'd been in the sport for a long time and treated me like a granddaughter. The topic of conversation just got a lot more awkward for me, but at least I had him on my side… I hoped.

"What was it you were saying about Blake?" Dad asked as he sat next to me on the couch, placing his arm along the back and essentially engulfing me in a protective stance. James and Mira sat in the two club chairs across from us, a coffee table in between.

Mira blanched, her face paling slightly as she glanced at me and then back at my dad. "Oh, just that if Blake had spoken to me about her relationships first, then this never would've happened." She turned to me, giving me a fake pout. "Blake, I really wish you would've trusted me."

"Interesting," my dad said, rubbing his jaw and nodding.

"I'm sorry her position didn't work out, Mr. Baker. I tried to help her, but she was more interested in the players than in doing her job. And since it goes against the policy to date players, it only makes sense to terminate her. I already have a list of candidates for interviews."

"Hmm." My dad didn't say anything else; he simply stared at Mira, and I watched in fascination as she dug her own grave. The silence was apparently her undoing, and each time Steven Baker didn't praise her for her excellent job or jump down my throat for my behavior, the more she panicked.

"Really, Blake, what were you thinking? Luke Olson is a known playboy, but I knew something was off when you let him bring his daughter to the stadium. Then, those two who are always attached. It's obvious they're using you so they can be together. And the tattooed coach. I've been saying for years he needs to cover them up and be more friendly with reporters," she spewed.

She rolled her eyes like she had a right to be offended. My blood boiled at each awful thing she said about my guys, and I had to dig my nails into my thighs to stop from saying anything. My dad said to trust him, so I would.

"And since I won't get to give you your review at the end of your term, I think it's only fair you know how subpar your work is. I don't want to be cruel, but I don't see you going far in this field." She glanced over at my father, insinuating that the only reason I'd gotten to where I had was because of him. She opened her mouth again, but thankfully, my father had heard enough.

"James, when did the dating policy change?"

"It hasn't. If there's a conflict of interest or hierarchy of power, then there's a form HR needs."

"So, in Blake's case, that doesn't apply, correct?"

"Correct."

"And nowhere does it state she must inform her supervisor?" my dad asked, making Mira squirm.

"I double-checked this morning. It does not."

Mira opened her mouth, but my father stopped her with his eyes. *Damn.* That was a move I wanted to perfect.

"You've had your time to talk, Mira. Now, it's mine." His words were laced with steel, and I saw the cutthroat man he could be emerge. He leaned forward, bracing his elbows on his knees as he stared down the woman across from him like she was a runner he was about to tag out.

"Despite not needing to, Blake informed me about the men she was dating a month ago. So, as far as I'm concerned, the bullshit rule you made up was, in fact, met. Unless I don't qualify as a superior?"

Mira swallowed. "Of course, Mr. Baker."

"Therefore, your claim that her position should be terminated is malarkey. Blake has done no wrong as far as this club is concerned."

"Understood."

"Now, in regards to her performance, I've had several people outside of your department report back to me about the excellent job she's doing. I know you aren't a fan of social media, but if you'd taken the time to check out the team account, you'd see how many followers and likes she's amassed in a short time. Ticket sales are up, game attendance has improved, and the overall satisfaction of the team is happier."

My dad steepled his hands together, his eyes narrowing at Mira as she squirmed across from him. When he said nothing, she glanced at James, who was also staring at her.

"So, what are we here for?" Mira asked, her voice cracking.

"Excellent question. James, would you?"

He bent down, pulled out a folder from his briefcase, and opened it. Shots of Mira and Seth were enclosed, and they weren't hugging. I averted my eyes, not needing to see that much of either of them. I had no clue how they'd gotten the photos, but I didn't care.

"Oh dear god!" she shrieked.

"While you were angling to take down my daughter, your bed partner was looking for his own payday. He took those and was going to blackmail you with them."

Mira's eyes bulged, her hand trembling as she covered her mouth. I wanted to feel bad for her, but she'd actively attempted to ruin me and outed my relationship to the world. While I was grateful we didn't have to hide anymore, she'd robbed us of the chance to tell people we loved first.

She'd taken our choice away, and that was never okay.

"And while Blake didn't break any rules of fraternization, *you* did."

"What? But?" she spluttered, apparently forgetting that part of her rant toward me.

"You're a director. He's a player. That is a power dynamic. Are there different rules for you? Did I miss a memo where you told me you were dating Davis? Does HR have the form?"

"HR was not aware," James offered. "In fact, while I was at Champion Field this morning, I stopped by Mira's office to touch base on the leak."

"Oh?" my dad asked, leaning back now and crossing his ankle over his knee. He now presented the epitome of calm.

"I—" Mira tried to say, but James ignored her.

"Funnily enough, her office was empty. But another lovely girl was there, Rue, I believe, and she let me into the office. I was going to leave a message, but then I discovered something."

"You can't go into my office. That's private!" Mira shouted, standing. Her fists were balled tight at her sides, and gone was the meek woman.

"Actually, it's *company* property," my dad responded, then motioned for James to continue.

"IT is compiling all the keystrokes right now, but from the notes I spotted on top of the desk, it's clear where the leak came from. Does Libbie French ring any bells, Mira?" James turned to his phone, which had a picture of a notepad with the name Libbie French and the note 'send evidence' next to it.

"She's my hairdresser," she tried, faltering.

"Huh. Weird coincidence then, since the author of the expose was also a Libbie French."

Mira's eyes widened, her face paling as she finally came to terms with her predicament.

"I can explain! It wasn't fair. She waltzed in here without any experience, and then they were all panting over her. *Her*! She doesn't even brush her hair most days!"

"Hey!" I shouted, finally having enough of her berating me. My father placed a hand on my arm, stopping me from standing and likely punching her in the face.

"Then she had the audacity to tell me she's 'Blake Baker,' and I needed to heel. I've had enough of you Bakers!"

"Mira, in case it's not obvious. *You're* fired. Your belongings have been packed, and your credentials have been stripped. You're no longer welcome on any YellowJacket or Blue Devil property. Should we press charges, the police will be in touch."

"What? No! You can't do this! I have rights!"

"You broke the law, your contract, and the NDA you signed upon hiring. If you try to speak to the press *again*, we'll have no choice but to file slander and defamation charges and wrap you up in so much red tape you'll be lucky to get a job at a fast food chain. Do you understand?"

Mira jerked back. Eventually, she nodded, the fight leaving her as tears streamed down her face, her mascara running.

"Please, show some mercy," she begged.

"Mercy? The baseball clubs are my family, and you went after that. The only mercy you get is the decency of me not outing you to the media."

"Good luck with your slut daughter." She seethed, yanking the pictures of her and Seth off the table.

"If being a slut means being in a committed relationship, then okay, I'm a slut. But you might want to look in the mirror, Mira." I traced my middle finger down my face. "You got something right there."

If her eyes could spit flames, I'd be incinerated, but it felt nice to speak my mind, even if it was a little juvenile.

Hey, I was still growing. There was only so much maturity I could do in a day.

Once the door clicked closed, the three of us burst out into laughter, and each time my dad looked at me, he would mimic my finger down the cheek and break out into peals of laughter again. It took a good ten minutes before we settled, wiping our faces from our laughter tears.

Damn. Second time today I'd laughed so hard I cried. I liked that. It was good for the soul.

"Now that the trash has been taken care of, where do we stand on clean up?" James asked, looking between me and Dad.

"This isn't how I wanted to tell the world, but I won't hide my boyfriends. I'm in a committed and loving relationship with four guys. That's all there is to know. Can you help me with that?"

"Absolutely." James picked up his phone, going into work mode and accepting my answer with no judgment or confirmation from my father, reinforcing my love for the man.

"Do we want a general statement from the team, a press conference, or something more personal?" he asked, looking up.

"What do you think, BB?" my father asked.

I chewed my lip. I didn't want to be in front of a crowd, but a general statement didn't feel personable enough.

"What if I use the account to set the story straight, with the guys' permission, of course? That way, it gets it out there, but we control it, and it's personable. People fear what they don't know, but if they see we're real people who care for each other, maybe it will be okay?"

"That could work," James said, nodding.

My dad's brow creased. "I think it's courageous of you, and you've discovered a way to connect with others without pushing your boundaries. Just promise you won't read the comments."

"First rule of social media," I said, making him smile.

"Never read the comments," the three of us said together.

"Now, I think it's time I talk to these boyfriends of yours."

"And that's my cue to leave," James said, stacking his papers. "I'll be in touch with candidates for Mira's position."

"Thanks, James. Tell Mimi I send my love, and I desperately need some of her shortbread cookies." My dad patted his stomach as James chuckled.

"Will do. I'm sure you'll have a batch on your desk when you return to Columbus."

"Yes!" He fist-pumped the air, laughing.

Smiling, I pulled out my phone and texted the guys.

> Blake: Everything's going to be okay.

> Blake: Time to meet my dad.

LUKE

Tucker and Graham spoke softly to one another as they walked ahead of me down the hall. Apparently, they weren't worried about meeting their death. Oh, to be that blissfully naive.

The walk to the suite door felt more like a trip to meet my executioner than meeting my girlfriend's father. Though, I supposed it wasn't every day that the girlfriend's father was also your boss *and* a baseball legend.

"You look like you might hurl," Hawk muttered, drawing my attention.

"You don't look much better."

He snorted but didn't deny it.

"I've known Steven Baker for almost twenty years. You'll be fine."

"And you?"

He grimaced. "I honestly have no clue. He told me one summer how I was like a brother to Blake; therefore, it was my duty to watch her as Bryce would. I don't think shoving my cock down her throat while she was impaled by another dick was what he had in mind."

Chuckling, some of the anxiety lifted as we reached the door. Graham glanced back at us and nodded, giving me that sentiment I'd had for the past few days—we were all in this together.

Swallowing down the last of my worries, I knew I could do this. I'd stopped drinking, met my daughter, and faced my past with Bryce. I could meet Steven Baker and pretend I hadn't made his daughter cum on a plane. Easy.

At least seeing Blake's face before her dad threw me from a window would be worth it.

Dramatic much? Maybe. But I still hadn't ruled it out.

"Hey!" Blake said as she greeted us, kissing Tucker and Graham on the cheek as they entered. Her smile fell when she got to me, her brows furrowing in concern. "What's wrong?"

"He thinks your dad's going to throw him from the team bus," Hawk said, stepping around me and dropping a kiss on her lips before continuing.

"The window, actually," I muttered. Sometimes, I really despised his ability to perceive things. It was about level with his cocky confidence.

Which was rich coming from me since I'd spent years being the cockiest asshole I could be.

"You'll be fine. I promise. I'll let you back on the bus," Blake teased, kissing me and pulling me into the suite.

"Wait, what?" I asked, her kiss distracting me from the words.

She giggled as she dragged me into the inner room, and I swallowed as I took in Steven Baker's intimidating form.

I'd met the man when I'd been traded to the Blue Devils, but it had been brief. A quick handshake and a 'welcome to the team' kind of deal. Now, he loomed ahead of me, his eyes narrowing on where Blake grasped my hand. I wanted to shake her off but decided that might be worse. I still tensed up every time I put on my jockstrap, memories of her IcyHot revenge always at the forefront.

"Sir," I said, my voice cracking. The others tittered at my discomfort, but I kept my eyes locked on him.

"*Dad*, you said you'd be nice," Blake warned. I glanced over, finding her doing some type of narrowed gaze that made her look as tough as a killer bunny. But apparently, it worked on her dad because when I glanced back at Steven, his eyes had softened.

"Fine, BB. You take away all my fun," he sighed, dropping his glare and posture. Steven looked at everyone before motioning for us all to take a seat. "It seems we have some things to discuss."

Blake pulled me over to the couch, sitting between me and her father. Tucker hauled a chair from the table, spinning it around to sit in, while Graham and Hawk took the two club chairs. We all glanced at one another, not knowing where to start or if we should wait for him.

"What was the outcome?" Graham bravely asked.

"Before we get into that, I have a few questions," Steven said, his eyes assessing everyone. I gulped, my hand sweating in Blake's as I awaited my fate.

"Dad," Blake admonished.

Steven ignored her, leaning forward and meeting the four of our eyes. "I need to know right now if any of you are dating her just to get in good with me?"

I jerked back, his words causing a physical blow. What the hell?

"Fuck no. I mean, no, sir," Tucker said, clearing his throat.

"It's a no from me as well," Graham said, covering his smile at Tucker's outburst.

"I'm not even going to answer that, Steven," Hawk said, giving him a bored look. I wasn't certain, but I caught Hawk swallow, his nervousness belying his calm exterior. Steven smirked before landing on me.

"Not in a million years."

Steven assessed me, noting my hand in his daughter's

before giving me a nod. I hoped it signified he accepted that, but I couldn't be sure just yet.

"And if I said I'd trade you for dating her?"

Blake groaned, placing her head in her free hand. The cap jostled with the movement, and I corrected it. She peered over at me, giving me a soft smile. I didn't even need to think about this answer.

"I'd play for whoever I needed to. I'd even quit if that's what it came down to," I said, holding Blake's eyes. Hers rounded, and she sat up straighter, staring at me open-mouthed. I didn't know if anyone else said anything; my focus was solely on her.

"You can't mean that."

"But I do." I nodded, the feeling spreading through me with certainty. "Before this season started, I believed the only thing I was good at was being a screw-up. Baseball had become harder than it ever had with the injury and age, and I'd used alcohol to numb myself. Learning about Willow was the first wake-up call I needed to change my life, and meeting you on that plane was the second."

"Luke," Blake said, her eyes watering.

"I thought baseball was my only dream, but it's not. Being a father and loving you are bigger than baseball."

Blake gasped, her hand covering her mouth as tears spilled down her cheek. I wiped it away and pulled her to my chest. The anxiety I'd felt earlier was now completely gone as the truth of my words sank in. I could survive without baseball, but I couldn't without Blake. I'd tried, and my life had been miserable. It wasn't something I wished to repeat.

"Fucking Olson stealing the show," Tucker muttered. I glared at him, and he gave me a wink. I still didn't understand him and Graham at times, but I realized I wanted to. And just like that, I became all in.

This was it for me. Blake, Willow, and the guys. The rest of it would work itself out.

I lifted my eyes to Steven's, shocked when I found acceptance and admiration there. I cleared my throat.

"Does that answer your question?"

"Yeah, it does. I'm glad my daughter saw the real you beneath all the cocky blubber."

I snorted. "Me too."

Steven reached over and gripped my shoulder, squeezing it. "Welcome to the family."

As a boy, I'd never had the acceptance of a father, and my mother routinely chose everyone else over me. Hearing Steven's words were the ones I'd longed to hear as a kid, but they meant even more now as a man.

Because I'd become the man I was on my own, despite my parents. Not only had Blake found me worthy, but so had her dad—an honorable and respected man. Turning my head into her neck, I let the tears fall for the little boy I'd been and embraced the future I had waiting for me.

I could deal with the reporters, the fans, and anyone else who disagreed with my choices as long as I got this.

Because for so long I believed control was what I needed to live, to survive even. But as it turned out, I only needed love.

TUCKER

Watching Luke own his feelings made my own intensify. Excluding the terrifying hunk of a man Blake's father was, I felt a sense of symmetry and stability I'd been searching for my whole life.

The smile I naturally wore on my face stretched wider, wrapping around my entire body in a warm hug. Or at least that was what it felt like as I rested my head on my arms, watching my family. Because that was what they were now. Mine.

Graham had been saying it all along, but until right this second, it had been just a word—family.

A whispered promise. A hopeless belief. An unanswered dream.

"Oh, no. What's that look?" Hawk asked, narrowing his eyes. "You're planning another prank, aren't you?"

"Me?" I asked, sitting up and peering around. "I'd never."

The room laughed, but I wasn't lying. As the sound died down, Steven Baker turned his gaze to me.

"What about you, Tucker?"

"What about me?" I asked, looking around, confused.

Had I missed something while I'd been off in my head? It wouldn't be the first time. Steven chuckled like I amused him. I liked that thought, but I usually preferred to know what I did that was funny.

"If I were to trade you, would that change your relationship with my daughter?"

"Hell, no. It would suck not getting to see her every day like I do now, but we'd figure something out. But if you traded me without Graham, then I'd refuse."

"You can't refuse a trade," Graham muttered.

"The fuck I can't!" I furrowed my brows.

"Tuck." Graham shook his head like he thought I was a cute puppy. Facts. But I wasn't joking about this.

"I'm serious. The last few games showed me that while I love baseball—which I'm pretty damn great at, if I do say so myself—but it's no fun without you. Hell, it's not even bearable. I was bored out of my mind the other day until you entered the dugout. I know they joke we're a package deal, but it's real. Maybe that's codependent." I shrugged. "I don't really give a flying fuck. I'd rather play for a losing team as long as we got to play together."

I held Graham's eyes, ensuring he understood what I was saying, before I turned back to Blake and her dad.

"I'm serious about your daughter, and I think I play better when she's around because she makes me happy, and missing her would be hell on earth. And I'm not above saying I'd do anything I could to bribe her to come to whatever team Graham and I were at. So, really, I think you should ask yourself where you're willing to send your daughter, sir. Because where we go, she goes."

"Tucker," Graham said, exasperated, but I caught the corner of his mouth tilting up. He could pretend he was annoyed with me, but he loved my over-the-top ass.

"That's a pretty big threat." Steven Baker watched me, his words hanging in the air. I held his eyes, noticing something akin to admiration there. It confused me, so I opened my mouth, spilling more words in my anxiousness.

"And considering Candi's now representing us both, our contracts will be ironclad moving forward. I'm not old like Olson, so I'm not ready to retire yet—"

"Hey!" Luke grumbled, and I chuckled but kept going.

"I still have a lot of baseball left in me. I love the game, and when I have those two people with me, it's even better. They're my future, even the grumpy and cocky one. We've made our own baseball team, a family I've craved my whole life. I'm serious about your daughter and believe I could be the pitcher this club needs. And hopefully, neither excludes the other because I love being a YellowJacket and, hopefully, a Blue Devil someday. But if I had to pick this club or your daughter, I'd pick your daughter every time."

Blake jumped up and threw her arms around me. I leaned back, giving her enough room to fall into my lap and avoid the chair back. Blake stole my breath as she kissed me, sealing every emotion in my heart. I wanted to turn her so she could straddle my lap and kiss her harder, but I remembered her father was in the room and pulled away. I kept her across my lap, helping to cover my erection, as my ass threatened to fall off the back with both of us backward in the chair.

Threatening your boss to steal his daughter was one thing. Popping an erection in front of him... too far.

"You're ridiculous, Tucker Jameson, but I'd follow you wherever you went just so we're clear."

"Thank fuck, because I was kind of bluffing."

Blake giggled, snuggling my neck, her arms wrapped around my middle. Steven's eyes were on me, and I swallowed as I waited for his decree.

"Hiring Candi was a smart move. She'll take care of you both and get you with an agent that supports all of your interests, not just their pocketbook." He paused, looking briefly at his daughter. "I shouldn't be surprised you'd surround yourself with men who value you, but I had to be sure."

"Does that mean Hawk and I are off the hook?" Graham asked.

Steven turned his direction, giving him a full smirk. "Not even close. I'll just have to ask you both different questions."

Graham gulped, shifting in his seat. I held Blake to me, relishing in how nice it felt to be accepted for who I was. I didn't need to perform around this group, and knowing that had my whole body relaxing.

"Choosing to stay tied together will limit you both," Steven said, and my body tensed right back up. "But I admire your commitment to playing together. Not many teammates would be willing to do that."

"We're more than teammates, sir," Graham said, stealing the words from my mouth.

"Now, who's stealing the show," I teased. Graham stuck his tongue out at me, and I chuckled.

"Is that new?"

"Yes," I said, not ashamed.

"Does the team know?" he asked, bouncing between us.

"They might assume, and the article painted the picture without saying it, but we've decided to come out and say it to them. It wasn't how I planned to announce that I've discovered my sexuality isn't as straightforward as I always assumed. Still, I won't let the media twist things either."

"Whatever support you need from management, let me know." Steven gave me a nod, and I felt that peace again.

"Thank you."

"Before you grill Graham and Hawk, can I share with them our solution?" Blake asked.

"Sure, honey." Steven smiled at his daughter, showcasing how much he loved and trusted her. She smiled, her whole face lighting up.

"You guys missed the best showdown ever with Mira," Blake started, telling us about the blow-by-blow of the meeting.

I held her with one arm wrapped around her waist and reached out my other hand to take Graham's. Now, *this* felt right.

I knew it wouldn't always be this easy. Baseball wasn't the most open sport, and plenty of people would comment on my relationship with Graham as being wrong. In the past, I would've avoided making this kind of statement so I didn't make myself a target. I'd been willing to hide to be accepted. I'd wrongly assumed being the guy people wanted would give me stability. But all it did was make me question myself and feel awful about who I was.

So, fuck that.

Graham had accepted me from the moment he walked into our dorm room and never asked me to be anyone other than my goofy self. And Blake had been so effortlessly beautiful and accepting from the start. She bravely opened her heart to me, and I wouldn't ever want to do anything that jeopardized losing it.

Bunting hell. *I'm in love with Graham and Blake.*

Which meant I needed to do something romantically spectacular to show them both just how much they meant to me. I did have a reputation to maintain. Grinning, I couldn't wait to see their faces when I told them.

Being in love was awesome. And soon, the two people I loved would know it.

Now, if only I had a cat to stroke and a chair to spin around in like an evil villain laughing...

"Wait, am I welcomed to the family now?" I blurted, realizing Luke had gotten the offer, but I hadn't. The others stopped, turning to stare at me. Steven laughed but nodded.

"Welcome to the family, Tucker. I have a feeling you'll be the one to match her humor. Good luck."

Blake laughed, and Hawk snorted, and I suddenly felt like I was missing something.

"What does that mean? Guys? Guys?"

"So, Graham," Steven said, everyone ignoring me.

Well, too bad. They'd regret that when I put my plan together.

GRAHAM

Steven Baker's gaze landed on me, and I gulped. I hadn't been nervous, but the second his eyes were on me, I felt the true weight of the man.

Two-time World Series Champ, MVP, and the Blue Devils/YellowJackets club owner. But perhaps the heaviest of them all, the father of the girl I was falling in love with.

I'd always been a romantic, filling my head with stories from an early age, but there had always been a part of me that believed I'd never have that for myself.

Yet here I was, living out the greatest love story I could ever imagine.

I got the girl *and* the guy.

"Yes, sir?" I asked, attempting to keep my voice steady. Tucker's hand squeezed mine, and I settled. His words about not playing baseball without me were the biggest 'I love you' he could give, and I wished I was out of this room already so I could kiss my man.

"You have two people speaking highly of your character, one of which I value greatly. My daughter told me the idea for this arrangement was yours. Was that only to get your cake and eat it, too?"

I scrunched my nose, my brow creasing as I digested his question. Um, what?

"Dad!" Blake hissed, but Steven held my eyes.

"I'm not sure what you mean." I glanced over at Tucker and Blake. "I never in my wildest dreams believed I'd be here, and when I suggested Tucker and I both date Blake, it was purely out of wanting to stay in the game. I'm not a man who dates a lot, and most women don't want to take the time to get to know me and that's a crucial part for me. Blake captured my attention right away, and I knew she was someone extraordinary. Even more amazing, she balances out Tucker and me, giving us both things we need in a relationship."

I squeezed Tucker's hand, smiling at the both of them. Blake stood from Tucker and moved to my lap, much to her father's annoyance.

"Seriously, BB? Is this your version of musical chairs? I'm scared to ask what happens when the music stops."

She turned, sticking her tongue out at him. "Tough cookie, Dad. You're grilling my boyfriends, so I get to sit in their laps when they say sweet things."

I chuckled, pulling her back to my chest. I let go of Tucker's hand so I could adjust, but apparently, he didn't like that.

"Oh, I want to play, too. Scoot over, Honey Bee."

Before I could protest, Blake and Tucker were both in my lap. "Tuck, you're too big for this."

"That's not what you—" Blake covered his mouth, her eyes laughing as she stared at him.

"Are you sure you want to finish that?" she teased.

I peeked out between them, giving Steven an exasperated sigh. "Do you honestly think I orchestrated this intentionally?"

"Ew!" Blake pulled back her hand, then slapped Tucker with it. "Don't lick me."

"That's—"

This time, I covered his mouth, elbowing him in the stomach for good measure.

Steven tried to pretend he wasn't laughing, but his whole body shook, and his eyes danced. When he recovered, he cleared his throat, giving me a nod.

"Fair point. I'd say you have your hands full, and no sane person would take that on, only someone who loved them."

I held his eyes but didn't confirm or deny it. I wanted to tell them in my own way.

"If I recall, you have a lot of sisters? A big family? How are they dealing with this?"

Blake and Tucker both turned to assess me. I accepted their comfort but didn't meet their eyes.

"My family has been accepting of me being pansexual since college, and I think they always wondered if there was more to Tucker and me so that part isn't the most shocking." I cleared my throat. "My sisters have called, and it's a mixed bag. Two of them are supportive and are proud of me for stepping out of the traditional path and living my life. The other two weren't as understanding."

"I'm so sorry, Graham," Blake said, kissing my cheek.

"It's okay. I knew it was possible, but I wouldn't change anything. I won't live my life scared my family might disown me."

"Do you think it could go that far?"

"My mom hasn't called. To her and my stepdad, being with two people is a bigger hurdle than being pan. It will take time. They don't always adjust to news immediately, so I need to be patient."

"Whatever you need, Teddy Graham, I'm there," Tucker said, kissing my other cheek.

Despite the fear and rejection brewing from my family, I

knew I was making the right decision for myself. These two were worth any risk I might endure. They were exactly what I'd been dreaming of when I realized I could like more than one person. And now that I had the chance to live it, I wasn't going to deny it just to make my family more comfortable. They'd either accept me and my relationship or miss out on knowing the two most important people in my life.

"Well, I hope they see the incredible man they have for a son before it's too late. Welcome to the family, Graham."

"Thanks, sir." I smiled, his words confirming my choice.

"Do you think seeing our video will help or worsen it?" Blake asked, chewing her lip.

"It doesn't matter, Sunshine. They either will or they won't. I can't control their reactions."

"But I don't want to make things worse. It's your family, Graham."

"They are." I nodded. "but they're not my only family. I'm building one here that means more to me."

Blake smiled, her eyes glistening as she leaned in and kissed me.

"Not to be the team owner here, but you four should change and get to the stadium. I'll be popping in to have a word with the team, so don't be alarmed later if you see me." He paused, glancing at the room, hesitating before he spoke the last part. "One of the hardest things about being a business owner is having dual relationships. I can recognize your role in my daughter's life, but in the stadium and diamond, you're my players. While my trading question was hypothetical, it doesn't mean it won't happen. I hope you can understand the two roles."

"Baseball's a business. And something we're all aware of. We wouldn't expect special treatment," I said, speaking for the three of us.

"I know. It's why I'm not trading any of you right this second."

"Dad!"

"It's okay, Slugger. It's the way of the sport, and your father is being honest. The fact he's giving us a chance says a lot," Luke said.

"BB, I'd like to shadow you today if that's possible. I think it's time you took your dear old dad to work."

"Sure thing, Dad."

She climbed off my lap and hugged her dad as the rest of us stood.

"Hawk, a word," he said, meeting the tattooed grump.

It was then I realized he hadn't been interrogated yet. As much as I wanted to be there to watch the big man sweat, I could understand the relationship was much different with Hawk versus the three of us.

Before this moment, we were just his players, but Hawk had always been part of the family.

Blake kissed Hawk, leaving him standing with her dad as she walked out with the three of us; she glanced over her shoulder once before we exited, worried lines on her face.

"He'll be okay," Tucker said, wrapping an arm around her shoulders.

"Yeah. I hope." Blake wrung her hands the whole way back to her room. We left her to change with Emory.

"I'm so glad you've come over to the fun side," Tucker said to Luke, pulling him into a one-sided hug.

"Fun side?" Luke quirked a brow.

"Oh, just you wait, my little porcupine!"

"Porcupine? What's your obsession with animals? You know what, I don't want to know," Luke said as we disembarked the elevator.

"Answering like a true porcupine," Tucker mumbled, following him.

Laughing, I watched the two as happiness flooded me. The pain of my family's rejection stung less than it had this morning. The road ahead wouldn't be easy, but it would be worth it. If the most mercurial man on the team could feel like a brother and friend to me after a month, I knew we'd fight whatever obstacles we'd face together.

"You know, Blake really gets out of the whole meet the family thing. We met her mother, father, brother, *and* best friend in the span of two days and had to pass the test. My family sucks. Sounds like your family sucks, and Graham's is on the fence. She already knows Hawk's family. We need to figure out someone she can meet so she can be grilled like we have been. I feel like I've fought on the frontline of two battles!" Tucker exclaimed, falling back onto the bed.

"I might have an idea," Luke said, his eyes shining bright.

"Yes, porcupine for the win!"

"Still not a thing."

"Totes a thing, just ask Teddy Graham."

I rolled my eyes. "This could be a disaster, but what the hell. I'm in. What's your idea?"

As Luke shared his grand idea, Tucker and I looked at one another, smiles growing as we nodded. Oh, yes, this would be perfect.

Now, to keep it a secret for a few days.

HAWK

I LET GO OF BLAKE AND WATCHED HER LEAVE WITH THE OTHERS, my eyes tracking her as I stood. Outwardly, I showed no signs of worry, but inwardly I was a fucking mess.

I'd maintained a calm exterior for an hour, watching Steven for any signs of displeasure. He'd avoided eye contact for the most part, only briefly glimpsing me when he would scan the others. Whether it was because he was pissed at me or trying to display a stern approach to others, I hadn't decided yet. Or which one I wanted it to be.

The door clicked shut, and the air in the room left.

Wait… that was just the oxygen in my lungs. I should breathe. Yes, breathing is good.

"Are you done freaking out yet?" he asked, eyeing me with a blank expression.

"That depends. Are you going to punch me like Bryce did?"

The blank mask broke, and Steven chortled. "He did?"

"Yeah, three years ago after the wedding."

"That's why you had a black eye," he said, moving to the

kitchen area to make coffee. He rubbed his temple, staring at the countertop while the coffee brewed. "I wish it was later in the day so I could have a real drink. My nerves are already shot, and it's not even noon."

I blinked, worried I'd missed something.

"So, that's a no on the punch?" I asked, stepping closer.

Steven laughed again, shaking his head. "The only reason I'd punch you, Hawk, is for taking so damn long to make a move."

I gaped at the man I considered as a second father. Though in a lot of ways, he had been the dad I'd needed growing up.

"Should I be insulted that you think I was too dumb to not notice how you looked at my daughter?"

"I mean..." I rubbed my beard. "But you told me to protect her like a sister," I challenged.

He smirked. "I couldn't do all the work for you. You needed to realize she meant more to you and make your own plan."

"I don't know what to say." I rubbed the back of my head, perplexed.

"You can start with 'thank you' for paying the plumbers to take longer and tell Bryce and Blake she couldn't return for one."

"What?" Now, I was truly dumbfounded. Had I stepped into a backward dimension? "But you just... What happened to making my own plan?" I sputtered, my body going back and forth like a sprinkler.

Steven rolled his eyes. "I gave you years!" He laughed. "I got tired of waiting, so I took an opportunity." The MLB superstar shrugged like he hadn't just changed the course of my life. Would I have made a move if she wasn't living with me? I'd like to think yes, but her forced proximity sped up the process.

Steven finished preparing his coffee and moved to the barstool. He patted the seat next to him, and I took it in a daze.

"Who are you?" I asked, chuckling.

"I know, I know. I shouldn't meddle. That's what Mallory always tells me. To let you kids figure it out." He grimaced before taking a sip of his coffee. "It's a little selfish on my part, but I wanted my daughter to stay here, and I figured if she was with you, she would."

"So you're not mad?" I asked, needing to hear it.

His brow scrunched. "Why would I be mad? I've loved you like a son your whole life. I'd be honored to have you as my son-in-law."

Tears pricked my eyes, and I fought to keep them at bay. Emotion clogged my throat, and I swallowed the cotton sticking along the sides. His words meant the world to me. Almost as much as Blake's love.

I cleared my throat. "Thank you, sir."

He narrowed his eyes, and I wondered if I misunderstood. "The deal still stands, Hawk."

"What deal?"

"I expect you to protect her with your life." He held my eyes, his words heavy.

"With all due respect, she doesn't need me protecting her. Blake's the bravest person I know, and I will love her fiercely until the day I die."

His shoulders dropped, and he nodded. "And that's why you have my blessing. You always have."

"Your what?" I croaked. I was back to thinking this was a weird pocket dimension.

"I'm beginning to think I overestimated your intelligence." He took another sip of his coffee. "My only advice is to ask her somewhere more private. That dodo Brandon picked the worst way to propose."

I snorted, relaxing. "When the time comes, I already know the perfect way. She told me once, actually."

"Good. She deserves the world."

"Is that why you're okay with her being with four guys?"

"*Okay* isn't the right word. Do I want to think about my only daughter with four guys? Hell, no. Do I like the idea of my daughter being cared for, loved, and cherished? Yes. Did I notice how happy and free she was? Also, yes. Am I a little selfish and secretly happy it connects her to me and baseball for the foreseeable future? Hell yes. If I take the part that no man should ever think about their daughter out of the equation, it's all upside for me." He shrugged, his logic so straightforward.

"How much of a mess is this with the team?" I asked, switching gears.

"It's not too bad so far. But it's why I want to stay. I'm trading Davis. I'd been working on it since I heard what he did to Blake, and it was official last night. Which is good for him because if I'd known he was part of the scandal, then I would've dropped his ass and not cared about the contract." Steven gritted his teeth, the ruthless owner coming out.

"Good. He's been a hothead for a while, and after Blake embarrassed him, he's been creating conflict amongst the team. The team was loyal to Bryce and saw her as the team's little sister. They respect her on their own, liking what she's doing for their careers. If he wasn't gone soon, it wouldn't end well. Ledger, especially, was about to explode on him. My message to Davis didn't seem to last long, either." I grimaced, wishing I could deliver another punch to the cocky asshole.

"He should be out by the time we get to the stadium. I wanted to let Blake have her say with the team before I stepped in. I think it's important for the guys to hear her before I put any mandates down."

I nodded. "I agree. I think you'll be pleased with the outcome."

"Is West ready to return?" he asked, switching gears.

"I'll double-check with the doctor, but I believe it's at least one more day, if not until we return to Wilmington."

He nodded, finishing his coffee. "The two of them really are something special. I might need them on the Blue Devils soon. There's been some… adjustments." He grimaced, and I wondered if it was connected to Bryce's issue.

"Anything I can do?"

"Keep working with them and get them ready."

"What about Olson?" I asked, curious.

"He started the season sluggishly, but he's been showing a different side of himself this last month. Do you think he and Bryce could be on the same team? BB said they'd made up, but that's off the diamond."

I thought it over, looking at it from a purely skill standpoint, not personal. "Bryce isn't going to like this, but I think they could. Their skills differ and offset enough that the two of them wouldn't be overkill on the same roster." I paused, weighing my words. "But honestly, one of them is better suited for a different position altogether, one you happen to be weak at."

"Hmph." He chuckled, the sound rough. "Yeah, well, that's a fight I've been having for fifteen years, and I don't know if I'll ever win it. You make one hell of a coach, Hawk. I'm glad to have you on my side." Steven clapped me on the shoulder, motioning to head to the door. "I'll let you get ready and see you in the clubhouse shortly." He dropped my shoulder, took a step, and stopped. "I don't think I need to say it, but for posterity, welcome to the family, Son. It's about damn time."

I gave a curt nod, my eyes welling up more as I pivoted and booked it out of the suite. I wasn't confident, but it seemed like Steven's eyes were glistening, too.

By the time I'd changed and headed downstairs, I was ready to take on the team and show the world who Blake was to me. The team bus was gone, so I ordered an Uber. As I climbed in, my phone rang, and my sister's name popped up on the screen. I wanted to ignore it, but Wren rarely called.

"Hey, Wren. I'm headed to the stadium, so I don't have much time to talk."

"So, that's how it's going to be, big Brother? Hmm? You decide to live a polyamorous lifestyle and don't think to tell your sister. You always did have to be cooler than me."

I laughed. Wren always was one to be over the top. "Hey, Sis, guess what? The girl I've been in love with forever likes me back, and we're going to be together, but she also has three other boyfriends," I said in a high-pitched and upbeat voice that sounded close to Tucker's, but I'd deny it. "How are the rugrats?"

"Nope. Nope. You can't just drop that and then ask me questions! I have so many," she rushed out.

"You get two." I leaned back, closing my eyes and preparing for the onslaught.

"Two! Two! But…"

"And that time is still limited."

"Ugh, I hate you."

"No, you don't.'

"Fine. Who gave in first?" she asked.

"Hmm, I was holding out for some obligation that now seems dumb and then finally caved."

"That sounds so romantic," she deadpanned. "I bet it was great. You two always had the best chemistry."

I ignored the flutter in my chest that lived there for Blake. "What's your next one, Wren? You got five minutes."

"Ugh. You're no fun. Hmm…" I could hear the girls in the background as she thought, and images of having my own kids running around someday hit me out of nowhere.

What the hell.

I'd never envisioned kids before. Maybe because I never wanted them if it wasn't with Blake. But now… now it was a possibility. I swallowed around the panic, knowing I needed to add more on to the house.

Or maybe I needed to look for something in Columbus. If Steven called the three of them up, Blake would want to go. I could follow them even if there wasn't a job. The future was open, and it no longer scared me because I knew no matter what, I'd have Blake. Even knowing the others would be there…that felt nice, too. They were like furniture I hadn't wanted, but now I was used to them, so there was no point in getting rid of them.

"Earth to Hawk!"

"Huh?"

"That's it, we're coming in for a visit next week. I need to see this for myself."

I rubbed my forehead, smiling. It wasn't the threat Wren thought it was. "I'd love that. We're having a baseball game party for Luke's little girl. She's turning five. Maybe you could come that day? I'll see if Bryce is cool with you staying at his place. Mine's a little full."

"Little girl? Full house? Oh my god! My brother's a real adult! I have so many more questions."

"And look at that, we're here. Text me later!"

I hung up the phone before she could go into another spiel. I wanted to argue I'd been a real adult far longer than she had, but I knew what she meant. I'd been going through the motions, following the rules, and doing the responsible thing for everyone else.

But now I was living my life and carving out a future for myself that didn't just consist of baseball, tattoos, and the occasional visits from my family.

The car dropped me off a minute later, the driver giving

me odd looks as I exited. I hoped it was because my conversation was so weird and not the article. It had been gone by this morning, but that didn't mean plenty of people hadn't read it before they took it down.

Stepping into the locker room, I didn't realize the silence until I turned the corner and came face-to-face with the team.

CHAPTER
SEVENTY

BLAKE

"WHAT ABOUT EMMETT? IS HE SINGLE?" EMORY ASKED AS I stored my gear and pulled out my camera.

"Even if he is, do you really want to be Emmett and Emory? Em and Em. M&M!"

Her face tilted as she thought about it. "It's a cute couple name."

"Nope." I laughed, pulling her out the door with me. To distract me from the stress of being on camera and telling the world to mind their own business, Emory had decided to ask me about each eligible bachelor on the team.

Not as fun as I'd imagined.

The YellowJackets had become pseudo-brothers to me, and it was weird to think of them with Emory. Mostly because Emory was the 'love 'em and leave 'em' type, and I knew most of the guys on the team were looking for something serious despite their reputations. Spending six days at a time with the players bonded you.

My phone vibrated in my pocket, and I pulled it out as I smiled. I'd worn a skirt for Luke and was eager to see what he thought.

But instead of Luke, it was Hawk.

Hawk: There's something you need to see in the clubhouse.

Blake: On my way. Emory's with me. Is that a problem?

Hawk: Nope.

"We've been summoned to the clubhouse."

"Ooo, that sounds kinky. Which guy do I get?" She rubbed her hands together as she bounced on her feet.

"Em, I worry about you sometimes." I chuffed as I dragged her toward the stairs.

"Why?" she asked, her brows furrowed.

"You think more with your vagina than your brain."

"And?"

I laughed. Emory was Emory, and I wouldn't want her any other way.

"Nothing. You're right. I just hope you let someone into your heart one day."

"Ew. Just because you're all loved up doesn't mean you need to spread it around. Wait, is this like herpes? Is love transferable?" she gasped, looking at me in horror and pulling her arm from mine.

"Oh my god!" I groaned as I continued down the stairs. "It's not like herpes. But you know what, just for that, I'm gonna good curse you."

"Good curse me? I don't understand, and I don't think it's a language barrier this time." She grinned.

"Ha! Funny. But yes, good curse you. I don't know what the term is for something that's like a curse, but good, so we'll go with gurse." I stopped on the stairs and turned to take her hands. She let me despite her earlier herpes comment. "I'm gursing you, my beautiful friend, to fall in love. It might not be the next guy or girl you sleep with, but it will happen. And when it does, it will knock you off your feet and strike you, that you won't be able to deny it because nothing else will have ever felt as powerful."

She frowned, taking one of her hands and patting me on the head like a little child. "Okay, sure. We'll go with that. Gurse me away, Lake. But this heart," she tapped her chest, "it only has love for moi!" She spun around, her arms wide as she skipped down the rest of the stairs.

Shaking my head, I followed her, hoping that one day she would let someone in.

"So why do they call it a clubhouse? Isn't it just a locker room?" she asked as we neared the visitors' area.

"Yeah. But it's baseball." I shrugged. "And baseball teams are part of clubs, and I guess back in the day, they liked the idea of hanging out in the 'clubhouse' before games over locker rooms." It didn't need to make sense; it just was. I pushed open the door and motioned for her to follow me.

The first thing I noticed when we entered was how quiet it was. I'd been in a clubhouse numerous times, and it was only ever this subdued when it was empty. Right before a game it should be filled with music, laughter, and chatter.

Goosebumps pricked my skin, and I turned back to Emory as wariness enveloped me. Either something terrible had happened, or they were about to jump out and scare me. I honestly didn't know which I preferred.

"Hello?" I said, hoping to get a response.

Hawk peeked around the side, and the sight of him unharmed eased my nerves. He motioned for me to come closer.

"Someone's not going to jump out and scare me, are they? Tucker's not waiting around the corner to show me—"

"Nothing scary about me, Honey Bee!" Tucker shouted, followed by a few chuckles.

It confused me more, so I stopped. Hawk rolled his eyes

and came forward, grabbing my hand and tugging me the last few steps around the corner. It opened into their cubbies with the showers off to the other side.

And while no one jumped out at me, the sight in front of me was odd, to say the least.

"What in the world?" Emory muttered, bumping into me.

I blinked, but the image didn't change.

"Did you do this?" I asked Hawk.

"Nope. I found them like this."

"We heard what he did, so we took action," Hector, the second baseman, said, his arms crossed.

I covered my mouth, attempting to hold in my giggle.

Seth Davis was surrounded by almost the entire team. His beard had been shaven, making that part of his face lighter than the top half, giving him a two-toned look from being out in the sun. His hair was dyed like a rainbow, and they'd dressed him in a white t-shirt. I squinted as I tried to read what they'd crudely written in black marker.

"I'm a douchenozzle in rehab, and part of my program is to say something nice if you ask. So, go on, ask," I read out loud.

"Oh, me, me! Say something nice to me," Emory said.

One of the outfielders pulled the tube sock in his mouth free, nudging him to perform like a monkey.

"Don't forget, Davis. It can't be superficial. So make it good, or we tell your new team, and *this* continues," Ledger said, narrowing his eyes at Seth with his thick arms crossed. It was the most I'd ever heard him say in front of the team, and apparently, that was scary enough for Seth because he didn't fight it. He swallowed, looking Emory up and down.

"You have the best energy."

"Aww, thank you." Emory smiled, then took two steps forward, bending down to stare into his face. "But it doesn't make up for what you did. In my country, we'd cut a man's balls off and then fry them up for the cows to eat. Do I make myself clear?"

"Yes." He swallowed as the team chittered like schoolgirls.

"Damn. That's hot," one of the other guys said, followed by a wolf whistle.

"Good." She patted Seth's cheek, stepped back, eyeing the team, and winked at a few before spinning and sauntering back to me.

I watched as grown men swooned, their eyes leaving their bodies as they transformed into hearts at my bestie.

"I think I just got pregnant," Levi whispered.

"Marry me?" Dalton asked.

I laughed as I processed Ledger's words. *New team.* "Wait… did you say new team?" I asked, turning to Ledger, but he was already gone.

Tucker walked over, wrapping his arm around me. "Yep. Your dad made it official last night. His stuff's packed, and we're ready to send him off. But we thought you might want to do the last touch?"

He tapped my camera, and I realized what he meant. Seth had shared images of us without our consent, so posting him like this would be a good payback.

But it felt dirty to me, and I didn't want that. Taking his consent away just because ours had wasn't the right message to send.

"I have a better idea," I said. Tucker smiled at me, kissing my lips briefly. I walked over to Seth and nodded to the guys to let him go. "I need to hear you admit what you did was wrong."

"I'm sorry," he gritted out like I'd been the one to wrong him. I shook my head, frowning.

"I don't want your apologies, Seth. Those words mean nothing to me because I highly doubt you'll change your behavior."

"Then what do you want?" he spat.

"To know you understand your actions hurt people. No one should ever have their safety taken away because of a choice *you* made." My words were firm, and I felt their resoluteness in my bones. He'd done that with me when he supplied me with drinks and with Tucker and Graham when he outed their relationship.

"The only person hurt here is *me*, daddy's girl. You wouldn't know what suffering was if it hit you with a ten-foot pole."

The chatter built around the room died as Seth's words echoed. I took a step back, the vitriol of his words punching me in the chest.

"Motherfucker!" Hawk roared. Chairs scraped against the floor as everyone moved.

I pressed my hand into Hawk's chest, barely stopping him from pummeling Seth to the ground. Hawk's chest vibrated, the rage a living and breathing entity. I swallowed, attempting to keep my anger and resentment from rising up. Seth jerked back in fear, and I could only guess the look on Hawk's face matched my emotions.

"The only thing stopping him is *me*. I hope you realize the gift I'm giving you here."

"Blazy!" Hawk roared, but I ignored him.

"I'd press charges if he touched me," Seth countered, some of his bravado returning.

"Oh yeah? With what witnesses? Anyone see anything?" I asked, not dropping my eyes from the weasel.

"Nope. Not me."

"I saw him run into a door."

"Yep, nasty spill he took in the shower."

I didn't know who said what; their words confirmed my trust in this team.

"Still feel as confident?" When he said nothing, I continued, already done with this man. "That's to show you the power *I* have. It's not my dad's. It's not my brother's. It's *mine*.

I've been around this league far longer than you, meaning I have allies in every stadium and every baseball club. If I hear an inkling you're up to no good, the reins come off." I dropped my hand, and Hawk pressed forward, his back pressing into mine.

"You heard my daughter, Davis. Get your ass out of this clubhouse," my father said, surprising me.

Seth scampered up, taking a wide berth around Hawk and me, and I choked back a laugh as I took in the rest of his outfit, my fingers itching to capture it. Whoever had been in charge of his pants had drawn poop emojis all over the back with "I'm a shithead" curving around his butt.

"Fucking bullshit of a team," Seth muttered as he turned the corner.

"Oh, and good luck finding your own way there," my dad shouted to his retreating form. The door slammed behind him, and the team turned to my father, waiting to see what he'd do.

"Whose idea was the pants?" he asked, shocking everyone.

Emmett raised his hand slowly. "Um, mine, sir."

"Good thing I pay you to play third base because you're a shit artist." My dad smirked, and the tension broke as laughter spilled around the room. Everyone relaxed back into their spots, no longer worried they were about to get chewed out by the owner. My dad cleared his throat once it was quiet, all attention snapping back to him.

"I'd wanted to talk to everyone before the game today, but it seems the team has already taken care of things." My dad's smile was proud, and I knew it was for more than just the team—he was proud of me.

"I'm still not sure why Blake didn't choose me, but she and the second-rate guys she did pick are family. We're a team, something Davis never understood," Hector said, blowing me a kiss. I chuckled, shaking my head.

"Second-rate? Coach, Suraz is benched!" Hawk yelled, making Hector's face go white.

"I mean, the others. You're top class, Coach."

Hawk glared at him as Hector shuffled his feet nervously. The guy was a huge flirt, so to see him buckle under Hawk's stare was comical.

"Lineup change?" Coach Phillips asked as he peeked around the corner.

"Never mind," Hawk said, and Hector deflated in relief, causing everyone to laugh.

"Anything you need to say, BB?" my dad asked once the laughter had stopped again.

"Oh, yes." I messed with the strap of my camera as I met everyone's eyes. "To battle Seth and Mira's story, we wanted to share our story on LiveIt. That is, as long as everyone is cool with that. It's the team's."

"I'm cool," several guys said; others nodded their consent. Only a few were quiet, but their teammates nudged them, and they relented, rolling their eyes.

"Thanks, guys." I grinned at them, my shoulders relaxing. "I'm sorry the team was brought into this. We're not going to hide our relationship, but we won't flaunt it either."

"Thank fuck. I was not looking forward to Coach making out with someone I consider a little sister," Levi said, winking.

"And everyone's cool with me and Graham?" Tucker asked.

"Honestly, we thought you were already together," someone said, followed by a lot of agreements.

"Right. Okay, then." Tucker blushed, but I knew he was happy no one would treat him differently. Graham nudged him with his elbow, and Tucker relaxed.

"Don't Baker and Olson hate each other?" another teammate asked.

"We're working on it," Luke said, taking my hand.

"Good enough for me."

After that, the team returned to their regular routines, falling into conversations as they pulled out their pre-game rituals. Emory spoke with some players, so I pulled Hawk's shirt so I could whisper.

"Watch Emory for me? I need to handle something real quick."

Hawk lifted his eyebrow but nodded. "Make sure Olson has his best game yet," he teased.

I dodged my father's eyes as he talked with the other coaches, and I tugged Luke out the door.

"What are we doing? Warmups are soon."

"Then you better be quick."

"Quick?" Luke asked, then swallowed. "Slugger. I appreciate it, but your *father* is here."

"Add quiet," I teased. I stopped, pulling Luke closer. "I finally followed directions." I pointed down, and he took in the skirt. Luke's eyes bulged, his eyes dilating.

"Yeah, I can be quick." He nodded, his voice cracked.

Laughing, I hauled Luke into the first room I discovered and locked the door. Our mouths were on each other in seconds, his hands gripping my hips. Lifting me up, I wrapped my legs around his waist as he devoured my lips, his tongue spearing into mine and sending desire straight through me.

When his fingers breached my opening, I cursed, my head falling back against the door.

"Holy hell," Luke moaned. "No panties, and you're already so drenched. You're gonna kill me." He plunged his fingers inside, not being gentle as I rode his digits.

"More," I begged, needing to feel him around me. It had only been a few days, but I missed each of them, no matter if I'd been with the others.

The sound of his buckle hitting the ground was my only warning before he surged up in me, filling me in one go.

We both groaned as his hands gripped my ass, neither of us breathing as we adjusted.

"I don't even have to try to be quick. Hold on, Slugger."

Bracing one hand on the back of the door, I gripped my other around his neck as he moved me up and down, impaling me deeper each time. My body exploded in pleasure as my pussy drenched him and my walls clamped down around him.

"This pussy," he moaned, stilling inside as he gave two more jerky moves before he spilled, sending me over the edge. I came so hard that my vision blurred, and every muscle trembled.

"Fuck, fuck," we both moaned as we came down.

Our breathing was loud as we returned to the normal plane, and I laughed as he placed me back on the ground, my legs shaky.

"Definitely a fan of the skirts. Though, having to walk around with your cum dripping down my legs... not so much."

"Jesus, why is that so hot?" He groaned, biting his lip.

"Hawk said to have the best game yet. But text me if you need a little support later." I winked. Luke gaped at me, his cock hardening at the thought.

"Come on." I grabbed some tissue from my bag that had landed on the ground, thankful I'd placed my camera in it. Once we were both cleaned, I slipped on the panties I'd put in there earlier.

Pre-sex commando... hot. After-sex commando... messy.

Looking both ways, we slipped out, and Luke headed back to the clubhouse and me to the stands. Emory found me a little later, a knowing smirk on her face.

"You're gonna have to teach me all these hidden rooms so I can get some ball player sex."

"I don't know what you're talking about."

"Then I don't have two players' numbers," she countered. Gaping at her, I chased her around as we both laughed.

At the beginning of the week, I didn't know if I could make this type of relationship work—out of fear for the guys' future and worry I'd disappoint my family. The truth was out now, and I'd never been happier, freer.

I wasn't deluded in believing this would be the only drama we'd encounter. There would be others like Seth who tried to break us down, but we had more support than I'd ever considered before—support I'd gained all on my own.

When Bryce asked me to return home, I'd been worried I wouldn't be able to handle everything I had to face. But with each obstacle and every stumble, I kept persevering, proving to myself that I'd grown and was ready for this. Life could pitch-slap me all it wanted, but it would never keep me down.

Because despite what others assumed about me, like Seth and Mira, my life hadn't been easy growing up, regardless if I was a baseball princess. That hadn't made my life a fairytale. Far from it.

But maybe that was the point.

Not every Cinderella had a glass slipper or a fairy godmother to save them, but it wouldn't stop them from slaying their dragons, or in my case, YellowJackets.

I might only be a Bee, but my sting was mighty.

CHAPTER
SEVENTY-ONE

TUCKER

I watched Graham and Blake climb out of the Uber, glancing at the mall in confusion. When I'd planned to tell them my declaration of love, I'd wanted to do it at a zoo. Unfortunately, Charleston didn't have one, and driving a few hours to visit one when our time was limited didn't seem like a brilliant idea. So, I had to rethink my grand moment.

Between the scandal, video, and Emory visiting, I hadn't had much time to enact my plan. Still, I was determined to do it before we headed back. Tomorrow was the away series' last game, so I'd jetted here right after the game and left a message for them to meet me at 9pm. I couldn't go one more day without telling them.

So here we were inside a mall after hours I'd paid to rent. I'd learned from Blake's ex that doing something grand in front of others was a no-no, so I kept this between us. Because there was no way I could do something this big on a small scale. That word didn't even exist in my vocabulary.

"I guess we go inside?" Blake asked, peering through the doors.

"If Tucker made us come stand in line with him for a sneaker, I'm going to be pissed," Graham muttered.

"No, you won't," Blake teased, laughing. Graham sighed and smiled.

"No, I won't."

Watching the two of them, I felt warm and tingling, and I knew I'd never feel this way for anyone else. They were it for me.

Time to show them.

They stepped through the mall doors and into the food court. There was a carousel and fountain to the right, which I hid behind. Rising with my Nerf gun, I fired two shots, hitting them both.

"What the pitch!" Blake cursed, swinging around. Her mouth dropped open, and she crossed her arms, trying to appear angry. "Tucker Jameson! You're in big trouble."

"Aw, babe. Is this our first fight? I guess you'll have to catch me first. Good luck!"

I hit the switch for the carousel and waved as it turned with me on it. As soon as I was clear on the other side, I jumped off and ran. I could hear them yelling at the sticky substance I'd placed on the floor, stalling their movements to where they'd have to leave their shoes behind. Coach would probably ream me a new one if he knew the risks I was taking but we wouldn't mention anything to him.

Chuckling, I ducked behind a kiosk and waited for them to reach the first stop. I wished I'd thought to record this so I could see their reactions and not just hear them, but I'd have to live off my own imagination for now.

"All is fair in love and Nerf war," Blake read. "What does that mean?"

"I think it means we're to have a Nerf battle in this mall," Graham said, picking up the two guns I'd left them.

"But it's huge!"

"That's what she said," I whispered, laughing at myself.

"You know if Tucker was here, he would've said—"

"That's what she said," Blake finished, laughing. "Ugh, fine. Do we team up or divide?"

"Let's stick together. Two is better than one," Graham said.

"Also, what she said." Blake laughed, and I had to hide a snort.

My body vibrated with laughter and exhilaration. This was already the most fun I'd ever had. If this was what planning dates were like, I couldn't wait to do it more.

"Never thought I'd be walking through a mall sock-footed with a Nerf gun," Blake muttered. "All right, Tucker, I'm coming for you!"

"That's what she said," I yelled, then ran again when I heard them take off. I hadn't been able to get any stores to stay open. Something about them being worried I'd damage the merchandise. Lame.

But that didn't stop my fun. I'd set up a few areas with ammo and mapped out where I wanted to stop, leading them to the end, where I had my big declaration setup. Sliding around the popcorn stand, I lifted over and took aim.

"Nailed it!"

"Tucker!" Blake laughed, shooting her gun at me before diving behind a kiosk. I fired a few more at Graham before I took off again. I slipped once and then righted myself laughing as Nerf bullets whizzed by me.

"You're gonna lose, Tuck-Tuck!"

"No such thing in a Nerf battle," I yelled back.

I refilled my Nerf gun at the next station before hitting my last hideout. I scanned the area, shooting off a few at Blake as she cursed, laughing as she found a hiding spot and then shooting at me. It was then I realized my colossal mistake.

"Gotcha, Mr. Studly Pitcher."

I'd forgotten to track Graham.

"Ah, babe. You got my name right," I teased, lifting my

hands and standing. Blake gave a battle roar as she zoomed toward me, pelting me with Nerf bullets. I covered myself as I laughed, loving this moment. This was what I wanted for the rest of my life.

"What do we get now that we've cornered you?" Graham asked, pressing into my back. Blake moved to my front, covering me there. Her cheeks were flushed, and her hair stuck to her forehead. Her blue eyes sparkled, and I cupped her cheek in my hand.

"Me. Forever," I whispered, watching Blake. There were no signs of panic this time, and I kissed her nose before glancing back and holding Graham's gray eyes. He smiled at me, squeezing my hips where he held me.

"I can live with that." His voice was husky, and it woke up every part of me.

"First, there's one more thing, and I promise not to ambush you."

"Disarm him, Sunshine, just in case."

Blake took my gun and checked my pockets, and then the two of them pointed at me with their weapons to move along. Shaking my head, I chuckled as I made the last turn to the display I'd set up. I gave a dramatic bow as I turned toward them.

"I might come off as the goofy one who doesn't always catch onto things right away, so I wanted to show you how serious I am regarding us." I stepped aside and revealed three pairs of white sneakers.

"Shoes?" Blake turned her head.

I laughed, then picked up the tablet. "Actually, they're custom ones I've designed. But apparently, doing three pairs in two days isn't possible, so they're white for now." I rolled my eyes and held my breath while waiting for their reaction.

"You designed us shoes?" Blake asked, blinking at me.

"Yeah. Is that dorky?"

"It's amazing."

"G?" I asked, turning to the quiet man.

He didn't answer but stepped forward and held my head, slamming his lips to mine. I stumbled back but braced myself by grabbing him.

"I love you, too," he whispered when he pulled back.

"You do?" I smiled when he nodded. "Wait, I haven't said it yet."

"You didn't have to. You're sharing something with me. That told me everything I needed to know."

"You love us?" Blake asked.

"Yeah. I was getting to that, but this one had to steal my thunder."

"Sorry not sorry."

"Teddy Graham, step aside, please."

Graham released me, and Blake launched herself at me, wrapping her arms and legs around me. "I love you too, Tucker Jameson. It's scary and big, but I've never been more excited than to find out where it takes us."

"You're amazing, Honey Bee."

I sealed my lips to hers, getting lost as our tongues twirled, sending tingles through my body. Another body pressed into me again, arms wrapping around me from behind, and I wondered if I could live the rest of my life in this position.

"I love you too, Graham. You both give me the courage to jump into the unknown, and I can't thank you enough for that." She held his eyes over my shoulder, her heart beating rapidly beneath my touch.

"Texting you was the best mistake I've ever made, Sunshine. I think I fell in love with you from the first moment you bantered with us. You slotted in so well; it was like discovering a part of my heart had always lived in you."

"Wow, that's hella romantic, G. You gotta kiss her after that," I mumbled.

"I would, but some brute is hogging her."

"Oh, right. I can fix that." I turned, bringing Blake and Graham closer, watching as they kissed. I didn't know which moment was hotter…watching them or experiencing it myself. I was glad I'd never have to choose.

"I have dessert, but I'm suddenly thinking we need to take this back to the hotel," I muttered, my jeans increasingly tighter.

"Mmm, dessert. What kind?" Blake asked, pulling back. Her lips were swollen and red, and I wanted to kiss them again, but her question broke through the lust.

"It's a build-your-own cookie station."

"How did you manage all of this?" Graham asked as I walked us over to the cart.

"I know some people," I teased.

"Do we have to pick up the darts?"

"Nah. The company I hired will get it once we leave." I placed Blake on her feet as I showed the cookies. I'd found a 'plan a date' company online that had helped me plan all the details for this. While I had the idea, they executed it all for a fee. Money well spent.

"Looks portable to me."

"Yep." Graham nodded, loading the cookies into the basket.

"Wait, what's happening?" I asked, confused as they took over.

"We're taking it to go. Now, did you bring a car, or did you Uber?" Graham questioned.

"I Ubered. Why?"

"Order another one. Now." The heat in his eyes had my body vibrating with need, and I suddenly realized their intentions.

"And this is why I love you both. You have brilliant ideas." Tossing the tablet and shoes into the bag, I quickly picked up everything outside the Nerf guns and bullets, dragging them to the front.

"Don't you need to order a car?" Blake asked, sliding on her feet as she tried to keep up.

"I planned ahead."

"Words have never been sexier."

Blake and Graham's shoes had been removed from the sticky substance and cleaned, sitting next to the door as we neared. They both quickly put on their shoes, and then the three of us hurried out the entrance to the awaiting car. It was the longest ride in history as the three of us attempted not to touch one another. When we pulled up to the hotel, I groaned at the sight of the paparazzi waiting outside.

"We can do it," Blake said, holding her head high.

We nodded, thanking the driver as we climbed out and headed toward the door. The video had done what we wanted, getting our story out to the world on our terms, but it didn't mean the paparazzi and media hadn't tried to get their piece.

While none of us were allowed online for the next week, the comments I'd peeked at on Levi's phone had primarily been supportive, as had the fans at the stadium. The team had been great, helping us field questions and focus on baseball instead of diving into our personal lives.

The second the paps spotted us, the flashes went off, and the questions started. The three of us huddled together, Graham and I shielding Blake as we hustled the last few feet to the door.

"Thank goodness we leave tomorrow. I didn't want to switch hotels again," Blake moaned as we headed to the elevator. After the news broke, the team split among a few hotels to thwart the media.

"Emory make it to the airport okay?" I asked. She'd helped distract Blake while I got the mall set up.

"Yep. She has another week of interviews, then she's gonna head to Wilmington. Bryce said she could use his condo."

"Is it me, or is there some weird vibe between them?" I asked.

Graham and Blake turned to me. "What do you mean?" Blake asked slowly.

"Just..." Graham gave me a look, subtly shaking his head. "It's nothing."

Thankfully, the elevator opened to our floor, and we headed to our room. The instant we crossed the threshold, the tension returned, and my back was pressed up against the door by both of them.

"Say it again, Tuck. I want to hear it," Graham whispered.

"I love you. I love you. I love you."

Graham's lips met mine in a fury of passion, stealing my breath as Blake's hands ran over me. They tugged me to the bed, pushing me back on it as they stared at me from the foot.

"How adventurous do you feel, Tuck?" Graham asked.

"I want it all, G."

Graham's pupils dilated even more, his gray eyes becoming like silver as he stared at me. He swallowed once, his Adam's apple bobbing with the move, and I became transfixed.

"Blake, grab my bag and bring it here."

My eyes stayed on G's as he pulled off his shirt and pants. His cock stood at attention, the pubic piercing glinting in the light. I licked my lips, the desire to taste him hitting me. The side of the bed shifted, and I caught sight of a naked Blake.

"You've got on too many clothes." Her hands pulled up my shirt, and I let her, enjoying the view of her tits in my face.

"I could get used to this," I moaned.

Just as I leaned forward to wrap my lips around her nipple, Graham unzipped my pants, palming my erection. My eyes rolled back as I moaned, pleasure racing through me. By the time I came to, Blake had moved, and I was completely naked.

"We need to prep you," Graham rumbled, nodding to Blake.

"Kneel, Tucker." I did as she asked, lifting up on my knees, and moaned when I felt Blake press her tits into my back. Graham moved forward, cupping my face and kissing my lips passionately.

"Okay, Princess, show me how good your tongue skills are."

Exhilaration lit up, and I leaned forward to get closer to my prize. Wrapping my hand around Graham's cock, I gave it a stroke before sticking out my tongue and tasting him. It was salty and musky and better than I expected. Graham's heady scent enveloped me, purely masculine, with a hint of spice. As I continued to explore his cock, I felt something cold land on my ass.

"That feels amazing," Graham cooed, distracting me from whatever was happening behind me.

Blake's hands smoothed over my ass, the cool liquid dripping into my hole as I continued to lick Graham. I soon became too distracted with the treat before me to pay attention. I took him further into my mouth, stopping when I gagged, and then tried again. His hands landed on my hair, and I tensed.

I suddenly felt awful for tugging a girl's hair and prayed Graham wouldn't touch mine. My hair was a masterpiece, not a steering wheel. Thankfully, Graham only cupped the back of my head, smoothing my curls away as he tenderly stroked my hair.

Pressure built behind me, something smooth and cool, and I remembered the two-sided dildo he'd used on Blake before. As she prepped my ass, I focused on experiencing everything Graham had to offer me. I sucked his cock, enjoying how he moaned, and gently thrust his hips as I pumped him with my hand. When Blake hit my prostate, my legs trembled, and I had to brace my hand on the bed to stop myself from falling headfirst onto Graham's cock.

"I think he's ready," Graham mumbled, and the pressure on my backside left me. I whimpered, already missing it, as Graham pulled his cock from my mouth. Cupping my cheek, he tilted my head up.

"Fuck, you look so hot like this, Princess." Graham bit his lip, his hand caressing my face, and I leaned into it, loving his words almost as the pleasure they were giving me. "Now, kiss our girlfriend."

Graham turned my head to Blake, who was lying back on the bed, the rainbow dildo we'd gifted her months ago plunging into her pussy.

"Fuck."

I dived on top of her, stealing her breath with my lips as I rocked against her naked body, my hands exploring every inch of her I could. My hand took over the dildo, pushing it and pulling it out as I watched her body tremble.

"Yes, yes, yes," Blake moaned, her head tossing back and forth. Tossing it to the side, I replaced it with my dick, lifting her hips and plunging in one go. Graham let us lose ourselves in one another for a few minutes as we rutted against one another, our bodies moving together.

"Tell me if it's too much," he whispered, kissing my shoulder as he spread my cheeks and nudged the tip of his cock at my hole. I slowed on top of Blake, holding her eyes as Graham breached my virgin hole.

"Just breathe and bear down. Your body will want to fight it, but go with it, and it will feel better."

I gritted my teeth, my cock softening as the pain surged. Blake pulled my lips to hers, kissing me and helping to distract me from the pain. When Graham brushed his cock over my prostate, my entire body lit back up.

He gave a few short thrusts, milking that magic button and bringing me back to full mast.

"I'm in," he whispered, his voice strained. "We'll move together."

I didn't know what he meant until he pulled back and then slammed forward, causing my eyes to blur as my cock went deeper into Blake.

"Fuck!" we groaned together, and I remembered to pull back this time when Graham did. There was so much pleasure around me that my body didn't know what to do as it trembled. Sex had never felt this great, but as I plunged into the woman I loved and felt the man who also held my heart press into me, I was done. Blake's walls tightened around my cock, gripping it so tight I had no restraint left as Graham hit that magic button again.

My orgasm exploded, my vision going dark as everything in me went off like a firework. My toes curled, tiny pinpricks of light lit up behind my eyelids, and I fell on top of Blake as all my muscles gave out.

"Wowzer," I moaned. "I think I forgot my name."

"Mr. Studly Pitcher, if I remember correctly," Blake teased.

"Or Punk Princess. Depending on how you're acting."

"Hmm, doesn't sound like me."

The three of us laughed, and I begrudgingly rolled over so I didn't squish Blake. "If this is what being in love is like, I never want to be out of love again."

"I think that's something we can arrange," Graham said, kissing my shoulder. This feeling right here, of being completely accepted and cherished, was the one I'd been searching for my whole life, and now I had it times two.

I wasn't sure if even winning the pennant would ever top this moment.

"Love you guys," I mumbled after Graham cleaned me and Blake up. The three of us curled up together, and I blissfully fell asleep, knowing I'd never forget this night.

Even if we did forget to eat the cookies.

BLAKE

Climbing off the bus, I shifted my bag on my shoulder as I yawned. We'd survived the last away game, bringing the season record to 50-10 as we entered week eleven. As long as the YellowJackets didn't lose over the next two weeks, they would clinch their division win for the first half of the season, meaning come playoffs, we'd host. My dad was super pleased, the stadium no longer in jeopardy.

But perhaps the better news was that we wouldn't have to travel for seven days. After next week's away games, the team got an extended break before the second half of the season resumed.

Oh, the plans I had for those days off... most of them were naked.

"What time do you want us to come over in the morning?" Luke asked, grabbing my attention as he took his bag from the travel manager. Tomorrow was Willow's birthday, so I'd asked Luke if we could have a special breakfast before she went to school. Her party wasn't until Friday at Champion Field, but we all wanted to see her and make her day special.

"What time does she have to be at school?"

"Whenever. It's not as strict as normal school yet."

"Eight works, then? I can make something." Hawk coughed behind me, and I rolled my eyes. "I can make pancakes," I protested. "And I'm great at ordering."

"Too bad Emory's gone. That girl can cook," Tucker said, patting his stomach. Emory had spoiled everyone with pastries after commandeering my dad's suite. The woman had impressive skills of persuasion.

"I'd be offended if I didn't agree. The Greek fifteen is a thing," I said, patting my hips.

"I need to doubly thank her then. Noted," Hawk said, shocking me.

"I'm no Emory, but I can make something that won't kill everyone," Graham teased.

"Hey! My pancakes are edible. It's hard to mess up a mix."

Graham groaned, shaking his head before turning to Luke. "I'll make real pancakes. What's her favorite?"

"I feel like I should be offended." I pouted until something registered. "Oh my god! I just realized something. Since you're moving in, does that mean your coffee maker is coming, too?" I hopped back and forth on my feet as I waited.

"The secret's out, G. She only wants us for our coffee." Tucker draped his arm over Graham's, winking at me.

"I'll take that as a yes!" I fist-pumped the air, making them all laugh. "Just wait! It's orgasmic," I moaned, their eyes heating as they turned to me.

Luke cleared his throat, stepping forward. "On that note, I better head out before I make things even more awkward with my teammates. I'll see you in the morning, Slugger." He kissed me briefly before walking away, waving over his shoulder at the guys.

I glanced around, noticing a few other players loitering.

Now that I could be open about my relationships, I forgot that not everyone was on board. Most of the team had been supportive, but a few weren't fans. Hawk added my bag to his, linking his fingers with mine as we headed to our vehicles.

"Oh! I sold my car while we were away," Tucker said.

"You did?" Graham's brow wrinkled. "I'm scared to ask what you got instead."

Tucker laughed. "Why would I get a car? You drive me everywhere, baby." Tucker kissed his cheek before opening his door and sliding in. Graham's face heated, but I caught the smile. I loved how surprised he still seemed at times when Tucker openly showed he cared for him.

"See you at home!" I said, smiling at the words. *Home.*

"That word never sounded sexier," Hawk mumbled, starting his car.

"I couldn't agree more."

He glanced over, his eyes tracking over my body. "I'm half tempted to find a dead end and have my way with you before we get there."

"Tsk, tsk. You know they'd just watch." I grinned as I buckled in.

Hawk grumbled but put the car in drive. Once he had the car on the road, he reached over and took my hand. It was simple, but it solidified the realness of this.

"It just hit me that there's nothing standing in our way now."

"Having second thoughts?" He looked over, his brow wrinkled.

"Nope. Only the best thoughts."

When he peered at me this time, nothing but love shone on his face as he took me in. "When your dad had everyone leave, do you know what he told me?"

"What?" I'd been dying to know, but I hadn't wanted to pry.

"He asked why I took so long."

I snorted. "You're kidding?"

"Nope. Apparently, Bryce's place has been done for a while, but he paid the contractor to tell you and Bryce it wasn't ready, so we were forced under the same roof."

My mouth dropped open at that. "You're kidding? *My* dad?"

Hawk smiled. "Yep. Steven Baker's a meddler."

Laughing, warmth spread through me. Life had a funny way of showing you how wrong you were sometimes.

He pulled into his driveway a few minutes later, and I'd never been happier to be home. This last away series had felt like a month. I climbed out of the car, smiling at the house that had become a home.

"What are you thinking?" he asked as he unlocked the door.

"Just how happy I am. This is my home, and I love that you've included them."

Graham and Tucker climbed the steps behind us, arguing about something as they neared. Hawk glanced back, his usual grimace gone and replaced with the warm affection he often hid.

"A home should be full, and now ours is. Go check on Sunny. I have plans for you."

He kissed my forehead, and I ran for the front room, scooping the fluffy hamster up and laying kisses on it.

"Sunny!" Tucker shouted, handing his bag off to Graham and joining me.

"Still questioning the team presuming you were already together?" Hawk teased, smirking at Graham.

Graham sighed, shaking his head as he headed down to their rooms in the basement, leaving Tucker and me in the princess room.

"I haven't had a chance to ask how you're doing with the video, Honey Bee," Tucker asked as we played with Sunny. I handed Sunny over, scanning his water and food. I knew Roxie had been by, but it had become a habit.

"It's about what I expected. I'm just glad the team is on board. Have you heard anything?"

"Your mom has some meetings set up this week. I'm hopeful."

"Good." I kissed his cheek, took Sunny, and put him back in his cage. "Now, show me your room."

Tucker's face lit up, and we raced downstairs, laughing the entire way. When we came to a wall of boxes, we stopped abruptly.

"Damn. I kinda hoped they'd unbox themselves," Tucker grumbled. "How much would I need to convince you to help?"

"None. Just tell me where things go."

Tucker kissed me, then took my hand, leading me to the back room. Graham was already unpacking a box, hanging things up in the wardrobe Hawk had added.

It took a few hours, but the three of us got everything unpacked and the boxes broken down. Tucker and Graham had decided to keep one room as their bedroom and the other as their showroom, as Tucker called it. It displayed Tucker's sneakers and Graham's books.

"Do you think Luke will ever move in here?" Graham asked as we headed up the stairs. Hawk had called down that he'd ordered pizza.

"I hope so, but it's more complicated with Willow."

"I'd give up my shoe room for her," Tucker admitted, surprising us all.

"Not needed. I have plans to add on if we stay here," Hawk said, setting the pizza on the coffee table.

"You do?" I asked, blinking. "Wait, stay here? You're moving?" His words left me speechless.

"You heard your dad. Anything can happen. I want to be

prepared for any option. I've been researching houses in Columbus, too."

"But you love this house," I protested, my mind unable to comprehend the gesture.

"I do." He nodded. "But I love you more, Blazy. And that includes housing all these knuckleheads."

"I think Hawk just proposed," Tucker whispered.

"Hush." Graham covered Tucker's mouth as I gaped at Hawk.

"Not proposing," Hawk said, lifting his eyes to mine. "Yet."

My heart flopped in my chest as I held his mismatched eyes. For the first time in my life, that didn't scare the crap out of me.

"Okay." I nodded, butterflies happily dancing in my belly. I could envision a future: the five of us, plus Willow and Sunny. Maybe even one day, we'd have a dog and a baby of our own. Yeah, that seemed nice.

I settled back on the couch, taking a bite of pizza as the three men stared at me. I didn't know if they expected me to freak out or what, but it was comical to watch them. Eventually, they broke their frozen state as Tucker slapped Graham's leg, his smile so big I thought it might pop off his face. Hawk sat back, his cheeks pink, and I felt like the real winner in this scenario. When he recovered, he cleared his throat and stared at my screwballs.

"Okay, house rules. First, clean up after yourselves. I'm not your maid. Secondly… "

Smiling, I sat back and listened, loving my life. Even if I had to deal with the media. My guys were worth it.

I'd been cutting up fruit for breakfast when Hawk stalked in, all sleepy-eyed and disheveled. He didn't say a word as he spun me around, lifted me onto the counter, and kissed me within an inch of my life.

"You weren't in my bed when I woke," he croaked, his voice hoarse.

"I wanted to get started on Willow's breakfast," I murmured as he assaulted my neck with his kisses.

"I had plans, and it's only six. There's still plenty of time to," he stopped, glancing over my shoulder at what I'd been working on. "Cut fruit?" He growled, sending shivers through me.

The truth was, I was nervous and hadn't been able to sleep. This would be the first time we wouldn't hide our relationship in Willow's presence. I was more concerned about her accepting us all than I'd been with my family.

"That's what I thought," Hawk murmured, capturing my lips again. He proceeded to kiss me, relaxing my body as he gripped my hips and pulled me to the edge. His cock nudged against my entrance, and I wrapped my legs around his waist, attempting to get more friction. I whimpered as I tried to pull him closer to no avail.

"I told you I had plans last night, Blazy. Then you fell asleep on me."

"Sorry," I gasped as he tweaked my nipple through my shirt.

"I was going to wake you with my tongue so you could wake up the entire house. But again, you thwarted my plans."

Hawk lifted my shirt, the cool air hitting my hot skin as he dropped it to the floor. My body was flushed with arousal, and I bit my lip to hold in the whimper that wanted to escape. Hawk stood before me, all tattooed and bronzed muscles on display. He wore only a pair of black boxer briefs that were very tight in the front as his cock pressed against the fabric. He kept staring at me, and I shifted on the counter, wondering what the delay was now.

"Well?" I asked when I couldn't take it any longer.

"Now, I punish you for making me miss out on all this twice."

Quicker than I could track, Hawk reached out and pulled me off the counter. I let out a squeak as my ass met air, and my body was turned. My feet landed on the ground a second later, and I was pressed against the table.

"Brace yourself. I'm not going easy." It was the only warning Hawk gave before ripping off my panties and lifting my ass. I felt the head of his cock a second before it plunged into me, stealing my breath.

True to his word, he gripped my ass, spreading my cheeks as he plowed into me. My elbows were braced on the table, the wood creaking with each thrust. It was hard to be angry when it felt so good.

"I'm not sure this is a punishment," I moaned.

"I was going to eat you out until you came all over my face first."

"Damn, that's hot," a voice from the stairs muttered, echoing my own. I glanced up and met Graham's eyes, the gray molten as he took in the view. He rubbed the outside of his sleep pants, his dick growing as he watched.

I kept my eyes locked with his as Hawk pounded into me, hitting me so deep it almost hurt. His cock stretched me wide, the metal of his piercings rubbing along my walls with each slide. My pants came out in choppy breaths, my orgasm building with each passing second.

"Why are you blocking—" Tucker stopped behind Graham, his eyes wide as he discovered the same scene. "This is what I call a good morning." He chuckled, wrapping his arms around Graham and running them over his chest. Tucker nuzzled into his neck, kissing him as he trailed one hand lower, pushing the joggers down and letting Graham's thick dick free.

"Holy fuck," I muttered, my eyes threatening to roll up as

intense pleasure coursed through me with each thrust of Hawk's and the erotic view in front of me. Graham gave in to Tucker, leaning back against him as his best friend stroked his dick. They were a vision to behold, bringing me close to the edge.

"Watch our girl come apart, G. See how good she takes it," Tucker whispered, stroking Graham in time with Hawk's thrusts, his hips moving forward as well as he slid his cock between his ass cheeks. Graham reached back, gripping Tucker's ass in one hand, and pulled him closer. It was the perfect balance of sexy and loving, and it was my undoing.

Letting go of the last remnants I held onto, I fell apart as my orgasm overtook me. Hawk's thrusts faltered, his hands gripping harder as my pussy squeezed him, his own release following. As I shuddered around him, Graham and Tucker came, their moans joining ours in the kitchen.

"New house rule," Tucker started, breaking the silence.

"No," Hawk said before he could finish.

"No fair, Hawkster. I was just going to suggest starting every morning with an orgasm."

Hawk paused, assessing Tucker as he pulled out of me. He walked over to the sink, dampened a cloth, and returned to me still bent over the table. My legs had become jello, so I hadn't moved.

When he tossed something to Tucker and Graham, my heart was close to bursting. He carefully cleaned me up and then himself, chucking the rag at the door to the basement.

"As long as mine comes from Blake. I prefer to pretend like you're not there," he said at last before stalking back toward his bedroom.

Tucker, Graham, and I all looked at one another, a laugh bubbling out of me at his departure.

"That's basically his version of 'I no longer wish to murder you in your sleep,'" I teased.

"Wait, that was a possibility?" Tucker asked, his face stricken.

Shaking my head, I smiled as I picked up my clothes. "Come on. We need to shower before Luke and Willow arrive."

They both moved after that, joining me in the guest bathroom, where we made it out and started the pancakes just as the doorbell rang, my nerves returning. Here goes nothing.

BLAKE

Tucker and I glanced at one another when the doorbell sounded, both of us taking off in a race to get there first. Past me wouldn't have run to the door, worried I'd look too eager, and past me definitely wouldn't elbow one of her boyfriends in the ribs, either.

Good thing I was no longer past me.

I jumped on Tucker's back, tickling his sides as he struggled, and then lifted his shirt from the front over his head as I jumped off, elbowing him in the ribs for good measure.

"What the fuck!" He laughed, struggling to get out of his t-shirt.

"I taught her that," Hawk said, beaming with pride as I skidded to the door and took a second to compose myself before opening it like I hadn't just maimed a man I loved.

"Happy Birthday, Lolo!"

"No fair. I wanted to tell her first," Tucker whined, coming up behind. "Bee is a meany."

"No, she's not!" Willow defended, putting her tiny hands on her hips.

I turned, sticking my tongue out at Tucker. Luke laughed

at us, pulling my attention back to him. Going with my gut, I stepped up to him, pulled his face to mine, and kissed him. It was brief, but it pinned that last piece of me that I'd been missing all morning.

"Good morning, Slugger," he whispered against my lips.

"Morning, handsome." I smiled, happy they were here.

"Yes!" Willow cheered, dragging my focus to her.

"Does that make you happy?" I asked, bending down.

She nodded, smiling so big she looked like a different kid. I took her hand, knowing I needed to say the rest, too. I glanced at Luke, and he nodded for me to continue.

"And what if I was also to kiss Hawk, Tucker, and Graham?"

She tilted her head, studying the men I assumed were behind me. "Would you still kiss my daddy?"

"Yes."

"Would they kiss anyone else?"

"No. Just me. Or well…" I turned to Graham and Tucker, letting them take this one.

"Sometimes I kiss Graham, too, but he's the only one," Tucker added.

"Like Braylin's daddies?"

"Um, yeah, maybe." I cringed, hoping I wasn't screwing this up.

"Cool. Can I have my birthday pancakes now?" she asked, her eyes big.

The five of us took a collective sigh of relief. "Sure thang, kiddo."

Willow ran to the princess room, Tucker hot on her tail, as they cooed and petted Sunny. Luke took my hand, dragging me further into the house and pushing up against a wall where he proceeded to give me a thorough kiss, one where I almost forgot a child was present.

"I don't know what I did to deserve you, but I'm so fucking grateful you see the man I want to be." Luke pecked my lips once more, blinding me with his golden smile as he stared down at me. I no longer had any reservations when it came to him, and I knew it was time he knew.

"I love you." His eyes widened, and he opened his mouth but was cut off by his daughter.

"I want strawberries!" Willow said as she skipped into the kitchen, breaking Luke and me apart. The five of us easily fell into a rhythm as we pampered Willow, making her the best birthday pancakes she'd ever have.

"Can we do this for all my birthdays?" she asked, licking the whipped cream off her fork.

"I like that idea. You know, Hawk's birthday is coming up, too."

Her eyes grew big, and she turned to him. "What kind of pancakes do you want?"

Hawk shot me a glare before melting under her stare. "I'm partial to campfire pancakes."

Willow quickly turned to me, her face stricken. She leaned close, putting her hand over her mouth to whisper. "Do you know how to make those?"

I nodded, giving her a wink. "I got you covered."

She smiled and sat up, giving Hawk a nod of approval. "Done."

"Is it time for presents?" Tucker asked, practically bouncing in his seat.

"Presents?" Willow made an 'o' with her mouth as she peered around. I'd never seen her so animated before, and I loved that she finally seemed to have come out of her shell with us.

"Let's move to the living room," I suggested, taking her hand. I led her to the pile of presents on the coffee table, where she stood stunned.

"They're all for me?" she asked, her voice small. I had a feeling this little girl was about to become the most spoiled five-year-old in a ten-mile radius.

Willow proceeded to open her gifts, oohing and awing over each item she opened. From Tucker, she received a pair of blue and yellow sneakers and tickets to the zoo. Apparently, he had a thing for zoos and wanted to take her. This led to us all complaining about wanting to go and Tucker grinning like he'd won the lottery.

Graham got her some books on baseball and a personalized apron. Willow then demanded her dad have one, too, so they could match, much to Luke's dismay. But secretly, I think he loved it. Willow had claimed him in her heart and wanted everyone to know he was her dad.

Hawk got her a new baseball glove and a sleeping bag that he said she could use for sleepovers, which immediately made her ask when she could use it. Hawk smirked as Luke panicked, and I didn't know which end of the feeling spectrum to fall on myself.

When there was only one bag left, I handed her the box. I'd found a camera like mine refurbished online, so I got it for her, hoping she'd enjoy it.

"It's mine?" she asked, looking up at me like I'd given her the most precious gift.

"All yours, Lolo. I'll teach you how to use it and develop the film. You can still use the digital one, but there's something about film that I love."

"I can be like you?"

"If you want." She nodded, smiling at me as I shrugged, trying to brush off the emotion. My cheeks heated as I pulled out the gift bag. "I also made you this."

Willow took her time pulling out the tissue paper before revealing the shirt I'd made that bore a baseball that said, "Run like you stole it" and "Olson" on the back.

"Just like Daddy's," she said, patting it in awe. I hadn't thought she'd love it as much as she did, making me well up as I watched her. There was no doubt in my mind I was already gone for this little girl.

"Okay, Willow, it's time to clean up," Luke said, clearing his throat.

"Ah, man. Do I have to?" She pouted, hitting me right in the heart.

"Matilda will be here soon to take you to school. You don't want to make her wait," he said, lifting his brow.

Willow sucked in a breath and nodded, jumping up to gather all of her things and putting the trash away. Right on time, a knock sounded at the door, and Luke jumped up to let her in. Willow gave everyone hugs and thanked them for her gifts, and we all wished her another happy birthday before telling her we'd see her at the game on Friday.

When the door shut, we all let out a relieved sigh. "How long did it take you to figure out the Matilda trick?" Hawk asked, studying Luke. "My nieces give me the pouty lip, and I'm a sucker for it every time."

"Too long." They chuckled together, finding a common ground.

"I don't know how you stand it," Tucker groaned. "That was the cutest and most heartbreaking pout I'd ever seen."

"Thankfully, Matilda is stern but loving, and Willow hates disappointing her, so it usually works."

"We're gonna have to figure out another solution at some point. Matilda can't always be the bad guy," I said.

"Why not? Let's have her move in too!"

Everyone laughed, but I expected they were all on Tucker's side. I could already tell I'd have to be the hard ass when it came to her. I needed to get better at my own levels of persuasion, apparently.

"Bee, I believe we have some unfinished business?" Luke lifted his brow, and I swallowed.

"On that note, Tucker and I will be out for a few hours. I'll pick up some things for dinner on the way back," Graham said, pulling Tucker out the door after they kissed me goodbye.

"I need to go and check on Bryce's place. Wren's visiting soon, and then Emory, so I want to ensure everything is in working order." Hawk eyed Luke before kissing me, leaving me breathless as he grabbed his keys and headed out the door.

"I can't believe I actually get alone time with you." Luke smiled, and I grabbed his hand, pulling him down to the couch.

"I'm glad Willow took the news well."

"It's hard not to see the upside from a five-year-old's perspective. More people to love her."

"I like that."

"Speaking of love…"

"I—"

"I love you too, Bee. I've never said that to anyone before. I know I mentioned something in your dad's suite, but I wanted you to hear me actually say the words to you."

"Crazy to think a little bit of vomit and a storm helped bring us together."

"Don't forget our game and the amazing orgasm I gave you," he teased.

"Hmm. I'm having a difficult time remembering the amazing part. Are you sure it wasn't panic-induced?"

His eyes heated. "I guess I'll have to remind you."

Luke pulled me into his lap, his tongue delving into my mouth as he kissed me, promising me everything he'd said with his lips. We slowly ravaged one another, relishing in the fact we didn't have to rush or be mindful of someone over-hearing us.

Our clothes fell to the floor as our hands explored, touching and caressing one another as we drove our arousal higher. I rocked on his fingers, my pussy throbbing with need as I threaded my fingers through his blonde hair. His thick thighs held me from below, and I lost myself in the pleasure as he kept his brutal pace.

"Would it be weird if I took you back to your bed?" he asked, slightly pausing.

"Um." I stalled my movements, tilting my head as the lust cleared so I could think. Technically, it was Hawk's bed, but it was also mine. Now, that was a predicament.

"Never mind, I'm too impatient."

Luke spread me open and thrusted up, sending me backward as I braced my hands on the coffee table behind me in a weird reverse crab position. At this angle, he hit me in a completely different way, and my legs trembled in moments.

"Luuukkee," I moaned. "I'm so close."

"Fuck, Bee. You always feel so good. I can never get enough. I think about being inside of you every moment I'm not."

I groaned, leaning forward and taking his cheeks in my hands as I kissed him. His thrusts slowed as we took a second to cherish one another. I stared into his green eyes. Summers spent at the ballpark flashed through me as I let go of the rest of my fear, giving myself entirely to him.

"I'm yours, Luke. Take me."

His hands gripped my ass, and I wrapped my arms around his neck, clinging to him as we chased our orgasms.

"I love you, I love you, I love you," he chanted into my neck, accentuating his thrusts with each word. It pushed me over the edge, my body singing as pleasure overtook me.

"Yes, yes!" I screamed, my voice hoarse as I came.

"Bee," Luke moaned, stealing my lips for a kiss as he faltered, his thrusts sloppy and uncoordinated now. We held one another, the sounds of our labored breathing filling the space as we returned from the high.

"I never thought I could love anything more than baseball, but I do. You and Willow. No matter what happens now in my life, it won't matter because we'll do it together."

"Together." I nodded, kissing his lips once.

I stared at my golden boyfriend, who was so broody in

the beginning that I wondered if he had two personalities. But now I saw it for what it was: a protection from the world around him. Luke, at his core, was a good man, wanting to be loved for who he was and not what he brought to the table. I could understand that, and I was glad I met the man beneath the bullshit first. Otherwise, I didn't know if we'd ever have made it here; too many obstacles in our way.

At least it wasn't something I had to worry about because we were here now, and it was my favorite place to be.

"Do you remember the first two truths and lie I told you?" Luke asked.

"Something about your tattoo, that you were an only child, and…" I tapped my lip as I wracked my memory. I tilted my head. "Was it volunteering?"

"Yep. Spoiler, but they were all true." He winked, and I pushed his shoulder.

"Yeah. I kind of figured out your game there, mister."

"Well, I was going to volunteer today. Would you want to come with me?"

"Really?" My face lit up, and I smiled, loving that he was sharing this with me.

"It's not glamorous, but—"

I smushed his lips together. "Don't finish that sentence. You had me at volunteering. The bonus is spending time with you. When do we leave?"

"Um, now?" He grimaced, seeing the time.

"Time for the world's fastest shower!"

We rinsed off together, and I changed before heading out, loving that I got to witness another side of Luke.

CHAPTER
SEVENTY-FOUR

GRAHAM

Tucker peppered me with questions as I drove, wondering where we were going. The more outlandish they became, the easier it was to ignore them. Internally, I chuckled, loving that I could still surprise him.

"Am I getting a puppy?"

"Do you want Hawk to murder me?" I teased. "Besides, he pretends you're a Golden Retriever, and you pretend he's a bulldog. I think we have enough dogs in the house at the moment."

"Good point. Though, if I were a dog, I'd be a chocolate doodle. The majestic and precised curls. Hello!" He dragged a hand down his frame, emphasizing his words.

I laughed, shaking my head at his nonsense. My phone rang a minute later, and my sister's name popped up on the dashboard. I rolled my eyes but hit the answer button anyway. I knew my time had been limited before they'd bombard me.

"Hello, Kadie, my lovely meddling sister. How are you today?"

"Hey now! I only meddle because I care."

"Is that what we're calling it?" I chuckled.

"Fine." She sighed. "But I think you'll like it this time. I got Mom and Leroy to watch the video."

Silence hung in the car at that. Kadie and Amie were the sisters who'd accepted me, no questions asked, while Nora and Clara had sided with Mom. I'd expected it, but it still hurt. Even though my family wasn't close-knit like Blake's, we'd always supported one another.

This had been the first time I'd been on the outside.

Though, in reality, I'd been on the sidelines for years. Being the only male, the youngest, and hours away from anyone had naturally made me excluded from things. I wasn't married, didn't have kids, and only visited a few times a year. Naturally, the physical distance created emotional distance over time. I just hadn't noticed it until I'd seen Blake's family in action.

She'd been in Greece for three years, but it had been clear how close her bond was with her dad, brother, and mom. I might not be able to get that with my blood family, but I was building it with one.

Suddenly, what she said didn't matter because I had everything I wanted. They'd have to work for it if they wanted to be part of it. I wouldn't cater to them anymore because I was happy to accept the scraps.

"Oh?" I asked, my voice croaking a little. I didn't know if the emotion was from my discovery or the fact she had to make them watch something. But regardless, it didn't matter.

Tucker squeezed my thigh, giving me all the reassurance I needed. I pulled into the parking lot and turned to him. His entire focus was on me. He hadn't even looked where we were. He'd foregone his own excitement to ensure I was okay.

God, I loved this man.

He smiled, and my heart leaped out of my chest.

"And they relented that they might've judged too quickly," Kadie said, reminding me she was still there.

I snorted. "That's one way to put it."

Kadie sighed. "You deserve better, Graham. You do. But it's a step."

She was right. I could give them that, but I would hold to my promise.

"And Nora and Clara?"

"Nora is still adamant she no longer has a brother."

"Harsh," Tucker muttered.

"Tucker, is that you?" Kadie's voice changed, a smile coming through.

"Hey, Kadie Bear."

"How's my favorite baseball player?" she teased.

"In love and living the life," he said, staring at me as he said it.

"It's about time. I've been waiting for you to wake up for years!"

"Say what?" He choked, his face turning red.

"You remember your junior year when you stayed with us for Christmas?" she asked.

"Yeah. What about it?"

"It was obvious then. Each time Graham left the room, your eyes would follow him, and your smile dimmed. When that friend of Clara's trapped Graham under the mistletoe, I thought you were gonna tackle him."

"Oh. Um. Hm." Tucker rubbed the back of his neck, his cheeks bright red.

I chuckled, cupping the side of his face. "It's okay, baby. We're here now."

Tucker melted beneath my touch, and it took everything in me to remember my sister was on the line. "Was there anything else, Kadie? Because it's my only day off, and I'm romancing my man today."

"Aww, I could just squeeze you two." She laughed, and I

rolled my eyes. "Okay, I can take a hint. Just one last question…"

"What?"

"I'm not promising anything, but if I can make it work, could you get me some tickets for a game this week?"

I swallowed. It had been years since anyone in my family had come to a game. "Sure. Just let me know what game."

"Thanks, baby Bro. It will be good to see you. Will I get to meet Blake?"

"You'd want to?" I asked, shocked. It wasn't that they didn't care, but no one went out of their way for me.

"Absolutely."

"Then yes. I'll talk to Blake."

"Perfect. Okay, I'll let you go. Love you and can't wait to see you soon."

"Love you too, Kadie."

"Bye, Tucker! Be good to my brother."

"Oh, I plan to!"

"Ew, gross!" She laughed.

"Buh-bye, Kadie Bear!"

The phone call ended, and I turned off the car, glancing at Tucker. He still hadn't looked to where we were, his focus entirely on me.

"I love your sister."

"You can have her," I grumbled but smiled. "She's not so bad."

"You good?" he asked, assessing me.

"A little shocked, honestly. But I realized something."

"What's that?" he asked.

"It didn't matter what my family thought because I was building my own. With you, Blake, and the others. That's the family that matters."

"I love that."

Our lips met as we leaned forward. The kiss was slow as

we took time mapping each other. We didn't have to hide or rush this, so we didn't.

Gasping for breath sometime later, we pulled apart. Both of us panted, our breaths labored as I leaned my forehead against his. Tucker's lips were swollen, his pupils blown, and I had half a mind to pull him into the backseat and skip this whole date.

But Tucker deserved more than a backseat blowjob, and I wanted to romance him.

"You ready for your date?"

His eyes widened as he looked out the window for the first time. "No way!" He was up and out of the car within seconds, leaving me to scramble behind him. "But... This..." He sputtered, apparently losing the ability to speak until he finally landed on. "Wow."

"I did good?" I asked, nerves ricocheting inside of me. I'd never cared this much before.

"The best." He nodded, smiling so wide it eclipsed the whole world. "I've always wanted to do this but never wanted to do it alone," he said as we walked into the spa.

"No! It's not like you haven't said a million times, 'G, take me to the spa.' 'G, I want to feel pretty.' 'G, if you loved me, you'd let me do a makeover.' Or, you know, something of that variety," I teased.

"I'm not even mad at that voice you just did for me because I'm too excited."

Pulling him to me, our bodies lined up until our toes touched as I held his hips, staring into his eyes. "I love you, Tucker Jameson. I'm even willing to let strangers touch me to show you that."

"You really do love me," he fake cried, wiping a tear. I smacked his shoulder as he howled, and we finished the last few steps to the counter.

"Hello, can I help you?" the clerk asked.

"I need to cancel," I started, and Tucker reached over to

cover my mouth, but it didn't stop me from talking louder. "My boyfriend ruined a perfectly romantic moment."

Tucker ignored me, putting on his best flirt for the girl. "Ignore him. It's under West, I believe," he said, smirking at me when she typed it in.

I narrowed my eyes, and he dropped his hand, wrapping it around my shoulder and nuzzling into my neck. He gave me a sweet kiss. "Thank you for loving me for so long, even when I couldn't see it. You're the best man I've ever known, G. This means the world to me. I love you for infinity."

My whole body relaxed into him, and my cheeks heated as his words cemented in my soul. The clerk looked at us with heart eyes, her smile beaming as she glanced between us.

"That was the most beautiful declaration I've ever heard," she whispered, clutching her chest. "This may be out of line, but I saw your video, and we're Team LoveBuzz here."

"LoveBuzz?" I asked, confused, glancing at Tucker and then back to her.

She smiled and nodded, her face changing when she realized we didn't follow. "It's the hashtag people are using in support of your relationship. Because you play for the YellowJackets, and Blake goes by Bee."

"We haven't been online," I admitted, wondering if that had been a mistake. We'd been so worried about the negativity we'd missed the positive.

"LoveBuzz. I like it," Tucker said.

"Yeah, me too."

"Right, well, you're all set for your day." The clerk led us to a private room where we changed out of our clothes into the soft cotton robe provided.

"Do I get to keep this?" Tucker asked, stroking his arm.

"You can probably ask."

"Score." He grinned, following the attendant as they led us to our first treatment.

Over the next few hours, we both had facials, pedicures, and, much to my chagrin, a manscaping wax. Tucker got some oil treatment on his hair, making his curls shine and bounce, and I got a trim, choosing to keep my hair short on the sides with a little length on top. It got too hot under a ball cap to deal with hair. Though Tucker disagreed.

We were at our couple's massage, and I found my favorite thing here. The others had been nice, but I'd only done them for Tucker. But this… this was my heaven. I didn't know who was more surprised. Me or Tucker.

"Ah, right there," I moaned as the masseuse got a deep spot on my lower back. All the crouching did a number on my back and hamstrings. I didn't usually like people touching me, but Sandra seemed to have the secret codes to my muscles.

"Do you not have a team trainer to do this?" Sandra asked.

"Not on the YellowJackets. The Major League teams do," Tucker answered, his voice relaxed and blissful.

"You should look into our memberships then. The stress you put on your muscles each day takes a toll."

"That's a great idea. We should bring Bee next time, too," Tucker groaned, making me laugh.

"We'll look into it. You're probably right," I agreed despite my abhorrence of massages. My body felt more languid and relaxed than it had all season.

"The showers are through there," Tucker's masseuse pointed. We gathered our robes and headed into the secluded showers as they cleaned their areas.

The second I stepped into the shower room, Tucker was on me. He pressed my back into the door, his lips taking me in a hungry kiss.

"This has been the most fun, Teddy Graham," he whispered, kissing my neck.

"I'm glad you enjoyed it." My head fell against the door,

and I prayed this room was soundproof. We both pushed off our boxers, moving closer to the shower heads. I turned on the water, jumping back with a yelp when cold water assaulted me.

"Holy shit, that's cold."

Tucker laughed, running his hands over my body as we waited for the water to warm. Soon, I didn't even care, our slick bodies rubbing against each other. Tucker ravaged my body like he couldn't get enough of me. A small part of me kept waiting for Tucker to freak out, but from the second he acknowledged his attraction, he'd been all in. I needed to credit him for that and stop waiting for him to pull away.

"We can't do what I really want, but let me show you something," I whispered, the steam billowing around us. Tucker nodded his complete trust, the best gift he could ever give me.

Taking our cocks together, I stroked us both with one hand. My hand didn't wrap completely around, but the added friction of another dick had me leaking already.

"Damn, that's hot," Tucker whispered.

I reached between us, tugging his balls and watching as his eyes rolled back. I came with his hands on me and the thrill of knowing people were on the other side of the wall. My orgasm rushed through me, my balls drawing up as pleasure coursed through me. I muffled my moan in Tucker's neck as he held me, our bodies trembling from the release.

"I'm not even mad my curls got wet."

"And you wonder why I call you punk princess," I teased.

"If the shoe fits."

Laughing together, we rinsed off the oil and dried, changing back into our clothes. I signed the bill, leaving a massive tip while Tucker flirted to acquire his own robe, promising to sign some YellowJacket merch as well.

The sun was shining bright as we left, and the fact there wasn't any paparazzi outside the spa told me everything I needed. This place could be trusted and would be worth coming back to.

"What should we make for our family tonight?" Tucker asked as we pulled into the grocery store.

Smiling at his phrase, I walked proudly through those doors, holding his hand and knowing this was exactly the life I wanted to live. I hoped to one day make it to the World Series, but I'd die a happy man if it never happened.

SEVENTY-FIVE

BLAKE

I handed out the last piece of cake, wiping my brow and praying I didn't wipe icing all over my face. I never knew little kids' birthday parties could be so draining. Willow's entire class took up the owner box, their happy chatter as they watched the baseball game, making the exhaustion worth it.

This week of games had been an adjustment with the added media presence, but we were all coping with it. Having Willow's party to plan had been a good distraction.

"Between the next inning, Jack will lead our birthday girl to the field for the birthday song, and then everyone can get pictures," Rue said, checking off the event's timeline on her clipboard. She'd been promoted to head of events since Mira's firing. They were still interviewing for director positions, but everyone else had been able to step up to jobs they'd wanted but had been held back by Mira.

Between the bullshit she tried to control with our hours, relationships, and job positions, the happier I was she wouldn't be returning here. Morale had already improved among the staff, especially when we could use the benefits none of us knew we had. Like taking one game off per month and the ability to flex our hours. With Willow's party today, I'd opted to use mine.

"Awesome. I'll corral them down there in a few."

She smiled, hip-checking me. "I'm still mad at you," she teased.

"I know, and I'm sorry. I didn't know how to talk about it. At first, it was just casual, and then it became everything." I dropped my head, hating that I had to lie to my friend.

She sighed, wrapping her arm around my waist. "Forgiven. I hate that she took your privacy away from you."

I smiled at her. "Maybe we could do a double date?"

Rue nodded, checking her watch again. "I'd like that. See you down there in twenty." She waved as she stepped out of the suite, heading to the next thing on her checklist. Wren walked over, taking her place.

"Kaylee wants her birthday here now. I hope you know what you've started."

I laughed, looking over at her two little girls. "They're adorable, Wren. And I would gladly throw them a party, too. They're family."

"About time," she said, giving me a hug. "I'm glad my brother finally pulled his head out of his ass. He needs you."

"Likewise." I grinned, my face becoming a permanent smile.

"Lake!" Willow shouted, running up to me. She grinned wide, one hand clasped with Lauren's, Wren's oldest daughter, and a little girl from her class, Alexis.

I dropped down. "What's up, Lolo?"

"Lauren said I can play with her tea set, and we're gonna invite Alexis. Do you think Daddy will let me have a sleepover? I have my sleeping bag."

I glanced over at Wren, who shrugged. "We'll need to check with Alexis' mom, but that would be fun."

"Thank you!" She dropped her friend's hands and

launched herself into my arms. "This is the best birthday ever," she whispered, kissing my cheek.

I held back the tears that threatened me as I stood. "You ready to have your picture taken with Jack?" I asked the suite.

"Yes!" the surrounding kids shouted.

Miss Staci, the teacher, nodded that she'd help get everyone together. "Okay, class, let's line up. Hands behind our back and try not to fall off the balance beam."

The kids hurried to do as she said, Willow and her two friends first in line. Wren and I followed them as one of the stadium workers directed Miss Staci. I snapped pictures as we went, mainly of the kids being cute.

Luke waited at the field entrance, and when Willow spotted him, she took off running, jumping into his arms. "Daddy!"

Luke barely caught her, taken by surprise at her exuberance. He gave me a hopelessly besotted look as he held her. She talked a mile a minute and told him everything about her birthday. Remembering how he thought their initial meeting would go and seeing him get it now was everything. I swallowed down the emotion as I focused on the rest of the kids.

Do not cry. Do not cry.

When Jack, the mascot, came out, he led Willow and Luke to the field. Hawk walked over, wrapping his arm around me as we watched. That was until Kaylee spotted him and tugged at his pants for him to pick her up.

"Uncle Hawk! Up!"

He smiled down at her, lifting her into his arms and placing her on his shoulders. Jack told the crowd it was Willow's birthday, and she was five. Everyone sang loudly, and Willow swung her arms as she listened. I expected her to be shy, but she drank in the attention, letting Luke spin her around. Some other kids saw Kaylee on Hawk's shoulder and tried to climb him, too.

I get it, kids. He's the best jungle gym.

Surprisingly, players from both teams came out and gave each kid a piggyback ride around the bases before taking the field. I remembered moments like this as a kid, where players took time to make you feel like more than a fan but part of the game. The guys all gave me smiles as they headed out to the field, the other team at bat.

I herded the hyper kids back to the suite with the help of Miss Staci and Wren after pictures with Jack and plopped down into a chair. Thankfully, the class seemed as tired as the three of us and sat and watched the game as they ate popcorn and Crackerjacks.

By the sixth inning, all the kids had been picked up by their parents, and only Wren's daughters and Willow were left. I'd spoken with Alexis' mom, and we exchanged numbers to set up a playdate for the girls. It hit me then how much Luke trusted me and the role I'd play in Willow's life moving forward. *Jaw drop.*

"Want to move closer for the last inning?" I asked. The three girls nodded in agreement, so I took them closer to see the field.

"Uncle Tuck!" Willow shouted, waving at him when he took the mound. His head whipped around, and he clutched his heart, blowing her a kiss. The three little girls giggled. Wren leaned closer, her eyes watching.

"I wasn't sure how my brother would deal with other guys in the relationship, but seeing the five of you together, I get it."

"Yeah?" I asked, curious what she thought. Wren and I weren't super close, but we'd grown up together in many ways. She was younger than me, but our paths crossed enough to keep us in the loop of one another.

"Hawk likes to pretend he doesn't like people, but really, he loves them too much. So to counteract his caring side, he protrudes this 'fuck off' vibe."

"Mommy said a bad word," Kaylee said, giggling. Wren stuck her tongue out at her daughter as I thought about what she said.

"It's why he loves coaching," I mumbled, putting the pieces together.

"Exactly. At first, I thought he'd struggle because he loves playing baseball. But then I watched him coach, and I got it. It's the complete package for him. He gets to help players, be around baseball, and can still pretend like he hates the world."

We giggled. It sounded like Hawk.

"Catch the ball, Daddy!" Willow shouted, turning my attention to the field. Luke snagged the ball out of the air, smiling over at Willow before he threw it back to Tucker. "Yay!" she cheered, dancing a little, and my heart soared.

"You ready to be a mom?" Wren whispered. I glanced over at Willow, knowing the answer.

"I hadn't planned on it happening this soon, but I'm not mad about it. She's special." I met Wren's eyes, letting her see my truth. She nodded, something like approval passing in her eyes.

"She looks at you like you hung the moon."

"Yeah?" I turned my head back to Willow, watching her chat with Lauren and laughing. Warmth spread through me, a yearning I'd never felt before opening deep inside me.

"What's the story with her mom?"

"Jasmine's a model. She's overseas at the moment. It doesn't feel like she's eager to return to motherhood."

"That's rough." Wren frowned.

"Luke's seeking full custody," I whispered. "He heard from his lawyer today that Jasmine agreed. He's gonna tell Willow at the end of the season."

Wren's eyes widened. "Wow. That's huge."

"It is. But it's the right call."

Wren turned back out to the diamond, her face thoughtful. "Motherhood will teach you so many things about yourself you never knew. An advantage you'll have is support. Growing up with all that love, that's something special."

"I think so, too." Our relationship definitely had challenges, but there were so many more positives. Family being the biggest. It multiplied out of us, bringing not only the five of us closer, but the people we all had as well.

The game ended thirty minutes later, the YellowJackets scoring two runs in the last inning to win. The five of us moved to greet the team on the field, the girls full of high spirits.

When we returned this week, the guys and I had been worried that the home community wouldn't embrace our relationship. It was actually anticlimactic how little people here cared. When I learned about Team LoveBuzz, it felt good to be rooted for and not against for once.

The staff had given us supportive smiles, and while there were some LoveBuzz signs in the crowd, most fans were here for baseball and not my love life.

Thank you, Babe Ruth.

It also helped that another scandal broke out from another team, taking some of the heat off us. Especially since we weren't hiding and were pretty boring when we went along with their claims. Honesty for the win.

"There are my girls," Luke said when he spotted us jogging down the tunnel. He was dusty and sweaty, but he'd never looked happier. His smile covered his entire face, lighting up those green eyes of his that reminded me of summer.

"Daddy!" Willow shouted, hugging him as he leaned in to kiss me.

"What do you think about playing baseball with the team, Slugger?" Luke lifted his brows, daring me to say no.

"You just finished a game and want to play more?"

"Duh, it's baseball," Tucker said. "Plus, we recruited a few more players, and the girls will get to run around the bases."

"Yes! Please, please!" Willow, Lauren, and Kaylee begged.

"Let's play ball." I laughed, shrugging my shoulders at Wren. We walked out onto the field, the sun setting just behind the field and casting everything in oranges and pinks. It was one of those perfect summer nights lit by the ballpark lights. When I spotted players from the YellowJackets and the Bruisers, I stopped.

"You got the other team, too?" I asked.

"We used to play with some of these guys," Graham explained.

Willow and Lauren picked the teams, splitting everyone into two sides. The rules were simple. Hit the ball, and you got to run to the base, but most of all, have fun.

That was it. Baseball at its finest.

Tucker showed off his skills by doing funny dance moves before pitching. Graham did cartwheels all the way to the base, and Luke caught a ball with his hat.

The whole time, all I heard was laughter from the players, the girls, and myself. A few fans stayed and cheered us on, making it even more exciting when you scored a run.

"You doing okay?" Hawk asked when I slumped onto the bench.

"The best."

"Wren hasn't been annoying, has she?"

"Not at all. It's been good, actually. Willow and Lauren are the best of friends and want a sleepover. And Wren's given me some great advice about being a mom."

"*A mom.* Why did images of you barefoot and pregnant pop into my head?" Hawk licked his lips.

"Don't know about the barefoot part, but I'm not opposed to the pregnant one," I said, shocking even myself.

"In that case, it's my turn to get some mid-inning luck."

Hawk tugged me through the dugout and into the meditation room, showing me exactly how much the thought of me being pregnant turned him on.

When we returned, the game was wrapping up, the other guys giving us knowing looks, but I didn't care. Having sex with four guys on the regular got you used to people giving you weird looks.

Everyone pitched in and picked up when the game ended, leaving the dugouts spotless so the crew wouldn't have to stay later because of our impromptu game. As we headed off the field, I turned and gave one last look out at the diamond.

Most of my life had been spent at the baseball diamond. There were plenty of times I loved it and others when I despised it, feeling like baseball had let me down. Dad held fast to his belief that baseball had the power to make anything better. And while I didn't believe baseball had magic abilities where it could grant wishes, I knew it had one of the most potent forces known to man: Hope.

Baseball made you believe in dreams and in the promise of the future. It lets you sit in the stands and cast off your worries with a box of Crackerjacks. It fostered a community and fandom, creating an environment where strangers bonded over losses and wins. It brought smiles to little boys' and girls' faces and could be shared from young to old. Baseball didn't care who you voted for, what tax bracket you were in, or whether you put your socks on first. The only thing baseball cared about was the love of the game.

Baseball made you believe in people; that was the real magic.

As the family I'd created for myself divided into cars to journey home and the baseball stadium lights shut off behind us, the only sound I could hear was contentment. I knew there was nowhere else I'd rather be.

As much as I'd run from it, baseball was my home, and these men were my future. It took a few swings and misses, along with a pitch slap or two, but this beauty had found her team, and now it was time to hang up the cleats.

EPILOGUE

BLAKE

I ADJUSTED THE LONG BLONDE WIG IN THE MIRROR AND PRAYED my skirt wasn't too short. It had seemed longer online when I'd ordered it, but now that I had it on, I worried everyone would be able to see all of me.

I was supposed to be Sailor Moon, not expose everyone to my full moon.

Cringing, I pulled it down one last time and took a deep breath. I could do this.

Luke, Graham, and Tucker believed I'd gotten off easy regarding meeting their families and friends. So, Luke had proposed an idea—one Tucker and Graham had jumped on. Comic-Con. Today, I was to meet Luke's Comic Con friends and see if I passed the nerd test.

No pressure.

The first half of the season ended yesterday, and the YellowJackets were sitting in first place in their division, giving them home-field advantage for playoffs in September, assuming they didn't lose from here out. Crackerjack!

Knock on wood, toss some salt, and whatever else superstitious thing will protect me. Right... I'll go and have sex with Luke. Take one for the team and all.

"Lake! Are you ready?" Willow shouted through the door.

It was the end of June, and we had three days off before the second half of the season started. So, we'd flown to Boston for the Fan Expo. We were here for two nights before we headed back to Wilmington. Willow had come with us, making it a family vacation. Though, she was staying with Wren and her girls tonight. They weren't getting here until later and then would spend the day with us as we explored the city tomorrow. The best part, we'd have the night to ourselves.

And the plans I had...

"I wanna go! Can we go? Come on, Lake!" Willow shouted again.

Taking one last look that I wasn't flashing people, I grabbed my camera and phone and opened the door.

The five pairs of eyes staring back at me blinked as they took in my cosplay outfit. I'd kept it a secret, wanting to surprise Luke, but in doing so, everyone else had decided to do the same. As their eyes traveled over me, I did the same.

Willow looked adorable as Vanellope Von Scheweetz. But perhaps even more impressive were Hawk and Luke. Hawk was dressed as Wreck-it Ralph and Luke as Fix-it Felix. If I ever doubted Willow's power over these grown men, it had just been confirmed.

Next, my eyes got stuck on Graham dressed as Geralt of Rivia. His white wig, opened shirt, and guyliner were doing things to me between my legs. I fanned myself as he smirked and took in the leather pants he donned. Hot Damn.

Taking in Tucker was also a lesson in restraint. He'd gone full superhero. Taking in the very tight spandex of his Spiderman costume, I gulped. While I couldn't see Tucker's face, I could imagine his heated gaze on me as he trailed up my legs.

"What time are we meeting your crew?" I asked, my throat suddenly very dry.

"You look pretty, Lake," Willow said, breaking my lustful thoughts.

"Thank you, Lolo. You look amazing. I love your Vanellope. I'm even more amazed you convinced these two," I said, gesturing to Hawk and Luke.

She swung her body, giving me a one-shoulder shrug. "It wasn't hard. I can teach you." She took my hand and pulled me through before I could respond. I sputtered out a laugh, loving how much she'd grown into her sassy side since April.

"Let's go, Fam!" Willow beckoned, heading straight for the door. She'd started calling us Fam when we were all together. She'd grown closer to all the guys, trusting they wouldn't leave her out.

"Yes, tiny Olson!" Tucker shouted, rushing and picking her up and smothering her in kisses.

"Uncle Tuck!" She giggled.

Luke came up behind me, his arm wrapping around my waist. His lips brushed the sensitive skin beneath my ear. "I can't decide if you look sexier in this or my jersey."

Shivers raced up my spine, and I had to forcibly control myself not to shudder. Now was not the time, or the right outfit, to get aroused.

"I take it you like it then?" I asked, attempting to focus on everything in front of me, not the feel of his hands on me. We'd started watching Sailor Moon together, and I knew it was the perfect option for my first cosplay.

He bumped his stiff cock into me, rubbing it between my cheeks. I sucked in a breath, closing my eyes.

"What do you think?"

"You're not playing fair." I bit my lip, barely holding in my groan.

"And you are?" He chuckled. The sound was almost as delicious as his moans.

"Uber's here," Graham announced, breaking the spell Luke had me under.

"Yes. Right. Uber." My cheeks heated as all my boyfriends smirked at me.

"I'm so excited!" Willow shouted. "Daddy, let's go!"

"You heard tiny Olson." Tucker winked, and we all followed him out the door. We'd rented an Airbnb so we could all stay together, but also for privacy. Things had died down tremendously since the beginning of the month, but the vultures came out to play anytime we were out in a large group. With Willow with us, we were all doing everything we could to shield her.

We all piled into the luxury van, my nerves returning as we headed to the convention's hotel. I didn't know why I was so nervous, but the trembling in my hand and bouncing of my knee said I was.

"I could rock a costume like that," Tucker said, eying my wig. "Next Con, we're doing a group one. We'd slay as the Scoobies."

"You gonna be Velma?" Graham teased.

"He's Scooby. Fight me on that," Hawk said.

"Don't be jealous, Hawkster. You know I'd look awesome in whatever I wore. Case in point." Tucker dragged his hand down his body, making us all laugh. I knew he was doing it to distract me, and it made me love him even more.

We pulled up to the hotel and climbed out, joining the line to get in with all the other guests. The detail some people went to in their cosplay was impressive. I stared wide-eyed as I took it all in. The sheer number of people was overwhelming, but it was also an incredible thing to behold. The only time I'd ever been around this many people was at baseball games. To witness this many people sharing their love of their favorite fandom was a bit mind-altering.

"This is incredible."

People were smiling, laughing, and commenting on each

other's cosplays. Occasionally, people would stop us and ask us to take a picture with them. Not because the guys were professional baseball players but because they liked their character.

"I think I've been asked to pose for pictures more today than I have as a player," Graham mumbled.

"That's because you're dressed as a popular, sexy character, and your rendition is spot-on." Luke chuckled. "You appeal to everyone. The die-hards and the casual goers, females, and males."

"You definitely are sexy," I whispered. Graham blushed, proving my point even more.

"We have an hour before we meet the group. Do we want to get in line to get signatures, listen to a panel, or do some shopping?" Luke asked us as a group.

"Shopping!" Willow cried, tugging his hand and pulling him to a booth filled with Lego figurines.

"Tiny Olson has spoken."

Over the next hour, the six of us walked around the booths, eyeing all the available merchandise. Everything from tiaras and swords to art, comic books, and even underwear was available. Every fandom seemed to be represented along with Legos, comics, DnD items, and books. I could see how you'd need multiple days in order to make it to every booth.

"Okay, the crew has assembled. You ready?" Luke asked, carrying a tired Willow. All the excitement had worn her out. I nodded, taking his free hand as he led me to an area out of the main doors.

A group dressed in various cosplay turned as we neared, watching our approach. They greeted Luke and eyed me, their expressions unreadable behind their masks and makeup.

"So, you're the woman that's tamed our Luke?" a man

dressed as Link from Zelda asked, circling around me and taking in every inch of my costume.

"Um, yes?"

"Eric, you promised to be nice," Luke admonished.

"I am being nice. Okay, Sailor Moon, first test. Who am I?" His eyes sparkled, and I wondered if he was teasing me or expecting me to fail.

"You're Link from Zelda." I raised a brow, finding some confidence when his smile dropped.

"You told her," he challenged Luke.

"Nope. I didn't know who you were coming as." Luke smiled over at me, happiness radiating off him.

"Oh, did you want me to say Zelda like a newb?" I teased.

The rest of the group laughed, the tension breaking. A woman dressed as Harley Quinn walked over, wrapping an arm around my shoulder.

"Stop pouting, Eric. She passed. Now, let's go mingle. I have a Joker to find."

Everyone introduced themselves as we headed to the others, asking me questions about Luke and telling me how brave they thought the LiveIt video had been. It was a little overwhelming but in a good way. I could tell how much this group adored Luke and how much their approval meant to him as well. It also showed me I could be the center of attention without becoming a bumbling mess. I was much happier when I quit focusing on what other people thought of me.

I couldn't control their reactions or even what the future held. Embarrassing moments happened. Period. Outside of avoiding life and hiding away, there wasn't much I could do to stop them. Except lean into them and not let the mortification control me. When I accepted these things happened on a global scale, it helped me not care as much. Especially when I had four boyfriends and countless others who loved me exactly as I was… disaster and all.

We trudged back to our rental, our movements slow after the long day. My body ached in places I hadn't known muscles existed. Willow had left with Wren an hour ago, and we'd grabbed some food before heading back to our rental. Eating in character had been funny, especially away from the Con, where people weren't dressed up.

"That was fun, but I'm exhausted," Tucker said, falling face-first onto the bed.

"Whoever said nerds didn't have stamina was wrong," Hawk grumbled.

"Someone said that?" I asked, yawning.

He shrugged, pulling off his costume. We'd somehow all walked into the primary bedroom on the first floor, the one I'd been using earlier. While they were all getting more comfortable being sexual around one another, we hadn't all been together yet. I believed it was partially because of everyone's schedule. We were rarely all at the same place outside of the stadium. The other factor was the room situation.

Hawk had put a queen bed in the princess room so Luke could use it to sleep over if he wanted, but he didn't use it often. And while Hawk's bed was the biggest, it wouldn't hold five adults—especially when four were professional athletes.

Enter my plan for this evening.

I'd found this place online under 'unique features.' This rental had one of those custom beds advertised as a family bed. It spanned the whole wall of the primary bedroom. I leaned back on the mattress and waited for them to notice. They hadn't been in here earlier since I'd commandeered it to change.

Graham noticed first, smirking at me as he kicked Tucker in the butt to get him to move. "Don't fall asleep. Peel your costume off."

"I don't wanna," he mumbled into the mattress.

Next was Hawk, his eyes widening as he took me in on the mattress, his movements stopping. His nostrils flared as he put two and two together, or in this case, four and one.

"Blazy, why does this room have a humongous-ass bed?"

"Oh? Does it?" I said, faking ignorance.

Luke stopped and turned, his eyes bulging as he finally noticed. Tucker picked up his head, blinking open his eyes to understand what the others were saying.

"Wait… is this one of those orgy beds?" he whispered.

I chuckled. "Orgy beds?"

Tucker sat up, more alert now. "Uh yeah. I've seen them on LiveIt." He fell back on the bed, starfishing. "Hawkster, buy me one of these, will ya?"

"Denied."

"What if I ask for it for Christmas?" he whined.

"Still no."

"Teddy Graham?"

"Don't answer that," Hawk warned.

I pulled off the blonde wig, hoping my hair wasn't plastered to my head. Next, I unzipped the side of my dress, lowering it and pushing it off my shoulders. The bickering stopped as I stood, pushing the tall boots off and shimmying the dress the rest of the way off. Standing only in my panties, I bent over and pulled them off before crawling up the bed. Groans echoed behind me as they glimpsed my pussy.

"You're right, Hawk. This bed is a horrible idea," I teased, turning around and spreading my legs.

At the sight of my nakedness, all of their reservations were erased, and it was a race to see who could undress the fastest.

Tucker fell over, getting his foot caught as he attempted to wiggle out of his spandex suit. Graham had almost the same problem with his leather pants. Hawk had already started undressing, so he finished first with Luke closely behind him.

"That's it, next costume won't have leather or spandex," Graham grumbled as he attempted to help Tucker.

I swallowed my giggle as Hawk grabbed my ankles, pulling me down the bed and suctioning his mouth on my pussy. All thought left me as his tongue speared me. Luke traveled up my abdomen with kisses, sucking my breast into his mouth when he neared. My body heated from their ministrations, and my skin flushed as arousal overwhelmed me.

When two more sets of hands touched me, I lost it. Hawk plunged his finger into my wet heat, sending me careening into an orgasm. Hands traveled all over me, leaving fire in their wake, and I struggled to focus on one thing.

Wet lips. Soft caresses. Nipples pebbled. Total assault on my clit.

My moans filled the room, and I couldn't hear anything other than myself. Desire flooded my mind, the edges of my vision blurring as my body trembled. When the pressure on my pussy stopped, I whined.

"More," I whispered, my voice already hoarse.

"Patience, Blazy. We gotta figure out how to do this without crossing lines," Hawk mumbled.

"You don't—" I started, but Luke cut me off.

"We know, Slugger. It's more that none of us want to wait or be left out. So, we're figuring out how to make that happen."

Hawk made some complicated hand gestures to the guys, and I blinked, wondering if the orgasm had made me hallucinate. The guys moved, and I gaped.

"You're using pitcher calls for sex positions?"

"It works." Graham shrugged, his cheeks pink as he took one side. Before I could protest more, Hawk flipped me around.

"On your knees, Blazy."

The second my ass was lifted, Hawk's cock was notched at my center and pushing in, his arm banded around my waist. Luke was to my right and took my hand, directing it to his cock. Graham was on the other side and did the same. I looked up, finding Tucker in front with his dick in hand, nudging my lips.

Hawk didn't slow as he pushed in, stretching me wide. His piercings rubbed me in the best ways, and my eyes rolled back as I wrapped my lips around Tucker. Gripping two cocks in my hands, I relished the fact that in this one moment in time, we were all connected through me.

The blow job and handjobs I gave weren't my best; Hawk's thrusts prevented me from focusing too much on coordination. Eventually, all three of the guys took over, fucking my mouth and hands as they rocked forward. Their gentle and loving touches gave me that perfect balance of my body being wholly used while cherished.

Pleasure tingled from every nerve, my body singing as the five of us worked together. The realization that this moment was about more than five people getting off, but the physical embodiment of joining together to be something hit me. The last strand of control I had snapped, and my body trembled as every muscle in me tensed and spasmed as an orgasm so big washed over me. Wave after wave of pleasure that had built crashed into me, and everything went white.

Blinding stars appeared in my vision as the big bang exploded in my body. Time and space ceased to exist, and only the five of us mattered at this moment, giving me a glimpse of our future.

We'd survive the odds and build something beautiful together. Not in spite of the hatred but because our love was too big not to.

"I love you all." I smiled, happiness wrapping around me sometime later. My voice was light and shiny, my love pouring out of me as I lay on the bed between my five men. I'd lost count of my orgasms at this point and what positions we'd tried. My body was tired but sated, my skin sticky with sweat and cum, and I'd never felt more beautiful.

"Love you," they said back, their words filling the space between us and tying us all together.

I knew with certainty that no matter what happened from here on out—trades, losses, pitch slaps—we'd conquer it together.

We were Team LoveBuzz, and we played to win.

AFTERWORD

I'll be honest. When I was writing this book, I wondered if I would ever finish it. The outline I had just kept growing, the book becoming longer and longer as the characters lived out their story. They had so much to say and didn't want to mince any of it, so I let them. This is by far the biggest book I've written to date. If I add in the prequel, it was around six months of writing and editing spent only in this new world. And what a ride it has been!

Blake spoke to me on a personal level, just as many of you have mentioned after meeting her in The Cleat Retreat. I think there's probably a part of Blake in all of us, making her journey even more powerful. Blake has a lot of stuff thrown at her, making her doubt herself at times, but she keeps going. She keeps persisting and never quits getting up, even when it's hard. I think we could all embody some of that and harness it for ourselves.

Friendship and family are also significant parts of this story, proving that we can choose the family we want for ourselves. From the sense of belonging the team provides to the friendships between the characters and siblings and the love they find together, this story thrives on that connected-ness at its core.

So, I hope you enjoyed The Pitch Slap. That it reminds you to keep persevering, to find your tribe, and never be afraid to explore—whether sexually, romantically, or mentally. It's never too late.

If you enjoyed this world, you'll be excited to know I have a bonus novella planned to give you all the happily ever after vibes you crave. (Megan has threatened me if I don't, so it's a promise). Next in this world is Bryce's book, which will be MMF with some taboo elements, followed by Ledger's book, which will be Enemies to Lovers MM. So, make sure to subscribe to my newsletter to stay up to date on all releases.

This book was a true labor of love, and I had a few pitch slaps myself along the way when it came to getting it published. I'm so thankful to my baseball bonanza crew for keeping me sane through it all. Emma—Resting Pitch Face—you breathed life into me with your comments, filling my author cup. Megan—Pitch Please—I love your thirstiness for the characters. Never change, even if Emma keeps her no-dibs rule in place. Melanie—Base-ic Pitch—thank you for joining my team for this series and keeping me straight on my baseball lingo. Your enthusiasm was exactly what I needed. Heather—Classy Pitch—you always know how to tell me if something isn't working without making me cry, so thank you for that. This book is better because of it.

A big thanks to The Blue Couch edits for stepping in during crunch time and ensuring this book made it to deadline.

To my husband for supporting me and being my biggest fan, even if it does make me blush. I couldn't do this without you.

And to all my readers—whether you ARC read it, are a die-hard fan, or a newbie- thank you for picking up this book and spending time with these characters. I would love to hear about your passion for them, so don't hesitate to reach out. If you can, leave a review, share it with friends, or suggest it to others. Your genuine love for a book is what helps others give it a chance, and you just might introduce someone to their new favorite book.

Lots of love,
Kris

ALSO BY KRIS BUTLER

BEAUTY AND THE CLEATS

#baseball #standalone series #heartfelt

The Cleat Retreat (Blake's prequel)

The Pitch Slap (Blake's book, MMFMM)

No Balking Way (Bryce's book, MMF)

Whiff it Real Good (Ledger's book, MM)

LUX BRUMALIS (COMPLETED)

#hockey #girlboss #nonbinary sibling

3 guys, no MM

Penalty Box

Dead Lift

Breakaway

THE COUNCIL SERIES (COMPLETED)

#figure skating #secret past #dark elements

7 guys, lots of MM with bi-awakening

Damaged Dreams

Shattered Secrets

Fractured Futures

Bosh Bells & Epic Fails

The Council Boxset

THE ORDER DUET (COUNCIL SPINOFF)

#secret agency #spy + hacker games #fashionista

4 guys, light MM (in book 2 at the end, and bonus)

Stiletto Sins

Lipstick Lies

The Order Duet Omnibus

DRESSED TO KILL SHARED WORLD (STANDALONE)

#female assassin #quirky & curvy #twins

4 guys, no MM

Raven

F*CK STEAL KILL (STANDALONE)

#morally gray #bestie unalivers #sassy

3 guys, biawakening, (FF in Joy's chapter)

F*ck Steal Kill

DARK CONFESSIONS (COMPLETED)

#mafia #therapist #foster kids + dogs #tattoos

5 guys with MM

Dangerous Truths

Dangerous Lies

Dangerous Vows

Reckless (Cami's Novella)

Relentless (Nat's Novella)

Dangerous Love

Truth Lies Vows Love: The Complete Series

TATTOOED HEARTS DUET (COMPLETED)

#tattoos #penpals #music #curvy fmc

3 guys with MM

Riddled Deceit (Part 1)

Smudged Lines (Part 2)

Open Road (Road trip Novella)

Tattooed Hearts Completed Duet

MUSIC CITY DIARIES (TATTOOED HEARTS SPIN-OFF)

#motorcycle club #age gap #TW #cam girl

4 guys, no MM

Beautiful Agony

Beautiful Envy

Beautiful Unity

VACATION ROMCOM

#romcom #social media experiment #besties

3 guys, no MM

Vibing

SINNERS FAIRYTALES (STANDALONE)

#Rapunzel retelling #dance #TW

3 guys, no MM

Pride

ABOUT THE AUTHOR

Kris Butler writes under a pen name to have some separation from her everyday life. Writing has become her second love, providing a safe place to normalize mental health through her characters. Kris enjoys writing emotional books with flawed characters, sassy heroines, and all the book boyfriends she loves to drool over. You can find her at home most nights reading with her husband and furbaby, trying to maintain her nerdy sock collection, or playing tabletop games with her friends. Kris loves to talk with readers about her books, even if it's just them yelling at her for that cliffhanger. If you enjoyed her book, please consider leaving a review. You can find her in her reader group or on social media.

Join my newsletter
Join my fan group
Check out my website

www.ingramcontent.com/pod-product-compliance
Lightning Source LLC
Chambersburg PA
CBHW061846310726
48972CB00004B/914